"WE ARE A PERFECT MATCH."

Ambrose reached down and took hold of her fingers, raising them to her own forehead.

Elizabeth let her hands trace lightly over the scar on her face.

"You are beautiful, Elizabeth," he said, pulling the cap off her head. His jaw dropped. "The devil . . . what have you done to yourself?"

"My lacerated face you find beautiful, but my shorn hair you do not?" she challenged.

"The first, I know, is the result of some brute's vicious act. But the hair . . . that must be self-inflicted."

"I'm sorry you find it so unattractive."

"Who says I find it unattractive?" Ambrose's eyes fell on her full lips. "My problem is I find everything about you absolutely fascinating."

She did not have to follow his gaze to know that he had every intention of kissing her. And that he did. Thoroughly.

And Elizabeth found that all she wanted to do was to yield to him. And that she did. Utterly.

◆ TOPAZ

TALES OF THE HEART

☐ **CAPTIVE by Heather Graham.** When sheltered Virginia belle Teela Warren gets a taste of the lush, exotic Florida Territory, her senses are dazzled. But when she glimpses halfbreed James McKenzie, the most attractive man she's ever seen, her heart is in danger. (406877—$6.99)

☐ **A TASTE OF HEAVEN by Alexis Harrington.** Libby Ross came to Heavenly, Montana, hoping for a new start, a family, children and a good place to raise them. What she found was terrible. The cowboy who duped her into being his mail-order bride had died, leaving her penniless with nowhere to go. That's when she heard about Lodestar Ranch and its owner, Tyler Hollins. (406532—$5.50)

☐ **ANGEL OF SKYE by May McGoldrick.** Alec Machpherson, famed warrior chief of the Highlands, has served King James IV of Scotland with his sword. Now he would give his very soul to protect Fiona, the spirited, red-haired lass from the Isle of Skye. But it will take Alec's Highland strengths pitted against a foe's cruel ambitions to prove, through blood and battle, which will reign—an army's might or the powerful passions of two lovers. (406745—$5.50)

☐ **PRINCE OF THE NIGHT by Jasmine Cresswell.** The Count of Albion, sequestered in an Italian villa, hid his secrets well—until the beautiful Englishwoman, Miss Cordelia Hope arrived. Irresistibly drawn to this cloaked, commanding count, Cordelia sensed his pain and, in all her innocence, craved his touch. He would become her destiny—the vampire whose love she was dying to possess. (405668—$4.99)

*Prices slightly higher in Canada

Buy them at your local bookstore or use this convenient coupon for ordering.

PENGUIN USA
P.O. Box 999 — Dept. #17109
Bergenfield, New Jersey 07621

Please send me the books I have checked above.
I am enclosing $_____ (please add $2.00 to cover postage and handling). Send check or money order (no cash or C.O.D.'s) or charge by Mastercard or VISA (with a $15.00 minimum). Prices and numbers are subject to change without notice.

Card #_____ Exp. Date _____
Signature_____
Name_____
Address_____
City _____ State _____ Zip Code _____

For faster service when ordering by credit card call **1-800-253-6476**

Allow a minimum of 4-6 weeks for delivery. This offer is subject to change without notice.

HEART OF GOLD

May McGoldrick

A TOPAZ BOOK

TOPAZ
Published by the Penguin Group
Penguin Books USA Inc., 375 Hudson Street,
New York, New York 10014, U.S.A.
Penguin Books Ltd, 27 Wrights Lane,
London W8 5TZ, England
Penguin Books Australia Ltd, Ringwood,
Victoria, Australia
Penguin Books Canada Ltd, 10 Alcorn Avenue,
Toronto, Ontario, Canada M4V 3B2
Penguin Books (N.Z.) Ltd, 182–190 Wairau Road,
Auckland 10, New Zealand

Penguin Books Ltd, Registered Offices:
Harmondsworth, Middlesex, England

First published by Topaz, an imprint of Dutton Signet,
a division of Penguin Books USA Inc.

First Printing, November, 1996
10 9 8 7 6 5 4 3 2 1

 REGISTERED TRADEMARK—MARCA REGISTRADA

Printed in the United States of America

To Pat Teal, Leah Bassoff, and Constance Martin;
three women who have provided the wings
that make flight heavenward possible.

Prologue

∾

The Field of Cloth of Gold
The English Possession of Calais,
on the coast of France
June 1520

The two knights collided in a shower of sparks, their metal-tipped lances exploding into splinters.

The snorting chargers rushed onward, carrying the men past one another, and Ambrose Macpherson glanced back over his shoulder in time to see his opponent bounce unceremoniously onto the soft earth of the lists. A roar went up from the French courtiers in the grandstands, but the Scottish warrior did not acknowledge the cheers until he saw the squires of the downed English knight hoist the angry fighter to his feet. Ignoring the glare of the King Henry's defeated champion, Ambrose stood in his stirrups and waved his shattered spear to the noisy and colorful crowd of spectators. Trotting over to the special box where Francis I, King of France, sat beside Henry VIII, King of England, Ambrose lifted his visor and saluted the two most powerful monarchs in Europe.

"Once again, well done, Sir Ambrose," the French king shouted. Turning to the burly king beside him, Francis clapped Henry Tudor on the shoulder and whispered confidentially, "This is the Scot you should have killed at Flodden, Henry. Not that we think you didn't try, seeing that scar of his." France needed more men like Ambrose as allies, Francis thought to himself. It was rare to find brains, courage, and power all in one man. "He's making the most of his opportunities here, don't you think?"

King Henry tried to look bored as he glanced down at this warrior-diplomat who'd been defeating his best fighters all month. Henry studied the hard lines of the man's face. The Scot's features were handsome enough, were it not for the deep scar crossing his brow from the top of his open helmet to his eye. The mark of a fighter, Henry thought somewhat wistfully, wondering vaguely what he himself would look like with such a scar. With a curt nod of his head, Ambrose wheeled his charger and galloped off toward the barriers.

"Aye, Francis," King Henry conceded. "But he has yet to ride against our man Garnesche."

"Come, Henry. With a lance, this Macpherson is the best horseman in Europe."

"Nay, these are empty words."

"Well, England, we have this golden ring set with a ruby the size of your eye that says he'll defeat your Garland—"

"Garnesche. Sir Peter Garnesche." Henry glared at his regal rival and removed a huge emerald ring from his finger. "Very well. This little trinket should hold its value against yours. Sir Peter will unhorse this Highland jester on the first course."

This friend of France is hardier stock than all of England's fighters put together, Francis thought. Perhaps we should up the wager. Calais, perhaps. Nay, we'd only end up fighting to take possession of it, anyway. "We'll just see if this champion of yours can remain in his saddle any better than the others. If he keeps his seat after five courses, Henry, the wager is yours." Handing the ruby ring to the nobleman standing behind them, the French king smiled wryly. "Would you trust our Lord Constable to hold the bet, or would you prefer to have one of yours do the honors?"

Henry glanced over at the stern-faced Lord Constable, then back at the broad, pale face of his ambassador, Sir Thomas Boleyn, standing attentive and eager at his shoulder. With a shrug, he tossed the ring to the French official. "You trust the worthy Constable with your kingdom . . . we think he can be trusted with a bauble. Sir Thomas, tell Sir Peter to arm himself."

* * *

The pale blue sky was warm, and Ambrose leaned his weary body back against the barriers, sipping water from a ladle while his squires attended to his mount. Looking across the open ground toward the grandstands, he thought to himself what a wasted opportunity this month had been for each of these two fiercely competitive monarchs. A wasted opportunity for each country. These great princes had come to the Golden Vale to discuss peace. To settle the differences that had kept their countries at odds for the past hundred years. Instead, they had spent the time trying to outdo each other in wit and shows of strength.

Thank God for their arrogance, Ambrose thought. Thank God for the incredible personal competitiveness that drove these two men. Thank God for the individual pride that had—so far, anyway—kept them from finding a way to come to an accord and forge an alliance that would seriously jeopardize Scotland's future . . . as well as the future of all Europe.

Ambrose smiled grimly, thinking of how these two kings so often acted like two spoiled adolescents, each trying to surpass the deeds and wealth of the other. Indeed, once, in the middle of the month, when Henry had suggested wrestling and laid his heavy arm on the French king's neck, only a massive diplomatic effort had stopped the two from going to war after Francis deftly tossed the English king to the ground.

And the Scottish knight had to make sure these two rivals would remain just that. For the good of all, the balance of power had to be maintained.

Ambrose scanned the fields outside the jousting lists. The rolling meadows were covered with the peaked tents and banners of the French and English nobles and their entourages. In planning this occasion, thoughts of expense had been discarded. And everything was for show. Covered with the golden tents and royal pavilions, erected to house the ten thousand lords, cardinals, knights, and ladies of each court, the sight was visually dazzling. It was intended to be. Even the fountain that stood by the great hall spewed wine instead of water. This was diplomacy at its most opulent . . . at its most futile.

Ambrose took in the sight with a twinge of disgust, for

his eyes also took in the hungry peasants being held back by soldiers beyond the grand gate on the far side of the field. Tents of gold cloth were being used by the nobles for these few short weeks, while many of these hungry villagers and their children begged for food and slept year-round in the open air. Politicians are largely blind men, Ambrose thought in disgust. And it's true everywhere. In England, in France, and even in Scotland. Once, years back, he'd thought the best course was to distance himself from politics. But along the way, he'd learned it was the profession he was best suited for.

On the surface, Ambrose Macpherson was a warrior without peer and the trusted emissary of the Scottish crown. He was a man of action and a man of learning. Though educated at St. Andrews and the university in Paris, Ambrose had mastered the arts of war fighting beside his father and brothers in the turbulent years of civil unrest that divided Scotland during his youth. Returning to the side of King James IV when war threatened with England, he had fought valiantly beside his king when Scottish blood was spilled on the fields of Flodden. That had been seven years ago, and Ambrose had received land, position, and fame for his continuing acts of valor and devotion.

But that hadn't been all. Being a free spirit, Ambrose had sought adventure and challenge. That had led him to every court in Europe. Renowned across the continent for his diplomatic achievements and his physical prowess, Ambrose Macpherson was respected as a man of honor in a world of treachery.

The sound of the heralds' trumpets brought Ambrose's attention back to the lists. These would be the final jousts of the day and of the tournament. Tomorrow he'd be riding to Boulogne, and from there sailing on to Scotland. He was looking forward to being home for the christening of his new nephew.

But first he had to ride against the Englishman Garnesche—a formidable opponent, Ambrose thought. He'd seen him unhorse every knight he'd jousted with. The man was as strong as a horse and as lithe as a cat. Ambrose moved toward his horse. The final joust of the day.

The two knights faced each other as the sounds of the drum roll and the blasts of the trumpets filled the air.

Peter Garnesche wore a cloak of cloth of gold over his full armor. Ambrose Macpherson was finely appointed in black satin and velvet. The razor-sharp blade of a Highland dirk could not cut the steady heat of their gazes as each opponent studied the other.

The crowd fell silent as the jousters made their way to their respective sides of the tiltyard. As he passed by the grandstands, Ambrose let his eyes roam the glittering rows of nobility dressed in their colorful finery. He saw the waving kerchiefs of the many young women who'd been beating a steady path to his tent these warm nights. He knew the ways of bringing pleasure to those he bedded. And, thus far, he was free of the scourge of pox that was running rampant. Having that reputation had made Ambrose a most popular courtier wherever he went. But lately he'd found himself somewhat bored with the selection of willing ladies at large. They all seemed the same. Too experienced and all too willing. There was no challenge. There was not even a pretense of innocence.

Ambrose shook his head to clear his thoughts of such nonsense. Concentrate, he thought to himself. Here he was, a moment away from facing the most challenging of his opponents, and he was still thinking from the proximity of his codpiece.

About to steer his courser toward the field, Ambrose was caught by the unwavering gaze of a young woman standing at the end of the seats. There was an air of power, of assurance in her glance. So much for being bored with the selection of the available ladies, he thought. Aye, some new blood . . . a new spirit . . . that's what I need.

Ambrose lowered his lance, saluting the unknown maiden, and wheeled his black stallion.

Elizabeth Boleyn blushed at the champion's sudden attention. And the heads that turned in her direction caught her quite off guard.

Since this was the French king's challenge, the English queen held her kerchief aloft, and Ambrose and Peter Garnesche waited like two great bulls, straining at their tethers in their impatience to do battle. Once more the heralds sounded their trumpets, and as the notes faded away, a deadly stillness descended upon the yard.

The kerchief fell, and the two warriors spurred their steeds into action.

As they thundered down the stretch, Ambrose began to lower the tip of his long lance. With a motion that had grown as familiar as a wave of his hand, the Highlander pinned the end of the lance against the side of his chest with his muscular upper arm. Watching the onrushing knight lower his lance, Ambrose realized immediately why the English fighter had been so successful. Garnesche's lance was not completely lowered; the metal tip was pointed directly at Ambrose's visor.

Fighting the instinct to raise himself in his saddle, Ambrose kept his spear pointed directly at his foe's heart.

With a deafening crash, the two warriors collided, the Englishman's lance exploding on Ambrose's shoulder, above his shield, while the Scot's weapon splintered in the direct hit to Garnesche's protecting shield. It took all of Ambrose's strength to remain on his horse as they passed.

The sounds of the cheering crowd rolled across the field as the two fighters turned and rode back to their positions, replacing their spent weapons.

"He cheated, m'lord," the young squire blurted out as he handed Ambrose the new lance. "He lowered his lance late!"

"Aye, but it just confirms the Englishman's reputation." Ambrose looked reassuringly at the lad. "I should have expected such tactics."

The two warriors faced each other once again, awaiting the signal. The heralds blared, the kerchief dropped, and the men flew down the course.

Leveling his lance early, Ambrose raised himself high in his saddle as the horse galloped on furiously. The crowd gasped. Despite the enormous weight of the cumbersome armor, the Highlander held himself and his lance rock steady as the courser raced toward the charging foe. Standing in his stirrups, the Scottish champion was sure to be unhorsed by the impact, or beheaded by the lance of his opponent should his strength falter.

Garnesche sneered through his visor at the oncoming Scot. The fool was finished.

An instant before the men closed, Ambrose sat hard in his saddle. The Englishman's lance was now aimed high . . . directly at his face. Leaning into the attack, Ambrose never flinched at the oncoming blow.

The impact of his lance against the center of his foe's shield resounded clear across the tiltyard, while the tip of Garnesche's lance whistled past Ambrose's head.

Raising his visor as he reined in his steed, Ambrose dropped his shattered weapon and turned amid the roar of the spectators to see the English knight sprawled flat on his back.

Cursing loudly and viciously, Peter Garnesche grabbed at the hand of his squire and pulled himself abruptly to his feet, glaring all the while at the Scot.

Ambrose's blond hair spilled freely over his shoulders as he removed his helmet. Dropping the metal armor into his squire's hands, the young warrior turned and trotted his stallion toward the grandstands and the royal box. He smiled at the grudgingly appreciative English crowd and gave a small salute to the cheering French. The two kings each greeted the champion, though Francis was clearly in the better humor.

"These are the finest of warriors, Sir Ambrose," the French king called out. "And you have vanquished every one." He motioned for the Lord Constable and took his winnings from the minister's open fist. Holding up the Tudor king's emerald ring to the light, he looked at it admiringly for a moment before handing it over the railing to the young knight. "I should have gotten England to wager Calais!"

Francis and Ambrose exchanged a smile while the surly English king looked on unamused.

With a nod of his head, the Scottish warrior turned away from the royal box and steered his horse down past the rows of French courtiers. Acknowledging the adulation of the still excited throng, he searched the crowd. He saw the women leaning forward in their seats, hoping for a chance to capture his attention. But his gaze swept over them all.

And then he saw her. She stood where she had been before. She hadn't moved.

Elizabeth studied the image of the warrior. He was all power, all elegance. She had seen enough. She was ready to start. She could feel the tingling, the excitement—in her hands, in the tips of her fingers. The sight of the man as he sat on the magnificent horse, watching her, would remain emblazoned in her memory.

Ambrose had never seen eyes as beautifully dark as hers. They were riveted on him. Studying him. He felt her gaze boring through his shield, roaming his body, studying him. She wanted him . . . he could tell. He would have her in his bed. Tonight.

Drawing his sword, Ambrose placed the great emerald ring on the razor-sharp point and extended it toward the young and beautiful maiden.

Elizabeth held out her hand as the knight deftly placed the token in her upturned palm.

The crowd fell silent as they watched the exchange. Then a thousand wagging tongues came alive with gossip.

Chapter 1

❧

Her mind raced, but her hand was slow to follow.

Elizabeth dipped the brush in the paint mixture and once again raised it to the canvas.

"What are you calling it?"

"The eighth wonder of the world!" Elizabeth murmured as she took a step back, studying her latest creation: *The Field of Cloth of Gold*. She had captured it. The sweep of the rolling countryside outside Calais. The grandeur and the majesty of the royal processions. The unadorned lowliness of the gawking poor. The blue skies overhead and the green fields of late spring. The thick, gray clouds darkening the distant skyline. The gaudy liveries of scurrying servants. The competitive thrill of the joust. The conquering knight. Her best work so far.

Mary shifted her weight on the couch as she stuffed more pillows behind her head. "May I see the ring?"

Elizabeth turned in surprise and looked at her younger half-sister. This was the last thing Mary needed right now, with this illness that was plaguing her. As if the sores from the pox were not bad enough, Mary had been unable to hold down any food for the past week. This once beautiful and robust young woman lay on Elizabeth's bed, exhausted and spent. Elizabeth held back her pity . . . and her tongue. After all, what could she say to this seventeen-year-old who had already endured more pain than others might bear in a lifetime? Elizabeth's mind wandered vaguely to thoughts of her other sister, Anne, and she wondered whether the youngest sister had been the source of Mary's knowledge about the afternoon's incident. The thirteen-year-old Anne was, for most part, Mary's eyes and ears these days.

"Where is the ring, Elizabeth?"

"I don't have it anymore."

"For God's sake, don't pity me." Mary turned her face away, speaking as much to herself as to her sister. "He took my innocence. He slept with me. He used me. So what if you are the one that ends up with his ring?"

"You slept with the Scot?"

"Don't be funny, Elizabeth. You know what I'm talking about."

It was no secret that Mary had been the mistress of Henry VIII, King of England, in the recent months. The affair had begun immediately after Mary and Anne were summoned to England and to the court by their father only four months ago. From what Elizabeth had been able to gather from Anne, their father had clearly encouraged Mary to respond in kind to the handsome young king's amorous advances, and Sir Thomas had even gone so far as to arrange private meetings in the hunting lodges away from court . . . and away from the queen. It was common knowledge that the king had long ago grown tired of the woman who could bear him no son.

Ten years back, after the death of his wife, Sir Thomas Boleyn had sent Mary and Anne to France to be brought up in the company of Elizabeth, his daughter from an earlier liaison. Growing up together in France in the household that their father kept in the court of Queen Isabel, the bonds had grown strong among the three young siblings. Elizabeth, then ten years old, was only three years older than Mary. Nonetheless, from the start she had taken on the role of guardian and had looked after and offered guidance to her newfound half-sisters.

It was a joy to have them. As a young child, before her sisters' arrival, Elizabeth had been an extremely lonely child. With no parents and no friends, Elizabeth had found other ways to capture the magic she missed in her life. The little girl had a God-given gift. Elizabeth Boleyn had the ability to see and depict beauty in the darkness around her.

She could still remember what it had been like the night of her mother's death. Dry-eyed, sitting by the burned-out hearth, she had held a fistful of warm ashes in one hand, a charred twig in the other. Using stick and ash, the young girl's small fingers had quietly, desperately swirled and traced a lifeline of patterns. Standing and moving to her mother's cold, lifeless body, Elizabeth had touched her ivory face, as beautiful in death as it had been in life. She left a smudge of ash on the high cheekbone.

Elizabeth had only wished the ash could make her warm.

The rest of her childhood was spent drawing on boards, floors, and walls—using whatever subjects she could find and then letting her imagination fill the void.

Years later, she began to paint. As long as Elizabeth made no trouble for her new guardian, she was allowed to run away from the confining prison of her quarters and spend countless hours with the craftsmen and the artists that visited Queen Isabel's court. None of the men had ever minded or questioned the bright-faced child who sat silently watching, her knees pulled up to her chest, her eyes intent on their every move. With apprentices bustling about, some of the painters had, in fact, shown interest in the little girl and, as she quietly told them of her interest, provided her with precious scraps of canvas or pigment for paint. She had watched the artisans fashioning their brushes, gazed with wonder at the mixing of paints, and studied the planning and the steps of each artist's technique.

Elizabeth had practiced all she learned. While other young children of the court might fear and avoid the dark corners of the grim castle keep, Elizabeth had taken sanctuary in them. Though the dark stone walls exuded dampness and cold, Elizabeth herself radiated the glowing vibrancy of life. The bold colors that she used in her paintings shone with sunlight and warmth. The lively detail of her work evoked smiles and good cheer in the few who shared her secret.

And then her sisters had arrived.

As time passed, the three black-haired daughters of Sir Thomas Boleyn had soon attracted the roving eyes of courtiers and knights from France and from many different countries. Of the three, Mary had always been the one drawn to the glamour of that fashionable life. Indeed, something in Elizabeth's sister had always cried out for the fawning attention of the court rakes, but nothing unfortunate had ever occurred. Not while Mary had been under Elizabeth's care.

Four months had now passed since her sisters had left. During the years Mary and Anne had been with her, Elizabeth had learned to discipline her creative urge. She would only paint when time allowed and when her siblings did not need her. After their departure, it had taken a long time to overcome her loneliness for them. But as time passed, Elizabeth had actually grown fond of her newfound solitude. It allowed her time to paint. With no disruptions, no one to baby, soothe, or look after, she was tasting the first fruits of freedom. But freedom was short-lived.

Suddenly Elizabeth found herself unexpectedly summoned to Calais by Sir Thomas. On arrival, she'd found Mary sick and bedridden. Her sister had contracted the dreaded pox.

She knew what it was. The scourge of every court in Europe. A miserable disease that attacked a lover's body first, and then attacked the mind.

Elizabeth tended to Mary with loving care. There was no need for scolding the younger woman . . . if the syphilis didn't kill her now, then Mary could look forward to a lifetime of suffering.

Though she herself had always shunned the allure of the court and its shallow inhabitants, something within Elizabeth kept her from condemning Mary for becoming the love interest of the most powerful man in England—the man who held their father's future in his hands. After all, Elizabeth had always had her talent, her painting, her secret life, and her hopes of becoming a great painter. Those dreams offered all the passion that Elizabeth sought in this life. They made her independent, even as a woman. Lost in her art, she needed no man to look after her, to protect her. But Mary was different. She needed attention. She wanted glamour. As Elizabeth strove to be the observer and to capture the image, Mary had always taken pleasure in being the object, the observed, the center of all attention.

Elizabeth thought now of the price her sister was paying. She picked up the brush and started to paint puffs of clouds scudding across the clear blue sky.

"Anne told me everything that happened today . . . at the tournament," Mary whispered, watching the smooth stokes of her sister's brush. "I have to warn you. He is a womanizer."

"You know him?" Elizabeth asked without breaking stride.

"It is hard not to notice him. That Scot is a good-looking man. But don't worry, sister. He is clean. I haven't slept with him."

The crash of the jug against the floor jolted Mary to a sitting position. She looked down sheepishly, trying to avoid the blazing temper of her older sister.

"I warn you!" Elizabeth took a step toward the cowering creature. "If I hear you even one more time . . . belittling yourself . . . as you have been . . ." She took a deep breath to control her anger before continuing. The walls of these tents were too thin for her liking. "You cannot hold yourself responsible, Mary. If someone should to take the blame, it is that king of yours for giving this god-awful disease to a mere child."

"Then you believe me that he is the only one I have ever slept with?"

"Of course I believe you."

The soft tears that left Mary's eyes did not go unnoticed by her older sister. Elizabeth moved quickly to her and gathered the young woman in her arms.

"Henry doesn't. He hates me. He called me ugly. He said he never wants to see my sickly face. The night before you arrived, I went to him. I was delirious with fever. He wouldn't even let his physician tend to me. He called me a . . ." Mary clutched at the neck of her sister and wept.

"Hush, my love. That's all in the past. That's all behind you now. Just think of the future. Of a beautiful future."

Elizabeth clutched Mary tightly in her arms—holding her, rocking her. She knew her words lacked conviction. She bit her lips in frustration as she thought of the cold and selfish king. But men were all alike in that respect. Born free to do as they wished. Free to take what they claimed was theirs by right, but never abiding by any civil rules.

"Oh, Elizabeth!" Mary wept. "What future? They once called me the fairest girl in France. Every man at court was after my affections. You know how popular I was. Now see what I've become. No man will ever want to look at me. I'll never have any place in society. No one will want me . . . not even as a friend. I'm already shunned. I just want to die. Why doesn't Death just come and take me?"

"Stop your foolish talk, Mary. That will not happen."

"Why not?"

"Because Death has to face me first before he gets to you."

"You think you could scare him off the way you scare me?" Mary asked with a weak chuckle.

"Of course!"

Mary closed her eyes and took comfort in the protective embrace. She should have asked Father to bring Elizabeth here sooner. Everything would get better now that she was here. Elizabeth would take care of her, the way she always had. She would never be alone. And she'd get better. Her sister had said so. Elizabeth had already sought the assistance of the French king's physician in examining her illness. The man had been here twice and was coming back this afternoon. He had sounded quite hopeful the last time.

The gentle footstep outside the tent separated the two. Elizabeth moved quickly to her painting and threw a sheet over it.

"Why don't you want me to see it?" The young girl stood in the opening of the tent, watching her eldest sister with a pout on her pretty face.

"Anne, you should not march in on grown-ups as you do. It is not proper," Mary whispered in her weak voice from the couch. "You know very well that Elizabeth doesn't want anyone looking at her pictures."

"I am not anyone. I'm her sister. And what you say is untrue. I saw her show her paintings to the Duc de Bourbon!"

"She saw what?" Mary turned to her older sister in surprise. Elizabeth had sworn Mary to secrecy years back. No one was to see her pictures. No one was to be told. Mary knew it was Elizabeth's greatest fear—that if people discovered her paintings, they would be taken away. After all, it was not proper for a young woman to pursue such hobbies to the extent that Elizabeth did. Mary had been shocked in seeing that some of Elizabeth's paintings actually portrayed nude men and women. Though truthfully, considering the builds of some of the men, she'd been tempted more than once to ask Elizabeth whom she'd used as models.

"I saw her with my own two eyes," Anne broke in before Elizabeth could respond. "In fact, I saw her accept a bag of gold coins from the duc and leave one of the paintings with him."

Mary jumped out of her place and flung herself at her older sister. "My God! You did it. At last! You sold your work. Which one? How did you convince him to buy one of your paintings? A woman's painting! How did you approach him? How much did you get for it? What made you do it?"

Elizabeth looked up and captured the gaze of her excited sister. She couldn't relate the truth. Not all of it. After all, she had done it for Mary herself. To pay the French physician's fee. But she couldn't let her know.

The Duc de Bourbon, for the past couple of years, had been a persistent pursuer of Elizabeth's. An admirer, true, but Elizabeth knew the duc loved to pursue every young woman who rejected his advances. The nobleman hated to be denied, and he surely thought that she, too, would fall to his charm and wealth——all the young women eventually succumbed. She knew the man had many mistresses. But that was a situation Elizabeth could not accept. She was simply not interested in becoming an ornament, tucked away and brought out from time to time for some man's pleasure as her mother had been . . . so many years ago. She had let the duc know her feelings on the matter. But the man was not giving up. In their most recent encounters, the duc had been most devious in his efforts to seduce her. She'd been regularly infuriated by his persistent antics and his pathetic tales. So now Elizabeth thought with some satisfaction of how she had earlier today been able to mislead the young nobleman over the painting. She had made up stories that were too unbelievable, but the duc had, for some reason, accepted her tale.

"Tell me, Elizabeth," Mary asked again, "how did you convince him to buy your work?"

"I lied. He thinks he's become the patron of a very talented, though as yet unknown, artist. An unknown *male* artist. He thinks I was just playing the part of the kind-hearted liaison."

"I would have thought he'd be a jealous monster at the thought of your acting for another man."

"I don't see why." Elizabeth sighed as she cleaned and put away her brushes. "My relationship with the duc has never been anything more than one of innocent acquaintance . . . at least on my part. I've never been attracted to him, and I've never led him on."

"No? Do I have to remind you how men think?" Mary moved back to the couch and sat down. This topic was one in which she had a great deal more expertise than her older sister. "It doesn't matter what you say or what you do. The fact is, Elizabeth, you don't belong to any man. So you are fair game."

"*Oui!* I know the poems . . . we women are the 'tender prey' for these overgrown, 'love-struck' boys. Well, I'm not. Though I guess I may have embellished the story to take that into account. I did tell him the artist is a crippled nobleman with leprosy who hides himself away in a priory and never sees visitors." Elizabeth removed her apron and tucked it away. "I suppose after hearing that story there was no reason for the duc to feel challenged."

For all her words, though, Elizabeth hoped she would not cross paths with the French nobleman for the rest of her stay here. With the heartache of her sister's ailment, she was in no mood to deal with a persistent courtier.

"Father wants you, Elizabeth." Anne's voice had the singsong quality of a child who knows a secret. The other two women both turned to her in unison.

"Father? What does he want?" Elizabeth had seen her father only from a distance since arriving in the north of France. There was nothing extraordinary in that, however. From the first day she had—as a child—entered Sir Thomas's household, their relationship had never been anything more than politely detached. In fact, unless it was due to Mary's illness, Elizabeth had no idea why her father had summoned her, a daughter he had always seemed intent on ignoring.

"I'll tell you for one of those gold coins."

"No chance, you brat," Elizabeth said curtly, her eyes twinkling. Taking the sides of the painting carefully, she moved it to the back wall of the tent. "I'll find out on my own."

"Perhaps," Anne responded. "But I'll get one of those

coins yet." As the words left the girl's mouth, she leaned over and grabbed a couple of Elizabeth's brushes, bolting for the tent's opening.

It took Elizabeth only a moment to realize what Anne had done. She turned and ran after her.

"You spoiled, greedy monster." The older sister chased Anne into the bright afternoon sun. There was no sign of the girl. She was as good at disappearing as she was at appearing.

Elizabeth's eyes roamed the setting before her. There were people everywhere. Squires and stable boys, soldiers and servants, some people dressed in finery and others in rags. Horses and dogs, dull gray carts and brightly painted wagons. The very air was vibrant with action. The gold cloth of the tents reflected the rays of the sun. It looked as though the ropes had captured that celestial orb, holding it down. Elizabeth made a mental note of that. Another touch for her work.

"I have to admit, lass, that I'm offended."

The soft, masculine burr of the accent made Elizabeth turn slowly in the direction of the voice. It was the High-lander. Uncontrollably, she felt her heartbeat quicken at the sight of the giant warrior, dressed in a Scottish tartan now, standing only a step away. His deep blue eyes were unwavering as they gazed into hers.

His long, blond hair streamed over shoulders that were wide and powerful. Like a great cat he stood, lithe and balanced and, she thought, ready to pounce.

Ambrose was stunned. She was even more beautiful up close than he had thought her to be. From the grandstand, where he'd first seen her, the young woman's presence, her confidence, her unwavering eyes had piqued his interest. But now, seeing her like this, he was taken aback by the full lips, the high sun-kissed cheekbones, the long luminous lashes, and the incredibly large black eyes that stared back at him in surprise. It was her eyes, black as coal, that had first captured his attention. She was taller than most women, but even in her unattractively sensible clothes, she was quite graceful.

"I'm Ambrose Macpherson. What's your name, lass?"

"Why did you say you were offended?" Elizabeth's mind was racing. Her next painting had to be of this man in his kilt. The sight was definitely too impressive to go uncaptured.

Ambrose smiled.

Elizabeth's heart skipped a beat.

"You were giving this dirt-packed alley more attention than you gave to the joust earlier today." Ambrose took a step toward her, allowing a horse cart to make its way past. He noticed that she didn't retreat from him. But he did see a gentle blush spread across her perfect ivory complexion. As her eyes wandered away from his to the groups of people moving by, the young warrior's eyes continued to roam the young woman's body. She had her hair hidden under a severe-looking headpiece, but from a loose tendril that lay against her forehead he could tell she was dark-haired. The dress, discolored in spots, was rolled up to her elbow and untied at the neck. The tease of what lay beyond the next tie was tempting. She had the stance and the boldness of a noblewoman . . . but the appearance of a maid. Ambrose let his eyes fall on her lips again. They were full, sensuous, inviting.

"You fought an exciting match." She caught his eyes on her.

"I had an exciting audience."

"I thought them dead," Elizabeth teased. "You surely deserved a better reception than what they gave."

Ambrose looked at her with a half grin. He'd thought the French reception quite enthusiastic—at least among the feminine members of the crowd. "Is it safe for me to assume that you were impressed?"

"By them? I prefer the living. The dead don't impress me much."

"I don't mean them." Ambrose frowned in jest. "I was trying to bring the discussion back to me."

This time Elizabeth looked at him appraisingly. "You think well of yourself, don't you?"

Ambrose laughed in response. Oh, no. He wasn't going to make himself a target by answering that question. Studying her closely, he tried to remember if he'd encountered her before today. No, he was quite sure he hadn't. This one was different. Beautiful, but different from the others. It was something in the way she held her head, slightly cocked, her eyes clear, alert.

"I haven't seen you before. Did you just arrive today?"

Elizabeth did not seem to hear him. He was handsome, incredibly so. But not proud and aloof. "You could have broken your neck at the joust, standing in your stirrups as you did."

"French or English?" he asked. She had watched from the French section during the joust, but the tent she had walked out of moments ago stood in the English quarter of the camp.

"Did you get that scar pulling a stunt similar to the one you pulled today?" Elizabeth studied the deep mark on the knight's brow. Though his loose blond hair covered some of it, it was clearly a badge of honor. She had to add this touch to her painting later.

"You are not married, are you?" he asked. She didn't seem too willing to answer his questions—not yet, anyway.

Elizabeth turned her eyes back to the activities in the alley. "There is so much more to see here than at the tournament field."

"Any jealous lovers?"

"Real people, in their element." She hid a smile. "They are so interesting to watch."

"Would you come to my tent? Perhaps tonight?" Ambrose reached out and took her hand in his. His thumb gently stroked the soft skin as he lifted her fingers to his lips. She was not wearing the ring he had given her earlier. "I will make it interesting."

Elizabeth shivered involuntarily at the feel of his lips against her skin. Their gazes locked. He was so beautiful and so openly sensual. And here she was standing in the midst of all these people, flirting with him. This was so unlike her. Besides, her father was waiting.

"I have to go." She pulled back in haste and, without so much as a backward glance, ran down the alley in the direction of her father's tent.

Chapter 2

❧

. . . the root, roasted and mixed with hog's lard,
makes a gallant poultice to ripen plague sores. The
ointment is good for swelling in the privities.
Indeed, the best of the Galenists hold that once
those afflicted with the pox expel the evil humors by
lying with the virgin, the decocted root will cure
the pustules with nary a scar.

—Camararius, *Hortus Medicus*,
"On the Treatment of the Pox"

The bloodied squire landed in a heap at her feet.

Elizabeth started, suddenly aware of the commotion she had walked into. She'd been intent on making herself presentable to her father. Now the dress ties and the condition of her hair were forgotten.

Pressed along the sides of the alley between the tents, spectators were taking in the activity wide-eyed, but with no intention of becoming involved. Elizabeth could see blood pouring from a gash above the lad's ear. She stared at the young man, who was groggily dragging himself erect, and instinctively put a hand out to help him up.

A voice filled with malice thundered from the center of the alleyway. *"Don't touch the lazy bastard!"*

Elizabeth's eyes flashed at the knight lurching ominously toward her. "He needs care," she shot back. "He—"

"You!" The knight stopped before her. His eyes had the glazed look of one either drunk or mad. Yanking the squire away from her, Sir Peter Garnesche's glare became a sneer. Casting the lad to one side, he spat his next words

over his shoulder, never taking his eyes from Elizabeth's face. "Go lick your wounds, boy. The . . . Scot's . . . lady wills it."

Elizabeth looked with loathing on the huge warrior. Like everyone else, she knew him to be among the English king's friends, but she also knew him as the man who, four months ago, had escorted her sister Mary to England—and to a lifetime of suffering. She turned away; she had no desire to converse with him.

"Wait, m'lady," the knight sneered, calling loudly as she walked off. "Perhaps you . . . or your sister . . . can give my squire the name of a good physician."

Elizabeth felt the prickly heat wash over her as she hurried from the ugly scene. The onlookers' laughs pounded in her head. Something brutal hung in the air around the man like a venomous cloud. She had to take Mary away from these vile people. She had to convince her father of that.

Though she was half-English by birth, Elizabeth Boleyn had good reason to feel no shred of loyalty to England or to its people. France was the country of her birth, and for Elizabeth, it was home.

Not that her childhood had been awash with sunlight. After her mother's death, and before Mary and Anne had joined her, Elizabeth had spent long, regimented years under the loveless supervision of her English nanny, Madame Exton. With the exception of the moments when she'd been able to escape to her painters, Elizabeth would prefer to blot this period from her memory. From early on, this manipulative woman had given her young charge a bad taste of English ways, particularly regarding the use of intimidation in child rearing. Even though Madame Exton had continued to run Sir Thomas's household in France through the years, life under the woman's iron rule became much easier to endure once the three girls had faced it together.

Sir Thomas Boleyn's tent was clearly marked with the banner depicting the family coat of arms, and Elizabeth paused before approaching the attendant standing outside. Running her hands quickly down her skirts to straighten her appearance, she thought through what she wanted to say to her father and wondered once again why he'd sent for her. She knew him to be a hard man whose ambitions had taken him high in the government of the English king, but he was also her father. And he had always provided for her.

Taking a deep breath, Elizabeth entered her father's tent.

"You don't know her, Thomas," Sarah Exton countered, never looking up from her needlework. "She won't do what you want simply because you command her. You must work her to your will."

Sir Thomas Boleyn stopped to glare at his cousin and then continued his pacing, pulling irritably at his gray speckled beard as he crossed the room. "This is no girl's game, Sadie. We are talking about the fortunes of this family. About—"

The shadows at the tent's opening stopped him, and he looked quickly at the attendant and the young woman who entered his spacious quarters.

Elizabeth's direct gaze captured the older woman's. The once-over look that her father's cousin gave her was clearly disapproving.

"Good afternoon, sir . . . madame." Elizabeth curtsied and stood quietly.

"Come here, girl, and sit." Her father waved at the chair by the woman and gestured for his squire to let them be. The elder man made no show of affection for the daughter whom he'd not seen in more than two years.

Obediently, Elizabeth seated herself by her overseer, who now bent over her work, seemingly ignoring all around her.

Sir Thomas paced the room, looking carefully at his daughter's intelligent, flashing eyes, at the strong set of her mouth and chin. Just like her mother's. But as Catherine had been gentle and forgiving when it'd come to him, Elizabeth was fierce and avenging. From the time he'd taken in the young girl when her mother died, Sir Thomas had never cared to be alone with her. Even as a child, she'd been able to turn his charity to guilt. Even now, her very presence was enough to prick sharply at his conscience, at the festering wounds that he tried to bury. Though Thomas Boleyn had been the one to walk away from Catherine, the pain of losing Elizabeth's mother still ached within him. It was a hurt barely contained beneath the layers of tough skin. An anguish ever-present, no matter how hard he tried to conceal it.

Elizabeth was tall, her complexion clear and healthy. She was not a voluptuous beauty, Sir Thomas thought. Not like Betsy Blount, Henry's first mistress, nor like Mary or any of the others.

"I don't know what he . . ." The courtier paused, his irritation turning to outright anger. "Oh! the hell with it! Who can understand such things?"

Elizabeth noted the furtive shake of the head that Madame Exton directed toward him. She sat quietly as her father turned and stalked to the table littered with official-looking documents. Sir Thomas lifted a tankard of ale and drained it, banging it on the table before turning back to her.

"Elizabeth, I have always been good to you, haven't I?"

"Oui, Sir Thomas—"

"Speak no French with me, girl!" he exploded.

"Y-yes, Father," she stumbled, surprised at the ferocity of his manner. She stared at him as he visibly contained himself, and when he spoke again, his voice was calm, controlled.

"Elizabeth, it's time you took your place in the world." The diplomat paused, turning his black eyes on her. "The point is, you have caught the eye of one who will raise you to the uttermost heights of society, and you will take . . . you would do well to take that place."

The young woman cursed the Duc de Bourbon under her breath. She should have known better than to be sociable with the nobleman this morning. The man had certainly stooped low. Now he was trying to force her compliance through her father. No chance, she thought.

"Father, I have to explain." Elizabeth paused, trying to gather together the words that were eluding her. "I have no wish to—"

Her father's glare silenced her. He was standing directly before her, his fists planted on his hips. "Girl, this has nothing to do with your wishes. This has to do with duty."

"Duty?" she exclaimed.

"Aye. Duty."

She blurted out the words before she could stop them. "What duty do I owe to a lust-infected nobleman?"

The power of the man's slap knocked the young woman from her chair, sending her sprawling into the middle of the room. There was a sharp pain in her head, and then numbness, ringing, and the taste of her own blood. She crouched before her father, her shaking hand pressed to her face.

"You will never, hear me, *never* again speak of your king in such terms."

"My *king*?" Elizabeth's eyes widened in disbelief. She glanced involuntarily at Madame Exton in her attempt to understand. The older woman's head never lifted. Her father's words brought her attention back to him.

"The king desires to take you into his bed, Elizabeth."

"*No!*" the young woman gasped, her hands clutching desperately at Madame's skirts. The tears rushed down her face uncontrollably. "No . . . he has . . . no . . . he has only seen me but once. This morning at the joust. It was only from a distance. This can't be. He has given his illness to Mary, Father."

"I know that!" Sir Thomas shouted. There was nothing he hated more than hysterical women. "She wasn't pure enough. He liked her well enough, but she wasn't pure enough to cure his pox."

Madame Exton laid her hand on Elizabeth's arm. "The king's doctors have told him that he must lay with only the purest virgins to rid himself of the disease." She looked at the young woman reassuringly. "It will bring great honor to you and to our family."

Elizabeth stared at the woman in horror. She was speaking so softly. No emotions. No excitement. Elizabeth could hear the words clearly. "It is a small sacrifice, Elizabeth. And as Sir Thomas says, it is your duty."

"I cannot. *I am not!*" she exclaimed, casting about in desperation for some answer, some reason that might halt this madness. "I am not pure. I've been raised in the French court. I've been with many m—"

The older woman's hand closed on Elizabeth's mouth roughly, smothering the words that were tumbling out. "Don't lie, Elizabeth. You are forgetting your company. If Mary were sitting here and speaking these words, I would have believed every one of them. But this is you. The pure and innocent Elizabeth. The one who has always hidden away from the glamour and from the temptation. The one who skipped even her own presentation at court." Madame Exton took Elizabeth's chin in her scrawny hands and jerked it upward. Her voice was as sharp as a dagger's edge. "I've watched you for many years, my girl. Don't waste your breath with lies. Just do as you are told. You owe that to your family."

"You have no option, girl," Sir Thomas added. "And just think of it, if you bear him a boy child, it'll be so much better for all of us, and for you."

Elizabeth slowly raised herself unsteadily to her feet. Her legs were shaking, and she wondered vaguely whether her knees would support her own weight. But then the look of disbelief on her face changed to something else as the terrible reality of her situation set in.

"But I—" There was anguish in her voice.

"There's nothing more to discuss, Elizabeth. Now go and prepare yourself. When the king's entourage leaves for Calais in the morning, you will leave with us." Dismissing her, he turned back toward the table.

The world had gone gray around her, its heavy mists swirling damply within. Her only sensation was the cloudy weight that was settling inexorably on her mind, her body, on her very soul. "But . . . what of Mary?" she asked in a daze.

Her father half turned to answer, his voice rough, his words clipped. "She'll go back to Kent. To the convent near Hever Castle. Don't you concern yourself about her. Go. *Go now!*"

Chapter 3

~

"You have the power to make your own future."

As Elizabeth hurried along the torchlit alleyways through the camp, Mary's words kept reverberating in her head. From a small knoll, she glanced across the tented field at the great dinner hall that had been erected out of canvas painted to look like stonework. Its glamour was only a veneer. At the approach of a roving party of men, weaving and lurching their way along, Elizabeth pulled the dark cloak low over her face.

"Hey, you pretty thing! Hey . . . there goes a woman!"

Elizabeth panicked at the sound of the drunk courtier and lengthened her strides. She would not let them know she was afraid. She would not be their prey. But then she thought of what she was about to do.

"This is insanity," Elizabeth murmured to herself. She could hear the anguish in her own whisper. "I've gone mad! The whole world's gone mad!"

The young woman put a hand to her face. The swelling had hardly subsided. She could still feel the ache that had made her eyes tear for so long after she'd returned to her tent. But it wasn't the physical pain that had torn at her heart; it was a pain that ran far deeper. She'd been sold out by her own father. Traded for . . . what? For another man's vile use.

When Elizabeth had returned, Mary had been there, waiting for her. Offering comfort, guidance. Coming here, at this hour of the night, had been Mary's idea. Her younger sister had given her the weapon that Elizabeth had desperately needed. Mary had shown her a way to fight their father.

The Scottish warrior's shield hung beside the tent's entryway.

Elizabeth stepped inside.

Sinking deeper into the warm water, Ambrose closed his eyes to the red glow of the coal brazier that had been used to heat the bathwater.

She had not come. He had expected her to. But then, he was no longer one to keep a vigil over any woman. Even one as fascinating as this one was turning out to be, he thought, glancing back over at the table—at the emerald ring that he'd given her earlier.

Lying there, soaking his bruised and tired muscles, he let his thoughts drift back over the events of the day, of their political importance. He thought again about the letter of false promises that had been signed by the two kings just a short while ago.

It was common knowledge in diplomatic circles that Henry had come to this meeting with the intention of breaking down the Auld Alliance between France and Scotland. The English king's chancellor, the crafty Cardinal Wolsey, had left no path untried in his maneuvering to gain some hold on the French king, in his search for some wedge to drive between Francis and the troublesome Scots.

But Ambrose had been unsuccessful in disrupting all hope of any real trust between the two monarchs. For, in a private meeting just before the signing, the Scottish nobleman had managed to convey to King Francis proof that his enemy the Holy Roman Emperor Charles was waiting to meet secretly with Henry in Calais. On hearing this, Francis had been ready to confront the treacherous English king on the fields. But with the Lord Constable and Ambrose's intervention, they had been able to restrain the French monarch from immediately embroiling himself in a war with England. In fact, Ambrose had been able to persuade him to go on with the show of signing the treaty with the double-dealing Henry while pursuing a different course—a waiting game—and meanwhile trying to gain some inside information regarding the details of Charles and Henry's upcoming meeting.

Ambrose had done what needed to be done. Based on the information he'd had, secret envoys of the Holy

Roman Emperor had met with the English king earlier today. Now it was up to the Lord Constable's contacts to reveal the details. There was one thing that was certain, though: The Auld Alliance between Scotland and France had survived the Field of Cloth of Gold. The Highlander had done his job.

Ambrose opened his eyes and reached contentedly for the tankard of ale that sat on the small stool beside the tub.

She was standing just inside the tent.

"I'm offended once again!"

Elizabeth hid a smile as she gave him a quick glance. Consciously turning her full attention back to the emerald ring that sat on the small table, she continued to stifle her urge to study his naked body. "You are far too sensitive for a man your size."

Ambrose's eyes traveled the length of her as she untied the dark cloak and let it fall to the ground at her feet. "I would have hoped that my present vulnerable condition might have attracted a bit more attention than that ring."

"I don't think there are too many things in this world that would attract more attention than this thing." She picked up the ring. The emerald caught the dim light of the brazier and lit up.

"If you were that fond of it, why did you give it up?" Ambrose watched her long, slender fingers, the tilt of her beautiful chin. Her midnight-black hair was gathered on top of her head. Stray tendrils curled against her perfect profile.

Elizabeth could feel the heat of his gaze on her skin. She wouldn't turn. She couldn't.

"How did you get it back?" she asked, though she already knew the answer.

Ambrose gazed at the lass. She was no maid-in-waiting. He had found that out earlier. And she was not used to answering questions. She asked her own. "Three of the Lord Constable's men dragged a poor village priest in here. He was caught trying to sell it to get his mistresses separate rooms." Ambrose grinned into his tankard as he quaffed the ale. Her sidelong glance was quick, but he saw it. "They thought he'd stolen the ring from me."

"I hope you made sure they dragged the wretch all the way to Guisnes Castle."

"I certainly did." Ambrose paused and then stood in the tub.

Elizabeth turned her back to pick up her cloak. Busying herself with folding the garment, she tried to ignore the image of him stepping out of the water.

"But not before I made him confess the truth." Ambrose tied the towel loosely around his waist as he moved behind her. She smelled of lavender and the fresh summer air.

"You wanted to know the whereabouts of his mistresses?" She could feel his breath on the back of her neck. He was standing far too close. She leaned over and placed the ring on the table. Elizabeth found herself suddenly fighting the urge to recoil, to run away. After all, wasn't this why she had come here? To lose her virginity?

"Hardly." Ambrose let his lips brush against her skin. It was as soft as it looked. He felt her body go tense. "Why did you give the ring to the priest?" he asked softly.

"Why did you offer him so much gold to take it back?"

"So you've seen him since." Ambrose let his finger run seductively down her back. He smiled as he saw the obvious shudder that ran through her.

Elizabeth clutched her cloak tight in her hand. She knew she had to relax. She had to let this just happen. She had to admit it had helped to get some glimmering of the kind of man this Ambrose Macpherson was . . . from Friar Matthew. This afternoon, when the priest had returned to her tent with word of Sir Ambrose's generosity, Elizabeth had listened closely to his story. She had known Friar Matthew for a long time, and she'd given him the English king's ring, knowing that many would benefit from it. The ring certainly had no monetary or sentimental value to her. Elizabeth had earned what money she'd needed for Mary's physician by selling the painting earlier. And if only for her sister's sake, she knew it would be far better if Mary's eyes never chanced to fall upon it.

And then the priest had come back, telling her—to Elizabeth's astonishment—that the Scottish nobleman had bought the ring from him. The young woman had never expected the priest to approach him. What must he have thought, learning that the ring he'd given as a token had been handed over to someone else the same day? But then, it had been too late to worry about such things.

Sitting there in her tent, beaten and fairly certain of what course she would take, Elizabeth had been surprised to hear that the Scottish knight had asked about her. And then the priest had told her of the man's generosity and compassion.

After hearing all that, Elizabeth had agreed with Mary that this was the right course, that this man was the one to come to. After all, she would never see him again. Never.

Ambrose reached up and pulled the pin that held her hair in place. The sliding mass of black curls tumbled caressingly over his hand. He breathed in the heavenly scent, wondered at the silken softness. He ran his hands down her shoulders, thinking back over what he'd managed to pry out of the priest. There was so much that fascinated him about this woman.

"Considering his tongue-flapping profession, your priest friend is not much on talking when he doesn't want to."

"That's very curious, coming from a diplomat." She watched as his hands confidently encircled her waist. She tried to hide her own trembling hands and hesitantly dropped her cloak on the bench.

"Hmm, so you know about me," he crooned, his lips a breath away from her ear. His strong arms pulled her tightly to him.

"Of course. You are the most charming courtier ever to wield a lance." Her soft voice carried just a touch of irony. "Your name is on the lips of every lady in France. They tell me that wherever you pass by, your squires have to sweep up the swooning maidens that are left in your wake."

"Oh, is that so? And are you feeling a wee bit lightheaded, as well?"

"Of course. Well, I'm feeling something." She looked down as his great hands roamed the front of her dress. Gently moving up to cup her breasts. "But thinking of it now, it may just be a touch of gas."

"We must be eating from the same pot." Ambrose chuckled as he turned her in his arms. He tensed. Even in the dim glow of the brazier, he could see the swollen cheek that she'd been keeping away from him. Immediately his brow darkened.

"Who did this to you?" His hand reached up to feel the lump, but she turned her face away, not wanting his sympathy.

"I had to fight my way through legions of women to get to you." Elizabeth winced as his hands framed her face and turned it to him. She reached up and tried to remove them, but to no avail.

"You must tell me who beat you this way." His voice was sharp.

"So much like a knight," she said with a sigh, trying to lighten the mood. "But I think she is even too tough for you. Rotund. Middle-aged. With a very strong right arm. But she may still be outside."

Ambrose looked at her askance. "That is no answer, lass."

"In fact, I think I might have suffered a blow to the head. My memory is a bit vague right now." Elizabeth tried to avert her eyes so she wouldn't have to look into his intense and beautiful blue eyes. Talking came easy to her. But looking at his handsome face made something inside her go soft. This close to him, she could smell his good, clean, masculine scent. She was very conscious of the massive chest that her arms rested against.

"Let me help. I know who you are." Ambrose knew a lot more about her than the priest had divulged. And he was not fooled by her quick tongue. Someone had hurt her, and he planned to find out who. The Highlander lifted her chin, forcing her to meet his direct gaze. "You're Elizabeth Boleyn. Eldest daughter of Sir Thomas Boleyn, King Henry's ambassador to France. Born of Catherine Valmont. You've spent most of your life in the French court. Not surprisingly, your beauty and brains are well spoken of. And, as the Duc de Bourbon knows, you are not one to share your bed openly with just anyone."

"He told you all of this?" she whispered. "I'm flattered, m'lord. You must have gone to a great deal of trouble to learn all these things. The truth is, I'm not what one might call 'well known' at this level of society."

"Did someone hurt you because of my gift to you? Because of my attention to you at the joust?"

Elizabeth thought back to the encounter she'd had with her father earlier. It was curious that Sir Thomas had not mentioned even a word about the attention she'd received from the Highlander at the joust. He'd been there and witnessed it, as everyone else had. Still, she shook her head in response. "It looks a lot worse than it feels. I'm fine m'lord."

"Whoever you are trying to protect does not deserve you, lass." Ambrose took a half step back and looked at her from head to toe. She was a striking young woman, radiating beauty, charm, and something more. Confidence. Even in her disheveled condition. "If you would allow me, I'd take great pleasure in teaching the man who did this a few lessons on how a woman should be treated."

"Please stop!" She took his hand in her own. "I didn't come here to discuss this . . . this minor mishap."

"Then why did you come?" Ambrose asked as he lifted her fingers to his lips. He paused as he gently kissed them. "Did you come to punish him? To get even?"

He turned her hand in his and stroked the soft palm before bringing it once again to his lips. The streaks of colors on her fingers caught his attention.

"Perhaps!" she whispered, coiling her hand and placing it in the folds of her skirt.

"Well, how far must your vengeance take you?" He stepped toward her, pulling her again into his embrace.

"My ven—" The words died on her lips as he leaned toward her. She felt his mouth possess hers. All at once hard and soft, demanding and giving, seductive and playful.

"How much does he need to suffer?" He whispered the question, tilting her head and deepening the kiss. Her mouth was soft, pliable, warm. Her sweet taste was intoxicating. Suddenly he couldn't get enough of her. With a silent roar, desire swept through him, desire for skin against skin, body against body. Ambrose knew it should matter that she wasn't there solely because she wanted him. But somehow, he simply didn't care. He knew that when the night was done, when their passion was—for the moment—sated, she would feel differently. Next time, she would come wanting him.

Elizabeth found herself short of breath. She could feel the hammer of her heart in her chest. She had not expected this. So quick. The kiss, this man's mouth, was undoing her, melting her. She felt herself going limp in his embrace, her mouth yielding to his mouth, her body molding to his body. She raised herself on her toes as her hands instinctively encircled his neck. She felt rather than heard his groan of pleasure as her body pressed involuntarily against his.

"Tell me, how much does he need to suffer?" Ambrose's hands worked their way through the laces of her dress front as his lips bit and teased her neck, her jaw, her lips.

"Endlessly!" she whispered.

Chapter 4

❧

Elizabeth had expected it to be quick, painful, and done with.

How could this happen? Her senses, now inflamed by the attentions of Ambrose Macpherson, cried out for release. And as far as she could tell in the amber haze that was swirling in her brain, she was still a virgin.

Elizabeth opened her eyes as Ambrose worked her fingers gently from their death grip on the sheets. She looked up into his passion-filled eyes as he kissed her palm.

"Hold me, Elizabeth. Don't be afraid. Touch me."

She watched in dismay as Ambrose lowered her hand and let it trace downward over the hard muscles of his abdomen. Her fingers played a dance of wonder over his skin. He shifted his weight off of her, to give her better access. She froze. He was naked, Elizabeth realized with a jolt. And so was she, nearly.

She had been so consumed with the magic of this man's beguiling touch, of his hands, his mouth, his searing kisses, that she had hardly paid any attention to her own circumstances. They were gone . . . forgotten. Elizabeth had only the vaguest awareness of his strong arms removing her dress, lifting her off her feet, and carrying her to bed. After that, she'd been lost to everything.

Now, looking down at her open chemise, her exposed breasts, she yanked her hand out of his grasp, trying to cover her flesh. But he was too quick for her.

"Not so fast." He lifted her hands above her head, trapping them there with one hand. "You have the most beautiful body of any woman I've ever laid eyes on. I want to savor every moment. We can't rush this." Ambrose's eyes lowered to the full breasts. To the raised aurora that invitingly beckoned his lips. He bent down and kissed the soft curves of the valley between her heaving breasts. Then moving on, he tenderly suckled her rose-colored nipples.

Elizabeth groaned uncontrollably in response. She wanted him. He was making her insane. But somewhere inside her head she knew she had to stop. She had to stop the rhythmic dance that was taking over her body, had to stop the liquid heat that was rushing through her. She could not go through with this.

Ambrose tried to control the pounding roar of his heart. He was losing control fast. She was incredible. Her beauty, her sweet taste were driving him wild. He wanted to take her now. But more, he wanted to extend this sweet torture. For his own selfish reasons, he wanted Elizabeth to remember him, to remember this night as the best lovemaking she'd ever had. Ambrose felt her hands work their way out of his grip and work themselves into his hair. She pulled at him. He rolled and brought her on top of him, stripping her of the open chemise as they rolled.

Elizabeth gasped as she found herself looking down at the handsome warrior. Her breasts, still tingling from his kisses, rested heavily on his chest. She was afraid. Afraid of her own body's responses. Something inside of her was taking over. Something she could not control. His hands were working across the skin of her buttocks, working their way toward the juncture of her legs. Against her judgment, against her very will, she thrilled to this act of lovemaking. She was ashamed of herself. But she could not deny it.

Ambrose couldn't hold back. Elizabeth's cascading waves of black silk framed her angelic face. Her cloudy eyes searched his face with curiosity, uncertainty. Her full lips, swollen from his kisses, drew his eyes. He wanted those lips on his body. He wanted to teach her things that her French lover obviously had not. The foolish man. He lifted her by the waist.

Elizabeth sat up slowly and watched as Ambrose's hands brushed her hair gently away from her breasts. Then he shifted her weight. Elizabeth looked down as she felt the throbbing member against her. Throbbing to enter her.

No, she thought in a panic. No! She had to get away. She couldn't go through with this.

Everything a blur around her, she leaned backward suddenly and, with a thud, fell heavily into the rushes on the floor.

Ambrose peered over the end of the bed at Elizabeth, shocked to see the naked beauty scuttling backward away from him.

His voice had a touch of humor when he spoke. "I've made more than a few women wild in my time, but I don't think I've ever driven one stark, raving mad."

"I'm not mad," she whispered, modestly turning to hide her exposed body.

"Here, lass," Ambrose called sharply, sitting up. "Watch out for the brazier!"

Elizabeth scrambled to her feet just before upsetting the coals.

"What's wrong?" Ambrose stood, taking a step toward her.

"Don't!" Elizabeth shouted, raising her hand pleadingly. "Please don't." She looked frantically about for her clothes, grabbing at the first things she could find. "I'm sorry, m'lord . . . I—"

"I'm not going to hurt you," Ambrose said, his tone soothing. She was scared. He couldn't believe it, but in an instant she'd gone from the heights of passion to the depths of cold desperation. He needed to calm her fears. "I don't know what that man has done to you. But, that's him. Not me."

Elizabeth fumbled with the oversized shirt as she tried to pull it over her head. "What man?" Her head just *wouldn't* go into the sleeve.

"You are young, beautiful. In fact, stunning. Any man would be a fool not to want you as his own. To treat you better."

"I am not just a rose sitting about, waiting to be picked, m'lord. I'll decide for myself what I want. I'll make my own choices." Damn, she thought, hearing the shirt rip.

"Then why do you stay with one who abuses you? Hasn't someone ever told you that you deserve better than that?"

Elizabeth's head finally appeared through the collar opening. Her hair was in total disarray. "If my well-being is truly a concern to you, then I have to inform you that I am quite self-sufficient."

Ambrose's eyes traveled the length of her as she tried to close the open collar. She looked wonderful in his shirt.

"You might think yourself as in charge, lass. But clearly you are not. Just look at you. You are a woman. A beautiful woman who—"

"There is nothing wrong with that." Elizabeth snapped.

"Let me finish," he growled, silencing her with a glare. "You are a *stubborn,* beautiful woman who obviously has not been told the difference between what she should tolerate and what she should not. You will never be in charge, Elizabeth, until you are able to recognize and act on that difference."

Elizabeth's head pounded with the thought of all that still lay ahead. "Simply, m'lord. Could you please tell me in simple terms . . . *what the devil you are talking about*?"

"I'm talking about you and your lover, my thick-headed English—"

"Don't you dare call me that you . . . you . . . *What* lover are you talking about?" My God, she was losing her mind. Elizabeth's brain whirled as she tried to make some sense out of all that was happening. Then her eyes widened as her gaze fell on the Highlander's imposing arousal. "I . . . Never mind. I have to go."

"The Duc de Bourbon. I should have known." Ambrose reached down, grabbed his tartan, and tossed it to her. "The man nearly went wild when I asked him about you this afternoon. The filthy knave. I can't believe I was so blind. It was he."

Elizabeth paused, gaping at the warrior. "Bourbon?"

"Aye. The coward Bourbon. I should have flattened his face before he did this to you." Ambrose ground his fist into his palm. "When did he do it? Was it after I questioned him? Did he come to you after I left?"

Elizabeth stared at the nobleman. "I don't know what it is you are talking about, but I don't need anyone to defend me. I can tell you right now that I will kill, with no hesitation whatsoever, any man who raises a hand to me again."

"Aye, lass. That's the spirit. And it's about time."

Elizabeth stood for a moment longer, now totally confused. She had no clue whether their discussion had reached its conclusion. In fact, she wasn't even sure if she'd heard half of what was said. She shook her head. She *had* lost her mind. "Good night, m'lord." Elizabeth turned as she pulled her hair back and tied it with a thong.

"Where are you going?" Ambrose asked. Though there

was something comical in seeing her wearing his baggy shirt and ankle-length kilt, his belt wrapped twice around her, there was also something quite arousing in the picture.

"I'm going in search of my sanity and perhaps even justice," Elizabeth murmured as she swept toward the tent's opening. "And my future. That's my only chance."

Ambrose stood by his bed and watched her leave. This had been, by far, the strangest encounter he'd ever had with any woman in his life.

Looking down at his still erect member, Ambrose thought about his would-be lover, even now wandering through the Field of Cloth of Gold, appareled in some very fine, albeit large, men's clothing.

Elizabeth Boleyn was, indeed, a strange creature.

Chapter 5

❧

The drunkards roaming the Golden Vale that night never imagined that the Scottish lad walking among them was a woman.

From the cloth great hall far off across the field, the sounds of merrymaking and music broke in gentle waves over Elizabeth's consciousness. Vaguely, she glanced across the knolls to the glow of the bonfire that lit the huge tent from within. With unseeing eyes, she continued on past huddling couples and men lurching about in various degrees of inebriation.

But as she strode through the torchlit alley, Elizabeth's attention was focused inward. Suddenly it was the noise of her own shoes padding along the dirt way that pierced her thoughts.

Twenty paces from her father's tent, Elizabeth stopped short. A cold wave washed over her as she considered what lay ahead. For the past quarter hour, she'd been arguing repeatedly with her father and had been able to convince him to rescind his earlier demands. Tomorrow, Elizabeth would return to France with Mary, where she could care for her sister and they would all forget what had taken place. Looking at the dimly lit tent, Elizabeth felt suddenly limp and tired. The problem was that their productive exchange had taken place only in her head.

The two reeling knights who now knocked Elizabeth to the ground did not even cast a glance at the toppled woman.

"Watch where you go, lad," one of the men growled roughly as they continued on their way.

Elizabeth peered up at their retreating backs in amazement. Rising, she shook the dust off the Macpherson tartan.

She stared down at the garment in her hands. At the plaid kilt. At the shapeless shirt draped over her torso. Lad! They thought her a man. She gazed back at the now-deserted alley and then back at her apparel. She'd walked through groups of them and not a soul had said a thing to her. These were the same hungry men who—in their present condition, at least—equated women to meat. Lad!

Shaking off the thought that was edging into her brain, Elizabeth turned her attention back to the confrontation that lay ahead. Dread flooded through her at what she thought might be her father's reaction. But what other choice had she left? Elizabeth stared at the attendant nodding beside the open entrance of the tent. The English soldier lifted his head and looked at her blankly. Not finding her stance a threat, the man nodded back to sleep.

Elizabeth took a deep breath and started for the opening. The die was cast; she must carry this through. Noiselessly, she slipped past the guard into the tent.

Sir Thomas sat at his table, a lamp flickering at his elbow. A few papers were spread before him, but nearly everything else had been packed up and stacked near the door for his departure the next day. Standing in the deep shadows, Elizabeth studied her father for a moment. Whatever her mother had seen in him, those many years ago, nothing remained that Elizabeth could discern. Though he now lacked any semblance of gentleness or feeling, she knew he once must have been different.

Sir Thomas was the younger son of a wealthy country squire. Hardly noble and in no position to inherit, he learned early that a man needed to use every resource at his disposal to get ahead in life.

Apparently a man of great knowledge and charm in his younger years, Sir Thomas had used his father's connections to enter King Henry VIII's service. Knowledgeable in several languages, Sir Thomas had taken his first diplomatic mission in France, where he'd met and perhaps loved the young and beautiful Catherine Valmont.

The noble lady's lineage was long and impressive, and her parents' horror at the thought of a penniless young Englishman in the family had forced their ultimatum: If she chose to marry him, she would forfeit all claim to her rank and wealth. Catherine had accepted the condition without a moment's hesitation. After all, she loved him, and that was all that mattered.

Then, to almost no one's surprise, Sir Thomas had walked away from Catherine, but not before he had planted his seed.

Catherine Valmont, cast out by her own family, was left alone, bereft and with child. Nine months later Elizabeth had been born.

For Sir Thomas, love was a condition that could not be allowed in the way of his own upward mobility. Marriage was a contract that allowed the committed parties the ability to improve their social position. Without her family, Catherine had nothing to offer him. So Thomas caught hold of a daughter in the noble English family of Howard. And by that union he attained the Earldom of Ormonde, a title far above anything he'd ever dreamed possible.

Marriage had been a joyless state, but it had produced the results Thomas had sought: wealth, position, and power.

Despite the glamour, Elizabeth knew that her father had paid the price. He had never been loved by his young bride as he'd been loved by Catherine. And after his wife's death in childbirth, the Howard family had made certain he knew he was an outsider. He didn't belong.

From what Elizabeth could gather, it was then that her father had set his course with the king. This grim man standing before her had shut out everything in life besides his mission as a diplomat and being a servant to his king. It was all he had left. They were words that defined him, for he never seemed to exist beyond that. Diplomat and servant. Outside of the presence of King Henry, Sir Thomas Boleyn became a hollow, miserable, bad-tempered old man who seemed to take very little pleasure in life.

Her father's hands rested flat on the table, his attention focused on a moth fluttering about the base of the lamp. Elizabeth could read no expression on his pale face. His eyes were black and empty.

Without warning, the man's hand flashed in the lamplight, and his wide palm smashed down with a thunderous bang on the unsuspecting moth. Lifting the lifeless insect by one shattered wing, Sir Thomas inspected the creature carefully. Then, with an expression of clear disdain, he dropped the moth's carcass into the flame, watching with renewed interest as it flared and sizzled before crumbling to ash.

Elizabeth stepped closer to the circle of light.

Sir Thomas's eyes darted toward her, and Elizabeth saw him master a quick look of fear that flashed across his face as he peered into the darkness at the Scottish attire.

For ten years Thomas Boleyn had been working to drive a stake into the heart of the Scottish and French alliance. Learning his craft under the Tudor kings, Sir Thomas had found that the handshakes of diplomacy were rarely effective without the sharp edge of a dagger visible in the other hand. Indeed, his position had often called for duplicity and ruthlessness, and Sir Thomas had long ago proved himself a master of the craft. But as a result, Thomas Boleyn was a man with enemies. Deadly enemies.

Elizabeth watched his hand go directly to his waist and to the short sword she knew he would be wearing.

"Who is it, there? And what's your business with me?" His tone was sharp and commanding, his face now hardened and bloodless.

"It is I, Father." Elizabeth watched the confusion muddle his stern expression. "It is Elizabeth."

Sir Thomas sat back in his chair and glared across the table.

"Eliz—Why are you here, girl?" His eyes swept over her. "What are you doing wearing those foul weeds?"

Elizabeth glanced down at her clothes and hid her trembling hands behind her. Fear shot through her like bolts of lightning, but she needed to go through with this. Now, while she was alone with him, without Madame Exton present. Sir Thomas, despite his crafty ways, hardly new Elizabeth well enough to question her word. But Madame would know.

"Speak, girl," the man roared. "Where have you been?"

"I've been to the Scot."

Sir Thomas sneered in disdain. "You've dined with the devil. Hasn't anyone told you how much I hate their entire race? They are worse than animals. They are mindless scum, cluttering our land."

"I've done more than dine with him."

The man's voice was cold and deadly. "What the devil have you done?"

"I'm no longer a virgin." She looked him straight in the eye. Her words were sharp, quick, and piercing. "No longer."

He gasped, staring. "Nay. Don't lie to me." Placing his hands on the table to support his weight, Sir Thomas stood. "Do you think me so simple?" Without taking his eyes from her, he shouted for his squire. "John!"

The young soldier stumbled at once into the tent. His sleepy eyes traveled from his master to the young Scot.

"Go to Madame Exton. Tell her to come here immediately." Seeing the boy hesitate and begin to draw a sword on Elizabeth rather than retreat, he shouted, "Damn it, boy! This is my daughter. And make no pretense of duty now. She passed your sleeping carcass to get in here. Now *go*!"

Elizabeth felt panic seep quickly through her body. Her scalp was prickling with fear. There was no time left. She had to convince him of this lie before her cousin's arrival. The older woman would be able to see the truth. Elizabeth knew Madame Exton all too well. She would stop at nothing. She would probably examine Elizabeth herself before believing her words.

She watched the squire disappear out the opening of the tent.

"Look at me," Elizabeth snapped, scorching her father's downturned face with her own unrelenting gaze. She waited until the older man's eyes focused on her, and then she continued. "I'm wearing the clothes of your enemy. I accepted his favor after the joust today. Hundreds witnessed it. *You* witnessed it. Ambrose Macpherson invited me to his tent. So tonight, I went to him. Your men saw me go. Every man in this Golden Vale saw me go. I went willingly . . . and I slept with him." Elizabeth paused, making certain that every word left its mark. "I lost my virginity. And I'm glad of it. I enjoyed it. Do you want to see the proof now, or would you are care to wait for your dear Sadie's arrival? We both know she is far more experienced in dealing with your daughters. But perhaps you should see the blood of lost innocence first."

Elizabeth reached inside the belt and began to draw out a kerchief.

"Hold!" Sir Thomas breathed heavily where he stood. His eyes were wild and bloodshot. His fists clenched tight. "How . . . how could you? No better than a common whore. How could you defy me this way?"

"Because my purity was not for you to sell. Damn it, *I'm* not for you to sell!" Elizabeth's eyes never left his face. As her voice had earlier conveyed a calm and resolute chill, it now bore her full fury. "I did what I had to do. To save myself. Now I am no good to you or your king."

"*My* king?" he stormed, sputtering as he careened around the table toward her. "You? With a filthy Scot?"

"Aye," she said, standing her ground. "I was willing to sleep with your enemy rather than allow you to give me over to that syphilitic goat."

With a roar, Sir Thomas lunged at his daughter, grabbing her by a long, thick lock of hair as she turned to evade his attack. Wheeling about, he smashed her face against the sharp edge of the table, and as he yanked her back again, Elizabeth saw her own blood flying in droplets into the darkness beyond the circle of light.

Sir Thomas turned her around in his rage and glared wildly into her bloodied face. His one hand still held Elizabeth by her mane. "Do you know what happens to those who defy me?" he rasped.

"Kill me," she spat, her blood running in rivulets down her face and spreading on the pure white shirt. "No one is going to stop you. Kill me!" She fought back the tears that stung her eyes. "And I tell you now, I welcome this death. But then again, that shouldn't surprise you. After all, I'm my mother's daughter. But remember one thing. She preferred death to being away from you. But I . . . I *long* for the next world to get away from you."

Elizabeth's eyes teared in anger. Wiping her hand across her bloodied cheek, she smeared it on her father's doublet as he stared at her. "People said she took her life with her own hands. The truth is that the stain of her blood, the guilt for her suicide, lies with you. And it has marked you for life. So go ahead. Kill me. Add another chain to the bonds that await you in hell. Go ahead, murderer. *Kill me!*"

Repulsed, Sir Thomas shoved Elizabeth away from him. His hands moved up to his temples as he tried to stop the pounding in his head. He still remembered that grim day so long ago when he'd walked away from his beloved Catherine. She'd stopped him by the door, a sword in her hand, and had begged for him to end her life. She loved him truly. Looking into her tearful eyes, he had known that for certain. But he had simply taken the sword from her trembling hand and walked out the door. Three years later, her servant had found her dead in the same room, her wrists slashed. And Thomas Boleyn knew—he had always known—that Catherine Valmont was the only woman who had ever loved him.

Elizabeth stood a step away. The pain and burning in her face didn't come close to the hurt and anger that she felt in her heart. "Draw your sword. Kill me where I stand." Her body shook as she moved toward him, reaching for his sword. "Come, I'll die with a smile. I welcome death over the future you planned for me."

"Get away from me!" he screamed, pushing her away again.

Elizabeth stumbled, righting herself as she saw the tent flap push open.

Madame Exton and the soldier stared, astonished by the sight before them. Before they could react, Elizabeth ran past them, pushing her cousin into the stack of boxes by the door.

Out into the night air she bolted, running blindly as her eyes adjusted to the darkness.

"Stop her!" Elizabeth heard the hysteria in her cousin's shrieking voice. *"After her, you fool!"*

Pressing her hand hard against the gash along her cheekbone, Elizabeth raced down the alley. The shout of the squire and Madame Exton's raging screams rang out behind her, but she never paused as she ran. She could feel the blood running through her fingers, but she dared not stop to tend it. Flying along the torchlit way, Elizabeth glanced back, catching sight of the soldier chasing after her. Turning corner after corner, she raced frantically in the direction of the clusters of French tents.

She couldn't let them catch her. Despite all that she had tried to do, Elizabeth knew if she was caught, Madame Exton would make sure Sir Thomas's plans were carried out. Elizabeth knew, with a certainty that seethed in the pit of her stomach, she would be lying with King Henry before the next sunset. She knew her guardian would see to it.

Panic swept through her as Elizabeth realized that her father's squire was gaining on her. A grove of trees beyond the next line of shimmering tents marked the division between the rival countries' courts, but Elizabeth suddenly felt weak, fearing she wouldn't make it to the tents beyond. She could hear the soldier's rasping breaths and pounding footsteps closing in.

Rounding a sharp bend, Elizabeth ducked between two large pavilions. They were deserted, but both were too well lit with torches to provide a hiding place. Pausing, she listened to her heart pounding so loudly she thought it would surely give her away. At the sound of the pursuer's footsteps, she held her breath and listened as he passed by. Then, by the light of the rising moon, she worked her way along the back of two more tents until she found herself at the edge of the wooded grove. Stepping into the shadows of the overhanging trees, Elizabeth paused to catch her breath.

Assessing her situation, she peered down in the dimness at her bloody hands. Her entire body ached. Her lips were puffy and sore, a good match for the swollen cheek her father had given her that afternoon, but what really concerned her was the stinging, throbbing cut that continued to bleed profusely. She would have a scar, she was sure. He'd marked her. Her own father.

Elizabeth looked up at the moonlit sky. Her problems were just beginning. She needed to get away from this place. But how? Everything she possessed was in the tent that she shared with Mary. All her worldly possessions, she thought, her derisive chuckle turning quickly into a wince of pain. Which meant her paints. But Madame Exton would be waiting for her. Elizabeth was certain of that. The only chance she had was to get a message to Mary. If she could just get her sister to meet her in secret. The ember of an idea was glowing teasingly in the corner of her mind.

The sound of raised voices somewhere nearby startled Elizabeth, and she crouched low in the covering darkness. Whomever the voices belonged to, they were not far from where she'd taken refuge. Elizabeth's first thought was to back out of the grove, but then a familiar voice caught her attention. Creeping forward through the underbrush, she soon spotted the flickering beam of a covered lamp. Following the glimmer of light and the murmuring voices, Elizabeth found herself on the edge of a small glade, and in the middle stood two men, one much larger than the other. He was speaking, and she recognized him instantly. The lamp shone faintly on them from a nearby stump.

"How dare you question me now?" Peter Garnesche growled angrily. "After all this time. Years."

"Then tell me what was said," the other man's voice broke in. "You cannot suddenly begin keeping things from us. We know your king met with the envoys of Charles. I need the details."

"I don't know what was said."

"You can find out. Don't play games with me, Garnesche. We know your tentacles reach into every corner of that English court."

"My sources provided nothing. I could find no information." The man's voice lowered to a dangerous drawl. "You will just have to accept my word for it."

"Your word?" Elizabeth knew that sneering voice. He was a Frenchman. She wracked her brain. From court. Someone from . . . Elizabeth remembered. The Lord Constable! The French king's counselor.

"You doubt me?" Garnesche scowled. "Do I have to remind you that it is in your best interest to continue relying on me? After all, who else could you find with such a wealth of useful information as I provide?"

Elizabeth watched as the Lord Constable studied the giant before him.

"I must admit what you say is true. We have been able to count on you in the past. And yes, we have watched you cut your own countrymen's throats. Naturally, that has occurred only when it suited you. When it improved your own stature with your king." The accusation was clear in the man's tone.

"I know what you're referring to." Garnesche glared menacingly at him. "The Duke of Buckingham was a pompous fool who spoke against me before the king in the Star Chamber. He was going to pay for that anyway. It just happened to be his misfortune that his claim to the throne was as good as Henry's."

"A circumstance that you were delighted to use to put

his head on the chopping block." The Lord Constable's voice dripped with cynicism.

"And that bothers you, suddenly? You gained more out of that than I did." Garnesche paused, but hearing no response from the Frenchman, he continued. "It was Buckingham who was pushing the hardest for an alliance between England and the Emperor Charles. It didn't take much prodding to make Henry think the two were in league together to take the crown away from him."

Elizabeth's mind flashed back to the year before, when the shocking news of the English nobleman's execution had swept across Europe. It had been the talk of every court in Christendom when the English king had imprisoned the mighty Duke of Buckingham on the charge of plotting to take his crown by force. Henry, lacking a legitimate heir, was acutely sensitive to any hint of revolt against his right to wear the crown. She recalled hearing the details from the endless stream of diplomats passing through her father's house: the accusations, the questionable witnesses, the trial by his peers, the finding of guilt despite his proclamations of loyalty. She recalled most clearly the talk of Buckingham's grisly execution. And now she knew what was behind it all. Now she knew who had caused it to come about.

"How you must have smiled to see Buckingham's neck go under the executioner's ax."

"His conviction for treason set back the alliance between England and the Holy Roman Empire two years, Constable. It was what you and your king wanted, and it was what you got. Why, even now the Emperor Charles must tread lightly with Henry. And it is due to me."

"Yes. It was due to you." The Lord Constable's stony gaze was unwavering. "But we have watched how your friendship has recently blossomed once again with the English king, and it makes us lose confidence in your willingness to deal with us. In so many words, there are some among us who don't trust you."

"Don't generalize, you coward. What you mean is that *you* don't trust me!" Garnesche snapped. Elizabeth watched as he drew himself up to his full height. "You and I both know *you* are the only one who knows of my dealings on your behalf."

"I don't have to trust you. I employ you and I pay you

to do our bidding." The Lord Constable's voice was cold, his tone bordering on disdain.

Garnesche paused, slightly considering the other's words.

Elizabeth stood as still as a statue, all her own problems now totally forgotten. From what she could gather, Sir Peter Garnesche's employment by the French government was no short-term affair. Though she certainly had no love for England or its king, this was treachery of the vilest kind.

"I've told you that the king is going directly to Calais to meet with the Emperor Charles. Of what happened earlier, I can't say. But if you wish to see your precious treaties with England honored, then you had better move quickly and keep that alliance from happening."

"What do you expect me to do, attack your king?" the Lord Constable snapped. "I know you are low, but I tell you, we will not dishonor ourselves by killing anyone under a flag of truce. Even if he is the King of England."

"This is all a farce." Garnesche took a step back. "Constable, I grow sick of you and your whining demands. I tell you what must be done, but do you ever do it? Nay, you lack the stomach for real action. Barbaric. Inhumane. Low. That's all I ever hear. Frenchman, you are a spineless coward."

"You are just a dog biting the hand that feeds him." The French nobleman stepped closer to the English knight and lifted his fist. "You are forcing me to put you in your place, and I, too, am growing tired of this game. Don't forget what happened to Buckingham. Treason. It cost him his head. The same could happen to you. But where the charge against him was false, yours will be well deserved."

"No one can bear witness to such an accusation. No one knows—"

"No one but me, traitor. And that's enough."

"Henry won't believe you."

"Fool, you have forgotten my connections."

Garnesche's hand came up so quickly that the Constable was lifted off the ground as the knight's viselike grip closed over his windpipe. The abrupt gurgling sound that the Frenchman emitted was quickly lost in his thrashing struggle for release.

Grasping his foe's wrist with one hand, he struck at the Englishman's face with the other. A cut opened on the bridge of Sir Peter's nose, and the Lord Constable struck at it again and again.

But the knight was not to be undone, and Elizabeth watched in horror as Garnesche slid his dagger easily from its sheath and drove the point upward into the bowels of the struggling Frenchman.

Unable to cry out, the Lord Constable writhed in silent agony as the knight twisted the blade about, tearing the life from the nobleman.

Elizabeth took a step back as she watched the final twitching moments of the most powerful counselor in France. The bile climbed into her throat as she espied the cruel, maniacal grin that crept across Sir Peter Garnesche's dark and bloodied face. He was mad. Truly mad.

Stepping back again, Elizabeth looked about her in the darkness. She had to get help. As she began to push through the undergrowth, the dragging hem of the kilt caught on the splintered branch of a fallen tree. She could see the giant murderer through the foliage, glancing about him as he lowered the Lord Constable's corpse to the ground. Panic struck at her heart as he wiped the blood from his flashing blade on the velvet cloak of the dead man. What if he came her way? What if he found her here?

Yanking at the kilt, Elizabeth stumbled backward as the cloth gave way with a loud ripping tear. Garnesche's head whipped around as she sat motionless and silent amid the soft green ferns. But she didn't sit for long.

The knight took a step in her direction, and Elizabeth was off through the woods, scrambling on all fours through the undergrowth. Bramble bushes and young saplings slapped at her face as she struggled to her feet. Throwing wild glances over her shoulder, she ran frantically through the dark glade. Flashes of light from a dying moon mixed in swirling confusion with the dark of the passing trees. Chaos had taken over her world, and Elizabeth felt her energy slipping away. Valiantly, she fought hard to keep down the sobs she felt rising in her chest. They were robbing her of her power to run. But on she ran anyway.

She could hear nothing from behind her over the sound

of her own pulse, pounding thunderously in her head. Then, as she turned to look for her pursuer, Elizabeth suddenly found herself tumbling in air, only to land with a sickening thud in the soft earth at the bottom of a diverted streambed.

She couldn't move. She couldn't breathe. She was lying facedown in the blackness of the hollow. Short, velvety leaves were brushing against her face, and her eyes were gradually focusing on the spears of dark grass that rose up and limited her field of vision. One ear was pressed to the ground, and she thought she could hear the dull thumps of receding footsteps. But, convinced briefly that she was in the last moments of life, she thought it probably the sound of her own failing heart.

She couldn't die. Images of her two sisters flickered in her brain. What would happen to them? With a massive effort, Elizabeth tried to take a breath. Painfully, the air pushed into her lungs as she rolled slightly to one side. Her left arm, she realized, was stretched out above her head. It was numb, though she only knew it when the dull pins-and-needles feeling started to creep into the limb, spreading gradually and more sharply from her shoulder to her fingers. Pulling herself slowly to a sitting position, Elizabeth lay her head on her upraised knees and attempted to take deeper and deeper breaths. Slowly, her senses returned to her, and only the throbbing in her shoulder remained. Flexing her arm, she knew nothing was broken, but she felt as if she'd been kicked by a mule.

Then she looked about her. The wooded glade was eerily silent and dark as death. She thought briefly of the Lord Constable. Of Garnesche. Her panic had disappeared, but a cold fear remained in the pit of her stomach. Pushing herself to her feet, she cocked an ear in the direction she thought she'd come, but there was no sound. Carefully, Elizabeth clambered to the top of the embankment and quietly pushed through the shrubs until abruptly she found herself standing on the worn path between the French and English encampments.

A young page boy eyed Elizabeth curiously as he passed. The sky to the east was just taking on the deep, purplish blue that preceded the dawn, and the air had the sharp tang of an early summer morn. Elizabeth looked up and down the path. A few late revelers were wandering along, and she stood a moment, undecided as to which way to go. Finally she made up her mind and started hurriedly down the path, looking over her shoulder at the graying canopies of the morning camp.

But she'd only taken a few steps when she slammed into the human wall that blocked her way.

Peter Garnesche stood before her.

Chapter 6

❦

Elizabeth recoiled in shock. Her breath caught in her chest.

Peter Garnesche silently watched the battered woman before him. He reached out and took hold of her chin. Despite her flinching response, he turned it to the light of the nearby torch. Elizabeth Boleyn's face was covered with blood. From the gash on her cheek that still oozed, he was certain her injury was recent. Looking down at her garment, a menacing sneer crept over the man's face.

"I'll have to remember to congratulate the Scot." Garnesche let his hand drop. "He is a better man than I thought."

Elizabeth tried not to look back at him or at his attire. In her mind's eye she could still see the Lord Constable's blood spilling darkly on the ground. She was sure the man's doublet must be spattered with it. She wondered if the hand that a moment ago held her chin was stained red as well. The smell of death suddenly permeated the air.

"I like this," the man continued. "Humility at last from the biggest prude in Europe. I never imagined that you liked it rough."

Elizabeth took a small, hesitant step back. Another group of drunken soldiers was approaching them, working their way back to their camp. Suddenly it occurred to her that the English knight had not connected her with the crime he'd committed moments earlier. She took another half step back, but Garnesche's hand shot out and grabbed her by the tartan, checking her retreat.

Elizabeth's blood ran cold in her veins, and the young woman glanced quickly and cautiously at the man's face. His eyes were not on her. Even though it looked as though he were conversing with her, his gaze was searching the faces of those passing by. But the men hardly gave them a second glance, and Garnesche looked back down at her, a foul gleam in his eye. Her blood ran colder yet.

"This is getting better and better." He smirked, pulling Elizabeth roughly to his chest. "Who would have thought that I could take a lesson from the Scot?"

Elizabeth turned her face at once as the man's foul mouth tried to close on hers. Instead of a taste of her lips, Garnesche's mouth roughly descended on her open cut. She cried out in pain. "Let me go," she whispered through clenched teeth.

"Where, my pretty?" His hands roughly grabbed at her breast through the baggy shirt. "We're just getting started."

Elizabeth struggled to get out of the man's grasp. "I'm . . . I'm his leftover, damn it. You don't want me."

Garnesche pushed her roughly against a nearby tree and moved after her. "Oh, I do want you, you arrogant bitch. In fact, I've always wanted to feel you writhe beneath me. I just can't see why I've waited so long."

"He'll kill you." Elizabeth moved swiftly to the side and escaped the madman's clutching grip. Turning quickly, she now had the path to her back. But she knew her speed was nothing compared to the English knight's. "I belong to Ambrose Macpherson. I slept with him. I'm his. Do you hear me?" She retreated as she spoke, but the man continued to follow. "He'll kill you if you touch me."

"That is, if he is alive after I'm done with him," the French voice growled.

The sound of the man behind her jerked Elizabeth around. The Duc de Bourbon stood a step away, his eyes blazing with anger.

Elizabeth stopped dead in her tracks. She'd never been happier seeing anyone in her whole life than at this moment. But the young nobleman's grim expression stopped her from showing any sign of it.

"How interesting." Peter Garnesche moved in behind her. "So much chivalry over a fallen maid."

Elizabeth stepped aside as the Englishman put a hand on his great sword. She was relieved to see five of Bourbon's men appear suddenly behind the young man. For one thing, the Duc de Bourbon never traveled alone. Elizabeth knew that from the past encounters. She remembered someone once telling her that a number of husbands had hired a band of fighters and put a prize on the handsome nobleman's head. It was about that time that the duc had started traveling with an entourage.

"She left the Scot's bed. I'm next in line." Garnesche leered in Elizabeth's direction. "When I'm finished with her, I'll send her to you. But I can promise you that it won't be for quite some time."

Elizabeth started to back away in small steps from the group and in the direction of the French quarter.

Bourbon ignored the Englishman altogether.

"You look a bloody mess, Elizabeth," he said. Pain showed in the Frenchman's handsome face. "Was I too gentle? Is this what you were after? A brute? Someone who would abuse you?"

Elizabeth shook with anger, pain, fear. How could she explain? She was alone. No one believed her, nor trusted her. She could tell Bourbon of what the Englishman had done, about the Lord Constable's body, but even the six of them might prove no match for this giant and whatever soldiers he could call for. If they failed to take the knight, he would know it was she who had witnessed the crime and heard the discussion of his treachery. But it was not only her own life that she feared for now. It was Mary's and young Anne's. Both would be prey for this vindictive madman.

"So you have nothing to say?" Bourbon's accusing voice cut in on Elizabeth's thoughts. "Will you just stand there and admit that you've been nothing more than a common whore?"

Elizabeth looked from one hardened face to the next. The Englishman stood a step away from the duc. The same distance he'd stood from the Lord Constable before cutting him down.

She took one last look at the duc. Her throat was tight as she straightened before his angry glare. "You are nothing to me. Do you understand? I don't have to explain a thing to you. Just leave me be." Elizabeth turned and ran. Ran as fast and as far as her tired legs could take her.

The Franciscan friar Father Matthew shook out the straw from his gray habit and rubbed his face to make sure he was awake. This is unbelievable, he thought, as Elizabeth ceased speaking. He must still be dreaming.

Beneath the loft where he sat, the horses crowded into the shed were shuffling hungrily. Unfolding his long, lanky frame, the friar tried to ignore the rumbling in his own empty stomach and concentrate on the story he'd just been told. This poor child needed his help, and he knew he'd be needing all his faculties to help her. He looked tenderly at Elizabeth's troubled and battered face. Washing the dried blood had not improved the looks of things. He cringed to think that she might need a needle to close the gash on her cheek. She would be scarred for life. Friar Matthew had known this generous young woman for a long time. Why, he still had the leftover gold from the ring she'd given him in the pouch bumping gently against his thigh.

Beatings, a father prostituting his own daughters, treason, murder. It was too unbelievable. He'd helped his flock in the area outside Paris with many problems in his many years as a priest—the hungry farmer who poached the king's deer to feed his family; the apprentice boy who got the landlord's willing daughter with child; the girl caught learning to read against her father's wishes; and a thousand other matters—but never had he been called on to deal with issues of this enormity, of this magnitude. Silently sending a prayer heavenward, he took a deep breath and let out a sigh.

"First, my child, we must decide if you are in any immediate danger." He sat down again on the straw. "Is there anything that you left behind that could lead the Englishman to you?"

She shook her head. "No, I don't think so, Friar." Gravely, Elizabeth thought for a moment. "Nothing that has to do with the murder."

"Thank God for that much, anyway."

"We have to let someone know about the Lord Constable," Elizabeth whispered as she stood and moved to the shuttered loft window. An odd breeze had picked up outside, rattling the wooden shutter. "We must expose Sir Peter as the murderer."

"I don't see how we can. At least not right now. That would certainly be the end of your life." Father Matthew paused and then blurted out his concerns. "It is not just

Garnesche that you will need to watch out for. Think of all his friends and allies in the English court. They will readily believe him when he says you are accusing him falsely. And then you'll be their target. You—and your family—will be the enemy. We must consider the risk to your sisters."

Surprised, Elizabeth turned toward the friar. Looking at the man's somber expression, she had to agree. Who was she, after all? She was more a member of the French court than the English. Born of an unwed French mother, raised so far from London. Everything Friar Matthew had said was true. Who would listen to her? Who would protect them? She couldn't trust even her own father. "I could send a message about the murder. No one ever need know whom it came from."

The priest shook his head in disagreement. "You don't know much about the king's justice, my child. The Lord Constable's death will undoubtedly be blamed on some passing beggar. Anything you say will be ignored right now because King Francis does not want war with England. So no Frenchman would dare accuse an Englishman of the murder of the Lord Constable without absolute proof."

Elizabeth returned to where the friar sat. "How can we let an innocent man's death go unavenged?"

Friar Matthew moved quietly, taking hold of her hand and nodding toward the Golden Vale.

"Out that window ten thousand wealthy men and women are sleeping comfortably in tents made of cloth of gold. But look beyond the vale, as I know you have, and you can see a million peasants and villagers living in the squalor of poverty. You're safe here right now because no one even imagines that any noblewoman would dirty her shoes in the muck of this stable."

Friar Matthew lowered his eyes and continued. "Elizabeth, the Lord Constable was no innocent. He was haughty and brutal and indifferent to the suffering of the poor. He was one of the worst. Everything he ever did was for the benefit of his fellow nobles. I believe he cared nothing for the real France, for the poor and hungry that populate every town and hamlet."

Elizabeth thought back of the few passing encounters she'd had with the Lord Constable. She'd really never known much about him. "Are you telling me his death will cause more celebration than grief?"

"Perhaps, my dear. Though he was no champion of the people, I think the peasants of France would celebrate his death only if they thought one of their own had done the bloody deed." The friar smiled grimly at her. "But you and I both know that is really beside the point. What the English knight did was treacherous and evil."

Elizabeth gathered her knees to her chest and rested her pounding forehead against them. At this time yesterday, her problems had been so much simpler. Other than thinking of a way to raise money for Mary's doctor, Elizabeth had been in control. What a mess things had become, she thought. "What am I to do?"

Father Matthew racked his brain—and his heart—for some inspiration, for some guidance. "First we must get you out of here. There must be someplace in Paris where you can go. Your father's house, perhaps."

"I can't." She shook her head violently. "I can never go back. He'll be waiting for me. I'm sure by now Madame Exton has convinced my father that everything I said was nothing but a lie. I just can't go back and wait to see whom he will try to sell me to next."

"What about your mother's family? There are certainly plenty of those left with enough money to feed the whole country."

Elizabeth shuddered at the thought of putting herself at the mercy of strangers she'd never met in her life. They had thrown her mother on the street with a babe in her arms. She could never ask them for help. "Never. I'll never ask for their charity. That's out of the question."

The friar paused. This was becoming difficult.

"The Duc de Bourbon! How about him?"

"I think he would probably take in a stray dog before he'd give me shelter." Elizabeth sighed quietly. "But that's probably for the best. He's always wanted something more than friendship from me, but now I'm sure we can't even be friends." Though he'd often tried, Bourbon had never become intimate with her. She had never allowed it. The closest they'd ever come was after a banquet last summer, when the young duc had tried to kiss away her defenses under a moonlit sky. She had escaped his attentions then and never allowed him so close again.

He was a friend and nothing more. But tonight, during those brief but incredible moments in Ambrose Macpherson's tent, Elizabeth had for the first time tasted the sweet, dizzying nectar of passion.

"Your choices are becoming more limited, Elizabeth," the friar pointed out, patting her hand. Then he brightened. "What about Sir Ambrose? He seemed to be interested."

Elizabeth blushed. She hadn't told the friar just how interested the Scot was. She also had carefully avoided telling him just how close she'd come to giving her virginity away. Elizabeth shivered unexpectedly at the thought of the man who had awakened feelings in her that she'd never before experienced. How tenderly he had caressed her. She could even now feel his lips upon her skin.

"You never told me how you came to be wearing his clothes."

"I . . . I borrowed them." She had not told Friar Matthew of visiting the Scot before going to her father. "I took them from his tent. It was much easier traveling through the encampment dressed as a man." Well, that was partly true.

The friar looked directly at the young woman. She was not telling him everything about the Highlander, but that was not what they needed to focus on right now.

"Then why not go to him for help? He's a generous man with a noble heart. And he has the resources to protect you from your father and Garnesche."

If life were a dream with no guilt and no consequences, Ambrose Macpherson's side would be the very place she would go. But the world she lived in was one in which the outcome of such a fantasy would undoubtedly bring betrayal and unhappiness. It was the way of the world. Elizabeth's hand unconsciously moved to her face. She did not have to see her wound to know she was disfigured for life. The Highlander would not even look at her. No man would want to look at her.

And then it occurred to her that this suited her plans. Quite nicely, in fact. The young woman straightened. Gazing down at the kilt that she still wore, Elizabeth brightened.

"Then you agree." The friar clapped his hands, seeing his young friend's face shed its grim expression.

Elizabeth bounced to her feet and moved to a bundle of worn clothing the friar had dropped in the corner of the loft. "I'll go to Italy."

"Who is in Italy?" the priest asked, watching in amazement as the young woman unfolded each item and held it against her frame.

"Some of these will fit!"

"Those are twice your size." The holy man leaped to his feet, moving quickly toward her. "Wh-what are you planning to do, Elizabeth?"

She ignored his question as she continued measuring the clothing. "But no more than twice. And some are quite . . . hmm."

"Young woman . . ." He didn't like the look in her eyes.

Elizabeth reached over and put her hands on the priest's shoulder, turning him toward the ladder. "Please get me a very sharp knife and some water."

The man dug his heels into the soft straw flooring. "I'm not going anywhere unless you tell me what you are up to."

"I will not tell you anything unless you go and get me those things." Elizabeth looked the priest squarely in the eye.

The friar stood a moment longer. Then, realizing he simply hadn't the heart to add to this innocent child's troubles, Friar Matthew grudgingly gave in and climbed down the ladder of the loft, muttering a complaint at every rung of his descent.

Chapter 7

❧

The man needed his face rearranged.

As the first rays of light crept across the roof of his tent, Ambrose pulled his traveling clothes out of the leather pack. Wrapping his kilt about him, he found himself getting angry again at the thought of the abusive Duc de Bourbon. The bloody bastard. Why was it that so many fine women put up with such treatment?

He had lain awake for what had remained of the night after Elizabeth left his tent. His thoughts had centered on her. Ambrose Macpherson had spent his entire life not wanting to get tied down to any place or to any woman. He liked his life. He enjoyed his independence. He could come and go. And he could pick and choose among the best, the bonniest. Ambrose enjoyed sampling, taking, and pampering the women he crossed paths with. But like a bee approaching any delicate flower, he liked to taste and then move on. After all, the world was filled with them. And why should he settle for one, when he could have so many?

Last night, though, had been bothersome. Ambrose forced himself to admit that Elizabeth's broken condition had been the cause. Damn the Duc de Bourbon, he thought.

The Highlander slammed his fist into his palm, then made a conscious effort to shake off the emotion. Such thoughts did no one any good. But perhaps before leaving for Boulogne, he would pay a visit to the amorous duc.

"Mac*pherson*!" the French voice shouted angrily from outside the tent. "Come out, you dog!"

Ambrose stiffened, recognizing at once the Duc de Bourbon's voice and the challenge in his words. Striding quickly across the tent, he threw open the flap and stepped out into the windy morning. The duc and five of his men were standing in the empty alleyway.

When the French nobleman saw the Scot, bare-chested and unarmed, come out of the tent, he quickly unbuckled his sword and tossed it to the retainer standing behind him. It was bad enough that Macpherson had bedded Elizabeth, but roughing her up the way he had was beyond endurance. And marking her face. He would pay dearly for that. The rage that had been seething, building within Bourbon since she ran, suddenly boiled over as the duc moved across the alley.

They were both large men, and when they collided in the middle, the ground shook with the impact.

Ambrose connected solidly with the nose of the duc, and Bourbon's head snapped back even as his fist fell like a hammer on the ear of the Scot. Either blow would have felled a lesser opponent, but the two men hardly flinched as they continued to attack each other with a violence so sudden and so unrestrained that it surprised even the trained fighters looking on.

The fury continued unabated, the warriors battering unmercifully at one another until suddenly the duc was lying dazed on the ground, blood spewing from his flattened nose. Ambrose stood over him, a raging pulse pounding in his brain. "Get up, you coward."

Bourbon looked up at the giant warrior through a haze. He pushed himself groggily to a sitting position. "I'll kill you before I ever let you touch her like that again."

"You are the one that needs to die, knave." Ambrose took a step back to give the man room to stand on his feet. He was not done with him. "How does it feel to get a taste of your own treatment?"

The French nobleman stood unsteadily and took a swing at the Highlander's face. "You cut her. You marked her for life, you animal."

The man's fist went wide of Ambrose's face by quite a distance, and then Bourbon once again lay flat on the ground.

In an instant the Scottish knight was standing over the Frenchman. One of Bourbon's men took a half step toward the two, but then backed off at the threatening glare of the Scot.

"What do you mean, *I* cut her?" Ambrose put his boot squarely on his adversary's chest. "You're the one who beats her for nothing."

Bourbon grabbed the boot and threw Ambrose to the ground. Scrambling on top of him, he grabbed the Scot by the throat. "Me? I've . . . I've never laid a hand on Elizabeth. Do you hear me? Never. I've admired and respected her since the time she was only a girl. I've even hoped to have her hand in marriage. We French take care of our women, you mountain pig. We don't beat them."

Ambrose pushed the man off of him and leaped nimbly to his feet. In an instant, Bourbon followed suit. Suddenly Ambrose had a gut feeling that his adversary was speaking the truth. "She came to me with a swollen face." He ducked, avoiding another punch thrown by Bourbon. "I was perfectly justified in assuming it was you who did it. Have you forgotten how angry you became when I asked about her earlier? I thought you had punished her for my attentions."

"If you knew her better, you scoundrel, you would understand that she is not one to be owned or punished or made use of in any form. She is a woman of character and talent. But before I grind you into the dirt, just tell me why did you do that to her. You slept with her. Why did you have to cut her?"

Ambrose reached out and grabbed Bourbon on the throat. "I did no such thing, you blackguard. She left my tent in the same condition as she arrived."

"She wore your tartan!"

"So she did."

"Then you admit you slept with her!"

"That is none of your business," Ambrose growled.

"I'm making it my business!"

"No one has given you the right." Ambrose increased the pressure on Bourbon's throat. "Where is she now?"

Bourbon pushed the Highlander's hands away. "There is no need for you to know where she's gone. You've used her as you use all your women. Just move on and throw out your line for the next catch."

"I'm asking you a question." Ambrose once again moved toward the Frenchman. "Where is she?"

"She's no longer your concern. Not that I think she ever was!"

"Listen to me, you pigheaded dandy!" Ambrose shoved Bourbon back a pace and walked threateningly toward him. "Someone beat her up pretty badly before she came to me last night. And you are telling me that after she left here someone cut her face. You claim you didn't do it. Now try moving your brain from your codpiece to your head and think. She could still be in danger. Whoever did these things to her could do even more harm. Now, where did you see her last?"

Bourbon's thoughts went back to his last encounter with Elizabeth, his anger toward the Highlander dissipating like a morning fog. My God, he'd been so stunned by the words that he'd heard her say that he'd paid no attention to anything else. She wasn't just standing with Garnesche; she'd been trying to get away from him! And she had gotten away, he remembered.

Ambrose watched in silence as the nobleman's eyes cleared, finally comprehending the meaning of what was being said.

"Do you have a drink in there?" the Frenchman asked quietly.

"Aye." Ambrose nodded, leading a pensive Bourbon into the tent.

Chapter 8

❧

She had nothing to lose and everything to gain.

Well, she had to lose her name, her identity, her family. And most important of all, she had to lose her hair.

As Friar Matthew looked on aghast, Elizabeth sliced off her ebony locks in chunks, talking quickly as she worked.

Elizabeth laid out her plan for him. She would go to Florence. The Medici family was back in power and stability had returned to the prosperous city of art and culture.

She would find a place, working as an apprentice, or as a laborer if need be, with one of the great artists who resided there. Brilliant, old Leonardo was dead, but perhaps with Raphael. Or with the young genius Cellini. Perhaps, if the heavens smiled on her, she might secure employment in the shops of the great painter and sculptor Michelangelo Buonarroti.

As she talked, Friar Matthew recalled that his order was building a church on the outskirts of Florence. Elizabeth told him she would need a letter of introduction to the friars there so that she could show her talents—her ability to paint.

She would travel there under the guise of a young man, she would get work as a young man, and she would live as a young man. She could do it. Elizabeth knew she could.

Friar Matthew looked at her with incredulous eyes. Elizabeth talked as if she had prepared this masquerade for many years, and he told her his thoughts. Elizabeth admitted that what he said was true. She had dreamed of doing this, many times before. But all that planning, all that preparing, had only been a fantasy. A wonderful, unattainable dream.

The friar knew very well about Elizabeth's paintings. Over the years, she had worked so hard to become the proficient artist he knew her to be. He had seen so many of her works, and he knew she was good. More than good, he admitted. She was exceptional. It had been a pleasure to be her accomplice in supplying the poor village churches around Paris over the past two years with the magnificent religious portraits signed only "Phillipe."

Like any other artist, Elizabeth had needed an audience. A group that would respond to her choice of subject matter, to her composition, her color choices, and her uniquely individual style. Without a master that she could learn from, Friar Matthew's tidings had been an indispensable learning tool.

"I can't watch any more of this, Elizabeth!" Friar Matthew cried. "It's unnatural, I tell you!"

The black hair slipped in silken cascades to the floor of the loft.

"I'm almost finished," she said, casting an adventurous eye around at her friend. "I need you to tell me how the back looks."

"You look like a . . . like a boy . . . God help me!"

"Come, now, Friar. You're acting like an accomplice to murder."

"Well, that's exactly how I feel," he moaned. "I feel as if I've just helped murder a lovely young woman who came to me for help."

"Such foolishness," she scolded gently, standing and straightening out her well-worn attire. She pulled an oversized cap over her newly cropped locks. Spying the friar's look of shock, she removed it for the moment. "Friar, this is nothing compared to what is yet to come. I'm just starting."

"I heard everything you just said, Elizabeth. But what we've done with your paintings is far different than what you are asking now. It is one thing to take a beautiful piece of artwork and hang it in a church for everyone to admire. But cutting your hair, dressing in these men's clothes, traveling God knows where . . . it's just too . . . well, too drastic! When I was encouraging the development of your talent in the past, my conscience was at ease knowing that you were protected from exposure. I knew you were in no danger so long as you were under your father's roof. But this has already gone too far."

"I see. You heard my plan, but you think I shouldn't go through with it." Elizabeth looked him challengingly in the eye. "What choice do I have, Friar? You've always told me that we must look beyond the trials of our lives. That we must forge ahead."

"I suppose I should have known better." The friar rolled his eyes. "Now I'm at the mercy of my own words!"

She scowled fiercely at her friend. "Well, do I look convincing?"

"Well, you sound convincing," he murmured under his breath.

"That's a good start, anyway!"

Matthew looked at the transformation before him. Elizabeth truly looked like a young man. The layers of baggy clothes covered her feminine curves, and the black tresses now fell in handsome waves to a point above her shoulders. Her bruised and swollen face, now a bit cleaner, lacked the whiskers of a man, but the cut on her face would leave a scar that no courtly woman would wear openly—uncovered and unpainted. Even the way she was standing! So confident. So self-sufficient.

"Walking all the way to Florence. Living the life of a man." Friar Matthew shook his head gravely. "I tell you again, young woman. It's unnatural."

Elizabeth laughed. It seemed to her that it was the first time she'd laughed in a hundred years.

The priest sat heavily on the straw, thinking over the journey that lay ahead of her. He weighted his responsibilities. Who needed his help more, right now—his flock or his troubled young friend? Thinking of whether it would be possible for him to accompany her, he vacantly picked up the Macpherson plaid that lay neatly folded beside him. The wet shirt lay beneath it. She had used the remainder of the water he'd brought to wash the crimson stains out of the blood-soaked garment. Her blood, the friar thought, shaking his head. Elizabeth had asked him if he could somehow return these to the Scottish nobleman. But knowing the man's generosity, Friar Matthew wondered if it wouldn't be better just to give away the clothes to a needy family.

"So, then. You think if I walked out in the open, dressed like this, the Florentines would think I'm a man?"

Hearing no answer to her question, Elizabeth turned in the direction of the friar. He was sitting with the Macpherson plaid in his hands, his face devoid of all color.

"What's wrong?" Elizabeth asked, hurrying to his side.

Friar Matthew held out the kilt that she'd been wearing earlier. "Do you know where this happened?"

Elizabeth stared at the torn hem of the garment. A large section of the plaid was missing, and she knew exactly where it was. She raised her eyes to meet his.

"In the woods, right after the murder. It was dark. There was a tree branch. You don't think he'll go back?"

"If he does, and if he finds the plaid, then he'll recognize it for sure and remember who was wearing it." The friar's face was grave. "And when that happens, Elizabeth, he'll come after you."

Elizabeth stared as her heart sank like a stone into the pit of her stomach.

"That means I have no time. I have to go." Elizabeth's eyes darted to the friar's face. She twisted the cap in her hands as she wrestled with her feelings. "But first I must warn my sisters. Would he harm them to get to me?"

"Only if he thinks you are in contact with them."

Below them, the horses in the stable were becoming perceptibly nervous and active. The whinnying caught the attention of the two friends, and then Elizabeth caught the scent that was being carried along on the strengthening wind. Fire.

Pushing against the stiff breeze, Elizabeth opened the shutter, and the two looked out. Over the encampment across the Golden Vale, black smoke was billowing up and racing across the tops of the tents. Something was burning, and Elizabeth felt a cold fear drive sharply into her belly. She and the friar exchanged a quick look, and then they turned hurriedly toward the ladder. Scrambling down from the loft, Elizabeth was off at a dead run, with the friar hot on her heels.

"Wait! You can't forget this," Friar Matthew called before Elizabeth could slip out the door.

The young woman paused an instant, and the friar

handed over the large hat. She pulled it hurriedly on her head, yanking it as low as she could over her eyes.

"We have to be careful. This could be a trap," Matthew cautioned, and Elizabeth nodded. Then together they dashed out into the early morning light.

Working their way through the horde of peasants now awake and moving about, the two hurried around the stockade barrier of the tournament field. Scores of poor still sat huddled against the wooden fence that for the past month had separated the peasants from the nobility.

Certainly no one could be left sleeping in the encampment, Elizabeth thought. In spite of the late-night revelry, everyone, it seemed, was awake and active in the face of the raging fire that appeared ready to engulf the entire English sector of the Field of Cloth of Gold.

Elizabeth and the friar ran past the companies of soldiers already hauling water in buckets of wood and leather. Some were even using steel helmets—anything to slow the crackling flames that the warm, dry breeze was pushing along.

The smoke became thicker as the two worked their way into the throng of gentility milling about in the alleyways. Nearing the source of the conflagration, Elizabeth looked wildly about at the panic-stricken crowds scattering before the hot sparks and thick, black smoke that was engulfing the area on the currents of the shifting wind.

"Mary!" Elizabeth gasped as they pushed through the mob. She looked ahead at the half dozen blazing tents. "She was in my tent. That's my tent." Her hands tried to open a path, pushing at the people ahead of her. She needed to get closer. But they were pressing in from all sides. Someone shoved a bucket into her hands; it was full of water. She held it tightly. A man in front tried to pry it away, but she wouldn't budge. Elizabeth knew she had to get to the front. Oh, please God, don't let her be hurt. "Mary!" she called at the top of her lungs. The shouts of the jostling men drowned out her words. She felt the crowd move. They were moving closer to the fire, and she let herself become part of that moving mass. Glancing around her, Elizabeth saw the friar a short distance behind. They were separated, but he was still there.

One instant she was blocked by a wall of human bodies all around, the next she was in the front row, preparing to throw the water on the burning blaze. It was her tent. The heat from the blaze was scorching the skin of her face, and the roar was deafening. Throwing the water on the flaming material, she took a step closer, then put an arm over her face as she prepared to run inside. Above her, she could see the fiery roof of the tent flapping in the grip of the wind. Beside her someone was chopping at one of the lines that held the shelter up.

If the tent collapses, Elizabeth thought wildly, Mary will be trapped in the flames. She started forward.

A hand from behind gripped her arm, holding her back. She cringed at the pain that suddenly shot down her arm from her injured shoulder. She squirmed, yanking herself free. The hand took hold of her again. She turned her head to see the one holding her. It was the friar. He was shouting, but Elizabeth could not hear him at all. Following his eyes, though, as he turned his head, she could see the cloaked figure standing amid the crowd of onlookers.

Mary.

Elizabeth let him draw her back into the crowd. Working her way toward her sister, she gave one last look in the direction of what remained of the tent. Mary was alive. Elizabeth rejoiced at the thought, wondering in the next moment how her sister had escaped. But as they pushed through the crowd, a lump rose in her throat at the idea of having lost so much. Glancing at the burning tents around her, she considered the losses that others were suffering. And she wondered if this had all started because of what she'd witnessed.

Nearing the place where Mary was standing, Elizabeth was opening her mouth to call out to her when a massive arm struck her brusquely on the side of the head.

"Make way," the rough voice shouted as the giant knight cleared his own path through the swarm of humanity.

Elizabeth stumbled to the side as Peter Garnesche passed by. She stopped dead, gaping after him. Sir Peter strode to a group of three soldiers who were busily surveying the faces in the crowd. Nodding his head curtly as he spoke, he said something to them that Elizabeth, though only a few paces away, could not hear. Then, turning sharply, he shoved his way through the crowd to another group of his men. His face was dark and smudged with soot, and his hard eyes darted from one face to the next as he went.

They're looking for me, Elizabeth thought in a flash of panic as she exchanged a quick glance with Friar Matthew. The priest's brow furrowed with anxiety.

Elizabeth tugged the hat down further over her eyes and peered over to where her sister stood. As she did, she saw Mary, the cloak of her hood pulled low, turn and melt into the crowd beyond.

Elizabeth saw Garnesche's men approaching. They were everywhere, searching the faces of everyone they could lay hands on.

It was then that Friar Matthew took charge. "Pretend you can't breathe, Elizabeth. Your sister is safe. Now we have to get you out of here."

She looked at him wide-eyed.

"Double over."

Seeing the soldiers only a few paces away, Elizabeth followed the friar's order instantly. She knew the ploy of dressing as a man might not work with the Englishman's cronies. After all, Sir Peter had seen and recognized her wearing the Highlander's clothes the night before. And the still fresh wound on her cheek was sure to give her away. Garnesche had seen that cut as well, and Elizabeth was certain he would have mentioned it as an identification mark for his men.

"Clear the way. Out of the way, there," the friar shouted as he put his arm around her, pushing his way through the oncoming men. Elizabeth held on to her friend's cloak, all the while keeping her head down and allowing him to lead her. Anytime Matthew came across an immobile knot of people, Elizabeth gasped for air and emitted the most heart-wrenching cough she could muster.

Within a few moments, Elizabeth could tell they were leaving the dense throng for a more open area. With the exception of an occasional brush of a passing shoulder, she could no longer feel the press of bodies all around them. Still, she dared not look up, for fear of being recognized.

"I think we've passed the immediate danger," Friar Matthew said quietly, coming to a halt. "I want you to go back to the stables."

"I have to find Mary. She is out there . . . vulnerable."

Elizabeth looked around; there was no sign of her sister. They had stopped at a crossing of alleyways, but they were still in the English sector of tents.

"I'll go after her," he replied. "I saw the direction that she went. You go back, and I'll bring her to you."

"But—"

"This is no time to argue with me, child. By now there are probably a hundred English soldiers looking for a woman with a freshly cut face. You'll be safe among the peasants. They'll never think to search among the poor French wretches." The friar looked about him cautiously. "I give you my word I'll bring your sister to you. Now go."

Chapter 9

❧

If only I *were* a man, she thought.

Pushing against the streaming mass of humanity, Elizabeth moved down the cloth-walled alleys toward the open fields and the stable. She hardly dared to look up at the oncoming faces, for fear of being discovered. She knew she had to leave for Italy. It was her only escape. But she had to convince Friar Matthew that she could survive on her own. The friar's last words as they'd run toward the fires had been that he would not allow Elizabeth to go alone. Even if he could bring himself to believe she would be able to protect herself on the arduous road to Italy, he believed that she would need fellow travelers, with a female especially among her companions. He was certain that would improve Elizabeth's chances of traveling successfully in the guise of a young man.

But Elizabeth did not want to disrupt any more lives. She and the friar both knew that finding a trustworthy female companion who would want to travel to Italy right now was nearly impossible. The friar did not have to mention it, but Elizabeth knew that, in spite of all that was happening, he was already considering going with her. She'd seen it in his face. In fact, he probably was thinking of finding her a safe place—not in Italy, but rather in some remote French convent.

That wasn't the answer. She could not remain in hiding the rest of her life, idling away her time and letting someone else take care of her. She could not sit, a silent observer, while the world moved on without her.

Elizabeth looked up as a young peasant girl banged into her side. The girl murmured a word or two and continued on. But something in the innocent face of the child washed away the thought of her own problems and reminded Elizabeth of her youngest sister, Anne. She wondered where she had gotten to in the midst of the fiery chaos. Mary obviously had been able to escape Garnesche's wrath, but would the man stoop so low as to bring his fury to bear on a defenseless child?

Anne was smart, though. Even at her age, she was capable of outwitting those around her on nearly every occasion. Elizabeth knew that the young girl had already made a place for herself at the English queen's side. And she had a way with their father, as well. No, Anne would be fine. Elizabeth could let her mind rest on that score. But Mary was a different story. Whatever would become of her?

Glancing across the alley, she saw him first.

Ambrose's eyes roamed the crowd before him. Suddenly he spotted a figure traveling against the tide. For an instant their eyes locked. Then she looked hurriedly away and disappeared into the surging throng.

The Scottish warrior leaped into the alleyway, pushing across the current till he reached the other side. Far off, he saw the large, floppy hat ducking along the edge of the path, and he quickened his long strides, cutting the distance between them in no time.

Rounding a bend, Ambrose saw her throw an anxious look over her shoulder, but he had nearly caught up to her. So with a quick lunge, the Highlander grabbed the shoulder of his scurrying quarry. Elizabeth pulled hard against his grip, trying to free herself, but the Scottish knight was not about to let her go.

Pulling her with him, Ambrose backed into a small gap between two tents.

"Let me go!" Elizabeth struggled against him, but he only tightened his hold on her.

"Nay! I'll not let you go. Not until you tell me who it is that you are running away from."

"That's my business, not yours." She looked up just in time to see a mixture of sadness and anger flicker across his face as he studied the wound on her cheek. She could feel the heat of his gaze wash over her skin. She felt scorched.

"Who did this to you!"

Elizabeth felt the viselike grip of his fingers dig into

her shoulders. She could hear the strong note of anguish in his voice. Then she turned her head, hiding the ugly gash from his stare. "It doesn't matter. Please let me go."

"I won't!"

Ambrose's fingers gently moved up from her shoulders and framed her face. He turned her head until their eyes met. He felt the tremble that coursed through her.

"You're frightened."

Elizabeth shook her head, trying to deny it. But the welling up of tears in her eyes spoke the truth.

"Seeing what he's done to you . . . I can understand why you are frightened. Tell me who it is. Let me help you, Elizabeth. Let me protect you."

She felt the caress of his thumb against her skin. *Protect you.* The words drifted about her in a haze of emotion. Her skin was burning at his touch, and she felt the heat shoot downward until it washed over her heart.

She fought to keep her mind clear. What was it about this man that gave him the power to wash away all the troubles that surrounded her, all the tribulations that were, right now, threatening her very life? "I'm marked forever. . . ."

She didn't know why she spoke those words. It was not like her. But Ambrose's attention made her feel vulnerable. Exposed. She did not have to look at herself to know what her wound must look like to a man. He had to be appalled, disgusted. After all, women were to be pleasing to the eye. And clearly, she was not. No, she would never be.

"We are a perfect match." He reached down and took hold of her fingers, raising them to his own forehead.

Elizabeth let her hands trace lightly over the scar.

"You are beautiful, Elizabeth." Ambrose reached up and pulled the cap off her head. His jaw dropped. "The devil . . . What have you done to yourself?"

"My lacerated face you find beautiful, but my shorn hair you do not?" she challenged.

"The first, I know, is the result of some brute's vicious act. But the second . . . this must be self-inflicted." Giving in to his impulse, he ran his hands through her short tresses. He actually liked the feel of them.

She shook off his unrestrained touch with the backs of

her hands. "Why do you do this if you find it so unattractive?"

"Who says I find it unattractive?" Ambrose's eyes fell on her full lips. "My problem is I find everything about you absolutely fascinating."

She did not have to follow his gaze to know that he had every intention of kissing her. And that he did. Thoroughly.

All Elizabeth wanted to do was yield to him. And that she did. Utterly.

She parted her lips as his tongue swept inside. The sound of the men and women rushing by, the roar of the fire in the distance, even the imminent danger of Sir Peter Garnesche, all faded away. Nothing else mattered as Elizabeth took refuge in his caress, in his touch, in his kiss.

Ambrose felt every muscle in his body harden as Elizabeth's hands rose to encircle his neck. He dipped deeper into the richness of her sweet mouth, and his arms brought her tight against his body. He remembered what lay beneath. The incredibly beautiful body, the full breasts, the intoxicating taste of her skin.

Elizabeth pulled away from the kiss. She felt weak at the onslaught of this man's attentions. She placed her head against his broad chest and tried to still her trembling knees, her pounding heart.

"How can I feel this way?" she whispered, fighting to keep her voice calm. "So quickly, I mean. I hardly know you."

"The passion that two people feel for one another cannot be explained in terms of time or place." Ambrose looked down and captured her gaze. "We are good together, Elizabeth. I can feel the passion that is raging inside you. Come with me. I'll never let him get close to you. Never again. I'll protect you. We'll find our own place . . . Scotland, perhaps. I'll take care of you. We'll find a corner of eternity for just the two of us. Think of the pleasure we could bring to each other. The passion we could share."

She paused, looking deep into his eyes, and then shook her head. This was an offer much like one she'd expected from Bourbon. But there was a difference here that made her hesitate. She would go to her grave before accepting the duc's offer; Bourbon was at best a friend. But Ambrose Macpherson's invitation carried a far greater temptation.

No. She shook her head resolutely. How could she even consider it? Had she already forgotten her mother's fate? Is that what she wanted? How long would it take Ambrose to tire of her? Where would she go once that happened? She was disgusted with herself for being even momentarily tempted by the man's words. "Please don't ask that of me. I can't."

Ambrose gazed silently into her deep, dark eyes. He had never made this offer to anyone. He had never sought a mistress that he might keep for any period of time. There were dangers in that. Dangers of getting attached, of getting caught up in a lengthy relationship. Of giving up one's freedom. But despite it all, he had made the offer. And she'd rejected it. This woman was so different from the others. Different from any woman he had ever been with in his life.

But Ambrose knew women, and he thought for a moment of pursuing the advantage he sensed he had right now. Ambrose Macpherson was a master of the powers of persuasion. Particularly when it concerned women. He knew if he tried again, if he set his mind to it, she would agree. But for the same reasons that he'd never asked another before her, he held back. Something inside told him he wasn't ready. Not yet.

Elizabeth searched for the right words. She didn't want to hurt him or seem ungrateful for his offer. But how could she explain to him that becoming someone's mistress was not the life she could accept? Even if that someone was as attractive and alluring as the man standing in front of her. Elizabeth looked up into the Highlander's handsome face. She could see the hint of disappointment in his eyes. But then her eyes were caught by the small gash along the line of his jaw.

"Was this self-inflicted?"

Ambrose caught her hand as she tried to probe the small injury on his chin. "Nay, lass. This was a good-morning kiss from your French courtier."

"Bourbon? You two fought?"

Ambrose let his hands fall to his sides. Even though the two knights had resigned themselves to the fact that neither was responsible for Elizabeth's injury, Ambrose still wondered if perhaps the duc was the reason Elizabeth rejected his offer. She had changed her mind and walked out of his bed last night. Well, fallen out of his bed. He wondered now if her willing attitude had not just been a way to make the handsome French nobleman jealous enough to propose marriage. women! Ambrose wanted to banish this new thought from his mind, but even as he pushed it away, he felt it taking root. He still remembered the Frenchman's words. Someday asking for her hand in marriage. *Someday.* That had been the emphasis. The Highlander didn't want to think she was simply trying to push things along.

"Aye," he replied. "We fought. But perhaps it will distress you to know that your friend got the worst of it."

Elizabeth smiled. "Hardly. It's about time someone caught up with the snake."

Ambrose have her a suspicious glance. "The gentleman seems quite fond of you."

"The gentleman is fond of all women, regardless of their wit, shape, or rank." She leaned down and picked up her hat. "But that's what drew me to you. You are not like that, are you?" she asked wryly.

"Of course not!" He was quick to answer.

"Of course not!" Too quick, Elizabeth thought. She placed the hat on her head and pulled it down over her eyes. "Well, I have to go."

Ambrose's hand shot up to her elbow. "Where to?"

"Paradise!" she whispered dreamily.

"With him?" Ambrose asked shortly. It wasn't Bourbon, but it had to be someone else. She must value the man greatly to continue guarding his identity from both the duc and him. "What he has done to you still has not convinced you to get away?"

"Aye, it has." She stretched up on her toes and kissed him quickly on the lips. "I'll always remember this Field of Cloth of Gold." She tried to turn toward the crowded alleyway.

Ambrose caught her by the elbow and pulled her toward him. "This was yours to keep."

Elizabeth looked down at the large emerald ring that the warrior placed in her palm. "I—"

"Think of it as a keepsake, lass. Just remember me by it."

As she gazed up into his eyes, Elizabeth closed her fingers over the gift. Then she turned without another word and disappeared into the throng.

Chapter 10

Dawdling is the thief of time, Friar Matthew thought.

"I'd been waiting for you, Elizabeth. Then you didn't come, and it was getting so late," Mary explained. "I must have dozed off." The dark-haired young woman gazed out into space as she recollected the events. Elizabeth sat beside her, holding her hand, while the lanky priest stood by the shuttered window, waiting less patiently for her to continue her tale.

Elizabeth urged her on. "And that's when you heard the voices?"

"Yes." Mary nodded. "Just outside the tent—beside my bedding—they were talking. There were two or three, I think. But I heard one of them clearly. He was giving commands to the others."

She looked from her sister's face to the friar's.

Matthew followed the young woman's gaze. How interesting that Mary hadn't once asked about how Elizabeth had come by the gash on her cheek. How typical of her.

"He said, 'Silence her,'" she continued. "'Cut her throat, or smother her, but don't let her cry out. And whatever happens, don't let her live.'"

Elizabeth shuddered at the moment of fear Mary must have experienced.

"So how did you escape them?" the friar exploded. "For God's sake, Mary!"

The young woman looked up in shock at the exasperated cleric. "Really, Friar. I'm telling you everything as it happened."

"Please, Friar Matthew, give her time," Elizabeth pleaded as she watched the priest throw up his hands with a sigh. "Go on, Mary. What happened next?"

The young woman collected her thoughts and gave the priest another quick look before continuing. "Well, when I heard that, I jumped out of bed. I assumed they'd be coming in the front, so I grabbed for my cloak. It was then that I knocked over the brazier. The hot coals spilled right across the floor of the tent." She looked wide-eyed at her sister. "The rushes on the floor lit up like one big torch. The flames and the smoke were everywhere . . . in an instant."

"Were you hurt?" Elizabeth asked quickly, glancing down at the ivory skin of her sister's hands.

"No. I ran!" she answered. "I scrambled as fast as I could to the back of that tent and slipped under the cloth wall."

"So no one saw you escape?" the friar asked shortly, turning then to Elizabeth. "It's just possible that if they don't find you in the encampment, they might decide you perished in the fire. That would be good for us."

"They were after *me*, Friar Matthew," Mary asserted with a note of temper in her voice. "Why would anyone want to hurt Elizabeth? Most of these people don't even know who she is. On the other hand, everyone knows me."

He tried to hold his tongue, but he couldn't. "Why would anyone want to use violence against a vain and silly ornament like you?" Friar Matthew scolded. Other than their similar complexions, the two sisters had nothing in common. And Matthew was losing patience with Mary. "After all, what use would there be in anyone coming after you? One just doesn't cut willow branches when there is a house to be built."

Perplexed, Mary looked up to her sister. "But I like willows."

Matthew shook his head. Brilliant she was not. But right now there was a much bigger problem at hand. While going after Mary, he'd heard from some peasants about a reward for anyone who could bring news of the whereabouts of Elizabeth Boleyn. Perhaps they did think she perished in the fire, but perhaps they did not. Friar Matthew knew that Garnesche was not a man to just sit and wait. From what Matthew had heard, the father of the girl was pretending to be heartsick over her disappearance, and Sir Peter Garnesche had taken the lead in the search for her. What liars, he thought. Clearly, the most important thing was to get her out of here . . . now. As good as many of these commoners were, to them Elizabeth could mean nothing more than a possible reward, and they all had empty stomachs and families to feed. She would not be safe here for long. "Elizabeth, I've already arranged for you to leave here on the hour."

Elizabeth looked up at her friend. There was no sense in arguing or in trying to find the whereabouts of the place he was sending her. She had to leave this camp. Once away from it, she could take control of her own destiny.

Elizabeth flinched as Mary's nails dug into the skin of her hands. She looked at her sister. The young woman sat, her face devoid of all color. Her eyes had welled up with tears, and as she watched, the glistening drops overflowed and coursed down her pale cheeks.

"I need to talk to you, Elizabeth." Mary's voice broke, and she threw a glance at the friar. "I need to talk to you alone."

Elizabeth turned to the friar. The man shook his head and took a step toward them. He had to stop Elizabeth from allowing her frivolous sister to continue using her. The elder sister had finally realized the value her father put on her. Why was she being so blind to the younger sister's manipulative ways? He opened his mouth to speak, but Elizabeth shook her head, stopping him. At his next attempt to intervene, Elizabeth frowned in response. He shrugged and turned to go, pausing by the ladder. "You're leaving in an hour, Elizabeth."

The two women watched as the friar disappeared.

"Elizabeth!" Mary broke into sobs, throwing her arms at once around her sister's neck. "You can't leave me. Please, don't. You promised to take care of me. You know how ill I am."

Elizabeth held back her own sadness, but reached around and hugged the young woman to her. "I'm not leaving forever, Mary. I'm just going in search of a place and work that I can do—yes, work. Once I find it you can join me there, wherever it is. I remember my promise. I'll take care of you."

"But whatever is going to happen to me?" Mary hiccuped as she straightened up, drying her tears with the backs of her hands. "My life is in danger, you know."

Elizabeth knew that there was no point in telling Mary that the assailants were not after her. By explaining the events to her sister, she would just put Mary in the same danger that she herself was in. In addition, Elizabeth knew that in her sister's highly dramatic and imaginary world, Mary might very well relish the idea of a life in jeopardy ... without really understanding the ramifications.

"Sir Thomas mentioned yesterday that he'll send you to Kent." Elizabeth tried to be convincing. "That won't be bad for the short term. Before you know it, you can leave and come and stay with me."

"Oh, Elizabeth . . ." Mary hid her face in her hands and broke down. Her cries this time were heart-wrenching. "I can't go to Kent. I can't go with Father. And I thought I could count on you. But now you tell me that I can't. I have no one. I should just take my life with my own hands and be finished with this misery."

Painfully, Elizabeth watched the suffering young woman weep. "That's not an option, Mary. So stop talking rubbish." She took a deep breath and tried to think things through clearly. It was her own fault. If she hadn't been, for so many years, so supportive and caring when it came to her sisters, she would be on her way to safety right now. Elizabeth knew the problem very well. For years now she had not simply been the older sibling; she'd been the only mother figure, the only nurturer that her sisters had known.

Mary saw her sister pause as she considered the situation. The young woman realized that she had to tell Elizabeth everything—before her sister had a chance to come up with some rational solution for the dilemma at hand. Mary didn't want to chance that. Elizabeth had to know the truth. "The French physician had some additional news when he examined me last night."

Elizabeth stared at her sister. Mary's face in an instant had gone from deep despair to utter happiness. She was sometimes difficult to keep up with.

Mary tucked her legs under her and sat like an excited child. "Don't you want to know what he said?"

"I do, but perhaps not at this moment."

Elizabeth had less than an hour left to decide on a plan that would be acceptable to her younger sister. She couldn't think, though, while Mary chattered away. "Can this wait?"

"Nay, Elizabeth. It can't." Mary sulked. "I don't care if you want to know or not. You're the one who brought that physician to me, and you're the one who will share my secret."

"Secret?"

"The upset stomach, the nausea, the endless naps . . . all those things were not a new stage of the pox. They've been happening because I'm . . . I'm . . ."

Elizabeth's eyes widened. "You're what, Mary?"

"I'm pregnant!"

"You're *what*?"

"Pregnant. With child."

"With child!" Elizabeth repeated, her head whirling with this news.

"When a man and a woman lie together, that's often the outcome." Mary looked into her older sister's astonished face. "You could be pregnant, too. I mean, now. As we speak."

"Me?"

"Aye, you." Mary nodded knowingly. "You slept with the Scot, didn't you?"

Elizabeth shook her head to clear it of all she was hearing.

"Was he as good in bed as everyone claims?"

"Stop!" Elizabeth yelled. "Stop this nonsense. Let's go back to what you said earlier. You said you were pregnant."

"I am. I'm carrying Henry's child." Mary turned on her tears once again. "I'm carrying the king's son, and I can't even come out into the open for fear of my life."

"The king's son? Mary, don't talk that way." Elizabeth scolded. "First of all, if you *are* pregnant, you don't know if you are carrying a boy or a girl. But that's not really important, anyway. Is it?"

"Of course it is. Just think of it, Elizabeth. If I had a boy . . ." Mary smiled dreamily. "He'd be the heir to the throne of England."

"Don't be ridiculous! The way you've been treated, you'd be lucky to have him recognized as Henry's bastard. And even if he is accepted as that, he'll never be heir to the throne. Not Cardinal Wolsey, nor the church, nor the noble families would stand for that."

"Stop being so perverse," Mary snapped petulantly. "You're supposed to be on my side."

"I am, Mary." Elizabeth turned away, shaking her head. Her problems were getting more complicated with each passing moment. Clearly, she had to get her sister out of here, too. Mary hadn't a clue how much trouble her wagging tongue could bring. To herself, and to her unborn babe.

Elizabeth sighed. As much as she would like to deny them, Elizabeth knew deep down that there were a few traits Mary had obviously inherited from their father. Being an opportunistic social climber was one of them.

She glanced back to see Mary eyeing her sulkily once again.

"You know, Elizabeth, if you would stop taking my head off and give me a chance, I could explain everything," Mary said.

"I'm sure you can."

"I have it all figured out." She looked hopefully at her older sister. "This is the way it'll work." Elizabeth sat silently while Mary hurried on. "I'm pregnant, but not everyone should know. Not yet, anyway. You can stay with me during my term. I will need you to look after me. The physician said yesterday that as long as I'm well cared for, I could have a perfectly healthy child. You can take me back to France, and we will stay there until my son is born. Then I'll send for Henry, and after he comes for us, I'll ask him to give you permission to paint. You won't have to hide your work anymore, Elizabeth. You might even get a chance to paint the portrait of the next King of England. A portrait of my son in his mother's arms. Isn't that exciting?"

All Elizabeth could do was stare at her sister. It was too early a stage for the pox to be affecting her mind.

"Mary, if this is your plan, then why don't you take it to Sir Thomas?" Elizabeth could hear her temper becoming shorter. "This is so much in line with his thinking that I'm sure he'll go along with any condition you would set."

Mary brightened before another thought crossed her mind, darkening her brow. "But . . . there are problems. . . ."

"Oh, there is more?" Elizabeth asked incredulously.

"I went to see Father already. This morning. He says he doesn't believe the child is Henry's. He says no one else will believe it, either. That dreadful cousin of ours, Madame Exton, told him that I couldn't have been pure when I lay with the king. That the child must be someone else's." Mary didn't want to tell Elizabeth everything that had been said in their father's tent earlier. It hadn't been a very genteel scene. Sir Thomas had refused to believe her and had told her in no uncertain terms that if Mary was pregnant, she would be sent away to some cloistered nunnery where she could be separated from all who knew her. Mary had walked off, stunned, confused, and angry, but Friar Matthew had found her and brought her back to Elizabeth. Mary looked into her sister's face. "But I know Henry will believe me. I was a virgin, after all. He'll remember that. I will be giving him the son that he wants so much."

Elizabeth waited until Mary finished speaking and then started for the steps.

"Friar!" she called, looking over the edge of the loft.

"Where are you going?" Mary asked, her eyes wide with alarm.

Elizabeth glanced back at her sister. "*We* are going to Italy."

"Italy! But I've never been to Italy." Mary looked about her helplessly. "What happens if I don't like it? Elizabeth? Elizabeth, I don't want to go."

Elizabeth turned sharply and, crossing the floor, knelt directly before her sister. She would help her in spite of herself. "You *will* go to Italy, Mary. That is your only way out of this mess. So you'll do it. And you *will* like it."

Chapter 11

∾

Art is long, life short. For man, his days are as grass, as the flower of the field, so he flourisheth. . . .

The sound of Pico hurrying up the ladder disrupted the painter's thoughts.

"Phillipe, hurry! He'll be here soon!" The handsome young sculptor looked anxiously over the top of the scaffolding at the painter and then scurried back down the ladder and across the room to look out the empty window of the newly constructed chapel. Two hours earlier, the room had been bustling with tradesmen of many crafts—carpenters, glaziers, stonemasons, and others—but the last few had left a short time earlier, cheerful with the easy camaraderie of those who work hard and who take pride in their skill.

"Don't worry so much, Pico. The master knows our work will be finished in time." The painter, lying back, cast a critical eye on the scene. The face on the angel directly above was smiling, but there was a sense of strain in the smile. The artist sighed aloud. I should be happy, Elizabeth thought. Why can't I be happy?

She gazed up at the fresco. Certainly the painting was not the cause of her melancholy. The colors were brilliant and true. The depiction of the angels bursting in shimmering streams of light through the summer clouds had turned out well. The thin coat of plaster was nearly dry, but it didn't matter . . . the painting was done.

Concentrate on your work, she told herself, consciously pushing all other thoughts from her mind.

Elizabeth Boleyn had a lot to be proud of. She considered the process for a moment. Frescoes presented some of the most challenging work done by the artists. Because you were painting on wet plaster, you had to work quickly and with a steady hand. Working on a wall was difficult enough, but lying on your back to paint ceiling frescoes was the most difficult of assignments, and only the two or three best painters in the studio were given those tasks. The old master was very particular about these works. Oh, yes, Michelangelo was very particular, indeed.

And that made Elizabeth feel especially good about being the one the maestro chose the most often. But still, she was living a lie. The maestro had picked Phillipe, the French painter. A likable young man with an exuberant talent and very little social life outside of his work. But in reality she was nothing more than a fraud. A deception. A man's exterior masking a woman's soul.

"He's coming, Phillipe," the man cried, clambering up the ladder. Elizabeth turned her head to see Pico's head appear, then disappear as he missed a rung, then reappear. "I don't like heights."

"Calm down, Pico," she said, chuckling. "I'm ready for him."

"But it isn't just the master. *His Highness* is with him!"

Elizabeth sat up on her elbows and began to edge quickly toward the ladder. "Don Giovanni? With the master?" This was a different story. Giovanni de' Medici rarely came out in public anymore, so she knew this visit must be an important one for Michelangelo. She glanced once more at the fresh painting, and prayed that the powerful ruler would find it pleasing.

"Quick, Pico!" she called, scrambling down the ladder after his friend. "Help me pull the scaffolding into the corner."

Two years earlier, Elizabeth had suggested that the scaffolding they used for the ceilings be built upon wheeled platforms, and right now, as she and Pico succeeded in their struggle to push the apparatus aside, she thanked God Michelangelo had seen the value in her suggestion.

She had used her brain, and the master greatly approved

of that. Starting as an apprentice, she had learned quickly that she lacked the physical strength that many of the other young men had. And not wanting to spend her time doing the physical labor that gave her the strength required, she saw immediately that she needed to make use of her ingenuity and invention. That had, indeed, been the key to being recognized early on.

The sound of the heavy oaken doors swinging open brought the two students to a halt. The aging master and the ruler of Florence entered the chapel with a train of several dozen men in attendance.

Elizabeth looked about in amazement as the room appeared to fill instantly. There were faces everywhere, and their attention focused on the work, not the worker.

Because the new stained-glass windows were not yet installed, streaming bars of golden sunlight washed the room with a radiant glow. Around the small central rotunda, rows of graceful columns rose straight to the ceiling, branching and bending like willows into an arch far above the resulting gallery. At the point where the pillars divided, Pico's decorative stone carvings adorned the supports in a petrified pattern of leaf, vine, and flower.

And at the center of it all, far above the floor, Elizabeth's angels appeared to burst downward through the dome, revealing a vibrant blue sky and the fair-weather clouds of a benevolent heavenly sphere.

Giovanni gazed upward at the breathtaking scene, enraptured by the sight of celestial creatures so real it seemed they might sweep down beside him.

"Michelangelo!" the powerful ruler murmured. "My friend! How could such a thing of beauty be wrought? What mind, what hand could conjure and execute such figures? . . ." His voice trailed off as he stared upward in wonder.

"Don Giovanni," the aging master responded deferentially, trying to keep the pleased expression out of his voice. Glancing around the room, he spotted Elizabeth and Pico standing unobtrusively beside the scaffolding. "We have only provided what you have asked."

"True, but with such exquisite mastery of color . . . of space . . ." The Florentine raised his arm and pointed as he spoke. "The face of that one. Look at how he looks into our eyes. And look at the rippling muscles on that other one. Surely strong enough to wrestle with Jacob. Ah, Michelangelo," he said, glancing at the artist. "This work ranks easily with your work in Rome."

The maestro pulled at his graying beard as he gazed critically at the painting. Elizabeth held her breath as he studied the work. With a smile, he turned back to Don Giovanni. "My friend, you honor a humble sculptor with your words. For this is the work of a young and talented artist. A man with the heart and the soul of a painter. The one I spoke of earlier . . . but let me introduce him. He stands here in the shadows. Phillipe, my boy, come here."

Elizabeth felt the knot quickly form in her stomach. She had known for some time now that her paintings spoke in a new and different language. She knew she had a gift that captured more than the exterior of her subject. She had the ability to seize the feelings within. Sadness and tears, joy and laughter, anger and greed. She had a gift; she could perceive the very essence of what she beheld—and it traveled through her fingers. It became alive in what she drew, in the colors of the paint. She knew, but never, never before had she heard her work praised so publicly by someone as important as he who stood with the maestro in the chapel.

Entering the rotunda, Elizabeth approached the group. Stopping before the two men, she bowed and dropped to one knee as Giovanni held out his hand to her. As the young painter kissed his family ring, the ruler appraised the lad before him. He had a small build and frail, delicate hands. The lad was fortunate to have the talent he did, since if he had to make a living by any other means, he wouldn't be long for this world. Then the lad looked up and gazed straight into his eyes, and the Medici padrone nodded approvingly. The young man had the brightest and most intelligent eyes he'd seen in a long time. A quite handsome face—almost beautiful—but for the pasty complexion and the puckered red scar along the high cheekbone. Giovanni raised him up and smiled, waving his plump, jeweled fingers at the ceiling fresco.

"Is it possible that a man so young as you could have produced such a masterwork?"

Elizabeth blushed at the compliment, turning her face skyward.

"He *is* a master," Michelangelo said proudly. "In my

studio, Phillipe is the youngest of the ten masters. He will be the finest." The maestro paused and put his arm around Elizabeth's shoulder. "Someday, he'll be another Raphael, Don Giovanni. This young man has the potential to surpass even the great Leonardo . . . God rest his old bones. You wait and see. It won't be long."

Giovanni de' Medici smiled encouragingly on the young painter and turned away. "What other marvels do you have in store for me today, Michelangelo?"

And as quickly as they had entered, they were gone, leaving an excited Pico gazing admiringly across the chapel rotunda at Elizabeth.

"How can you stand there so calmly?" The young man ran over and snatched Elizabeth's hat off her head and teasingly threw it into the air. "Look up there, Phillipe. Your angels are smiling at you."

Elizabeth looked up, but all she could see was a smirk.

"This calls for a celebration!" Pico caught the hat and placed it firmly on his friend's short-cropped hair. "I'll run and get the others at the studio, and we'll meet you at the baths off the Piazza del Duomo."

"Pico, you know that I don't—"

"Come on, Phillipe! This is a special occasion. It isn't every day that Giovanni de' Medici, the Duke of Nemours, gushes over your work. Come on!"

Elizabeth looked up at the handsome Genoan apprentice and smiled. She'd been working with him for two years, and he'd never even guessed that she was a woman. Pico was a young, squarely built man with large callused hands that showed the signs of his trade. From the first moment when they'd met, the young sculptor had taken the task of looking after the frail, boyish-looking painter. Elizabeth knew it would have been much easier for Pico just to call her weak and to ignore her, as some of the other artists in the master's studio had done early on.

But he hadn't. In fact, Pico had often been the shield behind whom Elizabeth had been able to hide during these very public years. He had the strength; she had the talent. He protected the young man he knew as Phillipe. And she shared with him a sensitivity for art that elevated him in the skills of his trade beyond his imagination. She spoke of the softness, the elegance, the way each curve of a sculpture must relay feeling, emotion, a story,

even. These concepts of art had been foreign to Pico until
he'd met up with Phillipe. And the two artists understood
one another in a way that was nearly spiritual.

"My sister is expecting me, Pico. Why don't you go on
without me."

"I won't," Pico said adamantly, turning on the surprised
painter and planting his fists on his hips. "Phillipe, how
long must this go on?"

"What are you talking about?" Elizabeth asked, raising
an eyebrow at the vehemence of the young man's tone.

"You have the right to live your life as much as she
does." The sculptor paused. He hadn't intended to speak
so brusquely to his friend. "Phillipe, everyone is talking
about you two."

"Talking?" Elizabeth face flushed angrily. "Who is
talking that has any right? No one, Pico. No one has any
right to speak about Mary or about me. I have never given
anyone reason to."

Pico grabbed Elizabeth by the shoulders. "Listen to me,
my friend. I'm about to tell you things that you should
have heard long ago."

"I don't want to hear." Elizabeth tried to turn and shrug
off the man's grip on her shoulders, but Pico's large
hands held her securely in place.

"It's too late, Phillipe. You must listen to what I have to
say."

Elizabeth pushed away the man's hands and walked to
the scaffolding, turning and sagging heavily against the
ladder.

Following her and leaning against one of the columns,
Pico looked down into the sad, black eyes of the young
painter. So talented, but so naive. For the entire time he'd
known Phillipe, he'd never once heard him speak of any
kin other than his sister and her child. It was true that the
three lived in the modest villa of Joseph Bardi, the wool
merchant. But Joseph and his wife, Ernesta, were not kin
to Phillipe. From what Pico had gathered, the lonely older
couple had taken in the three as tenants at first, and from
what Phillipe had said, they'd become close over years.
But what Pico needed to say to Phillipe was not something that those two people would have any knowledge of.
No, there was no one else who would do this. Pico knew it
was up to him.

"What I have to tell you regards your sister."

"You're about to bad-mouth her. Because she rejected your advances."

"I don't know what she tells you every night, but your sister didn't refuse my attentions. It happened quite a while ago, and it was wrong, I know. But I slept with her, Phillipe, as more than half of Florence has." Pico held up his hand as Elizabeth shot to her feet and began to interrupt. "Wait, my friend. Hear me out."

The sculptor watched as Elizabeth stopped, averting her eyes. "What she did reject were my half-empty pockets. But this was after . . ." Pico paused for effect, "*after* she came to my bed."

Elizabeth sat down on the pedestal at the base of the column and took her head in her hands.

"My friend, you have to put a stop to this. It is no secret that you are the highest-paid apprentice Michelangelo has. With the wages you make, you should be living in comfort, with a servant to attend to you. Instead, where are you? Still living under someone else's roof. You could marry and have a woman and children of your own. But instead, all you do is work. And for what? For wages your sister spends."

Elizabeth felt a knot in her throat, but she knew she wouldn't cry. Even if she were alone, she knew she wouldn't. She'd forgotten how to cry.

"Everyone in the studio knows that you are doing outside work. Everyone knows you need the money."

Elizabeth looked up in surprise. She had worked hard to keep her outside commissions a secret.

"Yes, the portraits. Everyone knows. Including Michelangelo. And don't be so surprised. Your style, your brushwork—it is so obvious, Phillipe. You can call yourself what you want, but everyone knows who you are." Pico looked earnestly into Elizabeth's face. "And tell me, Phillipe. What do you do with that money?"

"I keep what I earn."

"No, you don't. We see your sister spending it."

"Why are you doing this to me, Pico?" Elizabeth's face reflected the pain in her heart. "Why now?"

"Because I am your friend. Your only friend. Phillipe, what just happened here today is nothing you can simply ignore, nothing you can just forget." Pico had to get his friend's attention. "The word will be out in no time. Everyone will want you. You'll have opportunities, commissions far more grand than any you've yet had. But she could ruin it all. You need to put her in her place. She has to curb her . . . excesses. You need to talk to her. It's your right because you're her brother, and because you support her and the little one. You can order her to stop. Or at least to be more discreet."

Elizabeth had known for a long time about Mary's wildness. But there was not much she'd been able to do about it. Mary was twenty-one years old. A grown woman. Elizabeth could not lock her away, and she could not put her out on the street. Neither option was acceptable.

So all she did was divert what free time she had to Mary's daughter, Jaime. The three-year-old Jaime was the only bright spot that Elizabeth had outside of her work. Truly, the young child was the reason Elizabeth put up with all she did. Elizabeth had loved her sister once, but now she wondered if her love had not turned into an emotion closer to pity.

"She made a scene the night before last."

Elizabeth looked up.

"At the Palazzo Vecchio. Your sister was there . . . mingling with all the friends of the Duke of Urbino. From what Gino told me, her dress alone must have been worth half a year's wages."

Elizabeth knew Pico's friend Gino. The son of one of the wealthiest families in Florence. She doubted he ever paid for anything in his life. What could he know of the value of money?

"There were also a large number of foreigners there. Guests of the duke. From what I hear, your sister took quite a fancy to an Englishman. They danced and spent most of the evening together. Gino didn't know what happened or what was said between them, but suddenly Mary was screaming at the man to leave her alone. It was quite an embarrassing scene. The duke was mortified, and she left before anything more could be said. Gino said she was as pale as death, Phillipe. I don't think she'll be welcomed back there." Pico fell silent.

After a moment Elizabeth stood and walked toward the door. "I'm sorry, Phillipe." Elizabeth turned and looked at the sculptor. "I'll talk to her," she said quietly, before disappearing through the door.

Pico stood alone in the rotunda. Above him the faces of angels looked on gloomily as the evening's encroaching darkness began to settle on the room.

Chapter 12

❧

Don Giovanni waited for the strolling musicians to move on before continuing his conversation with Ambrose Macpherson, Baron of Roxburgh, Lord Protector of the Borders, Ambassador and Special Emissary of His Majesty, James V of Scotland.

"I tell you, my friend, the French king has an eye on Florence. My sources bring news of him moving his troops east."

"What makes you think it is your land that he is after?" Ambrose pushed back his chair and looked at his host, Giovanni de' Medici, the Duke of Nemours, perhaps the wealthiest man in Europe, and the uncontested ruler of the flourishing Florentine city-state. "You know it is more likely that he would be after the Emperor Charles. Francis's feud with him far exceeds any ill will he feels toward you or your family."

Giovanni paused, looking down into his jeweled goblet. Ambrose had arrived just two nights ago, after spending a week with Francis. If anyone could offer insights into France's intentions, that man was Ambrose Macpherson.

"It's true. Francis would be a fool to move into Italy, turning his back to Charles. This could work to my advantage. After all, the Holy Roman Emperor is the greater threat of the two. Just think, if Francis is busy fighting Charles, he might leave Florence alone."

"Except that Charles has a large number of troops guarding the Pope in Rome." Ambrose looked at the duke straight on. "Just remember, whatever happens this summer, *don't* let your guard down."

The duke's face creased with a slight smile. "What is this I hear? First you talk me out of my worries; now you fan the flames of my concern. So much for the politician I have learned to admire. You speak as though Scotland, Francis's oldest ally, is at last taking sides with me. Does this mean that you'll help the poor Florentines, my friend?"

"You are pushing your luck, Giovanni!" Ambrose stretched his long legs out before him, while a servant refilled his goblet. "I'm just making you think out loud. There is sometimes more than one way out of a predicament. We've known one another a long time—"

"And I know you to be a man of integrity," Giovanni interrupted.

"The obligations of friendship never outweigh the obligations of duty and honor."

"You can't change who you are, Ambrose. But I have heard some interesting news lately. Of Francis giving you yet another title to add to your property."

"You know I care very little about titles," Ambrose interjected. "And do not forget, my well-informed friend, that I paid for my estate there with Macpherson gold. Many years ago."

"I know, my friend. Everyone knows the truth. You can't be bought. All of these things—friendship, duty, honor—they all reside within you. They are not separable from you. They are the qualities that make you who you are. You know how much I've wanted you and Scotland on my side. Fight beside me. Help me."

Ambrose brought his cup to his lips and then, without drinking, placed it back on the table. He looked hard at the man beside him. "You continue to survive in these unsettled times because you are a sharp-witted, practical man. Scotland, however, is in a different position. We have a twelve-year-old king who needs all the alliances he can get. Most of all, though, James needs France. Our nations have been allied for centuries, and we are positioned such that we can keep England between us. But you, Giovanni, you need neither me nor my country. You will remain capable of defending yourself, my friend, so long as . . . so long as you remember never to trust an armed man who gazes longingly at your neighbor's fields. Now stop pestering me and use your brains."

The duke's dark eyes bore into the Highlander's. "Let me see if I hear you correctly." He paused for effect. "In a few weeks, depending on Francis's whim, he may be standing at my door."

Ambrose looked about the huge hall and let his eyes take in the series of sensational paintings that graced the room. Together, the works formed a series depicting the history of Florence and the triumphs of the Medici family. Before them six huge statues representing the toils of Hercules seemed almost trivial.

The Medici ruler held up his hand and smiled at the Scot. "I understand. We are done talking of politics and war." The duke sat for a moment, savoring the comradeship the two enjoyed. They were friends, and their friendship transcended the limits of borders and national alliances. This gave Giovanni de' Medici a warm feeling inside. No one else in Florence, perhaps in Europe, ever dared to address him the way this Scottish nobleman did. Good and honest men are so often fools, Giovanni thought. But Ambrose Macpherson was a man to listen to. He could almost picture it . . . Francis, giving Ambrose a title that the Highlander cared little about, then revealing to him his secret intention of attacking Charles. Of course, the French king would know that the Scottish nobleman was on his way to Rome to meet with the Pope. And naturally he would stop in Florence en route. It was no secret that Giovanni and Ambrose had been friends for years. Perhaps Francis cunningly planned on the Scottish warrior passing such information on to the Medici ruler. But that was what set Ambrose apart from other politicians. He would not allow anyone to manipulate him in any way.

"*Sí*, it is true what you say about my ability to live by my wits. The great sculptor Michelangelo says that, to grace a family tomb, he is planning a series of marble figures that will together be called 'Victory of the Mind over Brute Strength.' Isn't that wonderful, Ambrose?"

"So long as he doesn't plan on you filling the tomb too quickly."

A chuckle escaped Giovanni as he clapped his friend on the shoulder. "My thoughts exactly. Well, with what's left of this beautiful night, let's speak of more agreeable things. Of art and architecture, of love and women."

"Subjects Your Grace has far greater knowledge of than does his humble servant."

Don Giovanni brightened. "Ah, Ambrose. You are a delightful guest and an excellent storyteller. Such courtesy. But news of you often reaches my ears, my friend. I've heard that the fine collection of paintings you keep in that place of yours in France continues to grow. And from what I hear, the work is second to none."

"Just gross exaggerations and rumor, m'lord." Ambrose smiled. "You should stop by sometime and see the collection for yourself. You'd be a much better judge than those flapping tongues."

"Me! Step on French soil?" He shook his head. "Nay, to do such a thing would be to risk finding my head on the end of Francis's sword."

"There is a good chance of that, I suppose. And not one you would want to risk," Ambrose remarked seriously. "Considering how fond you are of it."

"I am. After all, it is the only one I've got—and a good-looking head, at that." Giovanni laughed. "But as I started to say before, I believe you are by far the finest courtier in the world . . . outside of myself, of course."

"Of course, Giovanni." Ambrose grinned and reached for the golden goblet of amber-colored wine. "But since you mentioned the topic of art, a courier came to me this afternoon with a message from the Queen Mother that touches on the subject. Perhaps you can advise me on the best way to proceed."

"Are you asking *my* counsel on the topic of art?" The duke looked sideways at the Highlander. "After all we hear of the things you have, Ambrose?"

"No one in Europe is better qualified to give counsel, m'lord, than you yourself." Ambrose cleared his throat. He would cut out someone's tongue if he could find out who had spilled his guts to the Medici ruler about Ambrose's estate. Friendship would not stop the extremely competitive Don Giovanni when it came to such collections. "I mentioned before that the message is from Queen Margaret. Needless to say, she is looking for the best advice. Must I repeat it, Giovanni? The best!"

"Well, since you put it that way . . ." He smiled. "It would be a pleasure, my friend. Unburden yourself."

"Actually, I have been asked to unburden you."

"Oh?"

"As you know, Giovanni, even though the king's

mother has spent more than twenty-one years in our barren and comfortless castles in Scotland, we have never been able to sway her. Queen Margaret is still bound and determined to bring civilization to us wild and barbaric Scots."

Don Giovanni laughed out loud. "So you'd like me to tell her that she is wasting her time. Is that it?"

Ambrose snarled at the duke. "I can see irony is lost on you. I happen to disagree with her, my effete, epicurean friend. Like you, she wishes to surround herself with—"

"With creations that raise man above the animals. That display the inner workings of the artistic soul. That render man as heroic, as the definitive proof of God's hand on earth. That shape our lives with a timeless aesthetic, a perspective that—"

"She wants pictures." Ambrose drained his goblet and put it down with a resounding clang.

"That's what *you* surround *yourself* with, my friend."

"Nay, there is a difference," Ambrose interjected. "My collection is the work of many fine artists. I don't take a fancy to seeing my own portrait on each wall." As the words left the Highlander's mouth, he spotted a new portrait of the Medici ruler that adorned the nearest wall. "Is that new?"

"I look especially fine in that one, don't I?"

Ambrose smiled. "She wants one of your artists to paint the royal family."

Giovanni paused and slyly scanned the Scot's rugged features. "I should think that France, that devoted ally, could supply Scotland with treasure troves of art—tapestries, lace, the finest cloth of gold and silver. Certainly Francis could send your queen one of his court painters. Perhaps you, with your fabulous collection, could come up with such a painter."

"This is Margaret Tudor we're talking about, Giovanni. She wants only the best; you know that."

"Oh, how I pity you." Margaret Tudor's reputation as a stubborn and coddled queen was well known all across Europe. "And I suppose her letter states *who* exactly she wants?"

"Of course. She wants Michelangelo."

The duke nodded, stifling his desire to laugh openly.

"I'm sorry to disappoint your king's mother, Ambrose, but really—"

"I knew you'd never let him go." The Scot put on a menacing glare. "But don't forget, she'll not forgive you. Just imagine me returning to Scotland with no satisfactory response to her request."

"He's a sculptor, my friend. And an aging one at that. For his own good, for the good of Florence, I simply couldn't let him make such an arduous journey."

"Well, you'd better think of something. If she doesn't get what she wants, Giovanni, there will be the devil to pay."

"I know, I know. And it will not be you that has to worry. After all, I understand that she likes you better than the air she breathes." At seeing Ambrose's raised eyebrows, the Medici ruler continued. "Of course, it *is* Scottish air. But never mind. I know if I don't help you, she'll probably send half of Scotland's warriors to join Francis as he attacks Florence."

"Hmm. I wonder if she'll let me lead them."

Seeing the scowl from the duke, Ambrose decided to let his friend think of a plan. Ambrose was a favorite at court with the queen, as he had been years earlier with her husband, James IV. But even at that, he did not want to risk facing her empty-handed. And unfortunately, what Giovanni had said about Scotland going to war with Italy simply because her request was denied was more than a jest. The queen had attempted in the past to send Scotland into battle for reasons far more trivial than this.

The Medici ruler laid his meaty hand on his guest's arm. "Wait! I have an idea." The duke looked excitedly at his friend. "I know just the man. One of the masters working in Michelangelo's studio. He is perhaps a better painter than the maestro himself. But it would be a great sacrifice for me to part with him, Ambrose. This is a young man with the potential of bringing great honor and prestige to my land. I would only loan him to the *closest* of Florence's friends. Do you understand me? And I would entrust him to no one other than you for safe-keeping. You must take care of him, Ambrose."

The Scottish nobleman laughed out aloud. "You are too clever for your own good. But I don't buy it, nor do I think Margaret Tudor will."

"I am not making this up just to suit your queen," the duke uttered, his expression serious. "Phillipe de Anjou is the finest painter Florence has to offer. You can see his work for yourself. In fact, as you make me think this through more, the more I realize I might not like to part with such talent."

Ambrose studied Giovanni with a deadpan expression. Though he would never admit it to his friend at this point, the Highlander knew the work of this Phillipe de Anjou. The man was, indeed, an exceptional talent.

"His name—he's French?"

"We try not to hold that against him."

"What should I know about him?" Ambrose asked, feigning ignorance.

"Nothing, other than the fact that I want him back."

"What happens if the queen likes the man too much and tries to keep him?"

"I'll side with her brother, King Henry, and attack Scotland."

Ambrose smiled. "I'm sorry to say, my friend, that you and my queen have far too much in common."

"*Sí.*" Giovanni smiled back. "The truth is, I don't think I would like Scottish air, either. Far too damp, from what I've been told. In fact, I'll need to talk to the young Phillipe. He might have objections to your climate as well."

"Too late!" Ambrose huffed. "Your offer has been accepted. Please arrange it with Michelangelo. I will stop and get the young man when I return from my discussions with your good cousin, the Pope."

"He'll be ready . . . with my regards to your queen, Ambrose!"

Chapter 13

She knew they had to go. It didn't matter where, but they had to leave Florence.

And then the miracle happened. As if the angels themselves had taken her plea to the heavens, Elizabeth was summoned to Michelangelo and told she would be leaving for Scotland in a week.

Scotland, the desolate northland. Cold, damp, barbaric, devoid of culture, a wasteland with more sheep than people.

Scotland. An absolute heaven. She could not wait to get there.

"Where is your sister, child?" An elderly woman charged breathlessly into the attic room. She plunked her heavyset frame on the closest bench, her ample bosom heaving from the exertion. Removing her kerchief from her sleeve, she mopped the beads of sweat from her brow.

"She's gone out to say her last fond farewells to friends." Elizabeth looked up from the packed trunks at her friend. "What are you doing up here, Ernesta? You should not exhaust yourself climbing those stairs."

"Humph! Look who's talking!" Ernesta smiled down at the black-haired child draped over Elizabeth's back. From beneath the linen shift, the child's arms and legs dangled comfortably around the painter. "Come here, little Jaime. Let your auntie finish her work. Lord knows, if she doesn't, no one else will raise a finger."

"Please, Erne—'Uncle'! We can't afford to have Jaime call me anything else in public."

Ernesta removed the cloth from the top of a small basket she'd brought with her. Catching a whiff of the fragrant smell of the cinnamon cakes, the three-year-old girl ran gleefully toward the older woman. "Go ahead, say what you will. Aunt or uncle. She's a lot smarter than any of us. Yesterday, when Pico came to say good-bye, you should have heard her. She chatted away about her uncle and his manly ways as if she were a grown-up taught to just say the right things."

Elizabeth smiled at the little girl plunked on Ernesta's lap. Little Jaime. So sweet, so loving, and so bright. Elizabeth would have expected the child to grow up so confused, living the way they did. After all, there had never been any mention of a father, and the mother, though present, had never shown the child even the slightest affection. It seemed as though, from the time Mary had given birth to her daughter, the upset of bearing a daughter rather than a son had been too much for her. Having a girl had ruined the woman's dreams of going back to England in pomp and glory. So the young child had nearly ceased to exist in Mary's mind. But not in Elizabeth's. Since the day Jaime was born, Elizabeth and Ernesta had done everything in their power to look after the child's welfare and to fill the gaping void with love and affection.

Elizabeth continued to cherish the young girl as if she were her own. And the young painter knew Jaime was the bright sunshine, the warmth and the strength that fueled her every decision. That pushed her forward.

Drawing her gaze back to the disorder of the room, Elizabeth let her mind travel back to the past. It had been almost four years since the first day they had stepped into this house.

Leaving the Field of Cloth of Gold, Friar Matthew had accompanied Mary and Elizabeth as they'd made their way southward through France to the port city of Marseilles. There Elizabeth had met the friar's old friends Joseph and Ernesta Bardi for the first time. A deal was struck between the two men, and to this day Elizabeth wondered how Joseph Bardi had so obviously gotten the short end of the deal. So, while Friar Matthew had turned around and returned to his flock outside Paris, Mary and Elizabeth and the Bardis continued on to Florence.

Joseph Bardi was an itinerant wool merchant, struggling to find a foothold in the thriving markets of the Italian city-states. Friar Matthew had known the childless and elderly couple for all of his adult life. He knew them to be people into whose care he could entrust the two sisters, and he'd been correct. Upon meeting them, Elizabeth had felt an immediate sense of kinship. They had never once ridiculed her masculine disguise, nor her dream of becoming what she had set out to be. In fact, during the sisters' first year in Florence, Joseph Bardi had been the one to find her first commissions in the small, remote churches in the rolling countryside to the north of the city.

Ernesta Bardi was a smart businesswoman who for over forty years had been an indispensable part of Joseph's life and his commerce. But even more than that, Erne was a woman—proud and full of life. Not having children of their own had allowed Erne to travel and be a part of her husband's life in the markets of Europe. As a result, she was the one dismayed at the prospect of having the sisters in her house. The last thing she wanted was to be tied to a wild, pampered, and pregnant Mary . . . and to the child that was due in the winter. But despite her reservations about the younger, Ernesta had grown to cherish and respect the older sister, as well as the child born of Mary. As difficult as it was for Ernesta to admit, she loved what chance—and the friar—had brought to her. A life that had once been so quietly focused on her husband's trade now bustled with the activity of the young family she had taken in as her own.

Elizabeth stood and dragged one of Mary's trunks into the corner of the room. Her sister would certainly not be happy when she found out they wouldn't be taking all her clothes on their journey.

The climate and physicians of Florence had been very good for Mary. The physician in France had prescribed the miraculous *unguentum Saracenicum*, a mercury-based ointment, and the doctors here had continued the treatment. Everyone knew that mercury was poison, and yet the medication reduced dramatically the horrible sores that Mary hated so much. Elizabeth worried incessantly about the irrational behavior her sister occasionally displayed, and about the bouts of stomach pain, but Mary would fight like a wild animal at any suggestion that she give up what she saw as a cure for her illness. She was more than willing to endure both physical suffering and an occasional mental lapse in exchange for the return of her good looks.

"Pain is the price of beauty, Elizabeth," she would say. "But, of course, how would you know that?"

So as the original symptoms of the disease disappeared, Mary had seemed to become as healthy as any other young woman of her age. But for Elizabeth, the most pleasing miracle of all had been that Jaime was born free of the pox.

Soon after the disappointment of finding that it had been a daughter that she'd borne and not a son, Mary had given up her foolish dream of returning to Henry's court in triumph. Faced with few options, she set her mind to make the most of their life in Florence and to enjoy her freedom.

Dragging a second chest alongside the first, Elizabeth sighed. She had sorted out Mary's wardrobe, and the one chest they would be taking contained only the finest, but most appropriate dresses.

She thought back over the steadily increasing amount of clothing that had been accumulating over the past few years. It amazed her that they'd been able to keep themselves afloat. She could no longer count the times she'd put her foot down and brought Mary to her senses—for however short a period. Somehow, however, Elizabeth had managed to keep up with the money she required the reluctant Joseph and Erne to take from them. That had been Elizabeth's condition from day one. She would accept the gracious hospitality of these generous people if, and only if, they would accept some pittance of rent for the space the sisters occupied. But Elizabeth knew better than anybody else that even though the Bardis had accepted her terms, the couple spent ten times the amount she gave them on their young charges.

"How did Mary take the news?"

Elizabeth looked up in surprise. She had been so caught up in her own thoughts that she'd totally forgotten Jaime and Ernesta.

"It's been so quiet up here." Ernesta continued, not waiting for the young woman's answer. "I would have thought that she'd have had at least one good crying fit over your decision."

Elizabeth had never thought it safe to tell the truth

about the circumstances that had driven them to Florence
and to the Bardis. And as if they understood, the subject
had never been brought up. Last week, after her discussion with Pico, Elizabeth had confronted Mary about
the details of what had taken place. That had been when
a teary-eyed Mary had at last confessed to her older sister the news of her encounter with an Englishman from
Henry's court. Upon hearing the story, Elizabeth had
known that it was time to run. Mary, shortsighted as she
was, had spent a great deal of time flaunting the story of
her past liaison with the king of England. After all, she'd
wanted to impress the young nobleman. The man, knowing Sir Thomas Boleyn and hearing of his daughters' disappearance years back, had taken a keen interest, asking
the woman more questions. That had been when Mary had
recognized her error and had fled.

For the past four years, the two sisters had been faceless, nameless—women lost in a time when war and
change threatened to unhinge the entire world. No one,
not even their own father, had any knowledge of their
whereabouts or even their existence. For four years they
had been safe. But on the other side, Joseph had kept
Elizabeth apprised of the news of England. She had even
overheard a conversation between two English merchants
once, about the power that Sir Peter Garnesche had lately
acquired in the shifting sands of English court politics.
When Mary had told her of being so foolishly discovered,
Elizabeth feared it was only a matter of time before Garnesche would hear the news of them. And to protect the
power and position he now held, he would come after
her—or send some assassin to do his dirty work.

"It must be really bad, child, if you don't even want to
talk about it."

Elizabeth shook her head in response. "She wants to go.
She really does."

"Oh? Well, I suppose I shouldn't be surprised. I could
never understand her, anyway." Ernesta stood up and took
the little child by the hand. "We'll go down to the garden
and give you time to finish up. Joseph said his men will
be over bright and early in the morning to pick up the
trunks. I wish we didn't have to go to the farewell party at
Condivi's tonight. But we won't stay long. We all need to

get our rest tonight. We'll be on the road for over a month."

"I still think you two are going too far to watch over us."

Ernesta clucked her tongue in response. "We would not have it any other way. You should know by now that Joseph and I will not let you three just go off into the wilderness."

"But you have a business to run. You should not just throw everything over just for us."

"Nonsense. You heard Joseph. We're going on this trip not just to see you safely ensconced there—it's good for us, too. The wool that has been coming out of Scotland in the last couple of years has been constantly improving. We *have* to go. With this trip and the one we'll take when we bring you back, we could build enough contacts to begin trading. Who knows, it could mean a fortune."

"I'm sure that's the only thing on your mind," Elizabeth said skeptically. "Erne, do you know if Joseph has gotten any response from Queen Margaret's envoy?"

"You know he wasn't planning on hearing any. But I don't think we need to worry. From what I hear, the Baron of Roxburgh's mission in Rome has nothing to do with us, so I'm certain he'll be glad to know we decided not to wait for him. He would have thought us a nuisance, anyway. You know these nobles—talking, feasting, God knows what else. It'll be fine. We'll be in Scotland before he even leaves Rome."

Chapter 14

∾

The ground shook from the thunder of two massive horses pounding side by side through the gathering dusk.

Ambrose Macpherson, Baron of Roxburgh, stared ahead at the lights of the torches that set the city of Florence aglow even in the midst of the growing darkness. He looked over at his friend Sir Gavin Kerr. From the giant warrior's expression, as black as the thick mane that ruffled in the wind, Ambrose could tell that the knight was still angry with him for setting them on the road before they'd planned. Gavin, newly arrived from Venice, had been ready to enjoy a brief but leisurely stay in Rome before the two started their long journey back to Scotland. But yesterday, as Ambrose finished his talks with the Pope, the painter's message had arrived.

So, before he could even get enough information to talk his friend out of any hasty decisions, Gavin had found himself on the road to Florence.

Ambrose Macpherson knew he was in no position to divulge to Gavin all that he'd been privy to in these sensitive discussions in Paris, Florence, and Rome. But he had to act. Ambrose knew if they did not stop the painter from traveling north, then the unsuspecting artist was certain to encounter the advancing armies of Charles as the Holy Roman Emperor moved south. And having such a small number of men in his company on this trip, Ambrose was in no mood to confront any larger forces just to save the stubborn hide of an impulsive artist.

Ambrose turned and shouted to his companion. "I have a shilling says you can't beat me to church at the top of the next rise, you gruesome son of a goatherd."

"Goatherd?" the giant roared. "I'll bury your ugly face in the dust of this horse before that rise."

Ambrose laughed and urged his steed a half length ahead.

The message from Phillipe de Anjou had said that he could wait no longer—he was leaving for Scotland. What's the rush? Ambrose thought with annoyance. Worse, his plan was to go north to the Rhine River, to Cologne, and across to Antwerp for passage to Scotland. Right into the middle of a probable battle between Francis and Charles, Ambrose cursed. In the painter's message, he had mentioned the name of a Florentine merchant—Bardi or something, a man obviously as empty-headed as the artist himself—who was going to escort him to his destination. So there was no need for Ambrose's service. Well, that was true enough. Taking that route, they'd all be dead in few days, the Highlander thought.

They had ridden hard since yesterday, stopping only to change horses, following the old Roman road from the sprawling congestion of the hill city northward. Through the moonlit night and the dusty, sun-drenched day, the two had ridden through a blur of towns and villages. Now the sun was low as Ambrose and Gavin crossed into Florentine lands. Driving themselves to reach the city before its heavy gates were closed for the night, Ambrose peered ahead through the dusky light as they neared the serpentine Arno.

"Do you think we can make it?" Gavin yelled, spurring his breathless steed ahead still faster.

"Just hide your ugly face, my friend," Ambrose returned, peering over at the giant. "I don't want you to scare them into closing the gates before it's time."

"You scurvy Highland blackguard. It's usually just one look at *your* scarred dog's face that makes people pass out."

"That's not passing out, you hideous beast. That's called swooning," Ambrose shouted with a grin as they made the last bend in the road before the straight run toward the gates. "And women like to languish at my feet. After all, I do have a remedy for their affliction."

Gavin shook his head. "One of these days, Ambrose Macpherson. One of these days."

Florence's ancient walls rose before them, and Ambrose and Gavin swept across the wide stone bridge and into the city as the company of armed men prepared to close the heavy gates.

Reining in his horse, Ambrose turned and eyed his dust-covered friend. "You do look like the devil, Gavin."

"Of course I do. It makes me all the more endearing. But you can sit here and talk all night. This handsome devil is going to find food and a bed."

"Very well. I'll go find the painter, and we'll meet at that inn you like—the Vista del Rosa—down by the cathedral."

"Aye, the Rosa." Gavin sighed. "I can see that bonny lass Pia right now, pouring me that bowl of wine. But how will you convince the painter to come with you? That is, if he's still in Florence."

"Well, his message said they were departing tomorrow, so he'd better be here. And as for convincing, the man has no choice. We are here, aren't we?"

Gavin looked around at the town, alive with people who appeared dressed for a feast day. Nightlife in Florence was far different than nightlife anywhere else in Europe. "Aye, we're here. But our men are not. They're still a day's ride behind us. And this Phillipe fellow seems to be in a bit of a rush. How do you plan to convince our impatient artist to wait around for a couple of days?"

"I'll talk to him first. But if that doesn't work, I may just tie and gag him."

"But, Ambrose, you always tell me that's my style, not yours."

"True." The nobleman shook his head. "I have to get away from you. You are clearly a bad influence on me."

"Flatter me all you want, Ambrose. You still owe me that shilling."

With only a scowl for an answer, the Baron of Roxburgh turned his steed around and headed across town.

Elizabeth quietly tiptoed away from Jaime's little bed. The child had at last fallen asleep. Elizabeth was hardly surprised, though. With all the excitement and the tumultuous goings-on surrounding the upcoming journey, the painter was amazed she'd even been able to coax the little girl into closing her eyes.

"Are you quite certain you don't want to go?" Mary called.

Elizabeth placed her fingers to her lips and moved closer to the center of the room. A wooden dividing screen, ornately decorated with birds and flowers, separated the private changing area from the rest of the large room. Mary peered over the top, watching her sister advance. At the last moment Mary stepped around the end of the screen and whirled about in front of her sister.

"So what do you think?"

Elizabeth gazed at the maroon satin dress, the bodice hugging the young woman's figure and the neckline cut low enough for a generous display of Mary's ample bosom. Stepping back to get a better look, Elizabeth could not avoid tripping over one of the piles of clothing lying about. "For God's sake, Mary! I already packed all this once!"

"I know, I know. But I couldn't decide what to wear." The young woman grabbed a black silk shawl from a nearby bench and wrapped it around her shoulders. "I was just trying to follow your advice. It would have been much easier to just go and have a new dress made for tonight, but you keep complaining about ... well, it doesn't matter. Because after all, there wasn't really enough time to have something nice made. And ... oh, well. I'm off."

"Don't forget, we are leaving at sunrise."

Mary turned her pouting face on her sister. "How could I forget? Joseph and Ernesta will be there at Condivi's house. I know the way they are—they'll be watching my every move. And Erne already told me right out—that I *will* be coming home with them tonight. Really ... as if I were a child! Oh, well. Ciao!"

Elizabeth watched in silence as Mary turned on her heel and disappeared through the doorway. Even now, Elizabeth found it difficult to blame her sister. Mary's life had certainly not turned out the way she'd expected.

Gazing about her at the mess, she sank onto the edge of a trunk. Life was nothing like she'd hoped it would be, either. Elizabeth squeezed her eyes shut and lowered her head into her hands. She had never imagined herself so unhappy, so unsatisfied.

This is foolishness, she chided herself, forcing her eyes

open. Don't pity yourself for choices you've made. For the things you yourself wanted.

The tub she'd carefully filled with water from the kitchen seemed to beckon to her from its spot by the open window.

Elizabeth stood and crossed the room to it. This was surely to be the last bath before they reached Scotland. Closing the double shutter slightly, she backed away and pulled her work smock over her head. Unlacing the tight leather corset she'd devised that bound her chest tightly, she sighed deeply as the familiar pressure on her breasts eased. Slipping out of the rest of her men's clothes, Elizabeth picked up the silk dressing gown her sister had carelessly discarded and held it to her lips. The smooth, slippery texture of the material felt so good and yet so foreign to her skin. Even the faint scent of rosewater struck her as exotic. Pulling the robe on, she walked to the looking glass behind the screen and gazed at the somber creature standing there. With her short hair and fiery red scar, she looked like a man. But the soft curves that showed beneath the silk told another story.

Oh, God! Elizabeth looked at herself in the mirror. In the reflected light a glint of metal flickered from the dark valley between her breasts. Taking the great emerald ring in her hand, she gazed down at the rich green of the stone, at the gleaming gold. Just like her own identity, her own true self that lay hidden beneath layers of false shields, after all these years, she still carried, hidden close to her heart, the precious gift. Of course, it was not the ring but the memory that went with it that Elizabeth cherished. She thought of him quite often—the man who had been the first and the last to make her feel as a woman should feel.

How odd that now she should be going to Scotland. Elizabeth wondered if she would see Ambrose Macpherson there. She'd recognize him, but he could never recognize her.

With a sigh Elizabeth slipped off the leather thong that held the emerald ring and hung it on the dividing screen.

The sound of people noisily making their way along the street wafted in the open windows and tugged her attention away. Yes, she had tried to pretend—to fool herself into believing she was happy. She wandered to the window and peered past one of the shutters. The crowd of revelers was just turning the corner at the end of the street. Above the darkened villa across the small street, a million stars glimmered like diamonds on the black satin fabric of night.

Elizabeth shook off the nonsense that cluttered her mind. She had reason to be proud. That, at least, was true. It had taken her four long years to achieve the status she enjoyed today—a status many men worked their whole lives to achieve . . . often without success. But she had talent. She knew that. She'd worked hard to establish herself, to display her gift while keeping secret the lie beneath it all. So in the process, Elizabeth Boleyn had fooled everyone, including herself.

Four years ago she had set her mind to do the impossible, to achieve something no other woman had ever done before. And she had done it. In fact, if it hadn't been for Mary blabbing her true identity and her past connection to Henry VIII to an English knight a week ago, they would still all be staying in Florence for a good long while. But even with Mary's public admission, tomorrow she would be traveling to the court of Scotland to paint the portraits of the royal family.

But now, standing alone in the dim light of her room—the same familiar ache settling in her chest—Elizabeth looked up into the star-studded sky and thought of the price she had paid. She could never bask in the warm glow of her successes. Not as a painter, nor as a woman. Never. But that had been her choice.

Impulsively, Elizabeth strode quickly to her sister's chest and rooted through it. Pulling out a small bottle, she turned to the tub and uncorked the vial.

With an air that was almost triumphant, Elizabeth poured out the rosewater into the bath. "Tonight, at least, you can be a woman!" she whispered, slipping the robe from her shoulders and lowering herself into the fragrant warmth.

Ambrose tied his horse by the small piazza and walked toward the front door. Peering up at the darkened house, he wondered if his friend Gavin had been right about the artist already being on the road to Scotland. But then, seeing a shadow pass by the partially open window on the top floor, the warrior stepped up and knocked at the door.

Ambrose hadn't run into any difficulty locating the place. Although those he passed had not known of a resident by the name of Phillipe de Anjou, they all had seemed to know where the merchant Bardi lived. Now, standing before the entryway, Ambrose looked back at a boisterous group passing by. One of the men paused long enough to shout in rather bawdy terms a specific offer for some female living within the walls. But then, seeing the huge Highlander standing on the steps, the man hushed his words and continued on hurriedly. Ambrose knocked at the door once again, but this time less patiently. This Bardi houses some interesting people under his roof, Ambrose mused.

The heavy carved door swung slowly open on its noisy hinges. A thickset older man peered out at the giant suspiciously.

"I'm here to see the painter."

The man continued to gawk wide-eyed at the warrior.

"The painter? Phillipe de Anjou?" Ambrose asked curtly. "Does he live here?"

"*Si*, m'lord."

"I'm here to see him."

"You can't, m'lord."

"Is he not at home?" Ambrose demanded shortly. He was tired and his patience was wearing thin. "Where has he gone? I need to find him tonight."

The porter shook his head, denying the request and trying to push the door shut.

Ambrose placed his heavy boot firmly in the doorjamb and stopped the door from flattening his face. The porter's face reflected his sudden terror.

"I mean no harm to anyone." Ambrose didn't need a hysterical servant on his hands right now. "I'm the Baron of Roxburgh. A friend of Duke Giovanni. I am to take the painter to Scotland with me. Now where is he?"

The man's face brightened with recognition at the Highlander's words. "Baron! We didn't . . . Signor and Signora Bardi were not expecting you."

Ambrose really had very little interest in the Bardis. "Then the painter Phillipe *is* at home?"

The porter's eyes involuntarily flickered upward, and Ambrose knew he had arrived in time.

"Signor Bardi is dining at Signor Condivi's tonight. We expect them back shortly. But if you will wait here, I'll get the letter that my master wrote for you. It's the letter that I was to give to you if you arrived after they had departed tomorrow."

Without waiting for a reply, the man disappeared inside the house, leaving the door ajar.

There was no time to waste. Ambrose was not about to let the merchant make decisions for him. The servant had said nothing about the painter being out with Bardi, and, following the direction of the man's gaze. Ambrose had a good idea where he was. He had not ridden like a madman for the past two days just to be left standing at the door.

Pushing through the entryway, Ambrose stepped in a large, darkened central hall. The embers in the large fireplace at the far end were enough to illuminate the room with a dim amber glow. The heavy furniture looked well made but not ostentatious. This Bardi was not a poor man, but he was clearly not one of Florence's merchant princes.

There was no sign of the porter. Quietly Ambrose worked his way across the room, easily finding the stairs. As he got ready to make his way up from the ground floor, his eyes were caught by the large portraits that decorated every wall.

Even in the dim light, they were magnificent. The bright oils gleamed in the flickering glow of the fire, and although the features of the subjects depicted were not discernible in the dark room, the bold colors and dynamic movement captured in the paintings were evidence of a master artist.

Climbing the stone steps to the first-floor landing, Ambrose paused before an open window and gazed at a painting on the wall. The waxing moon was just rising, and the Highlander's eyes lingered on the Madonna and Child. There was something familiar in the face of the Madonna. But it was not the customary depiction. The pout on the Virgin's face was subtle, but unmistakable. The Christ Child's round face, however, projected the joyful innocence of a child at play, and the tiny hands that reached up for the Madonna's face were so realistic that Ambrose could not resist reaching out and touching the canvas.

He knew this man's work. He looked closer. There was a signature on this painting. There wasn't any on the one that hung in his study.

Suddenly a sound from somewhere at the back of the house roused the warrior, and he continued up the stairs, taking them now three at a time. At the top, Ambrose stood and looked down a short hallway at a partially open door.

Like the first hint of dawn, a beam of golden light spilled into the unlit corridor. The Highlander slowly and carefully worked his way to the door. Noiselessly, he pushed the door open and entered the large room.

The silence that greeted him was complete, and Ambrose let his eyes roam, taking in the total disarray of the room. To his left, a tall, painted dividing screen stood, and on a small table against the wall directly ahead, a small oil lamp cast its warm light on the wall. The warrior's eyes were immediately drawn upward to the painting that hung above the lamp. It was a panoramic scene of noble pageantry, and around the equestrian figures at the center, tents spread out like nuggets of gold amid the rolling green meadows.

Ambrose smiled, recognizing the depicted event. Moving closer, he studied the painting. Calais. Obviously the artist had been there.

Elizabeth Boleyn. That was what Ambrose best remembered of the event. The Field of Cloth of Gold. She had walked out of his life without ever completely entering it. But standing there, lost in the picture, Ambrose felt in his chest that gnawing sense of loss. That same gnawing ache he felt every time he thought of the woman. For the life of him, he couldn't explain why he savored her memory as he did. Still, wherever he went—around the globe, in every court in Christendom, in the midst of street crowds—his eyes continued to search for her. He sometimes wondered if she was happy with the man she'd run away with. Yes, he had pursued her far enough to know that Elizabeth Boleyn had never returned to England with her father. Neither had she returned to her home in France.

This painter has more than just skill, Ambrose thought, shaking off his melancholy. The man has a social con-

science and real depth of understanding. Ambrose focused on the masterwork before him. The depiction of the
poor, the mockery of the class differences—these things
spoke volumes about the artist. And then the joust. Looking closer, Ambrose couldn't help the smile that was
creeping across his face. This man had painted Garnesche
and him, with the exception that Ambrose was wearing a
kilt. No armor, just his tartan and kilt. Ambrose didn't
recall meeting any of the court artists during his time at
the event.

Ambrose chuckled to himself and then turned. As he
did, his eyes were drawn to an object hanging from
the wooden screen. Hanging at the end of a leather thong.
A ring.

An emerald ring.

Chapter 15

❧

Elizabeth closed her eyes tight as the sting of the soap worked its way through her eyelashes. Finishing the work of lathering her hair, she reached blindly over the side of the tub for the bucket of clean water, but her hand failed to find the handle. Cursing quietly, Elizabeth tried to rub the soap from her eyes with the backs of her hands.

The shock of the water flooding over her head jolted Elizabeth upright. Forcing her eyes open, she stared up in alarm.

Then her heart stopped.

"You are as beautiful as I remember."

Her mouth began to move, but her tongue failed to respond.

Ambrose looked down at the incredible beauty before him. She was rising like some raven-haired Venus from the watery recesses of his mind. The smooth, glistening skin of her face, of her shoulders and arms, the curves of her full, round breasts threatening to emerge from the covering bath, the full, inviting lips, and the large black eyes, mesmerizing and demanding in their power.

Elizabeth gathered her knees to her chest and, crossing her arms, tried to cover her exposed flesh. Her mouth felt dry, her throat constricted. Ambrose Macpherson stood motionless before the tub in his Highland gear. She blinked uncertainly, somehow expecting that he would disappear at any moment. Her mind was playing tricks on her. The figure looming above her could not be real. The dark, handsome face was just a figment of her overly active imagination. But the giant simply continued to stand there, his powerful frame relaxed, his stance wide and confident. This was the way she remembered him: The knee-high leather boots, the kilted hips, and the Macpherson tartan crossing his chest. His dust-covered gear brought back another memory. The memory of a fighter just leaving the tournament grounds. And then the intense blue eyes—yes, he was just as she remembered.

"This *must* be a dream," she finally whispered.

"It must be," Ambrose repeated, as he knelt beside the tub and took her shining face in his large hands. Pulling her close to him, his eyes swept over her features and then locked onto her wet, inviting lips.

My God, he's real. The realization hit her as Ambrose's thumbs gently caressed her cheeks and his eyes roamed her face. Elizabeth's mind told her to panic, to pull away, to tell him to leave. But her heart wouldn't let her. She just couldn't. Since she had last seen him, there had been something growing in Elizabeth that she could not deny. Tonight, right now, there was nothing she wanted more than to be kissed by this man. She wanted to be touched, to feel as she'd felt once before.

Closing her eyes, she lost herself in the moment as he tipped her chin up, reaching for her lips. Hovering somewhere in the hazy cloud just above the subconscious, Elizabeth felt her protective shield, her armor peel away, only to be replaced by another garment. Soft, delicate, it was a fabric of sheer magic, it was a moment of release. Feeling his face descending to hers, Elizabeth knew she had no choice but to respond.

As Ambrose touched his lips to hers, he felt her hands reach up and caress his face. Their lips brushed gently in search of remembrance.

As if outside herself, Elizabeth felt her own body shudder as Ambrose's hands reached into the water and encircled her waist. His mouth was covering hers now, and she opened her lips willingly to his.

As his tongue delved into the depths of her mouth, a heat coursed through her body, scorching her with a sudden flame. Elizabeth's startled hands flew up to encircle his neck. Her tongue, her mouth molded to his and her body ached with the need to follow. A boldness took control of her as her hands traced his back, his neck. Her fingers were raking through his hair, while her mouth answered the seductive rhythm of his thrusting tongue.

Ambrose was oblivious to all that he'd come for. She

had awakened in him a desire so fast, so unbridled, that he was in near danger of falling victim to his need. There was only one thing that mattered. He could see the passion in her eyes. She was in his arms, and she was willing. He wanted her. One moment Elizabeth was half submerged in the tub, the next she was standing in his embrace, his arms about her waist. Ambrose's mouth moved insistently against hers as a rush of wild desire directed his action. His hands roamed her back, cupping her buttocks and pressing her against his hard arousal. He smothered her gasp with his kiss as she pressed her length against his.

He was losing control. Suddenly conscious of it, Ambrose forced himself to consider whether he wanted to take her now or slow down and prolong the pleasure he so enjoyed giving. Decisively, he dragged his mouth away, leaning back unsteadily and savoring the moment. His heart pounding, Ambrose looked down at the incomparable splendor of her naked body. She was more beautiful than Venus. His hands slid over the symmetrical perfection of her orb-shaped breasts, and then moved without hesitation downward. His mouth recaptured hers, again muffling her gasp of pleasure.

The cool breeze from the window enveloped Elizabeth's wet skin, and she started, suddenly aware of the moment. As if emerging from some other world, Elizabeth caught Ambrose's hand with hers and stopped its journey of exploration. Then, pulling her mouth away and looking down at herself, a shock of full realization struck her, and a dark blush covered her face, spreading rapidly to her neck and chest.

Ambrose, sensing immediately her mood change, sighed deeply. Not again, he thought. He seemed to remember them being here before. He remembered a night long ago, of being fully aroused. He remembered her, on the verge of giving herself to him and then putting a halt to their lovemaking.

"I want you, Elizabeth . . ." Ambrose began, but his words died away, his eyes lingering on her face. She had closed her eyes; she had turned her face away. She almost looked afraid.

Elizabeth tried to force down the lump in her throat.

Ambrose recalled the bruised and bloody face she'd

displayed the last time he'd seen her. The warrior could guess the reason for her fear. His voice hardened as he asked the question. "Where is he?"

Elizabeth opened her eyes and looked at him questioningly. The burning sense of shame quickly replaced her desire to understand, though. Turning from him, she stepped away and picked up the robe. Slipping it across her shoulders, she wrapped herself in the clinging silk before looking back at Ambrose.

A cold blanket of anger quickly replaced what had been flames of desire in Ambrose's mood. The Highlander's eyes swept over the room. Seeing her sitting in the tub after discovering the ring, he hadn't taken even a moment to scan the area beyond the screen. He had been so pleasantly shocked that his attention had focused only on her. But now, looking around at the open trunks, at the piles of paintings interspersed with the jumbled masses of women's clothing, Ambrose saw the confirmation of his first suspicion.

"It was he! Wasn't it?"

"Who, Ambrose?" she whispered, all too aware of his eyes searching the room.

"Phillipe . . . the painter. He was at the Field of Cloth of Gold. He was the man you ran away with, wasn't he?"

Elizabeth stared at him in silence, startled by his questions.

Ambrose watched her expression. Her face, clouded in a frown, was more beautiful now than it had been when they first met. The years had healed the damage of the brutality she had faced in the Golden Vale outside Calais. What had once been a jagged gash along her cheekbone was now only a thin line of a scar. Her bruises had left no mark, and the creamy complexion of her skin glowed in the lamplight. Oddly, she still wore her hair short, and the shiny, black locks were drying in soft waves around the black eyes that looked so intently into his own.

Unable to restrain himself, Ambrose reached up and smoothed the furrows that marred the wide, intelligent brow.

She stepped back from his touch.

Ambrose's expression hardened. He knew he should walk out and let her live the life she'd chosen. But his curiosity held him in place. The way she had softened in his arms, the way she had mirrored his own intense desire.

He was certain she had been responding to *him*. Unless, of course, she was all too accustomed to such casual attentions. He cursed himself for the softness he'd shown. Who was it the drunkard passing by had called for, anyway?

"How did you find me?" Elizabeth asked. Her sense of survival now demanded answers to a hundred questions. Had it been Mary's indiscretion that had led him to her? Did this mean that now everyone knew of their where-abouts? When would Garnesche's men arrive? A flush of panic colored her cheeks.

"You talk as if you think I was looking for you." His words were cold, and they were intended to hurt.

And hurt they did. For the briefest of moments she had assumed his presence had to do with their short liaison years back. Elizabeth had thought he'd valued her and had found her after a long search. But obviously she'd been wrong.

"Let me change the question. May I ask what Your Lordship is doing in my humble quarters?" Elizabeth asked, moving farther back and putting a distance be-tween them. "I don't recall inviting you here."

Ambrose let his eyes travel the length of her. The thin robe did little to cover the beautiful body beneath. He let his gaze linger suggestively on her breasts before moving lower. "If the way you greeted me was no invitation . . ."

"Don't!"

"Don't what, Elizabeth?" He took a step toward her. "Don't look at you? Don't desire you? Don't touch you? Don't hold you in my arms? Is that what you are asking of me?"

"Aye."

"Then don't look at me as you do. Don't melt in my arms at the first touch. Don't stand so provocatively near—"

"Stop!" she exploded.

Ambrose looked up in surprise. She stood facing him, challenging him with her glare. Her eyes blazed, her face flushed with her obvious anger. She looked ready to at-tack. This was the kind of physical fury a man might ex-pect from another man, but not from a woman. And she was hardly at the point of hysteria. Ambrose knew from experience that this was where most women would be breaking down, dissolving in tears, running away.

"I asked you a question, m'lord, that required only the simplest of responses." She felt the fire burning in her cheeks. "What happened between us just now was a mistake. I'd forgotten my place and your position. What happened should never have taken place."

He didn't believe her words, and he knew she didn't believe them, either.

"When last we met, I made a proposition." Ambrose studied her every move. "Was this man's offer so much better?"

"I try not to cry over what is past."

"Do you care for him?"

Elizabeth didn't know how much he knew about her life, but he clearly didn't know that Phillipe de Anjou and Elizabeth Boleyn were one and the same.

"Is that so difficult to answer?" he pressed.

Elizabeth peered at him from where she stood. She needed to get answers to her questions, but at the same time she didn't want to push him out prematurely. Was it attraction or need? She didn't know. But she was finding that the reality of having him in the room was a lot more difficult than dreaming of him nostalgically.

"I don't have to answer your questions. You, however, are still standing uninvited in this room, and I don't know why or how you come to be here."

Ambrose had come to convey a painter safely to Scotland. As he stood gazing on this strong-willed woman, the irony that she was the artist's mistress struck him. From what he had ascertained from Duke Giovanni, the warrior's understanding was that Phillipe was a shadow of a man, talented but frail. Here standing before him, however, was Elizabeth Boleyn, a woman of strength and beauty who seemed unable or unwilling to break out of the bondage of what Ambrose knew must been an unfulfilling relationship. Her response in his arms had been too immediate, too strong, too willing.

This was a challenge Ambrose would look forward to. Whatever the bond that held her to the painter, Ambrose set his mind to break it. As difficult as it would be to travel with the artist, Ambrose decided then and there that Elizabeth would accompany them during this journey, and before they reached Scotland, he would make her his own mistress. He had let her go once, but he wouldn't let that happen again. She presented a formidable challenge. One that he looked forward to immensely.

"Apparently you have no intention of answering my questions, either," Elizabeth concluded, taking the ring from the screen.

Ambrose watched the way she hung the leather thong around her neck, unconsciously laying the circle of emerald and gold gently between her breasts. The action, so innocent and yet so seductive, was a ritual that she'd apparently done a thousand times.

"Do you wear the ring against your skin like that when you make love to him?"

Elizabeth's eyes shot up.

"I find it hard to believe he's never asked you who gave it to you. What did you tell him? Have you told him about the passion we shared? Or does he even care how, to this day, you willingly accept my advances?"

Though Elizabeth felt her face burn with his words, she could not let him have the upper hand. He unnerved her, that was obvious. But it all had to end there. This was a conversation she dared not continue.

She turned her back and moved toward a pile of Mary's clothing. She needed to cover herself. Standing in the thin robe before him was too uncomfortable. Too revealing. Too vulnerable. She talked with her back to him.

"We have not even seen one another for four years, and yet you ask so many questions. I don't ask you matters of your personal life. Why not do the same for me?"

"I see I've struck close to the truth. You're running away. Hiding."

She gave him a sidelong glance. "I am doing no such thing." She picked up the first dress that she came across. "Remembering your passionate nature, I need to get into something more proper. That's all."

Elizabeth moved quickly behind the wooden screen. Assured that she was hidden from his view, she tried momentarily to make some sense out of Mary's clothing. It had been four years since she had last worn a dress. But looking at the garment, she realized she'd never in her life worn the style of clothes her sister now wore. With a sigh she removed the robe and stepped into the gown.

When the chemise flew over the top of the screen, Elizabeth bolted upright.

"If you're truly concerned about my unbridled passion, you'd do well to put on an undergarment first. There's no telling what I'll do if you step back over here dressed only in that gown."

Elizabeth looked down at herself. Oh, my God, she thought. The neckline of the crimson colored gown draped below her breasts. She was completely exposed. Hurriedly, she pulled the chemise over her head, working the garment under the dress. "You are certainly quite knowledgeable about women's clothing."

I've certainly had more than enough practice removing it, Ambrose answered silently. His eyes once again took in the room.

The painter had obviously gone out with Bardi. Ambrose knew other men like this Phillipe. It was typical that he would leave his beautiful mistress behind. Men like him were afraid of the competition. Afraid they wouldn't measure up among other men. Well, Phillipe de Anjou was about to face the toughest competition of his life.

Struggling to subdue the willfully revealing lines of the dress, Elizabeth again considered her guest, searching for a clue to explain Ambrose's presence here. Moving from behind the dividing screen, she brightened with an idea. "You must be in the service of the Baron of Roxburgh."

Ambrose scowled at her. "Who?" Grudgingly, he was beginning to understand why the painter would not take her out. She was simply too damned beautiful.

"The Baron of Roxburgh."

"Never heard of him." Ambrose moved to her side. He reached up and pulled at the chemise that covered the skin from her breasts to her collarbone. She slapped his hand away.

"Come, now, Scotland isn't that large a country," she scoffed, letting him turn her around and gasping for breath as he yanked tight the ties on the back of the dress. "The place has only six sheep and a dozen lairds to watch them, from what I hear. You must know him."

"I serve no one but the King of Scotland and the Regency Council that acts in his name. But your perception of Scotland is a bit off the mark." His voice was low and husky.

She turned and faced him. This was the proud and noble Scot speaking. "Is it?"

"Aye," Ambrose said with a drawl. "Scotland is a place like none you've ever seen. How can I describe the look of the storm tumbling across the moor? Or the torrents of a foaming Highland stream rushing through the deep green of the glen? I'm telling you, from the rolling river valleys of the Lowlands to the pine forests of the north to the wild, mountain peaks of the Outer Hebrides, it is a place that catches hold of your heart, your very soul. And once it has you, lass, it never lets go. It is a part of you, as you are a part of it."

Elizabeth paused and looked at him pensively. She hadn't expected this outpouring of emotion over his homeland. "It sounds lovely."

"It is lovely." Ambrose paused, his blue eyes intent upon her. "Like you."

She stepped back. He was charming her. Again. She felt herself melting inside. It was the same feeling. After all this time. When she answered, she could hear the slight tremor in her voice. "I suppose my knowledge of your home *is* a bit incomplete. Obviously Scotland is more than just sheep."

"Aye," he responded, his eyes piercing hers. "There are two cows, as well, wandering somewhere in the Highlands."

He watched as the dance of her smile reached her eyes. Her beautiful black eyes.

"Mama?" The child's voice called out uncertainly from the darkness beyond the dividing screen.

Elizabeth looked quickly into the surprised face of the Scot and held her finger to her lips. Without another word, she disappeared around the screen.

Ambrose, caught off guard by the child's voice, listened uncertainly to the murmuring voices for a moment.

A child. He should have known. She sounded like a small one. Of course! What else could have driven a woman like Elizabeth back to the painter? When she came to his tent at the Field of Cloth of Gold, he wondered, was she already carrying the child?

It took only a few moments for Elizabeth to settle little Jaime down once again. Casting anxious glances over her shoulder, she thought gratefully that it was a blessing Ambrose Macpherson was not in the service of this Baron of Roxburgh. It would be far too difficult for her to travel with him and keep up her disguise. He would probably see through it, in fact, and that would ruin everything.

But she could feel her heartbeat race at the very thought of being near him. No, she thought. Put it out of your mind. You must go to Scotland. You must paint. Phillipe de Anjou is expected, and Phillipe de Anjou must comply.

Hearing the steady breathing of the little girl, Elizabeth pushed her hair back away from her eyes and quietly crossed the large room. Smoothing the fine dress over her slender hips, she stepped past the dividing screen into the light.

"I'm sorry, m'lord. But you'll have to . . ." She stopped.

Ambrose Macpherson was gone.

The young maid's jaw dropped. She stood stock-still, the stack of dresses that she had been carrying scattered around her feet.

Elizabeth, hearing the footsteps, turned briskly from the window. She had opened the shutters and was looking outside for the Highlander, who had been standing in her apartment only moments before.

"I can't see anyone leaving the house," Elizabeth murmured, almost to herself. "Katrina, did you pass anyone coming up the stairs?"

The young woman continued to stare with her mouth open.

"What's wrong?" Elizabeth moved toward the young maid and grabbed hold of her two hands. "Have you seen a ghost? Has something happened?"

Katrina shook her head from side to side.

Elizabeth followed the woman's gaze. She was looking at her. At her dress. "You've never seen me in a dress, have you?"

The woman continued to shake her head. "No, I . . ."

All of Bardi's servants had been told the truth of Elizabeth's sex. After all, from the very beginning, it was clear that it would be very difficult to live under the same roof and not share the truth. But there had never been any question of their loyalty. "I look foolish, don't I?"

"You look stunning, Signor Phi . . . signorina. You are like a dream." The young girl's eyes scanned the painter's face. "But your scar . . . it is gone . . . your face is beautiful."

Elizabeth smiled. "Can I tell you something?"

Katrina crossed her heart quickly.

"I paint my face. I redden the scar to accent it. I darken under my eyes to look older."

The woman's eyes widened in awe once again.

Elizabeth shook her head in amusement. She had definitely made an impression on the young woman. "Katrina, did you see anyone leaving when you came up?"

"No one, signorina."

"Don't start calling me that. This dress hasn't changed who I am. Have you been downstairs? Did anyone come to the door?"

"No one, signorin—I mean, Signor Phillipe."

"Are you certain of that?" Elizabeth asked, her perplexity showing in her face.

"You know the porter, signor. He guards that door with his life when Signor and Signora Bardi are not here."

Baffled, Elizabeth turned and strode back to the window. The street was empty. Where had he come from? Where had he gone?

Had she conjured this man?

Elizabeth glanced about the room wildly for some trace, some sign, that Ambrose Macpherson had been standing here with her.

Nothing. She saw nothing.

Chapter 16

❧

Joseph Bardi quivered under the blazing words being directed at him. The nobleman had not stopped his tirade since entering the room. *Offending, dishonoring* Don Giovanni, the Queen of Scotland, and, even more, the Baron of Roxburgh. Joseph decided fearfully that he should consider himself as good as hanged right now. He only hoped his end would not be terribly painful.

"Please, m'lord," Bardi put in quickly, breaking into the other man's harangue. "We only meant to relieve Your Lordship of all unnecessary burdens. The last thing we intended to do was bring you rushing to Florence in the manner you've described."

"Taking a painter safely to Scotland is not a toilsome burden, so long as you know the safe route to travel." Ambrose looked at the nervous twitch in the merchant's face. He'd scared the man half to death. My God, he *was* getting too much like Gavin. "I have given my word to the Duke of Nemours to see to the task myself. The regions to the north of us are rough and dangerous lands. My anger comes from you taking on the task so blindly, without any advice."

Bardi heard the giant's voice lose some of its edge. Perhaps the worst was over. But the Scottish lord still needed to be told of the rest. "M'lord, I am not certain if the duke made mention of the painter's companions. You see, he won't travel without them. And we were concerned that you might have objections to taking so many, and—"

"And you thought if he arrived in Scotland with his entourage, then the queen would not send him back and they could all stay?"

The merchant wrung his hands, nodding disconsolately.

"The truth is, m'lord, he doesn't have many that accompany him. Just a young woman and a child. And perhaps a couple of servants. He is very attached to them."

"He is married?"

"Oh, no! No, it isn't that. You see—"

"I have no problem with that." Ambrose tried to suppress his smile. He had been correct in assuming that Elizabeth was only a mistress to the painter.

"And then there are the two of us," Bardi put in hopefully. "My wife and I. We hoped to be able to see them to safety and—"

"You don't trust them in my hands?"

"Oh, no! No, m'lord! That's not it at all. You see, I am a merchant, and I was hoping that perhaps I might meet and come to some bartering arrangement with wool merchants in Scotland. And as for my wife . . . well, she is very fond of the little child. M'lord, she could be . . . no, she *will* be a great help on the journey." The merchant watched a scowl darken the man's intimidating scar. "I know it all seems like so much we are asking. But I can assure Your Lordship, we are all well-seasoned travelers. We will cause you and your men no trouble. No inconvenience, I swear, m'lord."

He would take them; Ambrose knew he would. Elizabeth was definitely going, so he supposed he had to take them all. But so many people!

The warrior turned to the study's small open hearth and kicked at the embers. A small burst of sparks exploded as the fire flared up. What Ambrose really wanted to think about was how to break Elizabeth away from her lover. Well, first he had to size up his foe. He had to meet Phillipe.

"Get the painter."

The merchant looked at him wide-eyed. It was way past midnight. The household had settled in their beds long ago. In fact, Joseph himself had been awakened by a terrified servant with the news that the Baron of Roxburgh was about to break down the front door.

"Didn't you hear me?"

"Now, m'lord? You want to speak to him now?"

"Now!" Ambrose repeated.

Seeing the man's hesitation, Ambrose took a step toward the door. "If you don't get him, I will." Was Elizabeth lying in the painter's arms? Ambrose found himself getting angry at the thought.

"No, no that won't be necessary. I'll go after him myself." Bardi jumped quickly toward the closed door. This Scotsman certainly has a way of unnerving a person, he thought. He just hoped Elizabeth would be able to deal with him. She was often a lot better in difficult situations than he was. "Please make yourself comfortable. I'll awaken him and bring him to you, m'lord."

Ambrose watched the man's hasty retreat, then turned his attention toward the darkened inner room. The furnishings were well made here, too, but as he'd seen in the great hall and in the corridors, they were rendered practically invisible by the large number of portraits that dominated the walls and that drew the eyes upward in an impressive display. He strode to the closest one.

It was portrait of a child. A young child, still soft and round with ebony-colored hair. Against a harmonious background of light blues and grays, the face of the child stood out like a flower or a patch of sunlight in the dark room. Ambrose grabbed a candle from the desk and, lighting it in the fire, brought it closer to the painting. The eyes . . . the eyes of the child. He knew them. The large black eyes that stared back at him were Elizabeth's. Then he lowered the light and saw the brushes. The paintbrushes clutched in the tiny plump hand.

Elizabeth tripped over the tub and fell with a thud.

"Are you hurt?" Joseph whispered from behind the panel.

"Why, in God's name, must he come now?" Elizabeth hissed under her breath, standing up once again. She pulled the stockings up her legs. "Why couldn't he wait until morning?"

"Trust me, I tried. But he's a bear, Elizabeth. I'm sure the Baron of Roxburgh is one powerful and difficult man. When he wants something, he wants it *now*."

"I'm trying to sleep, if you don't mind," Mary called out, her complaint answered by a hush from the two standing in the dark.

"How am I going to paint my face?" Elizabeth asked softly. "I don't want to light a candle and awaken Jaime."

"You don't have to," Joseph whispered. "It's fairly

dark in the study. Let's just go down and agree to whatever he says. Then we can send him on his way. I think I've talked him into taking all of us with him."

"Why do we have to go with him, anyway?" Elizabeth pulled the loose shirt over her head. "We could travel on our own."

"No, no, Elizabeth! Please don't talk that way. I thought he was going to hand me over to the Medici's executioners for suggesting that. That is out of the question. We'll have to go with him. There is no other way."

Elizabeth cursed under her breath as she stepped around the wooden screen. "Do I look convincing?"

"Absolutely. Let's go and get it done with."

The Baron of Roxburgh was sitting in a straight-backed wooden chair in a dark corner of Joseph's study. His face was hidden in shadow, but Elizabeth could see from the man's long, muscular legs and broad chest that he must be an imposing figure. His high boots shone in the fading firelight, one leg crossed over the other. The doublet that covered his pure white shirt and hosiery was made of well-tailored black satin, and richly appointed with strips of black velvet. The glint of the jeweled broach clasping the man's dark tartan caught Elizabeth's attention. The size of the diamonds and rubies, even from a distance, was impressive. As he turned slightly in his chair, the light picked up the raised metalwork of the broach: a rampant cat sitting above a shield that had a ship depicted on it. Elizabeth felt a sudden stir at the sight. She didn't know how, but she knew the design.

This was a side of Scotland that Elizabeth had not experienced before. The image of wealth and power that was being displayed here was far different from the power that Ambrose exhibited. While Ambrose was rough-hewn, strong, and true, he always wore the gear of the Highland warrior he was. With the exception of the tartan, this man was dressed in the fashion of the day. He had the look of the perfect European courtier.

"M'lord, I'd like to intro—"

"Go!" the baron commanded abruptly, cutting Joseph off. "And shut the door."

Elizabeth and Joseph exchanged a quick look, and then the merchant bowed and backed out the door.

Elizabeth couldn't see the man's face, but his voice carried the weight of authority. This was clearly a man who meant to be obeyed, but the painter felt her temper flaring at the rough treatment of her friend in his own study. If this was a sampling of what they would have to put up with on their journey, then she would have to put this nobleman in his place now.

"M'lord, I am not certain if anyone has brought this to your attention, but this is Joseph Bardi's villa. As the rules of etiquette provide, it is discourteous to throw a man out of his own study."

The baron's boot slammed to the floor. "Into the light, you."

"I believe you came here to speak with me." Elizabeth tried to deepen her voice. "Not to order me and my friend about."

"I asked to see the painter."

Elizabeth clenched her hands into fists. Again. So many times during the past four years, people had only seen the frail build in their first encounter with her, and nothing else. And so many times, she had to give her sermon, as Pico called it, and lose her temper before they were convinced.

"I am the painter."

He disregarded what she said. "Do as you are told. Get the painter."

Angrily, she took a step closer to the man, her clenched jaw grinding. "Before we get started on this journey to your homeland, I have to make one thing clear. If you have any desire to arrive in one piece, then you'd better change that disdainful tone of yours. Now, *you* demanded to see me at this godawful hour of the night. So here I am. What is it you want?"

"In one piece?" Ambrose studied her anger. Elizabeth's face was now shining in the light of the candle. "That sounds like a threat."

"Take it as you wish."

"You are too puny for such swaggering."

"I have been known to split a man's head with my words and twist his body into a crawling, earthbound snake with my brush."

"And you think this strikes fear?"

Her hands were tight fists at her sides.

"Push all you want. But be aware the next time you walk inside some chapel or cathedral. As you stand looking up, admiring the scene as so many others do, don't be surprised when you see your own face looking back at you. In fact, everyone will see your features gracing the face of a devil." Elizabeth showed no sign of mirth. "And you can be assured, it will be a very lowly and very ugly devil."

Elizabeth waited for a response. But there was silence. An eerie, awkward silence.

"You *are* the painter."

Elizabeth watched him straighten in his chair. She wished she could see his face. "I am Phillipe de Anjou." As often as she'd said it before, the words still felt odd leaving her mouth. She saw him stand up, and her blood ran cold. Though his face was still shadowed in the darkness of the room, she knew. From his full height, from the way he stood. And then she glimpsed the colors of his tartan.

Not being able to control the gasp that escaped her lips, Elizabeth turned and ran for the door. But he was there before her, blocking her exit. She turned again and tried to run to one of the shuttered windows, but he grabbed her roughly from behind and swung her around to face him.

Elizabeth felt the pressure of his strong fingers crushing her arms. She would not scream or complain. She had no choice but to make him understand. She looked up into his eyes. They were cold, angry. Nothing like what she had seen in the past.

"Talk."

Elizabeth tried to shrug off his hands, but he would not let go. Suddenly the icy coldness of panic coursed through her. This was not the gentle and caring nobleman she had met before. This man was more judge and executioner, demanding to hear her final testimony. For all these years she had tried never to be overly concerned about the possible consequences of her life—of her work—in the studio. But now the truth, the ugly truth, was about to catch up to her. The Baron of Roxburgh, Ambrose Macpherson, was a close friend to Giovanni de' Medici. If he spoke out, if he revealed her secret, she would be hanged and then burned by the leaders of the Florentine guild. For, as a woman, she had lied and betrayed all the artists in the profession. She would be found guilty. She was a woman working as a man. This was a crime far worse than any they could ever pardon.

"What are you planning to do?" she asked quietly. She was working hard to hide the shiver that raced through her body.

Ambrose had to fight the urge to pull her into his arms and comfort her. That would have been so easy to do. She was afraid. Afraid of him, he could tell.

But he was angry. He had been taken for a fool by a mere woman. He'd never suspected it. She had not given even the smallest hint that Phillipe and she were one and the same. And then he'd seen the child's portrait. The softness, the love shown in the picture—this had disturbed him. For the few moments before she'd come down, he'd been confused. And then the painter had walked into the study. Not the man he'd been ready to challenge, but Elizabeth.

And now he didn't know what his next step should be. Not yet.

Elizabeth lowered her eyes from his intense blue gaze and stared at his broach. She could not take this long silence. He hadn't answered her. He would surely hand her over. She would never say good-bye to Jaime.

"Start explaining."

"Isn't it all to obvious?" she whispered. "And does it really matter? Is there anything I could say that would change your mind?"

"You think my mind is made up."

She looked down at the rough hold of his fingers on her arms.

"Isn't it?" she asked. "If I were to pour out my soul and speak the truth, would you give me a chance? Or are you just going to hand me over to be hanged?"

He eased the pressure of his grip. "I am giving you a few moments to present your case. But for a change, I need to hear the truth. And only the truth." Ambrose backed her to a chair and pushed her into it. "Start from the beginning, from the Field of Cloth of Gold."

Elizabeth looked up from where she sat. He towered over her. Once again his face was a dark silhouette of shadows and dying firelight. She wondered for a moment what "truth" he wanted to hear. Sitting there in the darkened room, she dared not even hope that this meant he intended to give her a chance.

"Silence will not work to reprieve your present situation," Ambrose growled ominously. "Do I have to remind you what your punishment would be for lying, for pretending to be what you are not, for delving into the secrets that your guild brothers protect so religiously? Do you know what these Florentines would do to you? To start, they would proclaim you evil—an abomination. Do you want me to just give you over to them?"

She looked down and shook her head.

"Then speak. I need to know when and for what reason you came up with this perverse idea."

"But . . . it is not perverse." She could no longer hold back her tongue. "I am not evil. I have never acted in any way that might bring indignity to anyone. If, as I have pretended, I really were a man, I would continue to be praised . . . rewarded . . . for my talent and my hard work. But now, being discovered, I am suddenly a demon. I am some unnatural denizen of hell simply because I have a God-given talent that I have chosen to employ. Simply because I needed to work to feed my family, to care for them."

Ambrose watched her blazing face, her power. It was obvious that she believed every word she spoke. "But you had a family. You had a place in society, a home. Why did you leave it?"

Elizabeth paused. She could not tell him everything. There was nothing that told her she should trust him. No, Elizabeth thought, there was no reason to trust him. After all, even if she had not been totally forthright, she was certainly not alone. Look at him. When he'd arrived in her bedchamber earlier, he had not been completely candid. The Baron of Roxburgh, indeed.

"I'm having a hard time believing you, Elizabeth, because you are saying so little." Ambrose watched as her face reflected some inner struggle. Finally she peered through the darkness and shrugged her shoulders.

"I had to run away from my father."

"Sir Thomas Boleyn?"

Elizabeth nodded slowly. "I don't believe he's ever considered me a true daughter. Not that it matters. But I had to get away."

Ambrose watched her shoulders drop in resignation. Well, she was willing to talk. This was a start.

"Why did you have to get away? I'm certain that your father's feelings for you were not an overnight revelation."

Elizabeth watched as he moved away and sat in a chair by the desk. He was keeping a distance between them. This woman is poison, she could almost see him thinking. Don't get too close to her.

But then, how could she blame him?

"It's true," she whispered, shuddering at the memory of all that had taken place that day. "But he'd never in the past tried to . . . dispose of me the way he was planning to the night before I ran."

"Dispose of you?"

"He was sending me to his master's bed," Elizabeth said, trying to keep the bitterness out of her voice. She watched as his eyes shot up to hers. "The King of England happened to take a fancy to me the last day of the tournament, so the disgusting, pox-infected blackguard summoned my father. Henry wanted me for his bed."

Ambrose thought back to the day. To how beautiful she'd looked in the grandstands. To the attention he'd paid to her after accepting from Francis the English king's lost wager. His face darkened.

"Aye, I was ordered to go. By my own kin."

"The bastard!" Ambrose cursed under his breath. The joust. He hadn't known who Elizabeth was when he spoke to her after the joust. But it was so typical of King Henry's viciousness. No Scot would make public advances to the daughter of one of his men without someone paying the price. Henry could not punish Ambrose for his attentions to Elizabeth. And Boleyn had his uses. But the daughter, beautiful as she was, would make a pretty plaything. And she would be made to suffer for Ambrose's advances—before he discarded her.

"Did you go?" He asked the question through clenched teeth. Elizabeth was not the one to blame—he was.

"No. I would have died before going to him." Elizabeth gazed at the single candle sitting on the worktable. A moth fluttered about the light. "I told my father that."

"Was he the one who beat you?"

"Aye. Both times." She turned her gaze back to him.

"As you can imagine, he was not at all pleased with my answer. That was when I knew I had to leave his house. He provided for me in Paris. As long as I stayed in his household, I belonged to him. Like a dog or a sword or a piece of furniture. He could trade me, barter my body." Her eyes flashed with anger. "I would have preferred death to such a life. I value myself more than to allow anyone to use me as he planned."

Mixed feelings for this woman pounded at Ambrose's brain. He couldn't tell what was worse, the guilt that was nagging his conscience that something he had done may have set all this in motion or the simple concern that was tugging at his insides. He shook his head. "Tell me, lass. How did I fit into your plans? Why did you come to me that night?"

Elizabeth looked down at her hands. She was not willing to admit to him the truth about her plan to lose her virtue. "You are a hero. Handsome, chivalrous, sensual. And you showed interest in me. Would you believe if I told you that . . . well, curiosity was the primary reason?"

"Nay." Ambrose suppressed his smile. "But if I did believe you, then I suppose I have to assume it was disappointment that drove you out." He watched a slow smile tugging at her lips.

"Quite to the contrary, m'lord." She could feel the heat of his gaze on her face. "Truthfully . . . I got scared. Scared of myself and my reaction to you. It was all so much at once. I knew I had to leave France, my family, everything I ever held dear. I could not accept any more complications in my life."

"You didn't have to run. I remember offering you protection."

You offered me your bed, she thought.

"It would have been wrong to impose myself on you or on anyone. I knew that I could take care of myself. I knew I had a talent," Elizabeth continued. "I had already sold some of my paintings, so I knew I could do it. It was my fate, my destiny to live by my own means, by my talent. I could feel it. That was my moment to try. If I didn't try it then, my chance would be gone forever."

Ambrose watched her entwined fingers on her lap. She was good. In fact, she was more than good. She was an exceptionally talented artist. From what he'd seen of her paintings at Giovanni de' Medici's palace, from what he'd seen in this villa tonight, and from the one piece that he had himself, Ambrose knew without question that Elizabeth Boleyn was indeed a gifted artist.

But what the hell am I going to do with her? he thought. He knew he couldn't expose the truth. After all, he himself was probably more responsible for the situation she was in today than anyone else. Henry had just wanted to use her and even a score—Ambrose understood the politics of court life. But could he take her to Scotland and present her to the queen? No, of course he couldn't. The men in Florence might be completely blind to a beautiful woman, but Ambrose knew that her ruse would never work in Scotland. She would be discovered before she stepped ten paces on Scottish soil. Perhaps even before— Gavin Kerr would probably spot her as a fake. Perhaps the best thing for him to do was simply to walk away and ask Giovanni for a different artist. He could tell the duke that he'd never seen this Phillipe fellow. She had hidden her identity for this long, she could continue indefinitely. Perhaps that was the best answer.

"Please take me with you."

Ambrose started at the request. He wondered, briefly, what she was asking. The possibility of her taking his offer, even after four years, still raised a stirring in his loins. And that was damn startling, considering.

"Please take me to Scotland. I won't disappoint you. I give you my word." The hesitation Elizabeth had seen in the nobleman in the past few moments had nearly unnerved her. She feared the silent argument that the man was having with himself. She could not let Ambrose Macpherson leave them behind. She *had* to talk him into taking them to his queen. There was not much time left. "I will agree to whatever conditions you set."

Ambrose watched her in silence. This was fear speaking. He had been involved with enough negotiations to know when desperation and fear had taken over. Elizabeth was not even trying to cover her fear. She was willing to throw herself into his bed in order to save her pretty neck. As much as the idea of having this woman for a short while appealed to him, this was not the way he wanted it to happen.

"I know your queen has been waiting for a long time

for a painter of some quality. Michelangelo told me that she had asked him to go to Scotland ten years ago to paint the royal portrait. But he'd been in the middle of a massive sculpting project for Pope Julius's memorial and used that as an excuse not to go. With the terrible troubles that Scotland had in that time, he said no painter he knew was willing to travel there." Elizabeth continued to talk fast. She needed to win him over. "The stories of the war between England and Scotland were dreadful—I remember when Flodden happened and you lost your king. Michelangelo said he even heard your queen blaming him for the death of her husband. It was rumored that she said if he had gone to paint them in the summer of 1513, the king might not have gone to war. The maestro says he heard she's become obsessed with the idea. I can remedy that."

Ambrose listened quietly to her words. He was certainly glad that he'd not spoken earlier. He would have had to swallow his words. She was not giving herself to him. She wanted him to help her with her masquerade. And everybody knew of Queen Margaret's superstitious ideas. They were no secret. She was more superstitious than the Florentines, and they were the most credulous people in Europe.

But more importantly, Ambrose did not believe a word Elizabeth said about why she wanted to go. There was something else.

"Please, no one needs to know the truth. I can do the job to your queen's satisfaction." Elizabeth wished he would say something. "It will only be for a short while. I promise not to be a nuisance, and I will stay out of your way. Please, give me the chance and let me try."

Ambrose had to admit this was much more to his liking. If she were throwing herself at him, he'd pass on the opportunity. But this had promise. It presented the possibility of challenge, of the charms of seduction.

"Nay, lass. She'll have my head on a pike over Stirling Castle if she finds out I've brought a woman to paint the royal family."

"She doesn't need to find out! She *won't* find out!"

Ambrose continued as if he hadn't heard her. "Did I hear you mention something about being agreeable to my conditions?" He stood and walked to the fireplace.

Leaning his broad back against it, he watched her confused expression.

"It all depends on what they are, m'lord." Elizabeth said, suddenly fearful of what was hidden in his words.

"The first condition of taking you with me is that you accept these terms."

"Are they many?"

"Possibly only a few." He crossed his arms. "It all depends on my mood during the journey."

"How could you expect me to accept them when I don't know what they are?" Elizabeth protested weakly.

"I am certain if I approached Don Giovanni with—"

"Agreed," Elizabeth broke in. "I'll accept your conditions so long as you accept one of mine."

Ambrose frowned at her. "You are in no position to bargain."

"I am in the position to ask."

"What is it?" he ordered. "What is your . . . request?"

Elizabeth stood as well and pushed the chair aside. "My family goes with me. To Scotland."

"Your family is in England. I'll not go there to get them."

"You don't have to." She leaned against the desk and stretched her legs in front of her.

Ambrose watched her shapely legs showing attractively through the thin hose. These Florentines are blind, he thought.

"Mary and Jaime are with me here. I am responsible for them, so they have to go with us."

"Mary is your sister," Ambrose remembered. "She disappeared when you did."

"You searched me out!" Elizabeth stated with surprise in her voice. The idea that this nobleman might have tried to find out about her whereabouts after they separated four years ago had hardly occurred to her.

Ambrose ignored her comment. "Your sister, as I recall, was trouble in the making. This is a long journey to Scotland. She'll be disturbing my men. I know already I don't like it. And this Jaime, who is she?"

Elizabeth paused. She couldn't go without them. How could she leave Mary and little Jaime behind? That was no option. And the way the Highlander spoke, he seemed somehow willing to take her and only her. Ambrose

Macpherson would not understand the bond that connected the three of them. Unless . . .

"The child . . ."

"Your daughter."

Elizabeth stared.

"I won't leave her behind. I have to take her."

Ambrose watched her face. "How old is she?"

"Merely three."

Ambrose pointed at the painting on the wall. "Is that her?"

Elizabeth nodded in silence.

"She looks like you." His eyes traveled from the portrait of the child to the face of the woman standing in the study. "Who is the father?"

Her eyes shot up to meet his. She had not expected him to ask. "He is not around."

"Who is the father?" He repeated the question.

"Why do you ask?" she protested. She had not expected to have to lie like this. Now, already, she was afraid. Afraid of getting caught in her own web of lies.

"One of the conditions," Ambrose said shortly, "is that you answer my questions."

"If I answer, does that mean that you'll take us with you?"

"I'll tell you once I have the answer."

It was impossible to reason with the man. Joseph was right—Ambrose Macpherson was used to having things his way and only his way. "He is dead. It doesn't matter who he was. He's dead."

Ambrose could hear that there was no regret in her voice. Had this man simply been another "curiosity" for Elizabeth Boleyn? As Ambrose himself had been? But there was a difference. She had been interested enough in this other man to stay and share her passion. After all, she had borne his child. The man was dead, but Ambrose still felt a gnawing pang of envy. It didn't make sense, but he did nonetheless.

"What was his name?"

Elizabeth panicked. What happened if she picked a name that he knew? She wished he would stop his questioning. "His name . . ."

"What was it? And how did you two meet?" Ambrose

was becoming less patient with his string of unanswered questions. "How did he die?"

She took a deep breath and resigned herself to going through with it. "Phillipe de Anjou." Seeing the surprised look on Ambrose's face, she felt encouraged and continued. "He was an artist. A French artist I knew in Paris. When I ran from Calais, we met in Paris and he brought me here. He died when we stopped in Milan, so I took over his name and his work." Elizabeth breathed a sigh of relief. "That's it. All of it."

"How did he die?"

"How?" she repeated. How the devil would I know? she cursed inwardly.

"Was he poisoned? Did someone stab him? Did he fall off a wagon? There are usually reasons for a young man dying."

"Oh!" she acknowledged. "But . . . but he wasn't young. He was old. He died of old age . . . and a fever."

"You slept with a rickety old man and gave him a child?" Ambrose nearly smiled openly. Now he understood her willingness in his arms.

"You have no right to talk about him so flippantly." Elizabeth looked away. "Phillipe was a good man, and he cared a great deal for us. I remember him fondly, and I cherish his memory. I would appreciate it if you would stop your mockery of something you don't understand."

Ambrose studied her downturned face. He could not see her expression. But from the small shudder of her shoulders, he guessed she was upset, perhaps even crying. Hell, he might as well take her and the whole herd of them. So what if she was discovered? If she was unmasked in Scotland, she'd have a better chance of surviving it than she would in Florence.

"You are going with me."

"You mean we're all going, m'lord." She turned her gaze back at him, wiping her eyes with the backs of her hands.

Ambrose could tell that she looked flushed. "Your daughter and you."

"My sister, my daughter, and I."

"Nay. Your sister is trouble."

Elizabeth faced him head-on. "I need her for my facade. Everyone thinks Jaime is hers. It's important."

"Where are we going, it won't matter. Be ready, we'll be leaving Florence in a week."

She shook her head in argument. "I cannot come up with a new charade in such a short time. Please, m'lord, I'll . . . I'll offer you a deal."

"You have nothing to offer," Ambrose reminded her.

"Conditions?" She watched his expression.

"Go on."

"I'll abide by your conditions—any and all that you state—until we reach Scotland. And in return you'll take my family and the Bardis."

He looked at her incredulously. "A moment ago it was your daughter and your sister. Now you've added your friends. I am starting to feel that with every passing moment, I'm losing a larger share of this bargain."

"Then accept," she said matter-of-factly.

Ambrose appraised his opponent.

"Aye. With conditions."

Chapter 17

❧

"We missed the damn boat!"

"I know! We all heard you!" Elizabeth was not about to be publicly humiliated by this man. She returned Ambrose's glare without so much as a blink. "Everyone in Pisa heard you!"

Standing on the dock beside the empty slip, Elizabeth looked back and saw her fearful traveling companions were keeping a safe distance away from the angry nobleman. It had been Mary once again, disappearing at the last moment for no apparent reason. She had no sense of the value of time or of schedules. But Elizabeth was not going to make excuses for her or anyone else. She saw no need to explain. Certainly not to the arrogant Lord Macpherson.

She had not seen him since they'd met in Joseph's study in Florence. His directions, as he'd departed that night, had been to be ready in a week and meet him in Pisa. But he had been courteous and offered to send his men to assist the group in bringing their belongings to the port city near the mouth of the Arno.

And she'd been daft and accepted his offer.

His men had indeed arrived this morning. But they were not there to help. They had arrived with specific orders from their master. Mary could not take her three chests full of clothes. Joseph could not bring his merchandise. Elizabeth could not bring her paintings. They were to travel light, with only enough to be carried on horseback. Those had been Ambrose Macpherson's directions.

And Elizabeth had disobeyed his orders. Every one of them. But he didn't know. Not yet.

It still amazed her, even hurt a bit, to realize how wrong she could have been about him. She had been so fooled by the facade of concern, by the sensual and passionate approach this man so easily used to overwhelm her. But that was before she'd seen the real man. She felt the tips of her ears burning at the very thought of the weakness he perceived within her—at the thought that she'd been so blind to the truth beneath his practiced technique. Ambrose Macpherson, the Baron of Roxburgh, was a pigheaded, bigmouthed, aggravating man who demanded things be done his way, and only his way. Joseph had been right about him from the beginning.

"We missed the damn boat!"

Elizabeth turned at the sound of the roar from the far end of the dock and watched as a second Scot came storming toward them. The wind was whipping the man's black hair about his face, so she could not see his expression, but his size, she had to admit, was more than intimidating. Ambrose was a giant, but this one looked half a head taller.

"I can see you Highlanders are very limited in your use of words," she whispered loudly enough for Ambrose to hear.

"Say that when he's closer, and he'll break you in half," Ambrose responded shortly. "Gavin Kerr's from the Borders—a Lowlander—and he thinks Highlanders are barbarians—"

"And he'd be correct, of course!" she broke in.

"This is a long journey, and you can be certain that I'll do my best to live up to that reputation."

She cringed at his words.

Ambrose gazed down and studied Elizabeth's face as his bearlike friend paused to look at the group of tardy travelers cowering near their baggage. She was extremely good at darkening her fair young skin under the masking pigments. But she still looked good. Damn good.

"Does he know the truth?" she whispered, not taking her eyes from the angry black-haired warrior. "The truth about me?"

"What truth?" Ambrose snapped. "Does anyone know the truth about you? I don't know what is the truth about you."

Elizabeth's temper flared. "I have answered every

question you've asked. I understand neither your harsh
words nor your sour mood." Her voice softened. "Why
can't you just leave the past behind? Why can't we just be
on our way?"

Ambrose looked straight out across the diverse collection of ships, galleys, and barges crowding the wide,
muddy river that would carry them out to the Ligurian Sea
and into the Mediterranean. He was still upset, and he was
having difficulty controlling his temper. This was a first
for him. Just calm down, he thought. They would get another ship.

"Gavin Kerr has no reason to think you're anything
other than what you say."

Elizabeth had chosen not to reveal her past liaison with
Ambrose Macpherson to the Bardis, and she had not told
them that the nobleman knew she was a woman, either.
This was a complication she did not want them to worry
about. But she had to tell Mary the truth. After all, her sister was still under the assumption that Elizabeth had surrendered her maidenhood to this Highlander.

"Gavin is a trusting man. I have not told him of your . . .
inventiveness."

"Thank you," she whispered.

Ambrose turned to her with wonder. He had not expected those simple words. Quickly regaining his frown,
he growled at the small painter. "Which means he'd as
soon kill you as look at you."

"Oh!"

"Is this the goddamn painter that has left us sitting on
our arses for the past two days?"

"Aye, Gavin. This is Phillipe de Anjou."

"What are you, a dwarf?" he rumbled, glowering down
at Elizabeth.

Elizabeth drew in a deep breath and glared back.
"There's nothing wrong with *my* size. But the baron tells
me you got to be the size you are by eating stolen English
cattle."

Gavin's eyebrows shot up, and he glanced quickly at
Ambrose. "Oh, he did?"

"Aye," she continued quickly. "He says you've even
been known to stop and roast the carcasses before devouring them . . . occasionally."

Elizabeth watched as the corner of the Border dweller's

mouth started to turn up. He was a huge man, as broad and as tall as Michelangelo's statues of Hercules. His face, as fierce as his expression was, had the handsome, chiseled features of the marble gods. What he lacked was the hint of humor that danced just behind the blue eyes of his Highland friend Ambrose Macpherson. Nor had he the easy smile. He hadn't the fluid confidence of his stance, either.

Nor, she decided, could she imagine him holding any woman the way Ambrose had held her.

"Tell me," she asked, pressing her advantage. "Is it worth your while sitting on your arses waiting for good meat?"

"Aye, lad," the Lowlander conceded thoughtful. "Particularly when it's stolen meat."

"Then, Gavin Kerr, remember this. You've just stolen me and my friends from the Medicis, and when your queen rewards you for what you've brought her, you'll see that the wait was worth your while."

A broad grin broke across the warrior's face, and with an abrupt movement, Gavin clapped Elizabeth hard on the back of her shoulder, launching her a half step forward.

"Well, Ambrose. This lad will be all right, I'm wagering. Though you *are* a scrawny thing, Phillipe."

Ambrose gave her a once-over look. But his face showed nothing of what he was thinking. He knew what was beneath.

"Perhaps we can fatten you up a bit during this journey. Make you strong. Like a man," Gavin boomed.

"He is a painter," Ambrose said under his breath. "He is fine as he is."

Gavin ignored his friend's remark. "I haven't seen any of your paintings. Though Ambrose tells me you've quite a talent."

"Has he?" Elizabeth remarked with surprise, casting an eye on the nobleman.

"Aye, though—nothing against you—I doubt he knows much about it," Gavin rumbled conspiratorially. "He is only a Highlander, after all."

Elizabeth watched as the two exchanged a glare. She had a strong suspicion that this bantering was constant between these two men.

"Well, Gavin," Ambrose broke in. "Did you find us

another ship? Or are we just going to sit around here for a week or so longer?"

"As a matter of fact, you see the bow of that galley about eight quays in that direction?" Gavin pointed at the ship. "They sail for Marseilles with the morning tide, and I was able to secure us a berth. Though it wasn't easy. The captain was not very excited about having two dozen Scottish warriors along."

"That's no surprise," Ambrose said under his breath.

Gavin looked at his friend. "And I didn't mention your name."

"Good."

Curiosity in her face, Elizabeth looked from one man to the other. "Is there something that you two would like to tell me before we get any farther along on this journey?"

"Nay," the two men answered in unison.

Without another word, the Scots turned their backs on her and walked away, and Elizabeth stood, her hands at her sides, looking after them as they moved together down the dock.

Elizabeth cringed as the two sailors dropped Mary's trunk into the hold of the galley. The sun was low over the western waters that extended beyond the wide mouth of the Arno, and though the troop of Scots warriors were drinking noisily on the dock, she was determined to keep a close watch on things as their luggage was loaded aboard the merchant vessel.

She looked at her friend standing beside her. "Joseph, do you have any idea why the baron would want to hide his true identity from the captain of this ship?"

Joseph turned his back to the high gunwale and smiled at the painter. "Aye, I do."

Elizabeth waited patiently as the merchant looked up into the rigging at the two masts of the galley. She knew it was the kind of ship Joseph had traveled on many times in his search for markets. From what Joseph had just finished telling her, she now knew that the two-masted galley was the workhorse of Mediterranean sea trading, and its design had not changed for as long as anyone remembered. The ship had forty-eight oarsmen who would propel the shallow-hulled vessel forward regardless of the wind's direction.

"This is one of the first of its kind," Joseph said enthusiastically, pointing toward the stern of the vessel. "From what I hear, beneath the high deck back there, they have expanded the cabin space."

"My friend, the cabin size of this galley is not my worry right now," she said quietly. "I am more concerned about putting all of you in jeopardy. Joseph, I need to know what information you have about the Baron of Roxburgh."

Joseph peered at the animated group of sailors gathering not far from where Mary stood pouting in the sun. An uneasy feeling crept through him.

"Well, Joseph?" Elizabeth prodded, still waiting for the details but not hearing any. "Would you care to tell me what you know?"

"No."

"Please, Joseph," she said shortly. "If you are planning to act like those two pigheaded Scots, then I'll be taking my complaints to Erne."

Joseph breathed more easily as he spotted his wife moving purposefully toward Mary through the throng of people milling about among the stalls of fishermen and farmers that crowded the stone quays. He watched as she sent the seafarers on their way with a mere frown. Then her face brightened as she glanced up at the ship and saw him, and he answered her nod with a smile and a wave.

"Well, in that case, I'll tell you what I know. But you must keep it to yourself. I just cannot afford having hysterical women on my hands during this journey."

"Is it that bad?"

"Nay! Not at all. But you never know how some people will react to something they've assumed for a long while was only just gossipy word of mouth."

She hung on his every word. As Joseph looked over the crowds moving about the pier, she nearly snapped. "Please, Joseph! The suspense of this is getting the best of me. Tell me what you know."

Joseph looked away from her once again, but this time his eyes searched for Ambrose Macpherson. He had no desire to be caught speaking about the baron by the man himself.

"The first night when he came to us in Florence, I

had no idea that the Baron of Roxburgh and Ambrose Macpherson were one and the same man."

And that makes two of us, Elizabeth thought.

"But seeing his broach and the colors of his tartan, I knew soon enough," Joseph continued. "I think that was when I became really frightened." The last words were spoken quietly, as if to no one but himself.

"At any rate, the stories go back some time and have to do with pirates in the seas west of England. Years back, as I remember, anyone who traveled the Irish Sea knew the names Macpherson and Campbell and feared them. They were the fiercest pirates ever to navigate those waters."

"He's a pirate?" Elizabeth asked with great deal of hesitation. She quickly lowered her voice to a hush as she looked around. "We're traveling with a pirate?"

"Not Ambrose. His father," Joseph went on. "He even had license for it. King James of Scotland gave exclusive rights to his most courageous noblemen. Their job was to defend the Scottish waters and to bring in whatever revenue they could by raiding passing ships."

"They were thieves!"

"No, my dear. Even today this is considered a legitimate—even noble—profession, and the practice is continued by every king in Europe. English, Spanish, French—they all do it. It is part of the shipping business. To trade in these dangerous waters, you have to protect your vessels and your merchandise. And the best way to do this is to be a pirate yourself. If you are not, then you'd better be prepared to pay large sums of gold and hope they will work on your side."

Elizabeth's eyes found Ambrose where he stood talking with the ship's captain on the stone quay. "Then he's one, too?"

"A pirate?" Joseph followed the direction of Elizabeth's gaze. "No one knows for sure. Alexander Macpherson's eldest son, Alec, now leads the Macpherson clan and, the word is, being married to the Scottish king's sister, he finds little time to sail the high seas. That leaves Ambrose and the youngest brother, John. Both these men have lived on the sea from the time they were children. They both could take up the father's trade. But now I find that Ambrose is the Baron of Roxburgh as well.

And from what I hear, the baron is known to have more castles—and more gold in them—than any king in Europe. So for him to continue in the family piracy business is a bit unlikely, although there are a few of us that hope he would."

"You hope he would?" she asked, turning to him in surprise. "Why?"

"The mystery. The adventure." Joseph smiled. "Macphersons have long been heroes. They are part of history. They're a tradition. No one wants to see the legends disappear. What man wouldn't want to tell his children of sailing with the Macphersons across the open seas? And, like everyone else, sailors are intrigued with legends. Particularly living ones."

Elizabeth shuddered involuntarily as she gazed at Ambrose across the dock. Once again he wore his kilt and his tartan, but now a black cloak was fastened around his shoulders. A long sword hung from the leather belt. His blond hair fluttered loosely about his face in the gentle breeze. He was tall, powerful, free. He was the very image of what she would have thought a pirate might be.

Even more.

Chapter 18

❧

The body lying in the small bunk shook with silent tears.

Elizabeth stepped inside one of the darkened cabins and looked about her in alarm. She had just left the stern deck and her companions, going in search of her sister Mary. No one had even seen the young woman since they had stepped aboard the vessel hours earlier. The oily taper that lay propped up in a tin box gave off a smoky light and filled one side of the room with a dim haze. Elizabeth peered into the darkness and then spotted her.

Mary lay facedown, wrapped in a rough, wool blanket. Even from where she stood, Elizabeth could see the young woman's small shoulders trembling with barely perceptible sobs that occasionally escaped her.

Elizabeth moved to the bunk and sat quietly on the edge. Her hands moved gently on her sister's shoulders, caressing her, trying to ease the pain the younger woman was feeling. Mary turned immediately and threw herself into Elizabeth's arms.

Now, once again safe in Elizabeth's familiar embrace, she wept openly. Elizabeth listened, unable to console her with anything more than the soft touch and the gentle rocking motion that had been part of them since childhood.

"I've never hated myself as I do now," Mary whispered bitterly, clutching her sister as tight as she could. "My name is a demon that precedes me. I am not a human being, but a disease. One to be avoided. To be cast off and shunned."

Elizabeth pulled her sister's face away from her shoulder and gazed into her tearful eyes.

"Did someone say something to you?" The painter's

voice shook with emotion. "I'll not allow anyone offend you in this way."

Mary just simply shook her head. "It is not what some-one else does to me, Elizabeth. It is what I do to myself."

The tears fell down her pale skin as she continued. "And it is not up to you to right what I continue to bring on myself."

Elizabeth stared at her sister in disbelief. She had never heard Mary speak words such as these. Something must have happened. "Tell me what has happened, Mary. Talk to me."

"Oh, how I wish I could just be a simple little girl again. Pure, untainted. Living again at a stage in my life when worldly possessions mean little. Then I would be free to choose . . . for love." She paused, staring at the shadows that flickered across the walls.

Mary's face became nearly trancelike as her eyes locked on the far wall. Elizabeth reached over gently and touched her brow. But there was no fevered heat on the skin, only cold. She was ice-cold. Elizabeth picked a blanket lying on the bunk and wrapped it around her sister, wondering if Mary was about to have another of her attacks. She had been so good for so long that they'd thought she had beaten the pox. Elizabeth wondered if her hasty decision to go to Scotland was the reason Mary was going through this right now. She winced at the thought that she may have put the young woman's life in jeopardy by dragging her along. Elizabeth ran her hands over her sister's arms, trying to bring back some of the warmth in her chilled body.

"You should have seen me. I was so foolish. I was standing at the pier with my heart in my hand."

Elizabeth listened in silence.

"He approached me. He was coming toward me. I saw his eyes, as large as life, were on me. His tartan whipped about in the wind, but he charged on. My heart stopped beating. I knew what he was about to say. He was about to . . ." Mary looked down at her hands.

Elizabeth felt a knot form in her own heart. It was pain. Dull and heavy.

"He stopped. He stopped just a breath away. I looked up, and I was lost in what I saw. Once again, here I was— a young girl, blushing madly, my breath caught in my chest and my temples pounding with the excitement. It was like . . . first love. Though I'm sure now that I've never loved any man, still I knew."

Elizabeth looked down at her own fingers as they clutched the blanket in her palms. She felt a burning ache in the back of her throat.

"He just stood there, looking at me with a half smile tugging at his full lips. I felt whole, cared for, sought after. It's been a long time since I've felt that when a man looked at me. He was like a dream creature that God had at last sent down to me. To awaken something in my soul. Something that has been sleeping. Or dead. Then . . ."

Elizabeth couldn't look up. She sat where she was, silent, waiting.

"Then his friend called him. Lord Macpherson called him away."

Elizabeth clutched her hands as she took a small breath. "Gavin Kerr!"

Mary looked up dreamily. "It was he. The man never spoke a word. But I . . . " The tears once again took control. She wept silently.

As Elizabeth pulled her into her arms, she thought back over all the time Mary had spent in the company of so many courtiers in France and in Florence. But she had never seen her so broken, not even when she'd discovered that her newborn child had been a baby girl and not a male as she'd hoped.

"This is the first time we've met, but I know him. He is the man of my dreams, Elizabeth. He is the one that I have waited . . ." Mary paused and looked questioningly at her sister. "But I haven't waited, have I, sister? I gave myself away in the first bed that I fell into. I was impatient. I was spoiled. Selfish. I didn't wait, did I? And now. Now I have found him, but now . . . I'm being punished."

Mary's eyes were glazed and unseeing. Elizabeth took hold of hands that reached out and clutched at the air. That scratched at invisible enemies. She didn't know how to calm her sister's fears, how to undo the torment she was bringing on herself. Mary's breaths were coming in short, quick pants. Her voice was thickening, as if someone had her by the throat.

"His friend called him. Took him away. Probably to tell him to stay away from the pox-ridden wench. They all know me. They know my reputation. And what they say is not even a lie. I know it. It is the godawful truth that I am nothing more than a diseased wench. A used-up old whore."

"Stop it, Mary," Elizabeth ordered, as she tried to hold on to her sister's hands. The young woman jerked them away and hid them behind her.

"You know it's true. And Gavin . . . he went by me again, later, while we were boarding the ship. But he never looked. Not once. Aye, he has been told, warned, reprimanded. For looking. Just for looking." Mary rocked back and forth on the bunk, her words coming out in moans now. "I want to wash myself. I want to get rid of this grime that I've accumulated over the years. I want to be wanted. By him. Is that so much? But I can't. I was no innocent, Elizabeth. I know. I knew. Standing there, I lost it. My dream! I searched for him, and then, after finding him, I lost him. I was dirty. I *am* dirty! Oh, God . . . so dirty!"

Mary began to rub her hands hard on the blanket, but Elizabeth caught her wrists and held them tight.

"Then I saw me. I saw my life. God helped me see. I never knew, for all this time. It was I. All this time. *I* sought out this fate, this destiny. After the first time, after Henry got me with child, I could have stopped. You told me it wasn't my fault. You said that. The blame was Father's. But he tried it on you, and you didn't let him. No. You were strong. I was weak. I was greedy. And then, after that, I still didn't stop. Always I knew someday I'd find him, but I was impatient. I still didn't . . ." Mary folded over and cried. She cried into the blanket. "I don't deserve him."

Elizabeth leaned over and held her. That's all she could do. Just hold her.

There was darkness and nothing else. Elizabeth clutched the side of the bunk and swung her legs over the edge, but the floor seemed to open under her. There was a lurching motion, and she was thrown into the air, rolling as she fell. And then she landed. She felt her skull crack hard against the rough wooden floor. From the above her, Elizabeth heard a sliding, screeching sound of metal against wood, and then the weight of the chest was on her. She flinched with a sharp pain that shot through her shoulder as she tried to push it away. But the ship lurched again, and the chest dropped onto her wrist.

She could hear the muffled, heavy, rattling sound of boxes being thrown about around her. The ship's cabin continued to rock, and Elizabeth, completely disoriented, began to crawl helplessly forward. Around her the darkness was deathly.

"Mary!" she called. "Mary! Are you here?"

Elizabeth had fallen sleep holding her sister. The troubled young woman at last had settled quietly to rest, and Elizabeth had stayed beside her.

Suddenly the cabin floor seemed to drop away below her, and Elizabeth heard the crash of another box a foot from her head. Her hands flew up instinctively, and she rolled away from the spot. She dragged herself quickly to her hands and knees, and scrambled in the direction she thought she'd come. But the wild motion of the ship fought to thwart her attempts.

"Mary!" she called loudly. But the hollow sound against the walls was answered only by the roar of the wind beating against the ship's sides.

So dark. There was no glimmer of light, no hint of which direction the door could be. And the storm. Panic began to crawl up from the small of her back. She had to open the door. Where was Mary? Where were Jaime and the others? She had to get out.

Elizabeth moved, pushed hard as she struggled to her feet. Her hand reached a wall. Good. The cabin was not that large. But then the boat shuddered and dipped and rolled her once more, downward and into the wall.

She heard the noise from above and behind her. The sound of more trunks and boxes ready to crush her.

As they reached the crest of another mountainous wave, Gavin scanned the rolling seascape for some sign of land, but there was nothing to be seen beyond the wind-whipped foam of a gray-green sea and the blackness of the low-hanging clouds.

"Damn the sky," the Scot cursed into the stinging salt spray. "It was blue not two hours ago."

As the galley slid uncontrollably into the trough between the waves, Gavin gripped the railing of the high stern deck. This is a lunatic's life, he thought. Give me a good battle and firm ground to stand on. He looked forward at the troop of Scottish warriors huddled in the bow and guessed more than a few of those brave men were thinking the same thing. Around the place where he stood, groups of travelers were sitting on the wooden deck, and the prayers of a number of them were as audible as the weeping of the old couple sitting directly at his feet.

Ambrose had just gone below again, having herded most of his own charges out of the tiny cabins. Gavin couldn't help but smile at the thought of the seamen's expression when the baron had so emphatically made his intention clear. Crowded deck or not, those in Ambrose's care were not going to be belowdecks if the ship went down.

Gavin glanced downward over the short rail in front of him at the painter's sister. She had been standing there looking out over the wild and frothy sea for some time now.

The Scot's gaze lingered on her as she clung to the railing on the far side of the ship and began slowly making her way forward. She was a bonny lass, and Gavin had heard her name was Mary.

Always uncomfortable in the company of women anyway, Gavin could only wonder now what could possibly be going through the young woman's mind. So unlike others, who needed a group of people to keep their company, this one was such a loner. So much like him.

Gavin had first seen her on the pier. From a distance, it had looked as if she were sanding there waiting . . . waiting just for him. Her eyes, her smiles had seemingly been directed solely at him. He had turned around—actually looked about—to make certain there was no one else she was looking at. But there wasn't. And then Gavin had strode toward her. She must know me, he thought. Perhaps we've met somewhere before. No, that would be impossible. Gavin was certain he would remember.

A step away, he had stopped. No, he had never spoken with her before, but he knew she was indeed waiting for him. Before he could even speak, it occurred to him that she seemed to need something—something from him.

But she was so beautiful, and his tongue had knotted up

in his head. He thought for a moment that she was about to speak. And whatever she had to say, Gavin was willing to hear.

Then Ambrose had called. They needed to finalize their agreement with the captain of the ship before they departed.

He had not seen her again before the galley sailed in the gray predawn light.

The ship heeled over slightly as it began its ascent up the side of the next watery mountain, and suddenly a crossing wave crashed over the gunwales, hammering free the great wood casks of olive oil that had been lined up and secured with such orderly precision. The galley's crew scrambled about, attempting to secure the huge barrels that now floated as free as twigs upon the flood. The shouts and curses came back to Gavin in snatches as the howling wind and the roaring sea overwhelmed all other sounds that struggled so feebly before them.

One of the wooden casks tumbled through the midsection of the ship, now awash with the deluge. All eyes in the stern were upon the barrel, but from the corner of his eye, the Scot saw another smaller wave break over the starboard bow, and the water swept aft, engulfing the black-haired lass.

As he watched in horror, the wave knocked the woman flat, submerging her momentarily before she reappeared, floating with terrifying speed across the deck toward an opening where the water was draining overboard.

Without a second thought, Gavin vaulted the short railing before him as the flood carried the woman ever nearer her certain doom.

The warrior waded powerfully against the surging current, driving his brawny legs against the thigh-high water. Gavin's black hair whipped across his face, blinding him for an instant with brine as Mary neared the gaping hole.

The giant was still a half dozen steps away, lunging wildly ahead, when the woman's body reached the side of the ship. The vessel tipped again, and the seawater rushed with even more force through the opening.

As the young woman's head disappeared, Gavin dived into the swirling foam. For a moment the giant thought the lass was gone, but then his fingers closed over one of her trailing ankles.

Driving his knees under him, Gavin Kerr struggled to his feet, dragging with all his strength the unconscious woman back into the ship. With a mighty heave, the giant hauled the young woman up into his arms and tossed her over his shoulder. Then, working his way back through the receding water to the short ladder to the stern deck, the Scot climbed quickly and lay the sputtering lass in the waiting arms of the huddled travelers.

Below, Ambrose kicked open the first door. There was no sign of her. After bringing the others up to the stern deck, he had realized she was the only one missing. Why doesn't this surprise me? he thought to himself. Holding the wick lamp in one hand, the baron held the door open with one foot and peered in. The room lit up slightly, but even in this light, he could see she was not there. He stepped backward into the narrow corridor and moved deeper into the bowels of the ship.

Ambrose's wide shoulders nearly scraped the sides of the passageway and he needed to keep his head low as he moved toward next cabin—the cabin he'd seen Elizabeth's sister Mary come lurching out of when he'd come below earlier.

Before he could reach it, though, the ship shuddered with the impact of a wave, and the hatch door behind him slammed open. A gust of wind and spray swept into the passage, killing the flickering light, and Ambrose was left cursing in the darkness.

Feeling his way toward the cabin door, the baron found himself thrown into one bulwark as the galley lurched again, seemingly dropping a yard as it did. Steadying himself, Ambrose found the wooden latch and shoved the cabin door open.

"Uh . . . Phillipe!" he called into the pitch-blackness of the room. "Are you in here?"

Straining to listen through the sound of the gale and the waves, Ambrose pushed farther into the cabin.

"Here." The reply was weak and small.

Ambrose stepped in, clear of the door, only to slam his hip squarely into the corner of a large chest directly before him.

"Damn," he cursed. But before he even had the word out, another abrupt shift of the galley threw the warrior backward against the closing door, leaving him staggered against the bulwark with the offending chest tipped onto his outstretched legs. "The devil!"

"Stop complaining and get me out of here." Elizabeth pushed the clothing that was inhibiting her breathing away from her face. She wondered vaguely whose chest had been opened by the movements of the ship.

"Where are you?" Ambrose called, as he took a step in the direction of her voice. His knees rammed the side of another chest. "What the devil is all this? I thought I said you were not to bring anything that cannot be carried on horseback."

"I don't recall discussing anything of the sort," she lied into the darkness. Gripping the side of a chest, Elizabeth pulled herself to her feet. She stretched her legs and flexed her hands. Amazingly, nothing appeared to be broken.

Another sharp dip of the vessel once again sent her flying, this time in the direction of the baron's voice.

"Ambrose!" Elizabeth called as she landed with a thud on the hard wood floor.

"Aye?" His voice now came from the proximity of the floor, as well.

"Please help me. I believe I've bruised every bone in my body." The cabin floor tipped once more and Elizabeth felt herself sliding across the floor, with the sound of luggage sliding after her. "Help me!"

Her hands fluttered about her wildly with the hope of grabbing hold of something. Anything. But to no avail. With another crash, the young painter hit the far bulwark a moment before a collection of trunks, furniture, and loose clothing came tumbling after her.

His hand found her ankle, and Ambrose pulled the limb toward him.

"You are turning me upside down," she called. "I don't need that kind of help, m'lord. My stomach is about to empty itself as it is, and it doesn't need any encouragement."

His other hand took hold of her leg as he searched for a better grip.

"Ambrose Macpherson, you keep your hands off of me.

This is no time to behave in this manner." While one of her hands tried to fight off his hand as it moved up her thigh, the other reached out in search of the rest of him. Elizabeth was buried under a landslide of baggage, and she needed him to get her out from under it. She struggled against the onslaught. "Where are you?"

"Make up your mind, my bonny one." His hand slid over her round backside. She tried to squirm away. "Do you want me, lass, or don't you?"

"Oh, Ambrose. I'm so glad you came for me." She now clutched him hard around the neck.

The vessel heaved and dropped again. Elizabeth leaped up and wrapped her legs around his waist, burying her face in his neck. "Please get me out of here."

"This is no way to behave, m'lady, if you want out of this cabin." His voice was hoarse.

"I can't help . . ." Another sudden drop made Ambrose lose his balance and fall backward. Elizabeth dropped like a sack on top of him. ". . . it."

"Really?" she whispered sheepishly as she struggled to pull one of her legs out from where it was pinned beneath his buttocks. "I thought I'd never get out of here, Ambrose. And then you came." She snuggled quickly beside him as she heard the sliding chest. "Though I'm beginning to think we'll never get out. Is the ship about to go down?"

"It might." He rolled quickly to his side and pushed her from him as another chest crashed into his back.

Elizabeth heard the groan that escaped his lips as they were pushed across the floor into a pile of clothing.

"We could die! Drown! Where is Jaime?" she asked in panic.

"Right now, everyone is huddled safely on the stern deck. I saw her in the arms of the merchant and his wife."

"My sister?"

"She came up as well." Ambrose reached behind her and found the solid wood of the bulwark behind the clothing. And right at the point where it met the floor, he found the rope. Running his fingers around it, he gripped it tightly.

"Are we the only ones left belowdecks?"

"The last ones."

The ship heeled over, but Ambrose held on to the rope and kept them where they were.

Elizabeth felt her body crush against his as the cabin deck sloped sharply toward him. She found her hands planted on his chest. She could feel his heartbeat. Her chest, her hips, the length of her entire body were molded against him. Her head gave in to the powerful pull and nestled against his neck.

It was almost as if the fear she was feeling had wrought some incredible change in the universe. She'd never felt her senses so alive. The smell of wind and salt water on his skin, the warmth of the cocoon that he'd made for her in his arms, the power of his muscular build—they were all so intoxicating. Seemingly unable to control herself, Elizabeth let her lips brush against the skin of his neck. She found herself wanting to touch him. Her fingers traveled gently over the smooth linen of his shirt and then, finding the opening, moved inside.

"I like your timing, lass," he growled, lowering his head and capturing her mouth. The kiss was hot and carnal, his tongue thrusting hungrily into her velvety recesses.

She took him in, suckling his tongue with a desperate longing. A longing to take him into her as deeply as she possibly could. She'd not known how much she needed him. Not until today, when she'd thought that the object of Mary's attraction had been Ambrose Macpherson.

Now the roar of the storm outside, the darkness that engulfed them, everything seemed to add to her overpowering need to have him, to experience him, to wrap herself around him. The world she knew, the solid world of precision, color, and light, was no longer the real world. It was another world, more dreary and unattractive than the undulating blackness she was a part of now. That other world was like some far-off dream, falling away farther and farther with every billowing wave of the sea.

She wanted him, and she would have him.

Elizabeth's hands tore at the fasteners of his shirt. Her fingers greedily devoured his skin, exploring and kneading every sinewy muscle.

"Is this it, lass?" the Highlander asked hoarsely. "Is this the way it's to be?"

"I want you, Ambrose."

"No stopping. No running off. No sudden fit of insanity." Ambrose paused. "These are my conditions, Elizabeth. If you want me, you will have all of me."

"I accept your conditions," she whispered, her mouth tasting his skin.

Ambrose released the rope with one hand and pulled at her doublet. He, too, had crossed into a world of desire. Of course, it was a realm that he was far more familiar with than she. But vaguely, hovering somewhere about the level of consciousness, the idea took shape that he was feeling these sensations as if for the first time. They had come so close before, the two of them. But not like this. The change, the urgency of their need was perhaps due to the place, to the time. Perhaps even to the storm that roared outside and within.

He wanted her now, and she would have him.

Ambrose wanted to feel her skin against his, as he pulled down at the shirt she wore beneath the doublet. Instinctively, one of his legs crossed over her hip, trapping her writhing body under its weight. Yanking the shirt open in front, he found yet another tight, thick layer of cloth frustrating his attempts. Pulling at the laces that held it in place, he pushed the material away. All at once his hand was filled with the full round orb of one of her breasts springing free. Hauling her toward him, he crushed her body against his—skin against skin, flesh against flesh.

Panting heavily, Elizabeth pulled her hand from his chest and took hold of his bare knee. Clutching his rock-hard thigh, her fingers delved uncontrollably beneath the folds of his kilt.

Ambrose slid his leg slightly lower, making room for his own hand as he slid his fingers into the juncture of her thighs. The thick breeches inhibited his search, but all the same he kneaded with the touch that he knew she sought. The moan that sounded somewhere deep within her triggered an even wilder desire in him, and as he stroked her rising pleasure, he slanted his mouth roughly over hers.

Elizabeth took his throbbing manhood in her hand, encircling his pulsing member with her fingers. Running her hand over its silky length, she trembled with anticipation of its size within her.

His head fell with a thud against the floor. "How did I

ever let you get away from me before?" he gasped. "I need you now, Elizabeth. I won't wait. You are driving me out of my mind."

She tightened her grip on him, hearing his groan of pleasure. "I want you, too. Once, before we die. Take me, Ambrose Macpherson. Make me yours."

Everything around them—the storm, the turbulent action of the boat, even the constantly shifting baggage around them—was forgotten, and he let go of the wall. Rolling toward her, Ambrose moved nimbly on top of her.

"You are not going to die, my sweet." His hand reached to pull open her breeches. "I'm not letting you die. There is far too much passion left for us to enjoy. And we just can't let all that go to waste."

Ambrose pushed aside the ring that hung between her breasts. His tongue flicked momentarily at a hardened nipple before moving to the other, where he settled, finally, suckling her tender flesh.

Elizabeth arched her back, gripping his hair and pulling his face tighter against her breast as his other hand made contact with the moist folds of her womanhood. She heard her own breath coming in gasps as his fingers began to stroke gently, rhythmically, while the colors of heaven danced like fire before her eyes.

The sound of running footsteps and the door slamming open froze the two at once where they lay. Elizabeth held her breath as Ambrose's mouth lifted from her breast.

"Damn."

Gavin peered inside the darkened room. His dim wick lamp only shed the dimmest light in the area by the doorway. All he could see was a room in utter shambles, the jumbled collection of clothes, trunks, and boxes scattered everywhere that the lamp illuminated.

"Ambrose? Are you here?"

The voice that reached him was muffled somewhat by the sound of the wind and waves hammering on the hull of the vessel. "Give me a moment, Gavin . . . to find my way."

"Have you seen Phillipe?" Gavin asked, raising his light to get a better look inside. "No one has seen him come on deck. His family is concerned. Ah, there you are."

Another lurch of the boat caused Gavin to brace himself against the doorframe. The young painter was standing with his back to him, and from what Gavin could see, Ambrose was holding the man and trying to steady him on his feet. But the movement of the boat was not helping the two. "You were gone so long, Ambrose, I thought you might have fallen and cracked that thick head of yours."

"I came after . . . Phillipe, but the damn door slammed shut on us." Ambrose put his great hand squarely on Gavin's chest and backed him out of the cabin. Elizabeth followed behind. "But why the hell am I explaining all this to you?"

"Because I have more sense than you." Gavin watched as Ambrose and Phillipe came fully into the light. His eyes widened. They were a mess. Ambrose's shirt was torn open in the front, while the painter's doublet was stuffed into his breeches rather than hanging over them, the customary way of wearing it. "You two must have had quite a rough time down here."

Ambrose glowered at him. But then he caught the painter by the shoulder as a dip in the ship nearly sent them all flying.

"I mean with all those boxes and loose things flying around." Gavin grinned. "You are just the right size to make a good battering ram, Ambrose. But Phillipe, I'd say, is not really strong enough."

"There is nothing wrong with him," Ambrose growled. "What are you waiting for? Are you going to stand there all night flapping your jaws or are you going to lead us out of here?"

Gavin straightened himself to his full height and snapped at him. "You foul-tempered Highland horse thief. I came down here to save your neck, and this is what I get in return."

"Just go," Ambrose rumbled more gently, slapping his friend in apology and turning him down the passageway. "You got me at a bad time, Gavin. Just go."

Gavin turned grudgingly away. "You might want to bring a blanket for your sister, painter," he said, directing his words over his shoulder at Elizabeth. "She is soaked through and needs a bit of comforting."

"Mary? Why, is she hurt?"

"Just wet. A wee bit of water down her gullet, that's all."

Elizabeth turned to go back into the room, but Ambrose blocked her way. "Go on up. I'll fetch it." He grabbed a cloak off the wall and placed it around her shoulder. The caressing touch that brushed her face went unnoticed by the other man, but Elizabeth felt it throughout her body. In the dim light of the passageway, she glanced up into his mischievous eyes, then turned quickly and followed the giant warrior out into the raging storm.

The force of the wind nearly knocked Elizabeth back into the passageway, but she shielded her face against the biting salt spray that drove hard against her. Squinting her eyes, she could see the galley's crew working to secure the huge casks at the forward end of the deck, and it looked as though they must have lost a number over the side. As she watched, a small wave crashed over the side of the gunwale and washed across the deck, but did no further damage.

"It appears the storm's easing up a bit," Gavin shouted at her. He jerked his head up toward the stern deck above them. "Your sister's up here."

As Elizabeth started up the ladder, the ship crested a wave, and she held tight to the rungs as the vessel dove into the next trough. When the motion of the ship allowed it, she scurried up to the top and grasped the low railing as soon as she could get her feet planted solidly on the deck.

Groups of travelers crowded the deck, but before she could search out her own party, a loud crack sounded above her, and she turned in time to see the very top of the closest mast break off. The sailors working forward stood frozen for a moment, gazing upward at the damaged gear. Then, springing into action, the men leaped into the sagging rigging of the aft mainmast and swarmed up the ropes, securing the dangling masthead and tightening the remaining lines. Though the two large triangular sails of the galley had been trimmed when the fierce storm winds had first blown up, those masts would be essential if the merchant vessel was going to complete the voyage to Marseilles. Without the use of the canvas, the sailors would be rowing the remainder of the distance—not a welcome thought for the experienced seamen.

Turning her back on the action above, Elizabeth searched the huddled groups for her family and friends. Finding them sitting out of the wind in the protective shelter of the high railing, she worked her way over to them.

Jaime was asleep in the arms of Ernesta, and Joseph sat beside Mary, his cloak rolled up beneath her head. The young woman's eyes were half closed as if she were about to fall asleep. The ragged looks of concern on her two friends' faces startled Elizabeth and she put her hand on Mary's forehead.

"What happened, Erne?" she asked quickly. Mary's skin was cold and clammy. "Did she have another attack?"

"We don't know," Joseph answered, glancing at his wife. "She didn't come up with us right away when the baron sent us up from the cabins. Your sister—"

"She was on the lower deck," Ernesta broke in. "She was at the railing and a wave nearly washed her overboard. She swallowed quite a bit of water. She hasn't said a word since Sir Gavin carried her up here. I am not sure if she is even conscious."

Elizabeth looked anxiously at her sister. Mary's black hair was plastered to her head, and her skin had a death-like pallor.

"Mary," she called softly. Removing her cloak and spreading it over her sister's wet clothes, Elizabeth rubbed Mary's hand between hers and tried to stir some warmth into her cold body. "Mary, can you hear me? Come on, my sweet. Open your eyes. Look at me, my love."

There was no answer but the occasional gusts of wind and spray. Elizabeth watched for some flicker of life on her sister's wan and vacant features. She ran her hands through the young woman's hair. Grabbing a corner of the cloak, she tried to wipe the water from her face. "Look, Mary. The storm is passing. It is going to be a lovely day. You'll see. Come on, my beautiful one, talk to me."

Gavin stood a step away, watching the careful ministrations and listening to the gentle words that the painter spoke. There was so much affection apparent in the young man's words. But he didn't like the pale look of the young woman. From where he stood, she looked ill. Terribly ill.

"Go to her."

Gavin turned at the sound of the Highlander's voice over his shoulder. "Go and help Phillipe, if you want. He could use the extra hand."

Gavin frowned at Ambrose. Was his interest in the young woman so apparent? "Why don't you go yourself?"

Ambrose handed the blanket over to the black-haired warrior. "I'll be of more use helping with the mainmast."

He watched his friend pause and then nod in agreement. But even as the Lowlander walked away, the baron couldn't move. Standing there as Gavin carried the blanket over to the travelers, Ambrose found he could not tear his eyes from Elizabeth. He ached for her. They once again had come so close to making love. But this time it hadn't been Elizabeth who had halted the onslaught of desire. Her passion had been as unbridled as his own. He had felt her spirit soar.

Ambrose wanted her. All of her. Body and soul.

Forcing himself to turn away, Ambrose gazed up at the brightening sky above the sailors working so far aloft. The sickly green of the heavens was giving way to shades of gray, and he knew that the back of the storm was broken.

Elizabeth. He wanted to call her name. Shout it so that all might hear. And know.

He knew there was more than just thwarted lovemaking behind his growing obsession with this woman. More than just the beauty that she kept hidden from the world. There was something even more mysterious about her. And its allure was driving him wild.

True, he had lied about helping the galley's crew with the damaged sail. The crew had everything under the control; he could see that. But Ambrose knew he needed to keep his distance from her right now. He had to keep a tight rein on his own desires. He wanted her. No, he needed her. In his entire life, he'd never become so fiercely attracted to any woman without having her.

And Ambrose knew Elizabeth wanted him, too.

Cursing under his breath, the baron cast a quick glance over his shoulder and then strode abruptly to the ladder. Dropping to the main deck, Ambrose moved swiftly through the tangle of fallen lines toward the bow of the ship, where his soldiers were beginning to stretch and shake out their wet belongings. As he neared them, he could hear their friendly taunting of one another. The sea was becoming calmer by the moment, and Ambrose knew the soldiers could hardly be sad about that.

A few moments later, the blond-haired giant stood gazing toward the stern deck. Patches of blue could be seen in the sky beyond the end of the vessel.

"Damn!" Ambrose banged his fist on the railing. It was under his skin, and he couldn't shake it.

He glanced around. He had to hide his feelings. She was pretending to be a man. He simply couldn't show his feelings or his interest. As much as he'd like to, he could not drag her away to his cabin or risk a stolen kiss.

They had to act . . . indifferently toward one another.

Try as he might, he simply could not understand Elizabeth's motivation for carrying on this masquerade. No matter how impossible her father's demands had been, that was four years ago. But even then, he found it difficult to believe that Elizabeth Boleyn had had no other options available to her.

As he stared out at the groups of travelers, Ambrose became more and more convinced there were things the young woman was hiding. There were too many unanswered questions. And the sight of the sister, Mary Boleyn—once a court favorite but now living alone with her sister—had also added to his suspicions. Why in God's name were these two living as they were?

Ambrose smiled grimly. Well, here was a challenge. Finding the truth. Finding answers to his questions—to all of his questions—before they reached Scotland.

But more than that. Ambrose also planned to have Elizabeth Boleyn in his bed before they reached Scotland.

Though the orange sun broke through the clouds low in the western sky, the seas remained high as the galley made its way westward toward Marseilles. The sailors unfurled what canvas the vessel's masts could handle in the still gusting wind.

On the stern deck, Elizabeth continued to sit beside her sister, while Gavin Kerr hovered over them by the railing. Mary, still lying motionless, seemed to drift in and out of a haze, oblivious to everything around her. Elizabeth tucked the blankets around her sister, talking continuously, her voice soft but insistent as she tried to keep her sister's body warm and her mind in the realm of the present. But Mary seemed unable to respond. Gavin just watched from where he stood, not knowing what to do or how to help.

During the short periods when Mary would fall into a kind of restless half sleep, they could see her face contorting in expressions Elizabeth had never before seen, even during Mary's worst bouts with the illness. It seemed as if she was dreaming, dreams of intense fear alternating with dreams of intense sadness. Even when Mary was indeed sleeping, there were tears. Elizabeth watched the crystalline drops roll down her sister's face and disappear into the black folds of her hair. Elizabeth wiped the shimmering tracks away tenderly.

"Do you want your sister to get a chill?" Ambrose looked back as Elizabeth and Gavin turned their scowling faces on him. They were concerned, but neither was seasoned in sea traveling. "It's bad enough that the movement of the boat has made her sick to her stomach. Look at her. She is green."

Seeing the startled face of Elizabeth, the Highlander knew he needed to take some responsibility. "Gavin, take Mary down to the cabin. Phillipe, you'd better arrange for someone to get her out of those wet clothes. Sitting around and letting the dampness settle around her bones will not help her."

"How about the waves?" Elizabeth asked. "Is it safe to go back below?"

Ambrose's look spoke volumes.

"I suppose it depends on who's going," he said in a low voice.

Elizabeth couldn't help the blush that spread quickly across her face. She glanced around quickly at the others, but no one even dared to question the baron's words.

"It should be safe enough now," Gavin said as he gently scooped Mary up and stood. She remained limp and immobile in his arms.

"Take her into the first cabin," Ambrose ordered. "Phillipe and I need to finish an earlier discussion in the other."

"You did say we are going to survive this storm, m'lord," the painter growled. "Perhaps another time."

Elizabeth glared at him before taking the sleeping Jaime out of Erne's arms and helping the older woman to her feet.

"Another time, then," Ambrose returned softly.

Chapter 19

❧

Feminine wiles, she thought scoffingly. What good are they to me? It is difficult to bewitch a man while you're among men, when everyone thinks you are a man.

And Ambrose Macpherson was an obstinate man. But she already knew that. Over Elizabeth's objections, the baron had refused to allow them to stay in Marseilles, insisting that they travel the two hours to a nearby monastery that served as a hostelry for travelers. In spite of her heated disapproval, Ambrose had hired a closed oxcart and herded Ernesta and Jaime into the conveyance. Laying the weak but conscious Mary carefully among the baggage, Gavin Kerr shared a look of concern with the painter while explaining the baron's plan for the younger woman. Mary was obviously still quite weak, and Ambrose had no intention of worsening her condition by forcing her to travel at their pace. The Highlander knew the monk in charge of the infirmary where they were headed, and based on past experience he knew that there was no better physician anywhere. The monks would look after the young woman and care for her until the time came when she would be strong enough to travel again. At such time she would be welcome to come and join the painter in Scotland.

Though Elizabeth could not believe what she was hearing, Gavin clearly agreed with everything Ambrose had proposed. She had begun to think, because of the attentions Gavin Kerr had shown Mary, that perhaps he was growing fond of her younger sister. But obviously she was mistaken. The black-haired warrior might be concerned about Mary's health, but his allegiance to Ambrose remained unchallenged.

Riding out of Marseilles, Elizabeth had wracked her brain for a way to convince Ambrose that leaving Mary behind was simply out of the question. Neither of the men knew the source of Mary's illness, but Elizabeth had lived with it for the past four years. Nearly every time, as quickly as the symptoms would manifest themselves, they would disappear. And Elizabeth knew the only lasting remedy lay in love and care and in being surrounded by those the afflicted one trusted. In Mary's case, that will always be me, Elizabeth vowed.

Mary's sickness was changing, and Elizabeth knew that better than anyone. No longer just the cause of hideous physical disfigurement and intense bodily discomfort, the pox was now affecting her sister's mind. In her moments of mad anguish, Mary now expressed a desire to die . . . to end it all. These were not the childish and dramatic displays of her adolescence, but the momentarily insane desires of one whose mind had become unhinged.

But Elizabeth had learned how to deal with these trying moments. And at a time when Mary was vulnerable to these attacks, Elizabeth would never leave her sister alone.

Elizabeth knew she had a formidable challenge on her hands. She had to convince Ambrose Macpherson, Baron of Roxburgh, that taking the younger sister with them on the rest of the journey was the best course of action. But she also knew that trying to bully him would not work.

Feminine wiles. That had to be the answer. Elizabeth was not blind to the heated attention the man directed at her. He wanted her. If she could only use that to her advantage, perhaps he would agree to her conditions.

Conditions, she thought with a smile.

Elizabeth nodded to the old monk who would watch over Mary through the night. Her sister was resting quietly in the monastery's infirmary. Gently, she pulled the door partially closed and stepped into the darkened hallway.

Since their arrival the day before, Elizabeth had not been able to leave Mary's side. Mary had been extremely nervous about Elizabeth leaving her alone, even for a moment, but her fears were beginning to subside.

Elizabeth headed down the stairs. She had to change his mind. The baron's message had said they were leaving tomorrow. With Mary, Elizabeth thought. That was the only way she would be leaving tomorrow.

The noise of the people crowding the refectory reached her ears before she even stepped into the room. She looked about her. The travelers crowded the long tables laden with an evening meal.

Elizabeth looked down at the little hands that clutched at her legs. Jaime. She picked up the little girl.

Ambrose watched the simple show of affection from where he sat.

Jaime jumped out of Elizabeth's arms and scampered off to play with a half dozen kittens that were rolling in the rushes in the corner of the room.

Looking back at the long tables, Elizabeth saw Ambrose motioning her to a seat beside him, and in spite of her dilemma she found herself blushing at the prospect of sitting beside the golden-haired warrior.

Moving toward the seat, Elizabeth paused briefly and gave Joseph and Erne the latest news of Mary's condition. Even they were under the impression that they would all be leaving the next day without the younger sister. Elizabeth assured them that such a rumor was false.

Turning toward the baron, Elizabeth realized Ambrose was watching her carefully.

"So at last she has given you permission to leave."

Elizabeth looked down at him and remained standing where she was behind the bench. He patted the seat next to him. She kept staring.

"You are angry," Ambrose said, amused.

"Nay, Ambrose. He is just tired. That's all." The hard slap on the back from Gavin forced Elizabeth to take her seat at the table. She had not realized that the Lowlander had been standing right behind her.

"I have to admit, Phillipe, after Ambrose you are the most loyal man I've ever met in my life. The way you care for your sister. It is a wondrous thing." Gavin seated himself on the other side of the painter. "Even though you and the baron here have very different styles, I'd have to say that you both have compassionate natures and great hearts."

Elizabeth snorted at his comment.

"You disagree?" Ambrose asked, grabbing her by the back of the neck and turning her face toward him.

"Am I to be allowed to answer the question, or perhaps you'd care to do that, as well?"

"By all means. I'm all ears."

She watched the young kitchen boy as he placed another platter of food in front of them. "I happen to take offense at the thought of anyone connecting your bullying approach and mindless decisions to my peaceful and reasonable ways."

Ambrose snorted. "Reasonable?"

"Actually," Gavin chirped in from where he sat, "what I said was meant to be an insult to Ambrose. Everyone knows he hasn't a great heart—it's about the size of a berry. But I never expected you to be offended, Phillipe, my friend."

"You be quiet," Ambrose snapped at his friend before turning to Elizabeth. "Would you care to dwell on why you take offense at my actions and decisions? This should be quite interesting, considering the fact that you've hardly had an opportunity to witness *any* decision that I have made."

"I have been around, m'lord. And I can hear." Elizabeth stared straight ahead, toying with the food in front of her. "And I can see."

"Nay, you haven't been around," he responded curtly. "You have been locked away with your sister ever since we arrived."

She turned sharply in his direction. This was no place to discuss what she had in mind. "Do you care to take this argument outside?"

"Nothing would please me more." He stood at once.

"Don't, Phillipe," Gavin advised seriously from where he sat. "He could beat you into bloody mash. And I think he is in no mood to argue."

"I can take care of myself," she stated under her breath, patting the surprised warrior on the arm before following Ambrose out of the hall.

Elizabeth had wanted to be alone with him. She knew she needed to get him away from the rest of his men so she could work on him, use whatever interest he had in her to take him in hand. It was the only leverage she had right now.

But now her eyes were riveted to his broad shoulders as Ambrose led her through the winding stairwells to his room—no doubt the finest in the hostelry—Elizabeth felt the prickly heat of panic surging through her, draining her of the strength to climb even the next step. She knew what he was after. But Elizabeth couldn't let him make love to her. She began to fall behind.

The man thought she was experienced—that she had lain with other men and had even borne a child. And he thought that she was as hungry for him as he was for her.

Of course, Elizabeth reasoned, why would he think otherwise? It was partially true. Elizabeth had given up the lie of telling herself that she could do without him. Her mind and body cried out for him. But she knew—she forced herself to know—that this yearning for him must be controlled. She had to hold him off.

If Ambrose were to find out that Elizabeth had lied, if he were to think that she was nothing more than an over-ripe virgin, all too willing to jump into the sack with the first man who showed some interest in her, then all hope of getting her family to safety would be dashed.

Elizabeth had seen the way men had treated Mary after they had taken what they wanted. Kings or commoners, men were quick to lose interest once their appetites were satisfied.

No, once Ambrose knew the whole truth about Elizabeth—once he had found out what a total fraud she was—he would not just leave Mary behind. He would go on without Jaime, without the Bardis, and without Elizabeth herself. How disappointed he would be, once he had her.

Somehow, Elizabeth knew, she had to put him off. Enchanting a man is easier said than done, she thought, her mind racing. But that was the answer. The only answer.

Ambrose pushed open a heavy oak door on its loud hinges and turned toward her. "After you."

She remained where she was but tried to peek past him into the semidarkness of the room. Not much was visible from where she stood.

"M'lord, I don't think—"

"After you." His voice was commanding, and Elizabeth stepped reluctantly into the bedchamber.

The room was larger than the cell that Elizabeth was supposed to share with Joseph and a half dozen of Ambrose's men. Not that she had spent any time there, considering the hours that she'd remained at Mary's bedside. Though she would have preferred to be closer to Ernesta and Jaime, they were closeted in a separate section of the hostelry, a section that Elizabeth doubted had any rooms quite like this one. For it was clear from her first glance that Ambrose was being treated like royalty.

The room, situated in the corner of the stone building, had been paneled below and plastered above, and the bright blue color of the woodwork shone attractively even in the fading light of day. A number of small wooden chairs were clustered around a well-made wood table, and a mat of woven rushes covered the floor. Against the far wall, a huge bed brooded ominously, its stuffed mattress high and frighteningly full. Elizabeth quickly looked away.

The shutters of the four small windows had been thrown open, and the young painter crossed the room to one of them. She gazed down at the walled garden, and at the orchards and vineyards that stretched in an orderly fashion into the distance. This was a prosperous monastery, of that she had no doubt.

"Long way to jump."

She turned around and saw him standing casually at the end of the bed. She could see the door to the room was already barred from the inside. "I came willingly, didn't I?"

He smiled. "If you call dragging ten steps behind and shuddering at every corner, willing, then I can't wait for what's to come."

Elizabeth fumed. "No one is forcing you to lie with me, m'lord. You were the one who came after me first, if you recall."

"You came to my tent."

"You came to my room," she retorted.

"I didn't know you were there." Ambrose shrugged. She was getting riled up, and he had to admit, he was enjoying every moment of it. He had been away from her too long. In fact, he had been somewhat startled earlier in the day when, after seeing that she was absent again at the noon meal, he'd realized that he was actually angry at the sister. Envious of a sick woman. That was bad.

"When I came to Bardi's villa in Florence, I came after a painter. Instead, I saw you."

"Such disappointment you must have experienced!" she said, her voice dripping with ironic concern. Bewitching and feminine wiles be damned, she thought. "Has anyone told you, m'lord, that you are the most empty-headed, insensitive, self-centered man ever to walk this earth?"

"Nay. No one . . . other than you."

Ambrose gazed at Elizabeth. At her arms crossed defensively over her chest, at her angry face, at the short hair that shone beneath the puffy hat and lay in waves against her face. His eyes traveled lower and took in the shape of her beautiful legs, showing so provocatively through the hose.

"Stop appraising me like that! I'm not some prize heifer."

"I thought that was the idea," he responded, as his eyes continued their journey. "I thought men were supposed to be able to look at you without any fear of detection."

"If, m'lord, all the men in Scotland are going to look at me the way you do, then certain questions arise. . . ."

Ambrose let his eyes slowly, ever so slowly, return to hers. "To answer your questions, all of your questions . . ." He took a step toward her. Elizabeth stepped back against the window frame. The Highlander swung a chair around and sat, straddling it and facing her.

She waited for him to speak, but he just sat silently. For the first time in years, Elizabeth felt the vulnerability of men's clothing. Her painter's clothing, as comfortable as it had been over the years, now felt strangely insufficient. She longed for the layers and layers of dresses that Mary wore.

A blush crept into her face as she looked away from the handsome nobleman. There were no barriers of modesty between them. But then, perhaps there never had been.

"You fascinate me, Elizabeth. You always have. No woman has ever called me empty-headed, insensitive, or self-centered. And certainly no man would dare to say such things to me. In fact, contrary to your opinion, most women think me intelligent, gallant, and considerably perceptive of the needs of others. But then again, I am not with most women. I am with you. So, I suppose, that explains that."

She bit her tongue in her effort to stay silent.

"And as far as my disappointment at finding you in Florence, you are once again wrong, of course." He paused, waiting for her to jump in, but she didn't rise to his bait. "From the moment I first laid eyes on you, I have been anything but displeased. From that day at the Field of Cloth of Gold, you have had a way of drawing me toward you. And I have advanced with pleasure—and anticipation. I have thought about you quite a bit. To be honest, I have spent four years thinking about this moment. You have surprised me, excited me, and enchanted me. Elizabeth Boleyn, you have driven me to a madness that no other woman ever has. It is time for you to supply the cure."

Elizabeth looked down at the weave of the mat under her feet. She could not trust herself to meet his eyes. "What would you like me to do?"

He stood up and walked to a bowl of water that sat on the trestle table. She watched as he soaked a towel and wrung out the water. Elizabeth held her breath as he walked toward her.

Halting a step away, he handed her the wet cloth.

"What I would like you to do is to be yourself. At least while you are with me. I want you to wash away the disguise that covers the truth about you. I want to see you for who you really are, as I've seen you in the past. I want to see the passionate woman who exists beneath these clothes." He took her chin gently in his hand and lifted it until her eyes met his. "You want me, Elizabeth. As much as I want you. And don't try to deny it. Your eyes have betrayed you from the first moment we met."

He spoke the truth. She couldn't deny his words.

"I want to make love to you, Elizabeth. I mean with no interruptions, no one running away, no life-threatening storms or anything else to stop us. Those were my conditions, you recall."

She nodded.

"That's the way I want it, as well," she whispered, still holding the cloth in her hand.

"Then"—he gestured toward the locked door with a half smile—"don't you think we are safe at last?"

Elizabeth raised herself on her toes and pressed a fleeting kiss on his chin before skipping around him. Then, throwing the towel across the room and into the bowl, she turned to face him.

"You are right about me and about the way I feel about you. I will not deny that." She whispered the words self-consciously. "But not here. We can't make love here. When at last we do make love, I would like us to be in a place separate from all these others. I would like to dress as a woman and come to you as myself. I would also like to have the peace of mind that we have more than a few moments that we could share. I am not being greedy. Perhaps a night. A full night to make love—as it should be made. That's not so much to ask, is it? We've waited so long, Ambrose Macpherson. We could withstand a bit more."

Ambrose moved closer to her again. "We could have that. All of what you ask for. But wouldn't it be worth our while to remind ourselves of the delights we have in store? Perhaps just as a token to hold us over for the far greater night to come? For the bliss that awaits us?"

Elizabeth circled behind a chair as he slowly, ever so slowly, stalked her. "Nay, m'lord. I don't think that is such a good idea."

"But I think it is," he continued. "And I think it will not take much for me to convince you, as well."

Elizabeth pulled a chair back and blocked his advance. "As I think more about this, I'm becoming more and more convinced that it's a terrible idea. After all, you're leaving tomorrow without me, and—"

Ambrose came to a halt. "You are not being left here, Elizabeth. We are all leaving tomorrow."

She stared at him momentarily, her eyes widening.

"Oh, thank you, thank you!" Elizabeth tossed the chair aside and threw her hands around his neck at last. "Thank you!"

Ambrose stepped back as she attacked him. She had lost her mind. "What are you thanking me for? This is no different than what we planned to do before we left Florence."

"Of course it is!" she whispered happily, kissing him squarely on the lips. "You just said we are *all* leaving tomorrow. That means Mary is coming with us. That means I won't need to stay behind and finish the journey to Scotland without your assistance. That means you and I will have our moments together. Moments to share—"

Ambrose grabbed her by the chin and forced her to listen to him. "You are going with me, my sweet. And your sister is staying here where she can be cared for properly. These people shall give her the best care there is. And when she is better, I will even send my men back to accompany her to Scotland. Now, is all that clear?"

Elizabeth slapped his hand away, her face flaming with anger. "Let me make something clear to you! I am not going to leave my sister all alone in a strange place with anyone else—and I don't care if Avicenna himself is going to doctor her! If she stays, then I stay. Is *that* clear?"

Ambrose stared at the young woman momentarily. "Is your skull so thick? Have the beatings you've taken in your life so damaged your wits that you can no longer think rationally? You are endangering your sister's life by taking her on so difficult a journey."

"I know my sister better than anyone else—and that includes you, these monks, and any other physician you might find between here and Paris." She took a step back. "Mary's illness is not of a physical nature that can be cured by medicine or by sleep. She needs love, care. She needs the knowledge that she is well cared for by people that she knows. The death of Mary will not be taking her with us across France. The death of her will be leaving her alone here among strangers."

Ambrose pushed her down in a chair. "You listen to me, young woman . . . ."

Elizabeth sprang back up. He pushed her down again, keeping his hands securely on her shoulders. She struggled for a moment, then sat, glaring up at him.

"Your sister is not a bairn. I might be able to understand your feelings if they were directed at your daughter, but Mary is a grown woman. And based on what I've witnessed in the short time that I've spent with you two, I can see that she is nothing more than a pampered, selfish woman who demands to be at the center of *your* attention. Elizabeth, she is using you."

She'd heard all this so many times before. She simply didn't need someone else preaching to her what she already knew was—at least in part—the truth. But it wasn't the whole truth. The baron did not have possession of all the facts. He only knew a small part of their past. Her voice softened. "But she is sick, Ambrose. She truly is."

"But you just said it yourself. She is sick in mind and not in body." He looked down into her troubled eyes. He had to do this as much for her as for himself. "Elizabeth, she is robbing you of your life. Of a time that you could be spending with your daughter, or with others if you choose to. Tell me one thing: Why is she with you? Why is she not fluttering about, enjoying English court life? It is where she belongs. Your father is very much in favor there."

Elizabeth shook her head. She couldn't tell him. She couldn't.

"She is unhappy, lass," he pressed. "That's obvious even to strangers. Must you pay for her unhappiness? Is she punishing you for the life she is leading? Why can't you send her back?"

"Please stop!" she pleaded, pushing him back. Standing, she took both of his hands in hers. She held them tight. She needed his strength. She needed him. "I know. I've heard all these things before. And I agree with much of what you say. Mary needs her own life, separate from mine. But leaving her here is not the way. I cannot cut her loose and leave her to drift here. Not here, where she knows no one. I promise you. I give you my word that I will find a place where she can live her own life. But let me take her to where she has friends. Where she won't be left alone."

Ambrose gathered her hands in his. The desperate pleading note in her voice was one he'd never heard before. This was a far different side of the strong and willful Elizabeth Boleyn. She was speaking from her heart. He couldn't let her down. As much as he believed that leaving the sister behind would probably be best for everyone, he knew he couldn't do it now.

"Paris," he said firmly. "We'll take her as far as Paris.

You have friends, family there. She can get the help and support you say she needs. But no farther. That is my condition."

"Thank you!" she whispered, throwing herself into his arms.

Chapter 20

He knows peace who has forgotten desire.

Ambrose wanted to place his fingers around her delicate neck. She stood leaning so peacefully against the low railing. A gentle breeze riffled through her black tresses. Her beautiful face—no longer hidden behind the concealing pigments—was now adorned with only the gentle color left by the early summer sun and the softly caressing wind. How could she be so content, he thought, while his own body burned so? Her constant nearness, the daily sight of her over the past fortnight was maddening. Ambrose Macpherson was on fire.

"The last time I traveled along this river, Mary and I were on foot."

Elizabeth gazed out at the rolling farms and vineyards that came right to the edge of the smooth-running Seine River. The midday sun was sparkling off the water, and the long, wide barge was gliding lazily through the countryside of Champagne northward toward the merchant town of Troyes.

Ambrose had been true to his word. And to make the journey easier for the still-weak Mary, the baron had hired a series of boats and barges to take them north along the broad, brown Rhône River to Lyons, and then onward along the Saône River, to Dijon, and finally to the Seine. Elizabeth and Mary had followed the same route, but southward, during their trek from the Field of Cloth of Gold to their new life in Florence. But it had been a long and arduous walk with a pregnant and complaining Mary.

Elizabeth knew that the Highlander's decision to travel the waterways had made for a slower journey, but it had been far more comfortable.

"Do you think your soldiers are already in Paris?"

"Nay, lass," Ambrose said, glancing over his shoulder to make sure Gavin was nowhere within earshot. He was below with Mary, the Highlander decided. As usual. An odd attraction. "If my men had already reached Paris, we'd see a glow in the sky at night from the section of the city they would've set ablaze."

Elizabeth cast a look past the massive body of the baron, toward the stern of the boat, where Joseph and Ernesta were sitting comfortably with the tillerman and a number of the boatmen. Jaime was playing on the deck with one of the kittens she'd received from the monks outside Marseilles. The little girl had a piece of line that, to the giggling delight of the child, the kitten was playfully stalking and pouncing on.

"Tell me." Ambrose spoke softly as he moved to her side, leaning against the same rail. "Tell me about the time you traveled this route."

Elizabeth could feel the brush of his shoulders against hers. It was an intimate act, but one that was noticed only by the two of them. She shivered in spite of the warm sunlight. She wanted his arms around her. The two of them were so close, his arms so inviting.

"There isn't much to tell. We set a pace Mary could handle, and we walked."

Ambrose studied her long fingers, the delicate hands of the artist that created depictions of life truer than the subjects themselves. He wanted to lift those fingers to his lips. He found himself wanting to trace a line with his lips from her fingertips to her wrist, up her arm, along her shoulder, down to the round fullness of the breasts he knew lay so tightly bound.

He still remembered the feel of her beneath him, the taste of her on his lips. Damn that Gavin. If he hadn't come down to the galley's cabin after them, they would have made love. Right there among the rolling trunks, in the midst of the storm. She had been ready then. They had come so close, but to no avail.

And then, at the monastery, he'd wanted her. But she'd asked him to wait, and Ambrose found it difficult to deny her anything.

So he found himself still waiting. And waiting.

"I remember swimming at that bow in the river,"

Elizabeth said excitedly, pointing to an eddy in the bend just ahead. "It felt so wonderful, the water so clear and clean."

Ambrose followed her gaze. "Did you swim with any clothes on?" His voice was huskier than usual.

Her head turned sharply toward him. She saw the clouds of passion lurking in his eyes. She smiled devilishly.

"No clothes. Nothing on. I was quite naked." She took a quick step to the side and gave herself some distance. "It was sunset. I rose out of the water and walked to the stony beach. There was nothing to dry my body with, so I let the summer breeze lick my skin dry."

She took another step back and stood facing him, somewhat amazed and amused by his reactions to her words. She looked at the clenched jaw, the way his eyes roamed her body as if she wore nothing now.

"Even then, I wished you there with me," she whispered.

"I want you, Elizabeth."

"We can't. Not yet." She eyed him steadily. "You promised, Baron."

Turning back toward the railing, she could feel his eyes still burning into her. Without looking at him, she reached up and slowly undid the top tie of her shirt, spreading the material with her fingers to let the soft breeze caress her skin.

"It's quite warm today. Don't you think so?" She threw a coy glance at him.

"I'll kill you, Elizabeth Boleyn. I'll kill you with my own two hands."

Below, Mary sat on the bunk, mesmerized by the tale, her back against the curved hull of the barge. The trencher of food lay untouched on her lap.

Gavin paused to take a sip from the bowl of wine that sat between them. His face was grim with the remembrance of so much destruction.

"Go on. Please go on," Mary prodded impatiently.

"I lay there, looking up at the sky. Well, at what passed for a sky that day. 'Tis true. It was more like night than day. The rain was pouring from a sky, thick and gray. Nay! It wasn't even gray—it was black with fog and with smoke from the German guns the damned English had brought up. They had been firing since morning—round after round. Boom! Boom! Boom! After a while, you don't know if the pounding of the explosions are coming from your head or from the next hill. It's a godawful thing, Mary—that cannon fire."

The young woman tried to imagine the fear Gavin must have felt.

"As I told you, it had been raining for two days, and the hills were slippery—they were thick with muck and with blood. Scottish blood, Mary. The treachery of that filthy Englishman Surrey and his vile henchman, Danvers, Satan's own brother—that was what defeated us. They'd agreed to a truce until the rain stopped. And then the bastards circled around, put their bloody guns in place, and lay waiting for us.

"It was a terrible thing, Mary, that battle, Flodden field. We, the men of the Borders, fought like wild men. We were faithful to the king and to our oaths to serve him. Each man of us fought like he possessed the heart of the Bruce and the soul of Wallace. But some, I'm ashamed to say, hung back when they were called upon. Many of the Highland clans—not the Macphersons, mind you, but many others—the motherless animals showed how long they can remember a slight. Those sheep in men's clothing watched as the Lowlanders and the men loyal to the king were mowed down like corn before a gale. It was a shameful thing, Mary.

"But a Scotsman fears nothing when his blood is up, and when the king took up the lance himself, we followed him down that muddy hill into the ranks of the English.

"For three hours, we fought with the valor of the auld heroes down there—knee-deep in bodies and in blood. But when King Jamie went down, fighting like the true warrior he was, our hearts were broken.

"They drove us across the hill. I saw my two brothers die like the gallants they were, and somewhere—not far from the king—some swine bashed my head from behind as I fought with another. I went down with the dying and the dead, and lay there unconscious for I don't know how long.

"I awoke, hearing a moaning sound and the noise of battle beyond. I tried to sit up and realized it was I who was moaning. All I could see was the dead and filthy sky. All I could feel was the rain pelting my face and the crack in the back of my head where my brains were trying to seep out. I pushed myself up and felt the ground spinning about me.

"The dead lay thick on that hillside. Thousands on thousands. It was a sight that defies telling, Mary. It defies telling.

"And then it struck me. The English guns had stopped. I knew what would come next. They'd be scouring the dead for rings and for gold. The camp followers and the shirkers. They'd be cutting the throats of those still living, and stripping all of their weapons and their armor. I tried to look down the hill through the smoke. I could see them at the bottom. Like vultures. But I couldn't stand. My legs would not move. I knew I was finished."

Gavin stopped.

Mary was suddenly aware of the tears silently coursing down her face. The warrior was silent his eyes closed. She moved the tray from her lap. "Please tell me."

He opened his eyes and returned her steady gaze.

"I lay back down to wait for the end. At any rate, I would die fighting, I decided, and readied a short sword that lay in the mud by my hand.

"And then I saw him. He was wandering in a daze among the dead, his broad sword dragging beside him. He appeared half blinded by the blood that was still running like a river from the great gash across his forehead. He was a Highlander, a man nearly my size. He was searching among the dead. I called to him, and he came to me.

" 'Where is the king?' he asked. 'Dead,' I told him. I saw his eyes flash with anger, with a silent, unutterable rage. Then he looked off down the hill before looking back at me. 'Go,' I said. 'Save yourself. It is finished here.' He just kept looking at me, but I knew he was thinking of the king.

"Then I saw his eyes clear a bit, and he took hold of my arm. Ambrose Macpherson lifted me up and threw me over his shoulder like I was no more than a bairn. He carried me, Mary. For all that night and for two days more, he carried me. Back into Scotland."

Mary Boleyn stared at Gavin as the raven-haired warrior drank down the remainder of the wine.

"He saved your life," she whispered.

"It was more than that. Much more." He looked up

toward the narrow sliver of light that was squeezing its way through a small opening in the plank ceiling. "He gave me hope, a chance for a future. He showed me what courage is. The strength that comes with compassion. He taught me that brotherhood goes far beyond the ties of kinship.

"And what took place on that bloody journey was only part of what Ambrose Macpherson has done for me. The greater part lay thereafter. I had lost my only family, my two elder brothers, the ones I loved and looked up to. I was a defeated warrior, and as my body healed, my mind's desires dwelled on hate and loathing. Hate for others like the treasonous Highlanders and the bloody English. Loathing for myself.

"But Ambrose changed all of that. He stayed by me as my legs began to work again. As I began to heal, he showed me that we must live out our lives, whatever our fate." Gavin turned to Mary and smiled. "I know you wouldn't think it, since I haven't stopped talking since I met you, but I am an extremely reserved man. I shy away from people. If left to myself, I would just crawl under a rock and remain there. When I was a child, my father contemplated sending me to a cloister to become a monk."

Mary smiled, the tears still glistening on her cheeks.

"I just can't see that," she replied quietly, watching him drifting off into a world long gone. She looked down at her hands. "Thank you, Gavin."

"For what? For boring you to death?"

"Nay, for making me see." Her eyes returned to his face. "So many times we only recognize the gallantry that occurs in the heat of battle. So often we are completely blind to the valor that takes place under our noses."

"You mean your brother?" he asked.

She nodded slowly.

"He is a fine man, Mary. Many might judge him hastily, based solely on his appearance. But I know they would be wrong. He might not be strong on the surface, but he has the spirit of ten warriors." Gavin remembered how Phillipe had so fearlessly faced Ambrose, time and time again. "But the most important thing for you to know is that he loves you. That is apparent in everything that he does."

Gavin looked carefully into the pale woman's expression before continuing.

"You probably know that Ambrose had planned for you to be left behind at the monastery outside Marseilles until you became well enough to travel." He saw her nod. "Well, you should have seen your brother. He raised hell. He was prepared to fight the baron if he didn't agree to take you with us. He has spirit, Mary. Phillipe stands up for what he believes in. That's real courage, if you ask me."

Mary leaned her head against the wooden hull. This was only a trifle compared to the things Elizabeth had done for her in her life. Gavin knew only the tiniest fraction of it. And Mary was beginning to see it all so clearly now. As if she were awakening from a deep and dreamless slumber, her eyes began to focus. Suddenly she could remember so many things. Recollect so clearly. Holy Mother, she prayed, forgive me for being so blind.

Mary considered for a moment what life with her must be for Elizabeth. She was very sick, perhaps more so now than ever before. This time was different. Mary knew that there could be no getting better this time. The physician at the monastery at Marseilles had confirmed her fears. She was dying. She knew it, though no one else did. She couldn't let Elizabeth know. Not yet.

She never slept. For two weeks now, every night as she had lain awake in her bed thinking, seeing her past relived before her eyes, she had felt the sickness taking over her brain. And then during the days, she'd listened, watched Elizabeth sitting so supportively, so lovingly beside her. Her sister, the one who accepted her as she was, in spite of her flaws, her ailments, her complaining tongue. Elizabeth had remained at her side for years—constant, true. Elizabeth had always been there. Been there for her. But what had Mary ever done, ever given her in return? Nothing.

Even sending Gavin—that had been Elizabeth's doing. Mary knew she was far beyond hope. Her time for first love was far behind her now, and the past weeks had brought that message home clearly to her. But she was not devastated by the realization. And when Elizabeth had sent Gavin down to her, she had found a companionship such as she had never known before. A camaraderie that she had never even thought of seeking.

But they had found that special relationship. They were friends. Other than Elizabeth, Mary had never even had a friend. But here they were. A man and a woman. Two people so different from one another. Two people who had gravitated toward each other's company. That had been Elizabeth's doing. Once again her sister had done that for her.

Mary's thoughts went back to the morning, when her sister had been beside her. She had not made any attempt to mask her complexion today. Even though Elizabeth still was dressed as a man, she had the undeniable freshness of a woman. And Mary knew the cause. Even from where she lay belowdecks, Mary could see the love that her sister carried for the Highlander. Elizabeth might not be ready to admit it to herself, but she was in love. In love with Ambrose Macpherson.

And Mary also knew her sister would never do anything about that. As long as Mary herself lived, she knew her sister would sacrifice every chance of love and of happiness to take care of her. She knew nothing would stop Elizabeth from continuing to provide her with the care and the companionship as she had always had.

Well, now it was Mary's job to cut the ties. She had to think of something. Elizabeth deserved some happiness of her own.

But first Mary wanted to see Jaime.

"I'm not going, Mary!"

"You *are* going," the younger woman ordered. "How many times do you think you'll have the opportunity to meet with the King of France?"

"But I have been presented at court before. You know that, and—"

"But never as an artist." Mary's voice shook with emotion. "Never as the painter all Europe is talking about. You have joined the top tier, Elizabeth. Your talent, your gift is finally being recognized. You deserve this attention. It is the moment artists work for their entire lives with only the slimmest hope of achieving. It's what you want, isn't it?"

Elizabeth let her head drop into her hands. "Nay. I

don't know!" The news that King Francis wanted to meet
Phillipe de Anjou at the Constable of Champagne's hunting lodge in the forest to the east of Troyes had caught
her off guard. "I don't know anymore. I don't know what
to do."

Ambrose's soldier had hailed the barge from the river-
side that morning. Word had gotten to the king of the Florentine painter's commission with the Scottish royal
family, and Francis wanted to greet this native son as he
journeyed on to the north.

"Please! For me, you should go," Mary cajoled as Elizabeth raised an eyebrow at her. "This is an opportunity for
me to live just a bit of it once more, through your eyes,
through your experience. When you get back, you can tell
me of the people who were there, the way everyone
dressed, the latest talk at court. Please, Elizabeth. Go!"

Elizabeth stood and moved to the side of Mary's bed.
The younger sister opened her arms and Elizabeth fell
into the embrace. The two hugged fiercely as they rocked
gently in each other's arms.

Mary was changing. Elizabeth could see it, feel it in her
heart. It had been three weeks. Three weeks on the barges,
traveling the rivers. With each passing day, Elizabeth had
seen her sister strengthen in her affection toward those
around her . . . while her body visibly withered. So many
times Elizabeth had questioned her own judgment in making this journey. But it was too late.

"I can't see how I could—"

"Elizabeth"—Mary pulled back to look into her sister's
eyes—"I heard you and Erne whispering about my health
last night." At seeing her older sister's protest, Mary
hushed her gently. "Please understand, my love. For once,
I am living my life the way I should have lived it all
along. I am happy." She paused. "I know I am dying,
and I know that all of you can see it, as well." She held
her sister's soft face in her hands. "And I want no sorrow
or tears from anyone. I've had a full life, and I was giv-
en a chance to . . . well, to correct it by coming on this
journey."

Mary gathered Elizabeth in her arms once again. "But,
God forbid, most of all I want no deathwatch around me. I
want to live to the last day—to the last breath. And I'll be
here, I promise you. I'll be waiting for you when you get

back. Go on this trip, Elizabeth. It will be good for me. Please."

Elizabeth lay her head against her sister's shoulder.

"And perhaps," Mary whispered smilingly in her sister's ear—she knew she needed to press her advantage now—"it would be good for you and Ambrose to be away from the rest of us for a few days. You two deserve some time alone. Just the two of you."

Elizabeth, color spreading like fire through her face, drew back momentarily from the sick woman's embrace and stared at her. She hadn't expected this.

"Do you think I don't see the way you feel about him? Come, now, my love. It's branded on your face anytime he comes anywhere near. Even anytime his name comes up. It is right there in your eyes."

Elizabeth looked away. Truly, she hardly knew how to hide—or deny—her feelings for him. Feelings that were growing more and more obvious with each passing day. How could she stop the way her blood pounded in her veins when he'd look at her in a certain way? Or the way her skin burned when he chanced to brush against her? Indeed, she knew she could hardly ignore the way her throat knotted when she'd seen him crouching so attentively beside Jaime while the little child showed the baron how her kitten's claws worked. It was difficult for Elizabeth to explain, even to herself, why tears had welled up in her eyes watching the Highlander unpin the broach on his tartan to show the little girl his family's coat of arms—a cat with outstretched claws sitting atop a decorated shield.

Elizabeth's heart and mind struggled as the desire to follow the path of love, if for only just this time, pulled hard against the sense of responsibility she felt for her sister.

"Such foolishness, Mary," she scolded, hugging her sister to her once again. But even to herself, the words of denial sounded feeble, at best.

The two women pulled apart and turned as the door of the cabin open lightly on its hinges. D'Or, the yellow kitten Jaime had named for its golden fur, was the first thing they saw as it leaped into the middle of the room. Then, behind her, the shadow of the little girl followed the animal in.

"D'Or wanted to visit," Jaime whispered shyly from the entryway.

Mary opened her arms as the young girl ran in and threw herself into her mother's embrace. Elizabeth choked back her tears. She loved them so much. Both of them. So many years she had hoped, she had prayed for this to happen. At last. Thank you, Virgin Mother. At last.

Elizabeth stood up from the bunk and started for the door. They needed as much time as they could have together, to make up for those years.

"Elizabeth!"

She turned at the sound of her sister's voice.

"Take that satchel with you."

"What is it?"

"Something for you," Mary whispered, her face aglow. "Something for your little trip. And Elizabeth . . ." She waited until her sister's attention was fixed on her. "You are going. Today."

"I don't think leaving you—"

Mary interrupted her, nestling her chin in Jaime's hair. Her eyes glowed with affection as she gazed into Elizabeth's face. "Believe it or not, we can do without you for a couple of days." The younger sister smiled happily and turned playfully to her daughter as she spoke. "Besides, Gavin has already told me he won't be going with you. He'll be staying with us. So you see, you don't have anything to worry about. We'll see you in Troyes. Gavin said we'll dock there and enjoy the market fair while we wait for you. I've always wanted to see the market fair at Troyes."

Elizabeth hesitated another moment, but her sister's gaze was direct.

"I need this, my love," Mary said quietly. "We both need to live every moment we have left. Give us both this time."

Chapter 21

❧

Frenchmen are as blind as Florentines, Ambrose thought, still somewhat stunned and hardly amused as he and Elizabeth rode along. If the armies of these two powers meet on the battlefield, he surmised, they'd better do so on a very sunny day . . . or they'll march right by one another.

The sojourn to the encampment of King Francis had involved an unexpected change in plans. Originally they were to travel to a hunting lodge in the forest to the east of the town, but that was not to be. Disembarking from the ferry on the east side of the river at Bar-sur-Seine, Ambrose and Elizabeth had been met by an emissary of the king, and they'd been escorted to the well-traveled highway that led eastward toward the Marne River and, eventually, to Geneva and Italy.

There, in a pavilion of cloth of gold that shimmered in the bright morning sun, the two travelers found King Francis trying on hats made by the craftsmen of Troyes, while twenty thousand armed men eagerly awaited his royal word to get on with their invasion of Italy.

And, to Ambrose's utter amazement, no one even guessed that Elizabeth was anyone—anything—but Phillipe de Anjou.

The painters that the king had brought with him to record his anticipated triumphs over the Emperor Charles's forces were uncommunicative but grudgingly compliant when Elizabeth reluctantly agreed to the king's request to do a portrait of him as he sat in armor at a camp table, the maps of conquest spread before him, chatting with Ambrose about his route. Working quickly—a skill the artist had honed through her extensive experience painting on rapidly drying plaster—Elizabeth created a treasure that won the praises of even the most reserved critic with its elegant structure, masterly brushwork, and astonishing display of color.

The entire visit was extraordinary, in Ambrose's view, but dining with the king would have been an ordeal for both painter and baron. Ambrose knew that, once ensconced in the dinner conversation with the French king, he would have been expected to elaborate in great detail on the results of his visit with the Pope in Rome and with Don Giovanni in Florence. And, Ambrose knew all too well, any involvement with Francis meant certain entanglement in more political intrigue. So the Highlander had been delighted when Elizabeth, professing sudden illness, had requested to be excused of His Majesty's gracious presence. Receiving a small bag of gold as a reward for his "wonderful work, and the honor he was bringing on France," Phillipe de Anjou had bowed his way out of the pavilion of the king, and the Highlander had joined in the escape.

They had not needed an escort back. Ambrose had assured all parties of that. So they rode in the golden light of the late afternoon sun, winding their way along the edge of the great forest east of Troyes.

Elizabeth grabbed her hat and yanked it off her head. She shook her hair loose in the light, early summer breeze. Her horse cantered easily behind the massive charger and its silent rider.

Before they had left the camp of the king, the Highlander had changed back into his Scottish gear, and Elizabeth gazed on him admiringly. His broadsword hung across his broad back, and his tartan's colors shone brightly in the evening light.

Ambrose Macpherson would cut a dashing figure in any company, she thought proudly. And every word he spoke, often so charged with his own wit, had been heeded very carefully by King Francis and his advisers.

Elizabeth wondered whether anyone had caught her gazing at him during their visit at the camp.

The painter tore her eyes away from him and looked around at the serene countryside. So beautiful, she thought. She glanced back at the baron and then out again at the rolling fields of flax. All the years she had lived in France, all those years growing up, she had never seen nor traveled in this land east of the Seine.

"You know these parts well," she called out, watching his back. He had hardly said a word since leaving the French king's camp. "Thank you for taking me back a different way. I don't know when I would have had an opportunity to see these parts again."

Elizabeth waited for him to turn around, to slow his horse, to acknowledge her words—but he never did.

She kicked her heels into the side of her horse, urging him on. Reining in at the side of the nobleman, she looked carefully at his grave expression. "What have I done now?"

Ambrose paused, then turned and returned her gaze. "Guilty conscience?"

"Nay," she said matter-of-factly, rising to the challenge in his tone. "This is just my advance movement prior to an attack on your cranky disposition."

Ambrose realized once again that her ability to pass as a man wasn't just due to the way she dressed. Elizabeth even had the aggressiveness. "I am not cranky."

"That's the truth. You are foul-tempered, disagreeable, and irritating. Does that cover it?"

"Couldn't have done it better myself."

Elizabeth shook her head as he once again fell into a brooding silence. She honestly had no idea what was wrong. Everything had gone beautifully at the king's camp—to her great surprise. It had been a short visit, but all the same, she couldn't remember doing anything that would have annoyed the baron, nor recall anything happening that might be the cause of his present sullenness.

Once again Elizabeth nudged her horse ahead, this time cutting in front of the baron and leaning over in an attempt to catch his steed's bridle.

"What are you up to?" He drew in the reins of his horse, bringing the animal to a halt. Elizabeth's horse followed suit. "Are you trying to break your neck?"

"Nay," she responded, reaching in again and making a grab at his reins. Ambrose yanked the charger's head around, but she persisted. "I'm trying to make you talk."

"I have nothing to say."

"Don't patronize me with such nonsense! You're a

chattering magpie. A flap-jawed diplomat. Nothing to say!"
she scoffed.

Ambrose scowled at her. "If you were a man, I would
consider breaking your neck for saying what you just
said."

"Well, I am not a man. So I suppose you'll simply have
to live with it."

"If I had ever had the misfortune of becoming involved
with you, I would have locked you away a long time ago.
For good, I mean."

"Well, that never happened, either, by the grace of the
Holy Mother. So you be damned. I am free to say what I
want."

Ambrose glared at her smug face. "Let me give you
some advice, lass. It is very dangerous business, trifling
with an angry man. And I *am* an angry man. Or are you
too blind to see that?"

"Blind? Ha! Why in God's name do you think I am taking all this abuse, you thick-skulled Scot? Of course I can
see you are angry! I just need to know why. Did I cause
it? Did I do anything that was improper? Speak to me,
why don't you?"

"Just let it be, Elizabeth."

"I won't!"

"I'm in no mood for this."

"Well, I am!"

Ambrose glared at her. She glared back.

"You are not going to give this up, are you?"

Elizabeth shook her head defiantly.

Ambrose took a deep breath and looked away, gazing
into the deepening shadows of the nearby forest. She was
the most stubborn woman he'd ever known. No, that
wasn't it. This woman cared for him enough to demand an
answer. Well, she did deserve that much. "You aren't the
one that's the problem, Elizabeth!"

"Not acceptable, Ambrose Macpherson. I am *not* accepting such an evasion for an answer."

"It's *me*, damn it!"

Elizabeth continued to glare at him. "If it's your own doing, then why must *I* take the brunt of your vile conduct?"

"If you would let me be, then you wouldn't need to
even witness my 'vile' conduct."

She tried to speak more calmly. "My good baron, I

think I've been around you enough in the course of this journey to know when I am the cause of your distress. And that certainly seems to be the case—"

"I lied," Ambrose broke in. As well she should know it, he decided.

"What?"

"I lied."

"To whom?"

"To Francis. To the King of France. Our host. I lied."

"Politicians always lie." She glanced away under the withering heat of his glare. "Never mind. Tell me, what did you say that was such a crime?"

"I lied to Francis about you. About you being a man. And some other grave political matter. And they believed everything I said." Ambrose had indeed lied to Francis about Duke Giovanni's power. He'd decided to buy his friend some time. Florence did not have a chance against the troops of Francis. This was the best help Ambrose could give Giovanni right now. "I made fools of all of them."

"You didn't make them fools, Ambrose. They are fools." She struggled to suppress a smile. To think that this man's worries were all over such a simple matter. "But m'lord, if this is the way you feel here in France, how will you feel once we reach Scotland? Are you going to take me to the closest tree and hang me once we get there, so you won't have to lie to your queen?"

"That's not a bad idea." He paused and considered. "I wouldn't need to put up with this kind of quarreling, and my conscience would definitely rest easier."

"Wonderful!" she responded, throwing her hands up dramatically. "But let's not stop there. After all, we still have a long journey ahead of us. Perhaps it is too great a distance to carry such a heavily weighted soul as yours must be. Aye, far too long a time to wrestle with such troubles. But what can we do? Alas, no priest in sight to lighten your burden. Are you certain there is nothing I could do right now to ease your suffering soul? To put your conscience to rest? Ah! I have it. Perhaps a sacrifice is in order, an offering to cleanse the soul. . . ."

Ambrose watched her extravagant act with growing amusement as she carried on her animated talk. Then his eyes began to see her again. Elizabeth. He studied her bright face; her intelligent, shining eyes; the very sensual woman who hid behind it all. Without even trying—perhaps without even knowing it—she had a way of clearing everything else from his mind. "I like the last one."

Elizabeth stopped midsentence. "Which was the last one?"

"The offering part."

She smiled brilliantly. "I'm glad that's the one. I was just moving on to maiming and immolation after that." Elizabeth reached into her saddlebag and removed the pouch of gold that she'd received from the French king. She tossed it to Ambrose. "The next church we pass by, drop this bag in as an offering."

The Highlander looked blankly at the woman.

"Offering?" she continued. "An offering for your soul?"

"There is nothing wrong with my soul." He tossed the bag back into her lap. "It is my body that suffers."

Elizabeth reddened and paused for a long moment before responding. "That's a dilemma. I believe I'll need some time to think of a remedy for that one."

Ambrose nudged his charger up close to hers and, without warning, slapped her horse hard on the flank. As Elizabeth's steed bolted, the Highlander spurred his own animal in pursuit.

"But wait!" Elizabeth yelled, holding her position firmly on the horse. "I need more time. I don't have an answer yet."

"Have no fear!" the baron shouted. "I know the remedy!"

The Marquis of Troyes certainly likes to hunt in comfort, Elizabeth thought, trying to look appreciatively at the things around her as she wandered somewhat apprehensively about the spacious bedchamber. And if this is how he accommodates his guests, how must he pamper himself?

"Honestly, I don't want to know," she said aloud, running her fingers over the fine lace-covered comforter that lay upon the huge damask-canopied bed.

This grand country manor—a hunting lodge, they had called it—was truly a palace by anyone's standards. Turning off the highway and plunging into the darkness of a forest road, Ambrose had led her, without any more words being said, to this place.

Now, seating herself on the edge of the bed, a recurring thought kept plucking at the strings of her anxiety.

His body! she thought. His suffering body! Sacrifice for his body? Elizabeth shook her head. No, he didn't mean it. This was just his way of tormenting her.

Elizabeth lay back on the comforter, a weariness suddenly overtaking her. Then, as if stung by something unseen, the young woman leaped from the bed.

Elizabeth moved to the middle of the floor, helpless as fears that lingered in the recesses of her soul flared up like the bunches of stars that shoot westward in the summer night sky. She felt them all, coursing through her in waves of heat and cold. All the anxiety of being a woman and yet not a woman. Complete and yet not complete. Experienced in the ways of the world and yet lacking all knowledge of courtship by men.

A woman still untouched. Wanting him and yet still not knowing if Ambrose's attentions focused only on the physical. She wondered if he'd missed her as she had missed him. If he even saw her as being worthy of his interest. Had he brought her here to satisfy their bodies' desire? Well, what of their souls? she asked herself.

Nay! Stop all this! Elizabeth shook her head and wrapped her arms around her. You're making more of this than there is, she told herself, finding cold consolation in the thought.

Crossing the room, she concentrated, trying to organize everything in her mind. This was the place where they were first supposed to meet Francis, so it was, after all, natural for them to stop. And it was getting late, so of course they would stay the night. Then tomorrow they would go on to Troyes. It was all explainable, logical. And after all, it was doubtful that the barge Mary and the others were traveling on would have reached the city by now. They would have to wait, so this place was as good as any others.

Listen to yourself rationalize, she thought guiltily.

Relax, Elizabeth reminded herself. This is a house full of servants. A house large enough to hide in and never be found by Ambrose. There was absolutely nothing to worry about. If she didn't want him to make love to her, then . . .

"What a lie!" she whispered with a sigh.

She could not deny it. She missed him. Pacing back and forth, Elizabeth realized she was fighting two battles at once. Battles she could not hope to win—at least not here. At least not now.

She shrugged again, pushing all thoughts of love from her mind. Moving to the spacious window, she looked outside. From the moment she and Ambrose had ridden up the winding path to the main house, Elizabeth had found herself admiring the lodge's design—the perfect balance of practicality and aesthetics. Modest-sized fields and pastures, carved out of the forest to produce enough food for the table of the marquis, eventually gave way to stables, kennels, and the most extraordinary gardens the young painter had seen anywhere.

And at the center of it all stood the lodge itself.

It was a magnificent building. Tall stone towers and turrets topped with conical slate-covered roofs adorned the multitude of peripheral wings that branched off with symmetrical grace from the main wing of the lodge. Though the towers were of stone, the walls of the lodge itself were of wattle and wood, and the X-designs of the supporting timbers created a strikingly picturesque look.

Elizabeth couldn't wait to see the rest of this architectural gem. Even the windows, luxuriously abundant and glazed with innumerable panes, had promised an interior that would be bright and airy.

And she hadn't been disappointed. The splendor of the place was truly inspiring.

Paintings, carvings, and tapestries filled the walls of the great rooms and the corridors leading to the bedchambers. Elizabeth turned around and faced the chamber she was occupying. This room on its own was a feast for the eyes in the glow of late afternoon light that spilled with reckless extravagance through the four open windows. Tables, chairs, a chest, and even a small fireplace—all part of the Marquis of Troyes's design to furnish each and every visitor with more comfort and hospitality than even a royal guest might expect elsewhere.

Very thoughtful, Elizabeth decided, smiling as she headed for the cheese, bread, and wine that sat so invitingly on the table.

The knock on the door stopped Elizabeth dead in her tracks. She stood in the center of the room, looking uncertainly at the great oaken door. Ambrose had his own bed-chamber. It was clear he was a regular guest here, for it appeared it was his customary room. It was just past the wide and gracefully carved staircase.

The sound of another gentle tap urged the young woman forward. Elizabeth moved quietly across the chamber and then stood listening, her hand steady on the decorative wooden latch.

"Who is it?"

The timid voice of the young woman on the other side of the door could hardly be heard through the thick wood. Elizabeth opened the door slightly and peered out at the young maid standing patiently in the hallway.

"Mademoiselle, I was asked to come and help you dress and also to bring you this."

Elizabeth looked down at the satchel the servant held in her outstretched arms. She recognized it as the one Mary had sent along. Then her eyes shot up to the young woman's face. "What was it that you called me?"

"Pardon me, m-madame," she stuttered apologetically. "I—I didn't know . . . no one told me if 'mademoiselle' is appropriate or 'madame.' I am so sorry. I—"

"No! No! That's not it!" Elizabeth swung the door open and gestured for the young maid to step in. "I was just surprised by . . ." She shook her head. Had Ambrose notified the household of her true identity? How curious, she thought. She turned and watched as the girl moved quickly through the room, opening chests and selecting fine chemises, hosiery, puffy-sleeved blouses of the whitest silk, and an elegant dress the color of a narcissus flower. "To whom does all this belong?"

"The marquis's mother, m'lady. The master's parents visit here quite often." The young woman held the dress up and cast a quick glance at Elizabeth, smiling happily at the evident match. She spread the garment carefully on the bed. "But she would insist upon you wearing them—considering that you have arrived without your trunks and servants."

The maid continued to bustle about the room as Elizabeth's hand caressed the rich texture of the yellow brocade cloth of the dress.

"We do this quite often. Though the seamstress will be disappointed that your size and Lady Elizabeth's are so close." The servant looked up quickly before continuing, and Elizabeth smiled, thinking how quickly the young woman had lost her shyness. The maid chattered on. "Oh, how interesting! You have the same names. Hmm. It is not always so. The sizes, I mean. Why, the last time Lord Ambrose brought—I meant to say, the last time—I'm so sorry, madame. I talk too much."

Elizabeth watched the young girl's reddened face.

"Does he travel here often?" she asked gently.

"I—I shouldn't . . ." She shook her head. "It is not proper to tell a lady about the one before."

"Does he come here with many ladies?"

"No, madame." The young maid shook her head. "I heard from the older servants that he used to. He and the duc. He is Lord Ambrose's close friend. But now, since the duc has married, Lord Ambrose has been coming alone. With the exception of this visit, madame."

Elizabeth listened quietly. She didn't care much about the duc or his pastimes, but there was one thing that the young woman had made clear—the purpose of this sojourn was to satisfy his desires, after all. Conditions. It all came down to this. The conditions that he'd spoken of in Florence. He didn't need to say anything. It was all so clear. All his "conditions" really just boiled down to one thing. They were here to share her bed.

Of course! What could she have been expecting? She would be a fool to think otherwise. Elizabeth walked to the satchel that the young woman had placed on top of the bed. The one she'd picked up in Mary's room. Something for her, Mary had said.

Pulling open the thongs that held it closed, Elizabeth dumped the contents on the bed and gazed down at a linen-wrapped package and a note addressed to her.

A note from her sister.

Elizabeth, my dearest! What pleasure this brings me, knowing you are—for at least one moment in your life—away from the cares you shoulder so unfailingly. For so long, my sweet, your thoughts and your actions have tended to everyone but you yourself. How different we are, my sister. For how many years now, you have lived so serious a life—while I have lived so frivolously. Well, for once, follow your heart's lead. For

*once be a woman as God intended you to be. And know
that we are secure and lovingly yours,
Mary.*

Elizabeth placed the note gently beside the package and
untied the ribbon that held the linen wrapping tight. Picking up the diaphanous silk nightgown that Mary had
packed for her, the young painter gazed silently at the garment until her eyes clouded over.

Then, reaching up, she found the ring that lay close to
her heart. Gently, she removed the leather thong from
around her neck and laid the emerald ring on the side
table.

For so many years she had kept and cherished this token as a symbol, as a reminder of Ambrose. So many
times, she'd held the emerald ring in her hand and
dreamed. But now, tonight, reality was pressing.

Tonight, this memento would serve no purpose.

For tonight, at least, there was no need for pretense.
Tonight, Elizabeth Boleyn would live as a woman. Would
have her chance to love. She would have Ambrose
Macpherson, body and soul.

For tonight, at least, Elizabeth would have no need for
this ring.

Chapter 22

Ambrose patted the gray, shaggy hound that lay by his feet and then stood up to go after her.

Too long. Far too long.

Stretching his long, muscular frame, the baron turned toward the door. He was growing old waiting for Elizabeth to come down to dinner. He was tired, hungry, and though he almost hated to admit it, anxious to spend time with her. The last servant he had sent up had returned with the news that she had finished with her bath and was dressing. But that had been an hour ago. He should have followed his instincts and gone after her himself.

Ambrose found himself once again becoming quite cranky. And justifiably so, he thought. She was doing it to rile him. He was certain of it. He could just see her sitting in that room, waiting—just waiting to see how long it would take him to reach the end of all patience.

Well, the vixen was going to find out.

By the time he reached the door of the sitting room, the Highlander was in a full rage. Yanking the door open, he took one step into the corridor and stopped.

There she stood.

The words he was forming to greet her with upstairs withered, forgotten on his tongue as he gawked helplessly at the vision before him. His eyes drank in the sight of her as if trying to quench some inexorable thirst. But somewhere deep inside him, Ambrose knew that there was no relief.

Though her raven hair was short and her expression challenging, she was all woman beneath. She was clad in a soft yellow dress that draped off both her shoulders, leaving them pleasantly—no, exquisitely bare. He was certain his mother had worn the same dress, but somehow Elizabeth looked quite different in it. And wonderfully so.

Ambrose's eyes traveled the surface of the exposed shoulders to the full curves of her breasts and then up again to the ivory splendor of her throat. And as he returned again to that beautiful face, so full of challenge, so full of life, he felt that familiar stirring in his loins.

Elizabeth smiled. Ambrose was wearing black. His blond hair was tied back, but the strands that spilled onto the ebony velvet of his doublet gleamed in the light of the room. The fine hose that displayed the thickly contoured muscles of his thighs and calves was also black, so only the gold chain that hung about his neck and the puffy white sleeves that pushed through slits in the arms of the doublet offered any contrast to the image of power that emanated from his richly dark attire. Just standing in his presence, Elizabeth felt her pulse quicken.

Ambrose had to control an overpowering urge to pull her into his arms at once and devour her whole.

Elizabeth pushed past him and stepped into the room. She did not have to look to know that he followed close behind. The sound of the door closing behind them made her shiver as emotion and anticipation mingled in a volatile mix.

Like some huge and fragrant oak with branches that spread around her, Ambrose Macpherson had, even in his absence, dominated her world for a long time—indeed, he affected her very senses. Now she could not stop herself from melting inside at the thought of how it would feel to hold him, to kiss him, to feel the very weight of him.

Elizabeth was obsessed with him.

Wrapping her arms around her middle, she gathered herself and stood waiting in the middle of the spacious chamber. The room was warm, and the small wood fire crackling noisily in the hearth was comforting and homelike. The shaggy gray hound trotted over to inspect her and, satisfied with the gentle pat he received, settled himself once again by the fire.

So what are you afraid of? Elizabeth asked herself. Four years ago, she had been ready to give herself to this man. She had even thought, momentarily, that the mere physical attraction that she had felt for him could carry her through the act. But now . . . now she felt a longing that far exceeded what she felt then. Now, something else pressed at the breath in her lungs.

Tonight, walking to this room, stepping within his arms' reach, was a dream. A long-awaited dream. She had waited long enough. She knew that. But she also knew that she had waited for *him*.

There were many things she had forgone in her life. But this was one thing she would not turn her back on. For now he wanted her, and she had made up her mind that he would have what he desired.

Ambrose bit back his smile as he leaned against the door and watched her turn and face him. She was struggling, he could tell. His silent scrutiny was unnerving her.

He let his eyes once again peruse every aspect of her dress, her body, her face. She avoided his gaze. There was a pink blush that had spread across her beautiful face. She looked exquisite and . . . so innocent.

"Do you approve?" Her voice trembled slightly as she glanced briefly at him.

He nodded silently.

"This dress . . ." She looked down and caught sight of her partially exposed breast. She looked away and quickly crossed her arms in front of her. "It's so beautiful. My wearing it simply doesn't do the garment justice."

Upon hearing no response, she turned her gaze to him. He remained where he was, leaning against the door, his arms crossed over his chest. She looked down at her own pose. Mirror images. They were standing the same way. She dropped her hands to her sides at once.

"You look beautiful."

She waited for more. But he said no more. Uncertain of what to do next, Elizabeth glanced anxiously at the baron again. Truthfully, she had come downstairs fully prepared to be ravished on the nearest table. And she had decided that would perhaps have been the easiest solution for both of them. That way, she would never have time to dawdle over the rights and wrongs of the act.

And there would be no time to reveal to him the truth.

The truth that she was not the woman he thought her to be. The truth that Jaime was not her daughter. The truth that she was a virgin. And the most troublesome truth of all—that she simply hadn't a clue about how to make love to him.

She was afraid.

And now she found that his flattering expression, his bold blue eyes, his smiling compliments were beginning to irk her. She wished he would do something.

"Hungry?"

"For food?" she questioned hesitantly.

"Aye, I'm starved."

Starved? For food? She nearly snapped. What's wrong with this man? she wondered. Let's get on with it! Elizabeth turned away from him, disgusted with herself for not having more knowledge of the game of love, more experience in dealing with men . . . on this level. "I have no appetite."

She glanced around again as Ambrose moved toward her. He was smiling confidently. "For food, I assume."

She held her breath. At last.

He took hold of her hand and placed it in the crook of his arm. "Too bad." He started toward a door on the other end of the room.

Unable to stop herself in time, Elizabeth held back, resisting gently. "Where are you taking me?"

"To a room beside the great hall. To watch me eat." He paused, taking a firmer grip on her hand. "Unless you would prefer to have dinner served here in this room."

Elizabeth scanned the room quickly. There were chairs, a table by the fireplace, a reed mat on the floor. Her eyes lingered on the mat. It looked comfortable enough. And they were alone. "Here. I prefer it here."

She allowed him to escort her to the table. He sat her in a chair and moved away.

Elizabeth watched him as he strode to a door and spoke briefly with someone just outside.

No longer having his intense blue eyes on her, Elizabeth felt she could breath once again. She had to get control of herself and her emotions. She looked about the room, noticing for the first time the marvelous paintings that adorned each wall. Rising to her feet at once, she crossed over to them and studied each canvas one by one. They were mostly the works of Europe's most renowned painters.

Ambrose gestured for the servant who had spread the food on the trestle table to leave them. With a cordial bow, the man departed.

As he moved behind her, the baron could tell that she once again was feeling at ease. Lost in the artwork of the lodge, she was in her element. He smiled. Fate had played a trick on him.

He studied her profile, the faint lein of the scar that barely showed on her perfect skin. She smelled of wild-flowers in an open field. His eyes caressed her slender neck. The soft curls that came short of hiding the exquisite splendor of her ivory skin. He could almost taste that skin under his lips. He wanted her so much that it hurt.

Elizabeth heard him come near. Then she felt the gentle touch of his lips on the skin of her neck. She looked down and saw his large hands encircle her waist. She leaned back against his strong body.

"It's time," he said huskily.

She turned slowly in his embrace. Facing him. Holding her heart in her hand.

"Aye. The food is here, Elizabeth. It's time to eat."

Elizabeth reached up, placing her fingers around his thick neck. She wanted to strangle him. "Why are you do-ing this to me?" The sound of his laugh soothed her heart.

"Doing what?" he protested coyly, as he pushed her hands behind his neck and crushed her to his chest. His lips came down and brushed fleetingly across hers.

"Making me wait like this. Why are you doing this? I thought you wanted to make love to me." She concen-trated on the cleft of his strong chin. "What are you wait-ing for? When are we going to . . . do it?"

Ambrose looked at her with raised eyebrows. "A wee bit impatient, wouldn't you say, lass?"

"If you're going to pretend that you did not bring me here to make love to me, then you are a liar, Ambrose Macpherson."

"Nay. But our lovemaking can wait, wouldn't you say? Perhaps until we've eaten some of this fine food. Then drunk some wine. Then we'll go for a walk outside. There is full moon out there, you know. Then I might be able to persuade the gardener to cut you some fresh flowers—"

"Stop it!" She yanked her hands from behind his neck and struck him solidly in his chest with her fist. "Why must you go on like this? And don't tell me this is some Scottish courting ritual. I know it's probably the same thing you've used on all the women you bring to this place."

Ambrose paused and looked teasingly into her face. "Nay, Elizabeth. I'm not courting you. And for your information, I don't play games like that with women. I have no need for it. In fact, by the time I've closed the door to this room behind them, we've already made love twice in the bedchambers and once on the stairway."

She pushed at his chest and tried to get away. He wouldn't let her. She punched at his massive chest once again. She was hurt. He ensnared her hands with his own. She gave up her struggle.

"Then why?" Elizabeth whispered. "Why are you doing this to me? If you are so disappointed—if you don't want me—then why don't you just let me go? Why did you bring me here, anyway?"

"To make love to you. To ravish you. To make you forget everything and everyone. To hear you cry out my name with more feeling than a she-wolf howls in the light of the full moon."

Elizabeth shuddered in his arms as she hung on his every word.

"But first"—Ambrose smiled mischievously—"I have to give you a taste of what you've given me. That's all. Waiting, Elizabeth. Waiting. The agony of wanting someone. The physical pain of languishing ever so patiently without really knowing for sure if she intends to go through with it. I've waited for you for quite some time now, my sweet. Shall we turn the tables? You see, two can play that game, lass. And now, shall I make you wait as I have?"

"This is quite different, m'lord. I'm here tonight of my own free will. I want to be here in your arms. This is no fate or accident that has thrown us together. I'm here because I want to be here."

"You have never been in my arms any other way, but still—"

"I want you, Ambrose." Elizabeth placed a hand gently on his lips, silencing him. "I want you now. Please take me."

He stood still, looking at her.

She moved her hand away from his lips and caressed his cheek. Her fingers traced the line of his jaw, the line of his cheekbone, and then she touched the scar that crossed his forehead. "I will not put a stop to this love-making. I'll not make you wait again. Ever. That I promise."

Elizabeth stood on tiptoe and kissed the point of his chin.

Ambrose tightened his grip. Whom did he think he was fooling? He couldn't wait any more than she could. He watched her eyes close as she brushed his lips, his face with light kisses. His body, coming alive at her nearness, pressed seductively against hers. His hand moved up and cupped her breast through the soft fabric.

Elizabeth shuddered at the feel of his hand and opened her eyes. Like the sky in spring, the blue of his eyes glistened as he gazed into her face. Reaching behind his neck and removing the leather thong that bound his blond hair, Elizabeth ran her hands gently through the thick flaxen locks.

Ambrose found himself lost in her eyes. He wanted her more than the air he breathed. What he'd said earlier of waiting all faded quickly into oblivion. What was it about this woman's touch?

But Elizabeth lowered her eyes, feeling her skin burn at her own awkwardness.

"I, too, have waited," she whispered, laying her face against the soft dark velvet of the doublet. "I, too, have suffered."

Ambrose lowered his eyes and placed his lips in her ebony hair. My God, he wanted her. He couldn't wait.

"We have such little time together," she continued. She turned her gaze upward again, her eyes searching his face for a sign. "Tomorrow we will be back with the others, and this dream will all come to an end."

"Is this a dream, lass?" he asked quietly.

"I don't know what it is!" she whispered. "I'm living the life of a man, but the feelings that threaten to burst out of my every pore tell me I am a woman. I don't know what is a dream or what is real. But I do know one thing, Ambrose. I want you."

"Waiting—" he began.

"Nay!" she broke in, her voice quiet but clear. "Let's not waste this moment with bad feelings and grudges."

As Elizabeth lifted her lips, his mouth descended on hers.

Ambrose slid his fingers into her hair as he crushed her mouth to his. He'd begun to say that waiting was a fool's game. But that thought was gone—dispersed in the moment like smoke in the wind. Now he had one purpose in mind. He wanted to make love to her. He wanted to show her the reality of what she should believe. She was a woman. A very desirable woman. Certainly she was a talented painter—she had that to be proud of. But now he wanted her to know how much they needed to be only themselves. A man and a woman. No pretense, no facade, just themselves.

They had so much time to make up for.

Ambrose lifted her in his arms as he headed for the door. She wrapped her hands around his neck, her mouth resting on the skin of his neck.

"Not here?" she murmured, a small smile playing on her lips.

"Nay, lass." The Highlander smiled back at her and pushed through the door. "Nor on the stairway, either."

Chapter 23

❦

The massive oak door swung easily on its hinges as the two swept into the room. Ambrose kicked the door shut with his foot as he carried her to the bed.

All the way up the wide stairway and through the long corridor, Elizabeth's mouth had never left his. Kissing him, biting him, she had been coaxing him on until they had burst into the bedchamber.

He was mad with desire.

There was no thought of gentle caresses, soft touches, beautiful words. Elizabeth tore at his velvet doublet, searching for the feel of his skin. She urged him on, and he followed her passionate demands with wild abandon.

Ambrose whipped the comforter from her bed and dropped her into the billows of down as he detached his mouth from her suckling lips. A momentary flash of conscious thought told him that he should step away, slow this reckless pace. If he could only pause for a breath, regain control of his discipline, of his desire. Then, gazing down at her, he could see the clouds of passion in her eyes. Her hair spread in disarray on the smooth white linen, and a perfect breast showed above the top of her pulled-down dress.

He knew there was no hope. Lowering himself onto her, his mouth latched on to the aroused nipple. He was ready to take all that she wanted to give.

Elizabeth couldn't lie still. Her mind raced into a thousand new worlds, worlds she'd seen only in her most vivid and wondrous dreams. Her heart pounded wildly, her blood roared in her head. She pushed at his clothes and grasped him by the neck, pressing him harder against her chest.

"Take me, Ambrose," she panted. "Please! Take me now."

There was no thought beyond the actions of their hands. Mindless to anything else but the fulfillment they each sought, they tore at one another's clothes. Elizabeth felt Ambrose rise from her and then saw him above her, stripping the doublet and shirt from his massive upper body in a single motion. She tried to reach for the tie that belted his hose, but instead fell back as she felt herself dragged by the ankle to the edge of the bed. There he stood, and Elizabeth looked up past the muscular chest to his handsome face, his eyes burning with desire.

Ambrose pushed her dress up to her waist as he freed his throbbing member. The soft silk of her undergarment tore in his hands. He was lost in his abandon. All discipline crumbled like spent tinder before the flames of carnal need.

"Elizabeth," he whispered, his voice raw with emotion. His fingers dug into her hips as he pulled her closer, spreading her legs apart and moving between them. "Only this once, we'll not take our time."

Clinging to the sheet, she raised her hips to him as he pressed into her soft, moist folds. "Take me, Ambrose."

In a single motion, he plunged his great shaft deep within her.

Elizabeth let out a sharp cry as she reached up and grabbed him around the neck. She was seized with a momentary shock of pain. She gasped for breath and held him as tightly as she could.

My God, he thought, she was a virgin. The thought cut like the cold, keen blade of a knife into a brain dulled and confused by the fires of desire. Ambrose took a deep breath and tried not to move. He was fully rooted within her. The tightness of her sheath—the way she had wrapped her legs around him—threatened to kill him. But still he remained motionless. His heart hammered against his chest, and his breath was coming in short, quick pants.

Then, gently, the Highlander lowered her to the bed. "You were a virgin," he growled.

"Don't hold it against me," she whispered, trying to lighten his scowl. The pain was beginning to subside. She ran her fingers caressingly over the rippling sinews of his chest.

"Why didn't you tell me?" he asked, pushing himself up onto his elbows. Looking down at her passion-filled eyes, he saw a tear break away from the corner of her eye and disappear into her dark hairline. What a brute you are, Ambrose Macpherson, he thought to himself. How he must have hurt her. Though he could not ignore his body, screaming for release, Ambrose tried to concentrate on Elizabeth and only her. But then another question edged its way into his thoughts. "Jaime. Whose daughter is Jaime?"

"Please don't be angry," Elizabeth pleaded in a ragged voice as she saw the fierce light in his eyes. "I'll tell you all you want to know. I'm sorry." She covered her eyes with the back of her hand. "I'm sorry I've disappointed you."

He looked down at the woman stretched in his arms. He was the first man to lay with her. Without being able to explain it, he felt a deep sense of pride.

"How could I be disappointed?" Ambrose protested, as he took her face softly in his hands. "Shocked. Pleased. Surprised. Curious even. But not disappointed, my sweet." He leaned down and slanted his lips over hers, his tongue probing the soft recesses of her mouth. Her hand once again encircled his neck, and he drew her up tightly to him.

Elizabeth arched her hips as he gathered her in his arms. Suddenly she could feel his member pulsing deep within her. He had her full attention.

Ambrose shifted his weight slightly, and Elizabeth gasped as a new sensation replaced the discomfort. As he partially withdrew his manhood, a feeling of intense heat, of torrid pleasure emanated from the very core of her. Ambrose slid into her again, and somewhere in her head Elizabeth felt as if a rod were being drawn across the taut string of a lyre. A single note resonated throughout her entire body.

Again, ever so slowly, he withdrew, and again the love tone played within her. Again he drove into her, and the sound that she felt more than heard reverberated through her. A rhythm began to envelop her, coming from within, and yet tied to the motion of her lover.

Higher and higher the pitch of the sound went, and

Elizabeth found her body rising and falling to the pulsating beat.

Over and over, Ambrose plunged, and Elizabeth's hips rose to accept him more deeply with every stroke. The moans coming from far down in her throat sounded more like the humming purr of a wild lioness. But he wanted to make certain that Elizabeth found pleasure before he did. He had to hold back, but the sounds she made were driving him over a precipice. She was making it impossible, and he strained against the overwhelming pressure.

Her fingers dug into his shoulders. She kept pushing, arching against him rhythmically, urgently.

Then she called his name. As if the earth shook, as if her existence depended on the hold of the arms around her, Elizabeth coiled around him. Within her brain a million notes exploded in a chorus of light and sound, color and music. Every singing fiber of her being on fire, her body lifted into his as lightning bolts of reds and yellows thrilled through her—elevating her, transporting her into a crystalline dimension she had only dreamed could exist.

As her body went taut as a wire, Ambrose plunged one last time, pouring his seed into her. Then, momentarily spent, he fell into her welcoming embrace.

Elizabeth caressed his damp skin, gathering him tightly in her arms. For her, the earth had stopped turning as they'd made love. But now, lying there with him, her breath shortened as a knot formed in her chest. Then, without warning, Elizabeth felt tears well up and wash down her face. In the span of a few precious moments, he had been able to release in her a world that had been hidden deep within. A wondrous world.

Because of him. Lying there, she knew it was because of this man, Ambrose Macpherson, that she felt as she did. From the first moment that he'd turned his attention to her in the grandstands at the Field of Cloth of Gold, he had changed her life. She needed him. She loved him.

Elizabeth brushed her lips against his hair as he rested so serenely on top of her. She could feel the pounding of his heartbeat beginning to slow. She cherished the feel of his weight. The strength that flowed from him.

Ambrose lifted himself and rolled off of her. Moving to the middle of the bed, he pulled Elizabeth to his side. She was a tangled jumble of dress and sheets. He looked down into her beautiful face and felt his heart tighten. She looked like a dream, curled up beside him. The burst of passion, the powerful explosion he'd felt only moments ago, had subsided now. But it had been a first even for him. Never in the act of lovemaking had he felt a commingling of spirits as he had felt with her. Never. Though there was something daunting at the thought of it, there was also something satisfying. A sense of completeness swept through him. A sense of oneness that pacified the body, soothed the soul.

But it wasn't only the strength of their passion that brought such peace; it was the way she felt now, lying in his arms. It was the feel of her body against him, as though she had been made to fit there and only there, where she lay at this moment. In his arms, beside him. She belonged to him.

His voice was gentle when he asked the question. "Why didn't you tell me the truth, lass?"

The young woman looked up and saw the softness in his expression. "I suppose I was afraid."

"Not of me!" he exclaimed, as his thumb wiped away the traces of tears that were drying on her perfect complexion.

Elizabeth found herself leaning into the warm touch of his hand. "A bit afraid of you, and a bit afraid of myself."

He looked up into the dark canopy above. "You were an innocent when you came to me that night at the Field of Cloth of Gold. What a fool I was for not seeing it." He turned to her. "But why did you come? Why did you lead me on so with your pretense of experience?"

She coiled the sheets between her fingers. There was no reason to continue to evade telling him the truth. He would know what she could share with him. "I've already told you of my father. Of his plan to send me to King Henry's bed."

He nodded silently.

"In part, that's why I came to you that night." She searched for the right words. She didn't want him to think her father's disgusting intentions had been the only reasons she had run to him. Deep inside she knew there was more. "That afternoon, after the joust, my father told me that Henry wanted my virginity. His foolish physicians had told the king a virgin's innocence could cure his pox. Unfortunately, I was there, at the wrong place. At the wrong time."

Ambrose cursed the stupidity of such backwardness. "You didn't believe them, did you?" he asked, already knowing the answer. "The arrogant bastard. Using his power over those too innocent to resist."

"I never gave my father a chance to go through with his threat." She moved closer to his side. "I came to your tent hoping that you would make love to me. It's true I was determined to teach my father a lesson. But my coming to you went beyond that alone. If I was to step into womanhood, I was bound that I would make that transition with the person of my own choosing."

"But you could have told me the truth. I could have taken you out of there without the hell you have put yourself through. It didn't have to be the way it was."

"How could I have done that to you?" she protested, raising herself on her elbow. "Here you were, the most handsome man in the entire Golden Vale. The most charming courtier, a champion among warriors, perhaps the most eligible bachelor in the Europe—"

"Perhaps?" he broke in with a smile.

"You had your choice of women," she continued. "And I should presume so much? Simple, plain Elizabeth Boleyn."

"The bright and beautiful Elizabeth Boleyn."

She clapped him gently on the chest. "There is no need to flatter me, m'lord," she continued, tracing patterns on his chest. "There I was. Wishing my innocence away, but deathly nervous about going through with it. I was just so afraid to reveal the truth and find myself thrown out of your tent."

"I never threw a woman out of my tent."

She dropped her head on his chest. "Please, don't depress me."

Ambrose smiled as he ran his fingers in her hair. "Of course, that was before I met you. I've turned so many of them away since."

"Liar!"

Ambrose laughed as he drew her face up to his for a kiss. "I was the real disappointment, wasn't I? It was I who didn't come through as you had wished."

"But you did!" She rolled on her stomach, propping herself on her elbows and looking at him with a twinkle in her eye. "As far as every one else was concerned, we did sleep together that night. They all believed me. Even my sister Mary."

"And that ruse served your purpose?"

"I ran away," she whispered quietly, growing serious again. "And here I am. So I suppose it did."

Ambrose turned onto his side and laid his hand gently on her back. "There never were any husbands or lovers."

She shook her head. "Nay, and there was never anyone by the name of Phillipe de Anjou."

Silent for a moment, the Highlander ran his hand over the curve of her buttocks, smoothing the dress beneath his wide palm. He stopped.

"But what about Jaime? She looks so much like you that it was only natural for me to assume she was yours." Ambrose gazed into her face. "She's Mary's daughter, isn't she?"

Elizabeth turned her head and looked him straight in the eye. She trusted him. There was no danger for the child in Ambrose knowing the truth. "Aye. Jaime is Mary's daughter."

"And the father?"

"Henry of England," she said quietly, taking hold of his other wrist. "This has been a secret between Mary and me. Only we know. And now you. But we must keep it that way."

Perplexed, Ambrose stared at her. "Even someone as heartless as Henry would care for his offspring. The child would be treated nobly."

"We know that. It's not Henry who worries us most." Elizabeth paused, searching for the right words. "It's our father. He bartered away two daughters. He'll treat Jaime no differently. She's happy with us. We have been able to provide for her. We are giving her everything she needs. She's better with Mary and me than she would ever be in the English court." Her voice took on an imploring note. "I just can't risk endangering her life. Please understand."

How could he not understand? Ambrose knew how illegitimate children were perceived in the royal families. They were the pawns of those in search of power—at best.

And Ambrose had enjoyed playing and talking with Jaime many times during this long journey. She was the spitting image of her aunt—in looks and in character. Jaime had spirit.

"You would do best to keep her as far away from that court as you can."

Elizabeth gazed into his blue eyes, confident in her decision to confide all in this man.

"Thank you," she whispered quietly.

He traced her lips gently with his fingers. Moving closer, he kissed her tenderly.

"Jaime is a lucky child." His fingers softly trailed over the silky skin of her chin to the hollow of her throat and along the line of her collarbone. "She's lucky to have you."

Elizabeth shook her head slightly, denying the compliment.

"Ambrose," she said quietly, after a moment's pause. "I have a question to ask you. Well, actually a permission, of sorts."

He laughed. "Permission? Elizabeth Boleyn asking permission?"

"Forget what I said," she scowled. "Consider it a question."

"Aye. That's more like my Elizabeth."

"The ring." She turned and reached over to the table and picked up the ring and leather thong.

"Aye. Henry's ring."

Elizabeth paused and gazed at it.

"Ambrose, I wore this for years as a keepsake. As a token of your attentions to me. Of what I carried in my heart." She lifted her eyes to his. "But now I'd like to put it aside . . . for Jaime."

The Highlander looked steadily into her misty eyes.

"She doesn't know her father's true identity. In fact, she might never know . . . but I thought it might be a good thing for her to have this someday." She caressed the sinewy muscles of his chest. "So what do you think?"

Ambrose's face was serious as he placed his huge hand over hers, holding her hand still.

"That is fine with me, Elizabeth. But I have one condition."

"Another condition?"

"Aye. Perhaps a final one."

"Very well. What is it?"

"You can't give me away."

Elizabeth smiled. "Never."

The gentle breeze kissed the two entangled bodies with its soft dawn touch.

Elizabeth paused for a moment, listening to the song of a lark outside, and then lifted her lips from Ambrose's naked chest. She brushed her black hair away from her face and smiled down at his tortured expression.

"What about now? Will you take me yet?"

"You're the devil's lass, Elizabeth Boleyn," Ambrose muttered through gritted teeth. "But I still say nay!"

With a growl that rumbled from a place deep in his chest, the baron threw Elizabeth onto her back and moved quickly on top of her. Securely pinning her hands under his, he grunted contentedly before letting his mouth travel leisurely along the soft skin of her neck, her shoulders, the firm white flesh of her breasts. His tongue made ever-narrowing circles around the broad, rosy aureole of one before finally laving and teasing the hardening nipple.

He cursed himself for the hundredth time for acting like an unprincipled knave, taking her the night before as he had. And what was worse, he'd silently promised to take his time thereafter. But the next time had been only a few short moments after the first time. And once again they had been too crazed to take and to give what they each had waited so long to share. Again there had been no gentleness, no taking their time.

So once again Ambrose had renewed his promise to go slower the next time.

It had been a wondrous night. How many times he had broken his promise, he couldn't remember.

Ambrose had to admit it was very difficult—nearly impossible—to go slowly with a woman like Elizabeth. In bed, the woman was a she-devil. A raging moor fire, one that incinerated everything in its path. Even now she continued to writhe restlessly beneath him. As he moved from one breast to the other, eliciting a low moan from her, he considered how the morning light would show nearly every inch of his skin gloriously scorched.

Indeed, he had awakened her out of her half-sleep only moments ago with a gentle touch, a seductive whisper. He

wanted to show her the ways—the many different ways—
that he could give her pleasure. But he also wanted to
show her there could be more to their lovemaking than
simply lust. He wanted to show her the dreamlike moments that could precede it. He wanted to show her the
tender side of romance.

But she had immediately taken charge. Her sense of curiosity, her need to discover had hours earlier laid waste
to any remaining vestige of constraint. In the graying
light, Elizabeth's lips and tongue had roamed freely and
extensively the length and breadth of his body—exploring
and delighting in the sweet torment she knew she was in-
flicting. Ambrose sighed deeply and took her taut nipple
firmly in his mouth. She had given him incredible pleasure, but now it was his turn.

Feeling like a goddess, Elizabeth wallowed in the billows of the soft mattress as Ambrose paid homage to her
body. Several times she tried to move, to follow his lead
in these acts of love, but each time his hands nudged her
gently back onto the pillows.

Still suckling her breast, Ambrose slid his fingers over
the soft triangle of her womanhood. Uttering a gasp, she
worked herself up once again onto her elbows.

"Just lie back, love," he ordered, bringing his face close
to hers. "This is my turn."

She gazed at him as his lips gently skimmed her cheeks,
her lips.

"This is just not fair," she whispered with a smile. "I
want to please you, as well."

His mouth covered hers, his kiss delicious and thor-
ough. When Ambrose was finished, there were no argu-
ments left in her. Indeed, sighing contentedly, Elizabeth
felt her body and her spirit growing ever more soft and
warm in his arms.

"Aye, lass," he growled huskily. "But you are pleasing
me by staying as you are."

She closed her eyes as he lay her back on the bed. Ambrose paused for a moment to note the look of trust in her
face. His eyes surveyed the smooth skin and the womanly
curves of her beautiful and giving body. Only he himself
truly knew the tenderness—and the fire—that coexisted
in that body.

They had only a short time remaining there at the

hunting lodge. Soon they would rejoin the others. Continue their journey to Scotland. Once beyond these walls, Elizabeth would again become Phillipe de Anjou. And then what? Ambrose thought. Perhaps she really could continue pulling off the deception. Pretending to be what she was not.

And he himself? Ambrose ran his fingers lightly over the sensitive skin at the top of her thighs, smiling faintly at the shiver his action provoked. What of him? He would go back to longing for her, and waiting for her.

Ambrose sighed, his face growing serious in the light of the approaching dawn. A sense of urgency crept into his soul. Suddenly it became overwhelmingly important that she remember what they shared here tonight. Crucial that she recall the night with longing. Essential that Elizabeth think of it often—and want it back again. More than that, she must want him. Again and again.

Yes, Elizabeth must give up this farce and be his. As a woman. She must belong to him. Only him. He would protect her, cherish her.

But he couldn't require her to give it all up. On every level, he knew that to be the truth.

Ambrose knew that art, for him, merely filled some void in his life. To Elizabeth, it was a love, an addiction far greater than any profession. To him a hobby and a pastime, no matter how great its value. But to her, painting was a passion. Ambrose knew he would have to compete with that.

The Highlander had a challenge before him. He had to show her a better way, a better future. He had to teach her love. His love. Then, perhaps, she would stop her pretense of being a man. Then, perhaps, she would be his.

She could paint. No matter if others frowned at her for being a woman—she could paint for him. She would always have a place beside him.

This was his chance.

As Ambrose lowered his mouth to her belly, Elizabeth's hands drifted carelessly to his shoulders. But her lips parted and her breath caught in her chest as he moved his lips even lower, his tongue flicking at the quivering skin and swirling into her navel.

He left nothing untouched. His lips and his tongue tasted the sweetness of her, lingering over every inch of her skin. Elizabeth's senses tingled, and inside, a bubbling mass of molten heat began to erupt and pour into every corner of her body, flooding her consciousness with a glowing white heat.

"Ambrose!" she called out weakly, her hands clutching at his hair as his lips and tongue reached her damp folds and stoked the blaze of erotic passion already raging within her.

She cried out his name again. This time in desperate need. The flames of desire threatened to consume her. Elizabeth's body arched, her breath shortened into pants. Her eyes could no longer see the objects in her chamber, for the lightning bolts of reds and yellows and whites were shooting across her face at incredible speeds, obliterating everything beyond. Her insides were coiling, melting, reforming.

"Ambrose!"

The Highlander raised his face slowly and moved with excruciating care up onto her body, trailing kisses that scorched her skin from her navel to her chin.

Then, once again taking possession of her mouth with his, he slid into her. Slowly. Ever so slowly.

As he did, Elizabeth's mind went white, a pulsating inferno exploding in the deepest recesses of her body and her soul.

Pressing her knees together to deal with the passing twinge of discomfort, Elizabeth put her hand out and leaned against the corridor wall.

Ambrose had warned her that she could be uncomfortable in the morning. He'd even suggested that perhaps they should take it easy.

Nay! she had responded. Too caught up in the delirious heights of passion they'd soared to, Elizabeth had been nothing if not definite in her unwillingness to put a stop to—or even slow for a moment—their hours of love. As far as she could see, this would have to be a memory she would savor for a lifetime.

So the longer she could extend this night of bliss, the better the remembrance, she thought.

And Ambrose Macpherson had gladly obliged.

But eventually, as the rising sun gently nudged the full

moon over the western hills, the private realm of night love gave way to the reality of the day.

Responsibility called to them. They had to leave.

"Could I get something for you, madame?"

Elizabeth nearly leaped out of her skin as the voice of the elderly man croaked quietly behind her. But the voice quickly registered. She'd met old Jacques, the estate's diminutive steward, yesterday on their arrival. Once again she wondered that none of the servants of the lodge so much as raised an eyebrow at her men's clothing. Elizabeth turned to face him slowly.

"Nay, but thank you." Her mind raced. "I was just admiring the collection of paintings on my way down."

"They are beautiful, aren't they?" He gestured toward the canvases that adorned every wall. "This is the work of some of the finest and best-known artists in Europe."

"Quite impressive," she murmured. "They are brilliant. I am a . . . I've a fondness for work of all painters. I just wanted to take a better look before we depart."

Jacques's face creased into a thousand wrinkles as he beamed at her interest. It was obvious to Elizabeth that the man took great pride in those things for which he was responsible.

"M'lady, what's displayed here in the main corridor and on the stairways represents only a small portion of the collection. The valuable pieces hang in the rooms downstairs."

The old man winked conspiratorially and nodded his head toward the stairs. The young woman smiled as the little man took hold of Elizabeth's arm, limping along beside her.

"If you would allow me"—he nearly cackled in a hushed voice—"I could show you my most favorite works."

"What are they? Raphael's original sketches?" she teased. Glancing back at the work hanging from the walls, she wondered how they could be any finer than what she'd been looking at. "You don't have Leonardo's notebooks, do you? There is talk in Florence that Leonardo kept secret journ—"

"You can see for yourself." Jacques pointed to a door as they reached the bottom of the great stairs. It was a room Elizabeth hadn't yet been through.

"These are what my master calls his 'hidden gems.' " The steward pulled a ring of keys from his shirt and opened the door with a flourish. As Elizabeth stepped inside of the giant room, her mouth opened in amazement. "They are all the early works of the world's greatest artists. The masterpieces of the—as yet—undiscovered. I believe this is the reason the master loves to spend so much time here."

The man continued to talk as Elizabeth stood in awe, her eyes taking in the hundreds of canvases that adorned the room. They were beautiful. All of different styles, some primitive, some using the new boldness of the Italian colorists. She walked toward one of the walls and began her survey of the works. Some were signed, but the signatures of the artists were clear from the styles and composition and the brushwork of the paintings themselves. Elizabeth could identify the creator of nearly every one. "He must have sent people around the world to have all of these brought here."

Jacques shook his head. "The master is very proud to say that he chose and purchased every piece in this room himself. Finding the work of genius, he says, is not something one delegates to others."

Elizabeth moved farther down the room. She paused before the startlingly realistic, and unflattering, portrait by someone she didn't know, a painter names Hans Holbein. His work hung beside the work of Dürer.

"And the master believes there is real value hidden within *these* pieces," the steward continued. "In spite of the fact that most of these paintings were done to feed an empty stomach, they are not—as you see in the use of colors and in the subject's depictions—traditional in any way. These painters' talents, these men's minds, were not limited by the restraints of set boundaries."

"Not these *men's* minds, Jacques. These *artist's* minds."

Elizabeth and the steward turned at once. Neither had heard Ambrose follow them in.

The elderly man bowed a greeting to the baron before heading for the door. Elizabeth watched with curiosity a silent exchange between the two of them. There was nothing said, but it seemed Jacques understood.

Ambrose glanced back as the door closed behind him. Then his gaze returned to Elizabeth. She stood once again in her men's clothing, her femininity disguised. In spite of the masculinity of her look and her attitude, his blood ignited. He knew what lay beneath.

Elizabeth blushed openly as she looked at his handsome face. Again Ambrose had donned his Highland gear for their ride into Troyes, and her pulse quickened at the memory of their bodies lying so closely together. She could remember every sensual touch, every bold act, every moment of joyous ecstasy. Nay, stop it, she admonished herself inwardly. She cast a quick glance at the closed door.

"Do you think anyone in the lodge guesses what we were up to last night?"

Ambrose answered her with silence.

She turned her gaze back to him. He looked suddenly dangerous. He took a step. She backed away. He followed. Elizabeth moved around the table, and he followed.

"Ambrose . . ." she warned in a low voice.

"They don't guess, love. They know what we were up to until dawn." He reached with the quickness of a cat and captured her wrist. "After all, I'm quite certain everyone heard you."

Elizabeth looked nervously at the door and then at Ambrose. He was smiling.

"What are you doing?" she asked, reluctantly allowing him to pull her from behind the table.

"I am about to make love to you."

"Here?" she whispered, her eyes widening at the prospect.

"Here, on this table."

Her heart hammered in her chest. She felt her face burn with heat. "You are not. Someone might walk in!"

Ambrose silenced her opposition. He crushed his mouth to hers.

"Ambrose," she protested, trying to catch her breath. Her hands halfheartedly pushed at his muscular chest. "You said we have to be on the road. We can't do this here." She shivered with excitement as his lips and mouth fastened on the skin of her neck. She could feel his hardening manhood rising beneath the soft wool of his kilt. "I—I have the wrong clothing. It won't work."

Holding her tightly, Ambrose pulled first at her doublet, then pushed at her breeches and her hose. Her gasp of surprise turned quickly to a moan of pleasure.

"Don't forget where we are, my love," he said, nodding smilingly at the paintings around them. He lifted her gently onto the table. "No boundaries."

Their love was fast and powerful, his strokes smooth and masterly, their release pure and complete. Spent, she gazed panting up to the ceiling, her limbs still tingling from their frantic lovemaking.

Ambrose placed a kiss on her lips as he straightened, offering her a hand up.

"We can't just do this anytime or anyplace you feel like it," she scolded, a smile tugging at her lips.

"Aye, we can." He tried to help her with her hose, but she slapped his hand away. "As long as we both want it and we both enjoy it."

She couldn't deny his words. She had enjoyed it. Fiercely so.

Elizabeth watched him from the corner of her eye as she tidied her attire. He wasn't tired of her. He still wanted her. Lying in the bath, she'd had her fears of how he would feel now that their night was through.

"We'll have breakfast before we get on our way." His words were so calm and self-assured. "Gavin will probably reach Troyes about midday today. If we ride hard, my sweet, we could get there this afternoon."

Ride hard. She cringed at the thought of it. Elizabeth was not sure she was ready to ride at all.

"Ready?" He stood, fresh as summer breeze, holding out his hand for her to take. "Let's eat."

She took his arm and allowed him to lead her toward the door. She imagined the faces of twenty servants plastered to the outer door listening to this latest moment of pleasure they'd shared. Uncontrollably, a flush of embarrassment colored her cheeks. Discreet. They needed to be more discreet. Approaching the door, she once again let her eyes roam the wonderful treasures that adorned every wall in sight.

Suddenly she came to a halt. There, to her left, between the two bright windows. Her eyes riveted on her own work.

Ambrose followed her gaze. He'd wanted her to find the piece herself. In fact, to make it possible, he'd asked the steward, Jacques, to be sure Elizabeth was shown into the study this morning. And he'd followed, unable to pass up the opportunity of seeing her expression when she found out.

He stood, beaming expectantly. Elizabeth whirled on him.

"You worm!" she burst out.

Chapter 24

She was thoroughly prepared to skin him alive.

Ambrose took a step back as Elizabeth advanced on him, an old broadsword in hand. She'd pulled the weapon from the display of armor before the Highlander could gather his wits. Her vehement exclamation was the last thing he'd been expecting. No, Elizabeth arming herself was the least expected response.

"Put that thing down before you hurt yourself," he ordered. She didn't even pause in her advance.

"There is only one person who is about to be hurt!" The long, heavy blade flashed in the sunlight. "And that's you."

Ambrose ducked as the weapon cut through the air only a hand span from his head.

"Well, why not use my sword, then? It will make for a quick death." He moved nimbly around the table. "At least it's sharp, lass."

Her eyes locked on the table.

The table! Elizabeth's rage flared to new heights.

"Nay," she seethed. She swung the blade again, as Ambrose pulled back. "That will be too kindly an end for you. I'd like to see you die a slow and painful death!"

Totally perplexed, Ambrose gazed wonderingly at the fury etched in her face. There was no question, she had to be rabid. "Can't we talk about this first?"

Elizabeth ignored his entreaty. "So," she hissed. "Is he late?"

He looked at her with raised eyebrows.

"Don't look so innocently at me, you pig! Was your plan for him to walk in while you had me spread on the table?" She leaned on the table and shook a fist at him.

"Or was it last night? You must have had them put me in *his* room. That way he could walk in on us there, I suppose!"

Ambrose put both his hands on the table and looked questioningly into her eyes. "Who are you talking ab—"

The sword arced straight overhead, the edge of the blade cutting deeply into the wood at the spot where the Highlander's hands had rested.

As lithe as a cat, the warrior grabbed her by the wrist and wrenched the sword out of her grip. As he looked up with a wry smile, Elizabeth punched him squarely in the face.

He hardly blinked as she held her hand in pain.

Ambrose reached over the table in an attempt to grab her by the shoulder, but she jumped back, tripping and falling clumsily on her buttocks.

"Let me ask this again. Who is this that you are talking about?" Ambrose moved around the table.

She shrank back from his approach. "Don't you come near me!"

"Who do you think was supposed to walk in while we were making love?" He reached down, trying to help her to her feet.

"Don't touch me!" She tried to fight off his hands, but he had the advantage.

"Elizabeth!" He gathered her in his arms, restricting her movement. But she fought in his grasp, snarling like a caged she-wolf. "What have I done? Who do you think was supposed to walk in?"

She tried to knee him between the legs. As he held her at arm's length, the legs of the two combatants tangled and they fell with a thud.

"The Marquis of Troyes, you fool!" She tried to bite him, but he pulled back. "Or whatever else you want to call him. The Constable of Champagne! The Duc de Bourbon!"

"Who?" he asked, dumbfounded. The baron grunted as she landed a kick to his groin area.

Elizabeth quickly rolled away from him and sprang to her feet. She pointed an accusing finger at the wall.

"He is the man that bought that painting from me!" She glared down at where he crouched in pain on his hands and knees, his head tucked into his chest. She reached out and touched him on the shoulder. "My God! What did I do? Ambrose!"

The warrior moved like lightning and struck decisively.

Elizabeth blinked up into his face. He had her flat on her back, his weight checking any movement on her part. "I can't breath," she gasped.

"Fine! That makes two of us."

Elizabeth tried to free her hands, but there was no hope. He had her. "I hate you!"

"Nay, lass. You don't," he returned. "But let's start from beginning. What was it you said about Bourbon walking in here?"

"You heard me, pig!"

"What the devil could have given you that idea?"

"Let me go first, you bully. Then I'll talk."

"Not a chance, my sweet. I value my . . . my life too much." He placed more of his weight on her body, and she gulped for air. "Ready to talk?"

Elizabeth grudgingly nodded, and Ambrose eased himself somewhat to the side.

She took in a deep breath and looked up into his serious expression. "My painting, you boor! The one on the wall. I sold that to Bourbon four years ago at the Field of Cloth of Gold. He is a collector of paintings."

"So?"

"Isn't this his place?" she asked through clenched teeth. "The title, the estate, the lodge. All these paintings—aren't they all his?"

"What difference does it make who all these things belong to?"

"Not a damn bit of difference!" Elizabeth snapped back.

"Well, then?"

She sighed deeply. "If you think I am simple enough to fall for this pretense of innocence now, you are mistaken." She waited for an answer. A protest. Something! But the baron said nothing. He simply continued to stare at her blankly. Finally she couldn't hold back any longer. "Wasn't it your filthy plan to bring me here, to take advantage of me, then to allow Bourbon to walk in and catch us in the middle of something? And don't give me that shocked look, Ambrose Macpherson. I know how men's minds work. I have lived as one of you for the past four years."

She took a breath to control her anger and disappointment. "You wanted to fling me in his face, to flaunt me like some rare animal that you'd hunted down and caught. I know your way! After all, the last time you two met, didn't you fight over me? Admit it, you just wanted to rub his nose in it. You wanted to show off your catch . . . before you discarded it!"

He stared at her in disbelief before a smile crept across his face. Suddenly his body began to shake hard with laughter.

She watched him in silence as he rolled off of her and wiped a tear from the corner of his eye. The knot that had grown in her throat now threatened to choke her as her eyes misted over. "What I've said is true, isn't it?"

Ambrose heard the heartbreak in her voice. It was hardly more than a whisper. She tried to sit, but he pulled her roughly to his side. Once again she tried to fight him, but he gathered her in his embrace so tightly that she couldn't move.

"Aye, I brought you here. But there was no taking advantage of you, my sweet. If you recall, you attacked me first. And secondly, I don't show off what's mine. In fact, I tend to be quite private with what I have. I think it comes from being a second son. So what's mine stays mine. And I don't flaunt those things in front of others. Finally, I'm sorry to disappoint you, but there will be no 'discarding.' Nay, lass, don't look so surprised. I'm keeping you. The question is, love, what am I going to do with you?"

"Don't try to fool me with cheap, endearing words, you fake. I know you don't mean them." Elizabeth turned her face away as a tear escaped, leaving a glistening track down her cheek.

"I can call you anything I like, Elizabeth." Ambrose took her chin in his large hand and gently drew her face back toward his. "Because I do mean what I've said. But that *was* an impressive story you just told."

"It was the truth!" she muttered, trying to look away.

But he wouldn't let her. "Nay, lass. It wasn't."

"Then it must have been close enough to the truth," she responded, pulling an arm free and gesturing toward the room and its contents.

"None of it was!"

She shrugged her shoulders. "Go ahead, continue to lie, if you like."

He started to reply, but she cut him off immediately. "But don't forget, Ambrose Macpherson, I am not believing a word of anything you tell me."

"Aye, Elizabeth," he said seriously. "I'll try to remember that. Your—"

"Let me up first," she demanded. "I am quite uncomfortable like this."

"Too bad. I don't trust you." He glared at her. "Now let me start—"

"Did I tell you that I don't trust you, either?"

"You did."

"And that I hate you?"

"I believe you said that, too."

"That—"

Ambrose's hand closed tightly over her mouth. "If you refuse to be silent and hear me out, I'll have to gag you."

She mumbled something into the hard flesh of his hand.

"Very well," he responded, not understanding a word she'd just said, but reading the flashing look in her eyes quite clearly. "We can do it like this if you prefer. At least this way you will listen to what I have to say."

Ambrose knew he had to make it short before she had time to decide on the next weapon she'd use to fight him off. "Elizabeth, don't be misled by a bunch of titles that are truly meaningless. Others might be misled into believing they mean something, but you shouldn't be. To you, I am and always will be Ambrose Macpherson. But, in the eyes of the world, anyway, I am also Baron of Roxburgh, Lord Protector of the Borderlands. Francis I of this fair land has also seen fit to bestow on me the title Marquis of Troyes, Constable of Champagne—more honorary a title than anything. But in any case, my sweet, the titles and this hunting lodge and everything else inside these walls—including these paintings—belong to me."

He gazed for a moment as the shock registered in her eyes, then let go of her mouth. "Well?"

"You are a liar!"

"Jacques!" he shouted, releasing her.

Elizabeth quickly scampered to her feet as soon as she realized he wasn't restraining her any longer. He was already on foot and striding away from her. Reaching the massive oaken door, he jerked it open, and the elderly steward scurried in.

"Tell her who is master here, Jacques. Tell her."

The older man looked questioningly from Ambrose's face to Elizabeth's. Then his eyes lit on the sword lying on the marred table.

"You don't have to lie for him," Elizabeth consoled, approaching the little man. "I'll protect you."

"Lie, m'lady?" The man looked wide-eyed at Elizabeth. "I never lie."

"Tell her about what we've done here, Jacques," Ambrose prodded. "Tell her everything."

Elizabeth stood still as the steward began to talk. He confirmed everything Ambrose had spoken of earlier. Of how the nobleman had owned this estate for quite a few years. He spoke with obvious pride of the construction of the new lodge. And of how the baron was a generous benefactor of artists and a true connoisseur of fine artwork. He spoke of Ambrose's parents, the good Lord Alexander and Lady Elizabeth Macpherson, and how they occasionally came to stay at the lodge, in spite of the laird's advancing age. He also talked about other lodges and town houses that the baron had built around the continent. Being a diplomat and traveling often, Ambrose was well known for the quality of his holdings and his ability to offer hospitality to kings and cardinals in places all over Europe.

The man continued to talk, but Elizabeth was not listening. Ambrose was leaning against his table, his arms crossed at his massive chest. His piercing eyes were on her, admonishing her. She looked down.

"That's enough, Jacques," he said commandingly. "You may leave us now."

The old steward turned with a quick bow to the two of them and crossed to the door, closing it behind him.

She studied the pattern of the wide oaken flooring for a long moment, then turned her attention to the glistening sweat on her palms. She couldn't recall a time in her life when she'd felt quite so foolish.

"Well?"

Elizabeth glanced hesitantly at his face. She nodded toward the table. "You can use that dull sword if you'd like."

"What good would that do?"

"Well, you must be about ready to cut out my tongue," she whispered.

"Knowing you, it would most certainly grow back!" Ambrose smiled at her. How could she go from so a fiery devil to so serene an angel in such a short span of time? "Come here!"

She looked up. He wasn't angry.

He motioned to her.

She walked toward his open arms and nestled inside. She laid her face against his chest. "I—"

"Next time we have a disagreement," he said, cutting off her apology, "would you please give me a chance to explain before attacking me with a weapon of war?" He rubbed his chin against her soft hair. He loved the feel of her in his arms. He loved the serenity of this embrace. Perhaps almost as much as he loved the heat of their battles.

Then there will be a next time, she thought with pleasure. My God, she loved this man.

"I'll try to remember."

"Are there any more questions that you might like to ask?" He pulled her away from him and looked into her sparkling eyes. His thumb brushed away a tear from her soft cheek. "Do you want to know about your painting? How I came to have it?"

She nodded slowly.

"I bought it. From Bourbon, that is."

"Did he charge you a lot?"

"A fortune, the bastard."

Elizabeth didn't know what to say.

He smiled. "We are friends. Bourbon and I have become friends since that day at the Field of Cloth of Gold. It is humorous to think about, but the fight over you did bring us together. But I think you should know that the duc's affection for you did not last too long."

"I am not surprised," she smiled. "He had little regard for women and the long-term relationships they sought."

"Aye, that was truly the way he was," Ambrose smiled wryly. "But he has changed. He just had to find his soul mate. And that he has."

"Well, I'm glad for him." Elizabeth kissed him on the chin and lowered her eyes again, not wanting him to know that thoughts of that nature were right now coursing through her own brain. "How was it that he sold you my work?"

"He is in trouble with Francis, these days. Political nonsense. I've been working on getting him a pardon. But the king doesn't forgive very quickly those who oppose him. So, for a short while anyway, Bourbon and his wife have gone to Burgundy. Since he needed all the gold he could get his hands on—and wouldn't take what I tried to give him—I offered to buy some of the paintings he's been collecting."

"And mine was among them?"

"Aye, but the knave never told me it was your painting. He didn't even give me a clue, other than saying that he'd bought it at the Field of Cloth of Gold."

"He didn't know." Elizabeth smiled. "I sold the work to him, but I never said it was mine."

"Ah. Well, I suppose I can't hold that over his head, then."

Ambrose wondered, though, whether Bourbon actually did have suspicions about the identity of the artist. There had been no secret between the two of them that the feelings Ambrose harbored for Elizabeth far exceeded any affection the Frenchman had for her. And when the two had discussed the sale of the artwork, Bourbon had seemed quite coy about parting with this particular painting.

She pushed her body closer against his, sighing contentedly.

"What do you think you're doing, Elizabeth Boleyn?" he asked huskily. Her soft, touch, so completely innocent, made his body hard and his blood roar.

"Apologizing." her hands roamed his chest. "I want to make sure that you won't hold what I did earlier against me."

"Hmmm. Perhaps, then, we should also consider what you did to me four years ago, as well." He pulled her doublet over her head in a single motion, smiling as he gathered her to him again. "And then you can talk me into staying here an extra night. I believe Gavin can use another day to show your sister and your friends the market fair at Troyes. Jacques tells me a great fire burned half the town last month, but that the fair has come back as strong as ever. It's really quite something."

"Then perhaps I can show you the nightgown Mary sent along." Elizabeth giggled, blushing in spite of herself. "It, too, is quite something."

"A bargain, then."

"A bargain," she whispered happily, lifting her lips to his.

Chapter 25

❧

Gavin Kerr looked about at the market fair of Troyes in grudging admiration. It did appear that there was almost nothing in this world that a body couldn't buy there.

"Come, Gavin." Mary pulled at his arm, smiling weakly. She drained the last of her cup of wine and handed it to him. "You should see your face. It can't be as bad as all that."

The nobleman glanced quickly at the young woman's frail body. She seemed to be growing thinner every day. She was not well enough to go through all this excitement. And he'd told her so before they left the barge. But Mary hadn't heard a word he'd said.

"I'd be contented just to watch, Mary. The people, that is." He pulled her to a low stone wall and forced her to sit beside him. She hardly ate anything anymore. For days she'd only nibbled at the food that he himself had brought to her. Only an occasional sip of something to drink. It was amazing she had enough energy even to walk.

Stretching his long legs before him, Gavin cursed inwardly for letting himself be talked into brining Mary to the market fair for the second day in a row.

When the barge had arrived the previous midday, Mary and the Bardis had pressed him excitedly to take them to the fields on the outskirts of town, which, for three months of every year, served as a major center of commerce for all of Europe. Now, gazing at the people walking by, Gavin was amazed at the sight of beggars and peasants roaming so freely with nobles and merchant princes. For these summer months, at least, the fields of Troyes belonged to all and had something for everyone.

So far the travelers had seen only part of the huge fair, but the Bardis had already seen a half dozen fellow merchants whom they seemed to know quite well, all working their trade. For the place was alive with the sound and smells of commerce. And the fair not only offered such exotic goods and spices and carpets from the Far East but also novel entertainments and unfamiliar foods at every turn. There were even three silent and mysterious men from the New World, on display inside the tent of a Spanish trader of precious gems.

Yesterday, Jaime had come to the fair with them. Gavin smiled, recalling how delightful the young girl's excitement had been to behold. But keeping track of the child on the day's excursion had visibly drained a considerable amount of energy from her ailing mother. Today, when Mary had begged to go again, Ernesta Bardi—clearly concerned about the young woman's health—had quickly stepped forward, volunteering to watch the child if Mary insisted on going to the fair once more.

But it was not just Ernesta who was worried. They were all quite concerned now about Mary. Bodily, she was frail and becoming obviously weaker with each passing day. But her spirits remained high. Though everyone, including Mary, knew that there was no getting better, they were amazed at her placid exterior. She showed no trace of fear.

But Gavin knew. For on the long voyage from Marseilles, Mary had told him of the disease and the mercury treatment she had been undergoing for the past four years. How strange, he thought, and how special—this relationship between them. Never, with any other woman, had he shared such trust, such confidence, as he shared with Mary.

And from the first, it had been special. The first time he had knocked shyly at her cabin door, she had asked him in and professed openly how much she loved him. Mary Boleyn had acted as though she'd known him all her life. She had known him from her dreams. She'd confessed that she'd waited all her life to catch up to him and that now she had somehow done it. But in the same breath

Mary had told him that she couldn't have him. Her sins and her past would not allow it.

He'd stood beside her bunk, speechless in the face of such openness.

And when she'd continued, asking for his companionship, his friendship, for the few days or weeks that she had left, how could he deny her?

Gavin Kerr couldn't deny her. And he hadn't. And now he was more than glad that he hadn't.

He and Mary Boleyn had matching souls. Different, and yet, there was something in them that drew them to one another. Like two halves of some ancient puzzle. How they could fit together was indeed a mystery. And yet, they each knew it was true.

As private a man as he was, Gavin Kerr had poured out his life story to her when she'd asked about it. Every triumph, every disaster. Every strength, every weakness. His tales had welled up inside him and spilled out . . . and she'd listened.

A few times, when he'd asked her questions about *her* past, about *her* family, she'd just shaken her head. "Nay, my friend. This is my turn to listen."

So Gavin had not pressured her. She'd told him enough. And if this was what she wanted, then he would abide by her wishes. He knew—they all knew—that the time she had left would not be long.

Mary leaned against Gavin's shoulder as a shudder coursed through her body.

"Cold?" he asked, placing his arm around her, rubbing her emaciated upper arm.

"Just the ghosts of the past, my friend." Mary quickly cast a weak smile at Gavin and then peered once again into the crowd. Though she had said nothing to anyone, lately her imagination had been playing tricks on her. The moments were not like the attacks she'd had in the past. These just involved seeing things. Trivial things from her past as well as things that had been incredibly important in her life. Things good and bad. Sometimes on the boat Mary had found herself dreaming, hallucinating in broad daylight. She had found herself experiencing events all over again. Moments from her early childhood—a wounded bird in a sunny garden; a long, wet ride in the growing gloom of a winter evening, wrapped inside the warm smell of a man's lined cloak. She sometimes became confused as people from the present and situations of the past would commingle in a whirling mix of time and place. And there were times when she couldn't tell what was real and what was not.

She stared at a group of men not ten yards from where she and Gavin sat. They looked at her; she peered back. Do I know them? she asked herself. She squinted as the sunlight flashed brilliantly off the silver buckle of one. Nay, she sighed to herself. Past and present. Keep them apart, you foolish thing.

She looked up to Gavin. At least he was real—of that she was certain.

"How can you enjoy this, Mary? Being in the midst of this chaos." His eyes were locked on a pair of arguing merchants.

"It's just for a short while longer, you gruff old bear," she teased, following his gaze. Her throat was strangely dry and an odd numbness was spreading through her back. She felt weaker than usual. Taking her cup back from Gavin, Mary looked into the empty vessel.

"I'm going to hold you to that, lass," he grumbled. One of the merchants appeared to be complaining about the location of the other's cloth booth, but Gavin could not get the details, since the two were speaking some language he was unfamiliar with. A crowd gathered quickly. The Scotsman glanced past a group of armed mercenaries at the booth in dispute. It looked like the young assistants of both combatants were hurriedly setting out trinkets atop makeshift tables. Gavin smiled wryly, nudging Mary. "If I'm not mistaken, these two noisy enemies are going to become fast friends as soon as this crowd of onlookers grows just a bit larger."

Mary looked vaguely at the warrior. The numbness had begun to spread into her shoulders and neck. Her eyes were drawn past his dark face to the sky above. The heavens were beginning to flash a number of different shades of gray and blue and green and red in a rapid succession of moments. Sounds of the crowd were fading in and out, and the young woman stared in calm wonder when she saw Gavin's lips move without any accompanying utterance. In fact, she was hardly even surprised to hear her friend's words tumbling unintelligibly through the air after a moment's delay. She was losing her mind. But her throat still felt dry.

"Are you all right, Mary?" Gavin asked in alarm. The young woman's eyes were glassy and unfocused. He took her by the shoulders and shook her gently. "Mary!"

"Aye, Gavin," she replied. "I'm here."

"Lass, we need to get back."

"Gavin, would you be kind enough to get me a cup of something to drink? Some more wine, perhaps."

The giant stared at her, uncertain for a moment what to do. He could hear the slight slurring of her words.

"Please, my friend. Just a cup of something." She handed back the cup to him. "I'll be fine here until you come back."

Gavin looked around him. They had bought Mary a cup of wine at a merchant's tent just before sitting. It couldn't have been more than two or three tents away.

"Aye." He nodded. "I'll be back before you know it. But, Mary, promise me you won't move!"

She smiled at him as he stood. As his words of concern for her registered in her brain, a warm feeling swept through her. "How solemn would you like that promise to be, Gavin?"

He gently took her hand and brought it to his lips. "Just a simple one will do. I'll return in a moment. It isn't far."

Mary watched him disappear into the milling blur of the crowd. She tried to focus her eyes but soon realized wearily that she simply couldn't manage it. Her head began to spin with the exertion, so she closed her eyes. Turning her body slightly, she let her face take the full warmth of the afternoon sun. The rays of sunshine were comforting against her inner chill.

Mary felt herself drifting. Suddenly she stood in her father's tent. He stormed back and forth, his hands cutting the air in his rage. "But it *is* his child, Father. Please. Believe me."

The shadow fell across her face and with it came the coldness. She opened her eyes and saw through the haze a number of men around her. Some stood behind the low wall, casting their shadow over her, while the others seemed to be blocking the crowds. She squinted her eyes.

One stood in front of her, his shining buckle hurting her eyes. She gazed up but could see no face. The radiant light dazzled her, but the shadowy darkness pushed through her like a rod of cold steel.

"Where is your sister?" The words echoed in her brain.

She didn't return to the tent.

"Where is—"

Nay. Father, I—"

"Where?"

A rough hand gripped her arm. So tight. He was hurting her.

She saw him. He wasn't her father. *What do you want from me?* Mary tried to scream. Her mouth opened, but she could hear no scream. There was no sound.

Where is Gavin? she thought with a panic. Where is Elizabeth?

She tried to look about, but everywhere colors streamed out of the blackness, crashing into her, and then swirling around her. Brittle glass rainbows exploded into glittering shards of whites and yellows and scarlets before melting into luminous pools around her feet.

Mary heard a man's voice. More than one was talking, but the noise of the fair crowded out all discernible meaning. And then one word penetrated her brain.

Poison.

"Where is . . . *tell us!*"

Poisoned. She listened hard. She'd been poisoned by the wine.

Mary waited for the bright, black space of unconsciousness to envelop her. Nothing. She waited for the heaviness that would dull her senses, but still nothing.

They were no longer talking to her. She tried to focus, to understand what they said among themselves. Elizabeth. These men were looking for Elizabeth.

I know you bastards, she thought bitterly. Killers. The same ones who came to the tent four years ago. They were English, too. Yes, she remembered. They were after Elizabeth. *But you can't kill her,* she screamed inwardly. *Not my sweet Elizabeth.*

And then there was silence. And sunlight.

Mary pried her eyes open. Once again she could see. There was no one around her. Peering through the bright mist, she could make out the shapes of people in the distance. No sounds, no one blocking her. No men around her. She felt the place on her arm where she thought the man's hand had been, but there was no pain. Only the numbness that was growing more profound with every breath. She gazed to the right, where Gavin had gone. She wracked her brain, trying to remember how long ago he'd left. Was it hours? Was it a moment? She stared at the dirt before her.

Weakly, Mary turned her glance once again up the pathway. She squinted at the shape coming toward her.

Elizabeth was walking toward her. The younger sister stared hopelessly at the approaching figure. At her wave, her smile.

From the corner of her eye, a movement drew her attention. Mary turned in time to see the buckle flash again in the sunshine. As the man walked past her, she could see the dagger hidden beneath his cloak. His hand was on the weapon, holding it to the side, away from her sister's view. But Mary could see it.

Elizabeth waved at Mary excitedly. Her sister was out among people once again. Even from a distance, she could tell there was color in her face. "Thank you, Virgin Mother. And thank you, Gavin," she murmured. Mary was getting better. She would improve. She had to. Elizabeth knew that there was so much that mattered now. So much for Mary to live for.

Elizabeth turned for an instant to look for Ambrose. He was not far behind, his big hand clapped on Gavin's shoulder as they walked. She gazed at his face as he listened to the black-haired giant's words. She turned back toward Mary, but the heavy cloak of a tall warrior blocked her way.

"Nice to find you at last, Elizabeth Boleyn." The clothing was French but the voice undeniably English. His hand grabbed at the shoulder of her doublet.

Elizabeth knocked his grip loose and jumped back, only to see the dagger coming right at her heart. She knew immediately that she had not jumped far enough.

As the dagger flashed in the sun, Mary stepped between them, shielding her sister from the blow.

The blade of the dagger slid through the thin young

woman, and the killer's thrust deposited her in Elizabeth's arms.

As the two sister fell to the ground, Elizabeth, stunned by the attack, held Mary instinctively.

The momentary calm that ensued was abruptly broken by the sound of shouts, and then the outbreak of total chaos around them.

"Mary!" Elizabeth cried, pulling her sister's cloak away from the wound. The cut in her dress was jagged and wide, and the dark stain of her blood was spreading rapidly through the material.

"Mary! Oh, God!" She pressed at the wound, trying to stop the flow. But as she did, she felt Mary's warm lifeblood draining out the wound at the back, covering her hand. *"Mary!"*

The young woman was gazing up into her face. She was conscious, and Elizabeth could see only peace in her face.

"You are not dying on me, Mary!" The tears rolled uncontrollably down Elizabeth's face, mixing with her sister's innocent blood. "You can't die, Mary! You saved my life. You can't leave me."

Elizabeth watched her sister's small, trembling hands reach up to her face. "Death had to face me before he got to you. Hold me, my love. Just hold me."

Weeping, Elizabeth gathered her sister in her arms and they rocked. Just as they always had.

"I am ready, Elizabeth." Mary's voice was weak. "It's time."

"Don't!" Elizabeth sobbed as they held one another. "Please, don't go."

"All will be well," Mary whispered. "I am ready. But Jaime . . ."

"Quiet, Mary," Elizabeth cried. "We need to get you back to the—"

"There is no time for that, Elizabeth," Mary murmured. "My sweet. Protect Jaime. Keep her away from Father. Keep her from Henry. Please, promise me."

A spasm of pain shook the young woman's frail body.

"I promise. By the Holy Virgin, I promise. Don't go. You just can't. Please."

"My love . . ."

Mary's eyes lifted to the sky beyond her sister's

grief-stricken face, and Elizabeth saw them widen, as if in surprise, before another look transformed her face. A look of joy, lighting her from within.

And then she was gone.

Chapter 26

❧

The shock of Mary's death stayed with them all.

The barge moved quickly down the Seine toward Paris, while the French countryside, still wet from the passing downpour, shimmered in the late afternoon sun.

Ambrose walked on the deck, solemn and silent. Leaving Elizabeth alone in the cabin below, sorting through Mary's belongings, had been difficult for him to do. But she had been clear in her request. She wanted to be left alone for a while. And he respected that. Elizabeth needed time to grieve the sister she'd lost. It had been difficult, but he'd come on deck. If she needed him, he would not be far.

They had buried Mary under a threatening sky among the wildflowers in the small plot beside the Church of St. Madeleine. The funeral mass inside had been a somber affair, and the grim, stony image of some saint—Ambrose wondered if it was St. Madeleine herself—had overseen the ritual with an immutable countenance of gloom. But for all, it had been a moving ceremony, and the clear and vibrant tones of the Offices of the Dead and the Te Deum still echoed in Ambrose's memory.

But as Elizabeth had tossed dirt into her sister's grave, Ambrose had been filled once again with anger about the unresolved crime. True, the man who had pierced Mary's heart with a dagger lay dead, cut down quickly by Gavin's sword. But there had been more to it. Things that Ambrose could not yet understand. Low as he knew many to be, English knights were not famed for drawing swords on an ill and defenseless woman. Ambrose could only guess what connection may have existed between the two. But even that made no sense. Had the dead warrior been

Mary's lover, it would still be unclear to Ambrose why the Englishman would travel so far to murder the young woman in so public a display of barbarity. Indeed, why murder her at all?

Ambrose was truly at a loss. The killing could also be somehow related to Mary's short-lived position as King Henry's mistress. But Ambrose knew that there was no talk of Mary bearing a child by Henry—not so much as a whisper of rumor had ever circulated. But if unseen powers were plotting to keep her away from the English court, why should they murder her when they knew she was en route to Scotland?

Ambrose was very aware of other rumors, though. Reports were spreading far and wide of the new infatuation of the restless English king. Everyone knew that Henry had recently been eyeing Thomas Boleyn's youngest daughter, Anne Boleyn. But even if this was true, the Highlander could comprehend no reason to kill the older sister.

Ambrose stared out at the road that ran alongside the river. That road, too, led to Paris. The baron had an idea that Elizabeth knew the answer to some of his questions. But the time was not right for him to ask. Not yet.

This morning, standing by the grave of the younger sister, all he had been able to think about was Elizabeth and her well-being. Mary, as pampered as she'd been all her short existence, had been the center of the older sister's life. Now Elizabeth's desolation was etched across her face.

Publicly, Ambrose had to keep his distance. She'd asked him to. As much as he wanted to, as much as his heart ached to reach out for her, he could not console her in her grief, could not hold or comfort her—that would have been improper.

He'd watched her face as she struggled to conceal the pain of her loss. It hurt him that Elizabeth could not show her grief in a way that would have been natural for her. His own heart tightened as he watched the young woman actually will herself to be a man. Against all odds, he watched her successfully hammer back the tide of emotions, burying the sorrow within her with only an expression of sadness on her face.

The Highlander ran his palm along the wet railing of

the barge. He was sick of this pretense. He could not go along with it anymore. Not after all that they'd shared on this journey. Not with all that they felt for each other.

Yes, he would wait. He would even help her, if he could, as she worked through her grief. But then it would be time.

Ambrose turned his face resolutely toward the bow of the boat and moved forward. They would find another way.

As the baron strode along, a movement on the forward deck caught his attention. A sad smile crossed his face when he saw it was Jaime, playing on a coil of thick line with her kitten.

"Good day, lass," he greeted her gravely. She glanced up at him with a shy smile but quickly turned her eyes away. He could see that she was still thinking of all that had occurred. Ernesta and Joseph Bardi had been keeping a close watch over her, but as far as he knew, no one had really spent any time talking to the child about the loss of her mother.

"And how is D'Or this afternoon?"

The little girl just shrugged her shoulders.

Ambrose studied the quiet child. He wondered if Elizabeth had given much thought to where Jaime's future would be spent. The court of King Henry appeared out of the question, and hearing what he had about Thomas Boleyn, Ambrose could only assume that Elizabeth would be drawn and quartered before allowing the child to spend so much as a moment under her father's care.

"She's turned out to be a fine sailor, hasn't she, now?" Ambrose prompted, sitting himself on the deck beside the heavy ropes. The kitten scrambled up from the inside of the low coil and eyed the baron curiously.

"My mama is in heaven."

Ambrose gazed at the little one's bowed head. Her words were matter-of-fact and carried a lot of conviction. He watched her small hands prying the kitten's claws free in a half-hearted effort to pick the little animal up.

"She won't be coming back to visit, either," Jaime continued. "Erne said Mama is never coming back. But she also said that Mama loved me very much and that she'll always be watching over me."

"What Ernesta told you is true, Jaime." Ambrose gathered

the animal up in his large hands and placed her on the child's skirt.

Jaime gently stroke the fur of the restless cat, quieting D'Or into a comfortable purr. "It's really quite pretty in heaven, you know. Ladies wear nice, bright dresses, and they laugh a lot."

"Did Signora Bardi tell you that, too?" Ambrose asked with a smile.

"Nay. That I figured out myself." She paused and cocked an eyebrow at the sky. "I remember the days before she got really sick. Whenever Mama wore a pretty dress, she was happy. And in Uncle Phillipe's paintings, the angels and the saints always wear nice, bright dresses. So I know that's what heaven is like."

"This is all very reasonable, Jaime," he conceded, reaching over and scratching behind the kitten's ears.

She looked up into Ambrose's face. "Have you been there?"

"To heaven?"

She nodded.

Ambrose shook his head. "Nay, lass."

"Nor I." She looked back down at her kitten. "Maybe someday I'll go and visit her there."

Ambrose gazed steadily at the child. "There is no hurry, Jaime."

"Is Uncle Phillipe going to heaven?"

"Perhaps someday!"

Jaime grabbed the baron's hand at once. "Please, tell her not to go!" The tears splashed onto her cheeks immediately. "She can't go. Not without me."

Ambrose lifted the child at once and hugged her tightly to his chest. The way she took an immediate comfort in his embrace, hugging him tightly in return, brought a smile to his face. "Don't you fear, lass. She is not going anywhere. Your Aunt Elizabeth is not about to go anywhere without you."

"Oh!" The child's tiny hand flew to her mouth. "I—"

"Don't worry," he whispered in confidence. "You didn't give her secret away."

"Then who did?" she whispered back.

"She did it herself. Your uncle . . . your aunt told me herself."

Jaime threw her arms around his neck, hugging him fiercely. "You know our secret. That makes you family."

Ambrose felt his heart melt at the show of affection. "Aye, my bonny one. That makes me family."

The great fist rapped gently at the cabin door once again. This time he heard the soft footfalls as she moved to open the door. Finally, he thought. Hanging the small lantern on the hook on the wall, he waited patiently, but when he glimpsed her tear-stained face, Ambrose's heart nearly broke. But before he could even say a word, the door started shutting on him again. Instinctively, he shoved his boot into the doorjamb and shouldered his way in.

"Please don't." She took a step back. "I—I can't see you now. I can't see anyone. I simply need to be alone. Please."

Ambrose fought his first impulse—to pull her into his arms, to comfort her in her pain. He fought his desire to take hold of her, to promise her that he would take care of her. He fought all of that, for he feared actions such as those would be misinterpreted. He feared words about the future would sound hollow while she struggled to let go of the past. He watched her continue to back away in the murky light of the cabin.

"You've been alone down here long enough, lass." The baron looked about him for candles. For two days she had remained locked away in this cabin. For two days he'd been trying to get her to open the door. Only Ernesta Bardi had gained access, but the meals she'd brought down remained untouched. "Elizabeth, it's time you joined the world once again. We need you."

She sat heavily on the hard bunk where Mary had spent so much of her last days on the journey. "Nay, you don't," she muttered glumly. "And I need more time to pull myself together."

Ambrose reached back into the narrow passageway for the lantern and used the flickering flame to light a number of candles, beating the cabin's gloomy darkness back. "I know of no reason that you should be in any better shape than the others. And, as I told you before, we need you. Jaime, the Bardis. My God, even Gavin Kerr does!"

"No one needs me!" Elizabeth gathered her knees to her chest. She was cold and empty inside. "And please don't lie to make me feel better. I know I will work through this myself. I guess it is simply a matter of time. Isn't that what they say? Time is the great healer, I've heard."

Ambrose nudged open the small window of the cabin with the heel of his hand and stepped back as the fresh night air rushed in. He filled his lungs with the cool breeze, leaning his broad back against the closed door.

"Elizabeth, tell me what you smell when you breath in this air." The Highlander watched as the young woman lifted her chin a fraction. "Tell me."

The painter paused for a moment. "I smell the night scents of the river. I smell the clean cold of the water, and the faint odor of fish that mixes with the good smell of earth."

"And the scent of grapes."

He paused as she nodded vaguely.

"Those are the smells of living things, Elizabeth. Growing things." He moved to the bunk and sat beside her. "You are alive. But she is gone. It is time now for you to accept this and let her go. We never know when our time here is finished, but I've seen many people in my life who walked around more dead than alive. I won't be letting you become one of them."

She leaned her head against her knees to hide the tears that rolled uncontrollably down her face.

"You don't understand." Elizabeth squeezed her eyelids shut. She wanted to tell him that the dagger that robbed her sister of her one chance to regain the happiness in her life was meant for her own fraudulent heart. Indeed, she struggled to tell him how she had put their lives in danger. All of their lives—including his. Those killers knew of her identity. They had tracked her down and found her. And they would find her again. Who would be the victim next time? She shuddered at the thought.

Ambrose placed his arm around her shoulder and pulled her to his side. "I might not have known your sister as well as I should have, but I know that she was a woman who was, perhaps for the first time in her life, beginning to appreciate the things that life had brought her, instead of mourning forever the things she had lost. Elizabeth, she could only have learned that from you. Right now I see you hiding yourself away, and I know this is not the Elizabeth that your sister finally learned to appreciate so much."

"I'm not hiding."

"Aye, you are. And you know you are." He gently caressed her back. "You are hiding because you don't want the world to know that you have a right to grieve. You are hiding because you are afraid of admitting who you are."

She looked up at him, her anguish showing in her eyes. "Please, Ambrose. This is not the time."

"But it is, lass," he continued. "You need to face the truth now, not sometime in the distant future. Out there, at this very moment, messengers are taking the news of your sister's death to the English court. And to your father."

She looked up at him in alarm. Her voice was low and guarded. "Did you send them?"

"To the *English* court? Nay, Elizabeth. Not I." He held her ice-cold hand in his. "But the man who killed your sister was an English knight. And he was killed by a Scot. Now, think. That market is filled with merchants from all over Europe. If the word is not being conveyed by English merchants, then the Flemish merchants are doing it. They all know how much money there is to be made conveying information. In fact, I heard your sister's name going through the crowd, though how that happened, I don't know. But the fact that she was an Englishwoman, the daughter of a member of the king's council, is no small matter. All Europe knows the power and influence Thomas Boleyn wields in Henry's court."

Elizabeth had heard all this about her father before. But she'd always assumed he would just count her long dead. Now a thought that had been nagging at the corners of her consciousness pushed to the forefront. "You think he had something to do with this, don't you?"

Ambrose said nothing, considering how far to take this.

"Tell me," she persisted, her voice flat and emotionless. "What interest would he have in me now?"

"His interest would be to destroy you, Elizabeth." The

Highlander decided to go all the way with this. To scare her. To bring her to her senses. "To make you suffer for your rebellion years back. He could feel he owes that to his king."

"We'll never cross paths. I am going to the Scottish court."

"Which is ruled by Henry's sister, Margaret Tudor!"

She paled. "Your queen . . ."

"Would she consider handing you over to your father?" he asked. "Aye, she would. You mean nothing to her, Elizabeth. But what's worse, you have lied to her. And betrayed her, as well."

"I have done no such thing. I've never even met her."

"By then you will have." He pressed. "By the time your father arrives at her court, you will have been presented to her as a man, even though you're very much a woman. You've pretended to be what you are not. But to make matters much worse—Margaret Tudor's a wildly superstitious woman. And you know how superstitious minds work as well as I. She'll think you've done all of this out of sheer witchcraft. To cast an evil spell on her, to bring her bad luck. Now that I think more on it, she might not hand you over."

"She won't?"

"Nay, she won't. She would want to keep the pleasure of burning you at the stake herself."

"You are cruel!"

"Nay, lass," Ambrose said sadly. "I just know my queen all too well."

Elizabeth felt a knot tighten in her gut as the thought of Jaime rushed into her mind. Whatever would become of the child if Elizabeth were to die?

"Perhaps he won't know," she whispered. "Perhaps my father won't find our trail. Perhaps he won't recognize me."

He shook his head. "What are the chances of that? As soon as he gets the news of Mary's death, he'll also learn that you are traveling with me. Pretending to be Mary's brother for years is all the clue he'll ever need." He took hold of her chin and brought her eyes to his. "I recognized you, Elizabeth, as soon as we met. Your father will, too."

"What will happen to Jaime?"

"She'll go to King Henry's court in the custody of her grandfather, Thomas Boleyn. And that will mean one more earldom for your father."

During those years in Florence, Elizabeth had always considered Garnesche to be the one they should fear the most. Peter Garnesche had been the villain to hide from. But now she knew—it had been her father that she had been running from all along. Indeed, perhaps this cowardly attack at Troyes had been set up by her father. By her own kin.

It was from her father's tent that she had been running, that fateful night at the Field of Cloth of Gold. That night when she had witnessed a murder. But perhaps after all these years, Peter Garnesche had pushed the entire event from his memory. Perhaps he no longer cared.

One thing was certain, though. Ambrose was correct— her father would never forget.

For a moment, Elizabeth considered telling Ambrose about Garnesche's treachery. She had never seen any reason to tell him before. She had never seen any purpose in involving Ambrose in a long-buried secret about a crime that had happened so many years ago. After all, even Friar Matthew had counseled her to let the matter rest.

She stared at the burning candle. Jaime was all that really mattered now. Elizabeth had to make the decision that was right for the child. It was up to her to do the right thing for Jaime.

"Tell me what you advise, Ambrose," she said simply. She knew she could trust him. She valued his judgment. With the exception of her encounter with the Englishman in the Golden Vale, the Highlander knew everything about her. And she knew he understood her.

Ambrose looked steadily into Elizabeth's alert eyes.

"To start with," he said calmly, "you can't go on sitting in the dark of a boat, mourning a sister who is gone and who entrusted you with her wee one."

"Aye. I know that, too." Elizabeth stood up and walked to the small open window. The night sky was clear, and she could see the moon rising through a grove of trees that ran right to the river's edge. The barge would soon be getting under way again, as soon as the moon rose high enough to cast sufficient light.

With the cold moonlight bathing her face, she thought about the life that she had been living. It had never been easy. But now she would need to carry on the deception when the price of being unmasked was so high. It was no longer just herself now that she needed to fear for if she should be caught. Perhaps—for Jaime—it would be best to try to forget the past four years. Perhaps it would be best to become, once again, faceless and nameless, a woman hiding this time in some remote corner of the country. The choice was clear.

"Do you advise that I become a woman again? Become Elizabeth Boleyn once more?" She turned from the window and faced him.

"I am saying you should leave this cabin." He stood and crossed the floor to her. "Jaime needs you. Your being hidden away has bothered her deeply. She saw her mother spending a great deal of time in this cabin before her death. I think she is afraid. She thinks she might lose you, as well. I don't think I have to tell you how she feels about you, but she told me that she wants her Uncle Phillipe to be her mama now."

Ambrose gently wiped away the tears that were rolling unchecked down her face. "Ernesta told me that the wee one depends on you more than she ever depended on her mother. She loves you, lass. And if all this means you should turn back to being who you truly are, then perhaps you should."

Jamie must be cared for, Elizabeth thought.

"And there's something else. It means less to you than it does to me, but there's Gavin."

"What?"

"Aye, Elizabeth. I'm deadly serious. Right now, the man is as broken in spirit as he was after Flodden. He blames himself for the death of your sister, and he sees your withdrawal as proof of it."

"Ambrose, I could never blame him. It was I who should have—"

Ambrose took her face in his hands. "Just tell him. Talk to him."

"Aye," she said. "I'll do that."

Change. She could already taste the sweetness and the bitterness that go with all change. But she'd had her moments in the sun. She'd had her opportunity to paint.

She'd felt the glow of success in doing the thing she wanted most to do. And now it was time to change. There were new pages that needed to be turned.

"I need to find Friar Matthew."

Ambrose raised an eyebrow. "Who?"

"The priest that sold you Henry's ring at—"

"I remember him. The one who helped you get to Florence."

"Ambrose, I'll give up the pretense. But I need a way to support Jaime and myself."

"Elizabeth, I—"

Placing her hand over his lips, she hushed his words. "I can't ask any more of you than what I have already asked, Ambrose. Friar Matthew helped me once before to sell my paintings, under a different name. He could do it again. Jaime and I could remain in Paris. We'll change our names. No one will know our whereabouts or who we are. Nay, perhaps it would be better if we moved to one of the villages outside the city. That way I could raise her in safety."

Roughly, he pulled her hand from his mouth and held it.

"Nay! I won't let you do that, Elizabeth."

She could see he was angry. "You've just said yourself that we can't go to the Scottish court after what has happened."

"Elizabeth, do the things that we've shared mean nothing to you?" He took hold of her shoulders. "Do you honestly think I could just walk away? Just leave you somewhere in France and forget about you?"

"Ambrose, I don't want you to do anything dishonorable. I don't want to see you shamed before your queen for protecting us. And I also don't want you to do something for us simply because it is the honorable thing to do. I know how men such as yourself readily sacrifice their own happiness because of some perceived sense of duty."

She looked straight into his cobalt-blue eyes. They burned her soul with their intensity. She knew she loved him. She hated the thought of parting from him. She could feel the ache of longing in her chest even now. But she wasn't about to let him hold on to them for the wrong reasons. "I won't accept your charity, Ambrose. We can look after ourselves."

"Damn honor and damn you, Elizabeth Boleyn! Can't you see what I feel for you?" No longer could he hold back the emotions hidden just beneath the surface, feelings straining to surge into the open. "Don't you know what you've done to me? How my life has changed since we first met at the Field of Cloth of Gold?"

His fingers were digging into the flesh of her arms. But she prized this mild pain. "Aye. I've ruined you."

"Don't jest with me, damn it," he growled, shaking her once firmly. Ambrose quickly let his hands drop to his sides as he realized what he was doing. "Look at me. I've become a raving madman. I used to be cool, controlled, even-tempered."

She reached out and brought his hand to her face, gently placing a kiss on his palm. "I like you better this way."

His hands framed her face. His gaze locked with hers. "Is that all you will admit feeling for me? Elizabeth, I think from the day we first met, your eyes have betrayed you. You care for me as I do for you. Are *you* willing to walk away, to forget?"

She shook her head as tears once again coursed down her face. "I am simply trying to do the best thing, Ambrose. That's all."

"The best thing for whom, lass?" he asked gently. "The best thing for Jaime? What you think is best for me? Forget the last, for what you've just suggested is as wrong as it could be. Elizabeth, in this room you are the one who is bound up by your sense of honor and duty to those who depend upon you. You place everyone above you. You think of everyone but yourself."

Elizabeth stood shaking her head. "Nay, I—"

"And also, don't try to talk as though 'honor' belongs in some male dominion. Nay, woman, you are living proof that it is not."

She couldn't stay away from him any longer. She slipped her arms about him, placing her face against his chest, holding him tightly. She needed his strength. She needed his love.

Ambrose held her trembling body against his.

"Elizabeth, it has taken me a lifetime to find you and

another lifetime to get you back." He kissed her soft ebony hair. "I don't know if you perceive this to be right or wrong. But know this, lass. I am not letting you go. The past two days have been worse than a thousand years in hell for me. I never want to go through that again. I never want to be away from you again. Never. Do you understand?"

He lifted her chin and looked into the shimmering blackness of her eyes.

"I love you, Elizabeth. Tell me that you won't leave me. That you—"

She reached up and silenced his words with a kiss—

"I never thought I would ever hear you say those words," she whispered, kissing him again and again. Her lips could not get enough of him.

Ambrose grabbed a fistful of her hair and drew her face back, forcing her to look into his eyes. His lips lingered a breath away from hers.

"And what about you, Elizabeth? I've waited as long as you have."

Elizabeth gazed longingly into the depths of his eyes.

"I love you, Ambrose. I need you."

Her simple declaration was all he needed to hear. The grip of his muscular arms tightened, his mouth descended. Their eyes, blazing with intent, never left one another as he drew her onto the bunk.

She needed him. Physically. Spiritually.

He needed her as he needed every part of himself. Deep within, he knew they were to be one, now and forever. Deep within, he knew the change had already occurred.

As the boat rocked in the restless current, Elizabeth moved past her grief, turning to life, to love. Like shipwreck survivors, starved for days, they clung to each other in a gathering storm of love.

Ambrose drew her to him, and her heart grew stronger with each passing moment. Caught up in the act of living, of loving, Elizabeth hardly felt herself shedding the weight of her grief. But she was, and the flames of her passion grew to a raging inferno, supplanting the darkness of death with the brilliance of being.

Together, they loved. The impatient hands, the roaming mouths—feeling, tasting—they were two paramours exulting in the quickening expression of their love. The radiance of their love soon dispelled all lingering shadow of loss.

In the lovers' frenzied desire, garments flew to the floor. Their clothing removed, Ambrose moved on top of her.

"Marry me, Elizabeth." His hands moved over the full curves of her breasts, the soft lines of her belly. "Tell me you will marry me."

She lay back on the bunk, her body quivering to his touch. While his tongue and lips teased and suckled the rosy nipples, his fingers gently slipped into her moist folds, finding within the nub of desire, stoking the flames.

Elizabeth groaned. "I think that . . . I think that I'd be in heaven . . ."

"A lovely place, no doubt, my love." Ambrose nipped at her jaw, kissing her neck, tracing a line with the tip of his tongue into the soft contours of the valley between her breasts. "Don't make me wait any longer, Elizabeth."

She pulled at his blond hair, pushing him onto his back. With a smile, the Highlander helped pull her on top.

"I am stubborn," she growled. "Opinionated, too. And headstrong."

She shifted her weight on him, moving her legs until she straddled him.

"I love that about you."

"I am emotional and short-tempered. I'll probably drive you out of your mind."

"I can live with that." His fingers played over the lines of her tender flesh. Her body was so perfect. He wanted her now. He wanted to feel himself buried deep within her. "And it will be an improvement over my present condition."

She gasped as he lifted her onto the crown of his throbbing manhood.

"Tell me, Elizabeth," he rumbled, his voice ragged with desire. "Tell me."

"Aye, my love." She lowered herself, gently pulsing her body as his shaft entered her. She whispered her response. "Aye, Ambrose. I'll marry you."

Joined in the love embrace, the perfect fit, they locked out any specter of fear and loss. At this moment all that mattered was the two of them. All that existed was the affinity of two hearts and minds. Two bodies and souls.

They would have time—a lifetime together—to face the enemies and intruders that awaited them. But for now, for tonight, each lived only for the other—together basking in the glow of fulfillment.

Chapter 27

Gavin remained behind when they left Paris.

Once Elizabeth surfaced from her mournful isolation, the warrior soon recovered from his sorrow over Mary's death. But he could not quite grasp the truth about his friend Phillipe de Anjou.

With Ambrose standing behind her, glaring at the black-haired giant, Elizabeth had told Gavin the truth—that she was a woman. Dumbfounded, the Lowlander had been unable to utter a word. But when he finally stammered out that he didn't believe it and required proof, Ambrose had been at his throat at once,

And Gavin had believed her.

They sailed out of King Francis's fine new port at Le Havre, going west around the tip of Cornwall and north through the Irish Sea to Scotland. The seas of the Solway Firth tossed their little ship, but soon the travelers found themselves making their way past the red stone walls of Sweetheart Abbey and the round towers of Caerlaverock Castle and into the calmer waters off the tiny village of Gretna. There Elizabeth and Ambrose, together with Jaime, the Bardis, and the baron's company of soldiers, secured horses and began their trek into the hills east of Gretna and on into the green, rolling valleys of the Borders.

On the second day's ride, they dropped down into the river valley of the Teviot and followed its sparkling waters east, toward the ancient Border stronghold of Roxburgh Castle. As they rode along, Elizabeth's eyes continued to survey the lush and fertile farmland, the broad expanses of forest, the rocky upland moors. The place struck her with its beauty, its wildness, its strength. She didn't know if she had ever seen a sky as blue as the one that covered the open spaces that they crossed.

To Elizabeth, the Borderlands between Scotland and England presented a study in pastoral beauty. Small, neatly thatched cottages stood side by side with rugged stone and sod huts. Flocks of sheep graced on craggy hills, while cattle roamed the river's grassy edge. As they rode along, farmers and fishermen doffed their hats to the passing baron, and children and maidens ran alongside the warriors, dispensing fresh bannock cakes and wildflowers.

Once, after riding between two high rocky outcroppings as they continued to follow the river, Elizabeth spotted a large group of buildings as she gazed south into the distance. That was Jedburgh Abbey, she was told, one of four powerful abbeys in the Borders. It was the good monks there, Ambrose told her, who centuries ago had begun to develop the land for agricultural use, raising their sheep and their crops, educating the local farmers, and bringing civilization to a vagrant people long beleaguered by marauders from the north as well as the south.

It had always been a hard place to live and prosper, and Ambrose had been sent there to bring about justice for the industrious and protection for the oppressed. And he had done just that. That was four years earlier, not long after his successes at the Field of Cloth of Gold. It was then that the queen and the Regency council had given the Highlander the title Baron of Roxburgh, Lord Protector of the Borders.

Finally, with the summer sun setting behind them and their own shadows stretching out before them, Ambrose leaned over and pointed at the four square towers rising on a tall hill above the river valley. Roxburgh Castle.

They were to be married in Benmore Castle, the Macpherson clan's stronghold in the Highlands. That was the tradition. Benmore was the place where Ambrose's parents had wed. It was the place where his brothers and he had been born. Where his older brother, Alec, and his wife, Fiona, wed and now lived with their children . . . when they were not in the Western Isles or at Fiona's own ancestral home, Drummond Castle.

Ambrose had sent a messenger to his family from Paris with the news.

Elizabeth had never been to the Highlands. She'd never been surrounded with a lot of family members, but the thought of it all appealed to the young woman. It appealed to her, and it made her a bit nervous. But if that was what Ambrose wanted, then she decided that she wanted it, as well.

However, Ambrose insisted that they stop in the Borders before going anywhere. They had business to attend to first.

So as the travelers neared Roxburgh Castle, the warrior baron thought over their plans and the best course of action. They had so much to do, and Ambrose wanted Elizabeth and Jaime safe while he took care of the immediate problems that only he could look after.

First, he thought with a wry smile, he needed to send a message to Giovanni de' Medici about the artist he would never get back. But he knew he couldn't tell the truth, not yet. Perhaps sometime, years from now, Elizabeth and he would make a visit to the Florentine duke. He would truly enjoy seeing the look on his friend's face.

And then, Ambrose needed to consider the Queen Mother. She represented the most pressing of concerns. Though the Highlander had deliberately overstated to his beloved what Queen Margaret's response might be upon learning about Elizabeth's sex, he honestly had no real assurance that the queen might *not* turn Elizabeth—and Jaime—over to her brother's ever-faithful counselor, Thomas Boleyn.

Margaret Tudor could be quite spiteful and completely capricious, especially if she felt she had been slighted in the least or in any way duped. She was a woman whom Ambrose knew it was a mistake to cross. When she decided she wanted something, she would stop at nothing to get it. And she wanted a painter. A Florentine painter.

The Highlander knew he would need to see her in person. He knew it was the only way.

"You don't know how sorry I am to have to leave you alone here, my love." He caressed the short waves of her satin-soft hair as they coiled around his fingers. Her hair was getting longer.

"I won't be alone," she whispered, smiling as she lay on her stomach beside him. "Aside from the five hundred and twelve sheep I've counted from our little window, you are leaving me with several hundred soldiers. I'm certain at least of dozen of them talk, and—"

"The last time I counted, there were only five hundred sheep!"

"Ah, well. You know how it is. Springtime in Scotland, love and . . . bairns is the word, isn't it? Well, there isn't much else to do, is there, my sweet?"

"Hmmm. Aye, lass. I like the sound of that." Ambrose drew the covers off her back, exposing her smooth ivory skin. He smiled as she moved right into his arms. "But this doesn't make it any easier for me to be going."

"It isn't supposed to," she whispered, snuggling closer.

Ambrose gathered her tightly to his chest. He still could not get used to the thrill he felt holding her close. The way she had taken possession of his heart, as if it had always belonged to her, filling it up until he felt that it might burst. Sometimes, like some wild coltish lad, he wanted to shout out her name across the valley and listen to the word ringing back to him, echoing off the rocky hills.

It felt so right. He watched her as she moved in, taking possession of his house and all who lived there. Yes, they, too, took her in, accepted her as their own, as if she'd always been there. One of them.

As Ambrose held her, he thought about the journey ahead. Amid all the uncertainties that lay before them, he knew one thing for sure. He would be the one at a loss when he left her tomorrow to go to Stirling to meet with the queen and the other nobles. He would be the one so utterly heartsick about being away. It was an odd, new knowledge for him, for he had always been one who lived on the road. Smoothing her ebony hair, he hugged her fiercely.

Five weeks earlier, when they had arrived at the grim and menacing Roxburgh Castle, Ambrose had sensed that Elizabeth was startled by the hulking mass of rough gray stone. The giant military fortification certainly had nothing in common with Florence, that lively city of art and culture where she'd been living the past few years. Indeed, the dark halls, the nearly empty rooms, and the

pervading attitude of constant vigilance were a far cry
from his own hunting lodge on the edge of the forest to
the east of Troyes. This was the place that had never held
any future for him. On the frontier border with England,
Roxburgh was simply a fortress designed and fortified to
keep the border skirmishes to a minimum, and it was a
place from which the Scots might offer a first wave of defense should the English decide to invade.

It was a place of war, a place of men. Aside from the
laundresses, no women worked in the castle at all. But
Roxburgh offered distance from the court, which Ambrose wanted for Elizabeth and Jaime, so here they would
stay for a short time. Rather than departing for the court at
once, the baron decided to stay around awhile and help
her get acclimated.

She hadn't needed much help from him, however.

Ambrose already knew. His men adored her. His servants respected and obeyed her wishes. Needless to say,
he and Jaime loved her, and he couldn't imagine life without her. Elizabeth Boleyn had a way with everything and
everyone.

"Ambrose."

He looked down at her soft and sober face. Her black
eyes glistened in an ivory face, glowing in the light of the
candles that illuminated the room.

"Tomorrow, when you leave . . ." Her fingers drummed
lightly on his chest. "Erne and I talked earlier today.
She'll be going on with you and Joseph to Edinburgh."

"I thought you enjoyed her company," he said with surprise. With Ernesta Bardi gone, Elizabeth would be alone
here with Jaime. "I thought she was a help to you, lass."

"I do, Ambrose! She is! But . . . well, I can't have her
wasting her life playing nursemaid to us."

"Is this Elizabeth Boleyn, the woman who knows what
is best for everyone else but herself, speaking now?"

"Nay! It isn't!" She slapped him on the chest. "Don't
make fun of me, beast. I am telling you this because I'm
certain this is truly the best course for her and for me."

"How so?" he pressed.

She paused to gather her thoughts. "Ernesta Bardi is a
merchant's wife; she is a smart businesswoman in her
own right. A person who has played a large part in her
husband's successes. And she had a life—a full life—with

Joseph, their business, their travels long before Mary and Jaime and I walked into it."

"She seems to have enjoyed filling it a bit more with the three of you."

"To some degree that might be the truth. But now, I guess, I want her to feel that she can go back once again to the life she chose for herself, without having to tag along after us. She should feel comfortable walking away from Jaime and me, with no fears or worries over our well-being. I'd like to see her traveling with Joseph and enjoying the time they have left together. They're not getting any younger, Ambrose. And I want her to be able to come back and visit whenever she wishes."

"So the two of you talked this out?"

"Aye."

"And she agrees that it is time to move on without you?"

Elizabeth nodded. "It took some persuasion. But I convinced her." She placed a kiss on his chest. "Erne is quite happy for us, you know. And she and Joseph will travel to Benmore Castle for our wedding."

"Oh, they will?"

"Aye, in spite of all the stories we've been hearing about those Highland rogues."

"So you've been hearing stories?" he responded, a wry grin tugging at the corner of his mouth.

"Aye, we have. So we'll all be seeing one another again in no time."

He combed his fingers through her hair. The silky black tresses tumbled over the back of his hand.

"Why are you doing this, lass? Why so soon? You hardly know anyone in this pile of rock. Why send her off now?"

She gazed steadily into his eyes. "Because I need to toughen up. And I need to prove something to myself. That can't be done with Erne here."

"Tell me, love. What do you need to prove?"

Elizabeth glanced away for a moment before turning her eyes back to his face. "I need to know if I can adjust to this new life. Operate on my own. Without anyone pampering me or taking care of me. Since we arrived here, Erne has done everything for me. In a way, she is treating me the way Mary liked to be treated. It doesn't matter what it is—small or large, minor or significant. She is always there for me, helping me. Running my bath, helping me dress, seeing to my meals."

"Perhaps this is the first chance she's had an opportunity to show you how much she loves you."

"That's what we talked about today." Elizabeth felt tears welling up in her eyes. "You are right. That was exactly what she was trying to do, and more. She's always thought I've been somehow deprived of even little luxuries, of simple comforts that I should have been enjoying for the last few years. So now she wants to make up for those times."

Ambrose gently wiped away a tear from her cheek. "Well, she's too late. It's my job to give you things, my love. Only mine."

"I don't need to be spoiled, Ambrose." Elizabeth smiled. "Ernesta loves me, and I love her. That came across today stronger than ever before. We were like a mother and daughter, sitting next to each other, holding hands, pouring out our insides, and retelling stories from the past. Sharing hopes for the future. After we were done, she was certain of my happiness. To her, that seemed to be all that mattered. So she agreed to go."

He watched as her face clouded with a frown. "You are unhappy, though."

"Not true." She took hold of his fingers and brought them to her lips. "I have never been happier than now—with you. But something *is* gnawing away at me."

"What is it?"

She rolled onto her back and stared up at the dark, rough-hewn timbers of the ceiling.

"I don't know if I still can function in the role of a woman."

The Highlander started to laugh.

She turned onto her side, propping herself up on one elbow. "I'm serious."

"Nay, lass. You can't be." He smiled and reached out, his finger tracing her full lips. "Elizabeth, you are a woman. All woman."

His fingers brushed over her cheek and caressed her ivory throat.

"I was a man. All man. For four years."

"Nay. You weren't."

Running along the smooth lines of her shoulders, his fingers grazed the skin of her upper arms and lightly moved onto the soft orb of her breast.

"I was too," she whispered, her eyes clouding over at his touch.

"You are obstinate, Elizabeth Boleyn."

Her voice was low and husky. "You've known about this quality for quite a while, Lord Macpherson."

"Aye, I have." His mouth descended on her lips and he kissed her hard. "I am not complaining. I love your flaws, my sweet. You can keep every one."

She tried to steady her voice after the shock of his kiss. "I have no flaws, only an abundance of talent." She watched the smile that pulled at his perfect mouth. "But if you laugh at me one more time, I'll . . ."

"Aye, lass. You'll what?" he teased.

"I don't know." She sighed happily, snuggling back against his side. "But give me forty years or so. I'll think of something."

Elizabeth considered for a moment how much she loved the way it was between them. They teased, they argued, they laughed for hours on end. Together, they rode out into the neighboring valleys, enjoying the late summer weather—more often than not, taking Jaime with them. Ambrose showed her the countryside, told her about the people of the Scottish Lowlands. About their history. About their heroes.

But as he talked, his stories always returned to the Highlands. When he spoke of home—of the wild, craggy peaks, of the rushing mountain streams and the storms so fierce and sudden, of the people so free and so alive—Elizabeth could see the faraway look come into his eyes. And she loved it.

In the daylight hours, before the other inhabitants of the castle, they acted so properly. Intelligent, reserved—two refined people who would soon marry.

But at night, their lives took on a different dimension. Enamored, reckless—two lovers who desperately, physically needed one another.

"Do you think I am making a mistake? In sending Erne away?" she whispered. "Do you think once she goes, your people will catch on to my facade and dislike me?"

"Hardly!" Ambrose hugged her hard against his chest.

"Do you really think *anyone* could dislike you, Elizabeth? Don't you see how they all love you? How could anyone not?"

Elizabeth rubbed her cheek against the warm skin of his chest. "Aye. It's true that your men treat me well. But when I think about the future . . . I want to say the right things, Ambrose. Do the right things. Be proper. I don't want to be a disappointment to you in front of your family, in front of your friends."

"You'll never be anything less than my greatest treasure, my love. Trust me."

"There is so much I don't know, so much I need to learn." She looked up and gazed in his eyes. "I want to fit. So desperately, I want to belong. I've never truly had a home. Not one that mattered, before this. But it matters now, Ambrose."

"You belong, Elizabeth. You belong to me, and I to you. And you've always had a home. You made that out of yourself . . . for your sister, for Jaime. Stone walls do not make a home. The warmth, the love you carry in your heart, that's what it makes it." He kissed the bridge of her nose; his lips brushed across her damp cheek. "I, on the other hand, have always had houses. Too many of them. Scattered across the continent. My friends laugh at me because of them. But I never felt tied to any of them. I could not make any of them a home." He kissed her lips. "Because I hadn't found my home. But now I have. I've found you, Elizabeth."

She missed him desperately, and for two weeks her mind and her blood had been racing. Almost frantic, at times she felt as if she only had moments left to get her life, and everything around her, in order.

Ambrose had gone two weeks ago. The Bardis had gone with him.

From the moment they'd left, Elizabeth had felt the rush of emotions surge through her. Things had to get done. Inside. Outside.

Robert, the tall, young warrior who commanded the battalion while Ambrose traveled, stood behind her, nodding his approval while she ordered servants here, soldiers there. He and Jaime followed her everywhere she went. She sent for masons, for carpenters. Roxburgh Castle would be a changed place by the time Ambrose returned. Elizabeth hadn't worked out all the details, but the creativity in her soul took flight. Her imagination soared.

And she moved as if there were no tomorrow. Frequently, thoughts of her sister Mary pushed into her consciousness, and she would think, wondering if her actions now were the result of some lingering guilt she carried concerning Mary's death. The true murderer who had sent the assassins, the real reason behind the attack, these things were still unknown. But the truth at the bottom of it all still haunted her—the dagger had been meant for Elizabeth's heart, not her sister's.

Garnesche remained in her memory as much as her father. Even simple things like the training of the men in the courtyard or the movements of torch-carrying soldiers along the paths in the evening would bring back memories of the crime she'd seen committed on a dark night in the north of France. And she wondered what tomorrow would bring. She wondered if there would be a tomorrow.

Mary was never given the chance to experience what the future would bring. But as violent as her sister's death was—Elizabeth knew—Mary Boleyn had died at peace with the world. She had been given a chance, perhaps a second chance, to bring a sense of harmony, of goodness back into her life. And she had taken hold of that chance with both hands.

As Elizabeth stood in the center of the chaos of renovation going on around her, she wondered if perhaps that same goodness was what she, too, sought after. For Jaime, for herself, and for Ambrose. Perhaps she, too, was looking for that sense of peace, of serenity.

"M'lady!" The warrior's voice was commanding and sharp. "You simply cannot go up there."

"I can, Robert. And I will," Elizabeth asserted as she pushed her way around the agitated Highlander. She turned to Robert as she climbed the first step. "Did the baron not specifically order you to see to it that my wishes were followed? *Didn't* you hear him say that?"

"I did, m'lady."

"Very well!" Elizabeth turned and started up the steps two at a time toward the top tower room.

"But wait," the man called out after a moment's delay.

She stopped and took a deep breath. She had to save her full fury for when he reached her. This was the last tower to be looked into. With dozens of workers busily working in the other sections, it was only natural for her to want to extend the effort to this final area of the castle. It was clear to her now, though, how cleverly Robert had contrived to keep her away from this corner of the castle.

The young warrior had been one of the first loyal friends she'd found at Roxburgh. Having trained years back as the squire for Ambrose's elder brother, Robert had been with the Macpherson family since boyhood. From what Ambrose had told her of the young man, Elizabeth knew Robert to be a prime example of the devotion and the courage that every Highlander aspired to.

"M'lady. I do need to talk to you about . . ."

Elizabeth turned slowly and faced him. Though he stood two steps lower, they were at eye level. "Robert. You haven't stopped talking since the baron left."

"Aye, m'lady. But this is important." The young man wracked his brain for some ideas. "This concerns the time when the baron was on the Isle of Skye with his brother, Lord Alec."

"On Skye?"

"Aye, m'lady. When Lord Ambrose was staying at Dunvegan Castle. It's a place that the MacLeod clan keep, a wonderful fortress, with—"

She rolled her eyes and then broke in unceremoniously. "It is amazing to me, Robert, that every time I have tried to come to this tower, you have managed to entertain and distract me with more stories about Ambrose's past. It's worked before, young man. But it won't work now. I am up to your tricks." She turned on her heel and quickly started running up the steps.

The young man cursed under his breath. Macpherson women! What was it about them? They were all the same. Headstrong and opinionated. The elder Lady Elizabeth, Lady Fiona, and now this one. Perfectly matched, they were.

Elizabeth quickened her pace as she heard the warrior once again chasing after her. She reached the landing, but he caught up to her at the last moment, moving in front of her and blocking the door.

"What is it now?" she asked impatiently. "Let me

guess. You just remembered I failed to stop for the noon
meal, and if I don't eat, then Lord Ambrose will have
your hide for that transgression, as well."

The young man brightened at once. "How did you
know, m'lady? You've read my mind."

"Get out of my way, Robert. Or else."

"It's for your own good, Lady Elizabeth. Please listen
to me. You don't want to be exposed to what is in there."

She matched the man's troubled expression with a sar-
donic look of her own. "Are there dead bodies lying
about? Is it a torture chamber?"

"Much worse," Robert replied, shaking his head slowly. "You had just better stay away."

She glared at him menacingly. "You know, of course,
that by trying—with these ridiculous ploys—to keep me
out of there, you've only succeeded in thoroughly piquing
my curiosity. Robert, it is no longer possible for me to
leave that door closed."

He nodded. "I know I've made it difficult for you,
m'lady. But you see, I'm not seasoned in the ways of
ladies of such quality as you."

"Don't flatter me. It won't work."

The young warrior dropped his head to his chest. He
wasn't certain to what degree he should go to stop her
from seeing what lay beyond the door. True, the baron
had instructed him to keep her away until he arrived. But
he had a pretty good idea that physical restraint was the
only thing left now that might keep her out of the tower
room. And Robert was not about to risk laying a hand on
Lord Ambrose's lady.

"And don't try to make me feel sorry for you. That
won't work, either." She crossed her arms over her chest.
"Now step aside."

He took one last look at her. She meant business. There
would be no distracting her. He stepped to the side, allowing her to approach the door.

Elizabeth let her gaze wander from the forlorn expression of the warrior to the metal key lock on the door. It
was one of only two in the castle. She took a step closer.
Her hand reached out and grabbed the door handle. Then
she took a deep breath. Robert had done a good job. She
paused, her outstretched arms still, her heart pounding.
She listened for a noise. For any sign of life. What was it

that was hidden inside the chamber? she wondered. Then she pulled hard.

The door would not budge. Locked. She set herself and pulled again. To no avail.

She turned slowly, ever so slowly, in the direction of the young man. "Get me the key, Robert. Go and get it now."

He nodded at once and headed down the stairs quickly.

"Thank you, thank you, thank you, Lord," he whispered. He couldn't imagine what had gotten into Evan Kerr, his second in command, to make him lock the door to the tower room. Lord Ambrose never locked that door, nor the door to his bedchamber, but Robert was glad it had been done this time. Robert took three steps at a time and disappeared down the circular stairwell. With any luck, he thought happily, Lady Elizabeth wouldn't be able to find him until Lord Ambrose returned.

Elizabeth watched him speedily depart, and then she turned once again to the door. The large keyhole might offer some view, she thought. Looking through the hole, she could hardly see. Dust and a spider web blocked the opening. It occurred to her that it didn't look like anyone had used a key in there in quite some time. She straightened up and grabbed the handle with two hands this time. The cold of the metal made her shudder. She pulled hard.

There was a give. A slight give of the door. She yanked harder. The scratch of the heavy door against the frame made a screeching noise.

She pulled again with all her strength. The loud scraping sound eased as the dark oaken door swung heavily on its hinges toward her. She stepped back, waiting for the door to come fully to a stop.

Her heart slammed in her chest. She looked straight ahead into the brightness. Light from the room flooded the dark landing where she stood. Hesitantly, she took a step in. And then she stopped.

It was a workroom. The most beautiful workroom she'd ever seen. Through windows larger than the thin arrow slits found in the lower rooms, sunlight poured over the freshly whitewashed stone walls. In the corner, three long and heavy rolls of canvas sat. There were benches and easels standing at the ready beside a brazier. A thick, clean mat of freshly woven rushes scented the room. A dozen small casks of what she knew would be oil and water and pigments lined one wall. Elizabeth turned around, taking in everything at once. She moved to the rolls of canvas. As she ran her fingers over the texture of the cloth, she knew immediately the canvas was of the finest quality. Growing increasingly dazed, the young woman worked her way past the casks of paint to a wall where a heavy sheet covered bundles of artwork. She laid her hand gently on the material and pulled the sheet off the rows of paintings stacked so carefully against the wall. Emotion clouded her eyes.

The sight of the first one unleashed her tears. The Field of Cloth of Gold. The second version of the one she'd lost in the tent fire at Calais. The one that she'd painted from memory in Florence. The only record that remained of where it had all begun.

Her fingers played over the depiction of Ambrose in the work.

"I love you," she whispered to him.

Then, carefully, she looked at the other works lying behind the first one.

They were hers. The paintings she'd thought had been left behind in Florence. They were all here, sitting in this room. He had them brought here for her.

She heard the sound of footsteps and turned at once. It was Robert. His body filled the door.

"M'lady, I need to speak with you."

"This room," she whispered. "You tried to keep me out."

"I'm sorry, m'lady. This is your room," he said quietly. "A present from Lord Ambrose to you. Your paintings from Florence had not yet come when he left for court. That's why he didn't bring you here himself. The casks of materials he sent for just arrived from Edinburgh yesterday."

She moved about, tears rolling freely down her cheeks. "It's a lovely room."

"Aye, m'lady. This is the castle's warmest room in winter, with a beautiful view of the valley. He wanted you to feel at home. He wanted you to have a place to work. But, m'lady—"

"I love this place," she broke in, standing in the middle of the room and looking at the young warrior. "I love him."

Robert watched the happiness that glowed in the young

woman's face. He didn't want to disturb this moment for her, but he had to tell her she was needed downstairs.

"You can leave me, Robert," she said gently. "I need some time to pull myself together. No one can handle this much happiness all at once."

"I'm sorry, m'lady. But there are people who need to speak with you."

"Can't they wait?"

He shook his head. "Our men have just escorted them in."

"What people?" she asked. "The masons from Edinburgh, the ones Ambrose was sending?"

"Nay, m'lady. Your father."

Chapter 28

❧

Elizabeth was out of breath when she burst into the hall. At once, her eyes scanned the great room in search of the child. Robert had said that her father, Thomas Boleyn, had been left talking with Jaime when the warrior came after her. The rest of her father's men had remained in the outer yard of the keep, under the watchful eyes of Ambrose's soldiers.

Panic began to sweep through her as she looked about the vacant hall. The room had been alive with artisans and workers an hour ago when she and Robert had left for the south tower. The dust of their efforts still lingered in the air of the hall, diffusing the light of the high windows. But only silence and emptiness greeted her now.

Then, at last, she saw him at the far end of the great room.

There he sat, on the baron's high-backed chair by the side of the vast, open fireplace. A goblet of wine sat on the floor beside him. He was speaking in a low voice with the child. Jaime sat on the hearth at his feet, playing with her kitten, D'Or, and obviously keeping her eyes averted from the visitor.

Thomas Boleyn's head swung around, and he came instantly to his feet.

With her heart pounding, Elizabeth took a step toward him and the child. She clenched her fists in an attempt to keep her hands from trembling at her sides. She watched as Jaime ran past the old man and skipped happily into her open arms. The sound of the little girl's footsteps echoed off the high walls.

Elizabeth crouched before the young girl and hugged

her fiercely. "Go to my bedchamber and stay there until I come for you," she whispered in the child's ear.

Jaime nodded silently but continued to hold on to her neck.

Elizabeth peered into the dark eyes that mirrored her own. They were filled with fear, uncertainty. "I'm frightened," the little girl whispered. Her voice was as soft as the drop of a leaf on a cool fall day. "He says he is my grandfather."

"That he is," Elizabeth returned softly.

"He told me that he's planning to take us away. To England. Just you and me. But we can't go, can we?"

"Nay, Jaime. We can't."

The young child nodded and leaned closer, whispering in her ear. "I didn't answer any of his questions."

"You did the right thing, love." Elizabeth ran her hands down the soft black tresses that fell to the child's shoulders. "Now, you go."

Jaime withdrew her hands from around her neck. "When is the baron coming back? I want him here with us."

"I miss him, too, Jaime."

"He wouldn't let anyone take us away." She cast a quick glance over her shoulder at the man waiting behind her. "I know he wouldn't."

Elizabeth brought the child's hands together and kissed them both. "That is true, love. And nobody is going to take us away while he's visiting the queen. We won't let them. Now be on your way."

The young girl raised herself on tiptoe and placed a kiss on Elizabeth's cheek before running out of the hall with her kitten at her heels.

Elizabeth didn't turn, but remained crouched where she was until Jaime's footsteps faded on the steps outside of the door of the great hall. Then she rose to her feet.

Sir Thomas looked frail and slightly bent with age. Elizabeth let her eyes take in the man whom she had feared and had run away from just four years earlier. The years—and the pressures of his life—had taken a visible toll on the man. He was much thinner than she remembered him. His body seemed to be wasting away, and his shoulders stooped as if he were carrying some enormous weight. Even in this fine summer weather, her father had wrapped himself in fine, thick wool and a fur-lined doublet of cloth of gold, with a heavy cloak that lay draped over the arm of the chair. His black eyes were set in a face etched with deep lines of worry.

Elizabeth's eyes widened as he opened his arms. The way she had opened her own to Jaime.

Surprised, she peered at him, not understanding. He took a step toward her, his hands still outstretched. She felt a pang in her chest. A deep, ancient sorrow sprang from within her, as sharp as the green blade of the narcissus cutting upward through the frozen ground of spring.

So many times as a child she had wished for this, dreamed of her father's affection, of his open embrace. But they had been only a dream.

He took another step toward her. She fought the urge to run to him, to seek that shelter. But shelter from whom? she thought. From whom had she ever needed shelter? From this man. Her eyes narrowed. It was this man—her own father—who had pushed her away, pushed her to the edge, to the place from which there had been no turning back. There was no turning back now, either.

He moved closer.

As much as she wanted to backtrack, to turn and run from him, she forced herself to remain where she was. To hold her ground.

Elizabeth looked straight into his eyes. She searched for the truth there, for some reminder of the reason for her anger. But there was nothing. No flash of power, no hint of temper, no fire of life. They were just the eyes of a very tired old man.

Suddenly she didn't know how to respond.

Sir Thomas reached her.

Elizabeth stood in silence as her father placed two hands on her shoulders and lightly placed a kiss on each of her cheeks. She fought her impulse to flinch, to pull back. She also fought the conflicting impulse to return the simple display of affection. She bowed her head, unsure of what it was that she wanted. His greeting had confused her, unnerved her.

"It does my heart good to see you, Elizabeth," he said, touching her hair and gauging its length. But his face was impassive, and he made no further comment, at last letting his hands drop from her shoulders. He took her limp and unresponsive hands in his.

"I cannot say the same," she whispered. Though her hands and her tone were like ice, she could feel her cheeks burning. Though she put on a face of stone, her insides were quivering. For the first time in a very long while, Elizabeth felt weak and vulnerable. And she didn't like the feeling.

He tightened his grip on her hand and drew her gently toward the chair where he'd been sitting when she came into the hall. She went.

"I didn't come all the way to Scotland to quarrel with you," Sir Thomas said.

"Then why did you come?"

"I have come seeking peace, daughter."

"Peace?" she asked shortly. "Peace between whom?"

"Between you and me, Elizabeth. Perhaps peace for the sake of Jaime."

She watched him pull a chair for her next to his. Then he gestured for her to sit. In a show of continuing defiance, she stood beside the chair.

"Jaime and I were living in peace. Before you came."

Sir Thomas gazed at her for a moment and then sat heavily in the large, high-backed chair. His eyes surveyed the empty hall, taking in the chaotic conditions. "He has left you already."

She felt her stomach go taut at his words. "We are to be married."

"Aye, your mother and I were to be married, too." His voice wavered unsteadily. "But I left her."

"You can make no comparison here," she replied icily. "You were after power, not her."

He looked vaguely into the embers of the small fire smoldering in the hearth.

"She had nothing to give. No dowry, no position."

"She gave you everything she had. Her heart, her love."

"Aye, that she did. But those things were not enough for me," he whispered. He turned his gaze upward to her face. "And they won't be enough for the Scot."

"You have a heart of stone," Elizabeth returned. "Ambrose has a human heart—flesh and blood, good and true."

"I am a man. So is he."

"You are a monster!" she replied, her voice on fire. She waved her hand at his garments. "You simply cover yourself with cloth of gold."

"Cloth of Gold," he said after a long pause, speaking almost to himself. "Where this all started."

Hundreds of words rushed into her brain all at once. There was so much she could say. These two men were light and darkness, joy and sorrow, heaven and hell. Words alone could not do justice in differentiating these men. But Sir Thomas sat there, hollow, expressionless. She turned her face toward the great fireplace.

"I thought you came in peace," she continued, her voice now calm once again. She was not about to expose her soul to him. She determined to control her anger, her hostility. She would learn his business first. "I have not sought your counsel for years. I do not need it now."

"Elizabeth," he said, gazing at her profile until her eyes turned back to him. "I don't blame you for feeling as you do."

She turned away again and moved to the fireplace. She shivered slightly at a coldness that was seeping into her bones. Placing a log on the embers, she watched the sparks and the small flames that licked the dry wood. Suddenly she winced as the pain she'd first felt so many years ago once again pierced her scarred cheek. With her back to him, she traced with her finger the mark he'd given her. She knew the scar was faded, hardly noticeable. But she wondered about the scar on her heart. The anger, the hurt that he had caused. She questioned whether time could diminish the memory of this man's selfish and hateful misdeeds.

"Why are you here?" she asked, still with her back to him.

"I told you before, to seek peace."

She stood and turned, facing him. "Why? Why now, after all these years?"

He paused and looked at the palms of his open hands. "I looked for you before this. But after your tent burned at the Field of Cloth of Gold, you disappeared completely."

She stood silently.

"I wanted to bring you back," he continued. "But I wanted you back for the wrong reasons. I sent people after you. I had them search everywhere. I sent men to

Paris, to the households of every friend and acquaintance
you ever had. I even went as far as to set a bounty."

She stared at her father. This was more the man she had
known.

"Aye, I wanted to get you back. To teach you a lesson.
Nothing would have made me happier than to drag you to
Henry and show the king how he mattered more to me
than my own child."

The silence in the hall was deadly.

"But you couldn't find me," she stated.

"Nay, daughter. I couldn't find you." Sir Thomas took a
deep breath before continuing. "But I know now that this
was the Lord's will. He wanted me to wait and to learn.
Some of life's lessons are long and hard in coming."

"And you think you have learned some lesson?"

He smiled bitterly. "Aye, I have, Elizabeth. I've learned
from my children."

"You mean from the only one left to you. From Anne."

"Nay. From all of three of you. Daughters that I looked
down upon for most of my life. Daughters that I simply
considered to be trifles, at best merchandise to barter
with. To trade away for my own prosperity, to improve
my own position. Nay, Elizabeth. It isn't just Anne whom
I've learned from. I've learned my lessons from all of
you."

She sat down before the fire, watching his faraway gaze.

"You were the first, Elizabeth. You, my strong and
high-spirited girl. You, who combined your mother
Catherine's goodness and her beauty with my stubbornness and drive. You were clearly the best of your mother
and me, joined in one person. And I hated you for it. I
couldn't stand you. From the time you were a small
child, I could see your mother in you . . . and I could see
myself. Aye, the better part of me. The good and gentle
Thomas Boleyn who existed once, long ago. The man
who wouldn't leave his true love for all the gold in the
world. But you were even stronger than I. You were
smarter. You had a belief in something greater, as well.
Something that I never had."

"And you still hate me. The person that I was. The person that I am."

"Nay, nay, nay. A thousand times I've cried out in my
sleep for forgiveness. It's true. You see, each night, your

mother is with me. She haunts me, Elizabeth. In my sleep.
And in my waking hours, as well. Oh, I know I can never
be absolved of the sins I have committed. Sins against
her. Sins against you, our only child. But still I beg her to
let you forgive me."

She looked down. The burning coals of sorrow showed
in his eyes. She didn't want to see that look. She could not
afford to pity him. Not now.

"What could you have learned from me?" she asked.

"You have an undeniable strength in you. Conviction.
You are like fire itself—pure and uncompromising. I tried
to compromise . . . nay, make you throw off your prin-
ciples. But you stood against me. You stood against your
king. I believe you have never feared any man, no matter
what power or position they hold." He shook his head in
admiration. "You are the strongest woman I have ever
known. You were willing to surrender your innocence to a
Scot rather than give an inch. Aye, you taught me a valuable lesson, Elizabeth, about the power of the human
spirit. After you left me that night with your face marked
and bloody, I knew that not even a sword to your throat or
a dagger to your heart could sway you to do wrong
against your will."

Elizabeth remembered that horrible night as if it were
yesterday.

"You showed strength like none I'd ever seen. In man
or woman." The old man's voice was barely a whisper.
"Strength that I have never had."

Sir Thomas leaned down and rested his head in his
hands.

"And then there was Mary. My pitifully young and in-
experienced Mary. She was merely a child, always a child,
pampered and cared for. She was forever what I couldn't
force you to become. Young, naive, malleable. If you are
like fire, Elizabeth, then she was like the clay of the earth.
So easy to mold to my own greedy ambitions. I never
loved Mary and Anne's mother. She was nothing more to
me than a steppingstone into a better class of society. I admit that with only disgust for myself. And true to my character, I manipulated Mary for my own purposes. Just a
pretty face to use and send to Henry's bed. And she went
willingly. To some extent for the excitement of it, I

suppose. But also because her father commanded her to go. She never questioned me. Never."

"You rejected her, Father. You didn't believe her when she came back to you with the news that she was carrying Henry's child."

"I knew she was telling the truth. But once again I allowed myself to be swayed by your cousin, Sarah Exton. Her and her conniving ways. Like a fool, I let her convince me that I would have more power over the king if I were to send Mary back to Kent, to keep her tucked away until the baby came. I always knew that was Henry's child. We just couldn't let her throw away a chance for real wealth. One thing I never expected, though, was that she would run away."

"You didn't know she was with me?"

"Aye, we did figure as much. After we found no trace of her in the tent. Nor any sign of her, alive or dead. Then we figured that was the way of it. We knew Mary was not strong enough to do anything, or go anywhere, on her own. And later, when I received her letter months afterward, we knew for sure."

"A letter?"

"Aye, the letter she sent me after losing the king's son in childbirth."

Elizabeth kept her gaze steady, fighting down the surge of feelings that coursed through her. She still remembered the days after Mary gave birth to Jaime. How Mary rejected the child since she wasn't a boy. It certainly fit. Sending a letter to their father would have been Mary's way of punishing him for making her run the way he had.

"I have had moments, Elizabeth. Dark and awful moments. When I would think of the terrible dangers, the misery that you two must have faced. Alone. With no kin to help you through the childbearing. To think that she bore a son of royal blood, the son that Henry so much desired. And then to lose the child. And my fault. No one's but mine."

The anguish in his voice was but a reflection of the ghastly despair that Elizabeth could see in his eyes.

"She taught me a lesson," he continued. "Her dealing with her fate the way she did. I saw Mary as easy and weak, but I see now I was wrong." He looked at Elizabeth with softness in his expression. "She grew strong, I suppose, by watching you. No longer the clay of the earth, but the earth herself."

"Mary learned from her own sorrows, Father."

"Aye. I reckon we all learn in just that way." The stone face turned again to the smoldering fire, but Elizabeth could see the redness of his eyelid. "I mourned her son. And no longer for what the child could bring me. I mourned losing my only grandchild. And all the while I never knew about your Jaime."

"Jaime." The words withered on her lips, and she dared utter no others.

"Until today, I didn't know of Jaime. I never suspected that you and Mary each left the Field of Cloth of Gold carrying a child."

Elizabeth steadily returned her father's gaze.

"The Scot's child."

Elizabeth said nothing.

"How typical of my life, daughter. What a mess I have made of it all. Because of my own selfish greed and ambition. All the while I mourned the death of one, I missed celebrating the birth of another."

Elizabeth remained silent. Mary had chosen this course of action. Up to the final moments of her life, the young woman had wanted her daughter to be kept safely away from the unfeeling malevolence of their father and his scheming ambition. Now, hearing of the letter Mary had sent earlier, Elizabeth was even more certain of the appropriateness of the decision. This was the way Mary wanted it. No matter what her father said to her now, this was the way it would be.

"Aye, Mary taught me a lesson." The older man shook his head. "Her letter was full of hate, full of anger. She blamed me alone for the loss of her child. I know she was right. I knew it then. I know it now. This was the same daughter who had respected me, followed my orders, and . . . perhaps even loved me in her childlike way. I brought it all on myself. I drove Mary to hate me. She had every reason. You have every reason."

Elizabeth watched his body seem to shrivel even further as he leaned back in the deep cushions of the chair. It was all so strange. These confessions, the pouring out of a soul in torment. The young woman had never dreamed that this moment would ever come to pass. It was certainly not something she would ever have asked of her father. But yet, here he was. Of his own free will. Seeking her out.

"You two were gone, and I felt the tearing in my heart that I knew I might never repair, a rending ache that I knew I deserved to suffer. But I'm only human, Elizabeth. So I turned to Anne. She was my only chance, the only one left for me after Sarah Exton's death."

"Madame Exton is dead?" Elizabeth repeated. The news of the woman's death, a woman she'd feared and hated for so long, did not bring her any joy. It all seemed so long ago, as if Madame Exton and Elizabeth's childhood belonged to some other life, to some distant past, somehow disconnected from the present. From Jaime. From Ambrose.

"Aye. She died a horrible death. A crippling pain that ate away at her. She died curled up in a corner of her room, fighting us off like a crazy woman. Screaming that we were devils come to take her soul."

Elizabeth shivered in spite of herself.

"And then, after she died," Sir Thomas continued, "I went to Anne. She was still a child. I thought perhaps I could undo what harm I had already done. I thought I had learned enough from the two of you, from the mistakes I'd made. I thought I had the answer."

"She must have wept to see you changed."

Her father stood and walked stiffly to the hearth. The smoldering fire was still giving off heat, but he hardly felt it. He shook his head without turning.

"Nay, daughter. I was too late."

"Too late for what? Is she ill?"

His laugh was short, devoid of any mirth. "Anne's ailment is not of the body, Elizabeth. It is her mind. Her very soul."

Elizabeth stared at her father as he turned and looked at her. Anne was only a child. It couldn't be that she, too, had contracted the pox. It couldn't be.

"You look horrified, daughter."

"Does she have the same sickness as Mary?" she asked at last.

"The pox?" Sir Thomas shook his head. "Nay. Well, not yet, anyway. Her ailment is that she is too much like me. Her mind is infected, poisoned with dreams of power and how she will wield it. Even at such a tender age, Anne has already planned her hard route carefully. She knows what she wants, and she has laid the groundwork to get it. Anne long ago planted the foul seeds of her desires. She is tending her weeds even now."

"I find it odd to hear you, of all people, speak so harshly of your daughter's desire for a place in society, Father. Who are you to find fault in anything she does?"

Their gazes locked, and Sir Thomas looked steadily at his daughter. And then he nodded.

"Aye, you are right. I am no one. And true, daughter, I've made mistakes. Many mistakes." He sighed deeply and shuffled back to the chair. Sitting down heavily, the old diplomat clutched the carved arms of the chair and stared into the fire. "Here I am, an old man. While others my age bask in the warm love of their families, contented in the happiness of their children and their grandchildren, here I sit, Thomas Boleyn, Viscount Rochfort, Earl of Ormonde, and member of the king's council, in another man's chair, in a savage and hostile land, begging my daughter for forgiveness."

Elizabeth could see plainly the anguish of this man's soul, etched in every line of his face.

"I must live the life that I have carved out for myself, I know. I am lonely and unwanted, and that is perhaps only just. But I see Anne asking for the same, and I must act. I turned my back on one woman I loved, married for power, and then turned again on the children who might have cared for me. Who might have loved me. Anne's future promises the same sad fate. She has watched me and her soul is corrupt, Elizabeth. God help me, I have helped her create the beginnings of her own ruin."

Elizabeth turned her face toward the small windows of the hall. She didn't want to know these things. Anne's life was her own business. The youngest sister had never been one to ask for help, even as a child. Elizabeth knew her little sister was smart. She always had shown a cleverness that far exceeded Mary's. But even if it were true that Anne had grown in the image of their father, perhaps that was a good thing. Perhaps a bit of that hardness was necessary to survive in the world of the English court.

"Elizabeth," Sir Thomas said, drawing her attention

back to himself. "Anne has set her mind to marry King Henry."

"Marry? But she is only a child."

"She is nearly seventeen," he replied.

Elizabeth's thoughts turned back to the events four years earlier. Mary had been seventeen when the English king first bedded her. Even though she was a child, Anne could see the pain that Mary had gone through. And what of marriage? she wondered. What of the future? Elizabeth shook her head slowly in disbelief.

"But the king has a wife already," she argued.

"Anne has set her mind to change that."

"Why?" she cried. "Doesn't she know what he did to Mary? Doesn't she know of his sickness and just how little he values the women he beds?"

"The king's physicians say his pox is cured."

A lie. That's all Elizabeth could bring herself to think. A lie. "Why is Anne doing this? Is she taken so with a man more than twice her age? Does she love him?"

"Love?" Sir Thomas laughed. A bitter laugh. "I once was fortunate enough to love. Aye, to be loved, as well. But I threw it away. Anne hasn't even had that. She cares for no one but herself. Nay, daughter. Anne doesn't love Henry. She wants to be queen and nothing else. It is power, Elizabeth, that your sister longs for."

Elizabeth stared in amazement at her father. "But you don't seriously think she could become queen, do you? M'lord, you are close enough to the king to know. Is there even the remotest possibility that Anne could succeed?"

There was not so much of a hint of triumph or even happiness in the man's words as he answered. "She will. Anne succeeds in anything she sets her mind to. The drones at court are already buzzing with talk of annulment. But—and hear me, Elizabeth—I want no part of it."

Elizabeth looked at him doubtfully. "You don't approve of her ambition."

"I don't." He paused and then shook his head. "Oh, I won't try to impress you with any newfound scruples I might have regarding Anne's plan. She is older than her years, Elizabeth, and she knows what she wants. But what she won't see is that she, and all of us, will pay a price. She thinks this is all just a lovely game of chance. She can spin the wheel . . . and ride only to the top. She will not consider the consequences, the potential for failure. Consequences that will be heavy for all of us when the wheel turns again."

Elizabeth tore her eyes away from her father's face and walked to the bench beside the open hearth. A coating of fine dust covered the surface. Absently, she pressed an open hand in the dust and lifted it, examining the distinct print her palm and fingers had left.

She couldn't care less about English politics and could not really see what effect Anne's actions could have on her own future. Elizabeth never planned to step on English soil for the rest of her life. But still, she knew that something in her heart longed for the youngest sister that she and Mary had left behind at the Field of Cloth of Gold. Right or wrong, Anne was still her sister, and Elizabeth cared deeply about her well-being.

"What kind of trouble do you think awaits her? You don't think the king would harm her?"

"Nay. Not the king. Henry is captivated by her wit and charm . . . for now." Sir Thomas picked up the goblet of wine from the floor beside the baron's chair and drank deeply. "From what I see, the king has already allowed himself to be convinced that his marriage to Catherine of Aragon offended the laws of God. After all, she was wed to his older brother, Prince Arthur, before him. The special dispensation he received from the Pope? Merely the result of political maneuvering. He now believes that the miscarriages that the queen has had over the years have been a sign. He has no legitimate son, Elizabeth, and he no longer believes Catherine is capable of delivering one. I believe Henry intends to make Anne his wife."

"Then what is it that bothers you? That will surely bring the family far more prestige. Far more power. The very things you yourself have worked your whole life to attain."

"The marriage cannot last. And if it doesn't, Anne will assuredly pay for it . . . somehow."

"How so?"

"Those who dwell in the corridors of power do not give up their place so easily. All the old noble families in England will align themselves against such a match. The Poles, the Courtenays, these are Queen Catherine's supporters. They will not soon forget if she is packed off to some convent. And they will not forget the woman who was the cause of the queen's banishment. The king needs the support of these influential families; they wield great power in England. A time will come when Anne will be a great liability to Henry, and then . . ."

Elizabeth stood stock-still beside the table, watching as her father shrugged his shoulders and averted his eyes.

"Cardinal Wolsey, the Lord Chancellor," Sir Thomas continued, moving back to the open hearth. "He has let it be known that if the king's marriage is annulled, then the king must marry one of the French king's sisters. That's the only way to put an end to the conflict there. Wolsey and the nobles do not see eye to eye on much, Elizabeth, but they will stand together on this. I have friends in every corner of the court, daughter, and I hear a great deal. They will fight the queen's annulment from every angle. From what I hear, the Pole family has even sunk so low as to seek the aid of one of the king's favored henchmen, a ruffian named Peter Garnesche. They will do anything to dissuade the king from proceeding the way he appears intent on going."

Elizabeth stared blankly, and Sir Thomas looked sharply at his daughter.

"You know of him, don't you?" Sir Thomas said, gazing steadily at Elizabeth's paling expression. "He cut quite a figure at the Field of Cloth of Gold—until your Scot knocked him down a peg."

"I remember him."

"Well, the somewhat hot-blooded Sir Peter has made himself quite indispensable of late to the king. In fact, I don't believe the king has made a decision in the past few years without talking it out first with Garnesche. I know the man employs spies that feed him information."

"The man is a brute."

"It is interesting that you should say that, Elizabeth. Because since his rise to power at court, Peter Garnesche has never been too excited about our family. And now, with the king's attraction to Anne becoming stronger every day, I have no doubt he will side with the old noble families. No one tells King Henry what to do, but Garnesche will surely try to steer the king away from Anne."

"Is that all?" Elizabeth's voice was tight. "Is that the extent of what he would do?"

The elder man shrugged his shoulders and sat down. "I just don't know anymore. I've written Anne off. She doesn't listen to me, and I don't want any part of her schemes. I don't."

Elizabeth watched Sir Thomas close his eyes and lean his head heavily against the back of the chair. He looked so old and fragile. Four short years had wrought an incredible change in this man. Her mind raced back over all that had been said. Despite all the bad blood that had existed between them over the years, Elizabeth somehow could not help but believe the things that her father had told her. She tried to think back, to remember everything that had taken place on the sad day when Mary had taken the blow from the dagger that had been meant for her. Sir Thomas could not have been responsible. He no longer had any motive for such an act. She knew that in her heart and in her soul.

It had to be Garnesche. It had to be. Perhaps, seeing Anne growing closer to the king, Garnesche was becoming wary of what information might be passed to the king through Anne. Information that might incriminate him.

Elizabeth shuddered at the thought. She had not been in contact with her sister Anne in the past four years. But now, with Anne's growing influence, perhaps the English knight feared a reunion between the two sisters.

That's it, Elizabeth thought. The sleeping dog is awake, and he's after me.

She had to keep her distance at all costs. That was clearly Elizabeth's best option.

"Are you happy, Elizabeth?"

"What?" she asked, roused from her thoughts.

"Are you happy, daughter?"

"Why do you ask now? You have never concerned yourself with such things, Father."

"You are the only one left."

"Anne is not dead."

"To my mind, she is," he murmured under his breath. "You and Jaime are all that I have left."

Elizabeth saw Sir Thomas's eyes glisten in the failing light. She felt differently now than she had when the old man arrived, but Elizabeth was not about to let her father fool himself into thinking the impossible.

"Father, neither I nor my daughter will go back to England with you."

"It doesn't have to be there," he said quietly. "You could go to Calais, or to France. I'll look after your expenses."

"I won't go," she said, her voice taking on an edge of determination. "I am staying. This is our home now. We are not leaving it."

Sir Thomas straightened his tired body in the chair. "I did not come here to uproot you for no reason. I came in peace. I want to see you happy, child. Everything I have is yours. I don't want you to stay in this wild and desolate edge of the world just because you have no place else to go."

"You don't understand, Father," she returned. "I am here because I want to be here. No one has forced me to it."

"But look at yourself, Elizabeth. Abandoned in this pile of stone."

She looked into Sir Thomas's face questioningly. Into his eyes, dimmed with age; his expression, saddened with remorse.

"I have not been abandoned here, Father. The baron and I are to be married." She tried to stay calm, to ease the tension in her voice as she answered his charge. "I know it is hard for you to believe, but Ambrose Macpherson loves me—and I love him. And our love is not bound by the endless quest for worldly wealth, nor by the corrupted politics of ambition."

He looked steadily at her. "You have nothing to give him, Elizabeth. No dowry, no title. Though, if you would let me, I could—"

"M'lord, he wants me. Only me. For who I am. Not for anything I have."

"Then he is a better man than I."

"Aye, Father," she whispered. "Far better."

Elizabeth watched as the old man's eyes reddened, welling up with tears. Sir Thomas made no effort to hold them back, nor to hide them as the glistening droplets rolled down his wizened face. She stared at the old man for a moment, struggling with her own feelings as her father's emotions spilled freely in the fading light. Thomas Boleyn, the same man who had walked away so easily

and so coldly from her mother, leaving her to a life so
wretched that only suicide could relieve her pain. Thomas
Boleyn, the same man who had shamelessly sent his own
flesh and blood to lives of disease and disrepute. Thomas
Boleyn sat before her now. But life had shown him the
vileness of his ways. And he had changed.

Elizabeth looked deeply into her heart. She knew she
could never be the doting daughter. She knew she didn't
feel the care and concern, the respect and trust, that one
friend should feel for another. She even wondered how
she could honor him as a man in the twilight of his years.

But gazing at the broken man, Elizabeth knew that she
could not deny the sorrow she felt for him. Pity pressed at
her heart, stirring in her an aching sorrow for a man who
had wasted his life in the pursuit of the wrong things. And
who knew what happiness he had thrown away.

Elizabeth walked to him and drew him to his feet. Placing her arms around him, she felt the ache in her own
heart disappear as he laid his head upon her shoulder.

He was punishing himself enough. She would not add
to his suffering.

Chapter 29

❧

Benmore Castle was a heaven plucked from the sky.

With only three days until their wedding ceremony, Elizabeth gazed somewhat anxiously out the leaded glass windows of her bedchamber, her eyes searching the distance at the purple heather-covered hills that surrounded the broad Spey River Valley. The rugged autumn Highlands in which the Macpherson stronghold was located offered breathtaking beauty, but even in the sunny, noonday light, they presented no sign to the bride of any approaching bridegroom.

"He'll get back in time," Elizabeth asserted firmly to no one, adding wistfully, "But the messenger said he would arrive today."

With a last look down the valley, the young woman turned toward the mirror, tucked a loose strand of hair into her lengthening braid, and started for the door. Lady Elizabeth, Ambrose's mother, had assured her at breakfast that, although the trip from Stirling, where the queen was holding court, could be slow in bad weather, she was certain that her son would appear anytime now. Elizabeth smiled as she pulled open the heavy oaken door. Never had she ever felt more welcome—more a part of a family—than she had been feeling since arriving at Benmore to the open arms of Ambrose's parents, Lord Macpherson and Lady Elizabeth. The laird and his wife had taken her and Jaime in as if they were their own long-lost bairns. Indeed, from the first moment they had ridden across the wooden bridge that led into the castle courtyard, little Jaime, clutching her kitten, had been treated like a precious princess presenting herself to her kingdom.

After all, Benmore Castle was the domain of men.

Elizabeth had watched in amusement as Jaime looked wide-eyed on the trio of young boys that scurried around the travelers' horses.

Ambrose Macpherson was the second of three sons. The eldest brother, Alec, was married to Fiona, a warm and wonderful woman who had immediately befriended Elizabeth. It was not until a week had passed that Elizabeth learned from the local priest that Fiona was also the half-sister to the king. The couple had three sons, as well as a handsome sixteen-year-old ward, Malcolm MacLeod, who had just arrived from the Isle of Skye for the wedding.

So, needless to say, with all the boys in the family, the attention and the treatment that young Jaime had been getting was exceptional. Elizabeth was not sure the little girl would be fit to live with after all this pampering.

The young bride also looked forward to the arrival of Ernesta and Joseph Bardi, who were due anytime now. Elizabeth couldn't wait to share with Erne some of the stories of Jaime's experiences en route to the Highlands. She knew that the older woman would be delighted to see how happily the little girl was adjusting to her new surroundings—and her new family.

Tripping lightly down the hall, Elizabeth considered how quickly the weeks had flown since she and her father had stood holding one another in the partially renovated hall at Roxburgh Castle.

A few days later, as Elizabeth's father prepared to depart for London, a stern-faced Ambrose had returned from the Scottish court, storming into the Border stronghold like a lion protecting his pride from a rogue intruder.

With little time to explain all that had passed between her and Sir Thomas, Elizabeth had been pleased, and a little relieved, to see Ambrose perceive quickly the change in the relationship between the two. Watching him proudly, the young woman was certain that her fiancé was calling into play all of his diplomatic skills as he assumed the role of cordial host, welcoming the aging Englishman. Elizabeth was convinced that her father had carried from Scotland great respect and ever perhaps a glimmer of fondness for his future son-in-law, Ambrose Macpherson, the Baron of Roxburgh.

As she moved down the corridor toward the circle of

stairs, Elizabeth paused and looked out a small window onto the courtyard. Not an hour earlier, on the stone cobbles below, she had seen Jaime being entertained by the MacLeod boy, who together with Fiona's lads had brought a number of falcons up from the mews.

Letting her gaze travel upward to the great Macpherson coat of arms carved into the stone wall across the courtyard, Elizabeth felt her eyes well up with tears again as she remembered how, after her father's departure, she had relayed to Ambrose her father's news of Mary's letter. And when she told the Highlander the tale she had told her father about Jaime's parentage, Ambrose had hugged her fiercely to him, telling her that he would swear by that story until the sun fell from the sky.

"I love you, Elizabeth," the blond giant had growled. "Jaime's our own now. And by God, that's how it will stay."

And she loved him. By the Holy Mother, she loved him more than life itself.

Dashing a tear from her cheek, Elizabeth hurried to the stairwell and went downstairs to the corridor below. She was running late. Fiona probably had the children all ready and waiting.

Elizabeth, on arriving, had taken it upon herself to do a portrait of the Macpherson grandchildren as a gift for Lord Macpherson and Lady Elizabeth. Fiona had been her accomplice from the onset, gathering all the children together for a number of sessions in the sitting room by Ambrose's bedchamber.

Collecting the children, Fiona had included Malcolm and Jaime, though at first Elizabeth had been uncertain as to whether it was proper to have Jaime there. But Fiona would not have it any other way. She knew the Macphersons well, and she'd told Elizabeth in no uncertain terms that Jaime was their granddaughter, and they, too, would not have it any other way.

Stepping into the dark hallway, Elizabeth picked up her skirts and ran down the hall. Passing by Ambrose's bedchamber, she paused, seeing the heavy oaken door standing partially open.

Accompanied by his brother Alec, Ambrose had left for court at once after bringing them to Benmore two weeks ago. From what he told her, Elizabeth knew that he still had unfinished business to tend to. Ambrose's first trip to court had been cut short by the news of Thomas Boleyn's arrival at Roxburgh Castle. After his brief stop at Edinburgh, Ambrose had barely reached the court at Stirling when word reached him, and he had ridden out without a moment's delay to get back to her.

And as much as Elizabeth's hours since arriving had been filled with activities and with preparations for the wedding, she missed him terribly.

Elizabeth glanced at the doorway. Knowing his quarters would be theirs after the wedding, she took a step toward the room. And then, unable to stop herself, she pushed open the door. The bright sunshine, pouring through the open windows, bathed the room and drew her in at once. Her eyes traveled over the fine furnishings and then came to rest on the large canopy bed that sat empty at one end of the roomy chamber.

She felt a flush of excitement wash over her at the thought of being able to share his bed once again. Their bed. She couldn't wait for him to get back. Crossing the room, she touched the fine cloth of the damask curtains.

Elizabeth turned with a start, hearing the door swing fully open on its hinges. The smiling figure swept into the room. He was back.

"Ambrose!"

He opened his arms as she ran and threw herself into them. He lifted her into the air, and they hugged fiercely in the open doorway. They had only been apart for a fortnight, but it seemed to Elizabeth as if months had passed since he had last held her like this. He kissed her hungrily, and she kissed him back.

"You are here." She pulled him by the hand into the room. He paused only long enough to push the door closed and to drop the heavy bar in place.

"At last." He held her tight. "I never want to leave you behind. Not ever again. From now on, wherever I go, you go."

She smiled. "I like that."

His large hands framed her face. His deep blue eyes gazed into hers. "Everywhere I went, wherever I turned, I was looking at you. Your beautiful face, your brilliant black eyes were always there before me."

"I've watched every traveler that has trod the path to

Benmore. I've studied every line of this valley through
my window." She raised herself on her tiptoes and kissed
him deeply. Pulling back, she felt her heartbeat hammer
in her chest, her insides becoming molten and liquid.
"These days have been the longest I have ever known,
Ambrose."

"And the nights?" Scooping her up in his arms, Ambrose carried his fiancée to the bed. "Have they, too, been
long?"

She nodded with a smile. Running her fingers through
his hair, she looked dreamily into his eyes. The jolt of excitement, the knowledge of what was to come, made her
quiver with joy. But she had to bank her fire. They had
time. From his slow steps, his graceful movement, she
knew he was savoring the moment. She had to control her
desire and do the same.

"When did you get back?" she asked. She could hear
the tremor in her own voice.

"Just a few moments ago." Laying her gently on the
bed, he stretched his long body beside hers and gazed
longingly into her eyes. "I missed you more than I would
have thought possible."

"I missed you, as well," she murmured, her fingers
pushing his heavy blond locks back from his face. "Every
day has been harder and harder to bear."

"I hope my family's been behaving," he growled. He
couldn't keep himself away from her inviting lips. The
very thought of her full breasts heaving beneath the cloth
of her dress was nearly enough to undo him. His mouth
descended on hers, devouring her attempt to answer. Her
lips opened to receive him, and his tongue thrust deeply.
Ambrose's hand found its way to her breasts, and he
cupped one gently as his knee moved against the junction
of her legs. Her moan of pleasure went to the very core of
him; her leg wrapped around his thigh, seeking more.

Suddenly he couldn't get enough of her. He found himself getting hard. He could take her that instant. But, as always, he wanted to enjoy this, to bring her to that
exquisite moment of pleasure. He drew back to look at
her. Under the round neckline of her mauve-colored
lamb's-wool dress, the ties at the neck of a white linen
blouse attracted his attention, and Ambrose gently
reached up and tugged at them.

"Your family . . ." Elizabeth whispered. His hand made contact with her bare skin. "They've been angels."

Gazing up at him, she felt a longing to recapture his mouth. But those thoughts were quickly forgotten as Ambrose trailed his lips downward over her chin and over the skin of her now exposed throat.

"Keep talking," he whispered. "Tell me."

A gasp escaped her as he softly buried his face in her neck. Elizabeth grasped the tartan that crossed his broad back as Ambrose took her earlobe between his lips and suckled it. His warm breath in her ear brought renewed shudders from her slender frame, and involuntarily her body arched even more tightly against his. She rocked herself slowly, ever so slowly against the hard muscles of his thigh. Her fingers worked themselves lower and lower until she reached his kilt. She began to pull it upward.

"Aye, they're perfect," she purred. "Just perfect."

"You drive me mad, woman. I want you."

Hearing the footsteps of someone passing in the hallway, Elizabeth cried out softly, suddenly alarmed. "Ambrose, we can't. We'll have your entire family banging on the door in a few moments. Everyone will want to see you, now that you've arrived."

He held her down.

"Nay, lass," the Highlander responded, brushing his lips sensuously over the soft ivory skin of her newly exposed breast. "My father is out hunting and my mother has ridden out with Cook to choose exactly what we will be serving at an upcoming wedding feast."

He drew his face back and smiled at her.

"No one saw us arrive, other than Fiona."

"But Fiona saw you."

"Aye, and knowing the way my brother Alec feels about his wee angel—and she about him—they're probably already locked away in their chamber, heedless to the goings-on of this world."

"I like her very much," Elizabeth whispered as she snuggled back into his embrace. "I know now why they call her the Angel of Skye. I don't think I ever met a person as kind, as gentle, and as beautiful as she is."

"I have."

She stared at him.

"You, my bonny lass," he responded, gazing into her

eyes. "You are every bit as kind, as gentle, and as beautiful. Far more so, I would say."

"I love you, Ambrose." Elizabeth hugged him tightly. "How did I ever live without you?"

He whispered his response softly in her ear. "I don't care to think of the past, my love. Only our wonderful future—and the next hour or two."

With the tip of his tongue, the Highlander traced a line along the skin of her velvety jaw to her waiting lips, finally reclaiming her mouth. His hands reached down and pushed her skirts up over her hips.

"I was thinking of this all the way back from Stirling."

"Then it must have been a hard ride," she whispered smilingly. "Very hard."

Elizabeth felt once again the surge of the raw desire that was swelling within her. Her tongue responded to his, to the heat that was coursing through her veins. Whatever discretion remained within her dissipated like a morning mist. Indeed, the full sun of desire burst recklessly through. She opened her legs as he moved between them.

Elizabeth's senses were filled with him. The scent of him, the taste of him, the warm and throbbing pressure of his body against hers. God, how she missed him. How she loved him. How she wanted him.

"An hour or two . . ." She moaned as he entered her. "But, Ambrose, that's the whole afternoon."

"Hmmm." He pushed himself up on his hands as he drove his manhood to the very center of her. "Just what are we going to do with all that time?"

Elizabeth smiled dreamily as she held him tight and gave in to the oncoming waves of pleasure.

The late afternoon sun bathed the two lovers in a golden light, and Elizabeth lounged comfortably on top of the blond giant. Her chin was propped up on his chest, and Ambrose ran his hands gently through the soft waves of her unbound hair. The silky black tresses reached her shoulders now. His fingers traced a frown that was lining her forehead. He smiled.

"Don't mock me, Ambrose."

"Never would I mock you, lass," he assured her, but the glint in his eyes undermined his words.

"You are mocking me." She lay her head down on his chest, averting her eyes.

He rolled her onto her back at once and propped himself up on his elbow beside her.

"Elizabeth," he said seriously, "I just don't understand what frightens you. That's all."

"I am not frightened," she snapped at him.

"Ah, now, that's more like my Elizabeth."

"Just . . . well, a bit nervous," she continued in a softer tone. "And perhaps a little apprehensive, worried, and maybe . . ." She rolled her eyes toward the window. "Very well, I'm scared." A tear escaped from the corner of her eye and dropped onto the down-filled mattress.

"But why, lass?" he asked, perplexed. "Elizabeth, think now. You've painted in the studio of the master, Michelangelo. You've received the accolades of Giovanni de' Medici, perhaps the greatest patron of the arts the world has ever known. You've painted the king of France, for God's sake. The leaders of Europe recognize your talent. Why should you fear such . . . mundane work?"

"Ambrose, it isn't the work itself that bothers me."

"Then what?"

"The queen," she blurted out, turning her gaze back to him. "Queen Margaret."

He paused and looked at her gently. As he considered, his fingers traced the line of her jaw.

"Isn't this what you've wanted? To paint for her? To be recognized by the world as a woman, as well as the artist that you are?"

She felt her eyes well up with tears. "You know that is what I want. But what I fear is what I don't know—what I might have to give up in return." She took hold of his hand as he brushed away a tear, and held his cool palm against her face. "I am happy now, Ambrose. Having you and Jaime. You two are everything to me. I won't give up this happiness for any dreams that I might have harbored in the past. I love you too much to throw away what I have for some fleeting moment of fame."

"And I love you, too, Elizabeth." The Highlander leaned down and placed a kiss on her soft lips. "What I told you before, when we were traveling in France, about Margaret thinking you could be a witch—"

"I know. I know. You were just trying to scare me. That part of it doesn't frighten me."

Ambrose gazed into her beautiful eyes.

"If you don't want to go through with traveling to Stirling Castle and painting the king and the rest of the royal family, that is fine with me, lass. But just remember this. The queen will exact no price from you. You are being presented to the Queen of Scotland as Elizabeth Boleyn Macpherson, a talented artist and the wife of her valued servant. I have brought her your work. She has seen it, and she loves it. She wants you at Stirling, for in becoming a member of her circle, you bring an added element of style to the Scottish court. An elegance, a bit of continental refinement. To her, the fact that you are a woman—albeit one with an enormous God-given talent—only makes it better. It adds a wee bit of notoriety to her reputation. Now Margaret can laugh at the other rulers of Europe and say, 'You are all fools. I have the most talented painter of all here beside me . . . and she is a woman.' Elizabeth, if ever there was a chance for you to demonstrate your artistic talents openly, it is in her court, my love."

Elizabeth gazed up at Ambrose, but her face was still clouded.

"But, Ambrose, she is sister to Henry, the King of England."

"Aye, she is. What's in that?"

"He is a brute."

"Well, lass, in many ways Margaret is a brute, too. But you were raised with your siblings—a condition, by the way, that Henry and Margaret did not share. Even though you three were all exposed to the same conditions growing up, each of you, as adults, took her own path. You, Mary, and the young one, Anne. Are you three the same person?"

She shook her head. "But what I fear is that she will turn me over to the English. That she will send me back to England, separating me from you and Jaime, fo r what I did four years ago. For disobeying King Henry's command."

Ambrose caressed her hair. "She is Scotland's queen, my love. Her ties to her brother are few. Sending you back would be treachery of the vilest kind. She would never treat an invited guest so inhospitably."

The baron paused before continuing.

"And what's more, lass, I don't think I'd be speaking beyond myself to say that she would never risk the wrath of the loyal Highland clans by sending one of their own to the south." His gaze was steady and warm. "And you are one of us now."

Elizabeth took his hand, and Ambrose brought her fingers to his lips.

"Then . . . then you think I should go."

"Not you, lass," he responded energetically. "*We'll* go. That is, if you want to do it."

Elizabeth could feel the excitement building within her. Her paintings had always presented her with a path to a new and different life. In doing what she loved, in practicing her craft, she had been forced to lose her identity. She had been required to live the life of another. That was why, when Ambrose had told her that she might still paint the Scottish royal family, she had recoiled in fear.

Elizabeth did not want to go back to being someone else. She was a woman. She wanted to remain a woman.

Phillipe de Anjou was dead. Elizabeth Boleyn was alive.

"I do want to go, Ambrose. I do."

Chapter 30

❧

For the tenth time today, Elizabeth folded the letter at its seams and placed it on the table.

Looking into the silvered glass, she gazed at the beautiful woman looking back at her. Never had there been such days of happiness, of joy.

Outside her open window, she could hear the crowds in the street below, the bells ringing in the distance. The autumn afternoon air was crisp and filled with the smell of mutton roasting over an open fire. Her mouth was beginning to water from the aroma.

She sat silently, her eyes taking in the flat stomach that would soon display the treasure it carried inside. She laughed quietly. Their child. Hers and Ambrose's. A sister or brother to Jaime.

And now, to top all this joy, she was to meet her sister Anne at last. Here, in this working room, within these walls, today.

"Keep working," she prodded herself aloud. "The time won't go any faster if you just sit and wait."

She roused herself from the three-legged stool and went back to the canvas.

A week after Elizabeth and Ambrose had married, the letter had arrived. Anne's letter. She had read it again and again.

Anne, the young girl she and Mary had left behind so many years back, had written with a heart full of love. Her words were not the words of the person their father had spoken of. No, this was a young woman who understood the pain of separation, the empty ache of loneliness. Anne wrote about how much she longed to see once again her only remaining sister, her beloved Elizabeth. She

wrote of the trials of life at the English court. She wrote
of Mary. Each time Elizabeth had moved through the text
of the letter, she'd felt her heart swell with emotion at the
sad lyric of her sister's words.

The letter had ended with Anne's heartfelt disappointment at not being able to attend Elizabeth's wedding, but
she had asked for some chance to meet—to reunite—if
only for a few moments. Anne had said she was sure she
would be granted permission to come to visit the court of
King Henry's sister.

If only, dearest sister, you could travel to Stirling . . .

Elizabeth had written back at once. Of course they
could meet at Stirling. At the Macphersons' new town
house there. Beneath the walled ramparts of the castle of
Queen Margaret, where Elizabeth was to be presented at
court.

Elizabeth's brushes flew over the canvas before her.
The black, mischievous eyes, the pale, reaching hand, the
last moments that she recalled of the time she spent with
the energetic little sister. Elizabeth hoped Anne would
like the portrait. It had been difficult to do a painting of
such detail just from memory. But Elizabeth knew it was
important for her sister to see the vivid image, and perhaps to know of the thoughts that the older sister, even
through the passage of time and distance, had retained of
the young woman.

Ambrose had brought Elizabeth and little Jaime to Stirling over a month ago. Elizabeth had been presented at
court and, to her surprise and dismay, had found herself,
after spending some time in the queen's company, accepting and even respecting Margaret as the strong survivor
that the woman was. Sent away at age thirteen to marry
King James IV of Scotland, Margaret—by her own
admission no more than a pampered child—had been
unhappy and lost for a long time. A stranger in a foreign land.

But the turning wheel of Fortune would soon teach the
young woman the hard lessons of life. Widowed at the
age of twenty-four, left in a wild and often barbarous
country in the midst of social and political pandemonium
after her husband's death at Flodden field, Margaret Tudor had quickly learned the skills needed for survival.

Elizabeth placed the brush with the others in the cup

and wiped her hand with the rag on the side table. All the fears she had harbored before arriving at court had soon washed away after her first meetings with the queen. Ambrose had been right in everything he'd said. Elizabeth could clearly see that Margaret perceived herself as a patroness, a great and generous benefactor of the arts and of artists. But the one thing about the queen that most surprised Elizabeth only occurred to her in her observation of the people who surrounded Margaret. The queen was the benefactor of intelligent women. Women of learning and accomplishment. The ones who took their lives and their destinies into their own hands. Women like Margaret herself. Women like Elizabeth. The survivors, the strong.

Then, yesterday evening, the man sent ahead by Anne had arrived with the news of her arrival by next noon.

Even though she'd done it herself, Elizabeth now wished she had not sent Ambrose and Jaime away this morning. She'd told Ambrose that she wanted to greet her sister alone, to have a chance to renew their bond of sisterly love before presenting Anne to her husband and her daughter. But there was something else, as well. The damp chill of anxiety had begun to creep into Elizabeth's bones. Even though their father had readily believed Jaime to be his eldest daughter's child, Elizabeth could not be certain that Anne would believe the same thing.

Even as a child, Anne had been intelligent beyond her years, and now Elizabeth was conscious of a nagging fear that her sister might discover the truth. After all, Jaime was Henry's child, and with the dreams that Anne had of becoming queen, Elizabeth worried now what discovering Jaime's true identity might mean to the ambitious young woman.

It had been difficult to persuade Ambrose to go. He'd not wanted to leave her side, especially, as he jokingly put it, in her weakened condition. Finally, after a great deal of cajoling on her part, he'd reluctantly agreed to take Jaime for half a day's ride and return at supper. But that was it. Elizabeth had known she would not be able to wheedle even a moment more out of him, and she cheerfully settled for their compromise. Indeed, since they'd wed, the Highlander had been true to his word—he had not left her alone for more than a day.

Elizabeth smiled and gave a small sigh, thinking of the

love that they shared. Life was bliss in Ambrose Macpherson's arms.

The painting was finished. Elizabeth stepped back and scanned the portrait with a critical eye. It was good work. And the young girl's depiction successfully captured the very essence of what she remembered of Anne. But the setting in which she placed the girl was purely the product of her own imagination.

Elizabeth depicted Anne standing before the high platform of an ornate altar. She was dressed in a crimson velvet gown, decorated with ermine, and a rich robe of purple velvet, also trimmed with strips of ermine. A golden coronet with a cap of pearls and stones covered her jet-black hair. Anne's face contained all the vibrancy of a young girl, but her vestments conjured the image of a queen. Indeed, on the high royal seat before her sat Henry. Elizabeth smiled at her representation of the English king. The man looked aged and heavyset, and Anne's arms were reaching out toward the king in a manner of confident entreaty.

The likeness of Henry was probably enough for a beheading, Elizabeth thought, if she ever dared step foot again on English soil.

The gentle knock at the door froze Elizabeth where she stood. She wiped her wet palms on her skirt and called quietly for her porter to step in.

She watched in anticipation as the heavy door swung partially open. Instead of the serious expression of the old manservant, the bright face of one of the younger servants peeked inside.

"They are here, m'lady."

Before Elizabeth could say a word, the door pushed open fully, and a tall, elegantly dressed young woman stepped in. Elizabeth recognized her at once.

Taking the few short steps to meet her, Elizabeth embraced her sister tightly, gathering into her arms the beautiful creature. "Oh, my Anne. You are here. Here at last."

The painter felt her sister's arms move around her, but she felt something else, as well.

Elizabeth felt ice. A coldness as solid and palpable as ice. And she felt it instantly. She felt it the moment that she touched her. Surprised and momentarily confused, Elizabeth pulled back, struggling to hide her disappointment. She had been expecting Anne to have some similarity to Mary. Their sister had been affectionate, tender. Mary returned affection the way she breathed air. It had always been natural, part of her.

Elizabeth realized instantly that she had been mistaken. That she had been wrong in expecting so much. She couldn't bring Mary back in Anne. Each one of them had her own individual traits that made her distinct. Anne was not Mary.

Elizabeth watched as her sister stiffly extricated herself from her arms. Then the younger woman turned to Elizabeth's gawking servant. "Leave us."

The serving girl nodded hurriedly and backed away at once, closing the door as she retreated.

Elizabeth gazed as the hard smile that seemed to be carved on Anne's face faded quickly. Too quickly. She wondered why the young woman had felt obliged to put on such a false show of joy. She stood silently, somewhat amazed at the hardness of the sparkling black eyes that were riveted to her own.

Anne's look was not one of sisterly affection.

Finally the younger woman turned from Elizabeth and unclasped the traveling cloak that she wore. Now Elizabeth could fully appreciate the bright scarlet dress that Anne wore beneath. Sleeves of silk interwoven with fine gold thread puffed fashionably from long slits in the arms of the garment, catching Elizabeth's eye.

The elder sister watched in silence as Anne straightened and fluffed the sleeves, assuring herself that the lines of each showed appropriately.

"You look beautiful in this dress, Anne. You've grown so much. So refined, so perfect." Elizabeth smiled unconsciously. Hardly the child she'd seen last. "And you wear the cloth of gold. The English king's—"

"It is about the least expensive thing that Henry gives me, Elizabeth." She nearly sneered at her sister. "How could I refuse him?"

Elizabeth bit her tongue. This was hardly the greeting—this was hardly the woman—she had expected. She again simply watched as the younger woman made her way around the room, studying every furnishing, every trinket in sight.

"Not bad, for marrying a Scot." She turned to Elizabeth

and gave a half-sarcastic smile. "I can see you've done well for yourself. He's certainly the best that this savage place has to offer, for what that's worth. But tell me, dear sister, what did you have to do to get him to marry you?"

Elizabeth stared at her sister, her anger gathering.

"*Not* what you are doing to get Henry to *marry you.*" Glancing away, Elizabeth moved quickly toward the painting she'd been working on. The canvas faced away from Anne. She'd be damned if she would show the brat what she'd done for her. Grabbing a white tarp from the table, Elizabeth tossed it over the painting.

"Temper, temper. I can see not much has changed after all these years." She walked casually toward Elizabeth in mincing steps, swinging her hips exaggeratedly from side to side. "I see I'm still not worthy of seeing your work. Still think you can hide things from me, don't you?"

Elizabeth paused. She had begun this meeting all wrong. Anne had no sooner walked in her door than Elizabeth had begun to judge her. Elizabeth admonished herself silently. She must give her younger sister a chance.

"I'm sorry, Anne," she said quietly. "I didn't mean to be so inhospitable. Perhaps we could begin again."

"You and I? Begin again?" The young woman stood facing her in the center of the room, her laugh short and joyless. "I wouldn't even bother."

"Why are you here, Anne?" Elizabeth asked shortly. "It must have been a long journey for you."

She smiled. "To pay you back, sister dear, for all your kindnesses of the past."

"You don't owe me anything."

"Ha!" Anne laughed again, loudly and without mirth. "Well, we do agree on something."

"Then?" Elizabeth could feel herself getting edgy as the young woman approached. Her sister's large black eyes were locked on her, and Anne looked like an animal ready to pounce.

"As I told you before, I came here to repay you." She stopped on the opposite side of the covered canvas that separated them. "But you are correct, Elizabeth. I don't owe you anything. It is you who owes me. So I am here to collect." Anne suddenly reached out and yanked at the sheet, unveiling the canvas as she moved beside her sister. Her eyes scanned the painting.

The young woman's laugh made Elizabeth cringe. It was a cold and hollow laugh. She could hear no ring of emotion, just an emptiness that reverberated throughout the room.

"I've heard people speak of your talent." Anne reached into the cup that sat on the small table and grabbed one of Elizabeth's brushes. Without hesitation, she dipped it into the paint of her sister's palette. "It's true, you do indeed have a talent for your art."

Anne jabbed at the painting with the brush and, hearing Elizabeth's gasp, turned and gave her sister another malevolent smile as she continued. "But you are blind, dear sister. Blind, blind, blind. And simple."

Elizabeth watched in horror as Anne used one stroke after another to cover with broad, black marks the portrait of Henry sitting on the chair.

"You see, if you had any wit at all, you would have depicted *me* sitting in the chair, and that pathetic old man standing with *his* hands outstretched in supplication."

"You cannot control the world with a stroke of a brush, Anne." Elizabeth reached out and grabbed the brush from her sister's hands. Anne released it without any struggle and turned her attention again toward the room.

"Aye, I can." She smiled with a backward glance. "I, unlike you, Elizabeth, live in the real world. It's true, I am not like you and Mary at all, you know. I am smart. I use my brain. I observe, I plan, and then I execute. And sometimes, just for the sport of it, I look for weaknesses in people; then I crush them. Just look at what I did to you. A soft, heart-wrenching letter. I knew that's all it would take to get you to meet with me. It worked."

Elizabeth scanned her sister's face for some recognizable feature. For some hint of familial feeling that might connect them.

We are sisters, she thought. Sisters. You don't have to lie, to pretend, in order to see me. But after hearing Anne, Elizabeth felt herself withdrawing. She did not want to deal with this young woman at a personal level. At any level.

"This English king is a great fool," Elizabeth whispered. "How could he—or anyone—be so blind as to fall for you?"

"You are so right, sister!" Anne swung around. "He is a

great fool. The greatest kind, a royal one. Oh, I have watched him for years. From the time I moved into his court circle, I've seen how he treats us. The new faces. The new mistresses. Each new woman tumbling into bed with the arrogant lecher. One after another they go. He relieves his lust in them, and then they are gone. Out of sight, and permanently out of mind. Henry is disgusting, Elizabeth, like all the rest of them. The man's brain is in his codpiece."

As she sat herself on the tall, three-legged stool in front of the mirror, Anne Boleyn pulled her skirts up above her ankles. Taking in the reflection, she raised her eyes and smiled at her sister in the glass. "I'll share a little secret, sister dear. I never, ever let him touch me. No sweet fondling, no tender caresses. Nothing. And after six months of this slow torture, he is mad about me. He is going crazy with desire."

"Why doesn't he just take someone else?"

"Oh, he does. I know he does. But, my dear sweet Elizabeth, those girls are simply substitutes for me." She cast a glance at her sister. "It's true!"

Elizabeth threw the tarp over the painting again and moved to the window. The streets were bustling with activity as laborers wending their way home now mingled with the street vendors. A woman hawking poultry called out to the passing crowd and held two live chickens aloft.

Elizabeth wished now that her sister had never come. Her eyes scanned the thoroughfare. She was glad Ambrose and Jaime had not yet returned. She was embarrassed. Embarrassed to present Anne to her husband the "loving" sister she had presumed her to be.

"I know he had a fondness for Mary," Anne droned on. "He used her body and then threw her out. And then he wanted you, but you ran. You *are* simple, Elizabeth. You could have had the most powerful man in the world at your beck and call, if you'd handled it correctly, but you ran away."

Elizabeth turned to face her sister.

"But me," Anne continued, not about to be interrupted. "I went after him. I used my charm, my wit. After the two of you, I knew he liked our looks, our builds. Henry is very particular in such matters, you know. So as I got older, I learned to become a predator, and he the prey."

Looking back in the mirror, she pushed back a loose lock of jet-black hair behind her ears. "I used seduction. I pretended to want him. And . . . I gave him a glimpse of what's to come."

She gave a loud laugh. "There are so many advantages to living at court. So many opportunities to give him just a quick glimpse of my maidenly charms. Aye, show him the curve of a breast, the shape of an uncovered leg . . . then hide it. What pleasure to simply stand there, to let him see, to let him drool. To watch the fool go hard. And then to blush, to back away. What matchless enjoyment to say, as he gets near, 'After our wedding, my great bear. We must save something for our wedding night, love.' Then I retreat—my 'honor' preserved, his lecherous desires provoked still further."

"This is a dangerous game you play, Anne. What's going to stop him from taking you against your will?"

"Ah, Elizabeth, you think I'm a fool? He won't," she said with conviction. "I have convinced him that there is something mystical about the feelings between us. The goat believes there is something almost 'holy' about me. And he is quite superstitious, you know. I've convinced him that Queen Catherine cannot bear him a son because heaven has frowned upon their marriage. I once even hinted that I have heard voices. Angelic voices that told me his marriage to Catherine is a reviled and incestuous union between a man and his brother's widow, and that the Tudor reign will end with Henry because of it. I've spend many an hour preaching to him the value of virtue and the utmost importance of my innocence on the marriage night. And he believes me, Elizabeth. He believes me!"

"Anne, think a moment of what you are doing. Whatever do you think will happen if you cannot give him the heir he is after?"

"There is no question," she said dismissively. "When I am queen, I will."

Elizabeth watched Anne as she gazed at herself in the mirror. In that fleeting, unguarded moment, she looked like the innocent child Elizabeth remembered. Whatever had happened to her, Elizabeth didn't know. But this was not the young woman she had expected today.

"Did your 'voices' tell you that, as well, Anne? That you shall bear him a son?"

"I weary of this discussion," she responded lazily. Then, pushing herself back sharply from the mirror, Anne stood and whirled, her face hard and sneering.

"And this brings me back to the reason for my visit today."

"I thought it was sisterly love that brought you here. The 'loneliness,' as you so artfully put it in your letter."

The young woman's expression went cold, her face paling at Elizabeth's words. "Nay, I got over that years ago—not long, in fact, after being deserted by my own sisters."

Then, for the first time since Anne walked through the door, Elizabeth saw a hint of pain in her sister's eyes.

"We *had* to leave you, Anne."

"You . . . you abandoned me! You left me behind!" She whispered the words, her eyes taking on a faraway look, as if she was reminding herself of what had happened. "One moment I had a family, older sisters whom I looked up to. Sisters whom I loved. Sisters who I thought loved me. And then, the next moment, I found myself rejected, thrown aside, forgotten."

Elizabeth took a step toward her. "My God, Anne. That's not the way—"

"Stop," she ordered. "Save your lies and your breath. You'll need them in a few moments."

"But you have to hear me. The reason Mary and I ran—"

"Mary and you," she repeated. "Listen to yourself. Mary and you. It always was just Mary and you." She took a breath and turned toward the window. "You two cared only for each other and no one else. You shared your affection, your time, your secrets with her. But I was your sister, too. What did you ever do for me?"

"You had my love. Whatever I felt for Mary, I felt for you. Whatever I did for Mary, I did for you. As far as my paintings, you were too young to be shown my work." Elizabeth felt sorrow creeping into her heart. She had been the reason. She herself. She was responsible for Anne becoming the woman she'd become. "You were strong, Anne. You were a smart child. At times it might have seemed that I gave more attention to Mary, but it was because she needed it. She was weak in so many ways."

"Standing in the Field of Cloth of Gold with an inferno of tents burning around me, I needed someone, too." Anne stabbed quickly at a tear that got away, dashing it from her pale cheek. "You ran to the fiery tent. I saw you. Wearing the friar's clothing. I ran toward you. Excited. Relieved. But you called for Mary. Only for Mary. Then I stood back and watched. You fought the flames, fought the people for the only sister you cared for. I stood there, scared . . . alone." Anne turned abruptly toward Elizabeth, facing her head-on. "Then you just disappeared. You and Mary both. You left me for good. No word, no message, no farewell."

Elizabeth moved quickly across the floor to Anne and took hold of her limp, ice-cold hands.

"I had to run, Anne. I was being followed. I had no other choice. But leaving that place, the Golden Vale, as we did—we hardly knew what was to become of us. Everything before us was so uncertain."

Elizabeth gazed into the downturned face of her sister. How could she explain fears that now seemed so distant?

"Meeting with you, telling you of all that had happened, all that was happening, would have meant putting your life in jeopardy. I loved you too much. I couldn't do that to you. And if taking Mary . . ." Elizabeth paused. "Mary had contracted the pox and, more than that, she was with child. King Henry's child. She had gone to Father, but she felt that he had turned his back on her, that he wouldn't help her."

Anne drew her hands out of Elizabeth's and stepped back. "Sir Thomas explained it all. I was a child, but still he explained it all."

"What did he tell you?"

"That you ran away in direct defiance of the king. That to spite the family you wouldn't become Henry's mistress. He said you took Mary, since you loved her best. And I was left behind because I was nothing to you. To either of you. He told me what I already knew, that I was not wanted."

"That was a lie!" Elizabeth blurted out. "It is true that I didn't want to go to Henry's bed. I didn't want my body to be sold by my own father. But I didn't leave you because I loved you less."

"It's too late for this." Anne cried in anguish, starting to back toward the door. "I had to learn, Elizabeth. I had to learn early on that I had no one. No one who would care for me."

"I cared for you. Believe me, Anne. You said you saw me by the fires. Well, did you see my face? The bloody face that our father had given me?"

Elizabeth pushed her hair back and showed her sister the still-visible scar on her cheek. She knew from the look in Anne's eyes that she remembered.

"That night," Elizabeth continued, "in that field, my world toppled. I went from being beaten by my own father to witnessing a vicious act of treachery and then murder. I was chased and nearly raped by the same brute who committed the murder. The same one who had my tent burned down. Aye, the same man who then tracked me as though I were some animal."

"It's too late, Elizabeth," Anne whispered as she reached the door. Her hand rested on the latch. "It's too late for explanations. The die is cast. It's time for you to pay."

Elizabeth stood, one hand stretched out to her sister. She didn't know what Anne meant, but a cold void in the pit of her stomach told her that something lay beyond the heavy oaken door. Nonetheless, she had to try to make her sister listen, to make her understand.

"I fled from the Field of Cloth of Gold without any word because of one man, Anne." She took a step toward her younger sister. "The same man who hunted me down years later in Troyes. The same man who is responsible for Mary's death. I was the one who was supposed to die there, Anne, but Mary stepped into the knife's path."

Anne stood at the door, silent, taking in every word.

"I want you to know the truth. It's time for you to hear what I couldn't tell you on that field." Elizabeth took another step toward her sister. "He had betrayed his king. Then he murdered the French Lord Constable, the one man who could reveal his treachery. But there was a witness. I was the witness. He has been after me ever since. Killing Mary . . . that was not enough. It is I he wants. And now I hear he stands in your way."

"Garnesche," Anne murmured.

"Aye, Sir Peter Garnesche," Elizabeth repeated. "Anne, you must use everything I have told you to threaten him with ruin. I . . . I cannot undo what has been done, but if marrying Henry is the thing that you most desire, if that is the goal you seek, then by all means use the truth to keep Garnesche at bay. But you must be careful; he is a devil— as ruthless a killer as ever walked on the earth."

Anne looked down at her hands, then her eyes ever so slowly moved up until they met Elizabeth's. "But you see, I have already found a way to deal with the man. He no longer presents any problem for me."

"He doesn't?"

Anne shook her head. "I told you before, I had to learn early, Elizabeth."

Elizabeth's eyes riveted on Anne's knuckles, white from her grip on the door latch.

"I've made a pact with him." Anne opened the door slowly on it hinges. "I want Henry. He'll stay out of my way, so that I can have him. Garnesche wants you, Elizabeth. So in return, I stay out of his way, so that he can have you. It's plain and simple. You owe me at least that much."

The door stood fully open now, and Elizabeth watched in horror as the giant Englishman stepped into the room.

"It was . . . very enlightening . . . seeing you, sister." Anne's eyes were troubled, but her voice was clear. "This time, however, I am the one who must be leaving."

Chapter 31

❧

Peter Garnesche gloated, his eyes full of malice, as the heavy oaken door swung shut behind the departing Anne.

Elizabeth backed unconsciously away from the door, her eyes scanning the room for something to use for protection. She could see nothing that might be effective in fighting off the giant. Elizabeth had been betrayed, and she was now at the villain's mercy. She looked into the knight's swarthy face, at the eyes that always hinted of madness.

Elizabeth's face hardened. Though her insides were quivering with fear, she was determined not to show it. No matter what happened to her, she would never give this animal the satisfaction of seeing the terror within her.

"Get out!" she commanded, her voice husky and forceful. "Get out of my house."

"Always the fighter," Garnesche sneered. "Well, I didn't come all this way just to leave."

"One step closer and a house full of men will come crashing through that door."

With an air that was almost leisurely, Garnesche pulled a dagger from his belt and held it out before him. The sharp point was aimed directly at her throat. "Your porter was the only man I could find. And I'm fairly certain he won't come crashing in."

Gazing at the evil smirk on his face, Elizabeth struggled to hide the shudder that wracked her body. She had been a trusting fool, and Garnesche's words struck terror into her heart. Here, in the midst of the bustling town, the house contained no soldiers—no one to protect her. And after all, she had not expected treachery of this magnitude.

"What do you want from me?" she demanded harshly.

"Not much." He took a step closer. "Only your silence."

She backed around the standing easel that held the canvas, cutting a wide radius to keep as much distance between them as she could.

"But that won't be enough, will it?"

"Nay, it won't. But there's no silence like that of the dead, you know."

"You are a greater fool than I thought." Placing one hand behind her, Elizabeth surreptitiously picked up a small palette knife from the cluttered table. She knew it was dull, but she held it tightly, hiding it in the folds of her skirt. "You think you can just kill me and then walk off."

"That is exactly what I intend to do." He continued to move closer to her.

"Then you might as well drive that dagger into your own heart right now, because you are as good as dead. Ambrose will kill you. He'll avenge my death with a fury, the likes of which the world has never seen. And your name will go down in infamy, for he will carve on your heart the names of Mary and the Lord Constable and all the others that you've slain in cold blood."

The fear that flickered across the back of his eyes was momentary, but Elizabeth saw it. The giant's hesitation was short-lived, however. A twisted smile crept back across his depraved features.

"Ah, you frighten me so." Moving toward her, he threw aside the easel and the canvas. Now nothing stood between them. "But right now, this exquisite moment is what I came to Scotland for."

Elizabeth looked about her in terror. She had nowhere to go. She backed away until she hit the wall.

"As we rode north, I envisioned this to be a quick death. A sharp twist of the neck or perhaps a quick slash at your pretty throat." He moved closer. "But being here with you now brings back certain . . . longings."

Elizabeth watched in amazement as the man quickly unfastened the belt about his doublet. Still holding his dagger, he dropped his sheathed sword to the floor.

"I've looked forward to this moment for quite a long time, Elizabeth. I know now that it is really the reason I came to this godforsaken country myself, instead of sending one of my men. It was meant to be this way. I didn't go to Troyes myself. That was why you didn't die there as I'd planned. Aye, I've dwelled on this many times before. Seeing, in my mind's eye, the moment when I will force you down. Listen to your screams. Feel your strong, tight legs fighting my entry. The moment when I drive my shaft deep inside you."

"It was never the murder that I witnessed that brought you after me. It was this sickness of yours. This insane lust for one you could never have."

Garnesche laughed. "You are so perceptive, m'lady." She moved quickly to the side as his hands reached for her. She backed up again as he steadily approached. "But it's not insanity. It's a dream. Call it a vision."

Elizabeth picked up the three-legged stool with one hand and flung it at his head. He ducked, avoiding it easily.

"I have seen it many times. I can see it now. Again and again driving my body into you, until your cries become moans, and I pour my seed into you. And then you lie in my arms and beg me for more."

"I will die first."

"You are nearly correct in that, Elizabeth. For as you beg, I *will* give you more. And that will be your death wish. Trapped in my arms, my shaft deep within you, I will wrap my fingers around your neck. Your tender, ivory neck. And shortly, when I hear you screaming for release, I will squeeze your windpipe. Tighter and tighter, squeezing and plunging until you won't know whether to scream for release or for breath. But you will get neither."

His hand shot out like lightning, and he grabbed hold of her wrist. Bringing her resisting body toward him, he smirked once again.

"You are sick." With her other hand, Elizabeth stabbed him hard in the wrist. The dull knife broke off at the hilt, the blade clattering to the floor, but the blow was enough to cause the knight to release her, bellowing in pain as he did. Elizabeth ran to the window. It was high above the street, but it was a chance.

Garnesche followed slowly after her, his eyes ablaze with madness.

"I will rest my full weight on your dying body, and you will sink into darkness, looking into my face, feeling me inside of you. You will die seeing my face! Aye, only mine!"

Elizabeth pulled open the leaded glass window so hard that it smashed against the wall of the room, shards of glass shattering around her. The violence of the crash stopped him for an instant, long enough for her to pick up a small strip of lead with a jagged piece of glass protruding from it. Garnesche paused and looked at the makeshift weapon.

"Ambrose will hunt you down," she whispered. "He'll make you die a slow and excruciating death."

"No one will ever know it was me." He glanced around at the rushes and the kegs of oil. "For when I'm done with you, your body will burn as your long-lost Lord Constable did. To this day no one knows what happened to the arrogant fool. That night in the Field of Cloth of Gold, he simply disappeared. And when this house goes up in flames, you'll disappear, as well."

Garnesche's back was to the door, but he heard it bang open as quickly as Elizabeth saw it. Whirling, the English knight thrust the dagger at Ambrose's chest with a single motion, and the weapon found its mark, sinking deeply into the Highlander's chest just below the shoulder.

Elizabeth screamed as Ambrose staggered back against the heavy oaken jamb, the point of his sword dragging across the floor.

Peter Garnesche leaped triumphantly to the place where he'd dropped his belt, and whipped his long sword from its sheath. As the Englishman advanced across the room, Ambrose straightened himself, the hilt of the dagger still protruding from his chest.

"Come on, you filthy cur," the Highlander challenged. "It is time this world was rid of you."

The Englishman paused, and the two giants eyed each other.

"The only regret I have about killing you, Macpherson," Garnesche sneered, "is that you won't have the pleasure of watching me take your woman."

"Then save your regrets, Garnesche, for you aren't man enough to accomplish either."

With a roar, the Englishman swung his great sword and the sparks exploded as steel crashed upon steel. One arm hanging limp at his side, Ambrose shoved his foe backward, sending him reeling across the floor.

Following as quickly as he could, the Highlander spun hard, his long blade arcing through the charged air. Again a shower of sparks rained down as Ambrose's brand hammered at Garnesche's weapon.

The Englishman stumbled under the blow, but as he went down, Garnesche kicked out with his boot, sweeping the Highlander's feet from beneath him. With a sickening thud, Ambrose's wounded shoulder hit the floor, and in a moment the Englishman was looming over him.

Malevolence vied with triumph on the face of the brute, and he drew back his sword to finish the fallen Scot.

"What a pleasure this is—" he began.

Elizabeth leaped onto Garnesche's back, grabbing his hair and yanking it back as she slashed with all her might at his exposed neck. But the Englishman's head snapped forward, and her jagged shard of glass found only the side of his face, ripping open a gash on his swarthy cheekbone.

Reaching back, the giant tore the woman from his back, throwing her like a rag across the room.

But Elizabeth had given Ambrose enough time, and the warrior lurched to his feet.

Garnesche turned his bloodied face back to the Highlander and, with a shout, raised his weapon to strike. But Ambrose spun once again, his blade slicing toward the madman's ribs, and this time his sword found its mark, cutting the very breath from the Englishman's roar.

Before Garnesche's body had ceased to twitch, Elizabeth was at Ambrose's side. Sitting the warrior gently against the wall, she knelt beside him, easing the dagger from his shoulder and pressing her palm tightly against the wound.

"Are you hurt?" Ambrose whispered, clutching her hand, searching her face for any mark of injury.

"Nothing happened to me, my love. But you . . . you are bleeding."

He brought her fingers to his lips while reaching in and wiping the tears that rolled freely down her face.

"A wee cut, lass. That's all it is. I've survived much worse than this." Ambrose smiled weakly.

"I am sorry, Ambrose. I am so sorry."

"Hush, lass," he whispered.

"I never told you before. I should have. I thought it was over. But it wasn't. He came after me. In Calais at the Field of Cloth of Gold, in Troyes at the market, and now here."

"Garnesche."

"He killed the Lord Constable, and I witnessed it. I was running from my father's tent, and I happened on Garnesche and the Lord Constable talking treason. I saw him murder the Lord Constable in cold blood. And he knew I saw it. So he came after me. I am so sorry, my love. All this would never have happened if I—"

"Nay, Elizabeth." Ambrose tried to smooth back her hair. "You can tell me all about it later. But remember this—nothing that happened here was your fault. Garnesche was a madman. And he is now dead."

Ambrose smiled. "And I am proud of you. You have the courage of a Highlander. The way you fought. You saved my life."

She kissed his lips. "Nay, you saved mine. I was foolish earlier when I asked you to go. I never want to be anywhere without you again. Never."

"That's a promise." His deep blue eyes locked in with hers. "I love you, Elizabeth Macpherson. And I, too, am sorry for what you went through."

"Don't, Ambrose," Elizabeth replied, caressing his face. "I just thank the Blessed Mother you came back when you did."

"Jaime and I were just coming up the hill into town when your sister came riding out under a white flag, at the head of a troop of English soldiers."

"Did she see you?"

"Aye. She was looking for us."

Elizabeth stared at him.

"She told me that your life was in danger. That Garnesche had you at the point of his blade in here. She pleaded with me to hurry. And then she rode away like the devil was after her."

Elizabeth listened carefully to his every word. Moments. A few moments more would have meant certain death for her. Anne. Her sister had gone after Ambrose. After she had betrayed her. A change of heart? she wondered.

"Did she say anything else?" Elizabeth asked quietly.

"Aye, as a matter of fact, she did. She said, 'Tell her I've forgiven her. And tell her I hope that someday she might forgive me, as well.' "

Chapter 32

❧

Benmore Castle, the Scottish Highlands
June 1525

The Highlanders charged with wild cries across the cobbles of the castle courtyard, their swords raised.

At the far end, the warrior queen and her official guard stood their ground, their fearless expressions unchanged in the face of the reckless charge.

"Your Majesty," Malcolm MacLeod said, turning to the little girl standing beside him fully armed with her own wooden sword. "Would you allow me the honor of dispensing with this horde of ruffians and rogues?"

"Aye, Lord Malcolm," Jaime assented sternly. "But they are my cousins, don't forget. So spare their lives when you can."

As the whooping brigands swarmed around them, the sixteen-year-old Malcolm lifted the littlest one onto his shoulder and fought off the other two with exaggerated displays of swordsmanship.

Finally, after her guard had wrestled the assailants into submission and was lying on top of them, Queen Jaime sauntered over and placed the point of her sword on the chest of her eldest cousin, Alexander.

"Yield, villain!"

"Never!"

Malcolm tightened his hold on the eight-year-old, giving the warrior an opportunity to surrender with honor.

"I yield," Alexander gasped. "But next time, *we* get the giant."

"Perhaps, blackguard. But first promise to give up your

plans to send my baby brother to the dungeons, and we will allow you to live." Her voice was commanding.

The young boy nodded grudgingly. "Aye, we'll leave him alone."

"Forever?"

"Until the bairn can carry a sword. But that's it. That's our final offer."

Jaime's eyes traveled to Malcolm questioningly. He gave a covert wink.

"We accept your offer, Lord Macpherson," she announced. "And you may keep your holdings in the king's name."

Ambrose moved behind Elizabeth and gathered her and the baby into his arms. He smiled, watching the tiny infant sucking gently on a closed fist.

Following Elizabeth's gaze, the proud father looked out on battling armies untangling themselves in the yard below.

"Another victory for the queen?" he asked.

"Aye," Elizabeth whispered, smiling. "With the aid of her heroic knight."

Ambrose placed a kiss tenderly on the silky skin of her neck. She snuggled closer to him.

"Jaime is going to miss Malcolm when he returns to St. Andrews," Elizabeth noted softly, watching the two cross the yard. The young girl's head did not even reach the young warrior's waist, but she held his hand as though he belonged to her.

"His education at St. Andrews is only a first step for him," Ambrose replied. "The lad has great challenges lying ahead."

Elizabeth turned in her husband's arms and gazed up into his deep blue eyes.

"As we all do." She sighed happily.

Ambrose leaned down and placed a soft kiss on the black, silky hair of his sleeping son. Then, turning his attention once again to the mother, he met her upraised lips with his own.

He was the happiest man alive. Gathering her tighter in his arms, he whispered words of love. She answered with fervor.

The noises of the stirring bairn between them disrupted

their moment together, and the two laughed as the infant stretched his tiny fingers upward toward their faces.

The sun shining on the Macphersons' carved stone coat of arms drew the young mother's gaze out the window, and she felt all around her the love and the strength of the family that was now her own. Then, her eyes traveling heavenward, Elizabeth's heart swelled with a happiness as infinitely vast, as infinitely deep, as the crystalline blue of the cloudless Highland sky.

Epilogue

❧

Greenwich Palace, 1533

Anne Boleyn, Queen of England, snuggled the red-haired infant closer to her and, taking a deep breath, nodded to the physicians and the Lord Chamberlain. The massive door to her quarters swung open, and the king led his Privy Council into the room.

Wordlessly, Henry strode over to the bed and sat beside the mother and child. His corpulent face folded into a wry smile as he poked a fleshy finger into the folds of the baby's soft covering.

The king did not look up into Anne's face, but she hardly expected him to, considering his disappointment.

"Well, Annie," he growled. "I suppose the wind must have been from the south, eh?"

"She's a healthy girl, Henry."

"Aye. She has my mother's coloring."

"Perhaps next time—"

Anne's comment was left unfinished as King Henry rose abruptly from the bed.

"We've a country to provide for," the king stated shortly. "We'll look in on you later."

As the king reached the door, a thought struck him and he turned back toward the bed, his entourage scattering before him.

"If you have a name you want considered, Anne, let us know." Without another word, the monarch swept out the door.

Anne watched, her face a mask, as the room cleared. Nodding to the Lord Chamberlain as he turned to go, Anne looked down at the infant in her arms. Gazing at the wisps of red hair, the round little face, and the nearly translucent skin, the mother wondered at the sleeping child, so peaceful and unaware of the world she had just entered.

Huddling her even closer, the queen glanced up defiantly at the closed door.

"A south wind, indeed," she whispered bitterly. Anne's eyes lowered again to her baby. "Listen to me, little one, and learn this now. They will tell you it's a man's world. But take heart. Fear nothing. You will carry the name of a great woman. You will carry her spirit."

In 1558, Elizabeth I, resplendent in her gown of cloth of gold, ascended the throne of Britain. For the next half century, she was to forge the glorious era of Sidney and Spenser, Jonson and Shakespeare, and in the end give her name to England's golden age.

Like a snake striking out at his prey, the sailor's line shot out toward the pitching longboat.

The small craft bobbed helplessly at the ship's side. Aboard the *Great Michael,* a crowd of seamen lined the rail and hung from the rigging, straining for a clear look through the thick, concealing mists—and ready for action. The occupants of the longboat made no move to board the larger ship, and the Scottish sailors waited impatiently, casting quick, questioning glances at their master for their next move.

"Where in hell did that boat come from?" John Macpherson exploded, pushing through the rugged throng.

"It looks like it's a solitary boat, m'lord," his navigator replied. "And only three men, at that."

"Bring them up!" he ordered sharply.

"Is that wise?" a voice broke in.

John did not even turn to acknowledge the question from the tall, blond-haired woman who glided quickly to his side. Caroline.

"What happens if they are armed?" she continued. "Even if they pretend to be friendly, isn't it possible they could cut all our throats as we sleep?"

Without answering, John turned slightly and frowned threateningly at Sir Thomas.

"Come, come, Caroline," her husband offered gently, taking his wife by the elbow and pulling her from the railing in an effort to avoid any unpleasantness with the angry Highlander. This was not the time or place. "There is not much to worry on that account, but I should think Sir John is capable of determining that."

John continued to peer over the side as a number of his men lowered themselves down the ropes.

"Women, m'lord!" came the return shout from one of the sailors. "Two women and a man."

The cry drew a slew of astonished men to the edge. John leaned forward, watching as another sailor scurried down the side. "Bring them up! Now!"

"They're bloody Spaniards, m'lord!"

"I don't care if they're the devil's own sisters!" John shouted angrily.

"This one's dead, m'lord. He's got a hole in his chest the size of my fist," the sailor called up, pointing at the male in the bow of the boat.

"Bring them up!"

"Even the dead one?"

"For God's sake, man!" John fumed, his patience gone. "Aye! Of course, the dead one, as well."

The sailors below, hearing the fury in their commander's tone, hastily secured the boat to the ship and started at once.

Seeing at last that his men were hustling, John stepped back, letting the ship's mate take charge. Turning around, he stopped short at the sight of the delegation crowding around him. For the first time since they'd left port, the noblemen and women had found something entertaining enough to draw them out of their comfortable cabins. Like a bunch of children, they were jostling one another for a better view of the newcomers.

He didn't like it a bit. His men didn't need the distraction. Not now.

Moving toward Sir Thomas, who was standing with Caroline by the mainmast, John spoke to him quietly. A few words were all that needed to be said, and the aging warrior leaped into action. John knew this was exactly what the gentleman desired. A chance to be involved and a chance to be useful.

Turning back to the railing, John ignored the cacophony of complaints resulting from Sir Thomas's blunt efforts to usher as many of the women and men as he could belowdecks.

Refusing the offers of help from the pushing throng remaining on deck, the Highlander silently thanked God that so far during this journey they'd been spared any attack at sea. Not that the *Great Michael* couldn't hold its own in any fight, but John was sure that the chaos he would have to deal with on board would be much more difficult than any enemy assault.

Moving through the crowd, John saw David and the mate carefully helping an elderly woman down onto the deck from the rail. From the blood-soaked cloak, it was obvious that she had sustained an injury. John held back an instant as she took the arm of one of his men and tried to walk a few steps. Not being able to support her weight, however, she suddenly leaned heavily against the sailor and sank slowly to the deck.

John moved hastily to the woman and crouched before her.

"She is wounded," a woman said from behind him. "Her shoulder."

John turned toward the strained voice of the other survivor who had just been brought aboard. He noticed how, once on board, she politely but firmly rejected the assistance of his men. As she crossed to where the older woman lay, she wobbled a bit but quickly regained her footing. This lass is a mess, he thought, giving her dripping clothes and jumbled tangle of her hair a cursory glance. And she, too, sported black spots on her torn, gray dress that he was sure had to be blood. These women had survived an ordeal that consisted of more than a row in the cold fog.

Taking his eyes away from the other, John pulled back the blood-soaked cloak gently and looked at the wound on the older woman's shoulder. He assumed these two must be survivors of the battle they'd heard earlier today. The older one had received what, from the burn on the surrounding skin, looked like a wound from a musket shot. But the damage was not life threatening, he thought, should the injury not fester.

"Ship's mate," he called over his shoulder. "Have the surgeon up on deck to look at her wound."

Then he stood and turned to look at the other woman, who now stood only a step away.

Maria saw him rise and her breath caught in her chest.

Crouching before Isabel, the man had not looked as intimidating as he did now. A fierce scowl clouding his swarthy face, he towered over every other man on deck. Quickly, she tore her eyes away from him and fixed her attention on her aunt's face. She did not dare to look up.

"And you," he asked shortly. "Any injury?"

"None," she whispered simply, turning and stumbling once more as she knelt beside Isabel.

John looked at the small, water-soaked figure at his feet, and his heart warmed to the bedraggled creature. He'd heard the tremble in her voice. There was a childlike quality about her—an uncertainty—that made him wonder for a moment from what depths she had conjured the strength to survive the ordeal of being adrift at sea.

Laying her fingers lightly on her aunt's cold, limp hand, Maria fought off the desire to run away from the eyes of the giant standing behind her. She could feel his gaze burning into her even as she tended to Isabel. For a brief moment, she thought that perhaps the mariner knew who she was, but her attention was diverted as her aunt began to murmur in her unconscious state. It didn't matter what this man knew or didn't know. There was not much she could do about it, and Isabel needed to be cared for. That was all that mattered.

The gray wool dress that the woman wore beneath her cloak must have been clean at one time, but it was now ruined with dark stains and seawater. Almost as if she could read his thoughts, the young woman pulled her heavy cloak tighter around her, making it nearly impossible for John to ascertain anything more about her.

She seemed quite young, but a strange bittersweet sensation swept over the Highlander as it occurred to him that nearly every woman he met now seemed to be quite young. The attention she showed to the other indicated that they must be related somehow. Mother and daughter perhaps. Even though she'd not said much, he could tell her young voice carried the lilt of a Spanish accent.

"There is blood on your cloak. Are you certain you have no wounds?"

"None," she responded evenly. "It's the sailor's blood. Not mine."

She did not even turn her head when she answered, but he could see the shiver. The shock, John thought. The cold and wetness and being left in a boat drifting at sea can test the mettle of the toughest men.

"Are there other boats coming?" he asked. "Other survivors?"

"None that we saw," she whispered.

"How long were you in the boat?"

"Long."

"How long?"

She didn't answer, only shrugged her shoulders in return.

"Did your ship sink?"

She didn't answer again. John found himself quickly becoming tired of speaking to the back of the woman's head.

"Where's the bloody surgeon?" he asked irritably, moving to the other side of the injured woman's body and crouching as well.

"He's coming, m'lord," the ship's mate responded, pushing into the circle.

"Who attacked you and how many ships were involved in the fight?" John asked, forcing his voice onto a more even keel.

Maria stared at her aunt's closed eyes. Isabel was resting, at least. But she still couldn't bring herself to lift her gaze and look at the man. She felt vulnerable, lost, and she fought to hide the tremors that were going through her body. She didn't have to look about to know that she was encircled by dozens of curious spectators who were watching her every more, hanging on her every word. Like a prize doe, hunted and injured and brought to bay at last, she felt trapped. What were they going to do to them? The giant, the one asking the questions, was clearly in command, and the others obviously feared him. She knew she should, as well. He had called them the devil's sisters.

"I need to know these things." His voice was sharper than he intended, but still John reached over and tapped the woman gently on the shoulder.

"Just one." Her eyes flitted briefly to his face, but dropped immediately.

Her eyes were the color of jade, and John found himself staring as she lowered her gaze. They were the most beautiful color, set in a face devoid of color. The paleness of her complexion only served to heighten the stunning effect of her green eyes.

"A French ship," she continued. "Only one."

John nodded. Looking into her face, he found himself at a loss for words. Letting his eyes drop from the young woman's face to her exposed hands, he could see them trembling as they clutched the elder woman's cloak. His eyes traveled up again quickly to her face. She was young, very young. Beyond the paled dirty face and a tangle of black hair, he could see there existed a terrified, young woman.

A thin, drunken rattle of a voice could be heard on the outside of the throng of men surrounding them. The surgeon, a member of the Douglas clan and a man that John was sure had been sent along as Angus's spy, slowly approached. A puffy, bleary-eyed monk with more of an interest in wine and a soft bunk than the welfare of his fellows. John's face clouded with anger once again as he watched him taking his time in answering his summons.

"We'll talk later," he growled, standing at once as the physician sidled up through the crowd.

Ignoring the man, John gestured sharply to the mate.

"The woman's been out in this damp long enough. Take her below; the surgeon can see to her there."

"May I stay with her?" Maria asked, quickly rising to her feet and turning to the ship's commander. The inflection of her words wavered between that of a command and a plea.

This time their eyes met, but only for an instant, before Maria averted her gaze in embarrassment.

"Aye," John responded. "Of course. I'll look in on you in a short while. My men will see to your needs. There are still questions that need to be answered."

She nodded, then stood silently, waiting for the men to move her aunt.

There was very little space in which to clean up nor to spread out her wet, soiled clothes in the small room adjoining the large cabin where Isabel was taken. A young boy had entered the cabin right behind them as they arrived and had, without a word, handed her a woolen dress and some linen undergarments. Maria had been thankful for the thoughtfulness of the gesture but had not really known who to thank. On deck, she'd seen many gentlemen dressed in the latest courtly fashions standing about. Thinking about it now, she realized that there would be a number of women in this welcoming delegation. Clearly, it was one of those ladies to whom she owed her gratitude.

Holding her wet garments up, she scanned the room helplessly. From where she was, Maria could hear the murmuring voices of her aunt and the physician and then the sound of shuffling feet moving out into the corridor. Finally giving up on the clothes, she placed them in a neat pile in the corner. There was a small washbowl and pitcher set into a board along one wall of the tiny cabin, so Maria carefully swabbed at the painful open blisters on her palms and fingers. Wrapping strips of linen dressing around her hands, she tried unsuccessfully to tuck the ends under. Having both hands reduced to nothing more than raw flesh made it almost impossible to succeed. Besides, even at this she was a novice. She shook her head with disgust. Unskilled in even the most simple of tasks.

With frustration and disappointment pulling at her, Maria tearfully jerked the wide, forest-green sleeves of the woolen dress down over her wrists. Then, dashing a glistening droplet from her cheek, she yanked open a narrow door and stepped into Isabel's more spacious cabin.

Her aunt's eyes traveled to her at once from where she lay. Maria watched as the older woman put her finger to her lips, hushing her for the moment. The young woman complied and stood back, waiting as the physician's boy gathered together the bloodied dressings from the small table.

"You were lucky, m'lady," the surgeon rasped, reentering the spacious cabin. "The ball just grazed you. But your sailor had no chance."

"Then he is dead?" Isabel asked.

"Aye. Dead and gone to his Maker." He glanced back at the older woman. "Sir John wants to know the man's name. For the prayers when we put him into the sea."

"I don't know it." Isabel said with embarrassment, looking at Maria.

"No matter, it makes no difference," the man responded. "Was it your ship? The one that went down?"

Isabel shook her head quickly in denial.

"Ah, well." The man started for the door, but then stopped before Maria and pointed to a small bowl of liquid and some clean dressings. "I'll leave these with you. You should change her dressing if she'll let you. And Sir John will be down directly. He appears to be impatient to have some questions answered. But don't worry about your mother, my dear. She is going to be fine."

"She is not—" Maria caught herself, "not going to die, then?"

"Nay, lass," the man wheezed, and turned again for the door. "I've given her something to make her sleep. I'll send the lad back in a little. If you need me, have him fetch me."

Without any further ceremony, the man shuffled out into the dark corridor with the younger boy on his heel.

Maria waited until the door of the cabin was shut behind them, then moved quickly to the side of her aunt's bed.

"They are Scots!" she said, her concern apparent in her voice.

"I can see that, my dear," Isabel concurred, her eyes taking in the elegant furnishings of the cabin. "And not just any Scots. No doubt, this is part of the fleet that your brother summoned to come and take you to back to their king."

"What am I to do?" Maria asked. "What would they think if they find out who we are?"

"Does it matter what they think?" Isabel chuckled as she yawned and stretched her body in the comfortable bed.

"If I am to be their queen . . ." Maria whispered.

"You are right." Isabel agreed, keeping her voice low. "If you *are* to be their queen, then I'd say, you have already lost any chance at their respect. After all, you're supposed to be sitting high and dry in Antwerp, waiting for them to arrive, not rowing in the open seas in an effort to escape them. But that's assuming you ever do become their queen."

Isabel patted the blanket next to her, and Maria sat down at once.

"I can't tell them my identity." Maria said matter of factly. "I am going to Castile, not to Scotland."

"You . . ." Isabel yawned again. "You are going to Antwerp, my dear. That's where they are headed."

Maria looked at her aunt helplessly.

"But I can't. Can you imagine the embarrassment? I wouldn't be able to face Charles. He would never forgive me. Being found adrift at sea by the same people sent to convey me to their home. By the Virgin, the shame that would result."

"I thought none of this mattered. I thought you had resigned yourself to accept your brother's wrath."

"I had," Maria said despondently. "But that was when I thought we could face him from afar. Not dragged back and handed right over to him. You know the power that he wields. How persuasive he is. Never in my life have I won an argument with him *tête-à-tête*."

Maria sighed. Since she was little, she had always let her brother have his own way. Charles was a bully as a child—he was just a more powerful one as an adult.

"Why can't go as we'd planned?" the young woman pleaded, fighting to keep the note of desperation out of her voice. "I don't want to go back, Isabel. I just can't."

Maria watched her aunt fighting off the drowsiness that was overtaking her.

"You ruined the longboat, child."

Maria could not help but smile.

"You know very well that I don't mean rowing." She turned her head and stared at the small window. "We must find another way. We are close to Denmark."

Isabel opened one eye and tried to focus.

"But it's too far to swim, Maria. And I'm just feeling warmer . . ."

Maria watched the smile tug at her aunt's lips before the older woman visibly gave in to the effects of the medicine.

"The commander," Isabel said, her eyes fluttering open a bit. "The Scot. Sir John, they call him. There is a young and handsome man. Certainly as good-looking as any sailor *I* ever came across in my life."

"What does *that* have to do with anything?" Maria

asked as she smoothed a silver tendril of hair from Isabel's face.

"Hmmph!" Isabel closed her eyes again. "And to think you've already been married once!"

"Isabel!" Maria protested. But her aunt was fast asleep.

BREATHTAKING ROMANCES YOU WON'T WANT TO MISS

Journeys of Passion and Desire

☐ **TOMORROW'S DREAMS by Heather Cullman.** Beautiful singer Penelope Parrish—the darling of the New York stage—never forgot the night her golden life ended. The handsome businessman Seth Tyler, whom she loved beyond all reason, hurled wild accusations at her and walked out of her life. Years later, when Penelope and Seth meet again amid the boisterous uproar of a Denver dance hall, all their repressed passion struggles to break free once more.   (406842—$5.50)

☐ **YESTERDAY'S ROSES by Heather Cullman.** Dr. Hallie Gardiner knows something is terribly wrong with the handsome, haunted-looking man in the great San Francisco mansion. The Civil War had wounded Jake "Young Midas" Parrish, just as it had left Serena, his once-beautiful bride, hopelessly lost in her private universe. But when Serena is found mysteriously dead, Hallie finds herself falling in love with Jake who is now a murder suspect.   (405749—$4.99)

☐ **LOVE ME TONIGHT by Nan Ryan.** The war had robbed Helen Burke Courtney of her money and her husband. All she had left was her coastal Alabama farm. Captain Kurt Northway of the Union Army might be the answer to her prayers, or a way to get to hell a little faster. She needed a man's help to plant her crops; she didn't know if she could stand to have a damned handsome Yankee do it.   (404831—$4.99)

☐ **FIRES OF HEAVEN by Chelley Kitzmiller.** Independence Taylor had not been raised to survive the rigors of the West, but she was determined to mend her relationship with her father—even if it meant journeying across dangerous frontier to the Arizona Territory. But nothing prepared her for the terrifying moment when her wagon train was attacked, and she was carried away from certain death by the mysterious Apache known only as Shatto.   (404548—$4.99)

☐ **RAWHIDE AND LACE by Margaret Brownley.** Libby Summerhill couldn't wait to get out of Deadman's Gulch—a lawless mining town filled with gunfights, brawls, and uncivilized mountain men—men like Logan St. John. He knew his town was no place for a woman and the sooner Libby and her precious baby left for Boston, the better. But how could he bare to lose this spirited woman who melted his heart of stone forever?   (404610—$4.99)

*Prices slightly higher in Canada

Buy them at your local bookstore or use this convenient coupon for ordering.

PENGUIN USA
P.O. Box 999 — Dept. #17109
Bergenfield, New Jersey 07621

Please send me the books I have checked above.
I am enclosing $_____ (please add $2.00 to cover postage and handling). Send check or money order (no cash or C.O.D.'s) or charge by Mastercard or VISA (with a $15.00 minimum). Prices and numbers are subject to change without notice.

Card #_____ Exp. Date _____
Signature_____
Name_____
Address_____
City _____ State _____ Zip Code _____

For faster service when ordering by credit card call **1-800-253-6476**

Allow a minimum of 4-6 weeks for delivery. This offer is subject to change without notice.

WE NEED YOUR HELP

To continue to bring you quality romance
that meets your personal expectations,
we at TOPAZ books want to hear from you.
Help us by filling out this questionnaire, and in exchange
we will give you a **free gift** as a token of our gratitude.

- Is this the first TOPAZ book you've purchased? (circle one)

    YES   NO

    The title and author of this book is: _____

- If this was not the first TOPAZ book you've purchased, how many have you bought in the past year?

    a: 0 - 5   b 6 - 10   c: more than 10   d: more than 20

- How many romances in total did you buy in the past year?

    a: 0 - 5   b: 6 - 10   c: more than 10   d: more than 20 ____

- How would you rate your overall satisfaction with this book?

    a: Excellent   b: Good   c: Fair   d: Poor

- What was the main reason you bought this book?

    a: It is a TOPAZ novel, and I know that TOPAZ stands
       for quality romance fiction
    b: I liked the cover
    c: The story-line intrigued me
    d: I love this author
    e: I really liked the setting
    f: I love the cover models
    g: Other: _____

- Where did you buy this TOPAZ novel?

    a: Bookstore   b: Airport   c: Warehouse Club
    d: Department Store   e: Supermarket   f: Drugstore
    g: Other: _____

- Did you pay the full cover price for this TOPAZ novel? (circle one)

    YES   NO

    If you did not, what price did you pay? _____

- Who are your favorite TOPAZ authors? (Please list)

- How did you first hear about TOPAZ books?

    a: I saw the books in a bookstore
    b: I saw the TOPAZ Man on TV or at a signing
    c: A friend told me about TOPAZ
    d: I saw an advertisement in_____magazine
    e: Other: _____

- What type of romance do you generally prefer?

    a: Historical   b: Contemporary
    c: Romantic Suspense   d: Paranormal (time travel,
       futuristic, vampires, ghosts, warlocks, etc.)
    d: Regency   e: Other: _____

- What historical settings do you prefer?

    a: England   b: Regency England   c: Scotland
    e: Ireland   f: America   g: Western Americana
    h: American Indian   i: Other: _____

- What type of story do you prefer?
    - a: Very sexy
    - b: Sweet, less explicit
    - c: Light and humorous
    - d: More emotionally intense
    - e: Dealing with darker issues
    - f: Other

- What kind of covers do you prefer?
    - a: Illustrating both hero and heroine
    - b: Hero alone
    - c: No people (art only)
    - d: Other_____

- What other genres do you like to read (circle all that apply)

    Mystery   Medical Thrillers   Science Fiction
    Suspense   Fantasy   Self-help
    Classics   General Fiction   Legal Thrillers
    Historical Fiction

- Who is your favorite author, and why?_____
  _____

- What magazines do you like to read? (circle all that apply)
    - a: *People*
    - b: *Time/Newsweek*
    - c: *Entertainment Weekly*
    - d: *Romantic Times*
    - e: *Star*
    - f: *National Enquirer*
    - g: *Cosmopolitan*
    - h: *Woman's Day*
    - i: *Ladies' Home Journal*
    - j: *Redbook*
    - k: Other:_____

- In which region of the United States do you reside?
    - a: Northeast
    - b: Midatlantic
    - c: South
    - d: Midwest
    - e: Mountain
    - f: Southwest
    - g: Pacific Coast

- What is your age group/sex?   a: Female   b: Male
    - a: under 18
    - b: 19-25
    - c: 26-30
    - d: 31-35
    - e: 36-40
    - f: 41-45
    - g: 46-50
    - h: 51-55
    - i: 56-60
    - j: Over 60

- What is your marital status?
    - a: Married
    - b: Single
    - c: No longer married

- What is your current level of education?
    - a: High school
    - b: College Degree
    - c: Graduate Degree
    - d: Other:_____

- Do you receive the TOPAZ *Romantic Liaisons* newsletter, a quarterly newsletter with the latest information on Topaz books and authors?

    YES   NO

    If not, would you like to?   YES   NO

    Fill in the address where you would like your free gift to be sent:

    Name: _____
    Address: _____
    City: _____   Zip Code: _____

    You should receive your free gift in 6 to 8 weeks.
    Please send the completed survey to:

    Penguin USA•Mass Market
    Dept. TS
    375 Hudson St.
    New York, NY 10014

"Do you think fate threw us together?"

*　　　*　　　*

Berry tried escaping Jason's searing mouth, but he placed one hand behind her head, clutched her tighter and kept kissing her. For an utterly mindless moment she was lost in sensation.

"Please," Berry whispered. Robbed of breath she pushed with both hands against his chest. Her knees, unreliable now, threatened to buckle. To her ears, both her voice and her breath sounded ragged, pitiful. Trying to recall what her speech coaches had advised, she strove for a light tone. "Why bother searching for reasons why we met again? Let's just enjoy the fact that we did."

The flippant reply deflated Jason, turning his thoughts inward. Maybe he had been wrong to suspect he was falling in love as they danced. The thought of a negative answer smarted, but he went on doggedly, ready if need be to challenge destiny. "Don't you feel anything for me?" he asked.

*

CREOLE MOON

Also by Myra Rowe

Cypress Moon
Cajun Rose
Treasure's Golden Dream
A Splendid Yearning

Creole Moon

Myra Rowe

WARNER BOOKS

A Time Warner Company

WARNER BOOKS EDITION

Copyright © 1991 by Myra Rowe
All rights reserved.

Cover illustration by Sharon Spiak
Cover hand lettering by Carl Dellacroce

Warner Books, Inc.
666 Fifth Avenue
New York, N.Y. 10103

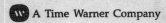 A Time Warner Company

Printed in the United States of America

First Printing: December, 1991

10 9 8 7 6 5 4 3 2 1

CHAPTER

·

One

*T*he first time Berry Cortabona saw Jason Premont, she was hurrying along Dauphine Street one Sunday morning in 1835. After pausing to stare in the predawn glow bathing the New Orleans French Quarter, she giggled.

Almost thirteen, Berry enjoyed a dreamy outlook on life and welcomed its diversions, no matter how bizarre. A wondrous ingredient of expectancy hummed within her consciousness, lending an inner sparkle to her eyes. Her hand shot up to cover her uncommonly pretty mouth, but failed to smother her laughter.

Cocking her head, she watched as a long-limbed young man a few feet away attempted to climb over a tall brick wall. The customary nails and shards of glass upended in mortar atop the wall—as a lifelong resident of the French Quarter, she knew they were meant to deter would-be intruders—gripped the seat of his stylish yellow trousers. At

1

the moment, he was stuck like some exotic insect impaled on the end of a giant pin.

Pulling her old shawl closer to ward off the chill of the February morning, Berry shook her head and mused at the inexplicable ways of men and women and love. She became aware that more light was coming from the huge moon now setting in the west than from the sun promising to rise over the eleven-by-seven-block area sometimes called the Vieux Carré, or Old Square.

Who in bloody blazes, Berry wondered when she quelled her laughter, dared sneak in or out of the famous gardens behind the Burgundy Street home of Auguste Soulé? He was one of the most prominent merchants of New Orleans in 1835 and a man said to own a short temper. A bit of a scamp herself, she grinned and eyed the dark-haired young man with admiration for his courage. He looked like a Frenchman and not at all like a thief.

"Are you coming or going, mister?" Berry asked in Creole French after the obvious interloper became aware of her presence on the banquette and jerked his head toward her. Had he heard her giggling?

Berry could not see the rascal's features clearly, for a trace of the fog rolling from the Mississippi River only four blocks away still blurred the light spilling from lamps hanging on the corner buildings. In fact, except in the block where she stood, she gained no clear view of the numerous brick chimneys sticking up through the tiled roofs, chimneys that she had learned only recently were taxed a whole dollar yearly to defray the expenses of the whale oil lamps lighting the city.

As she often did during her Sunday morning jaunts in the French Quarter, the girl sucked in a deep breath so as to inhale the fresh, damp smells coming from the river. Then she lost herself in admiring the way the mist softened even further the glorious tones of pink, blue, cream, and green paint gracing many of the closely spaced brick buildings.

Just then, with a curse blending with a horrendous, ripping

sound of heavy cloth, Jason Premont completed his escape. He dropped on his feet to the board walkway not far from Berry and straightened up. Pressing his backside against the bricks, he crawfished down to the far side of the neighboring wall before stopping. He showed no surprise when the slight girl followed, her eyes still asking her question.

"Can't you tell? I'm going," Jason replied in a deep, low voice, as if he might have been mulling it over before speaking. His teeth flashed white in his olive-skinned face. "I'm the number-one city inspector of fences and walls."

Berry relaxed her hold on the handle of her dagger resting as usual inside her skirt pocket. The smiling young man with the dimpled cheeks and laughing eyes seemed no threat at all. She adored jokes. She adored his low-pitched voice, too. "Did Mr. Soulé's wall pass inspection?"

Suddenly, Berry was recalling the scandalous tales about the Soulés she had heard at the Théâtre d'Orléans where she worked. So, she reflected with a wisdom belying her tender age, Mrs. Soulé, though well into her thirties, really *did* have a penchant for handsome young men and *did* entertain them in her boudoir during her husband's frequent nights spent with his mistress on Camp Street. He must have returned home early.

Berry's eyes sparkled with new amusement. She had not had such fun since slipping off to Peacock Corner one night last week with the current traveling troupe of actors. All had watched a bawdy dancer atop a bar shed choice pieces of costume while wriggling her hips and huge breasts in syncopation with a lively number from a band.

Before the entertainer got down to her bare skin, Berry recalled as she waited for the young man's answer, the proprietor, despite Berry's borrowed wig, had recognized her and sent one of his older waiters to walk her home.

As though he had given the matter considerable thought, the young wall climber replied with mock solemnity, "The wall passes." He lifted one broad shoulder in a shrug typical of a carefree Frenchman. "But I managed to rip the seat of my trousers."

Berry giggled again but stopped when she glimpsed his hands. "Bedamned! Your hands are bleeding." Compassionate by nature, maybe because she hungered for understanding herself, Berry rushed to his side, her soft French floating on the early morning air. "Oh, my! Do you have a handkerchief? I can split it with my dagger and bind your wounds."

Jason eyed the small, double-edged blade she had pulled from a pocket of her long black skirt. What kind of girl would be out alone at such an hour, cursing and carrying such a dangerous looking blade? None that he had ever run into during his twenty years. "Do you always carry that"— with a jabbing forefinger he indicated the obviously sharp weapon—"thing along?"

"Only for protection." Berry almost felt sorry for him. He must belong to the upper class and be unaware that evil stalked the French Quarter. "I was going to use it to make strips so I can bandage your hands."

"A Sunday kind of angel of mercy," Jason commented wryly. He glanced toward the Soulé wall before going on in that same low voice, one curiously furred and reminding Berry of midnight and whispering. "You may be just what I need, Miss . . . May I learn your name, angel? Should someone appear and ask if we're together, it would be best if we each know the other's name." As he talked and inched down to an even farther wall, he sent surreptitious looks all around, aware that the bright-eyed girl listened while following at a discreet distance. He guessed she was no more than ten or eleven, probably the devilish little sister of somebody living on one of the Quarter's meaner streets. "Mine is Jason Premont."

Berry shivered, feeling that she was caught up in something wonderfully dramatic. "I'm Berry Angelique Cortabona."

"Aha!" His dimples showed again. "I guessed right. You *are* an angel."

"Not quite. Everyone calls me Berry, Mr. Premont."

"Jason, please. Under the circumstances, we can't stand on ceremony, can we? Were a Charley to wander this way, I might need to pretend we're out for an early morning stroll."

Jason's dark eyes surveyed the girl's heart-shaped face, then lingered at the widow's peak centering her forehead before taking in the long dark hair spilling from underneath her pink kerchief and falling forward over her slender shoulders in an untidy cloud of curls. She was going to be a beauty someday, with her rich olive coloring and high cheekbones. Was that a hint of purple sparkling within her—?

Intrigued, Jason leaned closer. Yes, her eyes were black but there *was* a hint of purple when the pinkish light reflected in a certain way. "Your eyes remind me of ripe blackberries. Your name fits you, Berry Cortabona."

"That's what my mother used to say, I've been told." So, Berry reflected, he knew the nightwatchmen were called Charleys. He must not be a stranger to New Orleans, but his French sounded more American than Creole. She was not surprised that she had never seen him before, not when, as she had heard recently, some one hundred thousand people lived within the boundaries of the capital of Louisiana, making it the fourth largest city in the nation.

The way Jason's dark eyes studied her face sent ripples down Berry's spine. She imagined he might be seeing her as far more than a mere girl with only swelling buds for breasts. Who would have believed anyone would think of her as an angel of mercy? Aunt Maddy would have laughed.

Jason Premont was so handsome close up that Berry could understand why a married woman might choose to entertain him in her bedroom. He still stood with his back to the brick fence and was now holding his hands in front of him, apparently surprised to see that bleeding, jagged wounds marred his palms. Was he aware that his brown hair tumbled in profusion around his face and neck? "Don't you have a handkerchief?" Berry asked.

"Yes, but I can't think how I'll retrieve it from my pocket without smearing blood . . ." He frowned, obviously irritated. "Don't bother. The cuts aren't too bad. My townhouse is only a few blocks away."

"Which pocket?" Berry interrupted him to ask in a no-nonsense manner. She noted one of his wounds appeared quite deep and was oozing dark blood. Already she had eyed his beautifully tailored green satin waistcoat, unbuttoned as if donned in haste, and wondered if he had left his coat behind. Now she noticed he was not wearing the customary stock at the neck of his partially buttoned white shirt. The budding seamstress in her marked that the garment was expertly fashioned from the finest grade of cotton. In truth, even according to moderate standards, for one of his apparent upper class Jason Premont looked downright indecent, what with his chest almost bared and his hair tousled.

An angel of mercy would not allow minor details to keep her from ministering to the needy, Berry concluded with instant liking for her new title. It sounded grand and wonderfully grown-up, especially to one who hankered to rise to the rank of actress. "Do you want me to get your handkerchief or not?"

"No. I can manage." Gingerly he worked two fingers into his pocket and retrieved it.

Berry, who possessed both a practical and a fanciful side that constantly warred within, shrugged at what seemed inordinate pride on Jason's part and plucked the handkerchief from his grasp. She was eager to assume the role he had assigned her. Should she try for an impersonal sound, maybe like that of a nurse? From the utterance of her first word, she admitted that she had failed to harden the tone of her normally soft voice. "Let me bind your right hand first. The cut there seems the worst."

Berry went to work, thinking that Jason was most restrained and patient, behaving the way she had figured a gentleman would while having his wounds bound. Having grown up backstage at one of the most popular theaters in New Orleans and having peeped at the audiences, watched and listened to the callers rapping on the doors of the performers backstage, she knew that Jason's cultured French, easy manner, and well-tailored clothing bespoke gentry.

Without having to glance upward, Berry sensed that the rising sun was turning the clouds overhead into wondrous pink and gold masses and robbing the fading westward moon of its former glory. Just then she heard the Sunday call for matins chiming majestically from the steep bell towers of Saint Louis Cathedral. The familiar sound of the bells set her thoughts drifting into one of her favorite daydreams about growing up and falling in love.

Berry admitted to herself that she had been waiting to fall in love for a long time, or so it seemed to one not yet thirteen. Since she was a little girl, she had counted on finding a blessed kind of love, maybe the kind one discovered on a Sunday morning such as this. She wanted the kind of love that would lead to a home and children and a sense of belonging to someone who would love her forever in spite of her poor upbringing; someone who would never desert her as her father had deserted her mother. Until she discovered the man who could offer her that special kind of love, she had vowed never to marry.

Wouldn't it be wonderful, Berry reflected as she continued her ministrations there beside the brick wall on Dauphine Street, if within the next several years she could meet someone as darkly handsome and nice as Jason appeared to be? Of course, she could not expect the young man to come from the upper class. But she would expect him to have a better attitude toward women than Jason Premont did. Berry had already decided she could never consider marrying a man who skipped from the bedroom of one woman to that of another and did not honor marriage vows. Did such a man exist? She had plenty of time to find out, she reassured herself as she tied the top strip of handkerchief in a loose knot atop Jason's hand. Dollops of realism floated within the wealth of romance that flavored her being.

"There," Berry announced as she let go of Jason's right hand. He had kept his gaze fixed on what she was doing. Was he thinking about the Saturday night delights in Mrs. Soulé's bedroom? She squelched the urge to tease him as the theater folk joshed each other and maybe to ask if his night of passion had been worth the painful gashes. Often she had wished for a big brother and she had a feeling that one like Jason would have filled the bill perfectly. "I'll have you fixed up in a minute so you can be on your way."

Wanting to see Jason smile and flash his dimples again, Berry peeked up at him through her tangle of black eyelashes. His lean face looked forbidding, but she figured it was because he probably had a lot on his mind in addition to his smarting hands. "You must have many other walls to inspect before the sun gets up."

Jason grimaced a bit while Berry bandaged his other hand. "I do need to be on my way." He smiled at the girl in the shabby dress. The realization that she apparently possessed a tender heart warmed him. "Sunday is not the best time for a wall inspector to work, especially since I'll have to walk with my backside hidden."

"How bad is the tear in your trousers?"

"Bad enough that I can feel air."

"Let me take a peek."

He shot her an imperious look. "You're nothing but a child who has no business being out on the streets alone, much less talking to a strange man and asking to see his naked backside. I probably should yell for a Charley and have you taken home where you belong."

"I don't give a bloody damn about seeing anything you have, Jason Premont! Who are you to be talking down to me when you've just sneaked out of a married woman's bedroom?" Berry elevated her saucily shaped nose and shot him a fiery look, noticing that he stood several inches taller than her five feet and three inches. "Think of all I could report about you to the right people."

Berry told herself that she was relieved not to have a big brother like the suddenly arrogant Jason. He was not so special, after all. Come to think of it, what was he doing rutting after a married woman anyway—and one far older than he? Unless she missed her guess, he was no more than twenty and already a wealthy rake. She had seen plenty of his ilk hanging around backstage at the Théâtre d'Orléans trying to cajole favors from the prettiest actresses.

"Run along home, girl, before you get into trouble."

"I'm no stranger to trouble, and I've already learned it doesn't do any good to run from it."

Jason Premont, Berry's thoughts barreled on, was beginning to sound like everyone else who was trying to direct her life. Sometimes she thought that was one of the worst parts of having no parents or siblings—the way everyone, from Aunt Maddy down to the lowliest stagehand at the theater, chipped in with advice when she neither wanted nor needed it. Lately, she had been reading with new diligence the books that various theatrical folk lent her. Without verbal help from anyone, she was forming a plan for her life.

When Jason continued glaring at her and rammed his bandaged hands in his pockets, Berry huffed and said in a haughty tone borrowed from one of her favorite actresses, "I'm assistant to the wardrobe mistress at the Théâtre d'Orléans." There seemed no point in adding that the wardrobe mistress and seamstress was Maddy Quinette, her dead mother's only sister with whom she had always lived in two miserable rooms over a grocery store near the end of Dauphine Street. "If you weren't so cranky, I might be able to help you." Her snapping black eyes told of additional grievances held against him.

Tilting his head of unruly dark hair as if listening for sounds from behind the neighboring wall so recently scaled, Jason asked, "Are you on your way to the theater?"

"Yes. There's a matinee today and I promised Maddy I'd get to work early and start repairing some damaged costumes." She did not add that she nearly always worked early on Sundays so Maddy might sleep off her Saturday night gin and not come to work until afternoon. It seemed fitting, or so Maddy said, that Berry be free for the rest of the day.

Jason seemed to be reviewing his options and was finding them limited. Berry glanced up and down Dauphine Street, seeing nobody on the board walkways bordering both sides of the narrow dirt thoroughfare with its open, usually smelly sewers on both sides. A couple of dogs were chasing each other a few blocks down the way. Just then she saw a big black cat leap atop a brick wall across the street and meticulously follow a path across the shards of glass and upended nails.

"If you want," Berry said, "you can walk with me to the theater. We're not likely to meet anybody."

Jason bowed mockingly and with one bandaged hand gestured up the street. He had no wish to call further attention to himself by exposing his rear end to any others who might be out at the early hour. "Let's go."

Walking beside Jason on the banquette, Berry thought about how after work on Sundays she usually left behind the gay crowds strolling and shopping in the French Quarter. She preferred walking in the sedate Garden District across Canal Street. There she admired the beautiful homes of the Americans, set far back on block-sized lots along wide streets, some of which were already paved with handmade bricks or cobblestones used as ballast in some of the ships and discarded on the docks to make room in their holds for cargo. She often thought about how nice it was going to be when the city paved the main streets in the Vieux Carré.

On her walks, Berry also enjoyed seeing the homes in the American section that lay between Magazine Street and the Mississippi, especially the part around Annunciation Square. None of the stately residences—she had heard some had as many as twenty rooms!—resembled the walled-in, streetside homes of the Creoles, with their elaborately designed interior courtyards in the crowded French Quarter.

Some of the Creoles, those sometimes arrogant descendants of the early French and Spanish settlers who came to Louisiana before it became a part of the United States in 1803, had begun building large homes along the Esplanade. Many Creoles still owned and occupied the finer residences in the Vieux Carré. No matter that these old homes, many with intricately patterned wrought iron balconies and gateways set in brick walls, sat amidst the bustling commercial enterprises in the oldest section of the city; the clannish Creoles prized them highly.

Berry interrupted her musings when Jason's footsteps slowed, but when she saw that he was also lost in contemplation, she matched her steps to his and resumed her train of thought. She recognized that she had never felt the animosity that many French Quarter residents often expressed toward the "upstart" Americans. Since her mother had been born to second-generation French greengrocers in the Vieux Carré and her father had been a Spanish sailor, she proudly claimed her double heritage as a Creole. She found it easy to switch from speaking French to English, or vice versa, at the rounding of a corner or the opening of a door.

Drawing her shawl closer as she walked beside the still-silent Jason, Berry thought about how, on fair, temperate Sundays during the past two years, she had tucked a snack of bread, cheese and fruit in her pockets and begun wandering on the rutted roads passing in front of the mansions on the plantations fronting the Mississippi, both below and above New Orleans. Sometimes she followed Bayou Road that led to Lake Pontchartrain and admired the huge homes on her way to and from the enormous lake, with its enthralling, white-capped waves. How she loved watching the puffing engine of the Pontchartrain Railroad, as it carried people and freight from Elysian Fields out to the lake, and imagining what it might be like to ride in the open-sided passenger cars.

Gooseflesh still rose on the back of Berry's neck when she remembered the two or three times she had paused on Bayou Road and gazed in awe at the grove of moss-festooned oaks on the Louis Allard Plantation that had become infamous as the Oaks because of the numerous duels fought there. More than once she had seen groups of men on horseback in the area and had hidden in the underbrush for fear they might resent a girl seeing their faces and turn her over to the authorities. One time Berry had seen a cart carrying a tarp-covered form and, after making the sign of the cross, had shivered at the mysterious ways of men who apparently believed swords and pistols could settle disagreements.

Berry recognized that what fascinated her about the sights she saw on Sundays was more than the outward beauty of the lovely homes and their well-kept grounds. Her views of men, women, and children gathered on the verandas or underneath the moss-draped oak trees on the green lawns were what set her heart singing. To her way of thinking, such smiling family groups—handsome carriages sitting on the spacious driveways hinted of callers dropping by to partake in the Sunday gatherings—represented the blessed kind of love she dreamed of finding for herself. Not that finding it in such grand settings ever entered her mind; in fact, she found it disconcerting that she never could envision physical details in her dream—neither the man nor the background was ever clearly delineated.

Berry pulled her thoughts to the present and angled a sideways glance at her long-legged companion. What occupied his mind as they walked at dawn along the banquettes edging the narrow streets?

Ever since his escape over the wall, Jason had begun to regret his foolhardiness in accepting Mrs. Soulé's whispered invitation to come to her home after the party they both were attending. What was done, was done. He chalked up the rather sordid events of the Saturday evening as experience that a twenty-year-old man needed—or, he added with sobering hindsight, maybe deserved. "We're almost there, angel."

"Berry," she corrected him as they turned onto Orleans Street. She no longer favored his title for her, not when his manner implied mockery. "My name is Berry Cortabona."

"Isn't Cortabona a Spanish name?"

"What if it is? Yours is French or American, isn't it?"

"Both, I guess. It's just that I sometimes forget how many Spaniards live in New Orleans and speak French. Is your home around here? What does your father do?"

Berry considered spinning one of her lies about her sailor father who, during a three months' stay of his ship in port for repairs, had married her mother, and then had sailed off without ever coming back. Why not? Everyone at the theater had always told her she had a flair for the dramatic— but a voice too soft and feminine ever to project beyond the first four rows. She intended to prove them wrong about the latter.

"My father's a wealthy nobleman who returned to his hacienda in Spain. My mother died soon after I was born. He never came back after he learned about her death." When Jason looked down at her with apparent disbelief, taking in her shoddy clothing and shoes, she gestured in what she assumed was a regal manner and went on airily, "My grandparents loved me so much that they never told him I was alive, for fear he might send for me. Have you never heard of Count Cortabona?"

"Can't say as I have," he responded, amused in spite of himself, "but then, I stay in New Orleans only briefly."

Rolling her eyes and grinning up at him, Berry became herself again and replied, "It's easy to see why you might have to cut your stay short."

"Watch your tongue, little girl."

Berry felt herself stiffen at the derogatory term. Would she never grow up and be treated with respect? To hide her agitation, she retied the ends of her pink scarf underneath her chin and maintained a studied aloofness until they reached the Théâtre d'Orléans on Orleans Street between Bourbon and Royal.

After fishing fruitlessly in her skirt pockets for her key to the stage door opening on the alley, Berry muttered, "Bedamned! I must have left the blasted key at home."

"Don't fret. I'll make it to my townhouse."

"I need to get inside to work, anyway," she remarked while eyeing the drain pipe next to the door. She fixed him with a threatening look. "Promise you'll not gawk, or I'll have to have a curse put on you. I'm friends with a hoodoo queen."

Although he thought himself prepared for anything from this brash girl, Jason smothered a gasp when she brought the back edges of her long skirt up between her legs, tucked the ends into her waistband and began to shinny up a drainpipe to the roof from the banquette on which he stood. He reached to stop her, but too late; she was already clinging to the pipe like a nimble monkey holding on to a flagpole. "Good Lord, girl! You're going to fall and break your neck and get us both arrested."

Ignoring him from her lofty position, Berry pushed with one hand against the small glass partition above the door until it swung inward. Jason stared, open-mouthed, while Berry, as if she had entered the theater by that route before, swung a leg over the transom. Momentarily balancing herself with her hands on the outer frame, she then brought over her other leg from where it had gripped the drainpipe and dropped out of sight inside the theater.

Before Jason could decide whether or not to dash away from what seemed certain trouble, he heard the scrape of a key in the lock and watched the door swing open. Berry Cortabona, he reflected as she stuck her head around the door and grinned, was about the damnedest girl he had ever run into. For a moment, he felt her free spirit calling to his and was tempted to return her grin, but decided it best not to encourage her. He sent her a disapproving stare. Somebody should take her in hand. Maybe the part about her not having a father around was true. Though she was indeed devilish, he discarded his earlier thought that Berry was anybody's little sister. "Are you sure you know what you're doing?"

"A lot surer than you were when you were climbing over Mr. Soulé's wall," Berry retorted.

She motioned for him to follow her down the darkened hallway to the last room on the alley side, wondering what he thought of the musty backstage smells of greasepaint, sweat, and smoke. After striking steel against flint and lighting a lantern to add to the meager light available from the dirty little window set up high, she gestured toward the paneled screen standing in the corner of the wardrobe room. "Take off your trousers and I'll stitch up that tear."

"You're very kind, Berry, to help me out this way," Jason told her after she took his trousers from where he had tossed them across the top of the screen, which was obviously a shield for theatrical folk changing costumes. He stayed behind the shoulder-high contraption and watched her while she sewed. "I'm much indebted to you."

"You didn't have to give me this eagle, you know." From where she sat in front of a worktable piled high with yard goods and small boxes of sewing supplies, Berry plied her needle with accuracy and speed. The ten-dollar gold piece kept reflecting light from the lantern and tantalizing her with all it could buy.

First, Berry decided, she would insist Maddy go to the doctor and get new medicine for her persistent cough. The soles of Maddy's shoes were no more than multiple paddings of old newspapers; she would buy her a new pair. There would be enough left over to put aside for use when slow weeks at the box office delayed Maddy's pay envelope. She felt good all over. "I didn't offer to help you for the pay."

"I know, but I wanted to reward you. I'm glad you finally accepted it." Was she, perhaps, looking secretly pleased because she was envisioning the trinkets and baubles the eagle could buy? "Spend it on something to bring you pleasure."

"Thank you. I will. You said you don't live in New Orleans all of the time."

"No, I attend college in Virginia and will leave tomorrow to resume my studies. I came home to visit family and celebrate Mardi Gras. I grew up about fifty miles west of here near Calion in Saint Christopher Parish."

Sooner than he had thought possible, Jason was tucking his shirt into his repaired trousers. From over the top of the screen, he watched Berry shed her thimble and put away the needle and thread. Daylight was now poking through the soiled little window. In profile, she looked more grown-up than he figured she could be. Someday she was going to be a beautiful woman. Spirited and unorthodox in her manner and likely not a member of Spanish nobility, as she had bragged, but nobly beautiful in her own way. How could she not be with her black eyes and their unique tints of purple, her remarkably smooth skin, and her finely shaped features?

Jason could tell from the long fall of hair tumbling from underneath her pink scarf that it was as black as midnight. Not knowing much about theatrical folk, he wondered if the feisty girl with the apparently enormous heart would find happiness as she grew into womanhood. He found himself hoping she would.

He noted the way Berry's full lips met—the top one was not quite as full as the lower; it added a provocative curve to her profile. For some reason, the sight of her pink mouth with its uptilted corner made him think of her as terribly vulnerable—he who at twenty never before had given much thought to the vulnerability of anyone other than himself. He turned toward the door. "You'll be headmistress of the costumes one day, unless I miss my guess."

"You're missing it, then," she replied in her soft drawl.

With a quick, flashing smile, she faced him, then rose and stood with her back toward the worktable. "I'm going to be an actress."

He grinned as he had done when she had told him her father was a nobleman, then bowed slightly from the waist. If beauty, spirit, and quicksilver moods were the only requirements, Jason reflected, the girl might make it. Even he knew, though, that actresses must possess forceful voices. Berry's was like warm honey. "I wish you good fortune in all you attempt. Perhaps I'll be able to help you out someday. Goodbye, Berry Cortabona. I don't think I'll ever forget you."

Berry was delighted to have gained one more view of his dimples. She doted on scenes with happy endings. "Goodbye to you." Despite his being a rake and the glaring chasm between her place in life and his, he was handsome and easy to talk with, and she realized that she liked him. "Maybe I won't forget you, either, Jason Premont."

CHAPTER

*

Two

For the greater part of the next two years, Berry continued spending her weekdays as a day student in the nearby Ursuline Convent and her weekends and evenings as assistant to Aunt Maddy. Then without warning the spring before Berry turned fifteen, Maddy's persistent cough grew worse and forced her to bed for days at a time.

Berry stayed out of school and transported costumes back and forth from the theater, doing as much of the work as she could. Even so, Henry Zimpel, acting manager of the Théâtre d'Orléans, complained and withheld large portions from their pay envelopes. The coins left over from Jason Premont's generous reward did not last long.

The drastic change in finances forced the girl to question what would happen if her frail aunt never recovered enough to work fulltime again as wardrobe mistress. Berry refused to dwell upon what might happen if Maddy never recovered. The possibility of not having a place to live or a guaranteed

18

position at the theater, even at half pay, was frightening, but just thinking about life without Maddy proved unbearable.

"I'm sorry that you were ill, Maddy, but I'm glad it made me see that I don't need to go back to school," Berry announced one morning soon after her fifteenth birthday.

"Oh? I guess that's why you've been making up those ridiculous excuses about not returning these past few weeks," Maddy said from where she sat in the kitchen of their small apartment, hemming a skirt for a neighbor before it was time to go to the theater. Her normally soft voice sharpened as she asked, "You're grown-up already, yes?"

"You've said that I've matured during your illness." Berry gained confidence from Maddy's reluctant but thoughtful nod. "I can already read better than most of my class, and what else do I need to become an actress?"

Not since her first years at the private girls' school had Berry confided her misery at being ostracized by her classmates who, for the most part, came from wealthy homes, where theatrical folk were scorned. Maddy had wept and blamed herself for not being able to provide as well for her beloved niece as her parents had for her and her sister. Now that Maddy appeared vastly improved and able to go to the theater, Berry decided that a smattering of truth might lend weight to her cause. "Actually, I don't like school or my classmates. I love the theater and I would much rather spend my time there. Just think of how much more help I can be if I'm around every day." When Maddy's pale face took on a brooding look, Berry sneaked in the point that led eventually to success. "And best of all, think of how much more you can teach me about sewing."

From that day on, life for the two in the apartment above the greengrocer's store near the end of Dauphine Street eased somewhat. Though Maddy's illness had sobered Berry deep inside, she once again indulged in dreaming about the sometimes delightful, sometimes painful, aspects of growing up. The February evening of Mardi Gras in 1838 found her musing about her future. Her sixteenth birthday was close enough for her to taste. Savor. Celebrate.

"Maddy, don't you think this Puck costume is perfect? I'll blend right in with all of the other revelers, won't I?" Berry asked as they made ready to leave the wardrobe room of the Théâtre d'Orléans after the evening's performance.

When Maddy seemed more intent on brushing the wrinkles from one of the finer costumes than on listening, Berry thought about how Henry Zimpel, the cigar-puffing acting manager of the theater, had stomped around after the curtain fell, having one of his temper tantrums. "Bedamned if I'll go through this again!" he had thundered. "If even so-called civilized people want to wander up and down the streets in ridiculous masks and costumes, then I'll never again open my doors on Mardi Gras. I can't operate with an almost empty house."

From outside, the festive noises of the celebrants of the last night of Carnival seemed to be calling to the spirited Berry. What, she wondered, could have Maddy so quiet and sitting so still beside the worktable? Had she not heard the question about a choice of costume? Maybe she was regretting having allowed Berry and some of the others backstage to borrow wigs and costumes for Mardi Gras. She probably feared the articles might become damaged, despite the reassurances from all that they would exercise care and pay for any permanent losses.

Under her breath, Berry declared with the passion of one who thought of little else nowadays but becoming grown-up and an actress, "Perfect! This costume is perfect."

Lifting her arm dramatically and watching her slender image in the full-length mirror propped against the wall, Berry mixed together some lines from *A Midsummer Night's Dream*, the play she had been reading recently, and intoned, "Truly I am 'that shrewd and knavish sprite call'd Robin Goodfellow . . . I am that merry wanderer of the night.'"

In the glow spilling out from the lantern hanging over the worktable, Berry spun around. She doffed her elfin cap of green satin and bowed to her silent audience of one in the grand, flourishing manner of a courtier to his queen. The tiny silver bells interspersed among the red and yellow feathers that trimmed the elongated peak of her cap jingled energetically as she returned her headgear to perch atop her head. Her thick, single braid fell forward across one shoulder, its silky blackness gleaming. "A kind word for the merry wanderer of the night, if your grace agrees that I am Puck."

"Yes," Maddy replied with a fond smile, "I believe you very well might be whatever you choose to be."

Maddy nibbled her bottom lip as she watched her niece gather up the borrowed little pots of paint and powder and take them over by the mirror. Not for the first time during the past few months, she thought of how the girl had no idea how beautiful she was, how alive and temptingly innocent. Sure, Berry appeared wise in matters of the street and the theater because Maddy had set out from the beginning to allow her to gain such knowledge. She knew that inside, much like Berry's mother who had died before her baby was a year old, the girl possessed a shining, dreamy innocence.

Why, Maddy reflected from where she sat watching Berry, there she was, primping and painting her face, for all the world as though she was preparing to play grown-up the way she had done backstage ever since she was a little girl. How many years had gone by since Berry had started accompanying her to her job as seamstress, then mistress of the wardrobe as well? Now Berry served as her capable assistant and should be drawing more than the pittance Henry Zimpel meted out.

The fear that the girl might waste herself on some handsome, undependable rogue, as she judged her mother had done, troubled Maddy more each year, especially now that her health was failing. Estelle Berrone, fourteen years younger than Maddy and almost as beautiful as her daughter had become, had not had Berry's benefits of mixing and mingling with all kinds of people, benefits Maddy had ensured even when she might have had doubts as to her wisdom in providing them.

Even at eighteen, Estelle, the pampered, younger daughter of a Creole greengrocer, had been no match for the handsome, devil-may-care Spanish sailor, Leon Cortabona. He had laid his black eyes on her leaving Saint Louis Cathedral one Sunday morning while he idled in the Place d'Armes and had come courting that same afternoon. Within a month he was strolling down the steps of the cathedral with Estelle on his arm as his bride.

The way Maddy saw it, Estelle had begun dying of a broken heart after the dashing, black-eyed Leon sailed away when his ship was repaired. He never returned, never sent as much as a note. Although the doctors had told Maddy that her parents as well as Estelle had died from a mysterious fever as had many families in the French Quarter that summer, Maddy believed her sister had just lost her will to live.

A childless widow in her thirties by then, Maddy had lovingly devoted herself to rearing her niece in the manner she would have chosen for a child of her own. When she could not run her parents' produce store and tend to Berry as she wished, she sold it, retaining lifetime use of two small rooms over the store. Afterward, she was unable to provide the two of them with luxuries, but they had managed—until Maddy's cough appeared and reduced her capacity for work.

All Maddy's forty-eight years showed in the fine lines of her still-pretty face when a flourish from a trumpet outside jerked her back to the moment. "Berry, I'm beginning to doubt the wisdom of giving in to you on this matter of going out this evening. I know you sometimes sneak off after I've gone to sleep, but you've always heeded my warning about going out during Carnival."

Tossing her long braid impatiently, for she did not like hearing about the ways she sometimes worried her beloved aunt, Berry hastened to console her. "Ebon promised he'll stay with me every minute and see me to our door soon after midnight. After all, he's sixteen already.''

''I know, but unless the rains return, that mob out there won't be staggering off the streets any time soon. Some of them likely have already forgotten that Ash Wednesday follows Fat Tuesday and that Carnival is supposed to end at midnight. Haven't they had parties enough? From what I've been reading in *L'Abeille*, there must have been a thousand parties held all over town since Twelfth Night. Henry said the *Daily Picayune* reports a large number, too. It seems the Americans are beginning to favor Carnival as much as the Creoles.''

Berry spoke up defensively, though not harshly. ''As you're always telling me, don't be looking a gift horse in the mouth. Why, you and I made almost as much money sewing costumes for the rich American ladies and gents as we've made here at the theater.'' The thumb of Berry's right hand rubbed against the pads of her index and third fingers, where pricks from her needle over the past busy months formed little rough patches of skin. Would her own knuckles and fingers grow thick and gnarled like Maddy's if she continued to spend long hours hunched over her sewing? And would coughing spells leave her breathless and spent? Bedridden?

As if money were of little consequence, Maddy sniffed and elevated her fine French nose to a loftier angle. ''I never have condoned these Mardi Gras celebrations getting bigger and wilder each year. If you ask me, the city council was wrong to give its blessing this year for all those masqueraders on horseback and in carriages to parade through the main streets this afternoon. They would be wise to rule it out for the future and go back to outlawing masking in the streets. When people up to no good can hide behind a mask, they tend to become more daring. It's a pity tonight's rain didn't last long enough to dampen spirits and send everybody home.''

Berry leaned closer to the mirror and applied some more

kohl around her widely spaced eyes, then stepped back to admire the heavier black lines now outlining them. Wondering if the glow from the lantern might not be lending her face an added look of mystery, she shivered with excitement at being nearly sixteen and about to take part in her first Mardi Gras celebration.

Never before had Carnival appeared so inviting! Never before had it taken on such grand proportions, either, with a planned parade that afternoon and the blessings of the mayor and the councilmen. From outside Berry heard the banging of a drum, followed by raucous laughing and singing.

Maddy went on, her tone becoming increasingly aggrieved. "Back when I was a girl and Louisiana went from under the Spanish flag to the French for a few years, people celebrated Mardi Gras, but it seems to me that they did it without so much noise and disruption."

"Maybe because there weren't nearly as many people living in New Orleans then," Berry replied. "The French Quarter has stayed the same size and there's not enough room for so many extra people."

Without acknowledging the girl's sensible supposition, Maddy continued. "After the Americans came in 1803, they soon outlawed wearing masks and dancing in the streets. It wasn't till about ten years ago that authorities gave in to petitions and allowed Mardi Gras balls and street celebrations to resume. Each year it seems to get worse. I've never seen nor heard such a hubbub as the parade made, not to mention the racket coming from all those rowdy people following along behind. Why, the merchants had to shut their doors."

"Maybe they closed because they were in the parade," Berry rejoined softly. She reached for the container of rouge that Camille Hayes, her favorite among the theater's stock actresses, had lent her. Daringly, she brushed a round smear on each high cheekbone. Cocking her head this way and then that way before making up her mind, she grinned and daubed a lighter smear of carmine on the end of her nose.

Maddy frowned and shifted around on her straight chair. "I still can't believe there were so many men dressed up like women and acting like harlots. I can see why they wore full-faced masks to keep from being recognized."

"Oh, but all of them seemed to be having such a grand time, didn't they?" Berry enthused. She whirled around on the toes of her soft leather boots and clasped her hands together at the memory of what she had seen of the parade that afternoon before it was time to step inside the theater and help with the costumes for the evening's performance. "What harm can there be in wearing a mask and celebrating folly on the last night before Lent? I could just *feel* the excitement reaching out and touching me!"

"That's what worries me about you. You rely too much on what you call your *feeling*." Maddy's stooped shoulders sagged a bit more as a fit of coughing seized her.

"But, Maddy, you have to admit I'm seldom wrong. I always have my dagger"—she patted her loose blouse where her holster hung from a belt at her waist—"and I don't hunt for trouble, truly. With Ebon along—"

"I like Ebon Stringer all right, but he's not much bigger than you. He doesn't seem ambitious to be more than an errand boy, though. I still find it strange that he just up and appeared here last summer from Natchez and wangled a job out of that skinflint, Henry Zimpel." Maddy's gaze kept returning to Berry's long, shapely legs in their formfitting breeches. "How do you know Ebon could protect you if need be? What if some rascal finds out what's underneath that boyish costume?"

"Leonidas says he'll escort Camille and let us tag along."

Maddy sniffed and sat up straighter. "Leonidas Latrobe is pushing thirty and hot after anything in skirts. That was a sorry day last year when that traveling troupe dumped him on us here. He's far more interested in sleeping with rich wives around town than in improving his acting. I hear he takes money for escorting them to fancy balls while their husbands are out of town or indisposed. Camille Hayes is far too good to be wasting her time in stock here, or on Leo either.''

Maddy pushed back her straggling gray hair with a workworn hand and went on. "I've seen the way he sometimes eyes you. Watch out for sly ones like Leo with their pretty faces and perfumed breaths. They can love only themselves.''

"I've decided I'll not become interested in men that way for a long time." Berry laughed as she pirouetted and practiced a dramatic bow before the long mirror. "There seem to be so few concerned about anything but their own pleasures.''

"Funny," Maddy said with a thin smile, "you could talk of little else last year but falling in love. You had a crush on every leading man treading the boards.''

As she watched Berry, Maddy mused that the choreographer down from the East last fall was right. Berry does have the natural grace of a dancer. Where had she found her strange notions? Maybe she should not have been allowed quite so much freedom. Lately, she had begun spending much of her free time with Camille, who was nice, but probably ten years older. "I thought all young people dreamed about someday finding love and marriage," Maddy remarked.

"I did, as a child." Berry sighed dramatically, so lost in her theatrics that she missed the amused smile on her aunt's face. "Maybe I don't need a man to take care of me. You've managed quite well for the both of us. Camille and most of the other actresses aren't married, and they seem to get along.''

Worriedly, Maddy surveyed the girl in her tight green breeches and loose overblouse that hung well below her thighs. "Did you bind your breasts the way I suggested? I don't want anybody trying to run his hands—''

Berry laughed and jerked up her overblouse, revealing the wide strips of white material crisscrossing her chest and back like a giant bandage. "Stop worrying, will you? You can see I look as flat as I was two years ago."

"You're probably thinking that I sound like some old grouchy granny," Maddy said, pleased that her niece had taken her advice. With Berry, she never knew what to expect.

"The thought has crossed my mind," Berry retorted flippantly, meeting the frail woman's expressive eyes in the mirror and grinning.

"It's just that I love you so. I want you to be happy but safe. I've always known I'll have to let go of you one of these days, but—"

"You're a darling!" Berry rushed to throw her arms around the older woman and plant kisses on both her wasted cheeks. "I love you, too, and where would I be if you didn't care for me so much? Ebon says we'll walk you home first so the crowd won't crush you."

Berry dashed over to where both new and used costumes hung from two wires stretching across one end of the long, narrow room. The odors of greasepaint, perfume, and stale perspiration seemed to increase with each step she took. "There's a bottle of gin that Leo put here for you so you'll have something to share with Sergeant Harrigan if he drops by to toast the holiday." Berry emerged from behind a welter of musty smelling skirts and hurried back to where the frail woman sat. "Isn't Leo a thoughtful man?"

"Humph!" Maddy took the small bottle from Berry, noting right off that the label indicated high quality spirits. Maybe Dan Harrigan would manage to stretch his night duty as far as Dauphine and share a drink with her. He and his fellow policemen were expecting a hectic night; still—

A spirited knock on the door sounded. Ebon Stringer obeyed Berry's gay summons to enter, his smooth face blushing when both Berry and Maddy praised his costume.

"Do you really think I'll pass as a troubadour?" he asked in his boyish voice that contained a mere trace of bass. Holding out his lute with one hand, he swiveled around and showed his medieval-style black leggings below a tunic of purple belted with a yellow sash that matched the demimask hanging from a string around his neck. He nearly lost his balance when his purple slippers with their pointed toes crossed as he completed his turn. "I found this old lute at the pawnbroker's but I can't play a blasted thing on it."

"You look magnificent!" Berry said, "I thought you'd never get your chores done and come for us."

Berry tied her black demi-mask over her eyes and upper face, watching in the mirror while Ebon talked with her aunt. Maddy had been right. He was slight and not much taller than she. With her full breasts bound as they were and their costumes similar, they could almost pass for twins.

"We'll look like two boys out on the town," she told him as she laid aside her cap and began experimenting with coiling her braid at her crown and securing it with long hatpins so that she could tuck it under her Robin Hood hat.

Something about the way Ebon's red curls and dark eyes shone in the lantern light as he coaxed Maddy into a mellow mood reminded Berry of what he had told her in confidence not long ago about his growing up in the Chanticleer, a huge building serving as both hotel and whorehouse in Natchez-Under-the-Hill. The women who had worked alongside his mother before she died during his fourth year had looked after him. When Ebon grew older, they not only tutored him in reading and writing but also had secured him a job at the Chanticleer as flunky. Everyone tipped him for running their errands and treated him well, especially a woman called Flo.

What seemed horribly tragic to Berry was Ebon's more recent account of having visited last year with Flo in her room during one of her many bouts with lung fever. When a man's gruff voice demanded she let him in, Flo had ordered Ebon to hide underneath her bed. Ebon had heard him say he was planning on catching a riverboat for New Orleans at midnight. The man, evidently staying at the hotel and on his way to or from the bathroom down the hall, wore a dark robe and was barefooted. During an argument about money, one of Flo's coughing spasms seized her.

When all became eerily quiet that Saturday evening, Ebon had confided in a sorrowing voice to Berry, he watched the stranger kneel and fumble with the corners of the worn rug in front of Flo's dresser until he discovered the loose plank under which she kept her valuables hidden. The man took the little packet and limped from the silent room.

Ebon admitted to the sympathetic Berry that he was stricken with grief and fear when he found Flo smothered underneath her pillow. He knew little about her killer except that he seemed to be a big man with sparse, dark hair, a gravelly voice, and a slight limp. Berry could not forget the reason the man limped. The big toe of his left foot appeared to have been chopped off.

Berry made a final adjustment to the braid now coiled atop her head, thinking that Ebon had been wise—and terribly brave—to escape from Natchez soon after the funeral and hide on a steamboat headed for New Orleans. He had wanted to report what he knew to the police, but the women at the Chanticleer had discouraged him, pointing out that he was only a boy and had no proof.

Ebon's account of having known Henry Zimpel from his stays at the Chanticleer several times during the last few years explained why Henry had taken a chance on hiring him as errand boy and doorkeeper at the theater. Berry figured Henry probably was not eager for the mayor or his councilmen friends, with whom he did frequent business, to learn about his visits up the Mississippi. If there was a spot vying with the seamy sections of the French Quarter for the title of the Capital of Sin, it likely would be Natchez-Under-the-Hill.

Satisfied that the hatpins would keep her braid hidden underneath her cap, Berry sidetracked thoughts about her friend and aimed new ones toward the evening lying ahead. Soon they were dousing the lantern and stepping into the street.

"I thought Camille and Leonidas were going to be with

you two during your wanderings," Maddy said when they reached her door at the top of a rickety staircase. "The rowdy groups we saw were so busy frolicking, they didn't seem even to notice the muddy streets."

"Nobody paid us the least bit of attention, either," Berry assured her.

"Probably because they saw this gray head with you." The nearest street light hung a few buildings away and offered poor light as Maddy searched in her reticule for her key. After lifting out the pint of gin, she located it. "One of those men dressed like a harlot jumped out of the way in a hurry when he thought I was going to step on his foot. No doubt somebody had done more than step on his big toe, what with it being missing. It seems to me he could have found something besides sandals to wear. He and his two 'lady' friends had no business taking up the entire banquette that way."

Berry and Ebon exchanged startled looks.

"I didn't see a man without a big toe," Berry said. "Where did you see him?"

"What was he wearing?" Ebon asked before Maddy had time to answer.

"Lord's sakes," Maddy replied while fitting her key in the lock, "I don't know where I saw him. He was wearing a full mask with those simpering, painted lips, like all those men dressed like women. Seems like he had on a good quality red wig that he kept jerking to keep down, but I saw lots of wigs. Even sourpuss Henry said he might lend some to friends. What could I say, with him being the boss and all?"

Maddy frowned for a moment before going on. "I do recall the man was wearing some mighty pretty rings. On one of his little fingers was a big rectangular emerald that I vow looked real in the streetlight. I expect it was fake, though."

"Do you remember where we met him?" Berry asked.

"No." Maddy fixed the pair with a penetrating gaze in

the faint light. She fought down the impulse to ask what they were up to. "What happened to your plans to be with Camille and Leonidas?"

Ebon explained, his voice pitched higher than normal, "Camille and Leo left earlier, since I had to stay and clean up. They're expecting us to meet them at Shaughnessy's after we get you safely home."

Determined not to pour additional sour wine onto Berry's champagne mood, Maddy hugged the two young people and went inside.

"That may be the man who killed your friend, Flo," Berry said in a low voice to Ebon once they crossed over to Bourbon Street and were hurrying toward Shaughnessy's near Canal. The saloons and restaurants they passed overflowed with boisterous, masked revelers. Music and song blaring out from one crowded place of business scarcely faded before their notes clashed jarringly with more coming from another down the narrow street. Many of the two- and three-story buildings sported balconies filled with party goers making their own private merriment. "What are you going to do?"

"What can I do?" He took her arm so they could both dodge a handful of orange peelings being tossed from one of the balconies. "There might be other men around who lack a big toe. Anyway, who's going to believe anything I say—unless I could prove that might be Flo's ring he's wearing."

"Did she have one like Maddy described?"

Looking like two boys on a lark, they walked with their heads close together so as to converse over the din.

"She had a rectangular emerald as big as the top of her finger. It looked grander than anything anybody else at the Chanticleer had. She didn't wear it often. Once when she claimed she was having the mulligrubs, she showed it to me and pointed out the initials inside, F.J.M. She said it came from her husband, Diamond Maroney, who once was a big time gambler on the riverboats."

"What happened to him?"

"One of the other women told me she'd heard he got sent to prison and died there."

For a person expecting the evening to be one of gaiety, Berry confessed even she was feeling sadder by the moment, as they began meeting larger groups of masked, vociferous party goers. She was aware that Ebon seemed to be scrutinizing the groups of men dressed in feminine finery as carefully as she was. Not a single man wore sandals, though several were tall and sported wigs. "If we were to see the man with only one big toe, what could we do?"

"Nothing," Ebon replied tersely, reaching to hold her hand when a frolicsome party coming down the banquette threatened to separate them. The tipsy members of the group were trying to march in unison to the rhythm of the drum one of them beat upon with deafening impreciseness. A pack of dogs trailed along after the impromptu parade, cavorting and barking. "I promised Maddy to take care of you, not to let you get in trouble."

"If we were to see him, though, we could create some kind of diversion and you could slip the ring off his little finger and —"

"Hush up!" Ebon hissed as he slowed and jerked her from the banquette teeming with people to stand with him in the muddy but less-congested street. From a balcony down the way, a woman's scream pierced the jovial sounds, then ceased as if somebody had caught the sound inside a pan while it was still climbing and slapped a lid over it. Ebon dropped Berry's hand and began strumming on his battered lute. As he had hoped, nobody appeared interested in them.

"We're going to get muddy out here," Berry complained, glancing down at the black, well-tracked muck. The light spilling from the open doors of saloons on both sides of the street traced rainbow colors on the numerous oily patches.

Then her gaze followed Ebon's. Inside one of the saloons a trio of masked men grotesquely disguised as harlots leaned against the bar and seemed engrossed in listening to a woman singing with a band in the back of the room. One had two coconuts tied strategically around his chest and his shirt opened back to reveal his hairy, brown "breasts." He wore a red wig, the hair long and apparently of fine quality.

"I can't see his feet," Berry whispered, after the woman's song ended and applause, cheers, and whistles floated out into the street. "That looks like a green ring on his right little finger. Can you see it? Does it look like Flo's?"

Ebon nodded. He swallowed, as if his throat might be too full to allow speech.

"Why don't you go up to him and pretend to serenade him," Berry suggested, "and I'll pretend to flirt with him and get him to put his right arm around me and—"

"Are you out of your mind? If that's the man without a toe, then he's a killer. He'd just as soon kill you or me as Flo."

"But look at him," Berry insisted. An unsteady couple dressed as gorillas were bearing down on them and she snatched Ebon and herself to safety. "He's waving his arms around as if he's drunk. We can't see very well with our partial masks, but he can see even less because his covers his entire face and fits looser than ours."

"He can jerk off his mask if you start stealing his jewelry. You couldn't just take the emerald or he might figure out we were more than pranksters."

"Before he can remove his mask, he'll have to take off his wig."

Ebon considered her remarks. "Then he would yell for a Charley or a policeman."

"Not if he's who you think he is." Berry entertained the notion that the end always justified the means, and she cared deeply for her friend and his heartache over what had happened to Flo. "If that man is the killer, we can't stand by and do nothing. I'm going in there."

Ebon reached to grab her arm, but she escaped from him into a cluster of people entering the already-crowded saloon and pushed her way to stand near the man wearing the "coconut titties" and the red wig. Her scalp prickled when she saw he was wearing sandals. His left foot had no big toe!

Instantly Ebon appeared by her side, tripping over the long toes of his slippers, but managing to give the effect of one stupefied by alcohol. "A song, fair lady," he lisped to the masker in the red wig. "A song for the loveliest of creatures." His fingers fumbled over the strings of his lute and he made up a ditty about the joys of Fat Tuesday and the sights in the Vieux Carré.

Berry took advantage of the big man's interest in Ebon's performance and sidled up to him, touching his hairless chest with her forefinger, then running her hand down his shirted arm when the contact with his flesh made her skin crawl. Her heart was hammering. Trying to sound like a Puck, she deepened her soft voice as much as possible and said, "My, but you're an eyeful." The masker leaned closer to hear over the lute and Ebon's falsetto.

Relieved to note that the man's two companions were placing a new order with the bartender, Berry saw that showy rings adorned the fingers of both hands. All were unusual, but especially the emerald ring. She brought the man's right hand up near her lips and kissed the space right above it, then reached for his left and sent him what she hoped was a dazzling smile. She fought down the repulsive thought that the tops of his hands felt as hairy as the lewdly placed coconuts looked.

Never releasing the man's right hand completely or lessening her smile, Berry leaned closer and sent nimble fingers to slip the emerald ring off his little finger into her palm, then removed the one on his next finger. She managed to take one from another finger, too, before sensing his stiffening body. She darted toward the street.

"What the hell is going on!" the man roared when the boyish, green-clad masker made off with more than one of his rings. Before the words died, he was howling in pain. The red-haired troubadour had stepped on his stump of a toe and slung the fat bottom of his lute into his belly before turning and dashing after the fleeing figure.

The boy called over his shoulder, "I'll catch the rascal! Wait here!"

A late-arriving crowd of costumed revelers jammed the entry to the saloon, giving first Berry and then Ebon head starts on the stunned man with only one big toe. Ebon had trouble running on the muddy streets in his over-sized slippers but Berry, the rings tucked inside a pocket of her overblouse, made good time. Though the banquettes still held noisy revelers, nobody showed interest in anything but his companions. Chaos seemed to reign throughout the entire French Quarter and all present seemed willing subjects.

Down the way, Berry spotted a side street with noticeably fewer people on it and raced down it. For a moment she lost her sense of direction and almost panicked. Some of the lamps hanging from the corner buildings no longer gave off light. Ebon was not in sight. Which way to Shaughnessy's?

Blindly Berry rounded an unlighted corner and ran smack dab into a well-dressed party of six just stepping off the banquette into the street. She yelled "Look out!" as she took two of the masked revelers, one male and one female, walking close together, down into the mud with her.

"What in—!" came a breathy, masculine voice. Berry realized she must have hit the man and woman with almost equal force and that after a painful roll in the muck by all three, she had ended up lying across a man wearing a costume that had once been white satin. He gripped her wrists, bringing pain and a dollop of anger. "Have you"—he paused to suck in air—"no respect for decent people?"

Some other members of the group were bent over the woman who was lying in the street a few feet away and proclaiming in between sobs, "My costume is ruined! Call the police! Just wait till Father hears of this."

"Don't carry on so," one of the men kneeling beside the woman said loud enough for Berry to hear. "You aren't hurt, are you?'' He turned his head toward the other two lying in the mud and addressed his next remarks to the man with Berry. "Viola's all right, just mad and ruffled. Are you two all right over there?''

"Yo!" replied the man Berry had landed on, his voice still sounding strangled from lack of sufficient breath.

Gasping for air herself, Berry dimly heard the angry woman snap, "Help me sit up! You're the most unfeeling brother a girl could ever have, Ashley Breton!''

The man Berry lay against shoved her aside by her wrists and struggled to sit up, glancing over to where the young woman he had been escorting seemed to be recovering with the help of their companions. Holding both Berry's wrists with one hand, he jerked off her mask and peered in the near darkness at the muddied face. "Look here, young fellow. What in blazes did you think you were doing?''

"I'm terribly sorry, but I called to you to look out,'' Berry retorted. By the saints! Did he think she ran into them on purpose? A shrilly talking crowd was gathering around on where the accident had taken place. From the corner of her eye she looked for Ebon. He was nowhere in sight. Her breathing would not slow down, no matter that she ordered it to. Her pulse seemed to think she was still running.

"You've ruined my costume as well as that of my companion.'' His tone revealed pique and a decided note of indignation.

"So what?" Berry countered, able to think of little but that the awful man in the red wig might have caught Ebon. How important could ruined costumes and wounded dignity be at a time like this? She realized she had lost her cap and tried to spot it. "Mine's ruined, too.''

Somebody had fetched a man wandering around with a torch, and light from the dancing flame began flickering over the sorry scene in the mud. Everybody seemed to be talking at once.

From where he still sat in the mud facing Berry, the man with the aggrieved voice ripped off his own demi-mask then and stared at her face, her widow's peak. He dropped both of his hands to his lap. "Is that you, Berry Cortabona?"

Berry turned her full attention to the man who until that moment had held her wrists captive and scolded her. Recognition flashed like a streak of lightning in a clouded midnight sky. Tears of joy stung her eyelids. "Oh, Jason! My friend and I are in the godawfullest pack of trouble. Can you help us?"

CHAPTER

*

Three

Surprised and disconcerted, Jason Premont reflected that the slight, formless girl sitting beside him was apparently still free-spirited. Looking into her eyes, where tears seemed ready to start, he said with reassurance, "I'll help if I can, Berry. Tell me about it."

He motioned to his friends still gathered around the loudly weeping Viola Breton that he would be with them soon and returned his full attention to Berry. At least two years, maybe three had passed since that Sunday morning when he had first met her. Though he had never asked her age, he guessed that by now she must be twelve or thirteen. He noticed with amusement that a thick braid, apparently once coiled atop her head, now lay askew. He was surprised anew to note that she had restrained her tears within those remembered purplish black eyes, now rimmed grotesquely by smears of kohl. Berry Cortabona was still a spunky little thing. Despite the smelly mud mixed with the outlandish makeup, she was even prettier. She appeared to be searching for words.

Feeling protective toward the girl who once had volunteered kindness, Jason returned her demi-mask. "I can't possibly help unless you tell me what kind of trouble you and your friend are in. And will you please explain what you are doing out alone on this wild night?"

Berry recovered her senses then; and in spite of the milling, chattering crowd gathered at the site of the accident, she spilled out the major part of her story while Jason helped her to her feet. While they searched for her cap and until they found it, he took advantage of the time alone with her to question her further.

A night watchman was standing with his lantern near Viola and her brothers. They obviously didn't need Jason's help. From the sharp edge to her clearly carrying voice, he knew she was setting the Charley straight on what happened. Viola, a beauty at seventeen, still acted the only role he had ever known her to play—the spoiled daughter of a doting Creole planter.

"Do you still have the rings you took from the man?'" Jason asked Berry.

She fished in her pocket. "Yes, they're still here."

"Maybe the way I can help you and your friend is to keep the stolen goods for you so if the man shows up and makes accusations, the Charley won't find anything on you."

Her lips pursed for just a second before she placed them in his outstretched hand. "All right, but I don't how good I'll be at lying."

He smiled at her candor, recalling that she had tried out a fib on him about her father being a Spanish nobleman. "Didn't you tell me that Sunday morning you were going to be an actress?"

She nodded, her long braid completing its fall and flopping to rest across her bound, shapeless chest. Somehow it comforted her further that he remembered. She liked seeing his dimples play in his cheeks. Did she imagine it or had his voice really become deeper, more resonant? Incredible as it seemed, Jason Premont had become even more handsome during the past three years.

"Maybe you should pretend you're playing a part in which you've done nothing wrong," Jason advised, half serious, half tongue-in-cheek. Her quick smile told him that she had read his wry humor. He held up the rings in the dim light before slipping them inside his pocket. "I'm no expert, but this emerald does look valuable."

They returned to the vociferous group standing around the officer. After anxiously searching for a glimpse of Ebon among the thinning crowd and failing, Berry stood back while Jason edged his way to the side of the angry, tearful young woman someone had called Viola.

"Oh, Jason, here you are at last," Viola Breton said peevishly in a tear-filled voice shrill enough to soar above the unceasing clamor coming from the revelers passing behind her on the main street.

The masked man with the torch still stood nearby, and its eerie light illuminated Viola's unmasked face, one that Berry could tell, despite its streaks of mud, was beautiful. She experienced a twinge of guilt for not feeling greater remorse over having caused the young woman's disheveled appearance.

Most of Viola's high-pitched denouncement of Jason reached Berry's ears. ". . . and I thought you had forgotten you were escorting me. I hope you didn't let that little culprit escape after you managed to get disentangled."

Berry watched Jason murmur something close to Viola's ear and put his arm around her shoulders. When Viola hid her face against his chest Berry wormed her way through the curious bystanders and leaned back against the wall of the corner building.

Berry reflected after recognizing the Charley with Jason's party as Barney Deavers, a good friend of Dan Harrigan, that she didn't mind seeing Jason showing affection for the pretty young woman. After all, he was nothing to Berry but a friend. The reason she was feeling tense and miserable was that she was fearful about Ebon and was still rattled from bumping into the couple and ending up sprawled in the mud. She tried not to think of how much it might cost to repay the theater for the damaged Puck costume or how disappointed Maddy was going to be about her latest escapade. Or how much work it would require to repair the outfit of the "merry wanderer of the night."

Berry confessed she felt neither merry nor like a wanderer. Where was Ebon?

An off-key blast from a bugle out on the main street sounded to Berry like a catcall. Feeling for and then discovering a hatpin still stuck in her braid, she managed to refasten her hair atop her head and put her cap back on, although mud now clung to its once jaunty tip of feathers and tiny bells. Their tinkling sounded muffled, defeated.

Barney Deavers detached himself from Jason's party of six, ordered the remaining onlookers to return to the main streets and approached Berry with his lantern in hand. "What do you have to say—" The night watchman stopped in midquestion; he leaned closer and continued sotto voce, "How did you manage to get in this mess? Your Aunt Maddy ain't gonna like this and neither is Sergeant Dan."

"I was streaking to meet some friends over on Bourbon when those people stepped out in front of me." Berry lifted her gaze to both of the darkened lamps hanging from the buildings on diagonal corners. "If the lamps hadn't gone out, maybe we wouldn't have collided."

Repositioning his cap on his head, the Charley wore a troubled look on his face. "The captain could get mighty curious about that. We're not working tonight in our usual twosomes, so I haven't made this round recently. I don't know why the lamps are out. What you say might be true, but this Miss Breton is furious. She wants you hauled to the calaboose on charges of assaulting her and damaging her clothing."

"Assaulting—!" Berry sputtered and set clenched fists on

her hips. "It was an accident, I tell you. Besides, my clothing is ruined, too."

A stealthy movement up the side street caught Berry's attention, and she squelched the urge to squeal for joy. Ebon was hurrying toward her, his lute bumping against his chest. As if he heard her silent message to keep his distance, he slowed to an amble and blended in with those still standing near the intersection. She asked Barney, "How could I know they were about to step into the street?"

Barney reached as if to pat Berry's shoulder, then seemed to think better of it and sent his thumb to hook over the belt of his uniform. "Don't be getting riled. I'll try smoothing this over, but her pa's Clark Breton, one of them rich planters living up the river. To make matters worse, the two gents who didn't get smashed are her brothers. They said Mr. Breton and the mayor are good friends."

"Officer," Jason called after conferring with his five companions, "since nobody is seriously harmed, we're not going to press charges." When Viola sent Berry a venomous look and seemed about to interrupt, he patted the pouting young woman's shoulder, then took several steps through the dispersing crowd and joined Berry and the night watchman. "Perhaps, officer, somebody was chasing the youngster—"

"No," Berry broke in to say. Clearly the man in the red wig was no longer in pursuit. She had no wish to mention Ebon and get him involved, now that he was safe and only a few yards away. She warned Jason with a sharp look. "I couldn't see well enough while running, and I apologize to these people for crashing into them and mussing their clothes. Couldn't you just let me go, officer?"

"If Mr. Premont and his party ain't gonna press charges," Barney replied with a secretive wink for Berry, "then I reckon I got no call to keep you." Gesturing toward the man with the torch and two or three other maskers who were still hanging around Viola, her brothers and the two young women with them, he called, "Get on with you, now! Get back to your horsing around. Everything here is settled."

Ebon came to Berry's side during the ensuing commotion, and she quickly introduced him to Jason. Jason eyed askance the slight figure with the red curly hair. Was the boy Berry's only escort on such a potentially dangerous evening? It was none of his business, yet . . .

"Thanks for helping Berry out," Ebon said, as he reached for her hand and enfolded it in his.

Curiously uneasy about the girl, Jason acknowledged thanks from both, then told her, "It appears you've eluded the man chasing you. I'll give you back the rings now."

"I'll take them," Ebon replied. "I'm responsible for all this."

Not until Berry nodded her agreement did Jason drop what he held into Ebon's outstretched palm. "Need I remind both of you that you're dealing with something that could be more dangerous than you realize?" When neither made a comment, Jason continued in big-brotherly fashion. "If I could help you, I would, but this isn't a matter for ordinary citizens. A man who'll kill once won't hesitate to kill again. Will you promise to go to the police and let them handle this, Berry?"

"No," she answered, visibly huffed at his sounding dictatorial and all-knowing. Did he think she was still a green girl?

Jason went on, annoyed that Berry had asked for his help and was now ignoring his advice. "You're both liable to end up getting hurt. Will you drop the entire matter?"

When Berry and Ebon made no promises even to do that, Jason had no recourse but to respond to the calls from his friends and rejoin them. Even after they found some sedan chairs a couple of blocks away to carry them to his townhouse on Chartres, Jason continued to ponder his inexplicable concern for the black-eyed girl named Berry Cortabona.

Much later, in his bedroom, Jason thought again about Berry and hoped that Ebon had escorted her safely home—

wherever that was. He realized that he knew next to nothing about the girl, except that he liked her and believed her story. The business about a possible killer and a valuable emerald ring sounded far too serious for a pair of youngsters to be attempting to resolve.

If he had not already booked passage weeks ago and was not set to sail the next morning for Seville—the first leg of a year-long trek abroad with the two Breton brothers—Jason would have called at the Théâtre d'Orléans tomorrow and inquired about Berry's well-being. She was not easy to dismiss. She lingered in his thoughts; and when he finally slept, she strolled through his dreams, laughing at his concern.

Berry and Ebon waited until Maddy and Henry Zimpel had vented their anger and disappointment over what had happened to the borrowed costumes before putting their heads together about solving the mystery of the man who lacked a big toe. During the first week after Mardi Gras, they found time one afternoon to talk privately on the back steps of the theater.

"What's this for?" Berry asked Ebon when he dropped two silver dollars in her lap.

"Your friend, Jason Premont, put them in my hand along with the rings. I figured he was trying to help you pay for your costume or something."

Berry fingered the coins. She had already forgiven Jason for his remarks about the foolhardiness of their scheme to prove No Toe had murdered Flo and stolen her ring. Maybe he did not feel the same loyalty to people he cared about as she did. Ebon needed her help. "Jason is the nicest man, except when he's preaching." She held out one coin toward Ebon. "You take one."

"No. I didn't fall in the mud and I didn't have to pay as much as you to get square with Mr. Zimpel. Anyway, the man is your friend, not mine. He acted as if he'd always known you."

With a faraway smile and a contemplative nod of her

head, Berry slipped both coins into the pocket of her worn, black skirt. "Jason is real gentry, but he doesn't act as if he thinks he's one bit better, does he?" When Ebon made no reply, she jumped to immediate matters. "Do you think old No Toe is looking for us?"

"Don't worry. Even if he is, he won't recognize you dressed as a young woman. You didn't look"—he averted his gaze from her full breasts thrusting against her white blouse—"at all like yourself that night."

"But you didn't even have on a hat. He's certain to recognize you. Ebon, you must be careful."

"I didn't take his rings, though. Besides, I yelled to him before I left that I was going to chase you down."

Already having learned that Ebon had taken off in a direction opposite her own in order to throw off the man pursuing her, Berry said, "You were brave to lead him in the wrong direction that night until he gave up. Now that you know the ring has Flo's initials in it, what can we do?"

"You're not going to do anything but keep quiet about the other night. I'll think of something."

"You shouldn't have told Maddy about it. She got terribly upset. I'll bet my Sunday ribbons she's already told Sergeant Harrigan everything. She said you ought to go to the police, as Jason did. Camille keeps dogging me to tell what's bothering me, but I can't, even if she is my best friend."

Ebon looked troubled until Berry added, "The sergeant has never blabbed about things Maddy tells him."

Somebody called for Ebon then and they hurried inside. Henry Zimpel stood outside his office talking with a tall man with thinning dark hair. Both Berry and Ebon were wise to Henry's custom of selling tickets for choice seats to members of the seedier side of French Quarter nightlife for resale at exorbitant prices. They exchanged looks that said a new customer must have been added.

"Ebon," Henry said, as Berry and he came close to where the two men stood beside the large wooden box on little wheels that was used to cart small props around, "I'd like you to meet Mr. Warren Maroney. He's new in town and wants to handle some of our extra tickets for us from time to time."

In the dim light of backstage, the tall stranger stared at Ebon, then narrowed his small eyes to peruse Berry for a moment before returning his full attention to the boy. "I swear I've seen this redheaded kid somewhere before."

Maroney? Cripes! Ebon was thinking along with Berry, the man must be kin to Flo's dead husband, Diamond Maroney.

Despite his shock, Ebon picked up on the remembered tones of the man's voice, those he had heard from underneath Flo's bed that night in the Chanticleer. Warren Maroney had never seen him except at Mardi Gras. Ebon's heart threatened to jump into his throat. Leaning with one hand resting across the top edge of the prop box as he was, the man did not appear threatening. Ebon said, "I run lots of errands for Mr. Zimpel, but I don't believe we've ever met."

Henry chuckled, then showed what he was holding in his hand. "Maybe you saw him during Carnival while he was sporting this wig. He was just now returning it to me." He held it toward Berry, saying, "You might as well take it on down to the wardrobe room."

Berry reached for the wig, but shock was robbing her fingers of strength and it slipped through them to the floor. Both Ebon and she stooped to retrieve the wig. They bumped heads and Berry lost her balance. The next thing she knew, Warren Maroney was yelping and trying to jump back from where she had somehow landed on his feet and legs.

Henry and Ebon tried to keep the apparently wounded man from tumbling backward into the deep prop box, but failed. The screech of the wheels against the board floor, coupled with the raised voices, brought Leonidas Latrobe and several other actors hurrying from dressing rooms.

His vexation at the mishap showing in his face, Henry

leaned over the edge of the box and held out both hands to his visitor. "Damn, but I'm sorry these kids were so clumsy! Let me give you a hand. Are you hurt?"

Soon Henry and a helpful Leonidas brought Warren once more to his feet. While the actors and stagehands gathered around, staring and jabbering in low voices, Berry and Ebon blurted apologies to both men.

Berry stuffed the red wig into her skirt pocket and asked, "Mr. Maroney, are you hurt?"

"Young woman, I have two permanent knots in my calves and I feel blood running down the backs of my legs where they scraped against the edge of that blasted box." Clearly Warren Maroney was not a man who withstood pain or embarrassment well. He bent over and jerked up the legs of his trousers, gingerly testing his calves with his hands.

Somebody brought over one of the lanterns hanging from a post, and Berry knelt alongside Henry and Ebon, who were checking the man's injuries.

"Oh, Mr. Maroney," Berry exclaimed with genuine sympathy, "you do have nasty gashes on the backs of your legs. Could you come down to the wardrobe room with me where my aunt and I can bandage them? I feel terrible about being so clumsy!"

"And well you should," Henry Zimpel retorted.

"Let me help you, sir," Ebon said when the plainly indignant Warren Maroney began limping after Berry. He eased his shoulder underneath the left arm of the much taller man.

"You weren't much help to me the other night when you tried to catch that ring thief," the man grumbled under his breath. "Were you in cahoots with him? Is that why you never came back?"

"No, sir!" Ebon replied in what he hoped was an injured tone. "Maybe I had too much beer to remember much. I never realized till just now that you're the masker I saw. I never came back 'cause I was ashamed I let that culprit outrun me. If you recall, I was having a bit of trouble with my shoes.''

It seemed plain to Ebon that though the man he was escorting gave the appearance of being harmless, he was the masker minus the big toe on his left foot. Maybe he didn't limp badly without fresh bruises, Ebon reasoned, but he was doing so now. Had he deliberately pushed Berry against the man in order to see if he had a sensitive area in his left foot? Ebon was unsure if the tumble had been pure accident, but he was elated that things had happened as they had.

Soon the man, letting out little whimpers with almost every breath, was sitting on a cleared-off space on Maddy's worktable. Something about the way Warren winced and moaned from Berry's and Maddy's gentle ministrations struck them as being less than manly.

Ebon, who had stayed around after fetching a pan of water and some towels, was thinking along the same lines. To his way of reasoning, the man was acting at the moment more like a coward than a killer. He had never before thought that one person might be both.

''You must be in lots of pain,'' Ebon said when he began unlacing Warren's shoes. ''These two ladies are handy with cuts and bruises.'' His fingers trembled when he reached to pull off the last sock. He could feel the forces from the two sets of feminine eyes centering on the man's left foot. Sure enough, there was no big toe. The stump was an angry red where he or Berry had hit it a few moments earlier. His scalp prickled. ''Whatever happened to your big toe?''

''Never mind,'' Warren replied irritably. ''If it hadn't already been cut off, it likely would be now, after you and the girl stomped on my foot.'' He ended his sentence with a deep drawn out ''Oh-h-h!'' Then, ''What have I done to deserve this?''

Maddy exchanged worried, knowing looks with Berry as they tore strips from a white remnant found in the ragbag. What was the man Ebon believed had killed Flo doing in her wardrobe room? Did he suspect Berry had taken his rings? Both Berry and Ebon were acting more fidgety with each passing moment.

All the while Berry and Maddy cleansed and bound the slight abrasions, they crooned and sympathized as if the man had a bona fide reason to be moaning. Without any recognizable coaxing, he began telling about several of the injustices his family had inflicted on him.

"That's right, Miss Maddy," Warren replied to Maddy's gentle remarks that bordered on being questions. "A family can be a pain. My older brother caused me to lose my toe. He wasn't chopping wood the way our step-pa wanted, so the old man made me try. I wasn't but a boy and too little to hold an axe, much less use one."

"How dreadful! That must have taken a long time to get over," Maddy said.

"I suppose your brother got punished," Berry remarked, realizing that Maddy was learning about the man by being sympathetic and drawing him out. She found it hard to look at his hairy hands without remembering how it had felt to pull off his rings. Somehow she had expected his face to show that he was different, that he could snuff out a human life. He did not look evil, unless it was the way his small eyes, set unusually close together, seemed to blaze deep within when he was talking about his misfortunes.

"He didn't then, but he did later." Warren sniggered. "I hired a man to slip a shiv between his ribs while he was in prison up at St. Louis. And all the time he thought I was using money from his wife to hire him a new lawyer."

Berry and Maddy exchanged horrified looks before Berry said, "That sounds awful!" Evil did not always show plainly on people's faces as she had always believed, Berry reflected with a tiny shiver. What would he have done to her had he caught her the other night? She swallowed hard. Jason Premont had been right. She and Ebon should have reported the matter to the police.

When Warren shot Berry a testy, fiery look, she added in a

rush, "That sounds awful to have a brother like that, so unappreciative and all."

"Guess he got what he deserved," Ebon remarked. He had no wish for the man to stop talking, and Warren Maroney did seem to like talking about himself. "You must be a powerful man to arrange things like that."

"Yeah," Warren admitted with a grim smile and a noticeable narrowing of his small eyes. "Sometimes we gotta take justice into our own hands, boy."

"Not all people can make things work out to suit them," Ebon replied. He felt sick all over.

"Well," Warren said, "if they're too cowardly to stand up for themselves, they deserve what they get."

Berry spoke then, calling up all of her acting skills. "Stand on that leg and let's see if the bandage is too tight, Mr. Maroney. We don't want any pressure on the cut or it's liable to start aching in the night."

"Y'all are mighty kind to a stranger. Lots of people try to act like men don't feel pain," Warren said, as he let Ebon tie his shoes and brush off the legs of his trousers. "There's nothing like a woman's soft touch or voice."

"Now you're being kind," Maddy said. What were Berry and Ebon motioning for her to do? "A big strong man can hurt just as bad as anyone else. Don't you agree, Berry?"

"Yes," she replied, completely caught up in her role as dumb, sympathetic girl. "I feel bad about causing him to fall, Maddy. Since it's early yet, do you think Ebon and I could go with Mr. Maroney over to Paddy's for something to drink before it's time to get ready for the performance?"

Maddy bristled as she straightened up her worktable. What were those two up to? Judging from the crafty look inside the man's eyes when he wasn't slobbering like a baby, she figured if Warren Maroney were even to suspect that Ebon now had the emerald ring on a string around his neck, he would turn him into fish bait. As for Berry, if he were to discover . . .She was not about to let the youngsters go off with him alone.

Dan was off that day, Maddy mused. Maybe the big police sergeant would be hanging around Paddy's, helping tend bar as he sometimes did when not working his beat. Could that be what Berry was thinking about, too? Maddy was doubly glad now that she had shared with Dan what Ebon had told her, even if he had scolded her for not insisting the boy go to the police. "I think I'll go along."

When they went into the hallway and talked with Henry Zimpel, he seemed to like the idea that the three were trying to soothe Warren Maroney's rumpled pride. "Make sure you get back before curtain time," he called as they left.

"This is a nice place," Warren said after beginning his second shot of whiskey. The first one had lasted only long enough for him to toss it down. "Folks seem friendly and all, even to one who's not been in New Orleans long." He squinted across at the big man who had shucked his apron and walked from behind the bar to join them. Not many bartenders showed as much interest in a man's mishaps as this one was. "Reckon you like tending bar here, Harrigan."

"It's a good way to earn some coins," Dan replied. When Maddy came to the bar, ostensibly to get more coffee, she had quickly filled him in. He could hardly believe the man had shown up at the Théâtre d'Orléans that way. Dan had tossed his apron to Paddy, warned him to expect action, and sat down with the foursome. "I hope your legs are feeling better now."

"They still hurt mighty bad," Warren replied. He drained his whiskey glass and held it up for Paddy to see from where he stood behind the bar. "My ma always told me whiskey was bad for a fellow." He let out a snort, a harsh sound. "She didn't know much, and neither did my brother."

Berry explained to Dan that Warren's brother had caused him to lose his toe. Repeating Warren's self-serving theme, she asked the sergeant, "Isn't it awful what some people suffer at the hands of family?"

"Like I told 'em back at the theater," Warren said to Dan, "I got even with him."

"Served him right, didn't it, Mr. Harrigan?" Ebon asked, after Warren related, in more detail than time, how he'd hired an inmate to kill his brother in prison at St. Louis. "A man has to take care of the wrongs done against him."

Dan went along, watching the way Warren gulped a slug of whiskey from his third serving. "Maybe so, what with so many evil people around. Did you say you came from St. Louis?"

"Yeah. St. Louis. Evil," Warren repeated thickly, draining his glass and signaling to Paddy before going on. "That's what my sister-in-law was. A damned whore, that's all. She griped about giving money to lawyers to get my brother out of jail. Evil. Flo was shot through with it."

"I guess you got her straightened out," Dan said after clearing his throat and squinting across at the man.

"I did for a fact," Warren agreed drunkenly, while Paddy set down a fourth glass of whiskey and began wiping off a nearby table. "The world's better off without that Flo. She always looked down on me."

Berry asked softly, "Is she dead, too?"

"Why do you ask, girlie?" A steely note of suspicion crept into his voice and he narrowed his small eyes. "Damned if you don't have a fine set of lips on you. I could almost swear I've seen 'em before today."

Berry cleared her throat, forcing herself to meet his probing gaze. "I was just thinking how sad it is that you don't seem to have any family left, if this Flo's dead, too."

"That's right, but I'm damned glad of it. She's buried over in Natchez—if they got a place to bury whores, that is. The only thing I had left from my family got stole from me the other night. I get mad as hell just thinking about how Flo would like it that I don't have her fancy ring anymore."

"Are you talking about the rings that the masker took?" Ebon asked.

Aware that Warren was sipping again from his glass and that the glazed expression in his eyes was increasing, Berry blinked hard and toyed with her coffee cup. The tension she sensed brought prickles to her sensitive flesh. Why hadn't she heeded Jason's warning and talked Ebon into going to the police? It smarted, thinking of how right Jason had been.

Warren replied, "Yeah." He turned to Dan, slurring his words worse with each one uttered. "One of my rings was a emerald worth a small fortune, and some damned kid slipped it and a couple of fakes off my hand. Can you beat that?"

"Did you report the theft to the police?" Dan asked.

"Hell, no! I ain't aiming to have no police looking down my throat." Warren leaned closer to the big Irishman. "Don't be getting notions about telling the law any of this. Me and my friends down on Gallatin wouldn't like that."

Glancing over at Paddy, who was hovering around the table next to theirs, Dan signaled him with his eyes, then said, "I am a policeman, Mr. Maroney."

At a gesture from Dan, Berry and Maddy rushed over by the bar. When Warren tried to slide back his chair and rise, both Ebon and Paddy seized his arms and kept him seated until the sergeant hurried around and took charge.

"I'm taking you to the calaboose," Dan announced. "My captain is going to be interested in your stories."

"Can't y'all tell when you've been conned?" Warren countered, a drunken smile turning up his thin lips on one side. "I was just cadging drinks. You can't arrest me for spinning tall tales."

"I got a feeling you've been telling lots of truth," Dan told him as he took the handcuffs Paddy handed him and slipped them over Warren's wrists. "I'm taking you in because you're drunk in a public place and acting suspicious."

Angrily, Warren said, "Y'all been taking advantage of me." He sought out Berry and Maddy over by the bar and included them in his baleful look. "I'll get even! Wait and see!" Then he slumped and his voice broke, became whiney. "I can't stand being locked up, even for one night."

"Maroney, you won't be getting even with anybody. I figure after we do some checking in St. Louis and Natchez,"

Sergeant Dan Harrigan said as he led Warren out of the saloon, "you might be talking for a good while from the wrong side of bars."

Long after Berry had slipped under the mosquito *baire* beside Maddy that night, she was still remembering the frightening scene with Warren Maroney. Almost as hard to forget was the one later in the police station. Ebon had turned in the ring and told what he knew. Then Berry had explained how she had become involved in the sordid affair. Though she had not comprehended all about how Ebon and she would be appearing in court as witnesses at a later date, she had understood enough to know that the incident would not be resolved right away.

Along with Warren's threat to get even, Jason Premont's warning about a killer having no compunction about killing again kept coming to Berry's mind and hindering sleep. The partial comfort she gained from knowing the man was behind bars where he belonged seemed paltry, and she wished the unnerving events of the evening had not been necessary. She heard a whining nightwind from the nearby river rattling the sign on the greengrocer's store below. While watching the pale curtain at the dark window writhe, ghostlike, she shivered and moved closer to the sleeping Maddy.

Within Berry, a gut-wrenching fear coiled tighter. What if her spirited actions on Mardi Gras evening, though they had started out as a kind of lark fueled by good intentions, evolved into a matter of life and death for her and for people about whom she cared deeply?

CHAPTER

*

Four

Throughout the following months, the trial and the subsequent conviction and sentencing of Warren Maroney to life imprisonment for murdering Flo matured Berry Cortabona further. She felt relief after the ordeal that none of her earlier fears had materialized.

Ebon's unexpected return to Natchez afterward to work as porter at the Chanticleer shook Berry's equilibrium. A far worse blow followed, smashing her world. Death had snatched her beloved Aunt Maddy.

Not quite seventeen and on her own, Berry failed to wangle a decent-paying position as seamstress in any of the theaters. She read for understudy and minor roles but gained nothing beyond advice to work on strengthening her voice.

Actress Camille Hayes, who had taken Berry into her small room at a boardinghouse, suddenly found life in New Orleans unbearable. One evening about two months after Maddy's death, she came in from the theater and found the sad-eyed girl finishing up an alteration for their landlady.

"This was closing night. Let's get away from this town, Berry."

"Where would we go?" Berry had known that Camille was unhappy over something that she had not confided. However, she hadn't expected such a drastic proposal.

"The traveling troupe I've been acting with is leaving tomorrow for St. Louis and the manager offered me a role. When I told him that I wouldn't consider it unless he took you on as combination seamstress in charge of costumes and understudy, he agreed." Apparently encouraged by the gleam of hope shining within Berry's troubled eyes, she went on. "The pay is small, but they throw in lodging and one meal a day. When we reach a city where there are lots of theaters, we'll try our luck there."

By daylight a newly hopeful Berry and a wan-faced Camille were gliding on a riverboat up the fog-enshrouded Mississippi.

Berry and Camille returned to the Vieux Carré in the summer of 1842, four years after Berry's rash thievery during Mardi Gras and her subsequent meeting with Jason Premont. Though while away both had enjoyed degrees of success and good fortune, they recently had regained their former enthusiasm for life in New Orleans.

Nineteen now and cognizant of the fact that she would never be an actress, Berry had honed in on where her true talents lay. She was eagerly seeking success in designing costumes for the theater and for elegant occasions, such as the increasingly popular Mardi Gras celebrations in New Orleans.

According to Berry's optimistic viewpoint, there was only one major hitch. Until she sold at least one design, she needed a job as seamstress. With that thought in mind one pleasant summer afternoon soon after her return, Berry accepted an invitation from an old acquaintance from the Théâtre d'Orléans, actor Leonidas Latrobe.

"I'm proud to be escorting you to the subscription ball

tonight," Leonidas told Berry as they walked toward the ballroom at the new Saint Louis Hotel in the French Quarter. The evening was cool for June, maybe because the night breezes playing on the Mississippi had already begun blowing their damp breath down the cobblestone streets. Strollers were out in great numbers; frisky dogs and youngsters, too. "You look more beautiful and regal than the real Queen Isabella could have."

"Thanks," Berry replied, with a measuring look at the handsome actor from behind her purplish-red demi-mask edged with black lace and sequins. "You look quite royal yourself." Judging from the admiring glances others on the streets were sending them, she assumed that in their borrowed finery, Leonidas Latrobe and she appeared to be upper-class Creoles on their way to one of the private masquerade balls that always sprang into being after Lent.

Berry heard their footsteps resounding on the banquette and, as she had on the first day of her recent return to New Orleans, she mentally applauded progress. Either bricks or cobblestones now paved the major streets and walkways. Glorying in the nostalgic smell of river water tinged with a hint of fresh fish that rode the evening breeze, she lifted her face and welcomed the smells and sights of her childhood. Strange, but their redolence never completely left her even during the three years that she and Camille were gone.

Berry's smile widened and she felt her blood quicken when she detected the sweet, spicy fragrance of roses riding the latest breeze. Was it drifting over the walls of some nearby courtyard, maybe the one they had just passed from which the sounds of young children's laughter, counterpointed by rich, bass tones of a man's chuckles, had floated like phrases of a happy song? The city council's long planned renovation of the open sewers must have seen fruition during her absence, she reflected, for the trace of water in the shallow indentions running along the sides of the cobblestoned surfaces sent no foul odor to insult her sensitive nose.

A full moon beginning its ascendancy added new light to the star-studded sky above the two- and three-story buildings jammed together along the narrow streets. Berry saw a balcony up ahead with a giant bougainvillea spilling in artistic profusion over its wrought iron railing and wondered whether in daylight the blooms would show red or pink or purple. What about the baskets of geraniums hanging from other balconies with their clusters of blooms rising above fat leaves? What color were they? In the uncertain light coming from the sky and the street lamps, the familiar flowers looked pale and exotic.

Berry pulled her thoughts back to her escort and the festivities ahead. She truly loved dancing, though she had misgivings about agreeing to go out with the much older Leonidas. According to Camille Hayes, who had once known him well, Leo was in his mid-thirties. "Remember, Leo, this is merely a masquerade ball. You're not really King Ferdinand any more than I'm Queen Isabella."

"Didn't I vow to be a gentleman if you would come with me and act the part of a mysterious lady visiting our city?"

"Mostly you vowed you would speak to Henry about engaging me as wardrobe mistress."

"I'm sure he'll listen to reason now. He can't stay mad forever because you took off with Camille after your Aunt Maddy died. Even before Camille Hayes's name got top billing in the theaters in the East, you said you found employment as understudy or seamstress wherever she worked. If you had stayed here as wardrobe mistress, you might never have gained an opportunity to read for a challenging part."

"Well," Berry conceded with good grace, "it's obvious all of you were right in saying that I don't have the voice to be an actress. At least the lessons in acting and in diction from the seasoned actors helped me become more sophisticated."

"You are exquisite in every way, darling."

Ignoring Leo's smooth flattery and his blatant looks at her

low-cut gown, she continued in a musing tone. "I couldn't stay here after Henry refused to hire me as wardrobe mistress simply because I was only sixteen. Maddy's free rent lasted only as long as she lived. I didn't have anybody I felt I could turn to but my best friends, Camille and Ebon. He couldn't have helped me—not when he had already returned to the Chanticleer in Natchez."

"I hated hearing last year that yellow fever had taken Ebon." When he saw Berry's bottom lip quiver, he pulled her arm through his and added, "I really liked the little fellow. I know how close you two became during the awful trial of that fellow who killed the woman in Natchez. I never understood how he escaped execution, though I wouldn't count lifetime imprisonment at St. Louis as a pleasant sentence."

"I refuse to dwell on the man or that part of my life." Berry glanced down at the large emerald on her white-gloved finger as she thought of Ebon and how he had arranged for her to have Flo's ring. She never allowed herself to recall the details of Warren Maroney's trial or the way the man's fiery eyes impaled her while she was testifying about how and why she had removed the emerald from his finger that fateful Mardi Gras night.

Should she have given in to Camille's suggestion and worn the emerald tonight? Berry wondered. Was it a blessing or a curse? As Camille had pointed out, it did go well with the elaborate seventeenth-century costume Leonidas had obtained from the wardrobe room at the Théâtre d'Orléans. This was the first time she had worn the ring since Sergeant Harrigan had sent it and a note about Ebon's death in care of the theatrical troupe with which Camille and she were traveling. Fondness for Aunt Maddy's admirer had led her to contact the sergeant occasionally.

If only Maddy's lungs had not given out on her and caused her death three years ago, Berry reflected without the anguish that had plagued her during the first year after her aunt's death, she could have laid the matter before her for an opinion. She smiled. Maddy always had an opinion, bless her. Berry had decided a while back that being entirely on her own was not as grand as she had once imagined it might be. A word here and there from someone older who cared was not all bad. How young and foolish she had been!

Berry idled with the folded fan looped over her free wrist and pulled her thoughts to the conversation with Leonidas Latrobe. With renewed indignation she asked, "What did Henry think I was going to do after Maddy died? Sell myself on the streets or maybe marry the first thing in trousers who might propose?"

"To the best of my recollection," Leonidas replied with a strained smile, "Henry Zimpel was offering to set you up with a wealthy politician."

"Not as his wife, either, and probably for a hefty fee for himself!" Berry narrowed her long-lidded eyes at the memory of her last unsettling talk with the acting manager of the Théâtre d'Orléans. "He's a miserable skinflint without an ounce of feeling for anybody. He's a bastard, a skunk."

"It's nice to learn you haven't completely forsaken your colorful vocabulary. It's so ladylike."

Berry ignored his irony. "Maybe your report that he has run through three older seamstresses, who probably didn't do half the job with the wardrobe that I could have, means he'll at least give me a recommendation so another theater might consider hiring me. He's scum to try getting even by keeping me from getting a job. Since Mardi Gras keeps growing as an established social season here, I hope to contact some of Maddy's former clients and make costumes. But I had counted on steady work at a theater until I sell at least one design."

"Aren't you a clever little piece of baggage to divert your talents toward designing costumes? I always suspected you were more than a saucy beauty." When Berry's black eyes swept him a bit cynically, he cleared his throat. "Actually, Henry was mad at both Camille and you for taking off with that troupe. We've needed her talent in our group of stock players. She's still beautiful even if she is pushing thirty."

"You're right about Camille being talented and beautiful," Berry agreed. An image of the auburn-haired actress flashed to mind. How kind Camille had been to her over the years; Berry doubted she could love a sister better. "How long is Henry going to pout? We've been back three weeks and he still won't see either of us. Camille insists it's all right for me to continue staying in her guest bedroom, but after I finish her wedding gown, I need to find a job so that I can be independent. My savings won't last long."

Berry cocked her head and studied Leo's handsome profile as they walked arm in arm. For some reason, she recalled Maddy's warning her to watch out for egotistical men like Leo. She almost giggled. Did he really put perfume on his tongue, as Maddy had once said? His breath *did* smell sweet. "Are you jealous that Camille has found someone she loves?"

"No." Leo evaded her blunt gaze. "There was nothing between us but a professional friendship, even before she fell for that Ace Zachary. What bothers me is that after she ran away to get over the 'riverboat king,' she has returned now as little more than his paramour. He had no right to track her down. No matter that his ailing wife died last year; he will never marry Camille."

"I admire Ace for having stayed with his wife during her long illness. She might even have known about Camille and not minded that he had found a woman to love him after she was gone. You're wrong about his not ever marrying Camille. He will. And soon. I feel it."

"Feel it? Bah! Do you think the late Mrs. Zachary would have approved of his renting that townhouse for her on Chartres while he renovates his home and plans a fancy wedding? You're more of a romantic than when you left."

"I may be, but I'm no longer a child. True love doesn't have to follow strict patterns."

"Is that the voice of experience speaking? Did you find your—what was it?—blessed kind of love?"

"Where did you hear that?" Berry's tone was sharp.

"Walls between dressing rooms are thin, *cherie*."

"You eavesdropped on Camille and me, you reprobate!"

"Calm down," Leo said, patting her gloved hand where it threatened to desert its resting place on his arm. "If you still wear that deadly looking dagger, don't be reaching under your gown for it. At the time, I thought you sounded terribly sweet and pure. I hope you're less idealistic now." When she did no more than present him with her elevated profile, he added in a sly voice, "I assume you've been out with young men and know more what to expect now. Maybe you've kissed a few, too, and heard at least one proposal of marriage."

Blind to the secretive, prurient looks coming from her escort, Berry retorted, "Yes, I've been out with lots of young men. It's none of your business what we did. You can bank on it that I didn't find the one for me or I would have stayed with him."

For a moment Berry was tempted to tell the foppish Leo about Sir Reginald Cromwell, the dashing lead actor of the London Shakespearean troupe who had proposed to her last year in Boston after their first kiss. He had even dropped on one knee and quoted love sonnets. Heady stuff for her romantic side, she recalled while walking in step with Leo. Not heady enough, though, to silence the practical side that had warned her the British actor was not a likely candidate for the kind of love or marriage for which she longed. She had seen Reginald, less than a week before his dramatic proposal, sneaking from the hotel room of his married leading lady in the middle of the night, looking tousled and guilty as sin. It had reminded her of Jason Premont trying to escape over the wall behind Mrs. Soulé's garden. The fact that, in faraway Boston, she had remembered Jason's face, complete with dimples and engaging smile, as distinctly as if she might be looking at him had struck her as spooky. It had made her homesick, too.

No, Berry Cortabona reassured herself, she had no plans to marry a man who showed such flagrant disregard for marriage vows, no matter that he might be as handsome as Jason Premont or Reginald Cromwell. There had been other passionate kisses, vows of devotion and proposals, too, but she had even forgotten what the young men looked like.

Berry tapped Leo's arm lightly with her folded fan. "Jeer if you choose, but I still believe there's such a thing as a blessed kind of love. When it comes my way, I'll latch onto it in a Creole minute."

Even as Berry darted Leo a haughty look from behind her demi-mask, she realized that they were turning into St. Louis Street. She saw several masked couples in costumes walking toward the hotel and others stepping down from handsome carriages. "What possessed your latest paramour to offer you tickets for tonight's ball? Could it be that her husband is escorting her?" Berry asked Leo.

He chuckled and adjusted his black demi-mask. "You have, indeed, become an adult, Berry, with a woman's sharp tongue." Hungrily, he eyed her slender but voluptuous figure in the dim light coming from the street lamps, his lips curving into one of his most engaging stage smiles. "Tonight is a very special one for me, and I hope you also will remember it that way. I'm looking forward to dazzling both the Creoles and the Americans tonight with my mysterious Spanish queen. When everyone unmasks at midnight, who except I will realize that Miss Berry Angelique Cortabona is no stranger to New Orleans?"

"Cheer up, Jason," Ashley Breton said to his friend as the two walked down Chartres toward the St. Louis Hotel. "If you've passed the stage when the prospect of being with beautiful women doesn't bring on a happy face, then I'll know you're dead."

Jason Premont sent a quizzical look at Ashley. "Are you positive we'll be seeing beautiful women tonight?"

"Absolutely. Why else did I subscribe to this masquerade ball? I'm glad you finally got your knee in shape and came in from your uncle's plantation for a stay in the city. You've secluded yourself out there too long. You need to purge your mind of memories of our trek to Texas."

"You know as well as I, a man can't spend a year fighting alongside other filibusterers without thinking every once in a while about the friends he lost, or maybe about the men he killed in the name of freedom for Americans living in Texas."

Ashley's face sobered then, the still-pink scar on his left cheekbone no detraction from his good looks. "Yes, it was bloody hell when we had to bury my brother out there in that blazing hot sand."

At Jason's thoughtful nod, he continued. "Viola and Papa haven't completely forgiven either one of us for taking Clark Junior along, even after I told them that he never seemed happier than when we were following you on a charge. I've also explained that he had ignored your orders that all of us stay in camp the night he ran into those renegade Indians. I loved that brother of mine, but I realize he was always a bit of a hothead. God! How he loved yelling 'Remember the Alamo!' every time we engaged the Mexicans."

As Jason continued walking in silence, deep in reverie, Ashley asked, "How is your knee?"

"It hasn't bothered me in weeks." Jason glanced at the thin scar on his friend's face, and his dark eyes revealed a brooding sadness. "I doubt we'll ever forget entirely all the fighting and maneuvering we did to run those Mexicans south of the Nueces . . . and how we failed. After San Jacinto, Santa Ana should never have agreed that the separating boundary would be the Rio Grande if he meant to continue sending troops to defend as far north as the Nueces. The matter will have to be resolved before Texas can become a state, else a full scale war with Mexico to establish boundaries is likely.''

Both men walked in silence until Jason gestured toward a bar up ahead. "Let's take time for a drink. Since we're not escorting anyone this evening, it won't matter if we're late.''

Ashley glanced at their costumes, princely suits of pale satin left over from past Carnival seasons, and at their black demi-masks hanging around their necks. "It's all right with me if you don't mind that we might be setting a new style in this section of the Quarter. Some barmaid is likely to swoon right at our feet.''

Jason grinned. "We should be so lucky. Maybe she'll be as pretty as some of those Texan señoritas.'' Deliberately trying to lighten his mood, Jason went inside with Ashley, where they leaned against the bar and ordered bourbon and branch water. Both sipped their drinks before Jason asked, "Do you think Texas will be taken in as a state?''

"Talk in the coffeehouses indicates it will.''

"I hope President Sam Houston and his cause won't be defeated, even if some of his fellow citizens seem to prefer keeping their land independent. I like knowing I tried to help.''

"It seems to me," Ashley said, "that we did the best we could to help them run the Mexicans out of the disputed territory before we had to limp back to Louisiana and take care of our own business.''

Jason's thoughts raced to his uncle back in St. Christopher Parish. "Uncle Eduoard still thinks the filibustering groups should be outlawed here in New Orleans. He can't understand how those agitators at places like Banks's Arcade and the Rising Sun Tavern can get young men like us all het up over the rights of their fellow Americans and have them signing up before they have time to cool off. I suspect he never heard the right one cry 'Remember the Alamo!' at the right time.'' Jason smiled in a self-deprecating manner. "Sometimes I wonder if my mother's brother never was young and hungry for adventure. Uncle Edouard still thinks of himself as a Creole rather than an American.''

''Is he still riding you hard to marry and take over more duties about the plantation?''

''Harder than ever about the marrying.'' Jason held up his nearly empty glass and watched the reflection of the candle-light from the overhead candelabra come alive in the pale liquid. ''I've already begun supervising the renovation of the sugar mill and I'm working closely with the overseer. Uncle Edouard admits that after his wife died so young, he might have been wrong not to marry again and maybe have children.''

Jason envisioned the silver-haired gentleman sitting in his enormous rocking chair on the veranda of the mansion facing the bayou, his cultured voice spinning hunting and fishing yarns. ''I reckon when my father got killed and Uncle Edouard offered my mother and me a home, he put aside his personal goals to help us. I love the man like a father, but I wish he weren't so eager for me to bring home a bride. He seems healthy and is not yet in his sixties, so I can't see why he's so bent on pushing me into matrimony right away. I suspect he hopes marriage will settle me down.''

The handsome bachelors and longtime friends—Jason, twenty-seven, and Ashley, twenty-five—exchanged devil-may-care smiles. As they had been doing since they first tasted spirits, they toasted each other with a clicking of their glasses.

Jason went on, still serious but becoming more cheerful. ''What my uncle doesn't seem to realize is that I'm through with chasing around the world. I'm ready to learn how, as he puts it, to step into his shoes. Armand Acres is a prosperous sugar plantation, and I'll be proud to call it my own someday. My mother took what my father left us and invested it in the plantation. I feel it's where I belong.''

''I'll bet my little sister would be happy to make that old jesting agreement between your uncle and my father come true. She hasn't yet become betrothed. If anyone were to ask me, I'd say Viola is playing a dangerous game by keeping several men dangling. Two or three of her suitors seem nice enough, but there's a Roger Elton moved here recently from Cincinnati, a buyer for cotton brokers up East, who spells trouble.''

Plainly troubled by his younger sister's behavior, Ashley returned to the subject as he and Jason left the bar and continued walking to the hotel. ''Viola bragged to me that Roger says he's going to give her a key to his townhouse down on Dauphine for her to use on the days she's in town shopping. She walked away with her nose in the air when I scolded. I know Papa doesn't want her marrying someone from out of state—especially one who seems to be after her money more than her charms.''

''Maybe one of the others will sway her into accepting his proposal and settle the matter for everybody. I grew up with all three of you, and I can't see Viola as more than a mighty pretty girl. I don't know what kind of wife might be right for me. Maybe some young woman will knock me stone crazy one day and I'll have to marry her to keep my sanity.''

Ashley guffawed. ''I want to be there to see that.''

''Yeah,'' Jason said, with a grin as dubious as his friend's. ''Me, too.''

They had not covered more than a block before Ashley voiced more concern about his sister. ''Bayard Filhoil, from a plantation up near Baton Rouge, is crazy over Viola. He seems to be at the boiling point all of the time. I've learned he has resumed lessons at one of those fencing academies over in Exchange Alley. Hell! He's damned near thirty . . . and acting such a fool.''

''The signs of a man in love, or so we've always heard. Is this Bayard fencing at the same place where we used to go?'' Fond recollections of those carefree times during their college years brought a smile to Jason's face. Fencing had been only a part of the mad whirl in the capital city. There had been horse races and beautiful women—many of them married and eager to show a young virile man their expertise in the bedroom—plus gambling, partying, dancing, and flirting with the dark-haired Creole belles.

The whiskey, the reminiscing, and the talk about what was going on in New Orleans were lifting Jason's mood considerably. With each long-legged step he took toward the Royal Ballroom at the St. Louis Hotel, he felt a rising anticipation at the idea of attending a ball again. Maybe Ashley was right. Maybe he had stayed in St. Christopher Parish too long without making a visit to his townhouse on Chartres and again tasting life in New Orleans.

Before Jason tied his demi-mask around his upper face, he glanced up and saw a full moon rising above the rooftops. Wasn't that considerate, he mused in his increasingly mellow mood, of Mother Nature to be doing her part in turning the evening into one of promise?

Ashley answered Jason's question, after mulling it over. "I don't know where Bayard takes instruction. I hear there are even more academies and masters now than ten years ago. Jason, I'm afraid there'll be a duel over Viola and somebody might be hurt or killed before she realizes what her flirting can do."

Jason shook his head in quandary. "God! If those fops dying to duel could see what we've seen out in Texas, they wouldn't be so hotheaded and quick to find an excuse for a fight, would they?"

"You're right, but try telling that to the average Creole. Few seem willing to relinquish any portion of that era our parents and ancestors ruled before the Americans came."

"Maybe if my father hadn't been an officer from Virginia and lost his life in the Battle of New Orleans shortly before I was born, Uncle Edouard and his Creole ideas would sway me. Long before Mother died last year, she was leaning toward my view that if we hope to continue our prosperity, the interests of all in Louisiana now must take the same direction."

"She was a lovely lady," Ashley said as they turned into St. Louis Street and saw the hotel up ahead, "and wise."

"You're right and I thank you. She deserved to have her only child at her bedside when she died."

"How could you have known when we went to Texas that we'd be gone so long or that her heart would play out? You've often talked about how many friends she had in St. Christopher Parish. I'm sure she never felt alone or neglected. Don't punish yourself more than need be."

"I don't, not any longer. I have my thoughts sorted out now, and I'm ready to get on with the rest of my life." Jason paused and straightened his white satin coat, then checked to see if his matching trousers were still spotless. Sounds of dance music drifted down to the street from the second-floor ballroom and fed his rising anticipation. "I think I'll find the most beautiful woman there and propose to her on the spot. Even if she has me shot, that should prove to Uncle Edouard that I'm trying to find a wife."

Ashley laughed and clapped his friend on his back as they entered the appointed lobby and started up the marble staircase to the ballroom. "You're in fine fettle. I'm glad to see you acting more like your old self. After a few glasses of champagne, you should be able to dance the prettiest of the maskers out onto the terrace and steal at least one kiss before you get slapped."

"Lead on, my friend. I feel luckier than usual tonight."

The orchestra was in the midst of a Strauss waltz when the two friends handed their tickets to the doorman and entered the handsome ballroom with its domed ceiling and its three giant crystal chandeliers glittering from a myriad of burning white tapers. They exchanged pleased looks after they noticed the way that the mirrors down the long sides of the room reflected the elegantly dressed dancers gliding over the polished wooden floor. Fragrances of flaming tapers, fresh flowers, perfume, and heated, yet clean, bodies lent an additional festive air to the genteel scene.

"Who could that divine Spanish creature be?" Jason asked Ashley from where they stood near the entrance.

Lost in gazing at the costumed, masked dancers, especially the beautiful women dipping and whirling around in the arms of their partners, Ashley nonchalantly straightened his pink satin coat, then the matching stock rising above his ruffled white shirt. "Which one?"

"By the saints, man! There's only one truly divine creature out there." Jason's dark eyes followed the graceful figure dressed in a purplish-red gown with its enormously full skirt drawn back in front in an old-fashioned way that revealed a white petticoat embroidered heavily with gleaming pearls and crystal beads. When her partner again whirled her to face the entrance, Jason saw that the low-cut neckline of the fitted bodice revealed glowing, olive skin and high, rounded breasts. He felt keyed up, just from looking at her. "Have you ever seen such jet black hair? I wish it didn't droop over her forehead so low and keep me from seeing nothing but what shows below her mask. She wears her crown well, but she doesn't need one to mark her as Spanish royalty."

Ashley's gaze followed Jason's sparkling eyes. He located the beauty who was dressed like some of the women in paintings they had seen in the art museums throughout Europe during their extended tour a few years back. "You're right. She looks as if she's truly Spanish."

"I swear she makes the queens in the paintings in Madrid's Royal Museum of Painting look as if they might have been impostors." Noticing the dancer's partner for the first time then, and not particularly overjoyed upon finding that he appeared to be a handsome fellow, Jason added, "She must be Isabella and he must be Ferdinand. I wish I could tell if she has on a wedding ring. It's unfair that the married ladies seldom place their bands outside their gloves."

"When have you let that stop you?"

Jason shot Ashley a wounded look before lifting two glasses of champagne from the tray of a passing attendant.

"Look at the way she moves with the music." Absently, he handed one glass to Ashley, his gaze following the Spanish queen. "Such grace! It's almost as if she's inspired."

Ashley tried seeing what his friend was describing so passionately, but all he saw was an uncommonly smooth and beautiful black-haired dancer. What if he were to burst Jason's bubble of exhilaration by confessing he did not find anything inspired about Queen Isabella's waltzing? He was too glad to have Jason in high spirits to take a chance with such teasing. "She's remarkably beautiful." He had not had to lie about that.

While sipping his champagne, Ashley cast a testing look toward Jason. He never before had seen him carry on so over a young woman. Actually his friend had never had a reason to, Ashley reflected, when he thought of how women had always fawned over the handsome Jason Premont. In fact, back in their wilder days, women had sometimes made fools of themselves trying to charm Jason into smiling and flashing his dimples.

Though Ashley knew he was not a man poorly put together, either in face or form, and never suffered from a lack of female companionship, he freely admitted that Jason had always had a special appeal for women. Now that he was thinking about it, he doubted his friend's attractiveness to women had a hell of a lot to do with his having dimples. Anyway, Jason's face had matured and become so lean during the past couple of years that his dimples were little more now than vertical creases easing into his olive cheeks when he laughed or smiled.

When the waiter with the tray again passed close by, Jason returned his empty glass, then took a full one. The waltz was over and he craned his neck to see where the Spanish queen and her king ended up. Not believing his good luck that an intermission was taking place, Jason left Ashley chatting near a suddenly crowded refreshment table. He hurried to the terrace outside that ballroom where the mysterious beauty and her escort apparently had gone.

Jason observed the tall potted palms and rose bushes sitting in groups around the spacious terrace with its brick flooring and wrought iron handrailing. Had the defined grouping been designed for tête-à-têtes? The rising full moon and the lamps hanging at both sides of the French doors provided the only light. Now that the musicians had ceased playing, he could hear behind him the rising chatter of the dancers as they flocked around refreshment tables set against the long walls.

Jason frowned. Where in the devil had the Spanish couple gone?

CHAPTER

*

Five

With his glass of champagne in hand, Jason wandered among the pots of tall plantings spaced around the terrace, detouring around a few embracing couples. He reached the farthest corner and had about decided the black-haired masker and her escort had not come outside after all, when he heard what could be nothing but a hand smacking a cheek.

Following the *thwack!* came a woman's angry denouncement. Shamelessly, Jason listened, his smile widening at each word.

"Leonidas Latrobe, you're despicable! You promised that you were going to act like a gentleman. I came out here with you because you said you needed some fresh air."

"Can I help it if your beauty made me forget? What would one little kiss have hurt?"

"It might not have hurt anything, but I've no wish to kiss

you and you bloody well know it. Our being together tonight is nothing but a business arrangement.''

"Calm down, my queen. I'll fetch you some champagne and some dainties to eat. Will that make you feel better?''

So the couple were not married? Jason reflected while worrying his right earlobe with a thumb and forefinger for a moment. They were not even linked romantically, or at least the young woman with the musical voice apparently did not think so. A business arrangement with Leonidas Latrobe? If he had heard that name before, he could not place it.

Jason stepped behind a cluster of potted palms and roses until Latrobe, alias King Ferdinand, had stalked toward the ballroom. Then, as if he had no inkling that a young woman stood alone in the shadows a few feet away, he sauntered with studied casualness to the wrought iron handrailing.

"You're not fooling me," came the woman's voice, feminine, arresting, as she was herself. "Eavesdroppers sometimes hear what they wish they hadn't.''

Jason turned, wondering what kind of accent turned the lush voice into extremely well-modulated syllables. It was Southern, went well with the moonlight and the fragrance of the nearby roses, and yet...Perhaps a Southern adaptation of diction taught at an Eastern finishing school? "Was I eavesdropping? Pardon me. I thought I was enjoying looking at the Creole moon."

"I suppose I'm to ask what a Creole moon is. Well, I shan't.'' With the air of a haughty aristocrat, she snapped open her fan and waved it in front of her face, all the while leaning indolently against the handrailing and facing toward Jason. "You are like all other men—transparent.''

"Thank you, your grace." Jason bowed from the waist. He was delighted to discover that his guess was accurate. As young as she was, apparently she was no novice at fencing verbally with men. Not once had she even glanced toward the open ballroom door where the escort she had so ably put in his place had disappeared. Here stood a young woman confident both of her charms and how to guard them.

Jason's fascination with the black-haired queen soared to a new height. Back home in Saint Christopher Parish there were several beauteous belles whom he sometimes squired to local soirees and dinners at various plantation homes, but not one offered him more than outward beauty and the innocuous chatter of the very young and innocent. His pulse quickened.

"Sir, that was *not* a compliment!"

"May I accept it as one?" One step toward her rewarded him with a closer view of her beautiful mouth, chin, and exposed skin above her alluring décolletage. He felt wound up, somehow alerted all over, a bit like, when back in his fencing days, a match with a worthy opponent was about to commence. An inner voice advised: *On guard!* "I wouldn't want a lovely queen suspecting I have devious thoughts. I would much rather she see clearly into my mind. What do you read there?"

Queen Isabella laughed, a warm tinkling bunch of musical notes sliding down into Jason's heart and colliding with something tucked into a forgotten corner. Thinking that he could not be more spellbound were he in the presence of true royalty, Jason gazed at her full lips tilting upward in a tantalizing curve. The sight of her pretty teeth flashing silvery white in the moonlight and her crown of brilliants sparkling as if they truly might be diamonds dazzled him anew. For a poignant moment, the desire to throw caution to the night air and snatch the demi-mask from her face seized him.

Back in control as swiftly as the temptation had reared up, Jason noticed her hair was blacker than midnight and he realized that a few long, lustrous curls fell forward carelessly over one shoulder and grazed a full breast in a way that might well have been the studied effort of an artist preparing to paint Queen Isabella in a seductive pose underneath a full moon. His hands ached to touch those black curls, to brush against the gleaming magenta satin against which her voluptuous breasts strained. He gulped his champagne awkwardly.

The masked beauty was still half-smiling and leading Jason to suspect that mischief sparkled within her partially hidden dark eyes when she unleashed her riposte. "I read nothing in your mind but the alphabet."

"Zounds! I need help, don't I?" he parried with a smile. She was quick, an able opponent.

"Definitely." Gazing up at him, she hesitated, then returned his smile.

Jason marked the way the beautiful young woman seemed to be perusing his features, or what showed underneath his brief mask, before she let her fan dangle once more from its loop around her dainty wrist, a wrist his thumb and forefinger could encircle easily. With graceful gestures that he suspected might have been manufactured to give her time for reflection, she removed her ring, then her gloves, and, after sliding the ring on her bare finger, held the pale leather gloves in one hand. Was she a bit agitated? Had something thrown her off guard?

She said with open amusement, "I've never before heard anyone use the word, 'zounds!' I assumed it was one of those expressions meant only to be read or used on stage." Glancing overhead and fanning the air in front of her face with her gloves, the slender young woman remarked as casually as if they had been properly introduced and had dispensed with formalities, "The night has become quite warm."

"Yes, unseasonably warm." He felt drawn to her, much as the mindless, night-flying insects that were seeking the flames of the oil lamps hanging beside the ballroom doors. "Would you care to sip some champagne from the other side of my glass? The refreshment tables will be thronged, and your king might not be able to return soon."

To Jason's surprise she took a step toward him and reached for his glass. Even as he heard the rustling of silk from her graceful movement and thought about petticoats and the treasures they must be concealing, she was saying, "Yes, thank you. I'm unbearably thirsty."

Jason could not be sure, but he suspected the alluring Spanish queen was as shocked as he when their fingers grazed during the exchange of the long-stemmed glass. He dared not hope she felt the same spark of electricity that he had; still he could not discount the feeling that she had experienced something extraordinary. For one apparently as comfortable with the ancient game as he, she had severed contact too fast. Of that he was certain.

Jason reflected that his heartbeat had accelerated ever since her first words to him, but that now its pace was nigh dizzying. Of course, he rationalized, he had drunk quite a lot that evening.

While Queen Isabella sipped from his glass, Jason took advantage of her preoccupation to gaze at her more openly from behind his mask. She was slender, with full breasts thrust high in the confining purplish-red satin. She was not overly tall or short, about five inches over five feet, he guessed. A perfect height for his own six feet. Other than the delicately wrought crown perched atop her black hair, she wore no jewelry but the ring he had watched her slip on her right hand after she shed her gloves.

Even in the moonlight Jason could tell the ring flashed green fire. For some reason the emerald, a handsomely cut rectangle and apparently valuable, drew his attention. Or was it merely an excuse to admire her pretty hands with their long, tapered fingers and note again that her left hand was bare? "May I compliment you on your ring? It's a rare beauty—like its wearer."

Carefully, as if making sure that her fingers did not touch Jason's, Queen Isabella returned his empty glass. He had no idea why he made the rash movement, unless it was in hopes that he might hear her laugh again; but from where he stood leaning back against the wrought iron handrailing, he tossed the crystal stemware over his shoulder in the moonlight.

Her mouth flew open and she laughed deep in her throat, in an uninhibited manner that charmed him even further. She then clapped one hand over her mouth when they heard his glass smash against the tile roof of the ground floor jutting out below the terrace. Shot through as it was with half-smothered giggles, her voice sounded like that of a young girl's when she asked, "Why did you do that?"

He shrugged and returned her smile. "I don't know. Would you believe I'm testing glassware for the hotel?"

Queen Isabella shook her head with what Jason imagined might be more admiration for his daring than a negative reply to his ridiculous question. Her countenance thoughtful then, she looked down at the green stone in the moonlight, as if suddenly recalling his compliment. "Thank you for the champagne, and thank you for admiring my ring. It bears a special meaning."

Something lodged deep in Jason's mind had been trying to surface ever since he saw the ring and heard her laughter, but anything not connected with the moment seemed too trivial to consider. A sense of immediacy reigned. He did not want the game to slow, much less end. "May I ask for a dance after intermission, Queen Isabella?"

"How clever of you to guess my identity." After opening her fan again and bringing it up to hide the lower part of her face, she studied Jason with what appeared to him even keener intensity. The fan might have been the pale, artistically marked wing of an exotic butterfly at rest on a rare flower, so gracefully did it quiver before her face in the silvery light. Her eyes, moon-sparked like black water at midnight, remained fixed on Jason. "Who are you?"

Jason could not help but wonder if the Spanish beauty knew she was feminine fascination in its rarest form. He detected no trace of arrogance. "At midnight when everyone unmasks, I would like very much to introduce myself and learn who you are, your majesty.''

When she made no comment, merely continued to watch him from over the curved top of her lazily fluttering fan, Jason rammed his hands into the pockets of his form-fitting trousers to keep from reaching over and touching the pale gloves she held with her slender fingers. "Unless you would consent to our unmasking now. . . .''

Apparently accustomed to young men who tried pushing themselves on her, and eager for Jason to know she would do no more than banter with him from behind her mask, Queen Isabella removed her hand from the handrailing, drew herself up fully and inclined her head a degree higher. Her fan picked up speed. Jason wondered if she had any inkling how her regal pose suited her. God, but she was beautiful!

"I meant, sir, whom does your costume represent?''

Jason shrugged and glanced down at his leftover Carnival suit of white satin with its stylish frock coat and brocaded waistcoat over tapered trousers. He removed his hands from his pockets and tugged gently on his right earlobe. It had been some time since he had been enthusiastic about costumes to wear at masquerades. If his memory served him correctly, he had not worn the satin suit since Mardi Gras four years ago when the impish girl, Berry Cortabona, had knocked him down in the mud. Funny that he should think of that incident. "Maybe I'm Prince Charming looking for Cinderella—or for a Spanish queen.''

From the corner of his eye Jason spied King Ferdinand coming through the doorway and balancing a plate holding two glasses and a mound of party food. "Please, your grace, I need an answer before your king gets here. Will you honor me with a dance during the next interval?''

The queen brought her fan down from her face. With quick, susurrant notes it once more became a series of little folded pleats of lacquered silk shaped by narrow strips of ivory. "Yes.''

Before Jason faded among the shadows and potted plants and went back inside the ballroom, he said with what he realized might be bordering dangerously on truth, "I'll hold my breath until then."

"You dance like royalty," Jason said when at last he held the Spanish beauty in his arms and danced with her around the ballroom. His heartbeat was setting a faster pace than the three-four time of the Viennese waltz.

"How very gallant, Prince Charming." Berry Cortabona inclined her head in appreciation for the handsome masker's compliment, the movement setting the brilliants in her crown to sparkling anew in the candlelight reflecting from the multi-tiered crystal chandeliers. Was he, as she had begun to suspect out on the terrace when he first smiled, Jason Premont? She kept comparing his absurd remark about testing glassware for the hotel to Jason's equally ridiculous declaration that Sunday morning years ago that he served as wall inspector for the city.

Faint, elongated dimples played in the tall, dark-haired man's lean cheeks when he smiled and revealed his perfect teeth, Berry reflected, while easily following his masterful lead, but the Jason she recalled had not possessed such sculpted features. His dimples had appeared deeper, his cheeks rounder. Her dance partner's voice contained more bass than she recalled. Had Jason's shoulders been as broad and muscular, his hands as hard and manly that day she first saw him stuck on the garden wall? If the masked man were not wearing stylish white gloves, she figured she would be searching his palms for possible scars.

Four years had passed since she had run into Jason at Mardi Gras. She was positive that he had been wearing a white suit then. The light had been poor, though, and their time together brief; therefore she could not be certain about details lingering in her memory. She had already learned that the mind plays tricks on its owner.

If her partner really was Jason Premont, Berry's thoughts

whirled along as they danced, would he be surprised, maybe disapproving, to discover theatrical folk among those attending the upper class ball? And would he even remember having met Berry Cortabona? "I suppose that as Prince Charming, you've had experience in waltzing with royalty."

"Indeed. I had the pleasure of dancing with a princess or two while on the continent a few years back. And a few duchesses as well." Jason tightened his hold at the small of her back and pulled her as close as decorum permitted. She felt as right in his arms as he had imagined she would. "None could hold a taper to your beauty." With a slow, teasing smile, he added, "In fact, one had a mole on her nose."

Berry laughed, then pursed her lips and played at looking sympathetic. "Maybe the poor dear's patch slipped."

"Do you think I should have asked?"

"Not unless you wanted to get slapped."

"No gentleman wants to get slapped." Jason's impatience to remove her magenta mask and gain a full view of her eyes and face grew with each dance step. He marked again that a thick section of her black hair draped low over her forehead before being caught underneath her crown and robbed him of a glimpse of her face above her lace-edged mask. While appreciating the unrestricted view of her chin and full lips, he noted that the bottom was slightly fuller than the top. Both were alluringly moist and pink. The sight made him think about kissing. Could a man fall in love with a lovely stranger wearing a demi-mask?

"No gentleman is supposed to let on that he notices if his dancing partner has a mole on her nose."

"You were right in what you said out on the terrace."

"About what?"

"I do need help."

"I can offer you only pity."

"Don't you have any suggestions on how to arrange the alphabet in my head into words that might please the loveliest masker here this evening?" The realization that she too was enjoying their flirtation set Jason's pulse into a swifter race. "You truly are the most beautiful woman I've ever seen—though I've viewed only half of your bewitching face."

"What if I have a wart right between my eyes?"

Jason glimpsed the spark of mischief coming from behind the cutouts in her mask. Her eyes appeared more black than merely dark. Until he claimed her for the dance, he had not realized that her skin was so lushly olive, so tantalizingly smooth. He was deciding that it was possible to fall in love with a woman who had no name and kept the upper part of her face hidden. "Then I will know that warts can be beautiful."

She laughed and cocked her head to one side, so that the long curls cascading from underneath the back of her crown swung provocatively and grazed one of her naked shoulders. Unbeknownst to her, candlelight dipped into her black hair at intervals and lifted elusive blue lights. "You seem to be catching on quickly, now that you've discarded 'zounds.'"

"I could use private lessons. There's no telling how proficient I could become with you as tutor."

Berry pursed her lips as if in contemplation and shook her head, inadvertently sending an ebony curl to hug her neck and dangle enticingly against the expanse of silken skin above the daring décolletage of her gown. "That would be unfair to all womanhood."

"How so?" The masked beauty followed his steps easily, Jason noted with appreciation. From the start, he was as aware of the touch of her gloved hand on his shoulder as he was of the feel of the one he held in his left hand. His favorite point of contact, though, was where his hand rested on the warm satin above the small of her back and translated to his escalating senses the sensual sway of her hips.

Jason faced up to a dazzling discovery. No longer did a doubt befog his mind, which seemed to revolve in a dance of its own. He was falling in love with each stirring sweet note of the Viennese waltz.

"I get the feeling that you already know far more about the fairer sex than most men. You need no advice from me."

"Perhaps you've not known many men."

"Enough."

"But you aren't betrothed or seriously involved with someone, are you?" Jason held his breath for her answer, liking the way her full skirt belled against his trousers when, as now, they dipped and whirled in a loose circle among the other dancers on the gleaming parquet floor.

"No." Berry gazed over his shoulder. She had no wish for him to look into her eyes. What if he were to read in them her growing suspicion that she was dancing and flirting with Jason Premont? What if he were to suspect that she was fighting feeling something powerful for him, no matter who he was, and that she was leery about the outcome?

Even if the man were not Jason, Berry mused, he was a rake. During her three years spent traveling with Camille on the theatrical circuit in the East, Berry had learned to spot the handsome young men from the upper class who bore intentions no more honorable than a jolly good time for a fleeting interlude. Though she might enjoy the company of a libertine briefly—she never had denied she liked being around witty, carefree young men—she had no intention of allowing her life to merge permanently with that of such a man. Her old dreams of some day finding her special kind of love and marriage still nestled within her mind and heart. Though she had never put a label or face on the man she would love, her sensible side told her that a girl with her background could not expect to find happiness with a man from gentry. Even if he were not a rake.

Jason noticed that his partner's full lips wore a hint of a moue. If a view of her forehead were possible, might he see a tiny frown? Was she, perhaps, in deeper thought than she would have him know?

Berry returned her gaze to his, lifted her chin as if prepared for a blow, and asked, "Are you involved with someone?"

"No, and I never wanted to be until I saw you tonight." He realized that he meant both betrothed and seriously involved, that he was dying to know everything about her.

Berry rewarded him with a coquettish smile. *You handsome rogue! You must have said those words to a hundred women.* "That flowery phrase would gain you applause, maybe even a curtain call. You might become a star."

"Do you like theater?"

"Very much. How about you?"

"Yes, and I like opera in the winter when it's cozy being inside."

"So do I." Berry wondered if she had been wrong to imagine her masked partner was Jason Premont. The Jason she had met seven years ago would have cared little for any kinds of performances outside bedrooms. Unless he had changed greatly, he probably was visiting the bedrooms of married women where there was little chance of his becoming ensnared into lifelong commitment. "I would have imagined you liked calling on the operatic singers backstage better than listening to them sing their arias."

Jason chuckled. "Sly little minx, aren't you?" When she made no reply, he asked, "Will you allow me to escort you to a play tomorrow afternoon?" A wide smile seconded his invitation.

"We haven't even been introduced." Berry could not recall ever before having danced with a man as well put together in every detail. He could have been a young woman's dream come true. A part of her insisted he must be Jason.

Berry confessed to herself that since having met Jason back when she was twelve, she had always preferred tall, dark-haired men with resonant voices. She recognized that the main features she recalled about Jason were dimples in a laughing, handsome face. She thought about how her dance partner's well-fitting white costume showed off his broad shoulders and trim hips, even his muscled thighs and calves. From her considerable experience she judged his grace on the dance floor as unsurpassed.

For the life of her, Berry could not think of one outward attribute the man lacked. She was having too much fun to care that he was obviously a pleasure-loving scoundrel. Did that up the odds that he might be Jason?

"Prince Charming at your service, Queen Isabella."

In spite of herself, she giggled. "That hardly counts as an introduction."

"It's less than an hour before midnight." Jason glanced toward the terrace, turning them in that direction at the next full pattern.

"Unmasking doesn't count as a proper introduction." Was he going to dance her out onto the terrace? An exalted expectancy set Berry's pulse into a private waltz. None of the other young men she had known had flirted with her with more verve and daring than the tall Prince Charming. Fast behind that thought came the realization that she never before had so thoroughly enjoyed a flirtation with any man, rake or not. Had all her other encounters been preludes leading up to this evening?

To the last strains of the waltz, Prince Charming and Queen Isabella whirled onto the terrace. Laughing as he guided her around the tall, potted plants, they did not stop waltzing until they reached the secluded corner where they had talked earlier.

"I'm going to kiss you," Jason murmured as he released her hand and pulled her closer within his embrace.

"Don't promise," Berry whispered while lifting her face and sending her arms to curl around his neck. No longer did she doubt that the man setting her blood on fire was Jason Premont. She could think of nothing she wanted more than to have his mouth on hers. "Kiss me."

Jason tasted Berry's proffered lips reverently, then hungrily, pulling her body against him with impatient, masculine authority as the spicy fragrance of her skin and hair seeped into his being and wreaked havoc with his already tenuous control. The touch of her dance-warmed body close to his and the feel of her arms reaching around his neck fired his already heated senses. His kiss deepened, first searching for, then finding, the honeyed response he desperately craved.

The desire building within Jason since his first glimpse of the masked black-haired beauty on the dance floor surprised him with its intensity. For a crazed moment during their kiss, he felt lifted and weightless, as if, like the glass he had thrown earlier, he had been tossed off the second floor terrace into moonlit space. He entertained the thought that if the woman in his arms spurned him now, he might also splinter into jagged pieces.

Berry Cortabona knew about kisses, or so she had believed; but never before had a man kissed her quite like the masked Jason Premont was doing. Never before had she wanted to open up her entire being to the man kissing her. With muscular arms Jason was pressing her body provocatively close to his and she had no wish to retreat. Her lips moved under his with the same hungry wet ardor that his offered, now closing, now opening, half-retreating, then returning and slanting this way and that. He tasted of champagne and warm, virile man.

Accompanying each melting of their clinging mouths were ragged little sounds that Berry recognized were as much his as hers. Stars were shooting off behind her closed eyelids; she felt eerily transported up into the moonlit sky.

How was it, Berry wondered, that she had believed herself knowledgeable about the ways of young men and women? The thought zig-zagged across her befuddled mind that she could have understudied the part for years and still not been prepared for the raw reality of Jason's fiery kisses. She almost panicked when she opened her eyes and could see nothing but blackness.

"You've captivated my heart," Jason whispered after he forced his lips from hers and looked into her upturned face. Moonbeams played among the sequins covering her magenta mask and he smiled when he noted that it had slipped aside and covered her eyes. Loosening his hold on her, but not stepping away, he removed his mask. "Unless you scream for help, I'm going to take off your mask and see the face of the woman who has utterly bewitched me. Will it require a proposal of marriage to learn your name?"

Trembling, Berry slipped off her mask. Relieved to learn she had not gone blind as well as half daft from the effect of Jason's passionate kisses, she smiled up at him. Their marveling gazes met in the moonlight and savored all upon which they had feasted so hungrily moments before. "I would never insist on a proposal as the price for learning my name. And Berry Cortabona wouldn't dream of screaming for help, Jason Premont. I grew up in the meaner side of the Quarter and I've learned to take care of myself. You may call me Berry"—she arched an eyebrow provocatively, noting his shocked expression. Had he remembered their earlier meetings?—"or if you prefer something more exotic, Angelique."

"Berry? Berry Cortabona?" Jason could not add more for a full moment. His voice seemed as soft as the moonlight when he managed to speak again. "This is incredible. That saucy, sweet, adorable girl . . ." He laughed low in his throat and pulled her close in his arms before kissing her again, soundly, then reverently. "By the saints! Berry Cortabona is the queen who has been driving me out of my mind all evening! When did you guess who I was? I never had an inkling . . ."

They stood in loose embrace and invited the moment to overwhelm them. It was as if a benevolent force prevailed and kindly led them into calmer waters before the undertow of their churning emotions swamped them.

Slowly at first, then with haste, they told each other of the major happenings in their lives since their second meeting four years ago. His trek abroad, then to Texas. Her journey with Camille to the East. The loss of his mother. The deaths of Aunt Maddy and Ebon. Warren Maroney's trial. Afterward they began dipping farther back to that first predawn meeting.

"You looked like a bug caught on that wall," Berry told him, giggling at the memory. She felt unreasonably close to him, as if he might have been a silent but integral part of her life since that first meeting.

Accepting her teasing with good nature, he grinned at her and retorted, "And you climbed that drain pipe"——He leaned to plant a kiss on the tip of nose—"like a monkey. An adorable monkey."

She slid him a teasing look from behind partially lowered lashes. "Come to think of it, the bug was rather attractive, the only one I ever saw with dimples."

Suddenly there was so much to tell, so much to listen to, so much to ask about that they blocked out the rest of the world. Neither noticed when midnight arrived, the music ceased and the official unmasking took place.

Not until chattering, laughing people began wandering out onto the terrace did Berry and Jason step out of their light embrace and lean side by side against the handrailing, ardent gazes still joined. Their animated talk went on.

Leonidas Latrobe's trained voice intruded and jerked Berry and Jason back to the moment. "Berry," he said with apparent vexation, "I've looked for you everywhere."

"Not here," she replied with a giggle and a conspiratorial glance at Jason. "I've been here for quite some time."

"Don't try being witty," Leonidas retorted.

"I'm sorry, Leonidas," Berry replied. Quickly she introduced the two men, then said to Leonidas, "I thought you would hardly miss me. I noticed the blond matron wearing the Jezebel costume was keeping you charmed each time I danced by with someone else."

The actor affected an aggrieved tone. "You're being unkind, darling. I was merely showing my gratitude for her having sent me our tickets. I saw how the men stood in line to dance with you until you disappeared." He glared in the moonlight at Jason before adding, "I thought perhaps we would leave now and go for a stroll beside the river."

"I'm not ready to leave."

"I will see Miss Cortabona home safely," Jason offered in a hurry. "I can think of nothing I would enjoy more."

"Who are you to be stepping into something that doesn't concern you?" Leonidas demanded. With pronounced arrogance he lifted his chin and sent a hot-eyed look at the younger man. His lips formed a forbidding line.

"He's an old friend of mine," Berry replied with a teasing smile toward Jason. Then she noted Leonidas's air of wounded dignity and the disapproving, almost ugly set to his normally attractive mouth. Striving to conceal her annoyance, she said politely, "Thank you for inviting me to come with you, Leonidas. I've had a lovely time. Goodnight."

Plainly on the border of losing control, the actor declared, "You came with me. You'll leave with me."

"My part of our agreement is over," Berry pointed out in what she assumed was a reasonable manner. Why was Leonidas behaving so badly? "You don't need me any longer to convince Jezebel's husband that you have a lady friend. Don't you agree that we put on a good show during the first part of the evening? Thanks for escorting me and arranging for my costume. I'll return it to the theater in a day or two. I prefer to let Jason walk me home."

A group standing nearby and obviously eavesdropping began tittering and stealing glances at the threesome.

"I won't forget this insult, Berry," Leonidas said with force and a narrow-eyed glare. "I cannot abide women toying with me." Without another word, he wheeled away and lost himself among the plants and buzzing groups of revelers.

"Should I have kept quiet?" Jason asked when he noticed Berry's discomfort lingering. "I'm sorry if I've created a problem; but as you likely guessed, I did overhear your earlier disagreement with the man."

"There's no problem. Everything will be all right," Berry replied. "Leo and I are old friends, or at least I thought we were." What had caused Leonidas to become upset? He had known as well as she that their being together that evening was merely a mutual convenience. Surely he was not so angry with her that he would not live up to his part of their bargain and speak to Henry Zimpel.

Not until Berry felt the warmth of Jason's hand covering hers could she forget the venom in Leonidas's words or the fire in his eyes. Then she could think of nothing but the way Jason looked at her, the way his voice sounded, and the way her hand tingled beneath his.

CHAPTER

*

Six

On Chartres Street Jason indicated where his townhouse sat, and Berry was pleased that they did indeed live near each other. She had been walking beside him with her hand tucked in the crook of his arm and hearing the mismatched shuffles their shoes made on the brick banquette. Soft, sibilant sounds from hers, solid messages from his.

Throughout their walk from the ball, they had never run out of talk; sometimes they even paused on the street to complete a spirited discussion. His interest in her plans to become a designer surprised and gratified her, led her to feel that he might share her unorthodox view that she was more than a female destined to depend on a male. When she asked questions about the happenings on his uncle's sugar plantation, Jason was happy to enlighten her about a way of life alien to her.

Now that their identities were no longer secret, Berry reflected as they ambled along, she would not have been surprised if Jason had shown some evidence that their vastly different backgrounds had altered his initial attraction to her, but he seemed no more inclined than she to pay homage to social class. Actually, though, they had nothing in common but their zest for life. Maybe both could be categorized as what she thought of as "Impulse People." "You were right, Jason. Camille's townhouse is one of several small ones sharing a courtyard in the next block down. We *are* your neighbors."

Jason remarked with mock superiority and a pat on her hand that thrilled her, "Trust me. I'm nearly always right."

"How can you expect me to trust you when I know some of your tricks? Like hiding a stolen emerald for a thief." What fun to have something to tease about!

"But I know some of yours, too, like climbing through the transom of a locked building—"

"*Touché!*" Berry smiled up at him. Jason's kisses, his very presence, had ignited a flame within her that she had not suspected could be so volatile. Until meeting with him this evening, she had considered herself inured to the advances of handsome rakes. She felt a little frightened at how easily he was proving her wrong.

Without warning, Jason stopped and guided Berry into his arms for a sweet, slow kiss that added an extra note to her already singing pulse. It almost stole her breath.

Before they resumed their leisurely pace, Berry glanced up and down the narrow street, seeing nothing but fog sneaking in from the river and drifting into eerie halos around the street lamps hanging from corner buildings. Even the numerous dogs in the French Quarter had settled in for the night, she noted with the complacency of a native. Flashing him an insouciant smile, she asked, "Do you care that people might have seen the dashing planter kissing a seamstress with extravagant dreams of becoming a designer?"

"Not a whit. I hope they noticed and became jealous. No other woman I've known could entertain such dreams and expect to see them come true. And no other ever looked as gorgeous as you do tonight.''

"Morning is more like it. I adore your flattery.'' Berry laid her head against his upper arm, savoring the pleasure and security she felt in his presence. The exalted sense of expectancy she'd possessed since childhood was so strong in her still that she had not puzzled over the uncanny way the two had met again. Life was both good and bad, to her way of thinking, and it seemed prudent to enjoy the good when it came along so as to bear better the bad when it reared its ugly head.

"Would you like to come inside my house for a brandy and let me show you around?'' Jason asked, gesturing toward a walled-in, two-story brick building that was sandwiched in between two of similar Spanish architecture. "My mother and father lived here the brief time they had together before he was killed in the Battle of New Orleans. Actually, it's where I was born.''

"Thanks, but it's terribly late and I wouldn't want to disturb anyone.'' Berry knew that she was far more concerned with how much being alone with Jason was disturbing her, although she could not deny a keen interest in the place of his birth. In the light from the full moon and the street lamps, she could tell that the townhouse was large and U-shaped, a fitting city residence for a wealthy Creole planter. His earlier casual reference to his permanent home had lodged in her mind—Armand Acres in Saint Christopher Parish.

"No problem. My friend, Ashley, sometimes stays overnight at my place. I believe you heard him say that tonight he was returning to his father's plantation upriver.''

The image of the good-looking young man, wearing with grace a pink satin suit, a tiny scar on his cheek and a slightly lopsided smile, sprang to mind. "I liked meeting Ashley Breton. I was relieved you didn't remind him that I was the one who knocked you and his sister down that night. You two acted as if you've known each other for ages."

"We have. Our families have always visited back and forth. I grew up with him and his sister and brother. Since Ashley isn't staying here tonight, the only people in the house are the blacks who run things. They live in the wing behind the kitchen. We could take a quick look and maybe sip a brandy before I escort you on down to your friend's place. If you don't care for brandy—"

"Could I be a N'Orleans-born Creole and not like brandy, suh?" She flicked open her fan and waved it coquettishly in front of her face. Instead of settling down into a comfortable pattern, the initial excitement of being with Jason seemed to have escalated throughout the evening.

Jason laughed at her exaggerated drawl and gloried in the mischievous sparkle of her black eyes in the moonlight. "Then you must come in with me. The evening has been too perfect for us to let it end so quickly."

Observing Berry's hesitation, he added, "Of course if you're thinking a chaperone might be a necessity, perhaps my man, Alonzo, will do. He nearly always waits up for me, or pretends he does. Actually he falls asleep on the stairs so I'll have to trip over him when I get in."

"A chaperone?" Was he reading her mind, maybe, and discovering her uneasiness about finding herself alone with him in a room? His nearness was overpowering, her defenses teetering, but his invitation sounded much like a dare. "Don't be absurd! I've been on my own far too long to think along such lines."

When they reached a wooden gate set in a tall brick wall, Jason opened it and escorted Berry inside with a playful flourish. "Welcome to my home, Queen Isabella."

"Thank you, Prince Charming." The clank of the iron latch falling back into place with finality reminded Berry that she might have taken a step toward more than a casual visit to Jason Premont's townhouse. She hesitated and glanced upward. Though the full moon was not visible from within the walled-in space, she saw that its silvery light, aided by that from innumerable stars twinkling against their black velvety backdrop, was creating intriguing shadows all about. The witching hour had arrived. She shivered.

The night fog, its breath suggesting damp mystery, had not yet crept inside the walled-in courtyard, Berry noted with the discerning eye of one growing up in the Vieux Carré. Though no raucous sounds drifted over the block of Chartres where they stood, she was certain that there was plenty of riotous merrymaking going on in the saloons, beer parlors, brothels and gambling dens on Front Street and its neighboring thoroughfares. The faint, sporadic noises of metal scraping, of wood creaking and thumping against wood reminded her that the ever-present ships and steamboats tied up along the curving miles of docks were restlessly riding the Mississippi's night current.

From somewhere in the direction of the river, a dog bayed, the mournful notes belying her earlier presumption that even the dogs were asleep. Was nothing as it seemed at first thought, first glance? Remembering that Jason likely was awaiting her reaction to his home, she said, "I love your courtyard. I'll bet it's beautiful in the daylight, too."

Jason said, "I'm inviting you over for tea tomorrow afternoon so that you can see for yourself." By then they had crossed the flagstones and were passing the fountain splashing delicate watery notes in the center of the spacious open area.

"I accept."

She smiled at him and then they were lost, gazing into each other's eyes, pausing before stepping onto the shadowed veranda that followed the U-shape of the house. Just before Jason kissed her, he asked with a trace of shyness weaving in and out of his husky bass, "Do you think that fate threw us together again . . . for a purpose?"

During their fervid kiss, Berry clung to Jason with mindless joy, content to glory in the feel and taste of his mouth on hers, the warmth of his arms folding her against his tall frame. Her hands met at the back of his neck and tingled as they caressed his hair, his shoulders. The handsome man plumping up her awareness of her femininity must be sharing her mindless fascination, else why the question about fate? Her already aroused senses leapt like something going wild and fed the tendrils of flame curling and uncurling deep inside her womanhood. Then her mind stepped into the act.

Berry's stern, inner voice took her to task. What was she doing letting Jason's sweet words and kisses tempt her into believing any kind of relationship between them was worthy of consideration? She was being absurd! He was not the kind of man who could offer her the blessed love she sought. Jason Premont probably had spoken eloquently to numerous young women when he first became enamored of them. Probably such references to fate were a part of the games that wealthy young rakes played as they flitted from one new face to another. When she was back East, had not similar romantic innuendos been whispered in her own ear? And more than one proposal of marriage that would have dissipated along with the moonlight, had she accepted it.

Berry tried escaping Jason's searing mouth, but he placed one hand behind her head, clutched her tighter and kept kissing her, kept turning her brain into mush and her body into a hot, throbbing boneless mass. For an utterly mindless moment she was lost in sensation.

"Please," Berry whispered when she at last gained a space between their faces. Robbed of breath, she pushed with both hands against his chest. Her knees, unreliable now, threatened to buckle. Fearful that she might sink into a puddle of magenta silk at his feet, she held on to his arms. To her ears, both her voice and her breath sounded ragged, pitiful. Trying to recall what her speech coaches had advised, she strove for a light tone. "Why bother searching for reasons for our having met again? Let's just enjoy the fact that we did."

The somewhat flippant reply deflated Jason, turning his thoughts inward. Maybe he had been wrong to suspect he was falling in love as they danced. From what he had always believed, love unrequited was not true love. Evidently Berry had experienced nothing unusual. How was it that he had known many women and yet had few clues as to the way their minds worked? Had he been imagining all evening that she seemed as fascinated with him as he was with her?

Jason could not believe that, despite her apparent ease around men, Berry Cortabona was a shallow flirt. She seemed too forthright, too unaffected to practice deliberate deception. The prospect of a negative answer was daunting, but he went on doggedly, ready if need be to challenge destiny. "Don't you feel anything for me?"

Berry searched his dark eyes, all the while hearing the soft melody of the fountain behind them and thinking how marvelous it would be if she could accept what her runaway heart was pressing her to believe at that poignant moment. "Oh, yes, Jason, I feel something for you, something wonderful."

"I'm glad." He avoided her gaze for fear that his disappointment still showed in his eyes. She hadn't told him what he longed to hear, but at least she hadn't rejected him. "A man likes to know that the woman who has bewitched him at least finds him . . . special."

Her crown shimmered in the celestial light reflecting from overhead as Berry explained further. "I feel illuminated inside right now, feel as if I might be playing the lead role in a fantasy with the most handsome man in the world." His eyes delved into hers, seeking out her secret self, which seemed to have gone into hiding. "But I recognize it is fantasy."

A secret voice within Berry branded her a liar, tried to remind her that something electric had penetrated her being during their first kiss, during all those following. The tingling sensation had not yet gone away, but it could be nothing beyond physical attraction. Could it? Never! Jason was a wealthy rake, not the man for her. "Let's not spoil a perfect evening by baring souls."

Jason heard what he wanted to hear and felt his wounded heart surge with hope. Earlier she had called him "dashing," and now, "handsome." She did feel something for him, and in time . . . After all, she had told him that she was nineteen and also that there was no other man in her life. Berry was young, would require time to examine her heart. But he would court her as no woman had ever been courted and win her over to his way of thinking. "Forgive me. Perhaps I have rushed matters."

"Perhaps," Berry said, looking him straight in the eye, "you're mistaking physical attraction for something else."

Jason stroked his right earlobe. Berry Cortabona was sounding not at all like a naive young woman who might be easily persuaded into doing anything against her will. Was it her beauty alone that had captivated him? Or had her independent spirit also played a major role? "Have it your way for now."

Jason forced a smile and, taking Berry by the hand, led her inside his foyer, where an oil lamp in a wall sconce flickered and gave out a soft light. Sure enough, just as Jason had predicted, Alonzo lay sprawled up the lower steps of the staircase leading to the second floor, sound asleep with his gray-sprinkled head resting atop one outflung arm.

Grinning and putting his forefinger to his lips in the sign for silence, Jason led the amused Berry down the hallway. He showed her the rooms facing the courtyard—the candlelit parlor, the dining room, and the library in the bend of the curved house.

Then, with snifters of brandy in their hands and exchanges of secret smiles, they followed the hallway to a staircase directly across the courtyard from the one where the black man slept. After a low-voiced consultation with his beautiful companion, Jason lighted a taper in a brass-handled holder and led the way up the stairs.

"I like the balconies outside each bedroom," Berry whispered to Jason after he had shown her nearly the entire second floor. Somehow she was finding his elegant home in the French Quarter especially suited to candlelight and husky late-night voices. She sipped her brandy, wondering if the sweet liquid might not be flavoring her opinion. "Your townhouse is lovely and much larger than Camille's."

"You don't have to whisper any longer," Jason reminded her with a boyish smile. "Alonzo is slightly hard of hearing and usually he doesn't wake up unless I call him. Sometimes, when I come in feeling weary, I step over him and he never knows I came in until he rushes upstairs the next morning."

"Poor man. You're a rogue, just as I figured." Berry returned his grin, feeling like a co-conspirator. Talking with Jason was intoxicating. "I'll bet he wouldn't be shocked at all to find a young woman wandering about the place in the dead of night."

"What a devious mind you have, Queen Isabella," Jason remarked with a chuckle. Intrigued by the sight of her pink mouth curving against the crystal edge of her glass, he cleared his throat of a sudden fullness. "I'm almost afraid to confess I saved the best room for last."

Berry swallowed the globules of brandy nestling on her tongue and stepped through the door Jason was holding open into a spacious room. It was obviously a man's room—spicy, clean, and energizing. Refusing her eyes permission to do more than glance at the turned down bed, she admired the massive pieces of mahogany furniture with straight lines, the pale rug with geometric patterns in earth tones that were repeated in the trim of natural-colored linen draperies at the tall windows. French doors opened out onto a moonlit balcony.

"This must be your bedroom," Berry said. "It is strikingly handsome." She bridled her tongue to keep from adding, "like its owner." There was a time and place for everything, a sensible part of her pointed out, and a man's bedroom in the middle of the night was no place for handing out compliments.

Jason set both the candleholder and his empty glass on the mantel and turned toward his beautiful black-haired guest. His dark eyes sparkled mischievously. "Well, are you coming inside to see it all? Or are you afraid?"

"Me, afraid?" Berry retorted with false bravado. "Why should I be afraid?" Her pulse sounded so loudly she was afraid he could hear it. She darted unseeing looks around the room before her gaze centered on Jason who stood in the small circle of candlelight watching her. His expression warmed her even more than had the brandy. Clutching her glass with both hands as if it offered support, she said, "I like your room very much."

"Try the view from the balcony."

"Some other time, maybe. I think we should leave now. Camille might be worried about me."

"You told me earlier that she was out with her betrothed. Surely you don't suspect me of bringing you here with ulterior motives."

Berry attempted a lighthearted laugh. He looked serious, offended. Draining her snifter and setting it on the mantel beside his, she strolled on wobbly knees to the balcony with its wrought iron handrailing. The view and the sound of the fountain splashing musically in the moonlight mingled with the faint smell of roses and cape jasmine below, captivating her. Holding her crown in place with one hand, she craned her neck to see the full moon far above the orange tiled roof. "Oh, Jason," she murmured with unabashed awe, "it *is* lovely here."

"I ordered the moon just for this occasion."

She turned, to find him standing beside her at the delicately detailed iron handrailing. "What was it you called it on the terrace when you were being so brash and flirty—a Creole moon?" she asked. "I've never heard of a Creole moon."

"See how it's smiling?"

Berry humored him and leaned again to gaze upward, this time noting the faint, upward arching shadows within the silvery circle. "So?"

The sight of the lovely curve of her neck almost made

Jason forget what he had meant to say. "It smiles like that only when it's gazing down on Creole lovers."

So natural was the movement Jason made to draw Berry into his arms that she wondered if she might not have initiated it herself by turning then and looking up at him. His lips met hers with tenderness. When hers answered in like manner, he felt a rush of passion fire his blood. He gathered her closer, deepening his kiss, savoring the sound of the feminine rustles of her magenta gown and the feel of her body as she gave herself more fully to his embrace. He wanted to show her with more than words that the two of them were fated to become one.

As his tongue teased the soft inner edges of her mouth, Berry responded, clasping his head with both hands and running her fingers across the back of his neck, through the thick waves of his dark hair. The inner illumination she had told him that his nearness brought to her glowed ever brighter. The heat she had felt inside her earlier rose again, but this time it burst into a flowing liquid flame that could not be quenched. She ended the kiss but could not force herself from his embrace.

"Berry, you're the most beautiful, desirable woman I've ever met," Jason whispered. A bare inch separated their lips. He could not tell which quick breath was hers, which his.

Speechless, she struggled for control. Her pulse pounded. Escape. She needed to escape before . . . "That's quite a compliment"—oh, it was, and she treasured it, but—"coming from a man like you."

Jason chose to ignore the implication because he saw starlight mirrored in her eyes and realized that a fierce battle raged within those ebony depths. He wanted to make love to her—could hardly think of anything else—but not until she was as ready as he to recognize that what sizzled between them was more than raw passion. Torn between pressing for the advantage of the moment and setting her free to resolve the conflict that tortured her, he made one of his most difficult decisions and released her. "Perhaps it would be wise for me to walk you home now."

Berry looked into his handsome face, thinking that she was going to find the events of this Saturday evening hard to believe in the clear light of Sunday. At the moment, she felt like a sleepwalker caught up in a dream, vaguely aware of sensory perceptions but finding reality elusive. With an emotion unfamiliar to her and more than a little frightening, in a voice gone throaty all on its own, Berry replied, "I think you're right."

It had already occurred to Jason before he escorted Berry out to the street for the brief walk to her friend's townhouse that he had best leave off talk of feelings and concentrate on getting her to agree to see him again. If he were going to woo and wed Berry Cortabona—and by then he knew damned well that he was going to give the effort his all—he needed to keep open their lines of communication.

"Is that a boatswain's whistle?" he asked, when muffled notes penetrated the patch of low fog surrounding them at the moment. He strove to make small talk, but he was so aware of the feel of her hand resting in the crook of his elbow as they walked along the banquette that he might not have been wearing a coat and shirt.

"Sounds like it."

"I know you said you've been back only a few weeks, but have you and your friend met your neighbors?"

"Some of them."

"You must find New Orleans much changed during your absence."

"Yes."

Jason hoped that Berry's reticence was a sign that once she reached her bedroom, her earlier stated convictions might be in for a review. And revisions in his favor. She was obviously deep in thought.

When they reached the gate into the courtyard leading to several small townhouses, in one of which Camille lived, Berry looked up at him for the first time since leaving his place. "Jason, thank you for inviting me into your beautiful home and showing me around. The entire evening was lovely."

"It truly was, wasn't it? I would like to come for you tomorrow afternoon. What time is best?" When she tilted her head and gazed at him in apparent confusion, he added, "You agreed to come for tea and see the courtyard in daylight." The brilliants in her crown winked but he saw only the light in her eyes. "Perhaps your friend Camille would come along. I'd like very much to meet her."

"Oh, yes. I did accept your invitation, didn't I?" Berry replied, unable to decipher the look he sent her in the pale moonlight. She was also unable to figure out why her heart had begun to pound as it had during his kisses and caresses. He was standing at least a foot away, but the space between them seemed fraught with silent messages.

If Berry hadn't known better, she would have thought Jason was as puzzled as she about the emotion that had nearly overwhelmed them earlier. Had he also felt the need to escape? She regretted having agreed to come for tea before she had realized that she should not spend any more time with Jason Premont. For a man not even remotely resembling the kind she longed to marry, his effect on her was too heady, too frightening. She could offer the excuse about a forgotten appointment . . . "Unless Camille has made other plans, both of us will be expecting you to come for us around four."

"Goodnight. I'll see you tomorrow at four." After leaning and brushing her lips with a quick kiss, Jason watched Berry go inside and heard her close the door.

On his way back to the townhouse, Jason did not glance in the direction of the moon that was setting on the horizon. He did not dare because he feared it might no longer be smiling.

CHAPTER

*

Seven

A few mornings after having met Jason Premont and gone with Berry and him to his place for a delightful tea, Camille Hayes sat in her guest bedroom drinking coffee with Berry. She seldom lost her temper with her young friend who, in her opinion, already had endured a goodly share of life's heartaches. This morning, though, the actress felt her control slipping while listening to Berry's diatribe against rakes, Jason counted among them.

"Come now," Camille retorted with a toss of her long auburn hair when Berry's soft voice trailed off, "you try my patience with your childish attitude toward accepting invitations from that handsome Jason Premont. You've gone out with men like him before, though I'm not sure you were any more accurate about their being libertines than you are about Jason. Sometimes people pin unflattering tags on wealthy young man simply because they're different, especially when they're handsome and charming."

From where Berry sat beside the window in a wash of morning sunshine, she looked up from her sewing and frowned. "Why call my attitude childish? I think mature is more apt. Maybe I've outgrown such frivolities as going out with men who don't have a purpose more serious than to lure some young woman into their arms for a brief interlude before they dash off to someone new."

"Come now, Berry," Camille chided. "Why such cynicism from one not yet twenty?"

Berry pursed her lips and returned to her needlework.

Camille continued. "Ever since we went to Jason's for tea, he has called here every afternoon with little gifts of candy or flowers. I've yet to see him make one gesture of impropriety. He's too much of a gentleman to force himself on any woman. I don't intend to sit with you when he calls again. You've never before asked for a chaperone and you don't need one around Jason." She slid a knowing look Berry's way. "Not many women would need persuasion to be in his company alone. I figure he's about my age, and to me, he's quite good-looking."

"Looks aren't everything!"

"I never said they were, but you're a fool not to go out with him. After all, we're not talking lifelong commitment. I've never before seen you afraid of a man who has shown you nothing but courtesy and attention—"

"A fool? Afraid?" Berry interrupted sharply. Camille's innocent reference to lifelong commitment cut to the bone. If she but knew of Jason's romantic innuendos that evening of the ball . . . "I'm not afraid of Jason Premont. It's just that I know better than anyone else what's best for my future." She threw her sewing aside and took a sip of coffee, evading Camille's probing gaze.

"Your future?" Camille echoed, already sorry to have lost her patience with her friend. She was hoping to discover what was bringing sad looks to Berry's eyes lately, though, and she did not abandon her attack. "Do you mean your plans to work at a theater until you sell a design?"

Camille's dark eyes softened. "I thought we were discussing the rather simple matter of whether or not you should be turning down invitations from a young man who apparently is smitten by you. Are you depressed about not getting a wardrobe mistress's position? Perhaps you shouldn't be spending so much time working on my wedding gown. Perhaps you should be working on designs instead."

Relieved to have diverted Camille from the subject of Jason, Berry decided to share another concern. "That scoundrel Henry Zimpel is still making certain that I don't work in any of the theaters," she confided. "Maybe I made a mistake in returning to New Orleans. I'm lucky to have your gown to keep me busy until I find steady work or manage to sell one of my designs. I loved designing your dress and I'm enjoying sewing it. I want it to be perfect for your marriage to Ace."

Camille touched Berry's hand. "Forgive me. I don't mean to harangue you. I couldn't bear it if you weren't staying here with me, and I wish you'd not be so intent on striking out on your own. It's not as if you haven't any money, or talent to earn more, or a place to live for as long as you like."

Berry slid her an appreciative smile. "Thanks."

"You can always accept Miss Dilly's offer to help in her shop with Mardi Gras gowns. You'd probably earn more than if you were wardrobe mistress at a theater. I'm confident you'll make it as a designer soon. To me you're the younger sister I never had. You know as well as I that Ace adores you."

"Are you trying to cheer me on or up?" Berry asked with a mischievous smile. "Either way, I appreciate your efforts."

Camille watched Berry return her cup to its saucer and place it on the small table sitting between their chairs before she said, "Ace was saying only the other evening that when the renovations are done on his house in the Garden District, he hopes you'll stay in our guest wing until you marry and have a home of your own. I think I've told you that years ago, before Ace's wife became ill, they had a child. Had the infant lived, by now she would have been only a few years younger than you.''

For a moment a pensive expression claimed Camille's face as she thought of how much sadness her betrothed had suffered. First there had been the loss of his baby and then the lengthy, debilitating illness of his beloved wife that had taken her away from him long before her actual death last year. Three years ago, when Camille had first met Ace Zachary at a backstage party for theater patrons, the black-haired man with the haunted eyes had drawn her to him without a word. Who could have predicted that they would fall in love before the evening was over or that Camille would feel compelled to flee New Orleans in order to escape her desire to become his mistress?

With the June sunshine angling through the window and highlighting her blue-black hair, Berry smiled across at her friend. Sometimes, she mused, Camille seemed to step beyond the ten years separating their ages and assume a maternal air toward her. A measure of guilt for having kept secret all week her disturbing thoughts about Jason and causing Camille to be concerned sneaked up on her. Maybe she should have discussed the matter with one far more experienced with men than she. "You're forgiven. I have been distracted lately and I'm sorry if it bothered you."

Camille smiled her forgiveness.

Berry said, "I like your future husband as much as he seems to like me. It's hard to think of a man as handsome as Ace Zachary being father to someone old enough to attend school, much less near my age. He's lucky to be getting you, but I think you're lucky, too."

"I can't help but agree," Camille said, a tender expression gracing her flawless features. Her concern about Berry's welfare shadowed her glowing thoughts and led her to say, "It's not like you to brood and keep in all of your thoughts."

"One thing that troubles me is that Leonidas hasn't lived

up to his promise to speak with Henry about us ironing out our differences. I can't believe he's such a scoundrel!'' Berry's eyes flashed fire, and her chin shot up. "I'm so mad at Leonidas and Mr. Zimpel that I'd like to kick them both in the seats of their pants.''

"I'm sorry you're upset over anything that rascal Leo does. You never told me what his excuse was the other afternoon when you returned the Isabella costume to him at the theater.''

Picking up her needle again, Berry said, "You know how egotistical and peevish Leo can be. He seemed itchy to have me gone before Mr. Zimpel returned. He never said much that made sense. I'll not count him as a friend again.'' Camille had told Berry of some past instances of Leo's vindictiveness toward her when the two of them were close, and Berry did not want to reveal that she herself had angered Leonidas twice at the ball, once when she refused his kiss and again when she chose to leave with Jason. After all, Camille had a right to enjoy her present happiness in being reunited with Ace and planning their wedding without worrying about her friend.

Berry reflected that she was grown up and could do her own worrying—if need be.

Camille interrupted Berry's troubled thoughts. "Before Ace left on the shakedown outing of his new riverboat, I let him know about Leo's abominable behavior. He said he would like to wring his neck.''

"I love that idea!'' Berry giggled, welcoming the instantaneous image of the muscular Ace Zachary attacking the foppish actor. She knew the story of how Ace had started as a deckhand on a riverboat and moved through the ranks to become captain of a Mississippi side-wheeler before at last purchasing his first vessel. In his early forties now, he owned several riverboats and still chose to take an active part in their operation. She doubted Leonidas Latrobe had ever done anything more physical than help move around a few props. "I'll bet Ace would enjoy that, just because he hates the idea that once you and Leo were close."

Delighted at Berry's elevated mood, Camille laughed and admitted, "You're probably right." Deadly serious then, she asked, "Did you and Leo quarrel the other night before he brought you home? I wouldn't put it past him to try seducing you. I've noticed the way he looks at you since we've returned to New Orleans. He's quite vain, you know."

"No," Berry said with little more than a twinge of guilt for her partial lie. "We had no problems." There was no need in adding to Camille's anxiety. Everyone knew Leonidas was a moody egoist; he would forget all about being upset with her and seek out one of his many married amours. She picked up a handful of seed pearls and began stringing them on her needle. Soon she was attaching them to the heavy white satin of Camille's wedding gown, making certain that each pearl lay on the lightly penciled outline of her floral design.

Amused at the way Berry held the tip of her tongue between her teeth while making the intricate stitches, Camille watched her fondly and let her thoughts run on. Though Berry at first had been downcast from having failed to develop a stage voice and, thus, presence enough to become an actress, she seemed to have bounded back from that disappointment with her usual resiliency. Recently, Berry had astounded her with several perfected sketches of outstanding designs for ball gowns. All she needed was to show them in the right place. Camille, who could do little beyond thread a needle or jam a florist's bouquet into a vase, still found it hard to believe that the slender beauty had little conception of how talented and creative she was.

Camille's gaze wandered to the small table between them. Through the open window the morning sunshine bathed a slender crystal vase that held rewards from Berry's early morning visit to the potted plants on the balcony outside the stair landing—a single rose with sprigs of maidenhair fern serving as an airy background for the red bloom. In Camille's bedroom sat another, similar but with a flair of its own. Who but Berry Cortabona, or one with her abundance of energy and love of beauty, would go to the trouble of setting bouquets in rooms never seen by callers?

"Will you think over what I said about going out with Jason Premont and having some fun?" Camille asked after rising and preparing to leave. "It's my theory that while a woman is waiting for her true love, she might as well enjoy whatever opportunities come along. Maybe a harmless little romance is what you need to take your mind off your worries."

Irritated at Camille's scarcely concealed attempts at matchmaking, but more irritated at her own inability to come to terms with her feelings toward Jason, Berry sighed and caught the soft inner side of her lower lip between her teeth. Her earlier plan to avoid being alone with him and in time forget how meeting him again had turned her world upside down seemed doomed. Jason's persistence had caught her off guard, as had the silent but certain force that emanated from him each time he visited.

Certainly the rakes she had known in the past never would have returned after even one reception as cool as those Berry had been meting out all week to Jason. Had he, like Camille, suspected she was afraid to be alone with him? If so, was he reading into it the absurd notion that she might be fighting against feeling more than a physical attraction? Well, she concluded, it was time to lay suspicions to rest. She was not afraid of anybody. Neither was she about to fall in love with Jason Premont.

"You win," Berry said after Camille paused at the door and turned around to face her, plainly awaiting a reply. "If Jason returns this afternoon and mentions going out, I'll accept. But only to please you." Bedamned! Her needle pricked her finger then and she had to pop it into her mouth to keep the drop of blood from falling onto the white satin.

* * *

Jason leaned impatiently toward the mirror over his wash-stand, vexed with more than the fact that the cloth he was trying to fold in place kept trying to creep up from the inside of his shirt. His visit to Camille Hayes's townhouse this afternoon would be his fourth straight one, and not once had he managed more than a few moments alone with Berry. Did she intend to shove him out of her life before he gained the opportunity to win her love? Scowling, he ripped the strip of white cloth from his neck and flung it over his shoulder.

"Wait a moment, Mr. Jason." Alonzo's soft voice came from the doorway into the bedroom. He closed the door and walked lightly to where his master stood. "You don't have to throw the stock away and get another. I can fix that one up in no time. No need to get in a funk. Why didn't you call me when you started getting dressed?"

"I'm not in a funk!"

"You's in a funk."

"I'm not!"

"I recognize a funk when I see it." The black man picked up the stock from the rug and smoothed it with his nimble fingers.

"I don't need smart talk from you, Alonzo."

"You need smarts from somebody."

"One of these days I'm going to forget my mother gave you to me on my third birthday and kick you out on the street."

"I sho' hope you's gonna let me pick the street." Alonzo motioned for Jason to lean down so he could get the stock in place before lapping the ends of the white fabric and tucking them in at the back of his neck.

"I guess you'd choose Congo."

"Why not? I figure them hoodoo darkies got as good a chance at bein' right as bein' wrong. No tellin' what gonna happen to me if I choose the wrong way."

"Is that why you also send up prayers to the Lord?"

"Sho' is. I believe in playin' it safe. If'n I had suspenders, I'd wear 'em even with my belt."

Jason chuckled at the older man's kindly attempt at humor. Ever since he was a little boy, the black man had been around to see to his young master's needs. The two had become close friends, though both had become too wise to allow anyone to overhear their private exchanges. They knew that the usual relationship between slave and master was far removed from theirs and that if known, theirs likely would have caused criticism. In the presence of others, both played their expected roles.

"Now don't that look fine?" Alonzo asked, leaning around Jason's large shoulders and greater height to peer in the mirror at his handiwork. A small man neatly built, Alonzo had a smooth, unlined face of a rich chocolate hue and unusually even, white teeth for a slave in his forties. Once, when Jason was very young and had asked Alonzo why he smiled so much, he replied that it was because he had a contented soul and body.

"Contentment with your lot," Alonzo had told Jason that day, "goes a long way toward evenin' out life's mistakes. You gotta learn to tell the diff'rence between what's your lot an' what you's able to change. Best you hang on to that bit of 'Lonzo wisdom, 'cause you ain't gonna always like the hand life deals you."

As though he were back listening to "Lonzo wisdom" again, Jason thought about how he chafed at the cards he had held lately. After scrutinizing his image in the mirror, he said, "Thanks. The neckcloth does look better now."

"Miss Berry gonna have to give in soon an' go out with you."

"Well, she hasn't yet." Jason heard the grumpiness in his voice and blamed it on his not having slept well lately. Since Berry had refused to see him alone, he had spent too many evening hours pacing up and down in his library or his bedroom. Not even innumerable glasses of brandy helped him find answers to his heartache.

At times Jason thought of how lucky he was that he had never before fallen in love, else he would already be gray and bent from the agony. Memories of the ecstasy of his one evening in Berry's company—and her kisses—were the only things keeping him sane. Or so it seemed to the young man suffering the first pangs of true love at the age of twenty-seven.

In the past, Jason recalled several young women had set his heart to hammering and his blood to racing, but none had prompted him to associate the excitement with marriage and consider proposing. As his contact with each of the young women increased, he had found himself feeling less excited and a bit boxed in by what had at first intoxicated. His love for Berry Cortabona was like nothing he had ever before experienced. It gnawed at him constantly, showed no signs of letting up—not that he wanted it to lessen. Though Jason recognized his conclusion as irrational, he knew he had rather be thinking about her with pain than not be thinking about her at all.

"I saw Miss Berry the other afternoon when she come over for tea. She's sho' the purtiest young woman I ever seen you with. She and her frien', Miss Camille, gotta a nice, friendly way about 'em."

"You didn't have to keep fawning over Berry and running back to the courtyard every few minutes with hot pastries. I was afraid that any minute you were going to start showing your card tricks."

Nonplussed by the criticism, Alonzo decided he never before had seen Jason in such a state as he had been in all week. He was becoming concerned about his master. After Jason returned from Texas last year with no injury more serious than a bruised kneecap, Alonzo had vowed to do all within his power to make the young man's life happier. He agreed with Mr. Edouard back at Armand Acres, in private when nobody else was around, that what Jason needed now was a wife and children.

Maybe not all could believe it, Alonzo mused as he went

about the tidying up of the bedroom, but slaves truly could love their masters and enjoy serving them. At least he did. Of course he knew from the grapevine and from following Jason since he was a boy that not all blacks ended up with masters as kind as his.

Though Alonzo had heard other slaves talk behind the scenes at various house parties about how their young masters acted when in the throes of love, he had not believed anything could affect Jason that way. It amazed Alonzo to be dead wrong about the man he had felt he knew almost as well as he knew himself.

Turning his thoughts back to Jason's ironic remarks about his behavior during Berry's visit, Alonzo broke the silence and explained in his good-natured manner, "It was fun, watchin' you havin' such a good time. I liked seein' how purty Miss Camille an' Miss Berry looked all dressed up an' actin' like such fine ladies. How come you just now payin' attention to my advice 'bout findin' yo'self a wife?"

"I've tried to ignore your advice since the summer I was ten and you pushed me to fight that bully visiting in Calion."

"Well, I was right. You beat him up an' he didn't shove you 'round no more. An' nobody has since then, either."

"Don't forget that he blacked my eye."

Alonzo hooted. "He was a foot taller'n you. You can't 'spect to win a tough fight without takin' some licks. Besides, if I 'member right, you had a lotta fun knockin' him down with that right cross I learned you."

When he glimpsed Alonzo grinning at the memory, Jason confessed with a one-sided grin of his own, "I guess I did, at that. I've not been giving much thought to marriage because until now I've never found the right woman for me."

"How come she don't know she is?"

"She doesn't want to hear what my feelings for her are. She doesn't even favor my company. I can't figure out why."

"Well," Alonzo said after handing Jason a clean handkerchief from the armoire and brushing off a piece of lint clinging to the sleeve of the frock coat he had laid out on the bed earlier, "*I* can. You done lived a purty wild life up to now. She likely ain't interested in settin' up house with no jack-about-town."

"You don't know what you're talking about. She doesn't know anything about my life before I met her, except what I've told her." To Jason's way of thinking, the meetings with Berry before the night of the masquerade ball did not count. Not once did he imagine what kind of impression might have lingered in her mind after she saw him escaping from the bedroom of a married woman. After all, she had been a mere child then. And he now knew that he had been green behind the ears himself.

After slipping the handkerchief into the breast pocket of his white satin waistcoat and allowing Alonzo to help him into his frock coat, Jason brought his brush up to smooth the sides of his dark brown hair one more time. Should he wear one of his beaver hats with the fashionable tall crown? He stepped back from the mirror and eyed his image. "Do you think this blue coat will look right with my striped trousers?"

"I wouldn't a laid it out if I didn't." Lordy! What next? Never before had Jason shown much interest in his appearance. Jason had always left the details up to Alonzo. What else but love, powerful love, could have such a hold on him?

Feeling compassion for the young man—after all, Jason had spent a turbulent time during the past twelve months, what with having lost his mother while fighting out in Texas—Alonzo said, "You looks fine an' dandy. I gotta feeling you gonna make some headway this afternoon." He waited until Jason was about to open the door before saying in a jocular manner, "Maybe it wouldn't hurt for you to try showin' card tricks yo'self. I stuck a deck in your coat pocket."

* * *

When on the following Sunday afternoon Jason found himself riding one of the passenger cars of the Pontchartrain Railroad with an animated Berry by his side, he almost doubted it was true. He slid a sidewise look her way.

Yes, there she sat on the wooden seat beside him, wearing a red dress and a straw bonnet with red silk roses and red satin ribands tied underneath her chin. Jason could see occasional flashes of purple coming from deep within her black eyes and thought about how the first time he met her, he had told her that they reminded him of overly ripe blackberries. Luscious. Berry. God, but she was beautiful! A smile still tucked up the corners of her full lips from where she had been laughing at something he had just said. For the life of him, he couldn't remember what.

Ever since Berry had favored Jason with friendliness on that afternoon he had been close to despair, he had existed in a dizzying state, veering between partial happiness and partial fear that the headway he seemed to be making toward winning her heart might dissipate. Sometimes he felt foolish about having taken Alonzo's playful advice and shown her card tricks while Camille fetched fresh tea that afternoon. If that absurd business was what had broken the ice, why should he look back? Not that he ever wanted Alonzo to know.

"How did you guess that I've always wanted to ride in an open-sided car out to the lake?" Berry asked.

"I didn't. I wanted to ride it myself and thought you'd make good company."

"Were you wrong?"

"Not yet. I'll reserve judgment till I see if you're a passing fair companion on a picnic." Alonzo had handed him a rectangular basket when he left the townhouse, and he glanced down where it rested on the floor between their feet. Then he allowed himself a full-face view of Berry. "Why didn't you tell me you'd like to ride the train to the lake?"

"I never thought about it." Berry evaded his solemn gaze and watched the trees, fields and mansions glide by. She realized that ever since she had seen him at the masquerade ball seven nights ago, she'd seldom thought about anything but Jason, the man. Positively, negatively. Over and over. Maybe being with him would help settle her thoughts. A week was only a brief span of time, yet in one week she had succeeded in pushing back farther and farther the temptation to lose herself in his arms.

While the steam engine puffed and sometimes flung cinders into the open-sided cars, Berry's thoughts revolved along with the wheels noisily spinning along on the iron rails. Uncanny, how she was seeing those Sunday afternoon scenes that had filled her yearning heart with daydreams back when she was a youngster. She saw that families still gathered on their porches or under giant trees on their lawns, still had company joining them, still appeared blessedly contented with talk and laughter. Someday she would meet the right man and—Why did Jason have to be such wonderful company and such a handsome . . . rake?

Berry reassured the doubting part of her mind that Jason Premont was perfect for an infatuation. Along with an admitted physical attraction, which she was positive would fade in time, infatuation was all she intended should ever link them. And friendship. She admitted to liking Jason, an awful lot.

When the train stopped, Berry looked around with wide-eyed wonder at the growth of concession stands and tents that had taken place during her absence along the shores of Lake Pontchartrain. She took Jason's proffered hand and stepped down from the passenger car.

As on the four-mile journey to the lake, Berry was hardly aware of the other passengers also enjoying a train ride on a balmy June afternoon. Since Jason had come for her, she had felt buoyed up with anticipation. The touch of his hand on hers as he helped her to the ground revved up her heartbeat. Courtesy of her handsome escort, Berry mused, she at last had become a grown-up participant of the smiling, vociferous crowd spending a Sunday afternoon at one of the most popular gathering places for the fun-loving citizens of New Orleans. "This is like a dream come true!"

Jason smiled at Berry's obvious delight. "I was thinking that same thing."

With the handle of the picnic basket looped over his free arm, Jason held Berry's hand as he led her toward a pink tent where a fat man wearing pink-striped suspenders was selling lemonade. "Lemonades for my lady and me."

"*Moi*, I never before see such a handsome couple out enjoying *le bon temps*," the vendor remarked jovially as he dipped the sparkling liquid from one of the burlap-wrapped stone churns sitting in an enormous bed of Spanish moss on the ground. With an approving smile at the handsome Creole couple, he returned his gourd dipper to the churn and came up with small pieces of ice and dropped them into their tin cups, explaining with a Gallic shrug, "*Lagniappe.*"

Berry and Jason rewarded the vendor with "*Merci, beaucoup!*" and wide smiles for his "little something extra" before turning toward another tent down the wide shore of dark finely particled sand. The crowd milled around the couple amiably as they went about seeking their own pleasures. Several couples had children and dogs with them and the frequent sounds of laughter fell gently on Berry's ears. The lemonade tasted the way she liked it, both sweet and sour.

A hawk-featured man with dark skin and one gold earring, who Berry thought might well be a descendant of a pirate, sold Jason a bag of boiled shrimp and a jar of red sauce. At the last minute, the man laid a lemon alongside the shrimp and flashed them a one-sided smile. When Berry spied the loaves of French bread stacked like firewood on a low table behind the pirate, she gestured toward the one on the end with the darkest brown crust and watched the man add it to their basket.

Jason looked perplexed at the way the loaf angled upward like a fence post, then grumbled good-naturedly, "Wouldn't you know that my lady would choose a loaf too long?"

Berry giggled and said, "Let it be a challenge to you."

After giving her a mock bow, Jason broke off the protruding portion and settled the loaf in the basket. Laughing at her pretended protests, he fed her bits of the crunchy crust and soft center until she waved his hand away. He was finishing the remainder himself when they noticed that a tall, thin man wearing a voluminous white apron was motioning for them to visit his small stand.

"Could we?" Berry asked, her black eyes pleading without her being aware. "I've never had so much fun."

"Why not?" Jason lifted his shoulders in his version of the Gallic shrug. "The day is yours."

"No. Ours."

As they approached the crude little shelter made of driftwood and an odd assortment of grayed planks, Berry saw that the roof, which did not keep out all of the sun's rays and fluttered with each brisk breeze blowing in from the white-capped lake, was made of limbs from palmetto criss-crossing a flimsy framework of saplings. Delicious smells tempted them, and with wide smiles, they entered. Inside was a giant black cookstove with its rusted vent pipe angling through the palmetto leaves.

After ordering café au lait and triangular pastries, dusted with sugar and still warm from the oven, Berry and Jason bit into the buttery crusts and munched; they drank the hot creamy coffee until nothing was left but sugar crystals on their lips. He caught her watching him lick off the sugar on his mouth and grabbed her. To the delight of the baker and his other customers, not to mention Berry, he kissed away the crystals clinging to her lips.

"Before I went East," Berry remarked when they left the hut and began walking again, "I saw P. T. Barnum's company perform in New Orleans. I didn't care for all of the acts."

"I saw his show at Opelousas. It wasn't my favorite either."

Pleased that they had similar tastes, they stole satisfied

glances at each other. When their conversation later showed their differences, the covert looks turned thoughtful, but not for long.

"I adore the color red," she replied when he asked her favorite color.

"I once preferred blue, but that was before I saw you in red," he confessed with a candor that delighted her.

"This looks like a good spot for our picnic," Jason announced after they had left behind the popular stretches of hard-packed sand near the tents offering concessions and games. Within moments he had set down his cup and basket on the beach and was fishing underneath their purchases. "I know Alonzo told me there's a tablecloth—"

"Here, let me help." Berry soon found the white linen tablecloth. Despite the brisk breeze coming from the lake only a few yards away, she flipped it so that it lay smoothly on the sand.

"You're a woman of vast talent," Jason said.

"You're a man with marvelous ideas for an outing."

They sank upon the outer edges of the linen and began removing items from the basket. He surprised her by bringing out a bottle of wine and a round of soft cheese. Once the feast began, each declared that the food was ambrosia, the wine a perfect complement to such a sumptuous repast on a perfect Sunday afternoon. Their eyes spoke volumes that had nothing to do with anything as mundane as food or weather.

"Where are you going?" Jason asked when Berry shifted her position on the tablecloth as if to rise. Now that they had tidied up and had put everything back in the basket, he sat with his arms angled behind him for a prop, one leg stretched full length, the other bent at the knee. He was drinking in the sight of his beloved. Sitting in the sunshine with the breeze playing with the black curls escaping from underneath her straw bonnet, Berry had never appeared lovelier. Though he hated the idea of leaving, he glanced toward the distant tents. "Do you want to stroll back toward the crowd?"

"No. I want to go wading." With her back toward him, Berry removed her shoes and stockings and stood.

"Wading?" Jason sat up straight. He had attended many large picnics on lakes, rivers, and bayous, but he never before had seen any of the young women present go into the water. Along the way he had noticed some youngsters wading in the edges of the gentle waves, but the adults accompanying them watched from the shoreline. "Aren't you afraid some lake monster might nip your toes?"

Berry laughed and called over her shoulder as she walked barefoot toward the gently lapping water. "No, silly. I'm not going out where it's deep. But I did learn to swim in the Atlantic when we were playing in New Jersey."

Eager to join her in the water, Jason shed his shoes and stockings, rolled up the bottoms of his trousers, and sprinted after Berry. She was, indeed, one of a kind. When he caught up with her, she was lifting her red skirt up to her calves and splashing in the edges of the whispering waves. The blissful expression on her beautiful face was absolutely charming.

After rewarding Jason with one of the warmest smiles she had given him all day, Berry crowed, "Isn't this fun?" A gusty puff of wind lifted her long hair and tried unsuccessfully to steal her bonnet. "I never had half as good a time when I used to come out here alone." Should she tell him how much more alive she felt in his presence? No. Such a confession might lead him to think she was feeling something deep for him. She counted it a good sign that not since that first evening had Jason attempted to speak of feelings. Was he realizing, as she had, that what had drawn them together was merely a physical attraction? "Thank you for giving me such a lovely day."

"My pleasure. I've enjoyed the day as much as, or more than, you have." Jason barely felt the grit squishing between his toes or the tepid water washing against his feet and ankles. She was right. It *was* fun wading along the edges of Lake Pontchartrain—with her by his side. As certainly as each succeeding wave lapped the shoreline and defined it, Berry Cortabona delineated the parameters of his world.

Nothing felt as blessedly right as his love for Berry, Jason reflected, so how could she not come to return his love? He must continue to bide his time. Glancing down at the bunched-up edges of her skirts, he asked, "Does it take both hands to hold up your skirts?"

Though it seemed far wiser to keep her attention on objects distant and impersonal, Berry transferred her gaze from a faraway sailboat bobbing amidst whitecaps to Jason. She had not realized how close he stood, how intently he was watching her. The breeze snatched away her breath. The rhythmic sounds and motions floated off into another world peopled by only two. The way he was looking at her made her sense he felt as she did.

He smiled down at her. Even in the unstinting glare of June sunlight, he was darkly handsome. Would she ever forget the way he looked at this moment, with the wind tousling his hair and the sunshine dancing in his brown eyes, kicking up golden flecks of light . . . just for her? She swallowed and licked her lips before trusting her voice to be normal. "Why did you ask if it takes both hands to hold my skirts out of the water?"

"Because I want to hold one in mine."

Right off, Berry decided that Jason's idea was magnificent. She transferred the mass of red skirt and petticoats to one hand. They ambled hand in hand amidst the shallows of the warm water for the rest of the sunny afternoon, exchanging infinitely more smiles and wondering looks than talk.

CHAPTER

*

Eight

Throughout the following week, Jason managed to spend a part of each day or evening with Berry. He felt his heart expanding each time she smiled at him, then almost bursting when she began returning his good night kisses with a semblance of the passion he well remembered. Afterward, he would walk the block to his townhouse on Chartres Street without awareness of anything but the beautiful, black-haired Berry Cortabona.

Time and weather continued smiling on Berry and Jason for the next couple of weeks. Even the frequent summer rainclouds paused but briefly to shower the city. The familiar streets of the French Quarter seemed to take on new sparkle for the striking Creole couple as they strolled about, stopping and sampling specialties of first one popular eating place, then another. Neither would have wanted the other to know, but seldom did they realize what they ate, or if they ate at all.

To the delight of Berry and Camille, Jason and Ace

seemed to like each other from their first introduction. The foursome attended the theater together several times and dined afterward. One gala evening they boarded one of Ace's tied up riverboats and, as the only passengers, took a ride on the river while sampling the chef's offerings.

Berry and Jason had spent three idyllic weeks together when he came calling one evening to take her out to dine. Camille, apologizing for being on her way out to meet her betrothed, showed Jason into the parlor. Before leaving him on his own, she said, "Make yourself comfortable. Berry will be down shortly."

Though Jason felt at ease in the parlor, he paced about while awaiting Berry. A sheaf of what looked like large sheets of art paper lying on a reading table caught his eyes and he walked over for a look.

"What are you doing spying on my sketches?" Berry demanded from the open doorway. Anger swelled her words and brought fire to her eyes. Recently, Camille had persuaded her to show her work to Ace and he had praised her efforts. But the piercing fear of hearing Jason's laughter, or scorn, or some equally unacceptable response was throwing her into panic. The instantaneous anger may have been directed at herself for caring so intensely about his opinion; still, it was genuine.

"I hardly call looking at them spying," Jason replied somewhat defensively as he put back the sketch he had been admiring. What was wrong with Berry? Until now he had found her generally sweet-tempered, flexible.

Berry glared at Jason as she recalled the incident back East that had triggered her reaction. A young man from gentry, with whom she had enjoyed numerous outings, professed interest in her efforts, hinting that he would introduce her to a famous designer he knew were he to judge her work promising. When she showed him a sketch, he had wounded her by laughing and calling her balmy for thinking a young seamstress such as she could design. After slapping his smug face and sending him on his way, she had vowed never again to display her work for young men who knew nothing about art or design. "How dare you look at my work as if it were on public display!"

Stung by her inexplicable explosion, Jason said through tight lips, "I'm sorry. Camille invited me to make myself comfortable until you came down, and that's what I was doing."

Berry was too upset to acknowledge that her carelessness in leaving her work downstairs had led Jason to view it. Or to recall that any time she had mentioned her designing, he had evidenced support and encouragement. "I might have known that a man like you would presume he could rule wherever he happened to be." Like a black-haired dervish in long white skirts, she marched over to the table and snatched up the sketches. "You won't do that to me!"

"What kind of man is one like me? You've bandied that phrase around before. Perhaps you prefer that I leave."

She scarcely heard the question, much less its testy tone. "Leave if you choose."

Jason remained as he was, arms folded across his chest, dark eyes glaring.

Clutching the large stiff sheets facedown against her front, Berry lifted her chin as if for a blow. "I suppose you think I'm balmy for calling myself a designer."

"Not at all. It appeared to me from my brief look that you're very talented." His heart ached at the desperate expression on her beautiful face. Determined to make amends, he said, "You look particularly beautiful this evening." His practiced gaze lingered on her white gown with yellow trim on a modestly rounded neckline, capelike short sleeves, and a voluminous skirt. "I like your gown."

Berry placed the sketches back on the table, feeling her face flush. How could she have thought he was like the Easterner, quick to ridicule? She had reacted on impulse as she so often did. She had made a hasty judgment and was now regretting it. How forgiving Jason was; he actually appeared eager to overlook her display of willfulness. "Thank you for admiring my new gown," she said softly. "I finished it this afternoon while you were tending to what you called Uncle Edouard's business."

"A special gown for a special evening? I'm pleased that you wore it first for me. Shall we go?" He moved nearer and held out his hand.

"Wait, Jason. I'm sorry about losing my temper like that."

"Perhaps I don't understand creative people as well as I had believed. I'll try not to intrude again." Reaching her side then, he took her hand in his and glanced toward the sketches. "Just for the record, may I ask why the sketches were in the parlor if you don't like people to see them?"

"Camille was in here when I returned from showing them to Miss Dilly, one of the Quarter's best seamstresses. I guess I forgot them when I went up to my room."

"Well, don't keep me waiting any longer." With an impatient forefinger he tipped her chin upward so as to see into her eyes more clearly. A soft ebony glow seemed to have displaced the earlier anger. "What did Miss Dilly say? Even I have heard of Miss Dilly on Royal Street. Tell me."

To Berry's bafflement, Jason's huge smile and his apparent enthusiasm magnified her inner sense of accomplishment and she felt far more successful than she really was. Suddenly, the intimacy between them was back. Her eyes sparkled as she returned his squeeze on her hand. "Would you believe that she offered me a commission for a muslin sample of one sketch?" When he nodded, she smiled up at him. "As soon as I get it made up, she's going to show it to her clientele."

"Then this *is* a special evening." He leaned and brushed her lips with a tender kiss. "Congratulations. I'm disappointed that you didn't tell me first thing."

Honesty crept in and demanded Berry add, "It's only a small commission and there won't be more unless Miss Dilly can interest someone in having the gown made up."

"No matter. A first step is a first step. Let's be on our way to celebrate."

Despite low-flying clouds and an extra heaviness in the evening air, Berry persuaded Jason not to stop by his place for his carriage and driver to take them to a restaurant.

"I prefer walking when the weather is nice like this," Berry assured Jason as they ambled arm in arm past his townhouse. "After all, it's only a few blocks to the Place d'Armes. I love seeing the people there and strolling about before deciding where we'll eat, don't you?"

"I can't deny that." Jason noted that it was still twilight and that a decidedly lavender light was creating a magic along the narrow streets with their handsome brick buildings and walls sitting only a few feet back from their edges. The purplish sparkles in Berry's eyes intrigued him. But then, everything about Berry Cortabona intrigued him. "If we spot your friend Latrobe again, I hope you make him acknowledge our presence and speak. I'd like to see his face when you tell him you've sold your first design."

Her pretty lips set in a moue, Berry contemplated Jason's words. "I don't count him among my friends any longer. And I don't care that Leonidas appeared to have snubbed us the other evening. Of course, he could have been rushing to the theater and did not recognize us in the half light." She tossed back her head, unconsciously rearranging a cluster of long curls that had fallen forward over her shoulder. "Actually, I wouldn't give him the satisfaction of knowing that I'm no longer waiting for him to intercede with Mr. Zimpel."

Jason reflected that he knew Berry well enough now to judge that her declaration disguised hurt. When he had first learned of her conflict with Zimpel, he had racked his brain for the name of a friend connected with the theaters who might help clear up the matter. Later, when he confessed his failure to her, she had bombarded him with threats if he dared step into what she considered her business. The spirited, black-eyed beauty was unlike any other young woman he had ever known. And he fell in love with her more each day.

"I'm taking you to one of my old haunts that I've been saving for a special occasion," Jason told Berry as he escorted her toward a café near the river. "I hope they still cook pompano daubed with clay. You'll adore it."

Once they entered the small café, the maître d'hôtel and the bartender greeted Jason with smiles and warm welcomes. After introducing Berry as his "designer" friend— as if she were a celebrity, Berry reflected while her cheeks burned—he ordered the finest champagne be sent to a corner table in the tiny courtyard out back.

Throughout the meal—she did adore the baked pompano seasoned with herbs and crabmeat, and told Jason so— Berry kept feeling a blessed sense of being special steal throughout her being. In between glasses of champagne, ridiculous toasts and much banter with the exuberant Jason, she counted the contributing factors.

First, Jason's dark eyes—so quick to note her bare bread plate, her half-empty wine glass—his deep voice—rising with authority to order more butter, more coffee, whatever she might desire. That same resonant voice falling to relate a story, to ask a question, lowering into spine-tingling intimacy to tell her of his admiration. And, his slow smile that trickled down inside her like honey sliding down a sore throat in winter, his ready laughter that inevitably called up her own. Once, she found herself remembering the way it had felt when Aunt Maddy used to cover her on a chilly night with a welcome blanket.

Both Berry and Jason ignored the first raindrop. But when the drops kept falling and soaking through her thin gown, they had no choice but to dash inside, where Jason asked someone to fetch a hackney.

"You're shivering," Jason told her as they sipped café au

lait near the door and waited for the hired carriage. He removed his coat, which was of heavier fabric and damp only on the surface, and draped it around her shoulders. "Too bad all the rental coaches were busy. It seems that the opera has just ended and they're engaged. If one doesn't arrive soon, I'll hire a runner to go to the townhouse and ask Alonzo to send the carriage."

"I'm fine, really," Berry assured him. Keyed up from the day's excitement, the champagne and Jason's attentiveness all evening, she accepted his silent invitation to lean against him and let his arms pull her close. "Maybe it will let up soon and we won't need a ride."

Within a brief time, Berry's prediction came true and they hurried down the wet banquettes toward Chartres, skirting puddles here and there.

"This has been another perfect evening, Jason."

"Even with the rain robbing us of brandy under the sky?"

"We can drink brandy under a roof."

"I vote for my place. I have a bottle of a rare cognac that I've not yet opened. Such an occasion deserves a special ending, don't you think?" Before she could answer, an overhead rumbling led them to glance up. "We may be in for another shower."

"Let's make a run for it," Berry said, aware that she still wore his coat and that he had no protection. He was doubtless too much of a gentleman to take it back even if she insisted. "We don't have far to go."

They ran then in the new shower, laughing because she could hardly keep up with his long strides and because they kept stepping in puddles and splashing themselves. When they reached Jason's townhouse, both were noticeably damp. They agreed that even if they hurried down the next block to Camille's place, probably they would be drenched. Berry made no protest when he opened the gate and ran with her to the shelter of the U-curved veranda.

"We'll go in here and not disturb Alonzo's nap on the

main staircase," Jason said as he opened the door on the opposite side of the courtyard from the official front entry and escorted her inside. He felt her trembling and noted in the dim light from the wall sconce that her hair was mussed and damp. "Why don't you go up to my room and look in the armoire for something dry and warm to put on? You'll find towels on the washstand." When she became inordinately still, he asked, "You remember where it is, don't you?"

"Yes."

"I'll go find the cognac."

"But you're wetter than I and—"

"Go on up. The sooner you do, the sooner I can get dried off myself."

Berry realized that if she were to insist on waiting for a letup in the rain and then ask him to walk her home, Jason would indeed be chilled. She left him and hurried up the stairs. Recognizing that she was more than a little chilled herself, she welcomed the warmth of his bedroom. As on her first visit, a lighted candle sat on the mantel.

And, as then, Jason's presence was everywhere. Blatantly assaulting Berry's already aroused senses were the masculine scents of polished shoes, woolen garments, starched shirts, spicy soap; the sight of massive furniture minus curved lines, a pipe propped in a holder beside what she guessed must be a humidor, rug and drapes of muted design and color.

A soft rap at the door and Jason entered his bedroom. Wearing a blue dressing gown and slippers, he carried a fat bottle tucked under his arm and clutched two fat goblets in one hand. When Berry turned from where she had been brushing her hair and fixed him with a startled look that reminded him of a doe surprised while drinking from a secluded stream, he said, "Hey, I'm glad you found my robe and made yourself at home."

"I've just finished toweling my hair," she said, rather

surprised that his appearance had set her pulse into an even wilder tizzy. After all, she had been alone with him in this very room once before and nothing untoward had happened. She was no simpering plantation heiress who had never before seen a man in anything but street clothing. Oh, but seeing Jason Premont in dishabille was not the same as seeing actors back stage in dressing gowns or robes. She felt alerted all over. Deliciously alerted. "I was trying to arrange it before coming down to find you."

Truth to tell, Berry had not expected Jason to come into his bedroom while she was still there. Without having to glance toward the armoire, she could picture her white dimity dress and her three petticoats spread over its open doors. For the life of her, she could not recall where she had hung her stockings and left her shoes.

Jason curbed his impulse to go take her in his arms and kiss her breathless. "No need. I found you first. Go ahead and finish with your hair." He set the bottle and glasses on a round table beside the fireplace. "I'll open the cognac."

Despite her thundering heart, Berry returned to her task. When she saw her wide-eyed image in the mirror above the washstand, she wondered what Jason must be thinking about finding her with her hair brushed out, hanging long and loose like a young girl's. Her hand on his hairbrush was trembling. Though she had found her chemise dry enough to leave on, she felt naked under his engulfing robe. She had opted to stay barefoot rather than try to wear his outsized slippers.

Berry gave up pretending that the situation was normal and turned toward where Jason was pouring their drinks. "I see you found something dry somewhere. I hope your chill has gone."

"Actually, I never felt better." He poured a splash of cognac in each of the snifters. "Uncle Edouard always leaves a few items here for when he comes to the city."

Feasting his eyes on her glorious cloud of black hair, he asked, "Are you ready for your cognac?"

"Thanks, but no. I've lost my taste for it."

He gestured toward the chairs beside the small table. "Maybe you'd like to sit with me while I drink mine. I can still hear the rain pattering on the balcony."

Walking over to stand at the open French doors, Berry said, "Yes, so can I. At least the plants will be grateful for the night rain."

"So am I," he said from right behind her. "I like the smell of a summer rain at night—it's such a clean fragrance."

She sniffed and knew that the fragrance feeding her senses came from Jason. Spicy and vibrant. Masculine. Giving in to an impulse that would not be denied, she half turned and buried her face against his warm, silk-clad shoulder. "Did I ever tell you that I like the way you smell?"

"Not that I recall, and I'm certain I'd remember." Jason pulled her into a light embrace. Was it because she was barefoot and without her customary full skirts that she seemed fragile and especially vulnerable? Whatever, he couldn't recall ever having felt so protective, so masculine. "Do you remember the first time I kissed you that I warned you beforehand?"

She smiled teasingly and met his ardent gaze. "And I told you not to promise."

"No more warnings." And his lips claimed hers, again and again.

Then, like dancers in a sensuous progression made to a private love song, they moved while kissing toward his turned down bed, the silk of her borrowed robe whispering sensuous invitations against his. In the flickering candlelight her eyes gave him permission, and he sat upon the side of the bed and pulled her down on his lap. He loosened the belt at her waist, his hands claiming the satiny skin exposed above her chemise and sending thrills racing throughout her body. Her fingers nestled in his hair, curled around his ears, as the two became lost in exploratory touching. Lost in kissing.

When Jason ran his fingers through the curtain of blue-black silk falling over her bare shoulders and back, Berry sighed and rested her head underneath his chin. Was she in a land of make-believe?

Jason's gentle but searing caresses with his mouth and hands—moving now from her neck and throat down to the swells of her breasts—were transforming her into someone she hardly recognized. His embrace, his touch felt like magic, something precious that she might have been seeking forever. Suddenly, she wanted to surrender to the silent questions his lips and hands were asking.

With a low cry and a flurry of moist kisses she signalled her desire. His eyes queried, "Will you?" Hers answered, "Yes."

Still holding her on his lap, Jason slipped off her robe, then her chemise. He kissed each newly bared spot of olive skin, murmuring appreciation for her beauty and bringing delicious prickles to each patch of flesh against which his warm breath fanned. Berry was unprepared for the maelstrom of sensations when his mouth settled on her hardening breasts, his tongue laving first one tightening nipple, then the other.

The fluttering candle on the mantel sputtered out, leaving them in a darkness broken only by the reflection from a wall sconce across the courtyard.

Shivering from her rising ecstasy, Berry helped Jason out of his robe. Unable to restrain the desire, she kissed the spot beating wildly in the hollow of his neck.

"Come to me and let me love you," Jason murmured as he caught Berry to him there on the bed. Whispering endearments, he buried his face in her hair.

Berry marveled at the way her nakedness melded with his. Lying in his close embrace set off torrid sensations within her that defied comprehension. Her reasons for denying Jason permission to discuss what they might mean to each other vanished in the heat of their embrace. Maybe it was because he had already kissed her mindless before they sank as a pulsating tangle of smooth, supple arms and legs onto the snowy sheets.

"How perfect you feel in my arms," Jason told her between burning kisses, as he looked at her lying there on his bed in naked splendor. The sight of her perfection quickened his breath even further. "I'm madly in love with you. This is where you belong forever."

"Right now, I feel that I belong here."

Though Berry's words fell short of what Jason longed to hear, he rejoiced that she plainly was eager to make love. He found it hard to believe that his independent Berry would lie naked in his arms if all she felt for him was physical attraction. Perhaps she had feared his passion for her was only fleeting. But surely now, after three weeks of being together often, she must realize that he had sensed a truth that first evening when he spoke of fate. "Do you realize that I knew I was falling in love when I first waltzed with you?"

With eyes accustomed now to the faint light coming from across the courtyard, Jason gazed into her lovely face and stroked her hair, wrapping her thick curls around his fingers. She was looking up at him as if she had never truly seen him before.

She rested the palm of her hand on his cheek. "Can love strike like a bolt of lightning?"

"Yes, that's the way it happened. Will you marry me so we can make love for the rest of our lives?" He leaned and kissed her saucily tilted breasts.

"We need no spoken promises," Berry said, barely able to lie still during the warm, wet assault on her breasts. Had she ever before felt as alive? She brushed back a lock of his hair that fell across his handsome forehead. With the tip of her forefinger, she outlined the shape of his nose, his full lips, lips still moist from their kisses. His strong chin invited like treatment while she whispered, ''Just make love to me tonight as though we're the only lovers in the world.''

''Darling,'' he said in a velvety tone that feathered her spine with tingles, ''that's the only way to make love.''

With Berry's untutored help, Jason proceeded to make love to her in the way she desired. He wanted her to know that he loved her beyond anything physical. He brought into play all he had learned over the years about how a caring man can make a woman feel the most desirable creature on earth. His mouth and hands discovered, caressed, teased lovingly all the soft, silken parts making her a delectable woman.

Her breasts became his first pleasure center and hers as well. She arched her neck with ecstasy as he fondled them and laved their pebbled nipples with kisses. He claimed her flat little belly, even dotted her navel with the tip of his tongue. When she moved restlessly and clutched his shoulders, he said, ''I've marked you as mine forever.''

''You're driving me mad,'' she replied in a voice she did not recognize. Her hands fondled his ears, his neck. She had thought she knew a little about the sex act but now she was deciding she knew absolutely nothing. Wasn't he supposed to be pushing himself against her maidenhood by now? Something in that nether region seemed to be seeking.

''What about what you're doing to me?'' His hands and mouth roved lower, paying homage to her hips and at the same time fueling the flames licking in his groin. The feel and taste of the soft inside of her thighs fed his passion to trembling heights, heights to which her throaty moans seemed to be giving voice. ''You're so beautiful,'' he murmured again and again as his heart expanded and his blood became rivulets of fire.

Sometimes Berry sighed and moved her hips against him, hungry—no, starved—for contact with his firm nakedness, yet half fearful of that hot, pulsating hardness nudging against her down low. Without awareness, she moaned and flung her hair back behind her, turning it into a silky ebon shawl upon the sheet for his pleasure. Twice she seized his shoulders and pulled his mouth to hers, overcome with passion. Boldly her tongue engaged his, and the wondrous light within her that she had confessed to that first night when she was with him, burst into full glory.

Berry soaked up for safekeeping the feel of her lover's skin, his kisses, caresses, and words of adoration that slid right down into her waiting heart. "Jason, you're marvelous," she whispered in the low, sensuous voice she had not known was hers until that night.

With a daring as new to her as her surprisingly husky voice, Berry began imitating her lover's seductive movements. She sent her mouth and tingling hands to claim his muscled chest, his broad shoulders, back, hard buttocks, all of those manly parts that made him different from her, that initiated her into the secrets of making love. With each of her discoveries, her senses reeled ever faster, spinning her into new paroxysms of delight. When his swollen, searing manhood at last touched the pulsating juncture between her legs, she clutched at his back in undisguised frenzy and offered him all that she was.

Ecstasy blotted out thought as Jason made Berry his, as he probed on past her maidenhood in search of her waiting hot center. There was only now, only the two of them becoming one, the roaring throb of their joining hearts and bodies, the exquisite ache of it shearing off fragments of the loneliness lodged deep within two souls no longer content to be solitary.

Berry matched her lover's rhythmic movements with joy and curled one leg over his lean buttocks to hug him closer. Great realms of light irradiated her being, wondrous light that was scintillating, lifting both of them to a glowing crest too far out in space to measure. With breathless cries of jubilation they shimmered at that coveted peak in one giant blaze of splendor that threatened to blind. Their very beings seemed to soar before airily whirling, drifting . . . down.

In the afterglow, Jason continued to hold Berry close,

reveling in love for the woman in his arms and in satiation such as he never before had known. What an armful of passion she was! Her ardent responses not only had thrilled him, they also had convinced him that he had been right in telling her that he had fallen in love with her. Once he had heard, or read, that love knows its own time. Now he had proof. Had any man ever been as blessed as he?

Jason had given no previous thought to the matter, but he confessed he was glad he was the first man to make love to Berry. With the confidence of a young man having found the conquest of the fairer sex no true contest, he vowed that he would also be the only man to make love to Berry Cortabona, his woman forever. How could she not share his beliefs that the two belonged together? She might not yet recognize that she loved him, could come to love him as he loved her, but plainly she had enjoyed their lovemaking.

Even as Jason lay beside her while both were collecting breath and thoughts, Berry wondered if she might not be in a role plucked from a dream, a dream from which she never had stepped. Would the wrong gesture, word, blink of an eye even, shatter the sublime rapture? The springy feel of the hair on his arm thrown across her reassured her, felt dear and . . . familiar.

Dear and familiar? Berry turned to look at Jason in the pale light, not surprised to find him gazing at her with a half-smile turning up the corners of his mouth. Yes, Jason was both dear and familiar, but she must guard against letting other endearing terms apply to their relationship, else she might find it difficult to forget him when he made his exit from her life as quickly as he had made his dramatic entrance. This she knew to expect from a rake.

Maybe, Berry reflected with a smidgen of worry, she would find getting on with her life without him in it more difficult now that she had given herself to him, but she could summon no regret. The experience was too precious to label a mistake. She would tuck away the perfect memory to enjoy when life frowned. She would remember how caring, how tender he was—and how he had even told her he loved her and wanted her to become his wife.

It seemed to Berry, or at least to the sensible part of her trying to regain control now, that it would be far easier to avoid the possibility of shattering her perfect memory by sending Jason on his way before he became disenchanted with his current new face. Later there might be a confrontation or, worse, heartbreak. She had no intention of falling in love with a rake, even one named Jason Premont. A dalliance was all she could expect from Jason. Had she not told him—and herself—that first evening that she recognized that theirs was a fantasy relationship? Still she couldn't end it yet.

"Berry, I'm in love with you," Jason said, his tone forceful. "I want you to marry me as soon as possible. I know you feel something for me. Why are you being so stubborn about admitting it? Is there something you haven't told me?"

Berry refused him a reply or a direct look. She slid from his embrace and padded over to the washstand in the corner of the bedroom. After deftly cleansing herself she began donning her still damp clothing, achingly aware that Jason watched from where he sat leaning back against the tall headboard of his bed, one hand resting on the knee of a drawn up leg. She dared not allow herself to look at him directly for fear she might return to his arms.

Though Jason would have preferred having nothing to do but enjoy watching his beloved's graceful movements as she covered her feminine charms, he found himself suffering from a rebellious mind and heart. What was wrong with Berry Cortabona that she would willingly, passionately surrender her virginity to him and then ignore his proposal and declaration of love? "What's wrong? Didn't you hear what I said about wanting us to get married right away?"

"Yes, I heard," Berry replied, unhappy that her heart was unwilling to give up center stage for what her mind had decided. Maybe she had drunk too much champagne earlier.

She heard Jason move on the bed and almost panicked at the thought that he might come put his arms around her and wreck her determination never again to lose herself in his embraces.

Jason had never before proposed to a woman and Berry's cool replies distressed him. Unexpectedly, he became a man on the defensive, one who for the first time in his life had no offense prepared. He felt deserted, stripped to the bone, a bit like a solitary conch shell that he once found at dawn on a foreign seashore. A roaring tide obviously had deposited the shell and left it, high and dry, to the mercy of alien elements.

Berry's heart urged her to confess to Jason her fear that, to her way of thinking, he was not the kind of man who could be serious about love and marriage and that he could never give her the special kind of love she knew she must have for lasting happiness. The words that her brain superimposed over that cry from her heart lodged in her throat, but she managed to get them out. After all, she reassured herself, had she not trained to become an actress? "We don't need to talk about love or marriage. Let's go back to the way we were before tonight and go on having fun together."

"You're talking nonsense." Jason rose and began searching for clothing in the armoire. He took pride in his ability to walk past her and ignore his need to take her in his arms and coax her into saying what he longed to hear. Unable to see well enough to select a shirt to tuck inside his trousers, he paused and lit a candle. "All that's happened tonight is more than that inane term you used—physical attraction." He spied a shirt and yanked it on. He was so angry and hurt that this fingers fumbled with each button and buttonhole. "Why won't you admit there's love between us?"

"Why do you think you're right and I'm wrong?" She was trying her best to keep her tone light. Her hands trembled as she sat on the bed and pulled on her stockings. Once when she was a child, she had tumbled down the stairway outside Maddy's apartment and found herself lying on the ground wondering what happened. She felt a similar disorientation now. "It's late and we both need some sleep."

Each tried ignoring the intimate sounds of the other getting dressed. They failed.

Mystified that the evening had offered both his headiest experience as well as his most miserable, Jason came to her and, brushing aside her fumbling fingers, fastened the back of her gown. Then he said, "Come over to the mirror. There's enough light for me to see how to help you with your hair."

Berry looked at him askance, causing his carefully controlled demeanor to slip as he said, "My God! I'm not going to pounce on you."

"I never suspected you would," she retorted. Sometimes the way he seemed to be peeking into her mind was scary.

After he removed the worst of the tangles from her long curls, Jason fell in love with her all over again as she stood before the mirror above his washstand and returned enough pins to her hair to make herself presentable. Would he ever again be able to look in his mirror and not recall the way her reflection looked at that moment?

"Good night, Jason." Berry was relieved that he apparently had decided to accept her plan to return to their relationship as it had been before that evening. Maybe his realization that they could never have a future together was what had kept him silent on the walk to Camille's townhouse. The knot in her stomach lessened not a tad.

"Tomorrow evening we're supposed to go to the theater with Camille and Ace." Briefly recalling "'Lonzo wisdom," Jason thought about how he detested the final hand dealt him that evening. By damn, he intended to be present for those in the future! "I hope you're still interested in going."

"Of course I am." Avoiding his piercing gaze, she glanced overhead at the stars beginning to peek from behind the scattering clouds. "I'm thinking that by then, we both will have sorted out our thoughts and be happy that we didn't allow runaway passion to lead us into making rash promises."

"Berry Cortabona," Jason growled in a tone that caused her to jerk her face toward him, "you're enough to twist a man into a stark-raving lunatic." He pulled her into his arms and kissed her soundly, then stepped back. "Good night."

CHAPTER

*

Nine

Jason spent the greater part of the remaining night chafing over his failure to win Berry's hand or her confession of love. Her earlier tart words about "a man like you" kept circling around as a possible key. Alonzo once had suggested that concern about Jason's past amours might be influencing Berry's opinion about him. Whether he liked admitting it or not, Alonzo was often right. The question hurt but Jason asked it. Could Berry be associating the present Jason with the foolhardy Jason she had seen leaving a married woman's bedroom one Sunday dawn years ago?

Yes. Earlier that evening he had seen a display of her willfulness. And he had noted the first time they met that she possessed a natural flair for the dramatic.

Though Jason's conclusion disturbed him more than the question, he had little choice but to accept it as the most likely possibility. He could not believe that any beautiful young woman could so joyfully surrender her virginity to a man, plainly enjoy his frequent company, and yet feel nothing for him beyond infatuation. If for this foolish reason Berry was deceiving herself, or at least trying to, he vowed to prove to her that he was mature now and steady, both in his love for her and his determination to make her his wife. Surely she could not turn away from him then.

Jason did not rate the following evening spent at the theater with Berry, Camille, and Ace Zachary as more than a partial success. Berry had not invited him inside afterward and had permitted only one good night kiss. But after only minimum coaxing, she had agreed to dine with him the next evening. His burdened heart could not help but be lifted.

When Jason reached his townhouse, he found Alonzo waiting for him on the staircase. Only this time the black man was wide awake and wearing a troubled expression. Jason's happy daze from Berry's having agreed to see him tomorrow evening dissipated.

"What's wrong?" Jason asked, when Alonzo rose and came toward him. "Has something happened to Uncle Edouard?"

"No, nothin' that bad. Miss Viola is upstairs in a guest room. She done come here over an hour ago in a hired carriage, all upset an' lookin' mighty scared."

"Viola Breton scared? Has something happened to her?" Jason thought about the headstrong younger sister of his friend, Ashley. From having known her all her life, he found it difficult to imagine Viola Breton afraid of much. "Did you send word to Ashley or Mr. Breton out at Breton Grove?"

"Miss Viola wouldn't agree to me gettin' word to her folks 'bout her bein' here. After Jewel went upstairs with her an' got her to bed, I sent Ebenezer to the plantation on horseback with a message to Mr. Ashley. On the sly, I told Ebenezer, so her pa won't have to know."

"Good man!" Jason started toward the library, his long legs eating up the distance down the tiled hallway. He figured he would need a slug of brandy to listen to what Alonzo had to tell. Not until after he had splashed goodly portions in two snifters and handed one to the black man did he speak again. "Is Viola hurt?"

"Not that I could tell. When that carriage brung her, she tore in here lookin' for you. She was some upset you wasn't in yet. I went out an' paid the driver but he wouldn't say where he brung her from. Miss Viola said something 'bout how she was sick a men, 'ceptin' you." Alonzo took a sip of brandy, letting the thick, sweet liquid roll around on his tongue before swallowing it. "She said you was the only man with common sense an' she needed you bad. You know how she's always favored you."

"That's all she told? Wonder why she didn't get the carriage to take her out to the plantation?"

"Probably 'cause that's a fur piece in the middle of the night. Maybe that's what she wanted you for, to see her home."

Jason tugged at his earlobe, wondering what was going on and what he should do about the tempestuous beauty upstairs in one of his spare bedrooms. Ashley's recent confidences about his concern over his sister's flirtations kept popping to mind. "Mr. Breton likely will be crazy with worry when Viola doesn't return before daylight."

"She told Jewel she was supposed to be stayin' in town this week with some frens from schooldays. Jewel thinks she was out tonight with somebody called Roger."

Jason sipped his brandy, then frowned. "Ashley has been telling me about the man from Cincinnati whom Viola has been seeing. I believe his name is Roger Elton."

"When Mr. Ashley was here last week, I heard y'all talkin' 'bout Miss Viola's beaus. That was one of the names he told. The other was the Filhoil gent'man from that plantation up the river from Breton Grove, close to Baton Rouge."

"Bayard Filhoil. Damn, but you don't miss much, do you?"

"Y'all wasn't 'zactly whisperin', what with it bein' after midnight an' both of you layin' in a supply of brandy 'fore goin' up to bed."

Jason nodded, recalling the surprise appearance of Ashley at his place one evening last week. He had gained much pleasure from talking with his old friend until long past midnight. They had spent the next few days visiting the sugar exchange, talking with brokers and shippers, and looking over modern equipment available for sugar mills, or as some citizens called the larger operations, refineries.

Both young men, but especially Jason, were eager to learn all they could about new methods and equipment. Since 1795, when Étienne de Boré first perfected the granulation process and paved the way for Louisiana to become the nation's leading sugar producer, Louisianians had made vast improvements in processing the tall stalks of green cane into sugar.

Ashley had pleased Jason by agreeing to invite Jeannette Moreau, one of the local belles whom they knew because of her friendship with Viola, to accompany Berry and him one evening to the opera and dinner afterward. With pride Jason noted that Berry, Jeannette and Ashley got along well from the start. Later, the four had become engrossed in discussing the better points of the evening's performance. With a renewed appreciation of his beloved's charm, Jason became aware before the evening ended that Berry's easy manner and knowledge of theater had won over the initially haughty Creole, Jeannette.

"Alonzo," Jason said after draining his snifter, "there seems little to do now but get some sleep and wait till morning. I'll find out then what Miss Viola's problem is."

Agreeing, Alonzo put down his empty glass, followed his solemn-faced master up the staircase, and helped him get ready for bed.

* * *

"Oh, Jason," Viola scolded when she came downstairs the next morning and found him at the table in the dining room. "I needed you last night. Where on earth were you?"

Jason rose and went to meet the distraught young woman. Her normally large eyes seemed smaller because of swollen eyelids. He detected tears in their brown depths just before she buried her face against his waistcoat and put her arms around his neck.

Feeling protective toward the trembling Viola as he would toward a young sister had he had one, Jason held her in loose embrace until her weeping slowed and her slender shoulders ceased their heaving. It was too much to hope that her fit of tears was over, for Viola had always been prone to weep at the smallest excuse. He stepped back enough to lift her face with one hand. The sight of her contorted features and obvious distress called up the familiar term used by family members and intimates. "*Chère*, whatever is wrong?"

Flipping her long brown hair back from her face, Viola brushed away tears sliding down her cheeks. "I hate for you to see me looking like this, but you've got to stop a killing!" Her normally rich coloring was blotchy, and her round, pretty face revealed the ravages of a restless night. When Jason offered her his handkerchief, she took it and wiped her eyes and face. "Oh, it was horrible and I didn't have anyone to look after me. Men can be such beasts! After I finally fell asleep, I had the most terrible nightmares. You must—"

Jason interrupted her tirade to say, "Hold up! Slow down and tell me from start to finish what has upset you." Gently, he disengaged her hold on him and led her to a chair at the dining table. "Sit down and I'll get Flossie to bring you some coffee and some of that papaya juice she squeezed earlier."

At Jason's insistence, Viola drank some of the hot, black coffee and the pink fruit juice that the servant brought. "I was with Roger Elton at this place—"

"What place? Tell it all or I won't even pretend to help you. I'll just drive you out to Breton Grove and let—"

''Oh, no!'' Viola lay her hand on Jason's where it rested on the dining room table. ''Please, *chèr.* You can't get Father involved, or Ashley either. They wouldn't understand.''

''So far, neither do I. Now tell it straight or not at all. For the record, I'm not vowing to keep anything you tell me from Ashley or your father.''

Viola snatched her hand from where it lay on Jason's and elevated her chin. She fidgeted with her unbound hair, finally tucking it behind her ears.

Jason saw a pout forming on Viola's lips and found himself thinking about how such a little pouching of Berry's full pink mouth could twist his heart into a knot. Not that he had ever seen her pout more than once or twice, he amended as he cleared his throat and scolded himself for allowing his thoughts to wander. Berry Cortabona was in his blood, though, and he realized he did not even have to think of her for her to be a part of his mind and heart.

''Jason, I'd forgotten how ornery you are when you want to be.''

''A man has certain obligations, whether or not you call him ornery.''

With a sigh of resignation, Viola started over. ''Roger took me to the Coachman's Inn''—When Jason's eyebrows shot up in surprise and disapproval, she had the grace to lower her gaze to her coffee cup—''to show me real gambling, he said. I thought the idea exciting. I didn't know until we got inside that the place was little more than a dive. Don't look at me that way; truly, I didn't know. When I got bored and told Roger I was ready to leave, he kept on gambling. I was angry that he ignored my wishes, but what could I do but wait until he was ready to leave?''

With the coffeepot in her hand, Flossie stuck her head through the door from the kitchen, but Jason motioned her away. ''Go on.''

''I've been seeing a lot of Bayard Filhoil lately, too. I can't imagine how it was that he showed up at the Coachman's unless he followed us there. It seems that every time

Roger takes me anywhere lately, Bayard has a way of just appearing.''

When Jason remained silent but attentive, Viola continued. ''Anyway, I was angry with Roger and was wandering about the back room where he and some terrible-looking men were playing poker, when a man lurched through the curtained doorway. The man, a stranger, seemed drunk and grumpy. Before I knew he was aware of me standing in the shadows, he came over and tried to kiss me. I slapped him and screamed for Roger. At least Roger put down his stupid cards then and started for the corner where we were struggling.''

Jason shifted around on his chair, plainly not liking what he was hearing.

Viola went on. ''Before he reached us, though, who should dash in from the big public room but Bayard? It was horrible! Bayard was yelling at Roger all the while he was knocking the drunk stranger to the floor. I never knew Bayard could be so forceful.'' Batting her eyelashes, Viola sent Jason a wondering look. ''For a minute there, I could've sworn it was you, Jason.''

Jason kept a straight face. He had known for a long time that Viola was a born flirt. ''Did the stranger hurt you in any way?''

''No. I'm not a helpless schoolgirl, *chèr.* I managed to keep him from kissing me by slapping him and kicking his shins. By that time, Bayard was there punching him in the belly and on the chin. You should have seen the way he tore into that man!'' Her eyes sparkled.

Jason pursed his lips and leaned back against his chair. ''If Bayard proved such a hero, how was it you ended up taking a carriage here alone?''

''Oh, that's the truly terrible part! Bayard showed what a fine gentleman he is and dressed Roger down for taking me to such a bawdy place and not looking after me properly. Roger had been drinking a lot and he cursed Bayard for putting his nose into somebody else's business." Her eyes began to fill.

"Don't tear up on me now. Keep talking," Jason said.

"I begged Roger to get us out of there, but he just shoved me aside. Then I asked Bayard to take me away, but—can you believe it?—neither seemed aware that I was even there. Both were beastly, ignoring me like that. They said some awful things to each other, and the subject of my good name kept coming up."

Viola's voice was thick with remembering and with a new note of what Jason heard as genuine sorrow. He leaned closer as she continued. "Then Roger challenged Bayard to a duel at dawn on Sunday underneath the Oaks. A big crowd had come in from the public room. I was horrified. Men were acting like beasts, making bets like idiots on which man might end up killed or maimed."

By then tears were again tracking Viola's pretty cheeks. "I recognized the manager and asked him to find me a hackney coach. I couldn't stay there a moment longer and hear them threaten each other.

"Oh, Jason, you've got to stop them! I thought if I could get to you that you could talk some sense into them. But you weren't home. They both acted like maniacs. Roger will kill Bayard for sure. He may be an American, but everybody says he's as skilled with a rapier as any Creole. He's always talking about how he works out with some of the fencing masters here in the Quarter."

Jason tugged at his earlobe for a few moments before he rose and, clasping his hands together loosely behind his back, walked up and down the dining room sorting out his thoughts. He remembered Ashley saying something recently about Bayard Filhoil taking fencing lessons. Hotheaded fools, taking unnecessary chances with their lives over a beautiful young woman who had no business being where she was last evening!

Jason ignored the inner voice that told him that if Berry found herself in such an intolerable situation, he, too, might be acting with less than a cool head. It was an easy matter to dismiss, for he could not imagine Berry acting so foolishly as Viola or allowing anyone to back her into a corner. He recalled his concern for Berry at the time she had snatched the emerald from the killer, but her brief explanation about the trial when he asked that night after the masquerade ball had indicated that she and her friend had come out unscathed. "I must get in touch with Ashley."

"No. Ashley detests me. The only brother who cared for me got killed while gallivanting around with you two out in Texas." Viola shot Jason a spirited, accusing look and set her lips into another pout.

"Don't be any more absurd than you've been already, Viola. You don't know a damned thing about what brought about Clark Junior's death and if you did, you likely wouldn't believe it. You've always painted things the way you want them to be and that's how you've ended up in this mess. I know Ashley loves you. He's concerned about your well-being, and so am I. I need him to help me carry out a plan to prevent this duel. Obviously you came to me for advice and if you want me to help, you must let me do it the way I think is best."

Viola folded her arms on the dining table and laid her forehead on top of them. After a brief silence, she said in a little girl voice, "Do whatever you need to do. I can't bear the thought of two men risking their lives over something so ridiculous." She let out a tremulous sigh. "Why couldn't I have known before last night that it's Bayard I want to marry?"

Relieved that Viola kept her face hidden and could not see his vexed expression, Jason shook his head in disgust and rang the silver bell sitting beside his chair. Before Flossie could return with the requested fresh pot of coffee, a commotion sounded from the hallway and Ashley burst into the dining room.

"Thank God you're all right, Viola," Ashley exclaimed as he hurried to kiss her cheek. "When Alonzo let me in, I thanked him for sending me that message." He sank onto the chair next to his sister and took her hand in his. "Tell me what's going on, *chére*."

In an hour of earnest talk the three pieced together all available information and evolved a plan that bore the possibility of success. By then Viola was regarding her brother with new respect.

"We've agreed that Roger Elton loves money better than anything else," Ashley said. When Viola and Jason nodded affirmation, he went on. "If he'll accept my offer to sell him this year's cotton crop at today's prices instead of waiting until harvest in the fall when they're as likely to go up as down, maybe that will be incentive enough to keep him from showing up at the Oaks Sunday morning. I can't imagine being able to dissuade Bayard from answering the challenge."

"What will your father think about this arrangement?" Jason asked.

"He'll be for it if it will keep down talk about Viola and prevent the duel. I've heard him tell about being a second for my mother's only brother soon after they married, and how heartbreaking it was to watch the young man die on the ground. Father may take inordinate pride in being a Creole of French heritage, but since that time, he has never gone along with dueling."

Viola, still pale and visibly shaken, studied her hands where they lay clasped tightly in her lap. "Father has sworn he'll never sell any of his cotton to Roger. He seems to despise the man."

"He'll sell this time," Ashley assured her.

"Maybe," said Jason, "you can get this Roger Elton to return to Cincinnati as part of the agreement."

Ashley chuckled. "You've come up with a capital suggestion, Jason. I know Father will endorse that idea and won't mind if it costs him a bit." He turned toward Viola and sent her his characteristic lopsided smile. "Father is going to be so pleased to learn you're going to accept

Bayard's proposal that he won't be hard to deal with. I'm happy you've at last made up your mind about which man you're going to marry."

Viola slid a thoughtful look toward Jason before rising. "I need somebody to accompany me to Jeannette's home so that I can explain my change of plans and pick up my clothing."

"I was planning on taking you home today and then coming back to stay with Jason till we can meet with Roger and Bayard," Ashley said, his tone revealing his disapproval.

"I can't bear to be so far away until I'm sure everything is settled," Viola protested. "Besides, I told Father that I'm spending the entire week with Jeannette to shop. He isn't expecting me back until Sunday afternoon."

Ashley asked, "Wouldn't it be better, more seemly, if you stayed these next two days and nights with Jeannette rather than here with us bachelors?"

"No, I wouldn't be able to keep all of this to myself and I don't want anyone else to know what happened." Viola's face flushed and her gaze wavered between the two men watching her. "I fibbed to Jeannette and Mrs. Moreau about where Roger and I were going last evening. I told them that we were driving upriver to dine and likely would spend the night at Breton Grove before returning to town this afternoon. Maybe they won't ever have to know what a ghastly mistake I made."

Jason and Ashley exchanged resigned looks before Ashley said, "All of us need to keep quiet about the matter. If Jason doesn't mind putting both of us up, perhaps it's just as well that you stay here where I can keep an eye on you. I expect you to behave yourself, though, and not stir up more trouble. With any kind of good luck, we can have this problem resolved before Sunday and return home."

"What kind of new trouble could I stir up?" Viola retorted, plainly stung by her brother's words. "You act as if I purposely set Roger and Bayard against each other."

Ashley let out a sigh. "I think that you didn't realize

what could happen when you kept both men dangling. I hope that you've learned not to play with the emotions of others as if it's some kind of game."

Feeling sympathy for the sad-faced Viola and thinking that perhaps she had at last grown up, or at least was on her way, Jason said to her, "Jewel will be here to attend to your needs, and Flossie loves cooking for guests. I agree with Ashley that none of us should discuss with anyone else what is going on. Until the matter is settled, you're welcome to stay here with Ashley and me."

CHAPTER

*

Ten

Mindful of her plans to dine with Jason that evening, Berry spent the afternoon shopping and running errands. She returned home late, puzzled at the contents of the note she found waiting for her.

Camille, dressed for an outing, came down the stairs and found Berry standing in the foyer staring at a folded piece of paper. "Bad news?"

Camille's concern was genuine, but she could not keep her gaze from straying past Berry toward the parlor where Ace Zachary sat waiting for her. Her head seemed in a permanent spin now that the renovations to his home were nearing completion. Recently they had asked for the banns to be posted. They were setting tentative wedding dates. Their goal was to have the home ready for occupancy when they returned from their honeymoon on the East Coast. "I was out when the letter arrived and I found it slipped under the door."

"No, not really bad news," Berry replied, blinking away her disappointment before letting her eyes meet those of her auburn-haired friend. Sometimes Camille had a knack for reading her thoughts. At the moment they were scrambled and might signal distress. "It's just that Jason has had some unexpected business matters come up. He wrote that he'll be unable to take me out this evening."

"Why don't you come along with Ace and me?" Camille asked while surveying her image in the mirror on the hall tree. Twirling around, she checked the bottom of her long green skirts in the petticoat mirror tucked underneath the marble shelf. "You've not come with us in more than a week to see the progress being made at the house. We plan to attend the opera and dine afterward, but Ace won't have any trouble getting an extra ticket."

Camille pursed her lips, then added, "Or tickets. I can tell that our charming architect is going to hate it when the project is completed and he no longer gets to see you at the site. I'll bet Louis would leap at the chance to accompany you this evening."

"Louis Gerrard is nice but—"

"Add handsome, suave, and—"

"I'm not that fond of Frenchmen."

"Or at least those that come from Paris, *n'est-ce pas?*" Camille asked teasingly. When Berry remained solemn, she said, "We could return you here if you don't care to go out with us later."

"No, thank you. The idea is lovely, but"—she glanced down at the parcel nestling in the crook of her arm—"I think I should work on the sample gown for Miss Dilly."

The solidly built Ace Zachary appeared in the doorway leading from the parlor. After exchanging greetings with Berry and warm smiles with his betrothed, he said, "I heard Camille's invitation and I second it. Both of us would enjoy having you along."

"Thanks," Berry replied, "but I'm eager to get started on the muslin model of my design."

Ace said, "As you wish, but I wanted you to know you're welcome. I couldn't help overhearing what Camille was saying about Louis Gerrard being interested in you. He has asked more than once if I thought you might receive him, were he to call on you."

"I hope you told him I'm much too busy," Berry said.

Ace grinned, the accompanying twinkle in his blue eyes making him look years younger than he was. "I had to, else I might find myself answering to a certain hot-blooded Creole who lives in the next block. I heard several years ago that he can wield a wicked rapier." Then, with a concerned expression on his good-looking face, he asked, "Are you sure you won't be lonesome?"

"You're kind," Berry replied with a fond smile, "but I'm never lonesome when I'm creating something I love. Now that I've finished Camille's wedding gown"—she watched the lovers exchange soft looks and smiles—"I'm bursting to get started on the sample of my design."

Berry went outside with the couple to Ace's waiting carriage and waved them off, then glanced up the street toward Jason's townhouse. It was childish, she admitted while listening to the fading clip-clops of the horses' hooves as the matched bays pulled Ace's carriage around the corner, but she felt let down that she would not be seeing the handsome Creole that evening. Not since the masquerade ball some four weeks ago had she gone twenty-four hours without seeing him.

Now that Berry thought about it, she realized that she had already spent more time with Jason Premont than she had with any other young man. None of the others she had known had affected her as he did. None had ever tempted her to allow passion to beguile her and lead her into complete surrender. Not one had revealed much about himself as Jason had nor shown as keen an interest in her thoughts and feelings. And only Jason had made her feel so special, so desirable, so womanly.

Berry knew from Jason's frequent talk about his activities

that he had been spending the major portion of his days during the past few weeks tending to business matters for his uncle's plantation, Armand Acres. Poor man, she reflected, having to give up an evening of pleasure for staid business matters. His serious interest in and apparent dedication to the operation of the sugar plantation had surprised her; such purpose didn't fit her image of a rake.

With a small frown on her face, she moved across the banquette toward the gate leading to the courtyard. What kind of business engagement could require Jason's presence on a Friday evening, especially one he had already promised to spend with her? A jarring question formed: Could Jason already be weary of her company?

Even as she stood with her hand on the gate latch mulling over the matter, Berry glimpsed a carriage pulling up in front of Jason's townhouse. Unable to tear her gaze away, she watched the driver hop down and open the door of the vehicle.

Then Berry, refusing to believe what her eyes were telling her, watched an apparently young woman step down amidst a flourish of long blue skirts and enter Jason's courtyard through the wrought iron gateway. Worse, Berry thought as she dashed inside and peeped from around the partially closed gate, the driver followed after the young woman with a portmanteau in his hands. Bedammed! Jason's guest obviously had come for more than a brief visit.

When darkness began soaking up the twilight like a giant sponge, Berry still sat in the small courtyard serving Camille's townhouse, plying her needle on the muslin. She kept trying to rationalize what she had seen with the excuse Jason had given.

The final vestige of light from the overhead patch of sky was fading when Berry removed her thimble, folded her sewing, and withdrew the folded paper from her pocket. She required little light to read again the last lines of the note:

" . . . I shall contact you when I know for certain when I shall be free to call on you again. Until then, please accept my heartfelt apologies and know that I will count the hours until I am once more with you.

> Your devoted and most humble servant,
> Jason Premont."

Devoted? Ha! Humble? Never! The note was the first of Jason's writing that Berry had seen. After her initial indignation lessened, she found herself imagining his sturdy fingers with their tapering ends making each slanting letter, flourish, curlicue.

Suddenly Berry envisioned Jason's hands in detail, large manly hands that held her small ones eagerly, hands that sometimes selected choice bits of fruit or sweetmeats and plopped them into her mouth while they wandered about the Quarter, hands that had tenderly roved her nakedness only two nights ago and . . .Emotions in turmoil, Berry snatched up her sewing, hurried across the bricked courtyard and went inside.

What in thunder, Berry wondered with growing irritation, did Jason think he was doing, bringing a new young woman into his life and casting the old one aside with no more than a note? Had he become impatient with her because she had refused to discuss her reasons for dismissing his proposal? Or had he become irritated with her because she had insisted that their relationship revert to its former state? If lovemaking was all he sought from a woman, let the conceited rascal go to the devil!

While lighting the candles in her bedroom, Berry thought about Jason's declaration of love and marriage proposal. She recognized that she might be spoiled from having tasted and enjoyed more freedom than had the average woman reared in New Orleans. Most young women accepted, even desired, being completely dependent for their livelihood on a man. Berry did not. Furthermore, she completely rejected the thought of spending her life with a husband who could not offer her the special kind of love she sought. Was it too much to expect a man to love her alone, utterly and forever?

After putting away her sewing, Berry tried thinking of what she might eat for supper. Her mind played truant. It kept skipping back and forth between joyful thoughts of what it was like being with Jason and hateful visions of him with another woman. Another woman was at that moment in his townhouse! The mental game whittled her already meagre appetite to zero.

Berry acknowledged that truth was on a rampage, that it was searching for answers to questions she fought against forming. Had she secretly expected more from Jason than the good times they had shared? Had she, in spite of her determination not to fall in love with a handsome rake, lost her heart to Jason Premont anyway?

No! Berry reassured herself as she gazed out the open window at the night air. What she felt for Jason was a physical attraction, an infatuation, no more. A mosquito circled around her head, whining its woebegone melody. Berry waved it away in irritation. Maybe she was experiencing petty jealousy because, apparently unlike Jason, she had not yet overcome those base feelings that created physical longings. Longings and needs. She *would* overcome!

Her infatuation with Jason, Berry assured herself as she extinguished the candle beside her bed and drew together the mosquito netting falling down from the tester, could not turn into love without her willingness. She had her dreams to fulfill, didn't she?

A familiar high-pitched drone close by led Berry into opening the mosquito *baire* and fanning the pesky insect outside. Settling back against her pillow with contrived complacency, she mused that she was the one in control of her life. The mosquito was gone now, wasn't it?

Suddenly another notion flashed across her unsuspecting mind like summer lightning marring a serene night sky. Could the transformation of infatuation into love have taken

place in the same way as the air changed ⟨...⟩light, to
twilight, to darkness? Gradually, impercep⟨...⟩rably?

"Good morning," Berry said ⟨...⟩
when Alonzo answered the be⟨...⟩
Jason's couryard. He stared a⟨...⟩
and what she suspected r⟨...⟩
smile arrived late and n⟨...⟩
face as Berry rememb⟨...⟩
tea with Jason at ⟨...⟩
why I don't stop⟨...⟩
today is the ⟨...⟩
Don't you ⟨...⟩

"Mis⟨...⟩
gling ⟨...⟩

h⟨...⟩
Can⟨...⟩
about ⟨...⟩
pastries ⟨...⟩
Alonzo's su⟨...⟩
gone out for t⟨...⟩

"No, Miss Be⟨...⟩
voice, "Mr. Jason ⟨...⟩
opened the gate all th⟨...⟩

"If that's the boy fro⟨...⟩
annoyed tone from where he⟨...⟩
flagstones, "tell him we'll n⟨...⟩
also."

Berry saw what she thought s⟨...⟩
Alonzo's shoulder. Jason, his back tu⟨...⟩
stood with his arms around a young wom⟨...⟩
be leaning against his broad chest as if she⟨...⟩
Determined to ignore her runaway heartbea⟨...⟩
breath, Berry stared at the pale arms and han⟨...⟩

on something private." She sent Jason a look that he could
describe only as murderous.
Outwardly calm and making no move to leave, Berry
stood holding her market basket in both hands and quietly
observing the scene made by the brown-haired young woman clinging to Jason. With a trace of a smile at the absurdity
of it all, she wondered if she might not have stumbled on
stage during the second act of a poorly written melodrama.
"Perhaps I should come back later, for act three."
"No. Please stay," Jason hastened to say. Act three. W⟨...⟩
Whatever was Berry thinking? What godawful timing! W⟨...⟩
in the devil didn't Viola turn him loose and act like⟨...⟩
twenty-year-old Ashley hadn't had to go see his father⟨...⟩
to? If only Ashley hadn't had to go see his father⟨...⟩
glad you at last accepted my invitation to stop by⟨...⟩
morning for coffee." Surely Berry could tell that V⟨...⟩
in need of consolation.
Even before Berry appeared, Jason had alread⟨...⟩
wonder if there was enough consolation in th⟨...⟩
Viola. Each time she broke down and sobbed⟨...⟩
more prayers skyward that the entire business⟨...⟩
over. He loved her and had turned his back on⟨...⟩
that he was eager to return to his goal of p⟨...⟩
after the matter was settled, the admitt⟨...⟩
could summon no logical explanation. "Berr⟨...⟩
scene that Berry was witnessing. "Berr⟨...⟩
an old friend of mine, Viola Breto⟨...⟩
deal with, but she is somewhat reco⟨...⟩
Right away Berry recognized the⟨...⟩
Jason's companion that Mardi G⟨...⟩
snitched the emerald ring from W⟨...⟩
Ashley's sister was still in the⟨...⟩
She wore no ring on her left h⟨...⟩
truly have a sorrow? ⟨...⟩
Berry had always had a so⟨...⟩
but her anger at Jason tram⟨...⟩

she reflected with what she recognized as snide satisfaction, did not look a lot better with signs of weeping ravaging her face than she had with mud smearing it. As Berry had concluded the night of their collision, though, the young woman was a beauty—judging from what little of her face did not lie buried against Jason, that is. With an assurance she did not feel, Berry said, "Hello, Viola. I'm glad you're feeling better." Then she added, unable to resist sarcasm, "Jason probably knows a lot about making women feel better."

When Viola seemed unable to control her tears and downright reluctant to release her hold on Jason, he removed her clutching hand from his arm and looked down at her blotched face. It bothered him that she suddenly grabbed his hand and hid all of her face against his arm. Berry's cutting insinuation bothered him even more. "Viola, I'd like to introduce Berry Cortabona."

Jason moved his arm in little sideways jerks in an attempt to nudge Viola's face free, annoyed when she fought him till the last moment. Once Viola lifted her face, Jason slipped his hand from hers and rammed it in the pocket of his trousers. Not until after he had taken two steps away from her and stood halfway between the two women did he say, "Viola, Berry lives in the next block and stopped by to have coffee with me . . . us."

Jason recognized that his introductions and ensuing comments were going badly, but by that time, he was perspiring and fishing around for his handkerchief. When he spied it wadded up in Viola's hand, he snatched one of the napkins off the table, set as if for a morning tête-a-tête, and wiped his face. A single rosebud in a silver vase seemed a mockery, especially now that he had caught Berry looking at it and pursing her lips. "Let me get you ladies seated." He sent a pleading look toward the door leading inside as, in what he hoped was a carrying voice, he said. "Alonzo probably will be back soon with a fresh pot of coffee."

"I hope he brings an extra cup," Berry remarked tartly as

she pulled out one of the rattan chairs and seated herself in front of one of the places laid, "and a couple of napkins." She had not missed anything.

From Jason's obvious nervousness, Berry figured she had shown him that he had not gulled her with his declaration of love and his marriage proposal. He was still a rake. If the bitter taste in her mouth was one of victory, she decided while watching Jason seat Viola, then take the chair between his two guests, she had no desire to seek out the state again. She felt itchy all over and far too warm.

What puzzled Berry was why she kept hanging around. Probably both Jason and Viola were looking down their haughty noses at her, a mere theater girl without a single plantation in her background. She had to admit she was curious about what had upset Viola Breton, but she suspected her staying had more to do with a warped desire to watch Jason suffer a while longer. Somehow, remembering her last time with him as one where he was not in control pleased a devious part of her. How had the rascal signed his farewell letter? Devoted. Humble. He had not the least inkling of the meaning of either word.

"Isn't this a lovely morning?" Berry asked, tilting her face toward a breath of wind straying through the grills of the gate. Wonder why the music from the fountain seemed to be playing in a minor key? Berry mused. She silently thanked all who had instructed her in the art of acting a part. What she would have liked to do was blast Jason with her discovery of his inconstancy, his insincerity—and then wallop his handsome face before marching out of his life forever. "I've never heard the birds singing more sweetly."

Viola lifted her swollen eyes in response to Berry's lighthearted remarks. She stared across at the newcomer as if she might be viewing someone demented.

With her teeth set firmly into the role now, Berry said, "Viola, I feel ghastly for having stopped by during what is obviously a stressful time." She slid an accusatory look toward Jason who was watching her with an unreadable expression. Could it be pain from having been caught in a lie? Important business matters, indeed! Was his face pale? The look in his eyes suggested guilt. The thought that apparently he knew nothing about acting a part lent her strength. "If Jason hadn't insisted I stay, I would have gone on my way. Is there anything I can do to help matters?"

"No, thank you," Viola replied in a jerky voice. Her friend from school days, Jeannette Moreau, had told her all about Jason's latest *amour*. Viola had chosen not to believe Jeannette's declaration that when Ashley escorted her to the opera in the company of Berry Cortabona and Jason, she had ended up enjoying being around the vivacious beauty. Neither had she believed that, despite Berry's lack of social rank, Jeannette had found nothing lacking in her manners or appearance.

Jason cleared his throat and said, "Berry, you're most kind to be concerned about Viola. Everyone has times when problems seem overwhelming." Why was Berry refusing to meet his gaze? She seemed to be memorizing Viola's features.

"I quite agree," Berry responded with alacrity.

Somehow when Viola first glimpsed the beautiful black-haired young woman standing in the courtyard, she had sensed she was looking at the one who had captured Jason's heart, the heart too elusive for her to make her own despite her attempts ever since she could remember to win him as more than a friend. It irked her that Jason would choose an ordinary theatrical person over a Breton with a solid Creole background and wealth. For a selfish moment Viola pushed aside her genuine concern and affection for Bayard Filhoil.

Viola realized that she looked a pathetic wreck and had little true ammunition at hand, but she knew she never had been a good loser and never had seen any sense in trying to be one. She despised losing and was suspicious of anyone who did not share her views about such matters.

Sending Jason a coquettish look from beneath partially lowered lashes, Viola broke the lingering silence. "Actually,

Berry, Jason has always been masterful in cheering me up. I don't know what I would do without him. We've known each other for ages and ages, haven't we, *chèri*?"

Alonzo came rushing from inside then, a frown creasing his forehead. After setting down his tray and pouring cups of café au lait for all three, he addressed Viola. "Jewel sent word she's 'bout ready to help you get dressed for the day, Miss Viola."

"Tell her I'm not ready to come inside."

His smile deferential, Alonzo said, "She say I might needs to 'mind you that you gota 'pointment with the dressmaker this morning."

"I know that."

Alonzo gave a tiny shrug and turned away from the disheveled young woman. After sending Jason a what-more-can-I-do look, he asked, "Is there anything else I can do for y'all?"

"Yes," Jason replied. "You can pass the pastries that our guest was kind enough to bring."

Not wasting a movement, Alonzo did as asked. He was not surprised that nobody took one. He rolled his eyes heavenward, then returned the cloth to the sweet-smelling pastries and set the basket back on the flagstones beside Berry. After a silent exchange with his somber-faced master that resolved nothing, Alonzo hurried back inside.

While considering Viola's reaction to Alonzo's obvious attempt to give her an acceptable escape from the courtyard, Jason sipped his coffee. Why had she not jumped at the chance to get away? Surely she must know that copious weeping marred the beauty of her complexion and eyes. He had always thought of Viola as being uncommonly vain; yet, here she sat, drinking coffee with the stylishly clad Berry and him as if she had nothing more pleasant to do. Something did not ring true. Viola was up to something.

"Deep rose is a good color for one of your foreign coloring," Viola remarked after Berry had pursued the subject of dressmakers and the latest fashions and elicited some response from her. "I don't suppose that Miss Dilly made your gown. Almost all of my friends and I go to her shop."

"No, she didn't," Berry replied. Looking the brown-haired Viola squarely in her swollen eyes, she continued. "Miss Dilly is very talented, but I make and design nearly all my gowns myself. I can't tell what coloring you have under normal circumstances, but I hardly consider mine foreign. I'm a Creole with both French and Spanish heritage. If I recall correctly the history I learned from the Ursulines, the Spanish did far more for Louisiana than the French ever did."

Viola had the grace to blush and lower her gaze. Hearing from Jeannette about Jason's beautiful companion of the past few weeks had not prepared her for meeting Berry Cortabona and seeing such perfection in face, form, and diction. She possessed spirit, too, something Viola admired in anybody. Now that she observed the adoring gaze that Jason was sending Berry, Viola felt jealousy clawing in earnest. What she wouldn't give for him to look at her that way! If only she weren't all mixed up about Bayard and Roger and scared about the outcome of the duel tomorrow. . . .

Smiling over the top of his coffee cup at Berry and silently saluting her for setting Viola in her place, Jason said, "Berry is right, Viola. I fear our French ancestors were far more concerned with personal gain and comfort than in establishing a flourishing colony in the New World. It was the Spanish who set up a workable form of government and—"

"Botheration!" Viola broke in with a careless flip of her hand. "None of that matters anymore, so why discuss it?"

Jason looked admiringly at Berry, thinking that Viola had been right. The deep rose of her gown did set off her olive complexion and black hair. For the life of him he could not imagine any color that would not accentuate her beauty. Had her eyebrows always lifted in those delicate arches? He wished that he could explain this minute why it had been necessary to lie to her, why Viola had been in his arms.

"I had met Berry before your brothers and I visited Europe," Jason said to Viola. "When we reached Seville, I asked about her family. The Cortabona men were widely known and respected as builders of seaworthy ships. I managed to meet some who are her cousins."

Jason noted that though on the night of the masquerade ball Berry had appeared keenly interested in what he had told about her family, now she seemed not to be listening. He plunged on. "Berry's father was sailing on a Seville-bound ship that went down in a storm near the Canary Islands the year she was born here in New Orleans. None of the relatives ever learned of her father's marriage to the young Frenchwoman from New Orleans or about the birth of their only child. Some expressed their desire to write her, but other than through a local theater, I knew of no way to reach her."

Half-listening as Jason related the story about her relatives, Berry was reminded of how the first time she heard it, she had judged him thoughtful and considerate for bothering to inquire about her father's people. The memory also reminded her of the foolish boast she had made of having descended from Spanish noblemen. She squirmed in her chair and fidgeted with the bertha collar of her gown.

Now that Berry was intent on turning off her relationship with Jason, she deliberately began to entertain doubts about him. He might have searched out her family in Spain hoping to discover she had lied. He could have been lying about even having made inquiries.

To Berry's way of thinking, Jason was wasting his time if he was trying to make her look good in Viola's eyes. After she left his courtyard within the next few minutes, she never intended to be around him or his friends again.

In spite of Viola's earlier intentions to snub Berry and make her feel uncomfortable, maybe a bit jealous, she found Jason's deep-voiced story about Berry's background intriguing. Viola could not deceive herself any longer that she might worm her way into his heart. Even when he was speaking to her, Jason could not refrain from gazing at Berry. The man was smitten.

Viola recalled Berry's quick defense a brief time ago of her heritage and her obvious pride in being no more or no less than she was. The young woman's admirable qualities brought a grudging nod of approval from Viola. Since her introduction into society back when she was a mere girl, she had discerned that anyone possessing Berry Cortabona's remarkable beauty and spirit was worth getting to know, no matter her social status.

It went against Viola's nature to reverse her opinions quickly, but when Jason's story ended, she said, "Berry, I think it will be great fun for us to get to know each other."

Though Jason protested and Viola added her own wishes for her to stay longer, Berry left soon after Viola's remark. All the way to Camille's townhouse in the next block she saw red. Fiery red, as in anger and disappointment. Blood red, as in desire to strike out against a feared unknown.

Though Berry had read sincerity in Viola's eyes and empathized with her for whatever trouble had brought her to tears, she entertained no good will toward Viola Breton. How could she feel kindly toward the other woman in Jason's life? Let them both go to the devil!

CHAPTER

*

Eleven

*T*hat Saturday evening Camille had no trouble in persuading Berry to go with Ace and her to the ballet. Though Berry suspected both Camille and Ace were dissembling when they pretended ignorance as to how Louis Gerrard happened to show up in the lobby during intermission, out of desperation she accepted the French architect's attentions. She welcomed anything, or anyone, that might slow her churning thoughts about Jason Premont. When a waiter offered her a glass of wine, she took that, too. She sipped greedily.

The foursome stood conversing near the open double doors leading from the street into the large lobby, when Berry felt a tensing at the base of her skull, as if someone might be watching her. Jason! Was he present...with Viola on his arm?

With her pulse faltering and her mouth gone dry, Berry swept searching looks across the crowded lobby. She saw some familiar faces, returned some polite nods, but no dark eyes flecked with gold met hers. No stranger's piercing stare stabbed her.

When the prickling sensation remained, Berry turned and looked out into the night, seeing only a hunched-over old woman limping alongside another gray-haired woman on the dimly lighted banquette across the street. Both carried what looked like shopping baskets. Neither appeared to be doing more than gawking at the sight of the many elegantly attired people standing around during intermission and being sociable. Some tall oleander bushes down the street caught Berry's attention, but she saw nothing that led her to suspect somebody might be hiding in their shadows stealing looks in her direction.

Assuming she was just feeling edgy because of her sleeplessness of the previous night and the unsettling visit to Jason's courtyard that morning, Berry lightly rubbed the back of her neck. The flash of fire from her emerald ring caught her eye when she brought her hand down.

Why, Berry mused while the others discussed the merits of the evening's performance, did she never truly feel comfortable wearing the ring and never even thought about wearing it unless Camille suggested it? It *was* a tangible link with her old friend, Ebon. She really should forget how it had become hers and appreciate it for its rare beauty. At least now, with her earnings from her design and the potential for more, she would not have to consider pawning the jewel anytime soon. She forced her thoughts to the conversation about ballet.

"In Paris we have no more beautifully dressed dancers than I've seen during my year here in New Orleans," Louis Gerrard said knowledgeably. His lean Gallic face softened as he looked at Berry, so vibrant in her green gown, her black hair curled in tight little rosettes around her expressive face and caught high at the back of her head in looping braids and more corkscrew curls. "I have concluded that New Orleans has an abundance of beauty—in more than the costumes at their theaters."

"It was not until about ten years ago that women dancers began wearing the brief costumes that allow so much freedom of movement," Camille remarked, her dark eyes resting fondly on Ace Zachary before moving to Berry's pensive features. She was glad that she had insisted her young friend borrow one of her gowns and allow her to style her hair in the latest fashion. Yet Berry seemed aloof, as if removed from what was going on around her. Camille was fairly sure she knew the reason.

Ever since Berry had returned home that morning, raging about what she had discovered in Jason's courtyard, it seemed plain to Camille that her earlier suspicions were true. Berry had fallen in love with the dashing Jason Premont, whether or not she had meant to. When would she recognize that truth herself? Turning to Louis, Camille had more to say about costuming. "I think the new freedom of movement choreographed for women dancers and costume designs that allow that freedom have made ballet much more popular."

"So do I," Louis replied, and turned toward Berry. "What are your thoughts about the modern costumes being used in ballet, *Mademoiselle* Cortabona?"

"I'm for them," Berry answered, her interest in the subject drawing her out of herself for the moment. "I understand it was Marie Taglioni when she danced the lead role in *Les Sylphides* who first wore a ballet dress that reaches only to mid-calf. It must have been so difficult before then for women dancers when they had to wear adaptations of constricting fashions of the day."

The feeling that someone was still watching her covertly crept over Berry. Again she looked out into the night; even the two shuffling old women with their shopping baskets were gone now. Only a single carriage passing by lent movement to the summer night outside. Had she halfway hoped to see Jason striding toward her in his long-legged, straight-shouldered way?

"Do you suppose the present costume will become the

standard?'' Ace asked. He flicked an ash from his cigar into a sand-filled vase beside the door.

"I hope so," Berry declared with a flash of her usual vivaciousness. "It works so well and looks so ethereal. It captures the quality of the music."

"Then you as a designer," Louis asked, "would make no changes?"

Berry laughed. Was there no limit to what Camille and Ace would do to try making her look like more than she was? When had they told Louis about her first sale? "I'm only a novice designer, Mr. Gerrard, but the one change I might suggest would be to make the skirts even fuller and shorter."

Then the four fell into discussing the increased freedom that a briefer skirt could offer a ballerina, even a choreographer. What might be the reaction from the general public to such a blatant display of body and limbs in the United States in the 1840s?

"I suspect only in the East where the Puritan ethic seems still to reign would strong opposition be found," Ace concluded. With his customary air of authority, he motioned to a waiter nearby to bring over his tray and pick up their empty wine glasses. "Here in New Orleans I can't imagine many eyebrows would be raised. After all, life here takes on its own peculiar flavor. With its continental and regional cuisine, theaters and horse racing, New Orleans has a sophistication that makes it almost like a European city."

"Please do not omit fencing," Louis pointed out after the waiter took away their glasses. "There seem to be as many skilled fencing instructors here as in Paris."

"Yes," Ace replied thoughtfully. "Sometimes I wonder if their presence and popularity might not contribute to the growing number of duels fought here."

After drawing on his cigar, Ace continued. "A couple of years ago a Creole who was studying with one of our *maîtres d'armes* became angry with a visiting French scientist, Chevalier Tomasi. It was reported that Chevalier had made odious statements claiming the superiority of the French over Americans in almost every aspect.''

Ace waited for the expected exchange of amused glances before continuing. ''He even went so far as to write a series of newspaper articles in which he questioned the character of the correction girls and the revered casket girls sent over to marry the early French settlers. Then Chevalier began expressing his view that the Mississippi River should either be channeled into flowing peacefully in a designated course, as are the great rivers in Europe, or else be dammed up.''

''Obviously the man had never traveled on the Mississippi,'' Berry said, memories flashing to mind of her own journeys aboard riverboats.

''As the story goes, the Creole told him that,'' Ace continued, ''but the Frenchman sneered and bragged that European rivers are mightier than the Mississippi. After announcing to Chevalier that he would never permit the Mississippi to be disparaged in his presence by an arrogant foreigner, the Creole flung his glove in the man's face and was immediately challenged to a duel. They met at dawn under the Oaks where the Creole upheld the honor of the Mississippi by slashing the Frenchman across the mouth.''

''I shall be diligent in keeping my negative opinions about anything American to myself,'' Louis observed, with a quick smile. ''I plan to remain here. Preferably in one piece.''

Berry laughed. ''I once heard a man say''—she had no wish to mention Jason's name—''that he preferred the American method of settling matters by sending a swift punch to the jaw. Perhaps some men like dueling because it's theatrical.''

Indicating a group behind them, Louis leaned closer and said, ''*Mademoiselle,* you may be right. All during intermission, I've been overhearing fragments of a conversation about a duel. It will take place at dawn at the site Ace mentioned, the Oaks. I gather those speaking intend to drive out and watch.''

"I heard something about that this morning in one of the coffee houses," Ace said in a similarly lowered voice. "Sounded to me like a trumped-up affair between the heir to some sugar plantation and a cotton broker. Some headstrong Creole heiress was accosted in one of those dives down on Peter Street, and I gather one suitor accused the other of being lax in protecting the young woman's honor. Apparently both were hunting a reason to cross swords."

"How horrible!" Camille exclaimed.

"What in the world would they have been doing in such a place?" Berry asked. "Everyone knows it's dangerous there."

"Gambling, my dear," Ace replied as he jammed the glowing end of his cigar into the sand in the tall vase.

Berry pursed her lips. Heir to a sugar plantation? Jason had introduced her to several of his friends who were owners or heirs to plantations, some growing sugar, some cotton. "What are the men's names?"

Louis Gerrard, not a great deal taller than Berry, leaned nearer and spoke in little more than a whisper. "I believe I overheard the names Filhoil and Elton."

Just then a bell chimed, signifying the end of intermission, and the foursome turned to follow the crowd back inside the theater.

The reports of the duel kept cropping up in Berry's thoughts throughout the final movement of the ballet and afterward when they went for a festive, midnight supper to the Orleans Palace far beyond the French Quarter on Esplanade. She finally decided the topic fascinated her because of her many Sunday walks as a youngster in the vicinity of the grove of oak trees on the Allard Plantation. So many duels had taken place there that it had become known simply as the Oaks.

Berry's remembered fear of the Oaks, especially on the day when she had hidden in the bushes and watched a cart hauling away a motionless, tarp-draped figure, brought a little tremor.

"Are you cold, *Mademoiselle* Cortabona? May I offer you my coat as a wrap?" Louis Gerrard asked solicitously.

"*Non, merci.* Maybe a ghost is seeking my grave." When the Frenchman angled his head in puzzlement and reminded Berry of an adorable puppy seeking approval, she laughed and explained that her comment had no literal interpretation. Louis was quite handsome, with his smooth features and slender build. His excellent English bore only a trace of an accent. He did not remind her at all of Jason Premont.

Berry drank wine before, during, and after the sumptuous meal set before them, course after course. Soon she heard herself talking gaily, too gaily, about diverse topics and laughing wildly at remarks designed to be no more than amusing.

Before the foursome left the table for the return to the French Quarter, Berry realized that she was returning Louis's warm smiles with a movement of her lips that he might mistake for encouragement. Hadn't she made it clear that he was no more than a friend?

As they wended their way toward the exit through the boisterous crowd of late-night diners, Berry caught a snatch of conversation and stopped. Turning to Camille and clutching her arm, she asked, "Did you hear that? Who said it?"

"Hear what?" Camille regarded Berry's flushed cheeks and overly bright eyes. Perhaps, she reflected as they waited for Ace and Louis to catch up with them, she should have discouraged Ace from ordering a second brandy all around, or at least for Berry. Plainly, she was overwrought. Had her young friend drunk too much? Watching Berry looking searchingly around the dining room, she asked, "Who said what?"

"I heard someone say it was Viola Breton the two men are dueling over at the Oaks at dawn." When Camille looked at her blankly and Ace and Louis exchanged puzzled glances, she explained, "Ever since intermission I've had this strange sense of foreboding, and now I'm putting it all together. Viola Breton was at Jason's this morning. He must be dueling because of her. I need to find out who was talking about the duel and ask more. Jason may be in danger.''

"Nonsense," Camille replied, unobtrusively leading Berry toward the doorway as she talked. Berry was making no sense. "Remember how Maddy always said you rely too much on your feelings? You've always had a vivid imagination. You're just overly tired. You'll feel better after we get in the carriage and you breathe some fresh air. There's so much cigar smoke in here and—''

"You think I've had too much to drink, don't you?" Berry glared at Camille as if at an adversary. From the people in the restaurant all around her she could hear pleasant talk and laughter, happy sounds that grated against her rising trepidation. "I tell you there's something weird going on. I had a feeling at intermission that someone was staring at me, making me feel threatened. And then Louis overheard the conversation about the duel. I've good reason to be disturbed.''

When the three guided Berry through the door and onto the covered porch without comment, she spouted her indignation. "Stop treating me as if I'm a lunatic or a drunk! Can't you see that someone has made a mistake about the name of the heir to the sugar plantation? One of the men dueling over Viola Breton is Jason Premont! I felt something evil in the air earlier and I thought it was directed at me, but now I know it's connected with Jason's well-being. Please take me out to the Oaks before the sun rises!''

Even after Buford, Ace's driver, guided the carriage near the porch and Louis attempted to escort Berry inside, nobody had volunteered a response to her impassioned plea. Her words might as well have been the wind blowing from Lake Pontchartrain a few miles away.

"Please, Ace," Berry said, seizing his arm and looking into his eyes, "can't we just ride out to the Oaks before we start back to the Quarter? You're always saying you like to take Camille for rides in the moonlight. Maybe we could drive out to Pontchartrain and watch the waves. The Oaks would be on the way."

Ace looked from the apparently agreeable Louis Gerrard to Camille to Berry, then back at the troubled face of his beloved. When she gave an almost imperceptible nod, he said, "Very well, Berry. If everyone else approves, we'll take a moonlit ride out past the Allard Plantation. It isn't long before sunrise and if there's to be a duel, there'll likely be some people already waiting to watch the show."

"Yes," Berry replied in a rush, barely able to stand still now that Ace had consented, "that's what I overheard inside. There was a group talking about going on from here to the Oaks. I remember more now."

"The Orleans Palace *is* one of the popular places where people gather before going out to watch duels. I doubt your so-called premonition is more than a young woman's fancy, though. Even if what I heard years ago about Jason's skill with a sword is true, I can't imagine a sensible man like him getting himself in a predicament calling for a duel. If it means that much to you—"

"Oh, it does! It does!" Berry planted a swift kiss on Ace's cheek and, having seen Camille give her silent consent earlier, she gave Camille a hug. "Thank you both for being so understanding." Then she turned to the good-looking architect who had displayed adoration and gratitude for her presence throughout the evening's festivities. "You're not even an old acquaintance, Louis, and yet you're being so kind about indulging me. Thank you."

Louis smiled down at the lovely face lifted toward his and escorted Berry inside the carriage. "You're welcome. I think you are absolutely divine, Berry Cortabona. I have not had such an entertaining evening since coming here from Paris last year."

With each passing mile Berry watched the moon lose its earlier brightness as it inched toward the horizon. When

Buford drove the team of matched bays into the grove of moss-festooned trees located near Pontchartrain Road, Berry saw right away that, as Ace had predicted, carriages already sat among the shadows of the soaring oaks at the edge.

From the open windows of Ace's carriage, Berry strained to see up ahead. Were Jason and his party already gathered underneath the three largest oak trees in the grove? Would Ashley Breton be the one serving his friend as second? She had heard there was nearly always a physician in attendance, sometimes one for each duelist. The thought of Jason coming to harm set her trembling.

Drat Viola for putting Jason in danger, Berry thought as anger rose and her alcoholic daze diminished. No wonder Viola had been weeping and looking like death warmed over at Jason's home. Two men were at risk of being maimed or killed because of her and her careless behavior.

Berry's heart fluttered painfully. Jason must love Viola very much to put his life in jeopardy for her, especially when he had confided only recently that he classified duels as foolish and not nearly as good a solution to a raging disagreement as a fistfight. Whether duels were foolish or not, a man who would risk his life for the good name of a woman was proclaiming to her and to the world that he loved her. Berry, a confessed romantic, felt the sudden scalding of tears. She blinked them away.

Berry's jolting conclusions did not alter her determination to save Jason from his own impetuousness. She had begun wondering as they neared the Oaks and her head began to clear why she wished to rescue the rake. The only answer she could come up with was that she wanted the pleasure of walking out of his life in the hurtful way he had walked out of hers. But she would not even send a note full of lies; she would just refuse to see the arrogant rogue.

The faintest hint of pink was brushing the sky in the East when Buford halted the carriage and jumped down from the driver's seat to consult with his master. As soon as Ace agreed that the spot underneath a tree some distance away from the largest oaks was an acceptable stopping place, he assisted Camille in stepping down.

"We're going to stroll away from the Oaks," Ace said to the couple still in the carriage. "Would you care to join us and stretch your legs?"

Quick to realize that the betrothed couple had no time alone throughout the evening, Berry declined. Louis, the perfect gentleman, echoed her refusal.

"We'll not be gone long," Camille assured Berry.

As soon as Berry saw the couple, arm in arm, had sauntered a goodly distance, she picked up her skirts, stepped down from the carriage, and left Louis sitting in shock on the cushioned seat. Before Buford even knew she was gone and before Louis could climb down and deter her, she took off running through the shadows toward the large open space she recalled from her days of wandering in the area.

"Jason!" Berry called, holding up her long skirts to free her feet and legs for running. She glimpsed startled faces appearing in the windows of carriages parked here and there and heard mumblings, but she paid them no heed. She could hear someone running from a distance behind her and wondered if Louis would be able to catch her before she reached Jason. Louis was not very tall and she figured her legs might be nearly as long as his.

Berry's only fear was that she would not be able to get to Jason in time to save him. She slowed down long enough to snatch off her slippers with their bothersome two-inch heels and fling them over her shoulder. A protesting masculine grunt from behind reached her ears. For Jupiter's sake! Why hadn't Louis ducked? "Jason! Where are you?"

From where he had been sitting on a fallen log with Ashley Breton for the past hour trying to stay awake, Jason eyed the three men who were leaning against the trunk of a giant oak a few yards away: Bayard Filhoil, his second and his attending physician. How long before the hotheaded

Creole would admit there would be no duel and free all of them to go home?

Though Roger at last had succumbed to Ashley's tempting offer and agreed to depart from New Orleans this morning on the earliest steamboat, Jason reflected, Bayard Filhoil had stubbornly insisted that he would appear at the Oaks as agreed. At midnight, when Jason and Ashley had met with Bayard and told him about the late-minute resolution achieved, Bayard had retorted, "If Roger Elton chooses to act the coward and not show up, at least I will prove that I am a Creole of honor. Bayard Filhoil is not a man who makes idle threats or agreements."

"Did you hear somebody calling my name?" Jason asked Ashley. He peered toward the several carriages pulled up underneath trees not far away, then stood. As far as he could tell, the occupants were inside asleep, or at least quiet. Why anyone would drive out to watch two men dueling amazed him, but he recognized it was a popular pastime among the sporting men of New Orleans. Talk was that sometimes they brought along companions from the bordellos. "I know this sounds absurd, but I could have sworn it was a woman."

"Good Lord! Do you suppose Viola talked Alonzo into driving her out here?" Ashley asked, wide awake by then. Keeping his voice down for fear Bayard might take offense, Ashley went on. "I told her fourteen times that this is men's business and there's no place for women at a duel. Women seem to be the cause of most of them, but—"

"There," Jason interrupted him to say. "I heard it again. I swear it sounded like Berry."

Ashley chuckled. "You're out of your head. What would she be doing out here? You said you never once mentioned the duel to her when she dropped by and met Viola this morning—no, yesterday morning now." When he, too, heard a call, he said teasingly, "It appears that you might be the one to be embarrassed by a hysterical woman showing up at a dueling site."

Berry sighted Jason and Ashley then and made a beeline

for Jason, flinging her arms around him and sobbing. Close behind her came Louis Gerrard, the tails of his frock coat flapping against the backs of his thighs. In his hands he carried Berry's cast-off shoes.

"What are you doing here, Berry?" Jason asked. His arms went around her protectively. Was the stylishly dressed man who was chasing her trying to attack her? What in the devil was he doing with her shoes in his hand? "What's wrong? Who is that man chasing you?"

"Never mind him. Oh, Jason," Berry cried, "you're going to be killed!" Her breath was coming out in gasps. "I had this premonition and I came to save you!" She turned her head and glared at the trio of men, who were standing underneath a nearby oak staring at her with open disbelief.

In the first pink rays of dawn Berry saw the evil-looking sword held by Bayard's second, saw the black bag in the doctor's hands, and began wailing. Though Louis had caught up with her then and stood a few feet away struggling for breath, she ignored him. She ignored everyone but Jason. "Come away with us, Jason," she begged frantically while tugging on his lapels. Tears rained down her face. "Ace has his carriage down the way. You're going to be killed if you go through with this duel!"

Bayard and his companions exchanged amused looks and burst into laughter. Ashley, his hand on the pistol strapped underneath his coat, eyed the young man who had dashed up soon after Berry's dramatic arrival. He now stood trying to recapture his breath. Judging from the stranger's perplexed look that he had no intention of harming Berry, Ashley smiled at the ludicrousness of the situation. He would have laughed aloud, but he knew Jason's quick temper too well to risk it at the moment. A movement caught his eye and he turned to see another man, older and thicker, hurrying toward them.

Ace Zachary called, "Berry, I see you found Jason. Thank goodness you're not harmed. You shouldn't have run off like that. Camille didn't want to stay behind with Buford but I insisted." He was facing the small group then and heard the guffaws coming from the trio standing beside the tree trunk, saw Jason's companion smiling. When Berry seemed not to have heard, Ace addressed Louis. "What's going on?"

"Me, I cannot tell," the French architect replied, shrugging dramatically. With a puzzled expression on his face, where a reddening, swelling spot on his cheekbone marked the landing place of one of Berry's discarded shoes, he appeared engrossed in watching the little drama. Berry was still sobbing against the broad chest of the tall, dark-haired man. The second man was fighting back laughter, while the three men close by were openly laughing and talking among themselves.

Jason sent a cutting look toward Bayard Filhoil and his boisterous friends before explaining, "There isn't going to be a duel, Berry. The challenged man is probably at this moment boarding a riverboat for Cincinnati. Bayard showed up merely for the sake of his honor. Ashley and I came along to make sure all went as it was supposed to."

Disbelieving what she was hearing, Berry disengaged herself and stepped back from Jason, her face aflame. "Then you never were the one who was planning to duel?"

"No." Jason shook his head, amazed that Berry had learned about the duel, much less that she had believed him involved in it. Looking at her disheveled hair, her rumpled green skirts and her shoeless feet, he grinned. She looked good enough to eat. She had feared for his life and come to save him. What a spitfire! He laughed because his heart was overflowing with joy. Berry Cortabona cared for him whether or not she chose to admit it! "Even if I had been going to duel, Berry, you shouldn't have come tearing out here like—"

Not waiting for Jason to complete his unwelcome, humiliating reprimand and moving only enough to reach him, Berry reared back and slapped Jason's smiling face. Black eyes blazing, she hissed, "You rotter! Reprobate! You let me make a complete fool of myself by not telling me what was going on. Damn you! I'll never forgive you for this, Jason Premont. Never!''

With an agonized "Oh-h!" Berry lifted her skirts and whirled away. As quickly as she had entered the clearing, she dashed off on stockinged feet. On her way back to where Camille and Buford waited, she saw a startled face pop up in the window of one of the parked carriages that she passed. She stuck out her tongue. Damn Jason! Damn all men! She never wanted to see another man for the rest of her life.

CHAPTER

*

Twelve

"*B*erry," Camille called as she rapped on Berry's door. "Jason is here again asking to see you."

After Camille entered the bedroom, Berry rose from where she had been sketching and met her concerned gaze. "Please, Camille. I've told you for the past two days that I don't care to see him. Why can't he just go away and leave us alone? I'm sorry you have to be involved in this farce."

"Linnie asked him to wait in the courtyard. It's a lovely afternoon. She went to put on water for tea."

Berry sighed and rolled her eyes in exasperation. Apparently Jason had experienced no trouble in charming the pleasant black woman Ace had sent over recently to "do" for Camille. "At least you've always managed to keep him in the parlor near the front door. I guess I'll have to talk to Linnie again. She means well, but—"

"One of these days you're going to have to stop being

willful and face Jason Premont. Why not get it over?''
When Berry shrugged and returned her attention to her
work, Camille came closer.

Camille had saved as a last resort the ammunition that had
worked the first time Berry had tried shucking off the
persistent Creole. After all, Camille reasoned, before Berry
settled down to being sensible, she needed some time to
indulge her hurt pride and bruised heart. But now the time
had come for some realistic words. ''Are you afraid, Berry,
of what the sight of him might do to your determination to
shove him out of your life?'' Camille asked. ''Are you going
to shut yourself away forever?''

''I haven't been shutting myself away. Have you forgotten
that I received Louis yesterday?''

''Poor Louis. The heel of your shoe must have landed
smack on his cheekbone. His bruise looked monstrous, but
not much worse than his face looked all over after you told
him you wouldn't be going out with him. I'm afraid he'll
find other women dull after Saturday night's shenanigans.''

''You and Ace can share the blame. I never once encouraged Louis Gerrard.''

Determined not to become sidetracked, Camille went over
to the window. ''Jason looks better today.'' Still watching
the tall, dark-haired man prowling in aimless fashion about
the small enclosed area, Camille added, ''You can see for
yourself.''

Berry almost gave in to temptation. Instead, she wheeled
around with an angry swish of her long skirts and crossed
over to the dresser, where she began brushing her hair.
''Better? How does he look better?''

''That Sunday evening when he first came, the cut in his
eyebrow seemed certain to close his eye. This afternoon the
swelling is gone and there's nothing left but a purplish
bruise on that handsome face.''

Though Berry made a show of indifference, Camille did
not change the subject. ''Ace said he and Ashley had a

tough time pulling Jason away from Bayard, even after he had gained the apology he was after.''

Berry heard the unvoiced admiration in Camille's words and tossed her hair in what she recognized was a puerile fit of temper. She felt like acting childish, she consoled herself. Jason certainly had contributed his share to this ridiculous situation: writing lies, keeping secrets, and treating her as if she might be too imbecilic to hear the truth. Were the versions that Camille and Ace had offered after her ignominious retreat from the Oaks the truth?

How, Berry agonized, could she tell anymore what was true? She refused to believe that she had fallen in love with the rake. She insisted to herself that she had been infatuated with him and that the attraction would gradually disappear, especially if she stopped seeing him. Truth seemed to hide behind several masks, all of them tempting. The situation was frightening. Downright frightening.

"Jason acted like a fool," Berry protested to Camille. "There was no need to fight in my defense." She held a section of her hair in one hand and brushed the loosely curling ends with vigor. She brushed so hard that her scalp hurt and hot tears rushed to her eyes.

Berry could make no sense of her bizarre reaction, but even as she slowed the strokes of her hairbrush, she realized that she welcomed the fleeting physical discomfort. At least it was a distraction from the continuous pain that had assailed her mind and heart during the past three days and nights. Would tears offer relief from her inward agony? No, she had always viewed tears as a sign of weakness.

Clinging to her grievance, Berry said, "While you and I were worrying ourselves crazy about why Ace and Louis didn't hurry back to the carriage, that arrogant rascal was picking a fight. Don't men ever grow up?"

"What about women?" Camille's eyes met Berry's in the mirror with such directness that the younger woman dropped hers.

Not wanting the quarrel between Jason and her to spill

over into her friendship with Camille, Berry plunged ahead. "What did Jason expect to prove by socking Bayard Fihoil after I left—that he was quick with his fists like the Texans he fought alongside? I can understand why Bayard and his friends were laughing their heads off at me. Why would he start a fight with Bayard?"

"I think it was a matter of manly pride about—"

Berry butted in, remembered hurt and embarrassment honing her soft voice. "Manly pride? Ha! He was mad and ashamed of having a *former* woman friend come barging in to 'save' him from a duel he wasn't even going to fight in the first place. I guess he was furious at my slapping him in front of all those men, too."

"No. You're wrong. It was manly pride about being ready to defend your right to come anywhere he is and expect to be treated with dignity. Ace says"—in the mirror Camille noted Berry's stillness, the wishful look in her widely spaced eyes; plainly she respected Ace's opinion—"it was a way of defending your honor. Jason told me this morning when he came by with a bouquet of roses for you that he has never before been serious about any woman. He loves you so, Berry."

"Oh, my," Berry said in what she hoped was a teasing tone, "he has you cocked and primed with a batch of sweet words right out of a melodrama, doesn't he?" She lowered her gaze. Her heart was skipping around.

Berry's fingers no longer felt strong enough to hold her hairbrush. Letting it rest on the top of the dresser, she stared at it as if she never before had seen it. She felt childish for having refused even to look at the bouquets and notes Jason had brought daily. The memory of having ripped the paper into tiny pieces and strewing them like confetti made her feel even more foolish. An "Impulse Person," she rationalized, could expect no more.

"If I have any answers at all, and I'm not sure that I do," Camille replied in a voice thick with caring, "it's because I love you and not because of anything Jason or anyone else might say. If you choose to tell him to go straight to hell, that's your business. But do it, get it over with, and let all of us get on with our lives. I want you to face up to anything that knocks you on your elegant little *derrière*.''

Realizing for the first time that she might have piled too much of her own burden on her dear friend, and that the advice offered probably was sound, Berry straightened her shoulders and reconsidered Camille's words. Yes, she might be infringing on the rights of friendship. Her quarrel with Jason belonged only to the two of them. She let out a tiny giggle that bordered on sounding hysterical. ''I've never before heard anybody's posterior described as 'elegant.' I concede defeat.''

Within a short time, Camille had helped the suddenly nervous Berry arrange her waist-length hair in her favorite casual style, the sides and back hanging in loose curls with the top section pulled back and held in a cluster of curls at the back of her head. Aware that Linnie was hovering outside in the hall pretending to polish the handrailing on the staircase, Camille asked the black woman to go to her bedroom and fetch a red satin ribbon.

''Do I look like a woman ready to face the world?'' Berry asked after Camille had sent Linnie to make tea. Berry had tied the red ribbon around the fall of shining black curls at the back of her head and wondered if it represented her attempt to muster bravado.

Camille appraised Berry's red-checked gown with its basque top and slightly scooped neckline edged in white lace. She nodded her approval of the way the full skirt billowed out stylishly over several petticoats. Now that crinoline, a fabric made of horsehair and cotton or linen, was being used to make stiffened petticoats that could support the weight of several other petticoats, fashions were taking on a new look that both Berry and she welcomed. To Camille's way of thinking, Berry's decorative, half-apron of snowy organdy, which was trimmed with the same lace as the neckline and the brief, capelike sleeves, added a quaint touch.

With undisguised affection, Camille hugged the solemn-eyed young woman. "You're beautiful and ready to face anything." Stepping back to look into Berry's face, Camille added, "Would you rather I not leave right now? I could stay and have tea, maybe act as referee."

"No, but I appreciate the offer. Go ahead and meet with the people making curtains for your new home." Berry sent her friend a teasing smile. "Anybody with an elegant *derrière* can handle almost anything."

"You're being stubborn to make me suffer," Jason said to Berry. Teatime in the courtyard was over, as were the earlier civilities.

"I'm being honest. You're the one who's stubborn."

Berry and Jason had just rehashed the events of the past Sunday morning, plus those leading up to it. Their ensuing quarrel had made their infrequent squabbling during their previous four weeks together sound like a first rehearsal for opening night.

Both had let tempers and harsh words fly. Calming down was not easy. Letting go was no easier. Not for Jason. He recognized his goal and meant to attain it.

Berry still refused to acknowledge her life could include a man whom she classified as a rake. While Jason seemed bent on discussing the future, Berry had no desire to talk further. Having sidestepped messages from her heart, she considered herself generous to have allowed the confrontation to have lasted this long.

When Berry pursed her lips and pretended interest in the vase of roses he had brought and asked Linnie to set on the table where they had shared an amazingly sociable tea an hour ago, Jason sighed. Why in thunder did she have to be so beautiful? And obstinate? "You may call me what you choose, but you're not always right."

"Are you?" Berry leaned back against the tall fan-back of

her chair. She was exhausted. Camille was right. Acting a bona fide part scene after scene and letting out all stops was wickedly hard work. "I thought we were through fighting. I've said all I have to say."

"What makes you think you're the only one able to make judgments about us and our future?"

"Because there's not any 'us' in my future. There's just me, Berry Cortabona." Like the actress she had once yearned to become, Berry spouted the lines she had rehearsed as she lay awake the greater part of last night. "Please, let's drop the subject. I'm weary of it. We had some wonderful times together. If I choose to call a halt to our relationship, that's my right."

"Not," Jason retorted with a forefinger pointing toward her, "when it infringes on my right to court the woman I love and intend to marry." He watched her close her eyes and move her head restlessly against the back of her chair. Would it help if he got up and kissed the hell out of her lovely mouth?

Jason still counted himself lucky that when Berry had at last come down to the courtyard, he had been able to persuade her to accept the gift he brought. Somehow he had sensed that if he did not present it early on during their meeting, he might find her less receptive later.

"The thimble is lovely," Berry had said, holding the tiny silver object in the palm of her hand, admiring the engraved miniature leaves running around the tapering end and the smooth band encircling the lower edge. Engraved there in flowing script were her initials, BAC. Berry Angelique Cortabona. She remembered admiring the thimble in a jeweler's window when she and Jason had strolled toward the Plâce d'Armes on the evening that she had told him of her first sale. "You shouldn't have—"

"I bought it the day after we first saw it, and ordered it engraved. I wanted to commemorate the first sale of one of your designs. I know there'll be countless others, but the first is special. See if it fits."

Plainly moved, she slipped the thimble on the dainty third finger of her right hand, waggling it and watching the bright reflections. It fit. She smiled up at him. "I don't know what to say."

"I'll settle for 'Thank you.'"

While giving Berry time to collect whatever thoughts were going on behind her closed eyes, Jason congratulated himself for having at least begun their meeting successfully. Maybe his victory at the time was small, but it was the kind a man in love could savor. She had smiled at him with a touch of the old smile he adored. He liked knowing that his gift now lay inside one of the frilly pockets of her stylish little apron. How could she not think of him each time she used the thimble?

Framed in as she was by the tall, white wicker fan-back chair, Berry looked incredibly beautiful to Jason. How he had missed looking at her! Though direct sunshine no longer reflected into the courtyard, the singularly magic New Orleans light bathed Berry's sculpted features with a soft, ethereal glow.

Once Jason had heard a local artist declare that the air and light in New Orleans was unique because of the excessive moisture in the air filtered by the rays of the sun. "*Merci, mon Dieu!*" the ecstatic artist had interrupted himself to say with a Frenchman's thumb-and-two-fingered kiss blown to the heavens. Jason recalled the verbose fellow giving thanks then for the city's proximity to the Mississippi River and Lake Pontchartrain, as well as to the Gulf of Mexico. If at the time Jason had discounted the statements as being fanciful and without true merit—and he suspected that he had—he now embraced them wholeheartedly while gazing at the woman he loved.

As angry as Jason was about Berry's strangely false manner and words, he sensed he was falling more in love with her every moment. From the first time he had seen the pretty black-haired girl, he had sensed she had spirit. Still, he had been unprepared for what he had learned about her since they had begun seeing each other almost daily. He had been even more unprepared for what he had learned during the past few days. Yes, he mused, he had deserved her anger, her slap. He never should have lied to her.

"We would have a horrible marriage, Jason Premont," Berry said when she opened her eyes and discovered his gaze fixed on her. If she leaned across the table toward him, would she see the tiny golden flecks swimming within those brown pools?

Half in shadow as he was while leaning back against his own fan-back chair, Jason seemed lost in contemplation. She admired the way his pale blue frockcoat worn over a spotlessly white waistcoat, both tailored of fine broadcloth, set off his faintly olive complexion, his dark brown hair. As a concession to the summer heat, he wore a filmy white cravat over the neck of his shirt instead of a more restricting stock. The silent air of authority that always exuded from him had not dissipated, but she suspected he might have suppressed it for the moment. Had his anger diminished?

Earlier during the height of their heated quarrel, and afterward when he refused to drop his defensive mien, Berry had noticed how compressed Jason's sensuous lips were. She was accustomed to seeing them lifted in smiles, the sassy creases around them hinting at ready laughter. Despite her trying to chase away the unsettling memory, she recalled how his lips felt against hers, how they tasted, how they. . . Jason Premont truly was the most handsome man she had ever seen, likely would ever see, even when looking pensive, as now, and not revealing his dimples. There seemed to be something extraordinary about the light in the courtyard.

Oh, Berry chided herself, *you're being ridiculous.* The light was the same late afternoon light she had been seeing for most of her nineteen years. It was being with Jason again that had her brain scrambled. Soon she was going to have to ask him to leave so that she could get on with her plan to forget him. Was the silence really so filled with suffering? Nonsense, she was dramatizing again!

"Berry, let me be the judge of whether or not ours would be a good marriage. I need you. I love you."

"Your pride is wounded because I turned from you first. You just *think* you love me." If he truly did and if he could love only her—

"Dammit, woman!" Suddenly leaning forward in his earnestness, Jason said, "Stop trying to tell me what I feel and think."

The awful thought washed over Jason that if he had to leave before gaining some kind of commitment from Berry, he would have an even more difficult time seeing her again. Soon he must return to his duties at home. The shipments of needed supplies and equipment he had purchased were already on their way to the sugar plantation. In his last letter, Uncle Edouard had sounded impatient for his return, and justifiably so.

"See how angry you become when I don't agree with you? People who can't get along even before they marry don't have a chance to make a good life together. I've thought a long time about the kind of man I'll marry. As I've been trying to explain all afternoon, you don't come close."

"You do a lot to build a man's self-confidence." He was proud of himself for being able to adopt a light tone. The smile he sent her was purposefully cocky.

"Another proof that we aren't meant to marry."

"Are you saying that people in love can't overcome all obstacles?"

Berry sputtered, squirmed and busied herself with her curls, her forefinger making little corkscrew movements and winding hair over it until the mass was too thick and she had to release it. What was wrong with her? She never played with her hair!

With a practiced flip of her head, Berry tossed her hair back and declared, "I never said I'm in love with you. I admitted to being infatuated, yes, and feeling a physical attraction. That's not love. Anyway, it's over.''

The perceptive Jason had not missed Berry's rising color or her uncharacteristic toying with her hair. The only things that had kept his hopes up after their quarrel were such little telling signs that Berry's actions were out of character. He tugged at his earlobe. Berry was hiding something, maybe even from herself. Since she had appeared at his courtyard and found Viola in his arms, she had not been acting herself.

Inwardly Jason groaned at his gross stupidity in his handling of the note to Berry, his failure to tell her all. Though within the past hour Berry had verbally accepted his explanations about the need for secrecy in such a dire matter as a duel, he had read contradictory messages from her snapping black eyes: *Traitor! Liar!*

Jason clung to his tenuous belief that Berry loved him or else she never would have come to the Oaks. If she did not, at least she held an affection strong enough to blossom into love. Given the chance, he could win her love. He clutched at those straws of hope to keep from falling into despair.

How did a man who had lived an admittedly carefree life, though not one of debauchery, go about proving to a woman that she was the only one for him? Jason was beginning to suspect that to accomplish such a Sisyphean task was the only way he would ever persuade Berry to open her heart to him. And to herself. ''If you don't feel something mighty potent for me, why did you come dashing out to the Oaks and—''

''I don't care to be reminded of that awful business again. I've already apologized. I had drunk several glasses of wine and I must have gotten carried away.''

''What was the bit about a premonition that I was in danger?''

''Nothing. I made it up.''

''You're lying. I can tell by your eyes.''

"You can't tell anything by my eyes." Just in case, though, she lowered them.

"I have a right to know about the premonition. I paid for the privilege." Grinning, Jason pointed to the bruise showing purple in the upper edge of his right eyebrow.

Berry huffed and stood up abruptly, scooting her wicker chair back and then wincing at the keening sound it made while scraping against the brick paving. "You'll laugh."

Rising then himself, Jason joined her where she had gone to stand beside a banana tree growing in a triangular bed of loamy soil in the corner. "Try me. I want to hear."

"You make me so mad, I could just spit!"

"Go ahead, then tell me what made you think—"

"All right!"

Reluctantly Berry told Jason that she had sensed, during intermission at the ballet, somebody covertly staring at her. Her voice quivered when she described her eerie suspicion that whoever was watching her had a kinship with evil, or at least with something unpleasant.

Berry fumbled for words when she got to the part about how she had learned of the duel, how she had overheard Viola's name and somehow transferred her earlier misgivings about her own well-being to fear for his safety. Even to her, the story sounded lame. Lifting her chin daringly, she asked, "You think I'm fantasizing, don't you?"

"No. I know you better than to think that. You enjoy being dramatic, but you've no penchant for making up things. I suspect there really was somebody watching you. What puzzles me is who and why. As for your tying it into concern for my safety, I can't help feeling flattered."

"Don't. I acted a fool because I sometimes do tend to dramatize things, and because"—Berry almost bit her tongue to keep from confessing that her fear for his safety had driven her into a near frenzy—". . . because I've always been an 'Impulse Person.' It had been a long, trying evening, and I was upset. I've apologized all I intend to for slapping you, for maybe causing you to get into a fight."

To keep from meeting Jason's unsettling gaze, Berry separated a cluster of tall, upright leaves on the banana plant. Some disturbed mosquitoes whined and circled erratically before flitting out of sight. When she saw a tiny orange-spotted insect crawling up one broad, green leaf, she reached to remove it, only to have it lift its wings and fly away. How she wished she might disappear with the creature into the overhead blue sky where everything appeared to be peaceful, well-ordered.

"Berry, I accepted your apology and I don't care to talk about it anymore, either. The matter is settled, though Bayard's face won't be healing nearly as fast as mine."

Berry's lips turned up at the corners. Jason might have been a little boy telling about a fight at school and bragging about how much worse his opponent looked.

Encouraged by Berry's half-smile, Jason continued. "Bayard and I have met again and concluded with a handshake that our differences are laid to rest. Before Ashley left for Breton Grove Sunday afternoon with Viola and Bayard I had even agreed to attend Viola's and his wedding in the fall. You're going to be invited, too."

Jason flicked a sidewise look toward Berry, hoping to catch her off guard with the question begging to be asked. "Did you think that even though I was spending all of my time with you, I had a romantic interest in Viola?"

"What does that have to do with anything?" Peering at the small cluster of green bananas growing in their peculiar fruit-upward position, Berry flicked away an imaginary insect. She wasn't about to let him look into her eyes and discover she had been jealous. "Men like you often have an interest in more than one woman."

"Men like me?" All Jason could see of her face was her profile, but he did not feel cheated. He reveled in her beauty, side or front view. It seemed ages since he had kissed her. How his hands itched to encircle her tiny waist, pull her close and. . . . "What in blazes does that mean?

You've said that before, you know. What is there about me that's different from any other man?''

"You've always had lots of women friends"—his nearness, Berry realized in a kind of panic, was stealing her breath—"and you don't strike me as the type who would like settling—"

"Now you're making me so mad, *I* could spit!"

The sound of a door opening, followed by footsteps on the brick, allowed Berry to escape from the corner in which Jason was backing her. "What is it, Linnie?"

"There's a gentleman here. I put him in the parlor."

Jason muttered for Berry's ears alone, "If it's that French architectural wonder, I swear I'll—"

Berry's chin found a haughty angle and she tightened her lips, but she kept her attention on the young black woman. "Did he give you a card or his name?"

"Yes'm. He says he's Sergeant Dan Harrigan from the N'Orleans police."

Within a brief time Linnie was ushering the big Irishman into the courtyard where Berry and Jason stood near the table waiting. Perfunctory greetings and introductions took little time and after the three seated themselves around the small table, Berry said, "I'm delighted to see you again, Sergeant Dan. Would you like some coffee?"

"No, thank you."

Berry wondered if the expression on the Irishman's face might reflect uneasiness. Hoping to make him feel more comfortable, she said, "I came by your office one day to thank you in person for sending me word of Ebon's death along with his package for me. Some clerk told me that you were out of town."

"Right," Dan Harrigan said with a fond smile. "The boys at the station gave me your note. All of us are happy that you're back home. Lots of them remember you when you were but a wee lassie toddling along with Maddy, just as I do. It's good to have you back in the Quarter."

Berry returned the big man's smile and asked, "Did you

drop by to renew our acquaintance or is there a particular reason you called, Sergeant Dan?''

''Maybe a combination. I've some news to report. The newspapers will carry the story tomorrow, but I wanted to come in person and prepare you for the shock. I'd heard you were living here with your actress friend. I'm glad Mr. Premont is here now, since you say Miss Hayes is away.''

Filled with rising apprehension, Berry leaned toward the older man she had known and liked ever since she could remember. ''What have you come to tell me?''

''Warren Maroney escaped from St. Louis prison and is believed to be in New Orleans.''

Berry sank against the tall, enveloping back of her chair, fear bubbling up inside her.

CHAPTER

*

Thirteen

While Jason fired questions at Sergeant Harrigan and impatiently waited for answers before hurling more, Berry assembled her thoughts and her composure.

Was it necessary, she wondered with poorly concealed agitation, that Jason learn details about the grim trial in Natchez? Nearly four years had passed since Warren Maroney had been found guilty of murdering his sister-in-law, Flo.

Berry marked that Jason's handsome face took on an even fiercer expression as Dan continued, especially when he recited her involvement in the trial as the witness who had recovered Flo's emerald ring and thus, indirectly, led to the criminal's arrest. During the sergeant's relating of how Maddy, Ebon, and she had brought Warren to Paddy's where he was tending bar, Jason kept sending Berry such stormy looks that she squirmed against her chair.

Whether or not it was necessary for Jason to learn all, Berry concluded while Sergeant Dan was accomplishing the deed swiftly and efficiently, she doubted protestations coming from her would have hushed either man.

Berry thought about how upon questioning from Jason the night of the masquerade ball, she had not lied about the troubles resulting from her theft of the emerald ring. However, she had glossed over a great deal. She watched Jason tug at his earlobe, figuring that he was more than marginally upset upon learning from Sergeant Harrigan that she had skipped over many of the sordid details. She had deliberately omitted the killer's threats to get even with all who helped send him to prison.

"Do you think, Berry," Dan asked with his faint Irish brogue lending musical notes to his words, "as Mr. Premont seems to, that it could have been Maroney watching you Saturday night? Our first news was that he escaped over a week ago. The report coming today said that one of Maroney's prison friends told he was headed for New Orleans to settle some grievances."

Jason said, "Obviously the man would have had time enough to reach town by the latter part of last week since so many riverboats are floating down the river nowadays."

"I never put the two things together," Berry said, sending Jason a look of gratitude for his having believed her account of being watched. She added a look of admiration for his quick thinking in tying it to the news of the murderer's escape. "It never occurred to me."

Then Berry was relieved that Jason apparently was not going to say, "I told you so," or chide her in front of Sergeant Harrigan about her involvement in Ebon's affair. She had no regrets for having helped Ebon clear up the mystery of Flo's death, especially since he had expressed his gratitude time and again during his remaining short life. Even before this afternoon, though, Berry had come to view her actions as dangerously impetuous. She knew now that the best way to help Ebon would have been to insist he go to the police.

Aunt Maddy had been right, Berry reflected. She did have

a tendency to let emotions alone guide her. Was the realization of that weakness what led her from the start to attempt rationalizing what she felt about Jason? Feelings, as she had discovered out at the Oaks, could sometimes be dead wrong.

Aware that both men seemed eager to learn her thoughts, Berry forced herself to think back to intermission on Saturday night. "I saw two women shuffling along across from the theater with what looked like shopping baskets on their arms. It didn't occur to me then that it was late for two old women to be out. One was much larger than the other and seemed older—maybe with whiter hair." Recalling the absence of Warren's big toe and his tendency to limp, she added with a little shiver that sent her hair into shiny black ripples on her shoulders, "The way she moved could have been part limp and part shuffle."

"Right," the sergeant said. "You and Ebon said that Warren wore a wig at Mardi Gras. Maroney and a partner could have been rigged like women to avoid suspicion. We know he's got friends down on Gallatin Street and in other seamy places, too. Maybe he had just gotten into town and was following you that evening. He was probably trying to figure out who your friends are now and how you're spending your time. On your way over here, I stopped at the Théâtre d'Orléans to talk with the folks there who know you."

"Nobody there knows anything about me nowadays. I've not worked there since my return," Berry explained, a tiny frown of annoyance marring her smooth forehead. "Henry Zimpel holds a grudge against both Camille and me since our abrupt departure soon after Maddy died. I've seen very few of my former friends from there, though soon after our return, Leonidas Latrobe did come by here a few times."

Suddenly Berry felt a stirring of the initial disappointment and hurt created by Leo's having gone back on his promise to intervene with Henry. Now that she had delivered the muslin sample to the complimentary Miss Dilly, she was optimistic that she could sell more. She might not need a position at a theater now, but still it rankled that Mr. Zimpel had chosen to deny her request for an interview or a recommendation. Rankling even more was the thought that Leonidas, supposedly her friend, had turned against her for what seemed a trifling reason.

Sergeant Harrigan said, "Both this Henry Zimpel and Leonidas Latrobe pretended ignorance of your exact whereabouts."

Berry frowned. "That makes me wonder if Warren might not have already contacted his old friend Henry. I'm not sure if Warren ever met Leonidas, though he could have the day he fell backstage. I seem to recall vaguely that Leo helped Mr. Zimpel pull Warren from the prop cart."

From where her hands lay clasped tightly in her lap, Berry could feel the thimble Jason had given her. It felt warm and reassuring where it rested in the pocket of her frilly apron. "I believe it could have been Warren sending me those awful looks. The feeling of evil was powerful. I can't imagine anyone else harboring that kind of ill will toward me."

Wasn't it weird, Berry thought, the way she had transferred the tenuous threat against herself to debilitating fear for Jason's well-being? Thank the saints above that she had been wrong, even if she had made a fool of herself and caused Jason so much trouble.

Sending an imploring look at the big Irishman, Berry said, "Warren Maroney will be after you as much as me, Sergeant Dan. You need to be wary."

"Not likely he'll bother me." Dan smiled confidently. "I've got the whole force around and I'm a big burly fellow. Remember, Warren killed a sick woman lying in her bed. We have no proof, but he bragged about hiring somebody to kill his brother in prison. The man is a coward. It's my guess he'll be after you and that valuable emerald ring Ebon left to you. The ring could probably provide him with money enough to get far away."

With quiet authority Jason brought his hands together on

top of the table and leaned forward. "I think Berry should turn the ring over to me for safekeeping and stay at my place until the man is captured. My men, Alonzo and Ebenezer, can help me keep her safe."

After reading approval on the sergeant's broad face, Jason addressed Berry. "Actually you would be safer if you go with me to my uncle's plantation in Saint Christopher Parish." When she shook her head and set her lips into lines of what he viewed as stubbornness, he added, "Only for a little visit until Maroney is back behind bars. It's past time for me to return and I've been eager for you and Uncle Edouard to meet."

"Your offer is kind," Berry replied, "but moving isn't necessary." His invitation for her to go home with him appealed to her, made her feel warm and special, but she knew she could make no headway in trying to eliminate him from her thoughts and her life if she were staying under his roof. She needed more space between them, not less. Never before had she been so aware of the differences in their backgrounds. Home to him was a plantation. "There's no need for you to become involved. This affair is of my making. I have my designs to work on and—"

"Don't let foolish pride put your life in more jeopardy than it is already," Jason broke in to say harshly. "I don't mind saying in front of the sergeant that I care deeply about what happens to you. Your problems are mine because I want them to be. Sergeant Harrigan and his men have enough to do trying to locate the murderer. This Maroney must be mighty clever and have influential friends to have eluded the law this long."

"Pride doesn't affect my decision." Berry turned to her old friend who was sending thoughtful, plainly admiring looks at Jason. "Sergeant Dan, don't you think I'll be safe here? The Charleys are about at night and Warren isn't going to take a chance on being spotted in the daylight."

Dan rubbed his broad chin with one hand. "You have a point there. I like to think we can take care of our citizens.

Even so, I must say that Mr. Premont's idea to get you out of town sounds the safest plan. You're mighty special to me and the boys down at the station, too. Chances are it would take Maroney a while to figure out where you'd gone. By the time he circulated around enough to find out, we could catch him."

Choosing to overlook the sergeant's caring words, Berry announced to Jason in a withering tone, "I'm not a mouse, scared of my own shadow."

"Nobody's implying you are," Jason replied.

Berry stiffened. If she agreed to go with Jason, would she ever get over her infatuation? She had thought that once the unsettling afternoon ended, she would no longer have to face Jason, at least not on a regular basis. Nothing was going right. Her stomach felt fluttery. "The police will look after me. I can handle my own affairs without your help, Jason."

"Can you afford to think only of what you prefer? You might be putting both Camille and Linnie in jeopardy just by being in town," Jason said, tight-lipped and slightly flushed. Was her objection based chiefly on her avowed wish to oust him from her life? Maybe he had erred in thinking she cared for him, even a little.

While Berry was mulling over her responsibility to others, she heard a commotion coming from the passageway that led to the gate on Chartres. She started, then noticed with alarm that both Jason and Sergeant Dan had jumped to their feet with plainly wary expressions altering their features. Had the sergeant reached inside his coat for a pistol? A brassy taste filled her mouth. Was the suspicion that Warren Maroney was stalking her going to haunt her and everyone she knew?

Camille and Ace emerged from the shadowed passageway then, the smiles on their faces fading as they neared the solemn threesome standing stiffly near the little round table. Camille suffered through the necessary introductions before she blurted, "What's going on?"

Quickly Sergeant Harrigan explained the purpose of his call. Before Camille recovered from her shock, Jason told her of his wish to take Berry to Armand Acres for a visit until the murderer was found.

"Berry, you must go with Jason," Camille urged, tears forming in the corners of her eyes. "I remember what evil looks that man sent you during his trial."

Ace, who had been reticent and thoughtful throughout the telling, said, "Camille, you're in somewhat of a dangerous predicament yourself, simply because you're Berry's friend."

"I intended to try impressing Miss Hayes with that fact, Mr. Zachary," the sergeant said.

"I've decided I should go with Jason, either to his townhouse or to the plantation, where Warren isn't likely to look for me," Berry announced, her chin lifted and her face flushed. "If he didn't arrive in town until the weekend, chances are he never saw me with Jason. I realize now that I was wrong in thinking this is my business only. It affects my friends, too. I want to protect everyone as much as possible."

"Berry Cortabona, you're more than a pretty mavourneen," Dan said. "You've come to have a passel of wisdom, too." His smile showed his relief at her decision.

"Sergeant," Jason said, "I'll wait for Berry to pack and send someone back to get her things. When she's ready, I'll walk with her to my place. It's time for me to return home, so we'll leave for Armand Acres tomorrow. I'll tell you how you can post messages to Berry there."

Dan nodded his approval and entered Jason's information in a small journal that he pulled from his coat pocket. Addressing all then, he said, "Even though nobody will be spending the night here tonight, I'll go ahead with my plans to post a policemen in this block until Berry is actually gone from New Orleans."

"Camille and Linnie can move over to the big house with me within the next hour," Ace said. "My carriage is out front." He looked at Camille, a tender expression on his face. "Who knows? Maybe we can talk the priest into performing the ceremony right away and get out of town ourselves as Mr. and Mrs. Zachary. One of my riverboats embarks tomorrow at noon."

Sergeant Harrigan moved along with the chattering group toward the passageway leading from the courtyard. Before he made his farewells, he told Berry, "Try not to worry. I have a feeling you'll be in good hands with Mr. Premont. I'll get word to you when we catch the culprit. I'm sure the newspapers will announce it on their front pages."

That evening after dinner, Camille and Ace surprised Berry and Jason by appearing at his townhouse.

"We're going to be married in the morning," Ace announced after all had settled in the parlor.

After the exclamations of surprise and good wishes died down, Camille said, "We want you two to be our attendants. When we leave here, we'll stop by the theater. I want to invite my old friends from the stock company to attend." When Berry appeared concerned, Camille added, "Don't worry. I won't be asking Henry Zimpel, and I'll ask everyone to keep quiet."

Berry said, "I feel terrible about being the reason you can't go ahead with your plans for a big wedding."

"Nonsense," Camille assured her. "I never cared for a big ceremony. The special man that I wanted to like the gorgeous gown you created is going to see it." She slid a flirtatious look toward Ace. "I went along with the idea of a grand wedding because I thought that was what Ace wanted."

Ace's worshipful gaze at his intended supported his remark. "All I ever wanted was the privilege of slipping a wedding ring on your finger." He turned then to Berry. "This afternoon's events merely hastened the day that my wish will come true. Our house will be ready for occupancy within a week. Our month-long honeymoon to the East Coast will take us out of town longer than the police will need to do their work. We both like knowing that you and Jason will be safe at his home in Saint Christopher Parish.''

A summer storm moved into New Orleans before dawn. At daylight, which was bleak and dreary, the heavy clouds appeared set to remain all day. By the time Berry and Jason reached St. Louis Cathedral in his carriage, the low-lying clouds seemed to be releasing their load with increasing force. Claps of distant thunder threatened even more rainfall.

With the wary eye of a native, Berry noted the flooding of the narrow streets and the flat expanse of the Place d'Armes stretching in front of the cathedral toward the river. A clock struck, reminding her that it was only mid-morning. Only a bride and her groom, she mused as she visualized Camille in the white satin gown she had made for her, could consider the hour ideal for a wedding.

As soon as Berry and Jason dashed up the steps of the cathedral into the dim narthex and he saw they were alone, he kept his hand on her arm. ''We're a bit early. Before we go behind the altar to meet Camille and Ace as they requested, I want to know if you're sure you won't change your mind about marrying me before we leave town. I could petition the priest for a dispensation—''

''I'm sure I won't change my mind,'' Berry answered before he could complete his argument. She shivered, but not from the moisture-laden air.

What bothered Berry was Jason's deep voice washing over her there in the sanctity of the hushed cathedral. His insistence last evening after Camille and Ace left, then again just now, in talking about the two of them getting married before leaving New Orleans set her mind and heart into confusion. The remembered smells from childhood— damp mustiness, burning beeswax, traces of incense and sweet perfume lingering alongside less pleasant odors of perspiration from working men and women—reminded her that this was where her mother and father had married. Each time she came to the cathedral, she felt strangely in touch with them.

The storm raging outside, Berry decided, was no more fierce than the one tearing at her inside. Was she more afraid of what Warren Maroney might do to her and her friends or of what her heart was begging her to consider?

"Marriage to the right man," Berry said, her effort to control her voice barely concealed, "is very important to me." Hiding behind her lowered eyelashes, she breathed in the smell of Jason up close, the suggestive, mingling fragrances of summer rain and virile man newly shaved and dressed for the day. Heady! Dangerous!

"You've made that clear." He noticed that in the murky light her eyelashes, forming silky semicircles as they lay closed against her smooth skin, might have been fashioned from feathery particles of soot. Even as he watched her beautiful face, she opened her eyes. They, too, could have been of soot—smudgy soft, blackest black, reflecting no purplish light. "Marriage to the right woman is every bit as important to me."

Berry wished there were more light in the narthex. Jason had released her arm and seemed to be withdrawing into himself. A sense of being alone and vulnerable brought gooseflesh to her arm. Or was it the chilly dampness causing her discomfort?

"Jason," she said when the silence dragged on, "there's no reason to let my need to seek your protection for a brief time play havoc with our lives forever by leading us into a hasty marriage. I appreciate your being noble and trying to safeguard my reputation, but—"

"Berry, I'm not being noble." Stung by her latest refusal, Jason said through stiff lips, "I'll never bring up the subject of marriage again. When you finally figure out I'm the right man for you, you can damned well do the asking yourself."

"Don't hold your breath." She glared at him.

"Do I look like a fool?" He glared back.

Berry kept her eyes on Jason, even when he turned away

from her and peered down one of the aisles inside the cathedral where lighted candles near the prayer rail beckoned. Had she been too hard on the man who had gallantly offered her protection from a known murderer? It was not his fault that fears of what marriage to a rake might be like were plaguing her. Her conscience bothered her.

When Berry saw the priest coming toward them and motioning for them to come down the aisle to go with him, she rested one hand on Jason's arm. In a voice designed for his ears only, she said, "You look like a handsome man who has a most ungrateful woman friend. You may not be the man I want to marry, but I think you're wonderful, Jason. I promise not to make you sorry you invited me to go home with you." She shocked both of them—and probably the watchful priest as well—by planting a tender kiss on his lean cheek, on the very spot that would have been an elongated dimple had he been smiling.

Later, as Berry, Jason and Alonzo rode toward Saint Christopher Parish aboard a shrimp trawler, she kept remembering the simple but beautiful wedding ceremony that united Camille Hayes and Ace Zachary. She knew she would never forget it.

With Alonzo, along with Berry's and Jason's baggage, waiting afterward in the carriage and the rain still pouring down, there had been no time for visiting with old friends from the theater—nor for wondering at the stormy expression on Leonidas Latrobe's face. Neither was there time for sharing prolonged farewells with Camille and Ace. Teary-eyed, Berry had watched her dear friend lift the voluminous white skirts of the wedding gown that she had lovingly made and dash with Ace to his carriage. Her last view of the newlyweds was of them waving in the rain, laughing and, despite the absence of sunlight, managing to glow.

"We can be thankful that the storm has passed," Jason said, breaking into Berry's reverie. "The captain says we'll reach Nola soon after dark. That is the landing where we'll meet the packet in the morning. There's a decent inn there with good seafood.''

Returning her thoughts to the present, Berry realized that she hadn't heard Jason approach. It seemed ages since they had crossed the Mississippi on a ferry. She sat on a make-shift seat atop a hogshead on the foredeck of the small boat gliding along a canal leading to Barataria Bay and the Gulf beyond. ''I never thought I would be riding on a shrimp boat.''

''It's pretty smelly, but reliable. Riding in one with a hold full of shrimp is a sight worse. The captains are nearly always happy to pick up some extra coins from people who don't care to wait for a scheduled packet boat. How did you think we were going to travel?''

''I guess I thought we would stay in your carriage and cross the ferry in it. I hadn't realized you always left it in New Orleans.''

''I do so from necessity. You won't find many stretches of passable roads in southern Louisiana. Right now the land-owners along the waterways are responsible for building and maintaining roads in front of their properties, but the meth-od leaves much to be desired. On a long journey, riding horseback is the only alternative to traveling in some kind of boat. We have a wealth of waterways and we use them.''

Alonzo appeared on the foredeck then, apparently fin-ished napping on some sacks on the aft. When Jason motioned for him to join them, he did, saying, ''It's gonna be good to get back to Armand Acres. Miss Berry, you gonna like it.''

More perturbed about visiting her first plantation home than she cared to admit, Berry replied, ''I'm sure I will. Right now I'm happy just watching the sun chasing away the clouds.'' She used one hand to shield her eyes. Up ahead a giant cottonwood tree angled high above the muddy canal. ''What in the—!'' She screamed and grabbed Jason around the neck. ''There's a monstrous snake up ahead.

He's certain to fall on us when we pass underneath the limb he's on. Do something!''

The small crew exchanged amused smiles and went about their business of repairing nets and getting ready for a week's trawling in Barataria. Alonzo kept his eyes on the water moccasin. He figured that Jason was enjoying hugging Berry too much to pay attention to anything but her.

''That snake jes' be sunnin','' Alonzo told the frightened young woman. ''He ain't gonna be payin' us no never mine.''

Berry shivered. The wind was a mite cool since the rain and Jason's arms did feel comforting. ''Have we passed the cottonwood yet?''

''Not yet,'' Jason replied, liking that she burrowed her head closer underneath his chin and tightened her arms around his neck. It made no difference that they sat on wobbly barrels on the deck of a smelly boat. He was happy. Berry was not going to let yesterday's quarrel stand between them. He found himself hoping they sighted several more snakes.

''Surely we've passed the tree by now,'' Berry said after a few moments.

''Nope,'' Jason insisted.

When the question and answer were repeated once more, Alonzo spoke up. ''Miss Berry, we done passed that snake a piece back.''

''You're a reprobate, Jason Premont,'' Berry said after she lifted her head and glanced behind the boat at the cottonwood. When she saw Jason's devilish expression, she could not keep down an answering grin. ''That cottonwood is hardly in sight.''

''I'm sorry. I reckon I forgot to look,'' Jason said. His face showed no sign of apology. ''Something must have distracted me.''

Berry smiled across at the plainly amused Alonzo. ''You're an honest man, Alonzo. Maybe between the two of us, we can turn Jason into one. I'm going to hemstitch a linen handkerchief for you and put your monogram on it."

"That'd be some fine reward," Alonzo said. He flashed her his widest smile.

Jason felt his heart fill with unexpected warmth. Maybe his having invited Berry to go home with him was going to work out the way he hoped.

The next afternoon, Jason found Berry leaning on the handrailing of the packet boat as it chugged up Bayou Selène, the principal navigable waterway in Saint Christopher Parish. "We'll be at Armand Acres within an hour," he said in a voice loud enough for her to hear over the churning of the sidewheel below. She stood with her back to the wind, letting her long hair blow forward over her shoulders.

The rush of wind from the vessel's brisk pace pushed Berry's blue skirts against her petticoats and outlined the gentle curve of her slender hips. No matter how unaffected the pose, Jason mused, Berry Cortabona was ever the ultimate female. "Do you like my home parish?" he asked.

Berry turned from the handrail. She had been thinking about Camille and Ace while watching the sidewheel of the packet boat churn up the brown water. As she brushed her hair from her face to send it floating out behind her, she admitted that the sight of Jason in bright sunlight was rewarding. His finely chiseled features held the same appeal as they had in gentler light. "Yes. I much prefer the scenery here over that bordering the canals we traveled."

"I gathered you didn't care much for the tropical look."

"It takes only one giant water moccasin hanging from an overhead limb to convince me that living in a city has more advantages than I realized."

Jason grinned. "I was there to save you, remember?"

Berry remembered, too well. She also remembered how after supper last evening at the inn, she had hurriedly left him in the hallway and closed her door. Hugging Jason Premont could become a habit. She chose to ignore his comment and go on with her thoughts about his home parish. "I think I like the view better because I'm seeing more houses now that we've reached Saint Christopher Parish. They look so wonderfully private, set back under their own groves of trees like that."

Even as she spoke, Berry noticed Jason's widening smile. Did he have any idea how handsome he was?

Ever since those sticky moments in the narthex at St. Louis Cathedral, Berry thought, they had recaptured some of the easy camaraderie of their former relationship. They could not refrain from occasionally flirting. They really didn't try. She was glad. More than glad. She loved it.

Berry had stored up a number of things to share with Jason now that he had returned from his visit up in the pilot's house with the captain of the small vessel. Like Jason, she was glad that few passengers rode the packet and that he knew the captain and crew well enough to believe their assurances that they would keep quiet about their black-haired passenger and her destination.

Now that Berry had Jason's undivided attention, she spilled her thoughts, her words tumbling over themselves as they were wont to do when she was excited. "Back a ways, I saw some boys and girls stop playing chase with a huge dog and wave at us. They seemed to be having such fun. Then I saw a young woman pushing a child in a swing in the shade of one of the trees beside what must have been their home. It was small but pretty, with flowers near the front door and clothes flapping on a line out back. I thought about how contented . . . a woman could be"—she slid a wary eye his way, hoping he had not realized that she had almost used herself as example—"in such a setting. I got the feeling that I was seeing a mother playing with her baby and waiting for her husband to come home. I adore happy scenes, don't you?"

Jason nodded. He adored her.

"Have you noticed that some of the giant trees with their drooping moss are as spectacular as the finest mansions? And a time or two I saw some little furry animals come to drink at the edge of the water, then dart into the underbrush when we came near. Where did so many birds come from? I vow those brown pelicans have bills wide and deep enough to catch more than one fish at a time. I never expected to see such large fields of sugarcane growing. Everything looks . . .''—Berry glanced overhead at the blue sky for a moment, as if searching for words for her attentive audience of one—''and smells gloriously alive. But serene at the same time. I can tell you're happy to be returning, and I can see why.''

Jason smiled down at her. He loved seeing the return of Berry's former exuberant self. Maybe now that they had talked out some of their differences, he could go along with her idea to begin anew. Delighted that the beauty of the area he had always called home pleased her, Jason said, ''Yes. I'm glad to be going home. I was beginning to miss the place.''

''Please tell me again that your uncle isn't going to be upset when you arrive with a strange young woman in tow.''

''Uncle Edouard is going to like having you at Armand Acres, just as I am. Just as everyone else will, too.''

''Your uncle must get lonely living by himself.''

''He's not by himself.''

''Of course I realize that a sugar plantation likely has slaves and that he isn't alone.''

''Yes, but the blacks aren't his only companions. Friends and relatives visit often in these parts. When a first cousin's husband died several years ago, Uncle Edouard invited her to make her home at Armand Acres. Agnes Delange soon became indispensable. After my mother became ill, Agnes took over running the house. She never had any children and my mother used to joke privately that it was a good thing, that Cousin Agnes could not **have** settled down long enough to mother them. She's always flitting about from one task to another.''

''How nice that your uncle offered her a place to go when

she was left alone.'' For a moment she recalled her sense of utter loss when Aunt Maddy, her only known relative, died. ''He sounds like a very considerate person.''

Jason chuckled. ''Uncle Edouard is considerate, all right. And easily contented. Give him his dogs and his evening whiskey and he's happy. You'd have to throw in a full schedule of hunting and fishing to complete his contentment. I have a feeling he's going to take to you like a duck to a young June bug.''

When Berry felt the vibrations on the deck slow and heard the water falling more slowly from the paddlewheel, she had the eerie feeling that a curtain might be going up for a drama in which she was a central character. She wished for a script.

Up ahead on the left a two-story mansion thrust its slate roof through a grove of moss-draped trees and invited Berry's attention. About the time she heard the big bell outside the pilot's cabin clanging from its lofty perch, she glimpsed a wooden pier jutting out into Bayou Selene.

''That's my home,'' Jason said, noting that Berry's eyes were fixed on the white mansion growing larger with each slap of the paddlewheel. He took her hand in his, surprised that in spite of the warmth of the summer afternoon, it was cold. ''Welcome to Armand Acres.''

CHAPTER

*

Fourteen

A veritable storm of impressions attacked Berry as Jason escorted her from the sturdy wooden pier. After crossing the narrow dirt road, they passed a white pergola with an onion-domed roof of beautifully patined copper, splendid in the afternoon sunlight.

Ever the city girl, Berry marveled at the space surrounding them underneath the blue sky. The multihued greens of stately trees and shrubs limned the near horizon. Forming the lower periphery of the vast space were flowers and grass springing from black soil. She tried separating the marvelous fragrances she breathed in, some from gardenias and wildflowers nearby, others from succulent grass that their footsteps bruised. The smells blended with the air already sweetened by summer sunshine and moisture from fresh water.

Berry heard the bell clang aboard the packet, then the steam engine rev up as the small two-decked vessel nosed back out in Bayou Selene. When she turned with Jason to wave once more to the captain and the crew, she saw and heard the side paddlewheels speed up and push the small riverboat upstream toward a wide curve. Its twin smokestacks sent puny columns of gray smoke into the vibrant blue sky.

Then, sitting off to itself underneath the protective limbs of moss-laden oaks, a small octagonal structure drew Berry's attention. It was also white, with a copper roof of Moorish design similar to that of the pergola. The exotic looking building was small, she mused, only when compared to the imposing mansion standing at the end of the wide, tree-shaded driveway stretching before them.

"That's where I usually stay," Jason offered when Berry seemed unable to tear her gaze from the *garçonniere* with its narrow, encircling gallery. "One summer when I came home from school and found the main house overrun with a host of chattering female cousins and their young children, Mother suggested I might enjoy staying out here."

The sparkle of interest in her black eyes compelled him to go on. "Somehow I took a liking to the place and never gave it up. Mother, like most women living on plantations, was a great one for having friends and relatives come for extended visits. They had a way of aging along with her, though, and the need for the *garçonniere* to house visiting bachelors got lost. What do you think of it?"

"It's such a unique building." Berry realized that she should not have been surprised at the grandeur of Armand Acres, but she was. Could she fit in here? Too much had happened since learning that Warren Maroney was back in New Orleans for her to get her thoughts in order. Or was it being in Jason's continuous presence that kept her mind in turmoil?

"When you get settled in, I'd like showing it to you. Alonzo helped me turn the largest room facing the bayou into a parlor. There are a couple of bedrooms."

"Does Alonzo stay with you?"

"Not since I was a youngster. He has a room attached to the kitchen and has only to cross the whistlewalk when he hears the bell. I don't need him to help me get dressed except for special occasions, but he takes care of my wardrobe and helps me with personal matters. As you've probably guessed, we're the best of friends."

"Yes, I've noticed you two have an easy relationship." Not understanding much about life on a large plantation, Berry looked at him quizzically. Whistlewalk? Bell? She had a sinking feeling that she might be in the wrong place, that she lacked stage directions as well as script for the drama unfolding and drawing her in. Just how much did she really know about Jason? She had been aware from their first meeting that they came from diverse backgrounds, but . . . Her throat felt too full and she swallowed. "A bell? What bell?"

"You'll see out behind the big house a number of little bells hanging up high with cords reaching to various rooms inside. Each one sounds a different note, and the house slaves learn to recognize which is for them. When I'm staying in the *garçonniere,* I don't need a bell. Alonzo always shows up soon after sunrise with a pot of coffee, then comes back later with hot water for my bath and shave."

Glancing toward the mansion, which she figured must be at least a hundred yards away, Berry said, "I should think it would be inconvenient to be so far away from the dining room when it's raining, especially if it's cold, too."

Jason chuckled at her frankness, delighted when she sent him a feeble smile. Berry Cortabona would prove to be a new ingredient at Armand Acres, a spicy one that might be long overdue. How his mother would have loved her! How he loved her!

Was Berry, Jason wondered when he caught her sneaking little glances toward the mansion and nibbling at the under-side of her bottom lip, a bit nervous about what kind of reception she might receive? From what he had figured out since they had begun spending so much time together, Berry, in the careless manner of most people connected with the theater, seemed content to flout convention.

To Jason's way of thinking, society contributed to the somewhat unorthodox behavior of theatrical folk. The holier-than-thou attitudes people assumed toward those connected with the entertainment world alternated whimsically with lavish displays of admiration and gave performers license to live as they chose. He confessed he adored Berry's refreshing sense of self, her daring to be unique and fend for herself. Still, when it came to her showing up unannounced in the company of an unmarried man at his home, and without a chaperone or servant in attendance, she could be having misgivings about how she might be received.

"You're right," Jason replied. "Putting up in the *garçonniere* can be inconvenient at times. Ever since I returned from Texas, I've been using my old bedroom on the second floor. Uncle Edouard and I don't get in each other's hair because he lives on the ground floor in the suite of rooms he used when his wife was alive. Cousin Agnes has one of the bedrooms downstairs in the opposite wing near where my mother stayed."

When Jason saw Berry's avid interest in what he was telling, he scolded himself for not having realized before that she wanted to hear about what went on at Armand Acres. After all, she was a city girl, one without family. He recalled her telling him once that the yellow fever epidemic of 1832 had decimated her remaining cousins and their families and how her Aunt Maddy had barricaded the two of them in their quarters for weeks on end until the death bells had ceased their tolling.

Jason said, "I expect before cold weather arrives, I'll be back in the main house for good. In summer, it's nice and private down here by the water, though." He gave her a roguish grin. "You might like taking a midnight swim with me some time in the moonlight."

Berry felt her cheeks heating up at Jason's daring invitation. She chose not to reply. Instead she looked at the trees between the road and the bayou, the flowering oleanders and gardenias growing in artfully spaced patterns. Careful planning on somebody's part years ago, she mused, created a timeless beauty. Continuity. Family. Ambiance. Security. She sensed Armand Acres expressed those qualities, along with love.

Would she be welcomed? Berry wondered with a quickening of her pulse. Or would she be ostracized because of her unorthodox upbringing and her living as an independent young woman in a time when all young women were supposedly eager to leave the care of a father and seek that of a husband?

Berry's thoughts churned. Damn Warren Maroney! He didn't have the right to be interfering in her life and forcing her into making decisions she was not eager to make. Maybe news would come tomorrow that the police had already captured Warren and she could return to New Orleans where she belonged.

That Jason Premont might be more reliable and worthwhile than she had considered him to be seemed likely when she reviewed his recent actions. She batted down the notion, fearful that she might have to admit that she had fallen in love with him no matter what he was.

"Doesn't the passing traffic bother you when you live in the *garçonniere?*" she asked.

"Actually," Jason explained after Berry appeared more interested in her surroundings than in his overture, "there's very little traffic on the road and almost none at night, except for an occasional horseman. The majority of travel to points outside the parish has taken place on water ever since one of our local citizens on the other side of Calion, Luke Greenwood, started the packet line about ten years ago. As you saw on the way here, every house facing the bayou has at least one small boat tied up out front."

Turning to look back at the water, Berry watched as

Alonzo and the two young black men who had shown up on the pier, apparently in reply to the signal from the packet's jangling bell, deposited baggage on the gallery of Jason's little house, then returned to the pier to fetch the remainder. She noticed the leisurely pace of the three black men, the apparently easy conversation taking place, as if time were of no importance. She saw none of the hustle-bustle or the over-the-shoulder glances toward some foreman with a whip coiled over his arm that usually marked the activities of the deliverymen and dock workers in New Orleans, both black and white.

When Berry and Jason began walking up the driveway again, three big dogs came bounding toward them, barking hoarsely. She could not help thinking how freely and happily the animals moved underneath the towering oaks with their ghostly falls of gray moss that some people called Spanish moss. In the French Quarter, someone would have been trying to shush the dogs or shoo them off to another banquette or narrow street for their noisy cavorting.

"Here comes our welcoming committee," Jason said, fondness turning his deep voice even mellower. He took her hand and quickened their pace. "Uncle Edouard must have heard the packet's bell."

An elderly man was coming down one of the twin stairways that curved from the veranda. Minus the usual bannisters, the veranda reached across the entire front of the house. It sat high off the ground and had a two-story center section. Long, single-story wings spread out on both sides. As she and Jason drew closer, Berry could tell the mansion was made of bricks painted white.

In the deep shade the veranda, with its tall-backed rocking chairs and its slender white columns, appeared broad and inviting to Berry. As when she had first stepped from the packet, a sense of unending space overwhelmed her. Plants with large scarlet blooms rising on tall spikes above purplish leaves curled upward in the manner of young banana trees in front of the veranda. "What are those lovely red flowers?" she asked.

Jason's gaze followed hers. "Cannas. Do you like them?"

"Oh, yes. I love everything I see." She was unaware that she sent him an inclusive, sideways look.

The long-bodied hounds reached them then and Jason leaned to pat each eager head, calling each name in a caressing tone. "Berry, meet Kate, Pete, and Re-Pete."

Laughing and allowing the frisky, liver-spotted hounds to sniff her clothing and hands while she petted them, Berry asked, "Are you teasing? Nobody would name a dog Re-Pete."

"That's his name, all right. If there's a female in Kate's litter that's spotted like her, Uncle Edouard has already decided he'll name her Dupli-Kate."

Giggling a little and deciding she was going to like a man possessing such a crazy sense of humor, Berry watched as the dogs, their white tails lifted high and wagging sassily, trotted back to their master. For a moment they hindered his progress by jumping up on him, then chasing each other around his long legs. Was Edouard Armand as curious about her as she was about him? Had Jason brought women home with him before?

Berry was close enough now to see that the gray-haired man walking toward them was smiling. She tried smiling back. Birds overhead in the trees kept flitting about, calling back and forth. Were they also wondering what she was doing there?

"I wasn't expecting to find a place larger than the Cabildo," she told Jason. "It's beautiful."

"I'm glad you like it. I expect the house appears larger than it is because it's ninety-eight feet wide."

"Did your uncle build it?" The man coming to meet them was sizing her up; she could tell. The trio of dogs dashed back and forth from him to the couple approaching, as if they could not decide where their loyalty lay. She tried removing her hand from Jason's, but he held on.

"No." Jason felt her hand tremble in his when he refused to relinquish it. Tenderness swelled his heart. She *was* frightened. Her face looked pale in the deep shade.

"My grandfather built it," Jason went on when she appeared to gain comfort from his tightened hand clasp, "back when my mother and Uncle Edouard were very young. He evidently believed he was going to rear far more than two children. As you probably know, back then a lot more babies died at birth or soon afterward."

"There's plenty of room for a large family here. Oh my, yes, plenty of room for children." Berry recognized that she was prattling but she could not seem to still her tongue.

"Funny you should say that," Jason said with a wink and a teasing smile that brought the desired rush of color to her too-solemn face. "I've been thinking the same thing."

The trim, gray-haired man was close enough to be calling out greetings then, and the couple hurried to meet him and his playful dogs.

Once the initial greetings were over and Jason had introduced her to his uncle, Berry put aside the worst of her earlier misgivings. A lean man not quite so tall as Jason, Mr. Armand talked and moved like a person unaware that his hair was gray and receding. He led them to the veranda, where they settled onto rocking chairs and began discussing the merits of traveling by way of packets and other steam-powered vessels. Edouard Armand paused in mid-sentence and said to Berry, "I hope you're going to forget this 'Mr. Armand' bit. I answer folks quicker when they call me Mr. Edouard."

"Shall we make a pact then?" Berry asked. "You call me Berry and I'll call you whatever you prefer."

"I like the way you cut straight to the center of things," Edouard replied with a smile. "Jason has done me a double favor. Not only has he returned home, he has brought along a very delightful young woman."

Enjoying listening to the two men visit, Berry decided that Jason possessed the same kind of expressive brown eyes as his uncle. Jason exuded the same air of authority, too, but his more finely sculpted features and his dimples were uniquely his own. She admired the way Mr. Edouard spoke in a courtly, genteel fashion. He appeared to enjoy talking with her as much as with his nephew and looked directly at her when she spoke. She liked Mr. Edouard.

Soon a tall, thin woman came bustling from inside, hardly concealing her shock upon finding an unchaperoned young stranger on the veranda with Jason and Edouard. Agnes Delange tilted her head inquiringly and made little polite comments when Jason introduced his "friend from New Orleans, Miss Berry Cortabona." Accustomed to the easy familiarity among theatrical folk, Berry was surprised that the woman, who appeared to be little over forty, asked her to use *Miss* before her first name.

"Cousin Edouard," Agnes said after perching on the front edge of a rocker, "you really should have sent for me the minute you saw Jason arrive. I could have had somebody bring out refreshments, and I would have liked knowing we have another houseguest. I need to get one of the rooms upstairs readied. There's been so much happening around here lately that I meet myself coming and going. Sometimes folks tend to forget that being housekeeper in such a large place is quite demanding. I hope Jason will forgive me for not showing Miss Cortabona to a room as soon as she arrived."

"Thanks for your concern," Jason said. "We've been entertaining ourselves and enjoying visiting with Uncle Edouard. There's no big rush to get Berry settled in. I've invited her to stay for a long visit."

"How nice," Agnes managed, her eyes showing her puzzlement over what place the young woman held in Jason's life. She rallied and slipped into small talk. The weather, then the headlines of a recent *L'Abeille,* the French-language newspaper coming from New Orleans.

Berry's interest aroused, she asked, "Do you get the paper here?"

"Only if the packet has reason to stop," Agnes replied. "Otherwise we send someone into the nearest town, Calion. It's only twelve miles north of us." As if she expected one from New Orleans to consider the citizens of Saint Christopher Parish backward and uninformed, she fixed her bright eyes on Berry and added, "We usually receive our papers before they're more than one day old. The daily packet boats keep us from being isolated."

Though Berry attempted to erase the woman's suspicions that she might be judging the rural parish harshly, she suspected Miss Agnes's earlier words of welcome and her thin smile were false. Miss Agnes's hands fluttered while she talked, and her high-pitched, nasal voice, minus what Berry considered normal inflections, was unlike any that she had ever before heard. How could a person speak every word, every sentence, with so little variance in pitch?

Monotonous was the first description that came to Berry's mind as the woman talked on about her busy schedule during Jason's absence. Then she decided on a more apt term. Yes, Mr. Edouard's cousin and housekeeper *chirped* when she spoke.

After she had exhausted her account of her activities among gardens and fruit trees and ailing neighbors, Miss Agnes rose and addressed Berry. "I'll send someone for you as soon as we get your room tidied."

Almost immediately, another feminine voice sounded. Its timbre was soft and vibrant, not in the same family as *monotonous*. "Jason!" a lovely young woman squealed as she hurried across the veranda amidst a rustle of silken skirts and a cloud of perfume. "Aunt Agnes told me you had arrived. With a friend. I wish I had known it sooner so I could have been here to greet you. I'll bet you're surprised to find me here visiting—if you even remember meeting me that first time. I was nothing but a mere child."

Delinda Delange was no mere child now, Berry reflected after their introduction. A quick look at Jason told her that he also realized that the brown-haired Delinda was a beautiful young woman. Her gown was cut low enough to reveal ample quantities of skin as white and silky as thistledown.

Berry could not decide if Delinda's breasts were unusally large or if her waist was unusually tiny, or both. Certainly she was one of the most voluptuously shaped young women that Berry had ever seen. She noticed that a heavyset black woman wearing a black dress covered partially by a sheer, white apron stood near the front door. Delinda Delange, Berry surmised from the way the woman watched the brown-haired beauty, had arrived at Armand Acres with at least one attendant. Properly, she amended, the way the proper daughter of a proper Creole planter should arrive at a plantation. Berry knew all about upstaging.

Delinda returned her attention to the other young woman on the veranda. In syllables as thick and sweet as honey, Delinda said, "I do hope you're going to call me Delinda and let me call you Berry. I sometimes get plain bored up at my daddy's plantation. When Aunt Agnes's invitation for a visit came, I just couldn't resist coming down and seeing how things are in the southern part of our parish. Isn't it a remarkable coincidence that we both arrived the same week?"

Berry murmured she knew not what, for the brown-haired beauty was ogling Jason with almost every breath and not waiting for extended answers. It was as if Delinda knew she was playing the star role, Berry decided with sudden insight. Jason was winging Berry an imploring look. She ignored it. She was too busy vowing not to be an Impulse Person this time and become jealous before she learned all the facts.

"Though I'm kin to Aunt Agnes on her late husband's side," Delinda explained to Berry in her somewhat breathy voice, "I feel I'm almost blood kin to Jason and Cousin Edouard, too. Coming from New Orleans as you do, you might not realize all of us Creoles living on plantations feel like we're family." She flicked a tentative smile and a warm look toward the watchful Edouard, as if seeking approval. "I first visited Armand Acres one summer right after Aunt

Agnes came to stay. I declare, after being here only two days this time, it feels almost like home."

Jason cleared his throat and said, "As Uncle Edouard said, Delinda, Cousin Agnes's family is always welcome. This is her home now."

"How wonderfully kind of you, Jason," the soft-eyed young woman cooed. "Now that I'm seventeen, I can see that what I always thought about you when I was a little girl is actually true." With her limpid brown eyes sparkling, she smiled up at him. "I declare, you really are about the most handsome rascal in Saint Christopher Parish." Catching, then holding Jason's gaze with her own, Delinda asked, "Don't you agree, Berry?"

"I'm no judge, since I've not yet met any of the other rascals," Berry replied tartly, feeling Mr. Edouard's amused gaze tracking across her face.

"My goodness gracious," Delinda said, turning toward Berry then with a smile that displayed her perfect teeth, "I can tell you've got lots of treats in store. Why, up and down Selene Bayou there are some of the best-looking men you'll ever see anywhere. I attended the convent school in New Orleans until I just got bored outta my mind and quit, but I never saw any men in the whole city who could compare to our own Creoles."

Delinda slid a sideways look toward Jason that Berry judged as coy. No, she corrected, it was simpering. And Jason was watching Delinda of the spectacular bosom.

After sucking in a deep breath that caused her breasts to lift suddenly, Delinda sighed and added, "Not that we schoolgirls ever got outside the convent to be looking at young men, of course."

"Of course," Berry echoed with a trace of tongue in cheek. During Delinda's recital, gossip about countless schoolgirls sneaking from the boarding school within the Ursuline Convent had flashed to Berry's mind. Berry had no knowledge of all the places where the girls went on their outings, but from her peeping place behind curtains, she had seen many unchaperoned schoolgirls sitting in the Théâtre d'Orléans, laughing at bawdy jokes and casting wandering eyes among the audience.

Berry reserved final judgment for a later time, but she entertained the notion that the beauteous Delinda Delange was not so naive as she pretended.

CHAPTER

*

Fifteen

*T*hat evening, when Berry came down for supper—
the term apparently preferred by Mr. Edouard—she
was still feeling very much like an outsider. She
appreciated Mr. Edouard's special efforts to make
her feel welcome.

"Delinda made first claim to the place at my right,"
he said as they entered the dining room with its long
table formally set, "but you'll be just as close on my
left."

"And I get to sit beside you," Jason told Berry as he
pulled out her chair with smiling confidence. No matter
what his initial reaction to the lovely Delinda and her
ample charms, he seemed interested in no one now but
Berry.

Throughout the meal the stand-offish attitude of the other
two women puzzled Berry. Did they think she represented
some kind of threat? She almost laughed at the thought that
she might be cast as a villainess.

Berry did not have to look across the dining table to see that the beautiful Delinda Delange fit the role of Creole belle perfectly. While bathing and getting dressed for the evening, Berry had entertained a growing suspicion. Had Miss Agnes invited her niece for a visit so that she could flirt with Jason and perhaps wangle her way into his heart? Next would come the role of wife and mistress of Armand Acres.

Berry was grateful Mr. Edouard had insisted that she sit on his left, next to Jason, leaving Delinda to sit across the table next to her aunt. Of course it did allow the young woman freedom to flutter her eyelashes at Jason without having to turn her head. Where had she learned to flirt like that? Not inside convent school.

Generally the talk during the meal held Berry's interest, but frequently Miss Agnes's fluttery movements drew her attention. The thin woman kept sneaking jerky, sideways glances at the other four diners. Though Miss Agnes seldom initiated talk, she would yank her head in another direction if Berry happened to look up during her secretive appraisals. Apparently possessing a small appetite, Miss Agnes merely pecked at her food. Berry found herself comparing the nervous, brown-haired woman to a sparrow.

Sparrows had always held a fascination for Berry. She recalled once after mass on a sunny morning when she was a child, she had chased the little brown birds all over the Place d'Armes, but never had come close enough to use any of the salt Aunt Maddy had given her. A private smile twitched at the corners of her full lips. Playful as well as nurturing, Aunt Maddy had told her that if she could sprinkle salt on their tails, the sparrows would become her friends.

"Berry," Edouard Armand said, breaking into her musings while they were waiting for dessert to be served, "I'm delighted you decided to escape New Orleans for a while and spend some time with us. Jason tells me that you've already lived quite an exciting life, even for a modern young woman from our capital."

Berry's fingers tightened their hold on the stem of her wine glass. She looked around the spacious dining room with its magnificent mahogany furniture, then at Jason. Bedamned! What had he told his uncle? There were several matters that she preferred he not turn into dinner conversation. She felt like slipping her hand underneath the drop of the white linen tablecloth and pinching his leg, hard. "You're being kind, Mr. Edouard. I'm happy to be here and I appreciate the cordial way all of you have received me."

Berry inclined her head politely toward him and Miss Agnes, saving her last glance for Jason. Not a hint of politeness graced her silent question: *What in blazes did you tell?*

As if he heard Berry's unvoiced query, Jason slid her a reassuring look. "While you were getting settled in your room upstairs, I told Uncle Edouard about your traveling with a theatrical troupe in the East for the past three years. He was once quite a patron of the theater."

"How nice," Berry said, able to release her wine glass then. Did the looks Delinda and Miss Agnes sent her way indicate surprise or disapproval? "Mr. Edouard, you should consider coming to New Orleans this fall for the season. There'll be a British Shakespearean troupe coming in December. They're marvelous and speak with accents that Americans seem to have little trouble understanding."

"Sounds interesting," Edouard remarked. He waited for the young servant to set small plates bearing wedges of golden-crusted apple pie in front of the two women, then said, "Sassafras, before you serve me my pie, run out to the kitchen and ask Clementine if she has some clotted cream to put on it." Deferring to the others at the table then, he asked, "Would anyone else care for cream?"

When all declined, Agnes spoke. "Cousin Edouard, please restrain yourself." A frown pinched her sparse eyebrows even closer together and she inclined her head toward him.

"You know how you sometimes get a bad stomach from such overindulging."

"To hell with bad stomachs," Edouard remarked with a wink toward Berry. "I want to hear more about this British acting troupe. As Jason said, there was a time when I was a big fan of the theater, especially the works of the Bard." For a moment he seemed to slip into reverie as he looked at the empty chair sitting at the other end of the table. "Maybe I'd enjoy catching a play or two. It might spice up my blood."

Miss Agnes surprised Berry by sending open looks of disbelief and wonder at the gray-haired man sitting at the head of his table. Delinda appeared detached, as she usually seemed when she was not involved in a conversation or serving as its topic. Through her peripheral vision, Berry saw Jason's face break into a pleased smile.

Edouard continued, rubbing his clean-shaven chin with long fingers and narrowing his dark eyes in thought. "Up until a few years ago, I stayed for a couple of weeks each winter at Jason's townhouse. In between tending to business, I would treat myself to a bit of New Orleans society. When my wife was alive, we knew almost all of the old Creole families. We had some fine times together." He smiled at Berry. "You've reminded me that there's a world outside Armand Acres. Maybe now that Jason's taking so well to sugar cane, I should get away some, kick up my heels."

Berry, encouraged by her host's comments, entertained everyone then with accounts of the British troupe's performances that she had caught while in Boston and Philadelphia. Edouard appeared enthralled, as did Jason. Was she imagining it, or was Miss Agnes watching her with decreasing reservations? Delinda Delange might well have been a professional actress. Her pleasant expression revealed nothing about what was going on inside her pretty head.

Flipping her hand palm upward toward Edouard in a

dramatic gesture, Berry ended her little spiel. "You've never heard Hamlet speak until you've heard Sir Reginald Cromwell play the part. Reggie is the ultimate actor."

Jason had watched while Berry's olive-skinned face took on a more natural glow as she spoke with knowledgeable enthusiasm about the theater. Her reaction on the veranda at the unexpected appearance of Delinda had pleased him, made him think she might be jealous. He was feeling happier by the minute that she obviously was beginning to feel more at ease and—Wait up! Why had she referred to the actor as "Reggie?" "Did you know this Reginald Cromwell personally?" he asked Berry a bit irritably. Bedamned if he was going to acknowledge the man's title! Anyway, titles used in the United States were absurd.

"Why, yes," Berry replied, nonplussed at his question. Surely, she reassured herself, Jason could not tell from her praise of Reggie's talent on the stage that the two of them had enjoyed a mutual infatuation, one that had led to his dramatic proposal and her equally dramatic refusal. Reginald had insisted he was going to look her up when the troupe arrived in New Orleans and repeat his marriage proposal, but she had no interest in even seeing him again. "Back in the spring our troupes stayed at the same hotel in several cities."

"How divinely romantic!" Delinda remarked in a gushy tone. "You've lived such an exciting life, Berry. Actors have always fascinated me." When Agnes shot her a sharp, questioning look, she added, "Also actresses and everyone else connected with the theater."

Jason attacked his apple pie then and left the conversation to the others. Annoying questions were sailing around in his mind. Though he had guessed when he first parried with the regal Queen Isabella at the masquerade ball that she was no novice at flirting, he never had asked Berry about her past associations with young men. Maybe he should have. Jealousy was nibbling.

The memory of having seen Berry with the French architect the past Saturday night still lay fresh on Jason's mind. Could her refusal to marry him mean that her heart belonged to another? Or, maybe even worse, did she choose to remain single so as to enjoy the company of more than one man? The punishing questions formed an uneasiness within. Except for the fact that he loved her madly and knew that she had never surrendered to any man before him, what did he really know about Berry Cortabona?

Jason motioned for Sassafras, who was hovering around the sideboard in order to attend the needs of the diners. She might as well take away his dessert plate. He had lost his appetite for pie.

The next morning when Berry and Jason rode their horses up to the sugar mill, which sat a mile from the mansion, Jason told her, "For somebody who says she hasn't ridden much, you've done remarkably well." He prided himself on having hidden his jealousy when she told him how she had learned to ride. While she and Camille were attending a series of house parties on a large estate in New Jersey, she reported, their host's groomsman had instructed them in the rudiments.

"Thanks. Jewel is easy to ride." Berry patted the chestnut's gleaming withers. "Miss Agnes was kind to find me a riding outfit." She glanced down at the black cotton jacket and its matching skirt that draped gracefully over her legs as she sat on the sidesaddle. "I've never owned one but I've always been fortunate that my host made one available."

Jason decided that though he liked finding the woman he loved free-spirited and at ease around his family and friends, he would have preferred she not have learned so many of her social graces among people he had never known. Most of them male, no doubt. "Cousin Agnes is a kindhearted lady. There's usually an extra habit around for guests who might not have one along." As he reined Diamond to a stop near a grove of willows with patches of grass all around, he stroked the gray's withers. From the corner of his eye he watched Berry stop her horse without trepidation. She must be a born equestrienne.

"Why does Miss Agnes appear so nervous?" Berry asked after Jason helped her dismount. She was seeking something to think about other than the effect of his nearness. When they had ridden past the seemingly endless fields of green sugarcane, she had plied him with so many questions that she figured there were no more left to ask about the main crop at Armand Acres. "Does Delinda do that to her or is she always that way?"

After looping both sets of reins over the low limb of a black willow, Jason turned toward the sugar mill up ahead. The sight of Berry holding up the skirt of her habit and walking beside him pleased the part of him wanting her all to himself. He had fought against taking her in his arms and kissing her when he helped her dismount. Her lips looked lusciously soft. He reminded himself that he dared not give in to temptation each time they were alone and smother her with kisses.

Fixing his thoughts on ordinary matters then, Jason said, "I hope you didn't take offense because Cousin Agnes seemed edgy last evening. Uncle Edouard says she's concerned about Delinda's future, though he has no idea why. I've not seen the girl since she was in pigtails, but I gather she's headstrong and is giving her mother a bad time. When I visited with Cousin Agnes, she said she hoped to get to know you better."

"Really? I get the feeling she might be wary of me and I was wondering why." She sneaked a sideways look at Jason. Would he think she was crazy if she told about her comparing Miss Agnes to a sparrow? She was dying to confess her suspicion that Delinda's visit had been prompted by more than a wish for a change of scenery. Strange, the way she wanted to share her every thought with him—unless it pertained to her feelings for him.

"Cousin Agnes is not a sophisticated person. She might have felt out of place because she has never visited New

Orleans. I doubt she knows much about Uncle Edouard's former life. She might have been surprised at what he said."

"Why has she never gone to New Orleans?"

"She grew up on a small farm back in swamp country in a far simpler style than Mother or Cousin Edouard. When she married a farmer with a nearby tract, I reckon she just never had a reason to travel to the capital. I don't recall her visiting us more than once or twice until she was widowed several years ago. When she came here to live, she helped Mother run the house. Her biggest joy, she says, is running a big household efficiently. She does it well, I must admit."

As they walked on toward the sugar mill, Berry pursed her lips in thought. She was no threat to Miss Agnes. Soon she would be returning to New Orleans. "I told her this morning how beautiful everything looks. Maybe I shouldn't have launched into such detailed stories last night." She watched a bird soar against the inverted bowl of blue overhead. "I don't fit in here, Jason."

"Nonsense! You fit in anywhere." Though her tone had not invited sympathy and she had merely stated what she believed to be fact, he hastened to reassure her. "Actually, you were a huge success last evening. I've not seen Uncle Edouard so animated since I returned from Texas. You drew out more information about his personal life than anyone else has been able to do since Mother passed away."

"I noticed the sad looks he sent toward the empty chair at the other end of the table. Was that his wife's place?"

"Yes. Aunt Corrine died back when I was very young. It was a long while before he asked Mother to sit there."

"He must have loved his wife very much."

"Yes, he did. She was beautiful and full of laughter. As far as I know, their only sadness was not having children. After Aunt Corrine died in childbirth, along with their son, Uncle Edouard never quite regained his former enthusiasm for the activities they had shared."

Berry nodded sympathetically. Jason's apparent love and

concern for his uncle touched her. "I wonder if his wife would have wanted him to give up pleasure like that."

Jason shrugged, indicating he had no answer. "He hasn't left Saint Christopher Parish since Mother died last year."

"Maybe Mr. Edouard will follow through on what he said last evening and come over to see a few plays."

"Perhaps he will, if you'll agree to accompany the two of us. I can tell he likes being around you."

Berry let the subject drop as they approached the sugar house. Made of pinkish brick, the mill rose two floors high. She realized that because of their proximity, the tall smoke-stack poking toward the blue sky appeared taller than it actually was. A cloying smell that Berry could classify only as sweet yet fermented had been floating on the morning air a good while before they reached the mill. Now that the odor had become intensified, she knew the source.

When they paused inside the door of a huge room containing alien-looking equipment, Berry began asking questions about the process of refining sugar from sugar-cane. How? When?

"In October," Jason answered, "a crew of men and women will cut the cane near the ground with sharp mache-tes and knives and leave it lying. Others will be following behind loading the stalks on wagons and hauling them here to the sugar house. It's the busiest and most crucial time on a sugar plantation."

As he explained, Jason gestured toward the enormous press sitting across the large room. His voice took on an added note of excitement when her expressive eyes and face revealed her absorption in what he was telling. Was that a new, admiring look she was sending him? Had she not realized before that he had completed his youthful adven-tures and settled down to being a planter?

"The men," Jason continued, "will unload the cane and leave it for others to stack near the press. Another crew will strip the leaves off the stalks. Another will feed them into the cylinders where the juice will be extracted. The juice is collected in these huge kettles"—he gestured toward the monstrous, wide-mouthed vessels of cast iron—"and heated until boiling. Young boys supply wood for the fires. The syrup is allowed to simmer until it's almost too thick to be called a liquid.

"Either Mooney Snead, our overseer, or I will decide when the syrup is ready to take off the fire. When the syrup cools, it will granulate and be collected for packing in hogsheads. We channel our activities for the entire year toward the harvest season in the fall."

Berry's mind was racing to take in all that he was telling. "I recall your saying you were making purchases for the sugar mill while you were in New Orleans."

"Maintenance and additions are parts of the process. We save some cane shoots for the next season, 'heeling' them in soil until planting time. We have to make sure the coopers make enough barrels for the new crop. Extra wood must be cut to feed the fires. We try to finish up here at the sugar house by Christmas and ship our sugar on the packets for the New Orleans markets. Then it starts all over again."

Berry could well imagine the frantic, exciting activities of harvest season. She looked at the giant cylinders designed to roll against each other and squeeze the juice from the green stalks, then at the slanting, hollowed-out logs that would carry the cane juice into the enormous black kettles that appeared large enough to hold several people.

A plantation, Berry surmised, was far more than a place for easy living. With new admiration for the dark-haired man standing beside her, Berry realized that Jason was not the idler she had believed.

After Jason's voice stilled, several black men came from another part of the sugar house, their faces wreathed with smiles. Berry thought their greetings for the one they addressed as "Young Massa" sounded warm and laced with respect.

Berry felt cheated, somehow, that the slaves obviously already knew the side of Jason that she had just glimpsed.

Actually, she had not known him at all. Jason Premont was much more than a handsome, charming young man of wealth. The sense of power that he exuded was genuine, was directed toward worthy goals.

The slaves darted shy glances toward the black-haired stranger, then sent questioning looks toward Jason. Berry, after giving quiet greetings to each man when Jason introduced her, stood and listened as he and the slaves discussed the new equipment he had purchased in New Orleans. Jason's deep voice seemed to have taken on a new quality ever since they entered the sugar house, she thought, an authority and a subdued excitement she never had heard before.

"You'll be safe out here for a few minutes," Jason told her as he led her back outside, his teeth sparkling white in the morning sunlight. "The men want to show me some of the installations they've made during my absence. It will be messy in there with work in progress. I'll bring you back some time for a tour inside after everything is in place."

Acquiescing, Berry watched his tall, lean figure disappear inside the shadowed sugar house. She then found a resting place on a pile of boards stacked in the shade of the mill and sat down. Idly, she snapped off the long stem of a nearby weed, which she and her school friends had always called sheep shank. She placed the tart, sappy end in her mouth.

Last evening after going to bed, Berry had entertained the unnerving notion that maybe she had already fallen in love with Jason. The thought frightened her, then and now, as she let it take shape in her mind, but guardedly. Just because she was learning that he was no idler did not mean that his heart could belong to only one woman.

No, Berry reassured herself as she watched a puffy cloud drift lazily, she was merely feeling gratitude because Jason had brought her to his home for protection against Warren Maroney. The possibility that he could be a man with more on his mind than frivolity was so unexpected that it still astonished her.

Suddenly Berry flung the green weed away, her lips puckering and her black eyes growing thoughtful. Strange, the way things changed. She frowned. The taste of the weed's vinegary juices was not even close to what she recalled from childhood.

CHAPTER

*

Sixteen

New experiences continued to fill Berry's days at Armand Acres. If she had not paused each afternoon to scan the pages of the current *L'Abeille* for news of Warren Maroney's capture, she probably would have had difficulty in remembering when one day ended and another began.

Berry had not expected to find a sugar plantation existing as if it might be an entity unto itself. More than once she entertained the notion that the inverted bowl of blue that rested atop the forests on the near horizon might well have been the boundaries of the world.

Sometimes, as she rode Jewel alongside Jason's Diamond and, in passing, viewed the numerous outbuildings, the slave cabins set in neat rows off to themselves, the garden of vegetables and the orchards with their heavily laden fruit trees, she suspected she could almost hear and feel a palpable, throbbing energy coming from the black, tightly packed soil. She noticed that the half-rancid, half-cloying scent of the sugar house often drifted on the wind, especially in the early mornings before the sun chased away the excess moisture in the air. Within sight from almost all major points on the flat land, the vast fields of cane called to Berry's mind green-clad soldiers marching in precision. The burgeoning plants stood so close together that she wondered how the harvesters would find enough room to walk between the crisp stalks that were already taller than she.

Jason surprised Berry by putting away his stylish clothing during the daylight hours. As she secretly admired his lean body clad in tight-fitting trousers of yellowish-buff cotton called nankeen and white shirt of thin cotton with naught but a simple band at the open neck, she judged him even more handsome than when he wore his frocktail coats and fancy waistcoats. She figured he was seeking as much relief as possible from the bearing-down heat of the June sun, for he seldom buttoned his shirt above the middle of his chest and he wore his sleeves cuffed up to his elbows. To her delight, his olive complexion took on a golden tan that deepened with each stint in the sun. '

A time or two when Berry was waiting for Jason to talk plantation business with Mooney Snead, the overseer, or with one of the many slaves, she found herself imagining what it would be like to run her hands inside his partially buttoned shirt and feel again his furred chest and his muscles, maybe twine her arms around his back and hug his manliness close against her breasts. Although the sun's rays beat down without mercy, her sensuous musings brought shivers.

From the first day, Jason had insisted Berry accompany him when he left the mansion or its grounds for any length of time. When she showed her puzzlement, he had declared, "I didn't bring you all the way from New Orleans to leave you vulnerable to Warren Maroney or his cohorts."

Not that she objected to being in Jason's company most of each day and evening, Berry reminded herself at the end of her third full day at the plantation. In fact she loved the arrangement, had begun waking when the cocks crowed, and anticipating each new day. Never before had she found so many lengthy periods of time free for leisurely pursuits. There was no curtain time, no work, no clock chiming for Berry Cortabona. Was time standing still?

One night after stretching out on her bed with its lavender-scented sheets and listening to the rustle of the mosquito netting falling from the tester as Sheena, the slave assigned to serve her, pulled it into protective position, Berry allowed herself to philosophize. Why should she fritter away time trying to weigh her new life against her old—the transitory against the permanent?

The way Berry saw it, she would have plenty of opportunities to sift through her thoughts after the policemen caught Warren Maroney and she returned to New Orleans. Would tomorrow bring a letter from Sergeant Harrigan or an article in L'Abeille telling what she waited to hear? A mosquito whined its plaintive singsong from somewhere outside the netting. She stretched languorously against the smooth sheets, feeling blessedly safe, secure. Unbidden came the troublesome thought that the emerald ring that she had snatched from Warren Maroney lay hidden in her second floor bedroom among her gowns in the armoire.

Berry decided that living each moment fully was the only course of action for her to take. She yawned, stretched again, then lay still. The mosquito no longer threatened. Night callers from the trees outside the open windows of her second story bedroom supplied the only music. She welcomed the sensation that her head was sinking deeper into the down pillow, unaware that the ambiance of Armand Acres was seeping into her soul, much as her unacknowledged love for Jason was stealing into the caverns in her heart and finding a home.

Before giving in to her drowsiness, Berry winged wishes up the Mississippi that her friend Camille might be enjoying the kind of carefree happiness she was experiencing. Afterward she felt foolish, though still mellow from the thought.

As honeymooners on a luxurious riverboat, Camille and Ace would need no blessings from her to achieve bliss.

Embracing a tad of rare self-pity and thus forgetting the fact that when the couple first met and experienced attraction, Ace's commitment to his ailing wife had kept them apart, Berry sighed with a measure of nearsighted envy. In search of sleep she flipped to her favored side. Did Camille and Ace realize how fortunate they were to have fallen in love with the right people?

Late each afternoon after Berry and Jason returned to their rooms, bathed away the day's accumulation of perspiration and changed into fresh clothing, they would appear on the front veranda to visit with the others before supper. Never before having spent much time around women who did not travel in theatrical circles, Berry was uncertain about how to make friends with Delinda and Miss Agnes. Did they truly like her, or did the presence of the men demand their politeness? She sensed that in their eyes, she would forever be an outsider. Even so, she found the women's conversations interesting and was eager to accept things as they appeared.

From the first day, Delinda never missed an opportunity to complain that she would enjoy riding horseback with Berry and Jason some morning. "If only you would wake me early enough to join you. You seem to be having such a good time."

"You could join us later in the morning," Jason responded with cool politeness.

"Yes," Berry added with as little enthusiasm, "or in the afternoons."

"How can I?" Delinda complained, but prettily. "The sun is death to fair skin."

Berry reflected that Delinda probably was right. With its protective grove of trees, its shaded verandas, and its floor-to-ceiling windows opened to catch the errant breezes straying from the bayou out front, the large house provided an oasis of comfort on hot days.

"I'll never get to ride with you two because my Lexie won't allow me outside in the hot sun," Delinda announced late one afternoon after issuing her complaint again. All five sat on the front veranda, rocking occasionally and enjoying the quiet time before supper. "The poor dear would just die if I were to get a sunburn"—she stole a look toward Berry's smooth olive skin which had tanned noticeably since her arrival—"or get my skin tan and maybe look like a gypsy."

"Gypsies have a lot of fun," Berry remarked, smiling good-naturedly at the petulant young woman. She was finding that Delinda, in spite of her self-centeredness, possessed an appealing spontaneity and charm. Rather like a spoiled puppy. Then Berry remembered that that very afternoon when Jason had helped her dismount from Jewel, he had told her before he kissed her how beautiful her skin looked with its added color.

When Berry felt Jason's admiring gaze on her, she was grateful that Sheena had insisted on arranging her hair in a new style. The tight curls falling around her temples and in front of her ears bobbed with her tiniest movement and made her feel deliciously feminine—and perhaps a tad feline, too. "Actually, Delinda, I can see why you choose to stay inside. I might do the same if I had pale skin like yours that has a tendency to redden and get blotchy from sunshine."

While Miss Agnes added her chirping approval of her niece's actions and Delinda frowned at Berry's forthright description, Berry glanced toward the foyer where Lexie usually stayed when her mistress was in the central section of the mansion. Now that Delinda and the black woman had been at Armand Acres for several days, Lexie apparently had relaxed her guard and gone to the kitchen out back to visit with the slaves getting the evening meal ready.

From the few times she had been around Delinda and Lexie together, Berry concluded that the slave truly loved her young mistress. She had noticed that a kind of melting softness claimed the plump woman's face when she looked at the fair Delinda. Delinda's feelings about Lexie or anyone else were, as usual, too contained to be ferreted out. How was it, Berry wondered, that she had begun thinking of Delinda Delange not as a dangerous rival for Jason's affections but rather as a spoiled little girl? An adorable one, at that.

The next evening after all had gathered at twilight on the veranda, Delinda announced in her breathless manner, "I got bored doing tapestry this morning and Cousin Edouard was kind enough to take me in his darling little buggy to Calion." Her pretty face glowed as she sent the gray-haired man a sweet smile. "We ran into that handsome Alexander Oates from up the bayou. I met him last year when he came to an enormous house party in our part of the parish. He was ever so charming. Today he was telling Cousin Edouard and me that his brother and sister-in-law are holding a party this very weekend at his family's plantation."

Not waiting for a reply, Delinda continued. "Jason, Alexander said he hadn't heard you were back from New Orleans and he hoped to see you soon. He invited all of us from Armand Acres to spend the weekend, or at least come for part of the festivities. Cousin Agnes has consented to go with Lexie and me and spend Saturday night, but"—Delinda slid a pleading look toward Edouard who was fondling the ears of one of his hounds and showing little interest in what was being said—"Cousin Edouard hasn't agreed to go along . . . yet."

"Remember that I said I would go only after finding out how Cousin Edouard feels about the matter," Agnes reminded her niece. "My duty is to see to his comforts." She seemed agitated and kept glancing down the long driveway toward the empty road, as if avoiding eye contact with anyone.

"I suppose you told Alexander we have another houseguest," Jason replied. Both tone and mien revealed his annoyance. He wanted as few people as possible to learn of Berry's presence. Not that anyone would have a reason to get news of her whereabouts back to New Orleans, he reasoned, but idle talk often led to revelations best not spread. Uncle Edouard was the only person other than Alonzo in whom he had confided the real reason Berry had come to Armand Acres.

"Why, no," Delinda said, her innocent gaze sweeping over Berry, "I never once thought about mentioning another houseguest. I'm sorry, Berry. Please forgive me."

"You're forgiven," Berry replied, struck with the newest evidence of Delinda's total self-absorption. Maybe she truly could not think of anyone other than herself. Though Berry had found herself on guard against antagonism, covert or open from Delinda, she admitted she had seen nothing but a vain young beauty who smiled on the world and those around her as long as she was getting her way. Berry's custom of responding to Delinda's little barbs by tossing back some of her own seemed to please the headstrong young woman and lead her into eyeing the black-haired Creole from the French Quarter as even worthier competition. "There's no harm done."

Delinda appeared contrite and eager to make amends. "I'm sure it will be all right if you come along, since you're Jason's friend and all. Fernwood is an enormous mansion and there'll be lots of room and food."

"Berry and I have plans for Saturday evening," Jason said evenly.

"And so do I," Edouard added. His smile was bland.

Tossing her long hair as if it were a ponytail making a giant sweep at annoying horseflies, Delinda jumped up from her chair and went to stand by one of the columns. When she turned back to face the others—her audience, Berry mused, that awaited in silence her next lines—it was with an angry swish of silken skirts, lifted chin, and an audible sigh. Her pretty lips were pouty, her eyes fiery.

"What plans could possibly be better than attending a party at Alexander's place?" Delinda asked in a dramatic, high-pitched tone. Her gaze swept across all four faces, as if to make certain that nobody was missing her performance.

Before going on, Delinda waited until after the three hounds bounced up from where they had been lying near Edouard's rocker and, with tails drooping, disappeared down the steps to the grounds below. "From what Alexander said, everybody who is anybody in Saint Christopher Parish will be at Fernwood this weekend." One pretty hand shot out toward the bemused Edouard. "There's even going to be an orchestra coming from New Orleans to play for the dancing. From New Orleans, mind you!"

Berry, not daring to look at Jason or anybody else, hid her amusement behind her hand when Delinda drew herself up to her utmost height and, with her full breasts thrusting upward, placed her hands at the sides of her small waist. Recalling Delinda's impassioned comment at supper that first evening about adoring actors, Berry suspected the young woman had slipped away from the Ursulines at some time and watched a melodrama, maybe more than one.

Yes, Berry reflected, Delinda's overwrought actions could have been the direct result of orders being barked by a director with an eye to wringing the emotions of an audience. Was the pretty belle tapping one foot underneath the crinolines holding out her long skirts?

"Oh," Delinda wailed to nobody in particular as she pranced up and down in front of where her audience sat and watched, "I can't believe I'm the only one who can see what a wonderful time we could have. I'm not pleading only for myself. What do we ever do after supper around here but play cards or dominoes or some other silly game?" She brought the back of a fist to rest against her forehead, her arm held at an angle that left her sad face visible. "Oh, I might as well have stayed at home. Life is passing me by."

"I believe it's fitting that you and Agnes go and have a grand time, Delinda," Edouard said after a small silence that Berry was halfway tempted to break with applause.

"I'll have Ulysses drive you in the carriage whenever you like and stay until you're ready to return."

When Agnes recovered from apparent shock and seemed to be readying a protest, maybe calling Delinda's hand for her slanted remarks about life at Armand Acres where she was a guest, Edouard shushed her with a headshake and a motion of his uplifted hand. Berry wondered then if perhaps the astute Edouard had also seen through Delinda's theatrics and enjoyed them for what they were.

"Cousin Agnes," Edouard said, "I don't want you to feel you shouldn't leave your home here for outings that bring you pleasure. I do what pleases me, and so should you. You keep things around here running better than a new clock. I appreciate that fact, but you deserve free time when you want it. I'm not your jailer, merely your first cousin. All you have to do is speak up."

"You're too kind, Cousin Edouard." Agnes fidgeted in her oversized rocking chair as if trying to make a comfortable nest, her thin face flushing. Berry wondered what caused the woman's obvious agitation, the compliment or her niece's childish theatrics.

Edouard addressed Delinda again, his smile lighting up his eyes in the nicest kind of way. "You'll have to forgive an old man for forgetting that pretty girls like you are meant to go to parties and have fun. From the way Alexander was looking at you in town today, I figure he'll be relieved not to see Jason showing up and maybe robbing him of a few dances."

"Oh," Delinda exclaimed with eyes rounded and hands clasped to her generous bosom, "do you think he truly noticed me, Cousin Edouard? Truly noticed me?"

On the morning that Ulysses drove Delinda, Agnes, and Lexie to Fernwood for the party, Alonzo was keeping Jason company in the *garçonniere*. Jason was thinking about Berry's apparent, growing ease at being at his home and hoping that she might be coming to care for him in the way that he cared for her.

"Miss Berry can't help but see you ain't payin' no 'tention to Miss Delinda even though I hear tell she's done purt near everything possible to get you off to herself," Alonzo remarked while propping himself near Jason, who was scraping his straight-edged razor across his lean face. Each morning since their return from New Orleans, they spent part of their time together discussing Berry Cortabona and the possibility that she might be reconsidering marriage to Jason. "That's gotta tell her you ain't lettin' no other purty face charm you."

"I hadn't thought about it like that," Jason remarked, lifting the sharp blade from his chin and dipping it in the hot water Alonzo had brought from the kitchen behind the big house.

Little discarded blobs of lather mixed with the black of his beard rose to the surface of the water in the porcelain basin reminding Jason of the flotsam he had observed bobbing in busy ports in Europe and in New Orleans. Damn! but it was good to be home and find contentment. It was also good to be shaving before the handsome walnut washstand that had belonged to his maternal grandfather, to be dipping his shaving brush into the china mug that his father had used during his brief life.

Jason said, "Delinda Delange is mighty pretty but she's not my kind of woman." An image of his kind of woman formed: black hair, eyes like overly ripe blackberries, luscious pink lips, spontaneity in everything she did. Alive. Berry was excitingly alive like a river fed by an invisible source. Never static like a bayou or swamp. "If you want to know what I think, I think Delinda is in love with love and after any bachelor who might be ready to settle down."

"Whoo-ee!" Alonzo's unblemished teeth flashed white as his dark face broke into a smile. "Mr. Alexander Oates better watch out."

"Unless he's ready to get caught." Jason leaned closer to

the beveled mirror to inspect his handiwork. It came to him that he was looking at the reflection of a man ready—no, *eager*—to get caught. He grinned, then rubbed one hand over his smooth chin and, finding no scratchy stubble, laid down his razor and wiped his face on the towel Alonzo handed him. After slapping a handful of spicy lotion on his face, he turned away to finish dressing and left the blithely whistling Alonzo to tidy up the marble top of his washstand.

"You smell even better than the wildflowers," Berry told Jason later that morning when he helped her dismount from her sidesaddle near the edge of Alligator Swamp that bordered the back boundaries of the plantation. She had come to expect and enjoy Jason's habit, when nobody was in sight, of kissing her lightly each time he helped her from her horse. "Have I told you today that I think you're quite wonderful?"

Not waiting that time for Jason to tilt his head toward her, Berry boldly looped her arms around his neck and guided his smiling lips to hers. As she had anticipated, the taste and feel of his warm, firm mouth on hers sped up her heartbeat. Maybe it was because she knew they were unobserved in the remote area, or maybe it was because her heart was revealing more each day that what she felt for him was not a mere infatuation, but she did not step quickly out of Jason's tight embrace as had been her wont.

Instead, she savored the intimate moment. She enjoyed his fervent kiss, breathing in the tantalizing fragrances of freshly shaved man mingling with those of well cared-for leather and horseflesh. Jason always seemed vibrant, splendidly virile, but never more than now when he was holding her close to his barely covered chest. She soaked up the thrills his hands produced as they moved across her back in seductive patterns. His mouth worked wet magic on hers.

Their horses stamped their hooves impatiently then and switched their tails at the insects swarming from the over-head festoons of Spanish moss. Laughing at the intrusions and delighting in being alone and wildly enamored of each other, the couple finally parted and led their horses down to the water. Then, after the animals quenched their thirst, they tethered them in patches of green grass.

Hand in hand, Berry and Jason wandered near the water's edge. Protesting the rare intrusion with startled sounds, birds and small animals flitted and scurried about before finding hiding places. As they sat down on the large exposed roots of a gum tree not far from the water, Berry's questions about what they were seeing and hearing pleasured Jason. His deep-voiced answers pleasured her.

"... So now you can see that a fresh-water swamp is home to many animals and plants," Jason told her when she became quiet and glanced about, out into the unending expanse of tree-dotted water and up into the giant cypresses with their moss-laden limbs and their fat-bottomed trunks. Knobby cypress knees, as slick as if polished by hand, poked up as high as three feet above the dark, shallow water. "Our livestock in the back pastures drink from it. Many of our blacks like to fish and hunt back here, as do Uncle Edouard and his cronies."

"I was glad that you invited Mr. Edouard to ride with us today. Maybe he'll come along some day when he hasn't already made plans to go fishing on the bayou with one of his friends."

"I hope so. He says summertime is for fishing and wintertime is for hunting. I believe he likes you a great deal, Berry. He enjoys talking with you; I can tell from the way he seeks you out when we're at the house. I suspect you make him remember what it was like to be young."

"I like him, too. I can't imagine anybody not enjoying talking with him as much as I do. He knows so much about everything that I told him one day that he could pass for a Renaissance man."

"He told me, and he was beaming."

"I confess that since I hadn't grown up with a man around, I hadn't expected to find I had much in common

with your uncle. I was even a little afraid of him at first.''
She stole a glance at Jason to see if he might be amused. He
was tugging at his left earlobe.

Thinking how easy it was to talk with Jason, how easy it
had been from their first meeting, she continued. ''It's
wonderful that Mr. Edouard doesn't seem to mind that I
grew up in the theater. He seems not to care that I don't
have all the proper credentials for claiming to be a Creole,
or at least the kind of Creole living in Saint Christopher
Parish. When he and I talked privately the other afternoon,
he was so understanding about the way I got mixed up with
Warren Maroney.''

''He's a man who does his own thinking and bears the
consequences of both good and bad decisions. He expects
others to do likewise. I believe he can tell you're also one
who does.''

Berry pursed her lips in thought. ''I guess that does sum
up his attitude. I can tell he thinks about things a lot. When
I went into the library yesterday to find a book, he was
sitting in his chair by the window, so lost in his reading he
didn't even hear me come in the room.''

''He says he can't live long enough to read all the books
he wants to read. When Ulysses went into Calion yesterday
to pick up the mail and the newspapers, he brought back a
box of books Uncle Edouard had asked me to order for him
in New Orleans. I reckon his many interests keep him
young.''

''I was disappointed there was no letter from Sergeant
Dan. I meant to read the paper but—'' For the first time
since her arrival, she had failed to search L'Abeille for news
of Warren Maroney's capture.

''I would have already told you had there been news in it
about Warren Maroney.''

Berry let out a sigh; its cause puzzled her. Was it relief
that she did not have to leave Armand Acres yet? Frustration
that the murderer had not yet been captured? She was
unsure which and had no wish to dwell on either possibility.

"Jason, if people from the plantation like to fish in the swamp, why are there no boats"—when she realized her slip of tongue, she cut her eyes toward him and sent him a sassy smile—"no pirogues tied up here?"

Returning her smile, Jason explained, "Because I brought you to my private place, not the one commonly used for going out into the swamp."

Berry looked around more closely. Drooping limbs of many-branched oaks festooned with Spanish moss formed a deep shade. Fallen moss and castoff leaves from the overhead trees formed a partial covering over the black gumbo soil. What little of the sky showed through the thickly leaved branches seemed no more than a backwash of vibrant blue.

Somehow Berry never had thought of Jason as the kind of person who might wish to escape into solitude, might need, as she sometimes did, to commune with the inner self without intrusions from the outside world. What on earth, she reflected soberly, could he have to mull over and contemplate? She thought about how the loss of his mother last year probably had filled him with grief. Had he, as she had a few times, sometimes felt life had displayed a touch of deviousness by robbing him of his father before he even got to see him? Had he, too, agonized over finding the perfect mate?

Suddenly the desire to know all about Jason, to sit closer and ask questions, then listen to his deep voice giving her answers to fill in the blank spaces almost consumed Berry. Since they had left New Orleans, she had discovered numerous new facets of the man who, without question or logical explanation, had become an integral part of her life. Were there more facets yet to discover? Yes, Berry decided. The man looking at her with warm brown eyes was complex, and suddenly his very complexity evolved into one of his most beguiling qualities.

"Your retreat is lovely," she said. "Do you come here often?"

"Not anymore."

"Why not?"

"You're not expecting me to answer that, are you?"

"Not really."

Jason glanced overhead. "The sun has ducked behind a cloud but I believe it's noon. Are you hungry?"

"Not hungry enough to race back to the house right now. It took us an hour to get here."

"What if I told you I brought along food and a bottle of wine?"

"Jason, that's not one of your better jokes."

He leaned and tapped her nose lightly with his forefinger, then planted a brief kiss on the spot just favored. "Wait here, ye of little faith." He chuckled and with long-legged speed covered the distance to where his horse stood cropping green grass.

Sensing that Berry sat in the deep shade watching his every movement, Jason lifted the bottle of wine from his bulging saddle bags and held it aloft toward her like a trophy recently won. Had he ever felt happier? He would have loved being close enough to see her surprised expression when he reared back and yelled, "Yahoo! Victory!" At the moment he felt as keyed up as when he had led his men into battle against the Mexicans and Indians in Texas and urged them onward with that cry. With the shallow, flat-topped basket that Clementine had packed for him tucked under his arm and a folded blanket thrown over one shoulder, he hurried back to where she waited.

"If I were the suspicious type," Berry said as she watched Jason set everything down, then flip the blanket open and spread it on the ground, "I might suspect you're out to charm a woman and feeling mighty cocky about it. Even that yell sounded like a battle cry."

"Never would I appear so obvious." He faked looking humble. After motioning for her to sit on the blanket, he gathered up the basket and wine and joined her, sitting tailor fashion as she was. He leaned over and began stirring around in the shallow basket.

"And I'm not the suspicious type," she pointed out smugly.

Jason scoffed with good humor, bringing up a corkscrew from the basket. Once he had the cork impaled on the corkscrew and the bottle leaning safely inside the crook of his knee, he asked, "What about the suspicions you had about Viola and me?"

"All right! So I was suspicious *once*." He tossed her a napkin and while she used it to wipe off her hands, he did the same with his own. Sniffing at the tantalizing odors drifting over the damp air, she asked, "What has Clementine fixed for us?"

He checked the contents of the basket and ticked off what he found. "Some choice slices of roasted chicken. And what she calls a crust of bread—which is actually half of a loaf that must have been nearly as long as my arm. Here's a wedge of cheese from the keeping bucket in the well. *Voilà!* We have a *handful*—her word again—of ripe blackberries."

Her mouth watering and her heart overflowing with happiness, Berry watched as during his recital he slipped small plates from the fitted basket, unwrapped white chicken slices and bread, then stacked food on each plate. Next to last came a jar filled with blackberries. Last came two delicate wine glasses.

"Blackberries?" she echoed. Did he remember telling her that first Sunday morning that her eyes were like ripe blackberries and that her name fitted her perfectly? Of course not. That was seven years ago, back when she was not yet thirteen. "How marvelous! I thought you said all of the ripe berries were gone."

"When I asked Clementine if it would be possible for us to have blackberries, Sassafras spoke up. She knew of some bushes growing in partial shade that are still bearing and sent someone to gather them before the dew dried this morning."

Berry watched Jason tender a look toward her that made her wonder if he might not be vulnerable, might not be quite as sure of himself as he would have people believe. Strange, how the thought of such a possibility touched her somewhere deep inside, almost like a finger soothing a wound.

Jason said in a much lower tone, which sounded to Berry more like a love song than mere words, "I didn't let anyone know I wanted blackberries because of my lady love's eyes and her name."

Berry smiled across at the man feeding her soul and going about the business of getting ready to feed her body. When he poured the wine, propped the bottle inside the basket, and handed her a glass, she said, "Jason Premont, you're the most wonderful, thoughtful man I've ever known."

"Maybe you're prejudiced since I'm the only one around now that we've left New Orleans."

She looked down at the wine glass in her hand, hiding her eyes from him, savoring the warmth of the stem that lingered from where he had held it. Prejudiced . . . in his favor? Yes.

Her silence gave Jason time to admire the way the white of her blouse accentuated her tanned, olive complexion even in the deep shade. "I thank you, anyway. Can you think of a toast for this occasion?"

Berry shook her head, not ready to meet his eyes. Inside she had that same wondrous feeling she had experienced when they had made love that rainy evening.

Though at least three feet of blanket separated them and she was not even looking at him, Berry was conscious of Jason's every move, his every breath. He was watching her and smiling; she was sure of it. His dimples were forming shadows in his cheeks. His teeth were showing white, even between the lips she loved to kiss. If she lifted her eyes now to view those familiar sights, he might read within them the maelstrom of emotion sweeping over her and turning her into a woman hungry for love.

"Let's drink to the moment," Jason said in a voice that

he heard as being fuzzy around the edges. Damn! He had yet to take his first sip of wine. Just looking at Berry, her hair a dark cloud about her face and shoulders, her full lips parted slightly, as if poised for a kiss, was enough to stir his passion to fever pitch. More than enough.

"To the moment," Berry replied softly. She lifted her gaze to his and returned his half smile as she lifted her glass to meet his in midair: *Ping!*

For a moment that quivered with roiling, unspoken feelings, the little bell-like sound held Berry and Jason captive. The creatures overhead and out in the swamp might as well have suspended their normal sounds, for outside that single note, the man and woman heard nothing but their inner thoughts. They saw nothing but each other.

Somehow, Berry reflected, it seemed both natural and magical for her eyes to meet Jason's with tenderness over the rim of her crystal glass. In this private hideaway beside the water, they sipped wine and fell ever more deeply in love.

CHAPTER

*

Seventeen

*T*he wine was sweet; neither denied it. One glass. Serendipity reigned. Her skirts rustling, their heartbeats dancing, they inched closer. A second glass. They kissed, as if for the first time. Their kisses were more intoxicating than mere wine. Sweeter, too. Spirits soared. Eyes transported secret messages.

Then with a flourish, Jason laid a plump blackberry in Berry's mouth, sampled one himself and washed it down with wine. A minuscule drop of berry juice lingering on her lips became the most erotic sight he could imagine. Shaken, he leaned to kiss it away, savoring the taste of the tiny globule of tart sweetness, but savoring the taste of *his* Berry more. He fed her another, then greedily kissed away its tasty aftermath, laughing along with her when she freed her mouth and cried, "Enough, enough!" Jason covered her protest with yet another kiss.

Food lost its appeal. They returned it to the basket for sustenance of another, more provocative kind. A kiss here—

She sighed and closed her eyes in ecstasy—a soft nibble there; a button slipped free here—she sent him a look of pure longing—a garment cast aside there, and passion, a gleeful maestro gone mad, directed their symphony of love with abandonment.

Reveling in their daring, their intimacy, they were soon lying on the blanket, naked in each other's arms in the secluded, shadowy space underneath the trees.

"Kiss me there again," Berry whispered when Jason lifted his lips from her bare shoulder and looked into her eyes. Whispering seemed perfect. Anyway, she could not find enough breath to speak aloud. She imagined the thick falls of moss hanging almost to the ground on the outer perimeter might be a curly gray curtain shielding them from the world. She shivered.

Earlier Jason had discarded the hairpins holding her hair back from her face, and now, after propping up on an elbow, he drew strands of her unbound hair to cover the silken shoulder he had kissed, then leaned back to view his handiwork with the air of a painter posing his subject. "Lovely," he said, and smiled.

Smiling herself and joining in the game, Berry raised herself on one elbow and sent Jason a flirtatious look from underneath half-lowered lashes. She tossed her hair back out of the way with a provocative, ages-old gesture and lifted the shoulder to invite a kiss with blatant seductiveness. She felt her breasts ripple, and watched him drink in their sensuous movement with such warmth that she felt as if he had touched her suddenly tightening nipples.

"I love it when you flirt," Jason whispered before he kissed her proffered shoulder once, twice, then kissed the other one for extra measure. Her beauty and her obvious joy in lying with her limbs entwined with his overwhelmed him, almost stole his breath.

Trembling at the demanding passion rising in his loins, he drew her close. The feel of her soft breasts against the planes of his chest stirred the awesome fire threatening to burn out of control between his legs. When one of her taut nipples touched his, a lightning rush of desire consumed him.

It was all as wonderful as she remembered, Berry thought as she molded her tingling body to Jason's. No, it was more wonderful: She felt warm and soft inside, as if her bones had melted. She found herself thinking about how a ripe plum clings to its seed until severed and how even after it becomes two parts, the seed and the segments can be returned for a perfect fit.

Remarkable, Berry mused, that other seeds might come close to filling the hollow, but only one can do it perfectly. Were Jason and she designed by some mysterious force to fit together and make one whole? Sighing, she snuggled closer within his embrace.

It was then, while her nose nestled against Jason's throat and rewarded her with the fragrance of his skin, that Berry's brain accepted what her heart already knew. She was in love! She was wildly and blindly in love with Jason Premont.

She must be in love with him, Berry reasoned. Why else was she lying in his arms again and offering herself to him? There was no other explanation for the flouting of her well-intentioned promise to herself not to surrender to him again. Her love for Jason was real, was splendidly alive and leading her to the inevitable consummation.

Lifting her head enough to see his face, she caressed his lean cheeks with the backs of her fingers, aware that even such a small action filled her with abiding pleasure simply because it was *his* warm skin she touched, *his* eyes beaming brown, gold-flecked adulation from mere inches away. When he leaned his face against her fingers, she turned them over and formed a cup with her hand, a shallow cup that seemed to her to hold something far more precious than a part of a man's face. She knew why. Because it was Jason's face, the most handsome one that she had ever seen, and it belonged to the man she loved. Beyond that, she refused to think with any discernible logic.

Berry dropped a kiss on the bridge of his elegant nose, letting her lips track like a searching, fluttering butterfly down to the tiny indentation leading to the center of his upper lip, then to his mouth, his wonderfully sensuous mouth. She loved feeling the rush of his sweet breath on her skin, loved hearing his erratic breathing, loved opening her mouth anew to his probing tongue and savoring its mating with her own.

Jason's kisses and caresses were inviting her into a glorious symphony as violins in an orchestra sometimes did. A part of her was ready to soar into a burst of rhapsody. The note of music she and Jason had created when their glasses chimed together still resounded in her memory. With breathless anticipation she awaited a segue.

His mouth descended in slow time down the column of her throat—she trembled anew from the tenderness of his warm, moist kisses—across her chest, then he placed his hands as instruments of pleasure on her throbbing breasts. She felt and heard a moan from her throat join in the swelling chorus of sensations.

Her hands stroked lovingly across his smooth back—she sensed he stirred to let her know he loved what her caresses were doing to him—swept down to his narrow waist and flat buttocks—he groaned and pulled her closer against his tumescence.

The staccato drumming of Berry's pulse told her that the segue had come. His caresses and kisses were moving down from her breasts and she could no longer deny the demanding rhythm pounding hotly inside her womanhood. She writhed and flung her hair in wild abandon when he claimed the sensitive inner sides of her thighs. "Oh, Jason. Love me."

"Beautiful lady," he murmured in a velvety bass that seemed a perfect blend to the inner music driving her onward.

Jason moved then to make her his. Opening herself to his searching, pulsating shaft, she gathered him to her swollen breasts with hungry arms, sought his mouth with fevered lips and tongue. It felt so good to have him inside her moist womanhood again, so right, the way they fit together in sweetly throbbing harmony.

He withdrew his manhood almost to its full length and she felt her lips lifting to follow its path before she realized that he was not deserting her. With mastery he was orchestrating the final movement of the primal rhythm she had already felt building within, the movement that would culminate the inner music they were making together.

As Berry joined in his frantic quest for fulfillment, a glorious feeling of oneness with him filled her being. For that small space of time, Jason and she existed only as a part of each other.

For a brief moment Berry imagined that she was soaring along with Jason as an integral part of an elusive symphony created by their joining, heavenly music that would reverberate forever in space. She glimpsed behind her eyelids breathtaking flashes of colors—the purple of passion, the blue of love, the red of life, the fiery white of hope.

When the diapason of their thundering love song came, they hugged each other closer and called out in celebration of all that is precious and beautiful to man and woman joined in love. Sweet silence marked the aftermath. A welcome gentleness soothed the flesh now that feverish ecstasy had fled, easing the lovers into acceptance of the final note of their symphony, a note seeping into the marrow of their bones.

"You're wonderful," Berry whispered through love-swollen lips. She felt used up, deliciously soporific.

"You're even more wonderful," Jason replied in a voice as reverent as hers. When had he ever felt as in harmony with the world, with his beloved, with himself? Glorying in the satiation radiating throughout his being, he cradled her in his arms and drew her head to nestle against his shoulder.

Though it was a trying task to honor his vow not to be the one broaching the subject of marriage again, Jason reaffirmed his resolution and set his mind in other directions. Slowly he recognized there was a world outside the one of passion that Berry and he had just fashioned.

Jason became aware that the ongoing stirrings in the nearby swamp and the trees overhead were once more making themselves heard, that the world had not truly faded while Berry and he made love. A distant woodpecker's song of braggadocio, echoing eerily through the swamp, reached his ears and reminded him that he was feeling quite cocky himself. He was not surprised to hear follow-up echoes of the bird's bill rat-tat-tatting into the bark of a tree in search of hidden insects.

From the water only yards away, Jason heard a singular splash and wondered if a bass had surfaced in chase of a bug, or if a turtle had slipped from a floating log into the shallow depths. The sounds of horses making blubbery snorts and stamping their hooves as they grazed nearby told him that the real world was intruding again.

Berry's responses to his lovemaking, Jason reflected while letting their heartbeats and breathing return to normal, had been even more ecstatic than when they had first made love. He could not imagine a finer moment than when, as one, they had scaled the peak of their passion. His hand stroked her hair in silent adoration, unconsciously moving in rhythm with the ephemeral notes warbled by an unseen dove.

Surely, Jason reasoned, Berry would recognize now, or at least soon, that love, not infatuation, was what nourished her passion. Nothing as ordinary as aroused passion could light the fires burning deep within her eyes when she looked at him during their kisses and caresses—and at other times, as well. He imagined his happiness if her first words had to do with love and marriage. He felt unbelievably masculine, masterful.

Berry, while resting in Jason's embrace, did not welcome the thoughts swarming the edges of her mind and seeking her attention. Now was not the time to think about Jason and whether or not he was the special kind of man that she wanted as a husband, no matter that she now recognized she was madly in love with him.

Marriage, Berry thought as Jason's fingers combed tenderly through her hair and caressed her scalp, was for a lifetime. She had spent too many years dreaming of the perfect husband for her to lose sight of that dream now. She needed distance from Jason, and time. Besides, she who had always found words easy was discovering that in the face of the sobering reality of her love for the man she had always viewed as a rake, she was struck dumb.

Leaving Jason's embrace before his caresses tempted her again, Berry slowly put on her clothing, still mulling over their relationship. After Warren Maroney was captured and she was able to return to New Orleans, she could come to terms with her doubts about Jason's being able to commit himself to a wife.

Berry welcomed a scurrying noise in the trees overhead, welcomed something mundane to think about. She lifted her head and watched two red squirrels racing along a broad limb of an oak tree, their long furry tails waving playfully. "Do you suppose the squirrels enjoyed our little drama?"

From where he stood fastening the last button on his shirt, Jason chuckled. "Perhaps we should have charged admission."

It was unlike Berry, usually so ready with a comment about anything, to remain silent, Jason thought as he readied their horses for the ride back to the house. Somehow, and it smarted like the dickens to admit it, he knew he still had not completely won her heart. He stole a glance at Berry where she was standing near Jewel and stroking the animal's nose. She looked pensive. He no longer felt masterful. Alonzo's words about his less-than-impeccable past record among women came back and taunted him. Was it Berry's trust that he had not won?

Patience was not one of Jason's virtues. He struggled to restrain himself during the remainder of that Saturday and the days following. Undermining his efforts at times came a question born of frustration: What in blazes did Berry Cortabona want from him?

"You wouldn't believe what a marvelous time I had at the party," Delinda confided to Berry on Monday as if they were old friends. "The orchestra was divine!"

Berry, still surprised that Delinda had appeared at her bedroom door soon after breakfast and invited herself in, figured that likely no matter what she replied, the young woman was primed for a monologue. Since Jason had cautioned Berry to stay near the house while he rode the twelve miles into Calion to tend to some business matters, she had no excuse to cut short Delinda's first visit to her room.

Realizing that she actually welcomed something to distract her thoughts, Berry replied with easy friendliness, "I gathered from talk when you and Miss Agnes returned yesterday evening that it was a festive affair. I'm glad you had fun."

"I was in heaven! The entire time we were at Fernwood, Alexander Oates fairly fell at my feet. He's the most divinely handsome man I ever saw. He said he's going to come calling on me while I'm visiting at Armand Acres. I almost swoon at the thought of seeing him again."

Smiling, Berry went to sit on the sofa near her visitor. "You sound as if you might be in love."

"Oh, yes. I'm almost positive I am, and that's why I wanted to talk with you."

"About what?"

"About how a woman knows when she's truly in love and when it might just be something purely"—a becoming blush suffused her fair skin—". . . purely physical."

Having been bombarded nearly all of her nineteen years with what seemed like tons of advice from Aunt Maddy and then Camille, as well as from sundry folk among her friends and acquaintances in the theatrical world, Berry never had pictured herself in the role of counselor. She cleared her throat and sat up straighter. "First, it seems she needs to know how the man feels about her."

"I can tell he's wild over me."

"Did he say so?"

"Well—" Hiding her dark eyes behind a wealth of silky eyelashes, Delinda fidgeted with the ends of the rose-colored ribbons forming a sash around her narrow waist—"he didn't exactly say the words, but when he kissed me while we were strolling in the flower garden, he did say I was more beautiful than the flowers blooming."

Berry strove for an objective tone. "That hardly qualifies as a declaration of love."

"Do you suppose a man ever really says out loud that he loves a woman, especially the one he wants to become his wife and the mother of his children?"

Berry blinked at the question. "I can't imagine why he wouldn't. How else would he ever woo her into marriage?"

"My mama told me about how wealthy Creole planters can't help being fickle and letting pretty new faces turn their heads. She said it was their nature, that some men weren't meant to be tied to one woman. Except legally, so as to protect their legitimate offspring and heirs."

Though Berry sat motionless, her brain was reeling.

"What with their families making all the arrangements, Mama and her friends never had a choice about whom they might marry. I've heard of some parents betrothing a couple before they even learned to talk. Some say that Viola Breton from the neighboring parish was promised as Jason's bride back when she was born."

Plainly spurred on by Berry's wide-eyed expression of interest, Delinda prattled on. "I've overheard Mama and her friends talking about how lots of Creole husbands keep *quadroon* mistresses in those little one-story houses on Rampart Street and stay with them whenever they go to New Orleans. Why, anyone listening could have almost believed they were talking about something as ordinary as the weather or the size of that year's cane crop. I vowed to myself that I would never marry a man who doesn't care more for me than any other woman in the world. I begged Papa to let me choose my own husband when I grew up.''

A feeling of empathy for the beautiful young woman sitting beside her rushed over Berry. No matter that their social rankings stretched miles apart, their goals for marital happiness might well be living next door. ''I hope he gave his permission.''

''He did.'' With a tiny frown wrinkling her otherwise faultless brow, Delinda flipped her unbound hair over her shoulder and gazed out the open window toward the thick-branched trees where chirping wrens and sparrows proclaimed another sunny morning. With a self-derisive shrug, Delinda continued. ''It's downright disgusting, but I'm finding I like nearly all the handsome young men I meet''—Berry was thankful Delinda's troubled gaze wandered outside and that she did not glimpse her amusement—''and that it's terribly hard to tell when a man likes me the way I want him to like me.''

Turning to meet Berry's forthright gaze, Delinda added almost shyly, ''I don't want a marriage based on anything but love. I was hoping that with your considerable experience around men, you could advise me how a woman knows when she meets the right man.''

Berry thought about the inferences she could draw from Delinda's words, then decided she was being oversensitive. Here sat a young woman with troubles akin to her own, likely akin to those of countless women around the world. ''If I knew the answer, I would share it,'' Berry replied. ''It seems to me that each woman has to work out that problem for herself. The only thing I know for certain is that it takes time to discover the difference between infatuation and love.''

Sighing at the raw truth of her last statement, Berry went on. ''Aunt Maddy used to tell me that we ought to be careful when we start searching for something because most people find what they truly search for. Maybe that's true and you'll recognize love when it comes because you have looked for it. In the meantime, just enjoy being alive and pretty enough to attract a host of suitors.''

Rising and reaching out her hand toward Delinda, Berry said, ''Let's go down and ask Clementine to make a fresh pot of coffee. Maybe Miss Agnes will join us for a cup on the back veranda.''

Agnes Delange seemed as uninterested in coffee as she was in food at mealtimes, Berry reflected while the three women sat on the shaded back veranda and sipped their cups of coffee laced with hot milk. Or maybe the fidgety woman was too upset about something to relax against the back of her tall-backed wicker chair and enjoy the sweet concoction.

''Yesterday, Aunt Agnes and I were talking about the pretty bouquets of flowers placed around the house when we returned from Fernwood,'' Delinda said to Berry. ''When she tried to thank Sassafras for taking over her job while she was gone, we were surprised to learn that you had arranged the flowers before you went riding with Jason. I'm sure she has thanked you already.''

Agnes replied in the monotonous manner that Berry categorized as chirping, ''I hadn't given it a thought before now. I reckon as how I do appreciate your help, Berry.''

''Thank you. I enjoyed making the arrangements.'' While Berry stirred more brown crystals of sugar into her coffee and watched each swirl of the tan liquid, her peripheral vision told her that Agnes was sending peevish looks toward Delinda.

''I hope,'' Berry said, looking up then at the housekeeper, ''that you didn't mind my cutting some of the flowers. Mr. Edouard assured me it was all right for me to try my hand at arranging them. He explained that you'd probably be pleased. Jason said his mother used to take care of the flowers and that you never had liked taking on the job.''

''Just because I don't seem to have a knack for such doesn't mean that I shirk my duty of arranging flowers for the house. It's only one of many tasks for a woman in charge of a large household.'' Agnes twitched her long nose and jerked her head sideways.

''You did a marvelous job, Berry,'' Delinda said, seemingly oblivious to her aunt's coldness. ''You said once that you sew for yourself and design ballgowns. Wherever did you learn to do so much, so well? I feel I've accomplished a lot when I get a tapestry made without its being full of knots on both sides.''

Berry explained a little about her life with Aunt Maddy, ending with a self-deprecating shrug. ''But I learned almost nothing about cooking or managing even our small apartment. We had to spend most of our time sewing and caring for the costumes at the theater, so we never bothered about the condition of our quarters. When it came to eating, we made do by buying from the street vendors or stirring up something at the last minute.''

''That sounds like a deplorable way to live, much less bring up a child,'' Agnes remarked.

''Why, Aunt Agnes,'' Delinda scolded good-naturedly, ''that doesn't sound like you at all. Mama has always said that just because a person grows up in a way different from ours doesn't mean it's wrong. I'll bet if Cousin Edouard weren't off visiting some neighbors, he would say the same thing.'' Pretending interest in the contents of her cup, she added, ''And là! If Jason were here . . .''

''Perhaps I did sound more critical than I intended,'' Agnes amended, her tone still unyielding.

''All of us connected with the theater are accustomed to being criticized,'' Berry said, feeling her face heating up from the barbed words that the older woman had aimed her way. The sparrow had sharp claws, she reflected irritably. To hell with trying to tame her by sprinkling salt on her tail feathers. ''We don't mind being thought of as different. We *are* different—and contented to be that way. I, for one, would despise being one of a flock and exactly like every other bird in it.''

"That's one of the things that makes you so fascinating." Delinda gave Berry an especially warm look from over the top of her coffee cup. "I'll bet if Jason were here, he would agree."

"Delinda, you really should go write a letter to your father," Agnes said, after she discovered the coffee pot sitting on a nearby table was empty. "He needs to know that Alexander Oates might be calling on you while you're here at Armand Acres. I don't want him criticizing me for allowing you privileges he might not approve. You can't forget what's expected of a young Creole woman of breeding."

Apparently intent on telling somebody else about Alexander, Delinda bounded from her chair with a rustle of crinolines and hurried inside.

"Your niece is a charming young woman," Berry said. She had been right to suspect that the presence of the men had influenced the housekeeper's previous polite behavior. Now that Jason and Edouard were absent, Miss Agnes seemed openly hostile.

"Delinda can be charming when she chooses to be, like most young women."

"I'm enjoying getting to know her."

"You needn't waste your time trying to get Delinda on your side."

"My side?" Berry searched for a light tone. Her instincts had been right. Miss Agnes did not like her being at Armand Acres. Maybe her earlier suspicions that Agnes had meant for Jason to fall for Delinda were also right. "Is there a battle going on?"

"I think you know that I'm referring to your showing up here with Jason and trying to worm your way into his uncle's affections. I've noticed he takes you away from the house with him so that when friends drop by, he doesn't have to introduce you and maybe cause talk. Cousin Edouard never once has let on to our drop-in visitors that Jason isn't alone while he's away tending to plantation matters."

While sending guarded looks all around, Agnes kept her

unvarying tone low. "I can tell you a few things about Jason. Not only has he always had a taste for wild women, he calls on one living in a houseboat that stays tied up in a finger of the bayou not far away. You might want to ask him about his visits to Corrine."

"Why would I do that when you've already told me?" Berry's soft tone belied her inner turmoil. She fought down the impulse to lash out at the older woman for reminding her of Jason's past affairs. She needed no reminders. Because she agreed with Jason that the fewer people who knew of her presence at Armand Acres, the better, Berry could offer Agnes no explanation for Edouard's silence around callers.

Agnes sniffed. "I can promise you that when Jason decides to marry, it will be to one of the Creoles from one of the planter families. He'll be as particular about choosing the woman to bear his heir as he is about the horseflesh he breeds here on the plantation."

Summoning a haughty demeanor, Berry lifted her chin and watched a bumblebee drill into a cypress plank overhead. If she had a saltcellar at hand, she reflected with blind fury, she would not remove grains and sprinkle them anywhere near the attacking sparrow. She would throw the whole damned container at the infuriating Agnes Delange!

Suddenly Berry was able to view the situation with wry humor—would Miss Agnes croak like a raven if she knew that it was Berry who was saying "no" to marriage to the heir of Armand Acres?

Agnes Delange chirped on, apparently deaf to all but her own words. "I've heard Cousin Edouard telling Jason that it's past time for him to settle down and produce an heir for Armand Acres. You need not expect it will be one of your kind he'll choose to wed, no matter that you seem to have both those men hoodwinked. Under poor management, this place wouldn't please either man very long."

The sound of heavy footsteps coming from within the

house ended Miss Agnes's diatribe abruptly. Looking ruffled, she sprang to her feet.

Berry considered Miss Agnes's last statement, wondering if it might not contain the nexus of the woman's discontent. Was fear of losing her home and position as housekeeper if Jason married someone outside the social circle of planters what drove Miss Agnes to treat her with disdain? Even if someday she were to agree to marry Jason, Berry knew that she possessed neither the bent nor the desire to take over the woman's awesome job.

"Well, Cousin Edouard," Agnes said when a tall form appeared in the doorway, "you're already back from visiting the Langleys. I hope you found their children over their bouts of whooping cough."

Edouard nodded absent-mindedly to both women and reported the news learned on his morning's outing. "Yes, the worst seems over. The children gobbled up the gingerbread men that you sent and asked me to thank you. The report was that everyone at the Langley plantation is well now. Of course," he went on in a concerned tone, "that might not last long; the little slave children were exposed while playing with the Langley brood. I just hope our own don't catch it.

"Clementine gave Jason and me a scare yesterday when she said her youngest grandchild had coughed a lot during the night. We were relieved to learn this morning he'd slept last night undisturbed. Jason said he would stop by Doc Herbert's while he's in town and ask if he has something new to stop the whooping cough before it spreads all over the parish."

Berry nodded sympathetically, dismissing the veiled dressing down from Agnes. The woman's mistaken assumptions about the relationship between Jason and her seemed more pathetic than anything else. Now that she was thinking about it dispassionately, she judged Agnes Delange was pathetic herself.

It was easy for Berry to recall having had the whooping

cough and almost losing her breath during painful spasms while Aunt Maddy bathed her face and neck with a cool cloth. She had never before considered that the humane owners of slaves—like Jason and Mr. Edouard—might feel responsible for their well being and tend their needs as if they might be family. In a way, she mused with new insight, the slaves at Armand Acres were a part of the family.

"I don't have time to visit right now with you ladies," Edouard said, apologetically. "I promised Jason I would check over some figures of his before he got back from Calion."

Agnes took a step toward the kitchen out back. "It's time for me to see how Clementine is getting on with that roasting hen she was trussing up when I was last in the kitchen. Cousin Edouard, I'll send somebody to the library with a nice cool drink of water. I have a million things to see about before noon."

"Is there anything that I can do to help?" Berry asked, directing her question to Miss Agnes. The woman's thin face did look harried.

"Yes," Edouard replied in her stead before he disappeared inside the shadowed mansion. "I'd count it a big favor if you would fix some more bouquets and put one on the dining table. Cousin Agnes can use the help and I like seeing things around here looking pretty."

CHAPTER

*

Eighteen

That afternoon, while Jason and Edouard conferred about business in the library and Delinda retreated to her bedroom to attend to what she called her "shamefully neglected correspondence," Berry wandered around the spacious back grounds. The three frisky hounds frolicked at her heels. Never having paid particular attention to one of the small buildings set off to one side, she decided to take a look at it.

"I beg your pardon," Berry said when she stuck her head inside the open door and saw Agnes ensconced on a tall stool before an intriguing series of wooden beams and bars crisscrossed by numerous natural-colored threads. "I didn't mean to intrude. I was curious and the door was open."

"Come in," Agnes invited, ceasing her foot movements against long wooden pedals and turning to peer through the cool interior toward her visitor. A breeze wafted through tall windows with their jalousies opened back.

Agnes waved the nosy dogs away with a friendly "Scoot!" and watched as they trotted outside. "You've found me trying to catch up on some weaving. Tessie usually operates the loom but she's feeling poorly today and I sent her to the quarters to rest. Most of the slaves who normally work here are helping in the garden this afternoon."

Noting that the dogs were already flopping down to rest in the shade of a nearby stand of crepe myrtles, Berry wished she had kept quiet and backed outside. She had no desire to push herself in where she was not wanted. She doubted Miss Agnes had changed her mind one bit since insinuating that morning that Berry was cut from cloth unsuitable for fashioning into an acceptable wife for a Creole planter in Saint Christopher Parish.

"I'll come another time and look around when you're not busy," Berry said. Then she noticed that the small building apparently served as a center for crafting. That those living on plantations might manufacture many of the goods needed by its occupants never had occurred to her. She saw that, along with the fireplace they flanked, wide storage shelves holding a wide assortment of supplies and finished goods filled one entire wall.

She gathered up her white skirts, preparatory to stepping back down the few steps and leaving, but something held her in place. "This room intrigues me. I've never seen a loom before."

Agnes, her head cocked to one side, birdlike, pursed her thin lips and for a moment seemed lost in thought. "I'm surprised. I should think that anyone as interested in sewing and designing as you apparently are would know all about how fabric is made." As if warring within herself and winning a dubious victory, Agnes said, "Come over and take a closer look. I'm not any better at weaving than I am at arranging flowers. Jason's mother always performed such chores as if they were pleasure."

At the unexpected note of acceptance embroidering the housekeeper's usual monotone, Berry walked toward the loom that dominated one side of the workroom. She saw a spinning wheel sitting near the brick hearth and spools of thread lying in a rectangular basket beside it.

A round basket, wrought more finely of small reeds, rested on an armless rocking chair, holding scissors, folded garments or fabric, plus needles and pins stuck in a small red strawberry-shaped cushion. Berry smiled in appreciation when she noted that someone, apparently a long time ago, judging by the faded green taffeta, had stitched a couple of gracefully formed leaves at the top of the pincushion and turned an item of utility into a work of art.

What Berry judged to be candle molds hung from one of the several exposed ceiling beams; several devices propped against a wall defied definition. Could they be hoops and frames for holding quilts and large pieces of needlework, like tablecloths and coverlets for beds? Her hands itched and her imagination soared with the possibilities offered to anyone fortunate enough to spend time in such a place.

A worktable over in one corner held a partially woven basket that Berry guessed would end up big enough to hold vegetables from the garden planted near the slave quarters. A quick peek underneath the table showed her a bucket of water holding thin, coiled strips of wood, no doubt soaking so as to retain pliancy until someone came to resume making the basket. As a child she had sometimes knelt near a group of Indian women sitting cross-legged on the ground near the French Market. In between sales of the baskets brought with them, the Indians wove new ones while the entranced Berry watched their nimble fingers at work.

When Berry examined the loom, she found that it consisted of a series of wooden beams and bars fixed in a waist-high horizontal frame that held a host of threads running parallel with the frame's considerable length of nearly six feet. Two sets of natural-colored woolen threads were strung in place, their span measuring about four feet across. The section of fabric already woven lay rolled atop the frame facing toward where Miss Agnes sat on the stool.

Berry bent over, observing then how the weaving was taking place, how one set of suspended threads became meshed with the other and formed a design. "This is fascinating."

"See?" Agnes asked, pointing as she explained. Berry leaned closer, her face and eyes revealing her excitement at learning something new. "The spaces between the two sets of raised threads, called the warp, allow me room to run the shuttle"—Agnes held up with one hand the small, elongated block of worn wood that had thread coming from each end—"holding the cross threads, called the weft, through them."

When Berry nodded her understanding, Agnes sent the shuttle from right to left between the sets of taut threads, demonstrating how the weft strung out from the shuttle. Then she looped the shuttle over the farthest warp and brought the wooden device back between the raised sets of threads. Afterward she worked the foot pedals, which swung the batten—"the name of the board used to reinforce the weaving," Agnes explained—against the weft, pushing the two threads she had added tighter against the previously woven section of cloth with a solid, thwacking sound.

Agnes made several more runs with the shuttle and batten, her darting gaze revealing her awareness of Berry's eyes following every movement of her hands and feet and of the loom. "Would you like to try your hand at weaving?"

At first Berry meant to decline and leave the woman who obviously had little use for her and continue her exploring. The challenge to her creativity of adding warp and weft to the woolen fabric on the loom overruled her reluctance to stay. She wanted to know more about weaving.

Berry found herself wondering how the spools of thread were attached to the loom. Was the spinning wheel near the fireplace still used to turn wool and cotton into thread? Would it be possible to rearrange the spools of thread sitting atop the loom, insert some with colored thread, and create designs? Where could dyes be obtained?

With a catch in her breath and more fondness for the little sparrow-like woman than she would have thought possible, Berry looked directly at Agnes. Unknowingly she sprinkled salt on the birdlike woman's formidable tail feathers when she replied, "Yes, thank you. You're most kind. If you have time to show me, I would love giving it a try."

That evening, after a spirited game of dominoes with Agnes, Delinda, and Edouard, Jason turned to Berry and said, "I feel like stretching my legs. How would you like to take a stroll with me down to the bayou?"

Mindful that it was the first day since her arrival the past week that they had spent almost no private time together, Berry replied, "I'd like that."

At Jason's invitation and Berry's quick acceptance, Agnes shot them measuring looks. Delinda and Edouard merely smiled at the couple and reminded Agnes that it was her turn to shuffle the dominoes for the next game.

By the time Berry and Jason neared the pergola with its foreign looking onion top, they were holding hands under cover of partial darkness provided by the giant oaks. An occasional firefly flashed pulses of light against the luxurious falls of Spanish moss. Some birds had yet to settle on roosting places for the coming night and flitted restlessly overhead.

"You look so beautiful in your white gown with its sassy red ribbons," Jason said, leaning his head toward her and smiling in the light of the moon rising down the bayou. "What if I took you inside the pergola and kissed you?"

"If you don't, I might scream."

Hurrying then and laughing under their breaths, they dashed inside the small open-sided building. In the shadows formed by the lush bougainvillea climbing the supporting colonnades of the pergola, they kissed tenderly. Not once while Jason's mouth claimed hers did Berry think about Miss Agnes's suggestion that morning that she was not the right kind of woman to become his wife and the mother of his children.

Instead Berry banished thought to delight in the devastating thumps of her heartbeat, in his mouth that tasted even sweeter than she remembered. Her knees were turning into a substance no thicker than the bluish liquid she had seen left in the churn that morning after Sassafras had scooped out the yellow dots of butter floating on top. Whey. Her knees were turning into whey.

Jason led Berry to the slatted bench running around the inside of the eight-sided structure. As she sat next to him, her head resting on his shoulder, he said, "I missed being with you today and I wished I could have taken you into Calion with me. Were you bored?"

"Not for a minute." When he tipped up her chin with his forefinger and scowled in mock pique, she added with her characteristic candor, "Not that I didn't miss you, too, but I had a wonderful time this morning getting to know Delinda. She's not a bad sort. This afternoon, while I was exploring out back with Kate, Pete and Re-Pete, I discovered the craft house." She lifted her head and looked at him quizzically. "Wonder why the rascals didn't come walking with us?"

"Uncle Edouard keeps the dogs inside with him after dark. He says they're liable to wander too far at night and maybe get into trouble. One of his dogs was shot one night a long time ago after it chased a possum into a neighbor's chicken house and scattered chickens to kingdom come. Possums sometimes suck eggs and nobody wants his dog to learn that bad habit, so I guess it makes sense to keep them inside at night."

Her curiosity satisfied, Berry settled her head back against Jason's shoulder. It still amazed her that her body seemed to fit his from almost any angle. At the moment she felt like an over-ripe plum ready to burst from its skin. "Miss Agnes taught me how to weave this afternoon."

"I gathered as much from the talk at the supper table. She must be catching on that you're a most remarkable young woman."

When Jason looked down at her, Berry gazed into his eyes and decided that he had entertained enough serious matters for one day. She would not heap her little run-in with Miss Agnes on top of all that must have already wearied him. Besides, the woman had seemed downright friendly out in the work house, then again at supper. Maybe Agnes, as Delinda apparently was doing, was beginning to accept her for whatever she was.

Bullfrogs be-deeped out in Bayou Selene, and Berry heard full-throated answers from others up and down the stream. She had come to like hearing the persistent songs from frogs, insects and birds that began at dusk each evening. "It's so peaceful here," she said. "I was pleased today when Mr. Edouard asked me to make some more flower arrangements. Clementine's son was weeding in the rose garden and he seemed happy to teach me the names of some of the flowers. Their colors and shapes gave me so many new ideas for trimming ballgowns. I sketched a while before supper."

Jason rejoiced during her small recital. "Good. I'm glad you had a pleasant day." Was she finding a niche for herself at Armand Acres?

Perhaps, Jason reflected, he should leave Berry on her own more and allow her to explore by herself, get the feel of the place. His desire to be with her, more than concern for her safety, might have prompted him to keep her by his side too much during her waking hours. He did not expect even a known killer like Warren Maroney to approach her while she was at the plantation with family and slaves within hearing distance. "Cousin Agnes must be tickled silly to get the chore of keeping flowers in the receiving rooms off her hands. Mother was good at such things but she seems to have no knack for them."

"She told me she's not good at it but she never let on she liked my doing it."

"That's Cousin Agnes's way. She lacks your gift for warmth but underneath her brittleness, she's a very caring person."

"She said I can work at the loom any time I wish. Apparently Lettie is losing her sight and sometimes makes bobbles. Miss Agnes hasn't found time to start training another weaver. I'll like finishing that lap throw for Mr. Edouard's Christmas gift and I'm trying to figure out how I can make a design in one for . . ."—she jerked her gaze from his; now he would guess she was longing to make it for him—"for someone else."

Suddenly Berry realized how absurd her thoughts of that afternoon were. Why, she would be back in New Orleans long before such an undertaking could be completed. The newspaper that Jason had brought from Calion was two days old and contained no news about Warren Maroney, but any day now . . .

Jason's smile, complete with dimples, touched Berry's heart. As he bent to kiss her again, she wondered why he seemed so eager to have everyone at Armand Acres like her; he knew as well as she that she would be leaving soon. Then her heartbeat began to speed, and she could think of nothing but the way his slow kisses were turning her into a bowl of warm jelly. Plum jelly.

"What's that noise?" Berry asked, startled. She could go for hours on end and not think about Warren Maroney and his threats to find her and get even. Then suddenly fear would rise again. The thought of the murderer stepping foot on Armand Acres terrified her more each time she remembered why she was there. Had she been wrong to leave New Orleans and perhaps put even more innocent people in danger?

When Berry looked toward the bayou, she found that the tall oleander and gardenia bushes partially obstructed her view. The bullfrogs no longer bellowed. The tree frog that had commenced to sing was quiet, too. If only she had her dagger . . .

Jason cocked his head to listen and scolded himself for having become a bit careless since their arrival last week. After Berry asked him to return the emerald ring to her that first night and told him she would hide it among her clothing in her bedroom, he had tried not to think too heavily about the reason she had consented to visit. His almost constant thought since leaving New Orleans had to do with how much he wanted Berry to come to love his family, his home and his mode of living.

"Don't you hear something unusual?" Berry whispered.

Aware that Berry had stiffened in his arms and that the closest weapon lay in the *garçonniere* across the driveway, Jason listened with new intensity. With relief he replied, "It's only somebody paddling on the bayou."

From where he sat close to Berry in the pergola looking toward the moonlit water, Jason could make out two figures across the bayou dipping paddles from side to side of a pirogue at a leisurely pace. The water magnified the sounds of the paddles when they occasionally bumped the wooden sides of the vessel. He kept his voice low and gestured toward the water. "See? Two fishermen are trying their luck in the moonlight. They're probably after frogs or else setting out trot lines for catfish. From what I've learned about Maroney, I would expect him to arrive by packet rather than by pirogue."

Reassured, Berry nodded. "I heard the captain say he would check any strangers buying passage. He promised not to let anybody off here until you put out a signal flag letting him know the police have recaptured Maroney."

"True. It's unlikely that Maroney will ever learn you're here. I doubt any of the theater people at Camille's wedding would have suspected that you came home with me, even if they happened to remember my name from our brief meeting afterward. Try not to worry."

Looking out at the figures on the water for herself and

deciding neither appeared thick enough to be Warren as she remembered him, Berry shuddered and clung to Jason. At first the urging from Jason and Sergeant Dan for her to disappear for a while had seemed prudent. Now that Camille and Ace were safely away, the thought that Jason and all at Armand Acres might need protection, too, nipped at her earlier sense of peacefulness.

Berry waved away an annoying mosquito and sighed. "I can't help worrying. I'll be glad when we hear Warren has been caught and sent back to prison. Maybe I ought to return to New Orleans and ask Sergeant Dan and his men to stay close while I call attention to myself in the Quarter. I could draw Warren out from his hiding place. I'm beginning to feel it was selfish of me to come here and create danger—"

Jason crushed further words with another passionate kiss.

"Berry," Delinda called as she entered Berry's bedroom the next afternoon, fanning herself briskly with a palmetto fan. Excitement quickened the pace of her usual drawl and brought extra sparkle to her brown eyes. "I'm so glad you're back from the work room and that boring weaving. I would've died if I'd had to walk all the way out there in this godawful heat."

"I find weaving fascinating, not boring," Berry corrected with benign tolerance. "There's nearly always a breeze blowing out there."

"Well, whatever." Not waiting for Berry to invite her to sit on the sofa near the fireplace, its opening covered for the warm season with a tapestry hanging within a mahogany frame, Delinda lifted her skirts a bit and plopped down with none of the grace saved for audiences of opposite gender. Her fanning slowed. "You'll never guess what was in the mail when Alonzo fetched it from Calion a while ago."

Berry's welcoming smile became fixed at the thought that word might have come from Sergeant Dan. "Was there anything for me?"

"Yes, I almost forgot." Delinda laid her fan down and, after pulling a letter from the pocket of her skirt, handed the envelope to Berry. "I'll wait while you read it. Please hurry or I'll burst from my news."

Sending the self-centered young woman a vague smile, Berry settled on the opposite end of the sofa. The envelope bore her name in care of Jason Premont at Armand Acres. Word had come from Sergeant Dan! Who besides Camille and Ace and the sergeant knew her whereabouts?

While Delinda resumed her fanning, Berry read surprising news from, of all people, Henry Zimpel. He had urgent need of her services as wardrobe mistress, she read with disbelief. Would she please contact him as soon as she returned to the city? For a moment all she could think about was her disappointment that the message had not been the one she awaited from Sergeant Dan Harrigan.

"I do hope you haven't received bad news," Delinda said after Berry continued to sit and stare at her letter.

"No. On the contrary, it's quite good." Was it? Berry wondered as she slipped the letter into her pocket and tried to assume a calm air. For one thing, she couldn't imagine how the manager of the Théâtre d'Orléans had found out where she was. Why would he offer her the position he had refused to discuss with her only weeks earlier? Though Leonidas Latrobe had been among the few present for the wedding of Camille and Ace Zachary, he had done little more than exchange brief greetings with Berry and Jason afterward. In fact, he had appeared downright hostile.

If Leonidas had had a change of heart about his promise to intervene with Henry, Berry reflected, he certainly had given no indication that morning after the ceremony. She recalled his cold demeanor and she wondered that she had ever considered him a friend. She could not imagine that Leonidas had asked Henry to write her, even had he known her location. She folded the letter away and said, "Tell me your news, Delinda."

"An invitation came from Mrs. Bergerone for all of us at

Armand Acres to come for a supper party tonight. While Cousin Agnes and I were at Fernwood, she was ever so lovely to us. She and my mama were schoolmates, and she said she was going to make sure I meet everyone in Calion during my visit. Now that she's a widow, she owns the big general store with her son. Là! She knows everybody who is anybody, on the plantations and in the parish seat as well."

"And you're hoping Alexander Oates will be there." Berry sent the pretty young woman a teasing smile.

"Well, goodness gracious," Delinda said with a becoming blush, "I'm not going to deny it." Her lips formed a little-girl pout. "I do wish Jason wouldn't be so mean and insist on keeping you to himself. I told him I was dying to have you meet everyone, but he said he wasn't taking you anywhere anytime soon and that if he wanted the world to know you were here visiting *he* would be the one telling it. Whatever is wrong with that man to be acting so high and mighty?"

Obviously unaffected by Berry's silence, Delinda continued. "Why, you two aren't even engaged"—she shot a measuring look at Berry then, plainly hoping to gain information from her last words; Berry's expression remained composed—"or if you are, nobody seems to know it. The man acts as if he owns you. Pinch me if I'm wrong, but I think there's something mighty powerful going on between you two."

Berry smiled and smoothed the skirt of her blue dimity gown, amused at the young woman's dramatics and her attempts to discover the nature of the relationship between Jason and her. Delinda might be surprised if she knew that Berry was struggling with the same problem. "I've no inkling to pinch you, but you must realize that things aren't always as they appear."

"Don't you even mind that you haven't set foot off this plantation since you arrived last week? How can you stand it, being cooped up and not ever seeing anybody but the same folks all the time? You're always with him when somebody happens to drop by. Not that you've missed much, what with nearly all the callers being the ages of Cousin Agnes and Cousin Edouard. If you hadn't come and broken the monotony, I'd already be bored out of my mind! I'm mortified when I recall I wasn't very nice to you at first."

"Come now, Delinda. Don't be so melodramatic." Berry's tone was light, playful. "One week plus a few days is not a lifetime. I haven't yet seen all there is to see around here. You forget that this is my first visit to swamp country and that everything is new to me."

"I reckon you're right." Delinda wrinkled her nose in annoyance. "Even so, having Jason keep me company couldn't stop me from wanting to go to parties and dances and see what other folks are doing. Since Cousin Edouard says he won't be going to the supper party, either, Ulysses will be driving Aunt Agnes and me in the carriage before dark. We'll be spending the night. I'll just swoon on the spot if Alexander isn't at that supper tonight!"

Letting out a sigh and bringing her fan to rest against her bosom, Delinda went on in her non-stop, breathless manner. "I like you ever so much. I just know everybody else will, too, if Jason ever gives his approval for you to meet people."

Berry said, "I like you, too, and maybe before I leave, I'll get a chance to meet some more of the people in Saint Christopher Parish. It makes me feel good that you want me to meet your friends." It did, though Berry never before had given serious thought to the ticklish matter of how Jason's friends and social acquaintances might receive her. She had had no reason to, not when she had refused to admit until a few days ago that she was in love with him.

"None of my other friends is half as beautiful or talented," Delinda declared. "None of the women from around here that I know has ever been up East or knows one thing about what goes on behind a stage. All any of us has ever done is go off to school for a few years, then pine away on some moldy old plantation yearning to see and do half the things you've already seen and done. Life is just too terribly cruel!''

When Berry made no comment, merely looked comtemplative, Delinda continued in a more enthusiastic vein. ''Of course, we know that getting married will be the highlight of our lives. You don't seem to be giving marriage much thought. At least it doesn't pop up in your every conversation.''

''None of us can choose the way he or she is brought up, Delinda. Who's to say one way is better or worse than another? It seems to me that you've had a lovely, privileged childhood. As for marriage—like most young women, I've given it thought. I have a special kind of man in mind as husband.''

''And I'm betting you find him—if you haven't already.'' She smiled across at Berry, who was having a bothersome time pretending that Delinda's insinuation had not flustered her. ''Even Aunt Agnes has changed her mind about you. She's been telling the house slaves and me about how quickly you learned to weave and how you're making yourself useful about the place shows you're not a lot different from responsible young women growing up around here.''

Delinda toyed with the ribbon binding the curved edges of her palmetto fan, a contemplative look on her face. ''I think Aunt Agnes is disappointed in me for not knowing much about how to do anything useful. Alexander Oates might see me as the kind of wife he can't do without if I had some of your skills. Maybe if I started coming out to the work house with you, you could teach me how to do something more than make tapestry.''

''I'd enjoy that. I wouldn't worry, though. You undoubtedly have knowledge that I don't have, such as how to manage a big household and look after slaves. I can't imagine any young man thinking much beyond what his heart tells him when he courts someone as pretty as you.''

Apparently gaining little solace from Berry's reassurance,

Delinda said, "It might take weeks. Do you reckon you might stay on for the rest of the summer so you can help me?"

Berry laughed. Delinda's near-sighted view of the world was almost unbelievable. "Let's take each day as it comes."

After Delinda promised to relate all that happened upon her return the next day and left to get dressed for the evening in Calion, Berry pondered the young woman's statements. If she *were* to marry Jason and come to live at Armand Acres, would her different upbringing be an asset as Delinda had said? The budding friendship between Delinda and her was a sign that it might be. Counting as another was the growing approval from Miss Agnes.

"Should we leave Mr. Edouard alone?" Berry asked before taking Jason's proffered arm and strolling with him down the drive toward the bayou. "He seemed all right during supper but I've not seen him forego games afterward."

"Sure," Jason replied. "He wouldn't have insisted we take a walk in the moonlight if he had wanted company."

"I don't know," Berry countered with a smile. "Your uncle makes no secret of the fact that he's trying to do a little matchmaking."

"So you've noticed?" Jason laughed and gentled her head to rest against his arm for a moment. "I hope his influence is making inroads against your stubbornness."

Berry lifted her head, unable to respond to his teasing. How could Jason think stubbornness had anything to do with her deciding whether or not to marry him? It was the most difficult decision she had ever faced.

Stealing a sideways look at Jason, Berry conceded there was a minute possibility that he was right. Maybe it was stubbornness that kept her from telling him that she recognized now that she was in love with him. But what prevented her from telling him she worried that his declarations of love would prove to be empty words from a man accustomed to flitting from one woman to another? No, she was not stubborn; she was afraid. If the man she had fallen in love with was really a handsome rake, she needed to construct some kind of self-defense. In time, she would.

Deciding that Berry was in no mood for bantering about their future together, Jason returned to a safer topic. "I asked Alonzo to take Uncle Edouard water for a bath and help him get ready for bed. Actually, I think he might welcome the chance to go to bed early, since Cousin Agnes and Delinda are away for the evening. One of his cronies is paddling down the bayou at daybreak to fish with him."

Berry was concentrating on how much she liked looping her hand through Jason's politely bent arm, liked hearing their footsteps falling softly on the hard-packed earth. She sneaked glances at his handsome profile, drank in the sound of his resonant voice as he talked about his day. Sweet summer fragrances of honeysuckle, gardenias, and greening plants hitched rides on the moist evening breeze and rewarded her nose.

"How would you like me to paddle you up the bayou for a bit?" Jason asked when they neared the end of the driveway. Berry, usually bubbling with life, either positive or negative, seemed reserved that evening. Perhaps the letter from Henry Zimpel that she had told him about had upset her more than she had indicated. He hated thinking that now with a position assured at the Théâtre d'Orléans, she might be looking forward more eagerly to returning to New Orleans and its gaiety. "The trees growing in the edges of the water take on a ghostly appeal in the moonlight. Sometimes you can see big fish surfacing."

"I'd love to go out in a pirogue with you."

He took her hand in his and gestured with his head toward the small house where he stayed. "You'll have to come with me to the *garçonniere* while I change into something more suitable for paddling." He glanced down at his filmy cravat, brocaded waistcoat, and tight cotton trousers.

"No, I'd better not." Freeing her hand, she looked in the opposite direction toward the pergola where they had sat the previous evening. Her pulse was speeding up at the mere thought of being alone with him in his quarters. "You go ahead. I'll wait for you in the pergola."

"You don't trust me."

"I didn't say that." Berry started toward the pergola. Jason Premont was not the person she distrusted.

Still walking alongside her, Jason remarked, "You could wait on the gallery running around the *garçonniere*. I wouldn't want you to be afraid out here. We can walk back to the house and get Alonzo to come keep you company while I change clothing."

"No. You said he was attending your uncle. There's no need for anyone to be with me every minute." When they reached the pergola, Berry sat on the bench and leaned back, her head resting against one of the colonnades. "I like it here. I was being silly last night to let those fishermen frighten me." She almost confessed that since last evening's scare, she had begun wearing her knife holster again. "Besides, you won't be far away."

"True." He leaned over to give her a kiss, but she turned her head, directing the kiss to her cheek.

Displeased but unwilling to make an issue out of her deflecting his kiss, Jason took a few steps, then turned back. Sometimes, as now, he longed to shake her and make her tell him what was on her mind. She was not even looking at him. "Are you sure you prefer to wait here?"

"The sooner you leave, the sooner you'll get back."

"Right. I won't be long." With that Jason hurried toward the *garçonniere* some hundred yards away, his mind whirling with questions. What was bothering Berry, making her so aloof? Had the signs he had read during the past few days been dead wrong? The arrival today of Zimpel's letter must have upset her. Jason had been upset by the thought of her leaving. What if some handsome fellow won her away from him upon her return to New Orleans? Jason hated admitting it, but he did not deal well with jealousy.

Berry, leaning against one of the colonnades, had her eyes

closed, lost in thought. She was having some success in cooling her ardor for Jason when a footstep close by startled her. Her ardor died instantaneously when she opened her eyes. Swiftly a man sat down beside her on the bench, slapped a hand over her mouth, and jerked her close. The face only inches away belonged to Warren Maroney.

CHAPTER

*

Nineteen

"*A*re you surprised to see me, Berry Cortabona?" Warren Maroney whispered. His eerie tone increased the icy gooseflesh prickling on Berry's scalp and spine. "Where's my emerald?"

With her eyes wide and fixed on Warren's scowling face, so near her own that she smelled his whiskeyed breath, Berry watched him peer searchingly toward her hands. Her arms lay imprisoned within his cruel grasp. The painful pressure of his palm over her mouth pinned the back of her head against the colonnade. She should not have been deaf to all but her agonizing over her love for Jason. Jason! Had he been gone long enough to make it safely to the *garçonniere*?

Suddenly memories of her premonition that night after the ballet that evil stalked Jason rushed to Berry's mind. New panic seized her. A roiling at the pit of her stomach threatened to destroy her will to collect her senses.

Berry struggled, succeeding only in kicking empty space for a moment before Warren's leg clamped heavily over her lap. The leg holster holding her dagger above her knee pressed into her flesh, reminding her of her helplessness. A pleading sound reverberated back in her throat.

"Do you have my ring?"

Berry tried to shake her head "no."

Bringing up a long-bladed knife in front of her eyes, he said, "If you don't want my friends over on the bank to take care of your lover boy, you'll talk over our little problem with me. One sly word or move and I'll give them orders to stop him from butting in . . . forever. I'd like keeping this quarrel between us, wouldn't you?"

Berry moaned back in her throat, signaling "yes." A part of her rejoiced. Jason had not been harmed . . . yet.

"When I take my hand away, girl, I'll replace it with this sweet sticker"—he angled his knife threateningly—"if you don't come up with right answers. It's up to you whether you and your lover boy live or die."

Weird, Berry was thinking in her effort to hang on to sanity, how the bullfrogs had commenced bellowing and how the bass notes seemed especially doleful. Had she not been so wrapped up in her private musings, she likely would have noticed that when Jason and she entered the pergola, none of the usual sounds were coming from the bayou. How many men hid across the road among the trees and bushes awaiting orders from Warren? Gooseflesh was now a permanent part of her skin.

"Now," Warren commanded in the same low voice that he had used since first stealing close and seizing her, "where's my emerald? I've learned that slimy Ebon Stringer left it to you when he died of the fever last year."

Warren's hand eased from her mouth but his fingers hovered near her neck. Trying to conceal her fear and her repugnance, Berry had to clear her throat twice before words slipped out. "The ring is in my bedroom in the main house."

"I can see light coming from up there. People must still be awake."

His breath, sour with whiskey, washed across her face with each word. She said, "Yes."

"And I suppose there's a passel of blacks up there, too."

"Yes."

"I aim to have that ring, girl, because it's mine by rights. I can sell it down in Mexico and live damned fine out in Texas."

"I'll give it to you. I never wanted it. Honest. I'll get it for you as soon as everyone goes to bed."

"This here's a fancy place. I been hiding out across the bayou for a few days. I'd about given up on catching sight of you till last night when you and your lover boy came sashaying down the drive. Wouldn't it be a damned shame if you was to lie to me, maybe cross me up and I had to get my friends to help me burn the house down?"

"I won't cross you. The minute I think everyone is asleep, I can fetch the ring."

"Here to this fancy shed."

"Yes."

"You'll not be blabbing about me being here to anyone."

"Not to anyone. This is between you and me."

"I need more than the ring. I need a saddled horse."

"Did you come from New Orleans on horseback?"

"No. I rode on the same packet as you and your high-and-mighty planter friend, Jason Premont."

"But—?"

"You want to know how and when, don't you?" Warren giggled, a maniacal sound. "After Leonidas told me where you likely had gone, another friend told me about an orchestra coming up to play for a dance in this parish."

When the plainly shocked Berry sucked in a breath, he went on, a braggart with a guaranteed audience. "Even a captain aiming to do what Premont paid him for can't do much more than ask a few dumb questions of a band of hired musicians. He wasn't about to refuse the roundtrip fares from so many passengers. The captain was right pleased when I asked him to name and point out the mansions we passed. Can you think of a reason he'd bother counting heads when the musicians rode with him back down the bayou?''

"You're very clever." Leonidas Latrobe, conceited ass! Traitor! Aunt Maddy had warned her about Leo. Camille had, too. Her mind was whirling. One question demanded utterance. "Why would Leonidas tell you anything about me?''

Warren's low snigger made his broad shoulders jerk. "The way he told it after he learned I was asking about you, it was because you made a fool out of him in front of his friends at a masquerade by running off with that Premont feller. And his pockets ain't never full enough. Seems you have a weakness for masking and getting in trouble.''

Swallowing hard at her rising gorge, Berry said, "I have two conditions you must meet.''

From where he sat beside her, Warren snarled, brandishing his knife before her face and twisting her arm behind her back. "You're talking crazy! I want that emerald of mine. My Arkansas toothpick and I set the conditions.''

Desperate, Berry took a chance that the warped man desired the jewel more than he desired revenge. Or at least before he treated himself to revenge. After having hired his brother killed and murdering his sister-in-law, he would not hesitate to kill her or anyone else standing in the way of his freedom. Still, he did not yet have possession of the emerald. "Then go ahead and kill me and do without the ring. I'm the only one who knows where it is.''

"You *are* crazy.''

Twisting her arm free, Berry poured out her conditions before Warren could sort his thoughts. "As you pointed out, this business is between the two of us. If you want me to bring you the ring, you'll have to promise you'll give me time enough to get Jason away from here. You must also promise not to burn the house.''

Warren grinned lewdly and licked his lips while his small eyes raked over Berry's face and breasts. "So you've found yourself a loving man, have you? Hadn't noticed before how growed up you've got. You always did look like you'd be a bitch in heat if the right man came along.'' With a thumb and forefinger he pinched one of her nipples, grinning even more lasciviously when she sucked in a breath and slapped his hand away. ''I like my women spicy.''

''You're a level-headed man, Warren,'' Berry lied with forced calm. Inside, her belly was a quivering mass, her pulse a thing gone mad. He still sat with his body jammed against hers, still held the knife. Praying that her words might sound convincing, she continued. ''Jason is nothing special to me, merely someone who has shown me kindness. It makes sense to keep him out of the way. People say he was quick with a sword and a pistol even before he fought against the Indians and Mexicans out in Texas.''

Was the big man showing fear? Berry wondered. Sergeant Dan had called him a coward. Warren was leaning closer, obviously intent on hearing her every word. ''Jason might get curious about me wandering around down here at night, especially if I'm leading one of his horses from the stables. Then he might call on his slaves to attack you and your men and—''

''I just had a better idea.'' His gaze roved boldly over her breasts. ''Bring two horses saddled and I'll take you along with me to Texas. I'd be a plumb fool to kill you when you'd be such fine company for a man living on the frontier.''

Berry tried ignoring Warren and his nasty, insinuating smile. Perhaps if she could continue hiding her revulsion for him, she could gain a reprieve long enough to figure out some way to best him. And before he could do her any damage, he'd feel the sharp edge of her knife! Her years spent living close to the seamy side of life in the French Quarter had taught her much about the vulnerability of the human body. Too, she recalled the big man's intolerance for pain.

''If I agree to go away with you''—Berry heard her

voice wavering and thought about sinking to her knees and begging him to take the emerald and go away—"will you promise not to bother the house and leave everyone else out of this?"

"You bring the ring and the horses, girl, and we'll get along fine. Mighty fine."

Sending a searching gaze out into the moonlight, Berry saw nothing but the familiar. She heard mosquitoes whining, heard jagged breathing coming from both Warren and her. Was it only last night that she had sat on this same bench with Jason and heard similar sounds, sounds that told a different story? "Where are the horses for the others?"

"That's my business. None of yours. With this full moon, we can travel all night toward the border."

Berry summoned voice enough to whisper what she heard as her death warrant. "I'll be back no later than midnight."

"How do I know you won't tell your friend that I'm out here?"

Berry glanced across the road at the bayou, then toward the *garçonniere*. Any minute Jason might return. If only she knew how many men Warren had with him—

"Don't be trying to outguess me," Warren said, "or I'll march you over to that little house and take care of your man right now."

"Stay out of sight so that I can make certain Jason leaves." Despite the pounding in her ears, she heard her skirts rustle as she stood on legs barely sturdy enough to support her trembling body. "I'm not fool enough to cross you again, Warren Maroney."

"Just you keep remembering that."

Berry watched Warren limp to the edge of the pergola and turn back to look at her, the blade in his hand reflecting light from the fat moon rising above the trees. From somewhere the dizzying thought came that Creole moons did not always smile on lovers.

"Mind you," Warren hissed, "get back here before midnight or you'll be damned sorry." He looked toward the mansion standing white at the end of the long driveway and grinned. "I still say that place would make one helluva bonfire."

Jason was strapping on his holster over the waistband of his loose trousers when he heard someone entering his parlor. "Is that you, Alonzo?"

When no reply came, Jason panicked at his stupidity in letting Berry convince him she would be safe in the pergola. Just because she had seemed pensive was no excuse for him to forget the possibility, remote as it might be, that Warren Maroney could appear and cause her harm. Letting pique and momentary jealousy warp his judgment now seemed unforgivable. With his pistol in hand, he hurried from his bedroom.

"Why, Berry," Jason said with heartfelt relief as he slipped his weapon into his holster, "you surprised me." Smiling at her and wondering if finding him with a gun in hand was bringing that woebegone look to her lovely face, he went to give her a hug and kiss. "Did you get tired of waiting?"

"Yes."

Berry was unprepared for the pain she was experiencing as she looked at the dark-haired man she loved. She fought to pretend she was somebody else. That somebody else did not adore Jason Premont, did not want to melt into his welcoming arms and confide her fears. That somebody else was bent on making him so angry and confused that he would leave the premises for at least a brief time and prevent the fruition of her earlier premonition about evil attacking him. The real Berry was convinced that his life depended on her performance. "I got tired of waiting. I also got tired of listening to what my mind was telling me about you and me and this infernal plantation."

"Whatever has happened to you?" Jason was standing before her then, his brow wrinkling in puzzlement as he gazed at her pale face, her unnaturally bright eyes. "You don't look right and you surely don't sound right. What's wrong?''

"Nothing is wrong—and for the first time in a long while. At last I've gotten this absurd relationship between us straightened out in my mind. I came to tell you to forget the romantic ride on the bayou, forget all that has been between us. It's over."

"Darling, you're talking out of your head. What has upset you?" Jason took a step closer, his hand reaching out imploringly. "Let's go down to the bayou and—"

"No!" Not the bayou! Berry almost cried out a warning. "Get away from me. I'm not your darling. I won't ever be your darling. I've had enough of you and your boring country life. I want to go home tomorrow. I intend to go start packing right this minute." She backed up a step and half turned away. "Good-bye."

"Wait!" Jason's arm shot out and looped around her waist. He forced her chin up with one hand and looked into her face. Maybe if he kissed her and told her—

Though his touch almost did her in, Berry warned, "Don't be trying to kiss me and take me to bed as if I were a strumpet. I've had enough of you."

When Jason freed her and fixed her with a disbelieving stare, she rushed on with the kind of words she figured that other, uncaring Berry would be choosing. "Why don't you go saddle your horse and visit Corrine?" She managed a harsh laugh. "Don't try looking shocked. Your sainted Cousin Agnes told me all about you and your wild living. Not that anything she told was surprising."

"What's wrong with you? Corrine has been a past mistake for a long while. If you're jealous—"

Berry did not let him finish. "How can I be jealous over somebody who bores me? I figured that before now you would have already sought out a new face. Or was that why you spent yesterday in Calion, to line up the next woman to charm? I'll bet she's a true Creole, born and bred in holy

Saint Christopher Parish. Maybe she'll be good enough to bear your heirs and at the same time please your relatives."

"Now just a damned minute! How can you listen to talk from others and believe it without even discussing it with me? You're making accusations right and left and assuming nobody has anything to complain about but you. What about me?"

Despite Berry's genuine fear for Jason's safety and her immersion in her role of shrew, his question set her back. Suddenly she was not acting. Real pique set her eyes to glittering like polished jet. "What about you?"

"Is it so unbelievable that I might have a few complaints? You have no right to fault my family or where I live just because you obviously don't care to marry me. You talk about my having known other women. What about the other men you've known? A little honesty from you might could clear up this matter, might could have cleared it up weeks ago."

"Honesty?" Berry never before had seen Jason so incensed. What complaints did he have? He knew that he was the only one to make love to her. Why did he care that she had spent time with other men? He was looking stern, unyielding. She took a step backward, almost tripping over her long skirts. Her palms grew clammy. Bedamned! What a time for Jason to be demanding honesty.

"Yes, honesty. Is that a term you're not familiar with? Have you been around theaters so much that you can no longer tell the difference between being straightforward and play-acting?"

Berry gulped when Jason took a step toward her. Would he grab her if she tried backing up again? He seemed as angry as that other Berry had tried to be. She wondered if she might not be a clock about to strike.

She blinked, then couldn't force her gaze from his when his deep voice went on in something akin to a roar. "You've never once offered any reasonable explanation why you wouldn't consider my proposal. Why didn't you tell me to go to hell that night at the masquerade ball? I knew from the start that you've spent time with other men. How was it that you allowed me to be the first to make love with you if you felt nothing special for me? What gives you the right to make me the single villain in this absurd scene?''

Scene? Recovering then and applying herself to her original goal to get Jason safely away from her and thus from Warren Maroney and his cohorts, Berry parried, ''Because I've always known you're nothing but a rake and that even if your life depended on it, you couldn't be true to one woman.''

''Maybe you're the one who couldn't be true to one person.''

Inside, Berry's heart was whimpering. If Jason only knew how true she could be to him—painfully she played her role. ''A woman would be a fool to marry you!''

Jason's battered heart and pride joined forces then. ''So you think you're too good to be my wife, is that it?''

For a moment Jason's wounding words careened around in Berry's head and chased away all thought of the murderer she had promised to meet in the pergola before midnight. Not having to search for lines any longer, she gave full reign to her aroused emotions. ''Not too good. Too smart. Since I was a little girl and watched the goings on in the French Quarter, I've vowed that I won't marry just any man I take a fancy to. I want a husband who can offer me the kind of love that lasts past the fancy balls and sweet promises of Saturday nights. I want a man who will love me every day and every night. A man who loves only me. A rake doesn't fit the bill.''

Jason's dark eyes smoldered. He fixed her with a look that she felt was meant to slice her into unrecognizable pieces. ''A rake? What makes you think you're a judge who can determine if a man is a rake? Maybe at one time your unflattering term fit me. Even if it did, that doesn't mean I don't have deep feelings like other men, couldn't come to love the right woman and settle down with her. You seem fond of hanging titles on people.'' He leaned so close that she backed up a step. ''What's a good name for a woman who goes around judging men secretly against some asinine set of rules she dreamed up when she was a runny-nosed little girl? A holier-than-thou?''

''You're insufferable! You wouldn't recognize the decent kind of marriage I'm talking about if it marched right up to you and saluted. You make me so mad I could spit!''

''Don't talk about it. Do it!''

Berry sputtered. She had run out of words.

His face flushed, Jason added, ''Just for the record, I don't care to accept your standards as the ultimate. I happen to have my own ideas about what makes a good marriage.''

''Great! Try them out on the next woman you decide to favor with your sweet words. Whisper them to Corrine when you see her.'' Satisfied that she had riled Jason enough for him to stay clear of her company forever, but wondering how she could get through the awful hours that stretched ahead, Berry whirled around with a hissing flurry of long skirts and headed for the door. She felt like a self-contained tornado in a world gone crazy. ''I'm leaving.''

Following behind as she flounced out the door, Jason said, ''I'll walk you to the house.''

Berry stepped from the gallery to the ground, and he appeared at her side. Almost running then, and achingly aware that Warren and his men probably were watching from a hiding place near the bayou, Berry angled her chin haughtily. ''I don't want you near me. Go on ahead.''

Jason, his long legs easily matching her fast pace, remarked, ''I'm on my way to the stables to saddle my horse. Since we're traveling the same route, we might as well do it at the same time.''

From where she walked on the opposite side of the driveway, Berry noted how the moonlight barely penetrated the density of the overhanging trees, creating only dapples of milky light here and there. ''If you leave right away, you can get to Corrine's while your Creole moon still lights your way. How romantic!"

"Damn! but you have a mean mouth."

"It has served to steer me clear of people like you."

Berry knew that Mr. Edouard's bedroom lay on the back side of the left wing, and as soon as she got close enough to see for certain that his entire wing was dark, she let out a sigh of thanksgiving. She had hoped he would not still be up. She had no wish for Mr. Edouard to learn that something was going on and perhaps try going up against Warren and his men. Another stroke of good luck was that Delinda and Miss Agnes were in Calion for the entire night.

Lifting her skirts when she reached the nearer of the two curving stairways leading up to the veranda, Berry ran up the steps. Surely Warren, from his hiding place beside the bayou, would be able to see that she and Jason were going separate ways. He probably had heard them quarreling, too.

Jason stalked on past the steps toward the stables out back, saying over his shoulder, "You won't have to bother with me again. Go back to the kind of men who apparently suit your taste. I won't be present in the morning to walk you down to the pier and watch you load onto the packet."

Berry, almost to the front door then, aimed her final, barbed words at Jason's rigid back. "What a relief! I hope you and Corrine have a memorable night. I'll wave at you two when we glide by tomorrow."

Jason, tight-lipped, disappeared around the end of the veranda just as Berry slipped inside the front door.

Seeing that there were no candles burning anywhere but in the sconce above a marble-topped side table in the foyer, Berry picked up a handled holder, lit its candle from the flame, and climbed the staircase to her bedroom. She could not decide which calamity had her more upset, her tempestuous scene with Jason or the earlier one with Warren Maroney. Either was enough to flood her heart with raw pain.

Once she reached her bedroom, Berry stepped up on the

riser and lay back across the bed to catch her breath and give her runaway pulse a chance to slow. She knew that under ordinary circumstances she could have done with a friendly voice and a warm body for companionship, but she was glad that she had told Sheena not to wait up to help her get ready for bed. The folded-down sheet and her freshly laundered nightgown and peignoir resting across the foot of the tall bed told her that the soft-voiced slave had already been there.

Berry felt blessed that she had been able to convince Jason that she did not care for him. He would be safe now. She watched the shadows created by the burning candle dance eerily on the overhead canopy. Her tirade had driven Jason off in search of Corrine. Camille and her other former acting coaches would have cheered her performance. Tears formed as she relived fragments of her quarrel with the man she loved.

How could Jason have been so cruel as to fling such caustic remarks? She wished she could have told him how little the other young men with whom she had spent time meant to her. Was there any truth in his accusations that she was play-acting or being judgmental when it came to men? Of course not!

Jason's deriding words about her long-cherished dream of finding her special kind of love in marriage stung worse when Berry recalled them there in the quiet of the bedroom. He had no right to make her dream sound like a condemnation of men. And never could she rightfully be labeled holier-than-thou. Never!

Berry flopped over on her face and let the smooth sheet absorb her tears. Strange that since Maddy's death, only her love for Jason had brought tears. The clean fragrance of lavender scenting the bed linen added to her misery, for it seemed representative of the life at Armand Acres that she had come to love. The ambiance, the permanence, the warmth of caring people. Jason. At midnight all would be lost to her forever.

How wrong Miss Agnes had been to hint that Berry could never belong at Armand Acres. Mr. Edouard's liking for her seemed genuine, as did that shown by the house servants. Delinda was fast becoming her friend. Even Jason had remarked that since her arrival, Miss Agnes's manner had thawed.

That very afternoon out in the work house when Berry had met the black women who performed the various crafts and had operated the loom while they went about their jobs with what seemed normal banter, she had felt the same warm acceptance from them as from the other servants she had met. She had a feeling that she would have had little trouble fitting in well. The kind of home she had longed to call her own—and she knew it had nothing to do with size or luxury—could have been hers. If only she had—

"Stop it, you dolt!" Berry muttered under her breath. "Sniveling never has helped anybody. You would've had to deal with Warren Maroney, no matter what. It's time to get your things together and go. You've got to saddle two horses and you never have saddled even one before."

With renewed purpose, Berry rose and went to the washstand. After washing her face, she glimpsed her image in the mirror. Was she looking at the world's greatest fool? Probably. Who else would have refused to marry or even admit for ages that she loved the dearest man in the world simply because she found fault with his past behavior? An honesty that she figured even Jason would have admired made her alter her description to his *imagined* past behavior.

The most painful admission came then, sending her whirling away from the mirror to stand beside the open window and stare out into the night. As most truths are when faced, the admission was simple: she should have been far more interested in her beloved's current actions and his treatment of her than in what he had done, or supposedly done, in the past.

As if it were yesterday, Berry could see the young, debonair Jason smiling his gratitude at her that first Sunday morning after she had darned his torn trousers, could remember her warm glow of appreciation for the much-needed gold coin he had generously given her. Back then she had had a feeling he was somebody very special. And again, when he had come to her rescue that Mardi Gras night, a gentle man as well as a gentleman. She had met few of those in her nineteen years.

Why, when it came to the Jason she had met at the masquerade ball, had she not trusted her own good judgment of people to guide her? Had she somehow let her dream of finding somebody perfect, and therefore "worthy" of her love, get in the way of her being true to her instincts as a self-confessed "Impulse Person?"

Suddenly a new idea, one jarring and unwelcome, commandeered Berry's mind. Maybe the crux of the matter was that she was the one imperfect and unworthy of Jason's love. Perhaps she had deluded herself by presuming that she might be the kind of wife that Jason needed, that her dreams were the only ones worthy of merit.

For one as flawed as she now realized herself to be, Berry concluded with broken-hearted irony, she had done a masterful job of placing herself on a pedestal. Her pedestal was made of nothing more substantial than the sand along the beaches of Lake Pontchartrain.

The thought that probably right now Jason was making love to the faceless Corrine fired both Berry's jealousy and her memories of how glorious it had been to lose herself in his arms. She closed her eyes. A wave of desire washed over her as she remembered the taste of his warm lips on hers, the feel of his hands and mouth titillating her throbbing breasts, the ache of . . .

Berry's eyes popped open. Had Jason, perhaps, been a little too quick to quarrel with her and have an excuse to ride off to see Corrine? She scolded herself for letting jealousy shade her thoughts. Her goal had been to remove Jason from danger and that she had accomplished. Removing him from her heart and her thoughts was proving a

Herculean task. She whispered into the darkness outside, "Jason, what if I can never forget you?"

Getting on with the realities, Berry changed slowly into the black riding habit that Miss Agnes had brought her that first morning. If she left her fashionable gowns and petticoats behind, she might be forgiven for taking a garment not hers.

Despite her wish to equalize matters, Berry could think of no way to make it right that she was going to steal two horses and saddles. What little money she had would not be enough to replace them, but she dumped it out of her purse and left it on the dresser alongside the note she wrote offering a halfway plausible reason for her midnight departure. Maybe those at Armand Acres would believe her declaration that she could no longer tolerate being away from New Orleans.

By the time Berry had drawn the emerald ring from its hiding place in the armoire and slipped it on her finger, then placed her dagger and the thimble that Jason had given her in the pocket of her skirt, she had faced up to the possibility that Jason had known her better than she had known herself. Throwing a few articles of clothing in her portmanteau, she vowed that if she truly had been a holier-than-thou, she would be one no longer.

Berry crept down the stairs. Though she found it almost unbearable to face the fact that she would never see Jason again, that having lost him would diminish whatever contentment she might attain one day, she must concentrate on the distant future. If she ever again met a good man and came close to finding bliss, she was going to kick her old dream into a corner and fashion one in conjunction with his. Maybe together they could create a new dream that could lead to happiness.

After making certain that nobody was in sight, Berry stowed her portmanteau near the back door. Strangely, while stealing out to the stables, she had a powerful premonition that the events coming up would not lead to her defeat. The idea that she alone could best Warren and his friends, then catch a packet to New Orleans in the morning and get on with her life seemed farfetched. More like downright impossible, but Berry reassured herself as she let the flame of a lantern hanging just inside the open doors of the stable guide her, she had a feeling all might work out. The unexpected sight of the lighted lantern and the weight of her dagger in the pocket of her riding skirt boosted her spirits and she summoned up every available iota of courage to carry her through the coming ordeal.

The eerie call of a distant screech owl jangled Berry's manufactured bravado and slowed her steps. She swallowed hard. Reflecting that she could use some good luck to go with her sagging courage, she resumed her brisk pace and patted the small lump in her pocket. Maybe the thimble that Jason had given her would serve as a talisman.

CHAPTER

*

Twenty

*A*fter Jason left Berry at the front door, he strode toward the stables like a man whose senses had forsaken him. Glad to vent even a tiny portion of his anger, he kicked aside a small branch lying in his path.

Jason's whirling thoughts dwelt on Berry and her absurd notions about most things in general. Their quarrel, their parting forever—both were all her fault. She had never been honest with him, had no inkling as to the meaning of honesty. From his first sight of Berry Cortabona—God, but he had been insane to have viewed her as an angel of mercy that Sunday morning—he had known that hers was a free spirit, a stranger to discipline. How right she had been when she had called herself an "Impulse Person." How could he have been so blind as to have fallen for her?

"Wait up," Alonzo called. Having left Mr. Edouard after the old man began dozing over his poker hand and opted to go to bed, Alonzo had prowled around in the moonlight,

311

hoping to run into one of the comely young slaves who recently had begun casting flirty looks his way. He had seen nobody until he glimpsed the racing shadow of his master.

"What in blazes do you want?" Irritated at the entire world, Jason half glanced over his shoulder at the black man. He was reaching for lantern and flint by the time Alonzo caught up with him at the open, double doors leading to the cavernous stables.

"For you to tell me what's got you het up will do to begin with." Alonzo took the lantern from the plainly agitated Jason and soon had the wick burning. He guessed it was at least ten o'clock, late for Jason to be taking a horseback ride. Sizing up the tall familiar figure before him and noticing the holstered pistol, he hung the lantern on its hook just inside the doors. "Where you goin'? What you plannin' on doin' with that gun?"

No answer came. Alonzo had to stretch his short legs to keep up as Jason made his way past the tack room, on down the shadowy aisle to the second stall. Soft nickers and a few snorts came from some of the horses. "You ain't got wind of that scoundrel what's lookin' for Miss Berry, have you?"

"No." Jason stood in Diamond's stall then, a gentle hand soothing the searching nose of his horse. With motions made simple from years of practice, he lifted down the bridle from its hook, slipped the bit into the horse's mouth, guided the leather strips over the long nose and behind the alert ears before fastening the chin strap. "Nothing as simple as dealing with an escaped killer is on my mind."

"What you aimin' on shootin'?" In the spooky light coming from the lantern hanging up front, Alonzo could determine little about Jason's features other than that they showed strain. He did not like the look of things. "Or is it *who*?"

"Nobody. Nothing." To facilitate ease and speed in securing mounts, Jason had recently ordered the building of separate racks for holding tack in front of each stall. He grabbed a blanket from Diamond's rack and threw the woolen square across the gray's back, hardly waiting for it to settle before turning back for the saddle. "I just felt the need to be cautious, that's all. Go on to bed."

"I can tell somethin' is gnawin' at you."

"I can handle it."

"Sho' an' I ain't doubtin' that a bit, but I don't like seein' you worried." Alonzo smoothed a corner of the saddle blanket that Jason, usually considerate of the gray's flesh, had neglected, then dodged the flying stirrups as Jason flung the saddle over Diamond's back. After stooping and holding the dangling end of the cinch belt under the gray's belly until Jason's hand took it and pulled it toward him, Alonzo went around the horse and stood watching the younger man. "Have you an' Miss Berry had words?"

"God! but you're nosy."

"An' it's a good thing, else I wouldn't never find out nothin' what's goin' on." Only one thing, Alonzo mused, could have driven Jason to such a frenzied state. "Miss Berry an' you done had a bad fight, ain't cha?"

"I don't want to talk about it. It's over between us. There wasn't enough between us to float a dead mosquito."

"Where you goin'—or ain't it none a my business?"

"It's none of your business." Jason silently cursed himself for taking out his anger on his longtime friend. In a kinder tone he added, "I'm going to take a ride through the back pastures."

Walking beside Jason as he led Diamond outside, Alonzo thought about how it had long been his master's way to ride his horse hard in order to work off anger or frustration. Back before Jason left to fight in Texas, when he was far more hotheaded, he had often declared himself too restless to sleep and taken his horse out at all hours. Sometimes, Alonzo recalled, Jason had paddled a pirogue down the bayou to call on Miss Corrine. He figured that since Jason was not on his way down the bayou to the little houseboat tied up in a finger on the far bank, he was still crazily in love with Miss Berry.

Alonzo smiled to himself. The way he saw it, the couple seemed made to be a permanent pair. Though unmarried, he had been involved with enough women to know that love seldom ran a smooth course. Watching Jason put his foot in the stirrup and swing up into the saddle, Alonzo said, "I hope you ain't gonna be back to your ole tricks, jumpin' fences an' stuff."

"Don't wait up. Go get some sleep."

Jason leaned forward then and guided the apparently eager horse toward the broad moonlit pastures stretching behind the mansion. Giving the smooth-gaited Diamond his head, he succumbed to the need to immerse himself in something other than his inner turmoil. Relaxing, he synchronized his body with that of the galloping animal.

As Jason had discovered back when he was a boy growing up at Armand Acres, there was something infinitely soothing about listening to the rapid pounding of hooves against level earth, leaning forward into the night air and enjoying its rushing past his face, feeling between his legs the rhythmic, rocking motions created by powerful muscles of the horse as it galloped onward. He glanced around at the familiar landscape. He liked seeing the way that the star-studded sky, the full moon, and the shadows turned the daytime scenery into one of mystery.

Not until after Diamond slowed to a canter in one of the back pastures did Jason release his mind to dwell upon matters outside the night world that he and his horse inhabited. There was actually only one matter that he cared to think about: a woman. A beautiful, black-haired woman. Berry Cortabona. By the saints, how he loved her! He sucked in a deep breath. In spite of being mad as hell at her, he still loved her.

He had guessed from the first time he saw her laughing at him that Sunday morning that she was unique and moved to her own private rhythm. It smarted to admit that even now while he was angry with her, he gloried in the quirky nuances that fashioned Berry Cortabona into the exciting woman he wanted to live with for the rest of his life.

Never until earlier that evening, though, had Jason ever suspected Berry might possess a streak of cruelty. She had sliced up his heart with seeming relish. What could he believe but that she never had been honest with him, never would be? Dared he keep on hoping that someday he might win her love?

Not until after the moon had climbed higher in the cloudless sky and Diamond had slowed to a spirited walk did Jason's racing brain trot out telling reasons why Berry was the only woman for him. Her obviously heartfelt caring for people seemed as good a place to start as any other. The memory of the young Berry's compassion when she had bound his torn palms that Sunday morning rose up. And afterward, when she had insisted on mending his torn trousers before he made his way through the French Quarter to his townhouse.

What about that Mardi Gras evening? Berry had stood before him and staunchly refused to give up trying to help her companion seek justice for his murdered friend. She had brushed aside his warning that she and Ebon Stringer were heading for trouble.

Jason suspected that during Berry's pursuit of the wily Warren Maroney, she had shown as much bravery as fool-hardiness. Plainly her caring more about Ebon's peace of mind and the search for justice than for her own safety had directed her every step. Even the seemingly sensible Sergeant Harrigan, who obviously admired and respected Berry, had said as much when he related the details of the murderer's capture and subsequent trial.

Another asset to consider, Jason reflected, was Berry's outward beauty, her consummate beauty. He found himself gazing overhead at the stars and recalling how his beloved's black eyes twinkled, how her animated talk, her smiles and giggles brought flashes of white teeth. Her laughter was so deliciously infectious that once a man had heard it—or so it seemed to Jason as he looked at the starry sky—he could not think of anything pleasurable or frivolous without remembering Berry Cortabona. Berry with her graceful, feminine movements, her midnight hair, her olive skin, her widely spaced eyes, her full lips.

Was it totally wrong, Jason mused while fingering his left earlobe, for a young woman such as Berry to concoct a dream of finding a perfect man to marry and father her children? In conversations during the past several weeks— Jason's heart expanded, just from recalling her soft voice— he had pieced together the story of her rather bizarre upbringing in the theater.

Now that Jason was trying to be objective, he admitted that it seemed in keeping with Berry's unorthodox mode of life that she would dramatize almost everything and never realize she might be playacting, might be sidestepping truth. He acknowledged her tendency to mull matters over in her mind and come up with original ideas. Could he say he did not possess a similar trait?

Jason heard from somewhere deep in the woods, a dog baying, then another. Were they, like him, attempting to tree an elusive unknown?

Maybe, Jason decided, he had been too harsh in denouncing Berry's dream as childish, as a polemic against men— especially him. With his penchant for honesty during soul-searching, he acknowledged in the calm aftermath of their earlier, tumultuous confrontation that Berry Cortabona deserved the special kind of love for which she confessed she was searching. Why hadn't he gone ahead and told her the truth, that he was the man who could give her what she wanted?

Quick temper? Wounded masculine pride? Yes, Jason admitted both. Plus disappointment in her offhand denouncement of him and his style of living. Too, there was his edginess from feeling guilty about having left Berry unprotected in the pergola while he changed clothing. Unreasoning jealousy that he had not been the first man to spend time with her and despair that she might never fall in love with him played their parts in the tawdry scene.

Perhaps, Jason agonized, he was doomed to remember Berry playing out the sometimes absurd scenes that posed as integral parts of their being together. The first two, during which they had met as if by chance, still seemed incongruous. He recalled the night of the masquerade ball when he did not even know who she was, only that he suspected he was falling in love with the beautiful Spanish queen. Was that meeting also the work of chance? Or was it, as he had mentioned to Berry that very evening, ordained by something more awesome, like fate? He swallowed.

Then, with admiration for her daring, Jason was recalling the way Berry had barged into his courtyard that morning while he was trying to console Viola. Next came the memory of her running to him underneath the Oaks and weeping while telling of her premonition about him being in danger. His free hand lingered at his ear. A half smile turned up his mouth. She had created a scene that had—

Scene? With lightning quick motions, Jason dropped his hand, joined it with the one on the reins and pulled back. "Whoa!" he commanded. Diamond reared up, then danced in place for a moment before Jason guided the reins against the gray's neck and wheeled him back toward the mansion.

In a light clearer than the moonbeams lighting the path home, Jason recognized Berry's actions and words in the *garçonniere* as a scene orchestrated to get him away. Somehow Warren Maroney must have appeared while she was in the pergola. He probably threatened her with no-telling-what to get her to remain silent and fetch the ring for him. What would happen when she turned over the ring? Jason's heartbeat thundered along with Diamond's hooves. It would be like Berry to try some improbable scheme to best the man. . .

"Hurry, boy!" he yelled to the galloping horse as he half-stood in the stirrups and leaned close over the gray neck. "We may already be too late!"

* * *

"Humph!" Alonzo muttered to himself after Jason rode off from the stables. "That man ridin' off like he chasin' the Evil One. Or else runnin' from 'im." He watched horse and rider getting smaller in the moonlight, muttering to his disappearing master, "I ain't goin' to bed till you gets back or daylight comes. No tellin' what-all you gonna do, like jumpin' fences an' maybe breakin' your fool neck."

After making certain that the lantern had fuel, the concerned black man went inside the tack room and stretched out on a pile of old saddle blankets. He brought his hands up to serve as a pillow and lay watching the shadows flicker on the ceiling until sleep took him over.

Light but stealthy steps woke Alonzo. From where he blended with the darkness of the tack room, he cast wary eyes toward the open doors of the stable. Probably he shouldn't have called up the name of the Evil One, he reflected with mouth-drying respect for the unknown.

Though Alonzo, unlike many Louisianians in 1843, did not believe *loup-garoux* existed and could sneak inside the bodies of living people and animals, he could not swear that evil spirits did not stalk the earth late at night. When he recognized the figure heading down the aisle as Berry Cortabona, he expelled a breath of relief. He almost called out and asked if he could be of service.

Something warned Alonzo to keep quiet, though, and he stood and peeped through the cracks of the rough planks forming the walls of the tack room. Was Miss Berry really going to try saddling the horse she had been riding since her arrival? Maybe she was going to go in search of Jason. He didn't know how long he had been asleep, but he figured it must be close to midnight.

About the only things Alonzo knew for certain were that Jason had not returned and that Miss Berry was having the devil of a time saddling Jewel. Reflecting that if he were to go help her, she would be able to ride off more quickly, he convinced himself he was doing right by keeping an eye on her and keeping still. He knew that it wasn't fitting that a young woman be traipsing around by herself in the middle of the night. She and Jason must have had a tremendous fight for her to be trying to go somewhere at this late hour.

When Berry finally managed the feat of saddling the obedient mare and looped the reins over a post, she again surprised her hidden audience of one by going to the next stall. Alonzo called himself all kinds of a fool for having kept quiet even this long; but he had a feeling that Jason would return soon and that by reporting what Miss Berry was doing, he would prove to be helpful. It seemed plain that somebody needed to follow her and see which way she went.

Making decisions was not one of Alonzo's jobs, and even if it was, he fretted, he doubted he would know how to come up with a wise one right now. He could feel sweat beading his brow.

He covered his eyes with his hand for a moment, praying silently. "Please, Lord. Let my eyes be lyin'." Surely the slight young woman was not going to try saddling Trees! Why, that red gelding, favored by the overseer because he was tireless, was almost too frisky for a grown man to saddle and ride. Never would Trees allow a woman to mount him. The horse despised strangers, too.

Maybe, Alonzo thought when he opened his eyes again, he should step out and offer to help or at least say something polite, like, "Miss Berry, I just happened to be passin' by. If I was you, I wouldn't be messin' with that horse."

Since his smitten master seemed intent on telling Berry everything about Armand Acres, Alonzo reasoned, he reckoned that Jason told her how the horse had gotten his name from his habit of leaning against trees and trying to rub off his rider. More often than not, Trees succeeded with riders ignorant of his quirkiness. What to do?

Even as Alonzo wavered, he saw and heard the slender young woman crooning to the gelding. Bejesus if old Trees wasn't wiggling his ears friendly-like and nickering! A new question surfaced. Why would Miss Berry need two horses?

As soon as Alonzo saw that the mean-tempered Trees allowed Berry to slip on his bridle, he dashed from the tack room to the slave cabins sitting beyond the stables. He saw a light in the cabin belonging to Beesom. Within moments the four young men playing poker inside were sprinting back toward the stables with Alonzo and trying to digest the brief facts Alonzo had given.

"How come Miss Berry's leavin'?" Beesom asked in a low voice when the five black men peeped around the corner of the long building and saw no person or horse in the circle of light coming from the lantern hanging near the double doors.

Alonzo had finished whispering his suppositions when Berry came from the stables leading Jewel. She looped the reins over a post, then returned inside, emerging with Trees. Exchanging puzzled glances, the five black men watched her lead the animals to the side of the mansion. Still in the shadows, they saw her secure the horses near a thick crepe myrtle tree and disappear in the shadows on the back veranda.

"What we gonna do now?" Beesom asked Alonzo, who was older and held higher rank among the slaves because he was the personal servant of young Master. Beesom's eyes, opened so wide in the moonlight that their whites showed all around the dark centers, revealed uncertainty.

"Somebody gotta follow her 'round front an' see which way she goes," Alonzo replied. He was determined to carry out his plan. "Josiah, you saddle Buster for me so's I can try to find Mr. Jason. I knows 'bout where he rides at night."

"Wonder why Miss Berry got a extry horse?" somebody asked after Josiah hurried inside the stables to do Alonzo's bidding.

Alonzo had already puzzled over that question but as soon as he heard it spoken aloud and saw Berry returning from the veranda with a portmanteau in her hand, he straightened taller in sudden realization. How could he have forgotten the reason she had come to Armand Acres? She seemed to fit in so well, seemed so contented . . . What was the best thing to do? He didn't want any harm to come to the nice young woman. Keeping his voice low, Alonzo said, ''This ain't to be talked, but a bad cuss from jail been lookin' for Miss Berry to do her harm. Maybe he found her tonight. Could be he's makin' her go away with him.''

Beesom and the others showed puzzlement but Alonzo dismissed their questions with a sharp look that brooked no argument. ''Beesom, you an' Homer stay in the dark an' keep a sharp lookout. Follow her 'round to the front an' watch which way she goes. Try gettin' close enough to hear if'n she meets up with somebody. Don't let her outta sight. Be extry careful. Don't do nothin' less'n you think she's fixin' to get hurt bad. If that man's out there waitin', he's liable to have somebody with him.''

''I'se prayin' ain't nobody out there on the road,'' Abner muttered under his breath after Beesom and Homer, keeping to the shadows, crept after Berry and the two horses as they went around the big house toward the front. ''I'se prayin' all I'm seein' ain't nothin' but—''

''What you better be prayin' for,'' Alonzo advised soberly, ''is that I can find Mr. Jason an' get him back here soon.''

As soon as Berry reached the stables, she saw by the flickering light from the lantern that Jason's horse was not in its stable. She counted herself fortunate that Jason was still gone—still making love to Corrine, a part of her pointed out spitefully. She ignored her heart's threat to buck and overthrow her confidence.

Determined not to think about anything but the task at hand, Berry tucked the trailing skirts of her habit inside her waistband. While stroking Jewel's nose and withers, she talked to her in a soothing tone and tried to recall the steps in readying a horse for a ride. After a few trial attempts, she at last coaxed Jewel into accepting the bit.

"Thanks, girl," Berry murmured, encouraged that her small success was boosting her confidence. To her surprise, she did not have to fuss with the saddle blanket long before getting it to look right.

Berry was not quite so lucky when it came to getting the saddle positioned. Though the wooden stirrups slapped her chest and arms each time she attempted to swing the heavy saddle over the horse's back and made her arms grow trembly, she kept returning to tiptoes and aiming the saddle toward the blanket until the leather skirts lay in position. When she at last cinched the belly band, she rested her head against Jewel's withers. She breathed a shaky sigh while waiting for the horse to let her stomach go flat again.

Then, as she had seen Jason and the ostlers do, Berry quickly tightened the band enough to secure the saddle. "Thanks, Jewel, for letting me practice on you."

Berry struggled harder and longer to saddle the feisty Trees. Afterward she leaned weakly against the big horse and caught her breath. "There, there, big boy," she murmured when the horse turned his head and fixed her with what she deemed a puzzled look. Could the horse be any more surprised than she that she had been able to sweet-talk him into submission? "Everything will work out just right. You can have yourself a fine time swiping your rider off on a tree."

Even after Berry retrieved her portmanteau from where she had stashed it on the back veranda and led the horses around the mansion toward the bayou, she was still cheering herself by thinking maxims that Aunt Maddy had favored. *A poor beginning doesn't mean a poor ending. Might doesn't always make right. Where there's a will, there's a way.* Unbidden came Jason's encouraging words that night she had told him of her sale. *A first step is a first step.*

Berry decided to lead the horses across the deeply shadowed grounds instead of down the packed-dirt driveway where their hooves might make more carrying sounds. Because it seemed to her that each squeak from the saddles and each heavy hoof step was loud enough to wake the dead, she stopped at intervals to look and listen for signs that her escape had been discovered. A night breeze stirred the leaves overhead.

What Berry guessed might be the restless wandering of some small animal was the only other noise she detected. She welcomed the heavy shadows. They made her feel safe.

After Berry neared the pergola with its bluish green onion top gleaming in the moonlight, she became aware that the night callers were slowing their songs and figured the noise she and the horses were making was intruding on their privacy. She entertained the eerie notion that she might be caught up in the hollow of a dark saucer and that when she left its safety, the dazzle of the moonlight waiting outside its rim might blind her.

Nothing so dramatic happened. When Berry reached the unoccupied pergola, she looped the reins around one of the graceful colonnades and stepped inside. She did not dare treat herself to a look in the direction of the *garçonniere* sitting across the driveway under its own little grove of moss-bearded oaks. Thoughts of Jason Premont would be unbearable. The sound of her footsteps on the wooden floor echoed the hollow feeling in the bottom of her stomach.

Berry looked across the road toward the bayou and its screening trees and bushes, almost giving in to panic. Sliding her hand into the pocket of her skirt, she gained a measure of confidence by touching her thimble and her dagger. The prickling at the base of her scalp seemed proof that somebody was watching her. Where were Warren Maroney and his cohorts? Had he tired of waiting for her and sneaked off to do mischief at the mansion?

Shivers of apprehension shook Berry. She turned to make certain that the tall dwelling still serenely thrust its roof and chimneys above the surrounding trees. Its beauty threatened to dislodge her carapace of control. As reassuring as the sight of the apparently unharmed mansion was the thought that Jason was safely out of Warren Maroney's reach.

Relieved then, but unable to be still, Berry fidgeted in the silence. Over the hammering of her pulse, she listened to the restless movements of the horses, the droning of mosquitoes. How long before she learned if Warren hid in the shadows between the pergola and the bayou?

"You took your own good time getting back here," Warren's voice came from somewhere across the road.

As if an invisible string manipulated her, Berry's head jerked toward the sound. Gooseflesh alerted her all over again that evil awaited. She watched Warren emerge from behind an oleander bush. Had he kept quiet all this time to see if she came alone?

"Bring the ring and the horses over here."

"No." Berry doubted she could move. Her legs had become boneless. "You come to the pergola. You can see that I'm alone."

"Don't try my patience, girl." Warren removed his long-bladed knife from a holster at his waist and motioned with it. "Get over here with them horses!"

Unable to think of another hedge and commanding her courage to the forefront, Berry took her time freeing the reins and leading Jewel and Trees across the road. By then she could see Warren, knife in hand, coming toward her. Both horses shied but Trees snorted and strained against his reins. Berry consoled the bad-tempered animal, managing to calm him somewhat by the time she and Warren met.

"What's wrong with that fool horse?" Warren was eyeing the big red gelding with misgivings and making sure he kept a safe distance.

"Nothing." Berry noted the way Warren hung back and thought about how he would naturally be cautious about keeping his feet out of the way, especially the one having only a tender spot for a big toe. "He's jittery, that's all."

"Maybe I'll take the smaller one."

"You could, but she's not as well-gaited and she's accustomed to having only women riders. I can tie them to the willow tree behind you and let them calm down.''

Berry was surprised but grateful that Warren made no objection. His steady gaze, though, added to her fear. When the horses continued to hang back, she figured her nervousness must have transferred itself to the animals. She was not eager to begin her journey and, despite Warren's watchful eyes, she took as long as possible in talking the horses into a semblance of content and securing the reins around the slender tree trunk. Where were Warren's friends hiding?

''Quit dawdling and bring me the ring,'' Warren commanded. He appeared more concerned now about the restless red gelding than about whether or not Berry was alone. ''I want it in my hands.''

Berry, her free hand sweaty and itching to use the dagger from her pocket if Warren took time to ogle the jewel, had just dropped the emerald in Warren's outstretched palm when it seemed that a wild fury descended. From out of nowhere, or so it seemed to the stunned Berry, Jason came running and slammed a fist against Warren's jaw. With lightning-like precision, he buried the other in the killer's belly. A giant ''Whoof!'' issued from Warren, and his frame jerked forward into a right angle.

Wondering if either man was aware that Warren's knife and the ring had dropped to the ground and skittered out of sight on the grassy slope, Berry heard Jason demand in the deadliest voice she could imagine, ''Get away from her! Leave her alone!''

''A-ar-gh!'' Warren yelled, still bent over and struggling for breath. After being spun halfway around from a new series of blows that straightened him up, he let out a bigger bellow of pain and stumbled backward toward the bayou.

Gasping for air and barely fending off Jason's new attack, Warren sparred weakly with both fists. Berry, clutching her dagger in her right hand openly now and wondering how it was that Jason had appeared, noted that Warren was much thicker than Jason. She feared that Warren might rally, knock Jason down and hold him until his friends came rushing from the shadows.

Not so, she realized only seconds later. Nobody was coming from hiding places. Still halfway expecting somebody to sneak from the shadows and grab her, she moved nearer where the men were exchanging staggering blows on the angling bank of the bayou. If there was anyone to summon, wouldn't Warren have called for help by now? The whinnying horses were stomping around, pulling against their reins, adding to the general frenzy.

Berry wavered. Would it help if she tried to jump on Warren's back and send her dagger home? What if she missed and made matters worse? By the time Warren had landed some grisly sounding punches to Jason's jaw and belly and visibly slowed Jason's attack, Berry realized with thanksgiving that Warren had lied about having friends along. The gory fight was between Jason and Warren.

Then the struggling men, both with bloodied faces, fell to the ground. Berry saw Jason's pistol drop from his holster. When they grappled with each other and rolled nearer the edge of the bank, she ran on wobbly legs and picked it up. Its handle felt cold and merciless in her hand. She never before had been this close to a gun; she never before had seen two men fighting with such ferocity, such obvious intent to maim or kill. What if they rolled into the deep water? What if Jason were to strike his head on one of the piers?

Berry jammed the pistol in her pocket. With more bravado than she felt, she rushed to where the men lay locked in struggle, panting and grunting in their efforts. It seemed to her that Jason was tiring from the heavier man's weight atop him. He no longer rolled easily from underneath Warren's bulk at intervals to ram in extra punches.

The loud sounds of the men's ragged breathing punished Berry's ears. They tore at her heart and reminded her that she was the reason that Jason's life was now in jeopardy. Something within rose in awful indignation that the man she loved should be made to suffer because of her past folly. While Warren's fists jabbed at Jason, his back showed in the moonlight as a clear target.

Suddenly Berry recalled how the big man had sniveled and carried on about minor flesh wounds on his legs that afternoon at the theater; and she stabbed Warren's upper back with her dagger. Aghast at the quick flood of blood staining his shirt when she jerked her small blade free, but sensing that her wound had slowed Warren's fists, Berry stabbed again. This time her knife sliced where his shoulder muscles strained while his arms gripped Jason in a fierce deadlock.

"Ow-w! Lord! but—" Warren's guttural complaints broke off as Berry jumped back. Now that Warren had relaxed his hold, Jason had recovered his position on top and was pummeling the man's contorted face, even as the two of them rolled down the bank into the bayou.

Berry wondered if she would ever again hear anything that sounded as final as the giant splash that came when the men hit the water some eight feet below. Terrified, she opened her mouth to scream for help. Before any sound burst loose, Alonzo and three other blacks dashed past her.

"We'll get Master Jason," Alonzo called. "Stay back!"

Shock held Berry silent, transfixed. She watched the men dive into the churning water where Jason and Warren Maroney had disappeared, locked in what she feared might be a mutual death grip.

CHAPTER

*

Twenty-one

N ot until after Jason surfaced with Warren's body did he place Alonzo in charge. "Here," he gasped while treading water, "get him out."

Jason then dragged himself up the bank where he lay struggling to regain breath and strength. Without a word, Berry sank beside him and gathered him into her arms. Her tears blended with his wetness.

Berry held Jason fiercely for a time, then nudged his head across her lap. From his resting place he questioned her about her earlier encounter in the pergola with the escaped convict. By the time Berry had told all, the men had hauled Warren's lifeless body from the water and laid it on the grass across the road.

"Hey, Berry," Jason said teasingly after all was somewhat calm again, "you must have cried a barrelful. Something got us both all wet." Still feeling somewhat drained, he wondered if any other young woman could appear as unaware that his clothing and hair had soaked her riding outfit. When she made a visible effort to smile at his feeble joke, he thought about how they might never have quarreled, might never have played their farewell scene. He welcomed the thought that all seemed right between them again. "Did I imagine it, or did you stab Maroney?"

"Yes. I slashed him across the back to slow him down. I was afraid he was going to kill you." Berry glanced toward where some fifty feet away Alonzo and the other three blacks were wrapping Warren's body in a blanket that Alonzo had fetched from the *garçonniere*. All evening, time seemed to have moved in uneven segments. The moonlight and the sporadic screeching of an owl across the bayou enhanced the eeriness of the macabre scene. Although Warren had seemed the epitome of evil, she could not rejoice at his death.

Berry shuddered and returned her gaze to Jason, reaching with one hand to brush his wet hair back from the bloody wound on his forehead. Her premonition about his life being in danger had been all too true; only the timing had been in error. The lifeless body that Jason and the others had recovered from the murky water could have been his. Tears rose to the surface again. The knot in her belly still twisted. "I should have used my dagger sooner and maybe you wouldn't have rolled into the bayou."

Hoping to erase the pinched look from her lovely face, Jason maintained a light tone. "If I had known Warren was such a rotten swimmer, I might have pushed him in right off."

"I heard Alonzo say he found a huge bump on his head, as if he might have hit a piling underwater."

"By the time we landed in the bayou, we had broken loose from each other, so that's likely. I know that water and I headed for the channel before surfacing."

"I'm grateful you're all right and that you came back in time to—"

"It's a long story, but I think it will wait."

"Not," she retorted with a toss of her hair, "if you came back only because that Corrine turned you away."

Jason managed a faint smile. "What you don't know is that I can't even get to Corrine's houseboat on horseback. If I had wanted to see her, I would have gone by water. You're jealous over something long lost in my unscrupulous past. Surely a man is allowed to make a few blunders while growing up. I'll bet you've made a few yourself."

Berry huffed and dabbed at his bloody nose with his soggy handkerchief. "You're impossible."

"I'll bet I'm right, too."

"More often than I like to recall," Berry conceded. "One mistake I made was becoming involved with Warren Maroney."

"You couldn't have lived with yourself had you not helped your friend Ebon seek out justice for the murderer of the woman who helped raise him."

"But you said that Mardi Gras night that I was acting like a dolt—"

"Does it matter now what I said? You did what seemed right. Besides, you were terribly young. I can't help admiring people who have gumption and strike out for what they believe in. I'm relieved that it's all over now and that you don't have to be worrying about Warren Maroney any longer. Did you give him the ring?"

"Yes, but he dropped it and his knife when you attacked. They must have gotten lost in the bushes, or else fallen in the water."

"I'll ask Alonzo to look for them. He might have to wait until daylight to find them."

"I have no desire to see that emerald ever again. I wonder if it might not bear a curse. Even if Alonzo finds the ring, I don't want it." Berry shivered.

"Warren is gone now. You don't have to be afraid any longer."

At the memory of the sheer daring of his rush to step

between Warren and her, her voice became little more than a hoarse whisper. "Thanks to you, Jason."

"I'm not so sure that before you got very far away, you and your dagger and Trees wouldn't have bested him." Jason grinned up at her, aware that he was feeling more like himself with each passing moment. "That was a sly trick, saddling old Trees for him."

"I was desperate."

"Just as you were when you put on that ridiculous scene in the *garçonniere*?"

"Ridiculous?" She watched a firefly, dipping and rising among the oleander and gardenia bushes, blink yellowish green spurts of color in the moonlight. The bullfrogs had been quiet for some time. "It worked, didn't it?"

"At first."

"You weren't pretending, though, and you made some strong statements," she countered.

"True, but I was angry and hurt. You were mighty good in your role."

"Do you really think I'm a holier-than-thou?"

"Not for a New Orleans minute."

"You sounded convincing."

"Maybe I took acting lessons, too."

Alonzo approached and bent over Jason. "Are you still feelin' all right?" When his master said he was and sat up as though to prove it, the black man asked, "What you want us to do with that body?"

"Put it on one of the horses and take it to the tack room till Sheriff Bodron gets here. Don't you think Josiah ought to be back with the sheriff within a couple of hours?"

Alonzo nodded. "He oughta, since you sent him the back way soon as you rode up an' saw him leadin' Buster outta the stables."

"You and the others should stay around the stables till they arrive. Since I told Josiah that he and Sheriff Bodron should return the back way in case secrecy was needed, they'll show up there first." Jason glanced toward the covered corpse lying across the road. "We'll wait in the *garçonniere*."

"While I was out there gettin' a blanket, I opened the spigot to the cistern enough to start fillin' your bathtub."

"Thanks," Jason replied. "You're a good man, Alonzo. I think it's best we stay as quiet as possible and keep away from the big house until daybreak. I don't want to disturb Uncle Edouard until I have to."

Looking toward the big house at the end of the long driveway, Alonzo said, "I guess it's lucky he sleeps on the back side. I speck his brandy got him dreamin' sweet dreams. He ain't never been one to wake easy."

Jason nodded his agreement. "When I was in town the other day, I explained to the sheriff about Maroney being an escaped convict and perhaps hunting for my houseguest. I expect when the sheriff gets here, he'll want to question all of us."

Berry accepted Jason's outstretched hand and rose on legs steadier than she had expected. "Alonzo, I want to thank you again for doing such a fine job of looking after me without alarming Warren."

"You's welcome, Miss Berry. I still can't figure how you managed to saddle ole Trees, much less think up the idea to take him 'long for the man to ride."

"It was a smart move in more ways than one," Jason pointed out when Berry appeared ill at ease. He suspected it might take a while before she could rationalize the events of the evening. Her account of what had taken place before he arrived had sounded disjointed.

On the other hand, Jason reflected, Berry's avowed disinterest in the emerald sounded sincere and well thought out. Maybe she was right. Maybe it was better to leave the gem where it landed. If nobody could find it in daylight, he would dismiss it as quickly as she apparently had. He already had in mind the ring he wanted to place on her finger.

Attempting to boost Berry's confidence in the way she

had handled the situation, Jason said, "If Trees hadn't been acting a blamed fool and keeping Maroney's attention fixed on the horses, the man might have noticed us slipping from underneath the trees and entering the pergola."

"You put us in a worrisome spot," Alonzo complained good naturedly to his master, "when you tole us we wasn't to leave the pergola lessen a whole bunch of men showed up or you called for help. When we saw you tumble in the bayou, I tole the others we wasn't waitin' no longer."

Before Alonzo turned away, Jason said, "Tomorrow I'll tell all of you again how well you took care of matters. Thanks."

Then, hand in hand, Berry and Jason started across the road toward the *garçonniere*, leaving Alonzo and the other men to their task.

Was she imagining it, Berry wondered as they neared his living quarters, or had Jason and she truly become closer because of their brushes with evil and having cleared the air in their earlier quarrel? The hour was late and Berry entertained the weird thought that the night might have already stretched past its allotted time. She sensed that, like her, Jason was remembering their spirited departure from the *garçonniere* earlier that evening. Was he also feeling a bit awkward about returning?

"How thoughtful of somebody to bring my portmanteau here," Berry said when they stepped inside the parlor and saw it sitting on the gateleg table where tapers burned. "I had forgotten about tying it behind my saddle."

"Alonzo must have brought it when he came to find a blanket. Now you won't have to go to the big house to find something clean and dry to change into before the sheriff gets here." He remembered another time when they had need of dry clothing and smiled.

She glanced down at her soiled riding costume. How could she bear another disrobing in his living quarters? Memories tortured her. "I hadn't realized I was this wet."

With tenderness, he explained, "That comes from hugging a man dripping with muddy bayou water and letting him rest his head in your lap. Do you recall doing that?'' He wanted to wrap her close and keep her safe forever. The thought that Warren had come close to harming her still plagued him.

''Yes, I recall.'' How could she ever forget the wonderful feeling of holding him and reassuring herself that he was alive and not seriously harmed? ''Let me tend your bruises now.''

''No need. My nose and the cut on my forehead have stopped bleeding and my knuckles need washing before we can tell if they're really cut up.'' He held his hands out for her perusal, flexing his fingers and showing that no fresh blood appeared on the skinned knuckles.

Berry leaned for a closer look in the candlelight, frowning a bit. When she pursed her lips in silent sympathy and unwittingly tempted him to kiss her breathless, he sucked in a deep breath. Even disheveled, the woman he loved was temptation. He felt his pulse picking up speed. Doggedly he went on. ''I think the best thing for us both is to get cleaned up before you take a look. Grab a candle and come with me.''

''I hate admitting it, but your idea sounds better. You don't seem to be as banged up as I had feared. Moonlight can be deceptive.''

''True.''

Berry refused to meet his gaze. She had meant for her last comment to be taken literally and she suspected that he had read double meaning into it. She needed no reminder that their first flirting had taken place in moonlight. Her heartbeat remembered, too. It was dancing a jig.

After Berry took up a candle, Jason picked up her small bag and led the way into the spare bedroom. ''While I go check on the tub that Alonzo said he was filling, you can get tidied up in here.'' He peered into the fat-bottomed pitcher sitting in its matching china wash bowl atop the washstand. ''There's water in the pitcher and—''

"I'll be fine," Berry assured him.

After waiting until Jason went on into the room next to hers and closed the door, Berry removed the combs from her hair and shucked her clothing. She discovered everything was either sodden or damp, even her shoes and stockings. Moving as if she were a sleepwalker, she took her time washing away the remnants of the muddy water.

What to wear? Berry wondered as she held a lavender-scented towel close to her breasts and recalled the contents of her portmanteau. Along with a simple skirt and blouse, she had taken only a few undergarments. When she thought about having to wear the packed garments around that evil man, she let out a tremulous sigh.

Berry could hear the faint sounds Jason made as he moved about in the adjoining bedroom. She found herself tingling just thinking of what he might be doing at that moment. Had he already washed away the grime? She felt her pulse skip as she imagined him standing naked from his bath. She smiled dreamily. He would be tall and straight and looking maddeningly virile with his heavily muscled arms and legs, his broad chest tapering abruptly to his narrow waist and hips. Was he looking in the mirror over his washstand and inspecting his face for bruises? His dear face! She envisioned his lean features, elongated dimples, his expressive eyes with their intriguing golden flecks. In her mind she had given Jason up earlier that evening, but chance or fate had stepped in and served up new choices.

Berry paused. The candle sputtered. What *was* she going to do about Jason Premont?

C H A P T E R

*

Twenty-two

*B*erry leaned closer to the mirror. Approving the black cloud of unbound hair, some of which reached down to her waist in the back while the remaining loose waves and curls formed a partial curtain over her breasts, she dropped the hairbrush back to the washstand. Then, with her bare feet making whispering noises against the wooden floor and her hair caressing her nakedness, Berry crossed the room and turned the doorknob. It would lead her to the man she loved.

Jason looked up at the sound of the door opening and almost lost his breath. Berry, her black hair and eyes shining, stood there wearing nothing but a radiant smile and a look that seemed to promise forever. She said, "I don't see any major mutilation, thank goodness."

"There isn't any. I'm tougher than you believed." He returned her smile and, clothed only by a towel draped around his lean hips, he moved toward her like a man who knew where he had been, knew where he was going. "Darling, did you read my thoughts?"

"Maybe." She noted the way the candle behind him on the washstand outlined his beloved form and threw his features into mysterious shadow. The heart-stopping sight of Jason smiling and walking toward her smoothed her intention to tell him that she wanted to make love with him once more before returning to New Orleans on the morrow and leaving him and his family in peace.

Berry in no way considered her planned departure as an attempt to be noble. She judged it a self-styled act of benevolence designed to ensure that Jason and his beloved Armand Acres would exist free of the taint her presence had brought. It was her way of restoring to him what she had taken, her way of thanking him for saving her from Warren and giving her back her life.

This time, Berry assured herself, once she worked Jason out of her heart, she would make her life count for more. Never again would she draw those she cared about into her miserable mistakes. She would guard against being an Impulse Person. If she were truly fortunate and had learned half as much as she believed, her mistakes would be fewer.

Suddenly Jason was close enough for her to touch, to smell, to hear breathing. Her every pore became alerted. She sensed that the small space separating them quivered in rhythm with her wildly beating heart.

Berry grew breathless just looking at the drops of water glistening on Jason's neck, his shoulders. On the dark hairs of his chest. With the force of an incoming tide, the desire to kiss away each tiny globule crashed over her. It left her restless. She felt trembly all over, like the surface of deep water lying in the path of a summer breeze. Then she was laying her hands in his outstretched palms and feeling as if she might be standing at the edge of something as far-reaching and unfathomable as the sea.

When Jason's lips inched so close to hers that even in the pale light coming from the candle behind him she could see their texture, see the tiny lines defining their sensuous shape and kicking up at the corners, Berry said in a breathless rush, "You may think I'm brazen because . . . the more I'm around you, the more I want to . . . get lost in your arms. Well"—his luminous gaze dipped into hers bringing a warm spurt of tingling deep inside in her womanhood— "I'm not denying it."

"Not brazen, but beautiful, desirable woman," was all he could manage before drawing her exquisite body nearer to his damp nakedness. Meeting her lips and feeling the caress of her taut breasts against his chest released a storm throughout his being. "I could kiss you forever, Berry Cortabona," he whispered.

Jason's mouth seemed to become an entity of its own as it savaged hers, hungrily, masterfully. If a world existed outside their embrace, he could not acknowledge it, had no wish to. Unrelenting waves of passion buffeted him into a sweet oblivion.

Berry, weak with want, leaned against him and clutched him closer. She welcomed Jason's bold assault on her mouth and, just as ferociously, sent her tongue to duel hotly with his. Her fingers crept up under his hair and stroked the back of his neck. How good it felt to touch him, to be touched in return, to feel the warm proof of his existence. She reveled in the stormy pace of her heartbeat, in the swelling of that first warm spurt of heat inside her belly into a rivulet, hot and tantalizing.

Jason's breath sounded loud and ragged when he lifted his mouth from hers and, from where her breath fanned across his chest, he could hear it matching up with his on a softer note. One of his hands had found a silken refuge in her hair, and now his thumb caressed the base of her skull in a slow, circling pattern. The flames first kindled in his loins at the sight of her entering his bedroom now blazed in earnest. Hot. She made him hot. God! How he loved the feeling. "You're everything a man could ever hope for, dream about."

From where her head rested against his furred chest, Berry felt the vibrations of Jason's declaration at the same time that she heard his whispered words. Shivering with pure happiness, she lifted her head and gazed up at him. Her eyes brimmed over with love, even as she squelched the voice that tried to remind her that she was a fool not to tell him of her love. "You're wonderful, too."

Berry became conscious that a drop of Jason's bath water had transferred itself from his neck to a spot above her upper lip. This, their last night together, she decided with a bent toward indulging fantasy and stamping out reality, would be one for both to remember. Aware that he watched her in the wavering candlelight, she sent him a flirtatious look from behind half-lowered eyelashes. Slowly, as if tasting nectar, she sent her tongue to capture the drop of water above her lip. He swallowed. So did she. "Jason, I'm glad you didn't dry off very well. I like the way you taste."

"I like everything about you." As if he might be indulging an adored imp set on making delicious mischief, he flashed his dimples and loosely looped his arms around Berry, letting his hands meet at the small of her back. Her perfect back, satiny smooth with wondrously curved flesh captured underneath his worshipful fingers. A fever was brewing inside him and he was loving each heated moment of excitement. How he loved her!

Berry leaned and kissed Jason's neck, letting her lips track an erotic path down to his chest. When she discovered another drop of water clinging to a tight curl near his nipple, she took her time in sucking it into her mouth. She felt supremely powerful when Jason flinched slightly, then shivered at the touch of her tongue on his skin, on his tightening nipple. By the time her exploring mouth found another drop nearby and worked a like magic there, she felt the warm bulge of his manhood growing and pressing closer against her nakedness. His body was as hot as hers.

"I want nothing between us," she declared, teasing and solemn at the same time. Holding his gaze with hers, she loosened the towel around his middle and tossed it on the floor. When she heard it land with a soft plop of finality, she trembled. She saved for later a full view of his visible desire because she feared that once she saw the straining shaft, she would be begging him to sheath it inside her that instant.

For the time being, Berry ordered herself be content to adore the way their eyes made secret promises, the way Jason's arms supported her, and the way his fingers splayed across her buttocks, caressing her skin just enough to remind her that his hands would not have to stray far to send her into throes of ecstasy. In fact, she could feel, deep inside, the molten desire increasing and trickling downward from where it had begun first as a tingling spot of warmth.

Driven by her rising passion, Berry stood on her tiptoes and with her breasts grazing the hair on his chest, she trailed her fingers up Jason's arms. Throughout the small journey, he favored her with a slow smile that reached into her heart. Her hands moved across to his throat; he arched back his neck for her loving perusal. She felt and heard a manly vibration deep inside that she deemed *lagniappe*. She fondled his lean cheeks, his temples, tenderly grazing the bruises earned in her protection. Then while his brown eyes, heavy-lidded and awhirl with golden flecks, gazed down at her, she cradled his dear face between her palms.

At each of Berry's soft caresses the sense of Jason's latent power had transferred itself through the sensitive skin of her fingertips and filled her heart with renewed awe for all that he was, both inside and outside. She lowered her eyelashes. The realization that she could exercise power over such a magnificent man merely by touching him with her fingertips titillated her further. She hadn't even needed "further." What must he be thinking about her wanton ways?

"You're driving me crazy," Jason murmured just before he swung Berry up into his arms, delighting in the way her hair fanned over his arm and brushed against his body with each step. When he passed the washstand he paused long enough to blow out the candle. "I like making love to my woman in the moonlight."

Tucking his hoarse *my woman* inside her heart for safe-keeping, Berry felt soft and quivery when Jason laid her down on the snowy sheet and knelt beside her. Silvery beams from the moon already low in the West shone through the jalousied windows, bathing the lovers and highlighting their long-limbed splendor. As though an agreement had been reached, Jason took a turn in playing out fantasy.

It seemed to him that the shadows in the room served as a feathery backdrop for the celestial light and lent mystery to the slender young woman lying on his bed. She watched him, with an arm flung back over her head, one shapely leg lifted slightly and bent at the knee. Her widely spaced eyes, sultry and luminous, and her kiss-swollen lips curving into a sensuous smile signaled that she was a woman ready for loving. His loving.

Jason spread out her long hair behind her head and face like an exquisite, ebony frame. Then he drew some strands forward over her shoulders and, with seemingly careless abandon, he looped the black curls lightly around her full breasts until only her nipples lay fully exposed. Then, without touching her anywhere else, he leaned and kissed her erect nipples into tighter buds, laving them with his tongue and tenderly suckling.

Berry arched back in undisguised ecstasy. Restlessly she moved her hips and legs until they collided with his kneeling body. After brushing aside her hair from her breasts, he bestowed loving treatment on the satiny mounds. The storm within Jason rose with each loving stroke he gave, pushing him onward to invent new ways to show her with his hands and mouth that he worshiped her, loved her, only her. Her sighs and moans—how sweetly they enhanced his desire—and her convulsive caresses assured him that he was pleasuring her.

"I adore it when you kiss me like that," Berry whispered.

Jason's mouth had centered around her navel and his fingers were stroking her secret places into agonizing, scalding desire that threatened to blast her into oblivion. When he kissed the little indentation again and dotted it with his tongue, she grabbed him around the neck fiercely and guided his head toward hers. She feared she might drown from wanting. "I love what you're doing to me but—"

Jason's mouth claimed hers then. No longer could he resist giving in to the raging need to feel their naked lengths make full contact. As soon as they touched, he reeled from the impact and, with a satisfaction beyond belief, felt her body tremble anew and her limbs entwine with his. His manhood throbbed with anticipation. The knowledge that the gateway to her womanhood lay warm and enticing before him drove him into a frenzy. Her hips tilted in invitation. Jason accepted.

Their passion built and climbed as though it possessed an energy all its own. They wondered if more than their bodies were being joined. Though neither mouthed anything coherent, both sensed a remarkable truth: He was the only man in the world; she, the only woman.

There in the moonlight ecstasy brought a roaring to their ears, shouts of joy to their lips, and animal strength to their limbs. Afterward, the roars faded into blessed silence. The shouts became murmurs. The strength of passion melted into delectable, quivering lassitude.

After a long silence, Jason recovered his breath and spoke. "I lied to you, Berry"—how was it that her breathing pattern seemed connected to the cadence of his words? —"when I told you that I fell in love with you at the masquerade ball."

Leaving his embrace and sitting up in the bed, Berry felt a shiver snake over her nakedness. A rake. She had known from the beginning that he was a rake. Earlier that evening she had made up her mind to leave tomorrow and tell him goodbye forever. Then why the pain, the awful, slicing pain?

"You see," Jason went on, half-wounded that she had turned away before he made his point, "I realize that I love you so much more now than then that I couldn't have been telling the truth." When her curtain of shimmering black hair kept her face hidden, he also rose to a sitting position. "Look at me. Give me your hand."

Wanting to believe Jason's solemn declaration more than anything else in the universe, Berry looked at him, then down at his outstretched hand. Her carefully wrought plans seemed to have jigged off with a moonbeam. If she let herself follow her heart and—

Gave him her hand? Why, she would give Jason her life. He had already offered his for her. With tears stinging her eyelids and a monstrous lump crowding her throat, Berry laid her hand in his and felt his fingers close over hers. The comforting feel and singularly unspectacular sight of their hands joined held her entranced, told her uncompromisingly that she had found a blessed home.

In husky bass Jason said, "I need you beside me forever. I'm the special man you told me you had dreamed of finding."

"No." She shook her head, her hair a mesmerizing cloud that he watched settle across her naked shoulders and breasts. "It was a childish dream. You said so yourself. I was painting myself as perfect and worthy of happiness without doing anything to deserve it."

"I'm the one who was wrong. Dreams are always cast that way," Jason replied. The grateful, almost shy, look Berry gave him in return reminded Jason that in sharing her dream with him, she had laid before him a private part of herself and he had not honored it. As he saw it now, such a precious gift transcended all others a woman could present to a man for consideration . . . or destruction. Physical beauty and pleasures succumbed to the tyranny of time. Dreams were forever, and, he suspected, too often kept secret. He wanted her never to hold back anything from him. "I want to be that man you dreamed about. If I'm not already, I will be. Won't you marry me and let me show you that we belong together, that—''

''Yes. I'll marry you, Jason, but only because I love you, too. I've lied both to you and myself for a long while and for all the wrong reasons.'' Berry sucked in a hurtful breath and let it limp out before continuing. ''I meant to leave tomorrow and let you get on with your life. I find I can't leave you now . . . not ever. Maybe I'm not the kind of wife you need, but I'd like to be. I want to try to be.'' Tears blinded her as she leaned into his arms and kissed him long and hard.

Then Jason was murmuring against her lips, ''You *are* my kind of woman, have been from the time I first danced with you. I'll love you every day of the week, every week of each month, the way you dreamed. Darling, I'll love you forever because that's the way I want it, too.''

When they lay again in close embrace, Berry knew she would never tire of feeling his heartbeat pulsating throughout his warm flesh. Her heart seemed near to overflowing, and she hugged him tightly for a moment before trying to share some of the emotions welling up inside. Would he understand if she told him she felt wondrously star-tuned to the universe?

Berry was surprised that her words came out as no more than whispers there on the moonlit bed still redolent with the spicy, moist fragrances of glorious love. ''I'm glad you offer me such a blessed kind of love. I was wrong to think it could be mine simply for wishing it. I'll do my best to deserve it all over again every day. I do so want our love to be special, to last past all the trite aspects of life. Will you help me keep it that way?''

''I promise.'' With a tender forefinger Jason brushed away the tears beading her black lashes. He swallowed the sudden hot lump in his throat, then searched for a light, loving tone to ease his heart-bruising tension. ''I can just see our children down through the years, whispering—behind their hands politely, of course—that their mother and father don't act at all like old married folks, always sneaking kisses and holding hands at the dining table.''

"I love the way you talk to me."

"I love the way you do everything."

"You won't love the way I run a house. I don't know about things like that." She tensed. "Oh, Jason, what if I'm wrong for you? What if—"

"You're perfect for me. You don't need to run a house. Cousin Agnes does a fine job—unless you want her to show you how."

"Actually what I'd like is for her to keep on doing what she does and let me spend my time weaving and designing gowns and—"

"And making your husband happy." His words sounded like a fierce yet tender command.

She laughed low in her throat. Pleasing Jason could never be a task. "That will be my main job and my greatest pleasure."

Smiling and snuggling closer to his hard body, Berry let her eyes climb up the bedazzling wash of moonlight bathing them until her gaze got lost along the star-filled horizon. She felt wise, womanly, yet deliciously new and challenged. "We have such different backgrounds, have such different mixtures of blood in our veins. I wonder what kind of babies we'll make?"

"The blessed kind, darling." Jason brushed one of her saucily tilted breasts with the back of his lightly fisted hand, then leaned to kiss its hardening peak. He loved the way she sighed and moved sensuously against the sheet when, as now, his caresses apparently stirred her deeply.

Jason went on. "I believe it's time to get started right now, else we'll have to wait a few weeks. After we tell Uncle Edouard in the morning and go visit the priest in Calion, we'll have a party and I'll proudly introduce you to everyone in Saint Christopher Parish. I love you madly, but it wouldn't do in proper Creole circles for the engaged couple to be alone in his quarters."

"Oh, my, no!" She shook her head in mock horror and giggled in that throaty, lilting way he had come to cherish.

Jason kissed her other breast, savoring the streak of lightning firing within his groin. The sight of beautiful, black-haired Berry Cortabona in the moonlight fed his soul and played havoc with his heartbeat. Mischievously he glanced toward the window where the moonlight shone the brightest, then back at his beloved. "Remember how I told you once that a Creole moon smiles only on Creoles in love?"

Berry sighed with unadulterated bliss and reached high with one hand to catch a moonbeam dancing above their entwined nakedness. Then, with her fingers cupped, she laid her hand over one of his dimples as though bestowing a private benediction. "Do you suppose, Jason Premont," she asked with a teasing smile and a flirtatious look, "that I'll ever get used to your always being right?"